PRINCESS KNIGHT

part 1

Osamu Tezuka

Translation - Maya Rosewood
Production - Hiroko Mizuno
Jill Rittymanee
Tomoe Tsutsumi

Published by Vertical, Inc., New York

Originally serialized in Japanese as *Ribon no Kishi* in *Shoujo Kurabu*, Kodansha, 1953-56;
reworked and serialized anew in *Nakayoshi*, Kodansha, 1963-66.
This translation based on the *Tezuka Osamu Manga Zenshu* edition, Kodansha, 1977.

This is a work of fiction.

ISBN: 978-1-935654-25-4

Manufactured in Canada

First Edition

Vertical, Inc.
451 Park Avenue South, 7th Floor
New York, NY 10016
www.vertical-inc.com

PRINCESS KNIGHT

part 1

Table of Contents

Chapter 1

Once Upon a Time

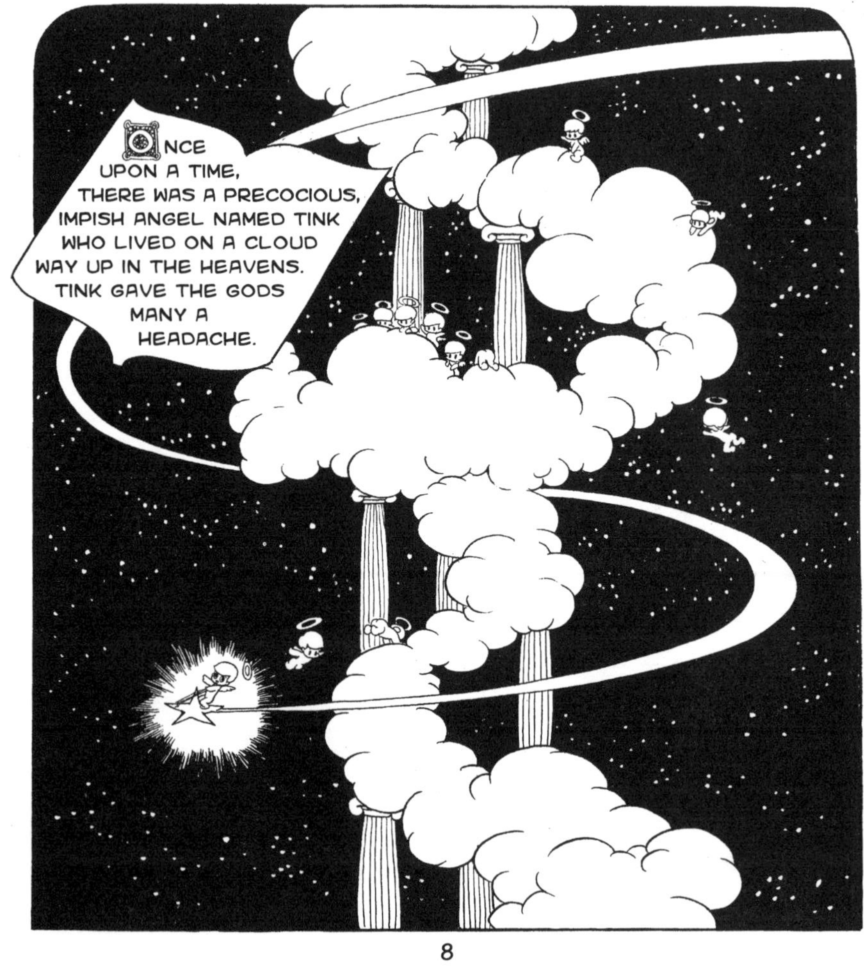
ONCE UPON A TIME, THERE WAS A PRECOCIOUS, IMPISH ANGEL NAMED TINK WHO LIVED ON A CLOUD WAY UP IN THE HEAVENS. TINK GAVE THE GODS MANY A HEADACHE.

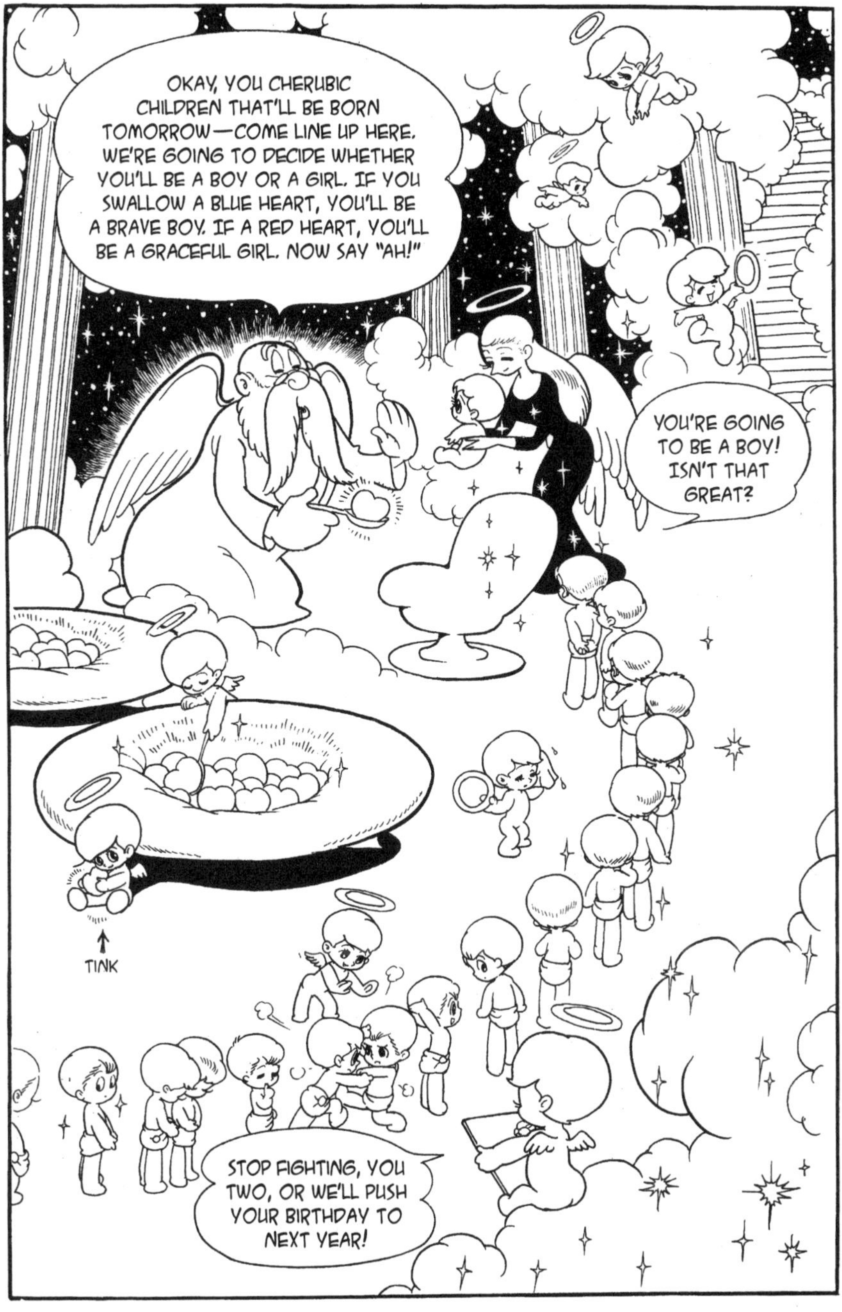
OKAY, YOU CHERUBIC CHILDREN THAT'LL BE BORN TOMORROW—COME LINE UP HERE. WE'RE GOING TO DECIDE WHETHER YOU'LL BE A BOY OR A GIRL. IF YOU SWALLOW A BLUE HEART, YOU'LL BE A BRAVE BOY. IF A RED HEART, YOU'LL BE A GRACEFUL GIRL. NOW SAY "AH!"
YOU'RE GOING TO BE A BOY! ISN'T THAT GREAT?
TINK
STOP FIGHTING, YOU TWO, OR WE'LL PUSH YOUR BIRTHDAY TO NEXT YEAR!

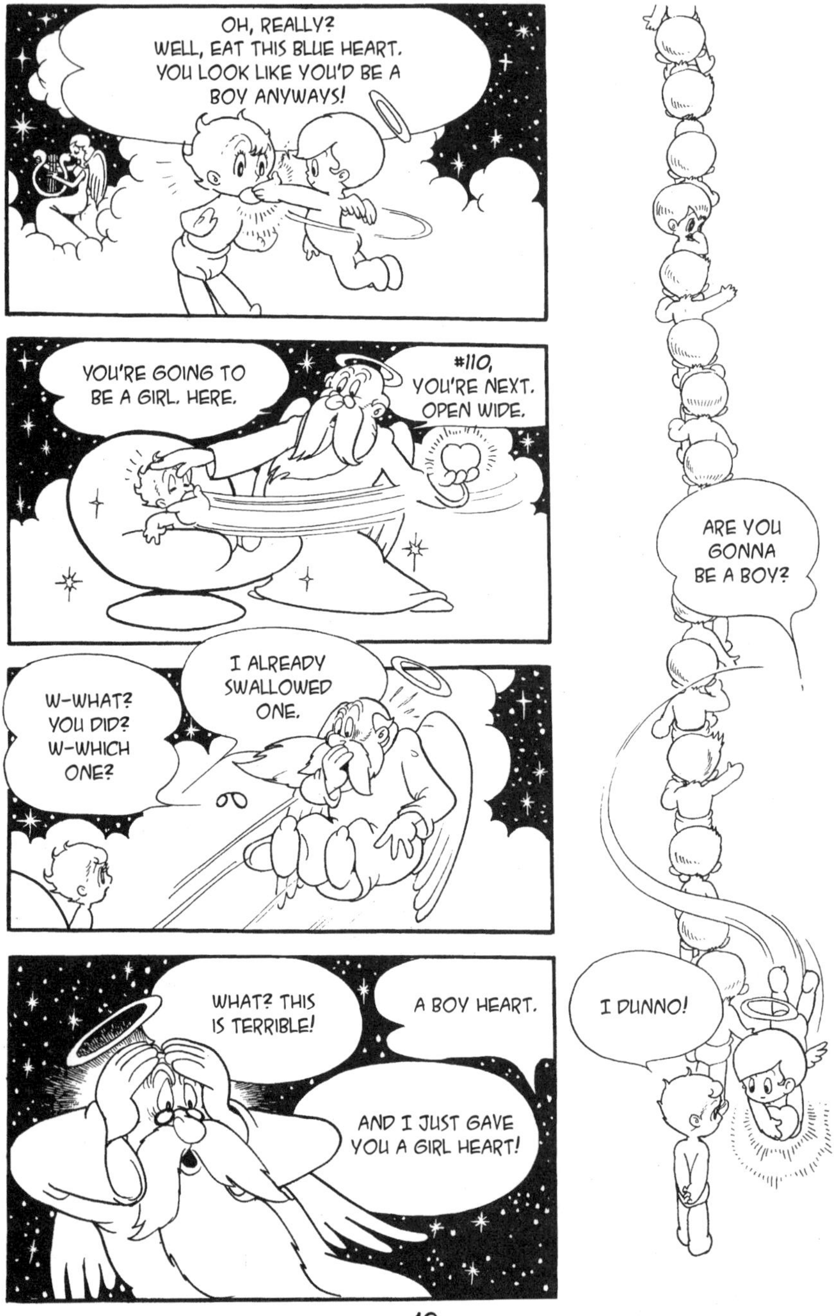
ARE YOU GONNA BE A BOY?
I DUNNO!
OH, REALLY? WELL, EAT THIS BLUE HEART. YOU LOOK LIKE YOU'D BE A BOY ANYWAYS!
#110, YOU'RE NEXT. OPEN WIDE.
YOU'RE GOING TO BE A GIRL. HERE.
I ALREADY SWALLOWED ONE.
W-WHAT? YOU DID? W-WHICH ONE?
A BOY HEART.
WHAT? THIS IS TERRIBLE!
AND I JUST GAVE YOU A GIRL HEART!

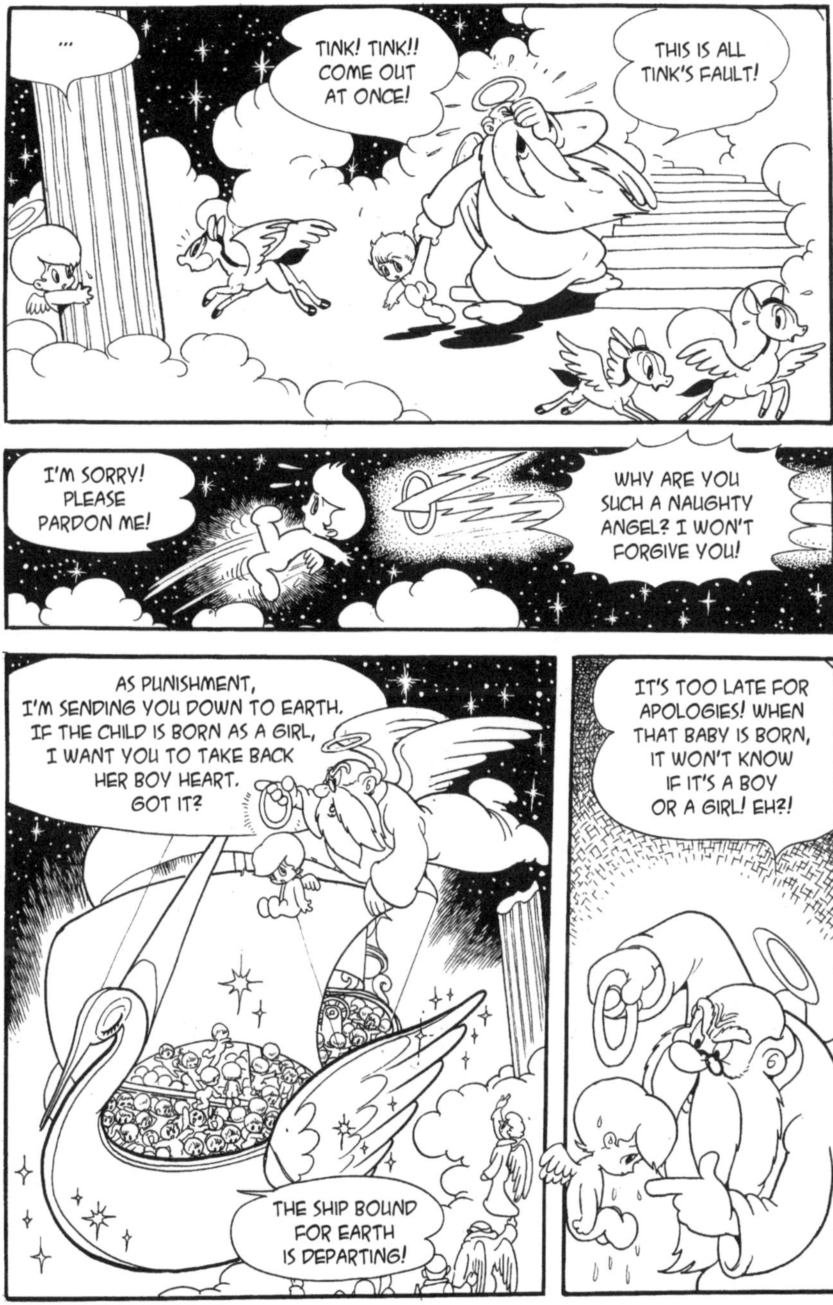
THIS IS ALL TINK'S FAULT!
TINK! TINK!! COME OUT AT ONCE!
...
WHY ARE YOU SUCH A NAUGHTY ANGEL? I WON'T FORGIVE YOU!
I'M SORRY! PLEASE PARDON ME!
IT'S TOO LATE FOR APOLOGIES! WHEN THAT BABY IS BORN, IT WON'T KNOW IF IT'S A BOY OR A GIRL! EH?!
AS PUNISHMENT, I'M SENDING YOU DOWN TO EARTH. IF THE CHILD IS BORN AS A GIRL, I WANT YOU TO TAKE BACK HER BOY HEART. GOT IT?
THE SHIP BOUND FOR EARTH IS DEPARTING!

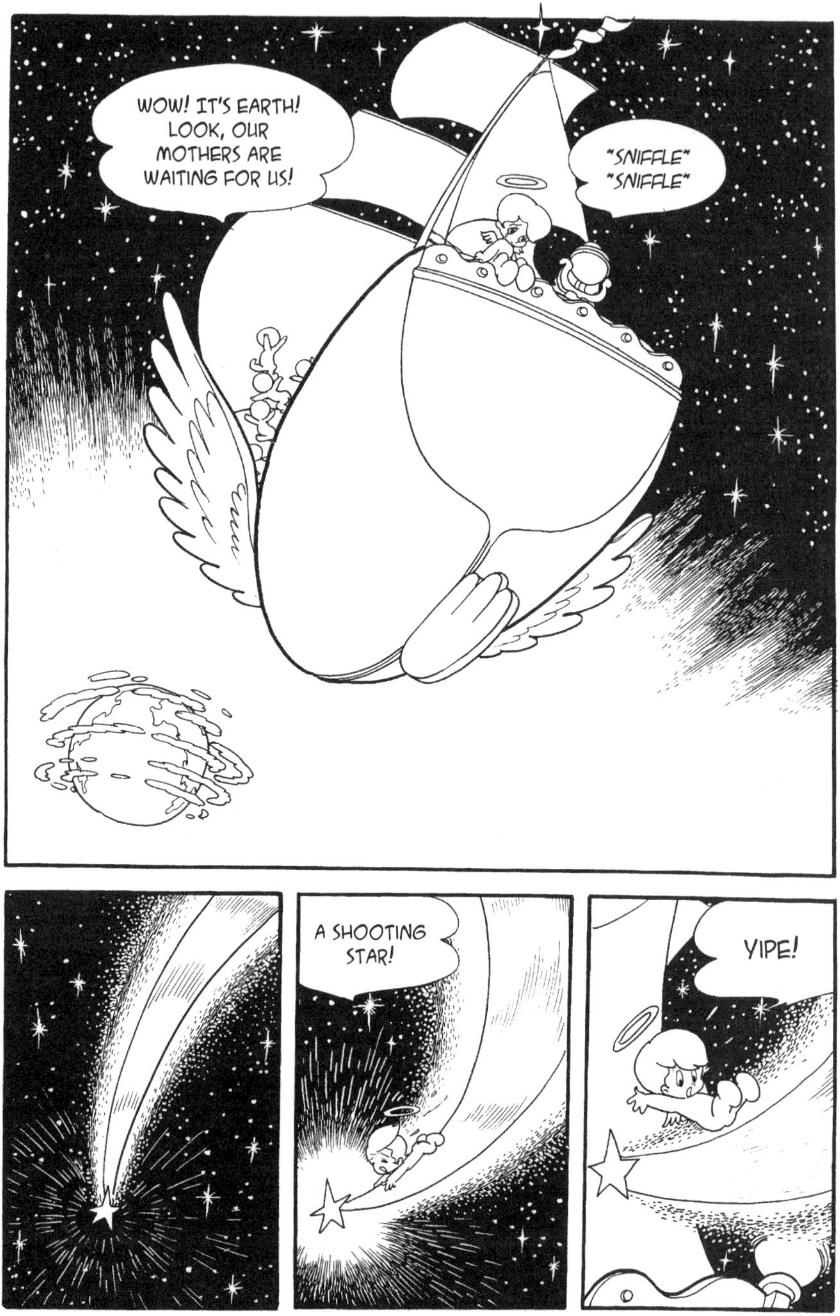
"SNIFFLE"
"SNIFFLE"
WOW! IT'S EARTH! LOOK, OUR MOTHERS ARE WAITING FOR US!
YIPE!
A SHOOTING STAR!

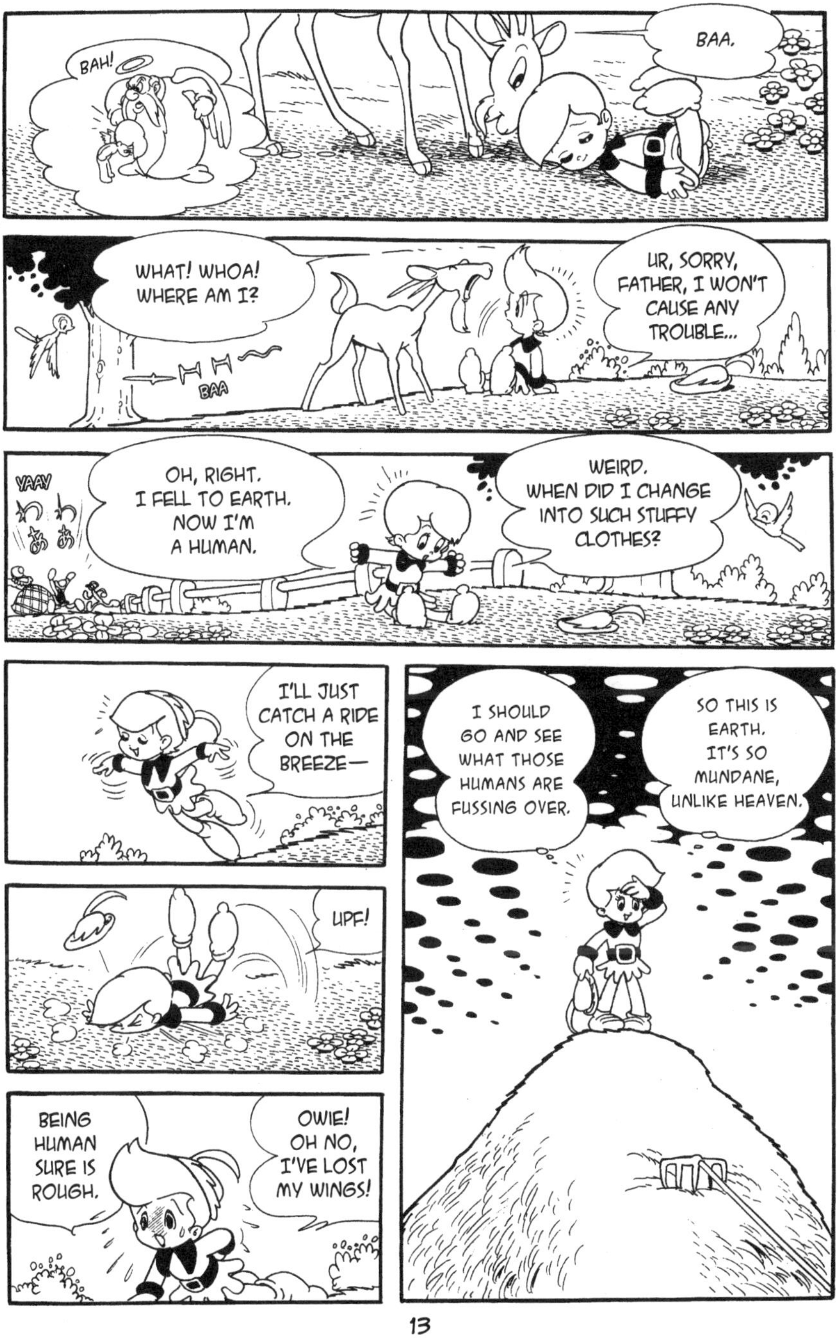
BAA.
BAH!
UR, SORRY, FATHER, I WON'T CAUSE ANY TROUBLE...
WHAT! WHOA! WHERE AM I?
BAA
WEIRD. WHEN DID I CHANGE INTO SUCH STUFFY CLOTHES?
OH, RIGHT. I FELL TO EARTH. NOW I'M A HUMAN.
YAAY
わあわあ
SO THIS IS EARTH. IT'S SO MUNDANE, UNLIKE HEAVEN.
I SHOULD GO AND SEE WHAT THOSE HUMANS ARE FUSSING OVER.
I'LL JUST CATCH A RIDE ON THE BREEZE—
UPF!
OWIE! OH NO, I'VE LOST MY WINGS!
BEING HUMAN SURE IS ROUGH.

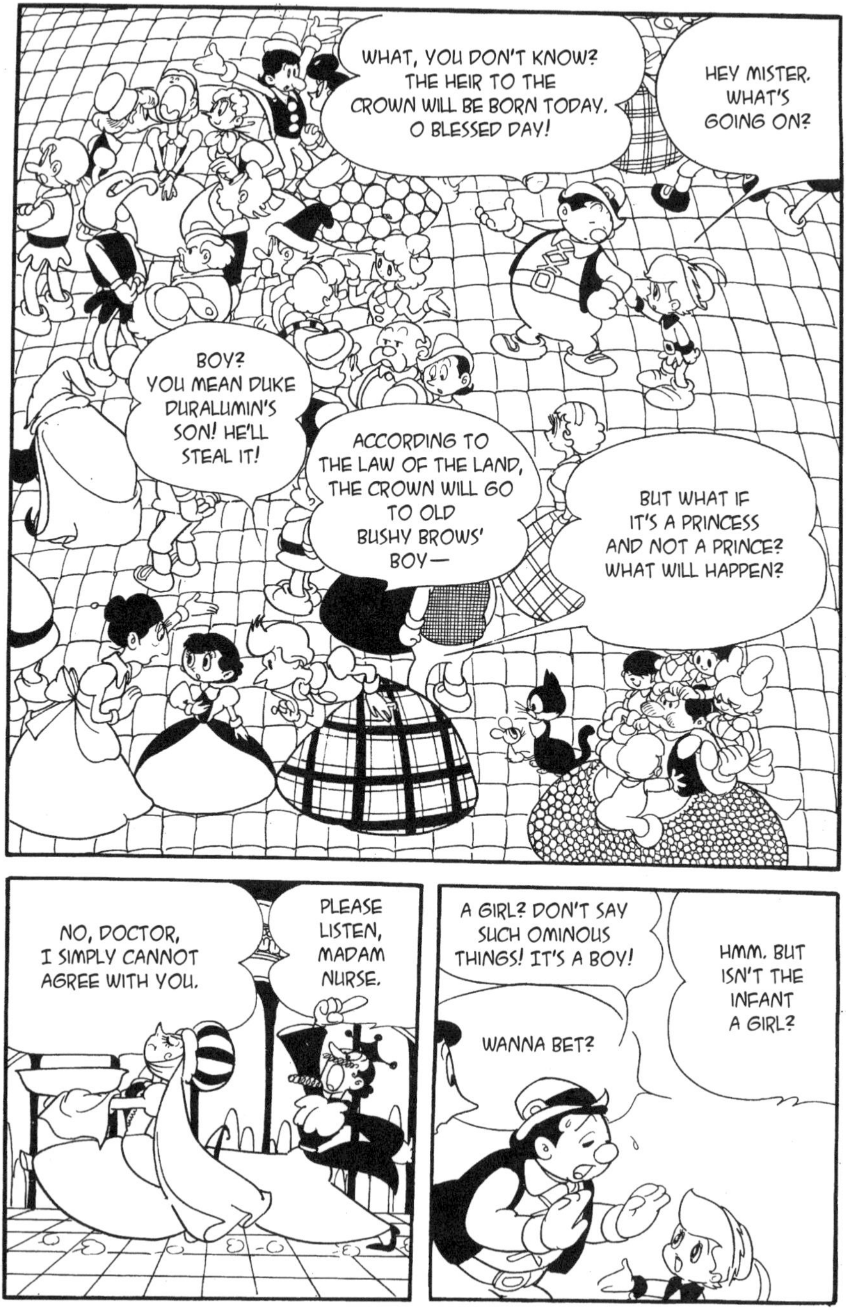
HEY MISTER. WHAT'S GOING ON?
WHAT, YOU DON'T KNOW? THE HEIR TO THE CROWN WILL BE BORN TODAY. O BLESSED DAY!
ACCORDING TO THE LAW OF THE LAND, THE CROWN WILL GO TO OLD BUSHY BROWS' BOY—
BOY? YOU MEAN DUKE DURALUMIN'S SON! HE'LL STEAL IT!
BUT WHAT IF IT'S A PRINCESS AND NOT A PRINCE? WHAT WILL HAPPEN?
HMM. BUT ISN'T THE INFANT A GIRL?
A GIRL? DON'T SAY SUCH OMINOUS THINGS! IT'S A BOY!
WANNA BET?
PLEASE LISTEN, MADAM NURSE.
NO, DOCTOR, I SIMPLY CANNOT AGREE WITH YOU.

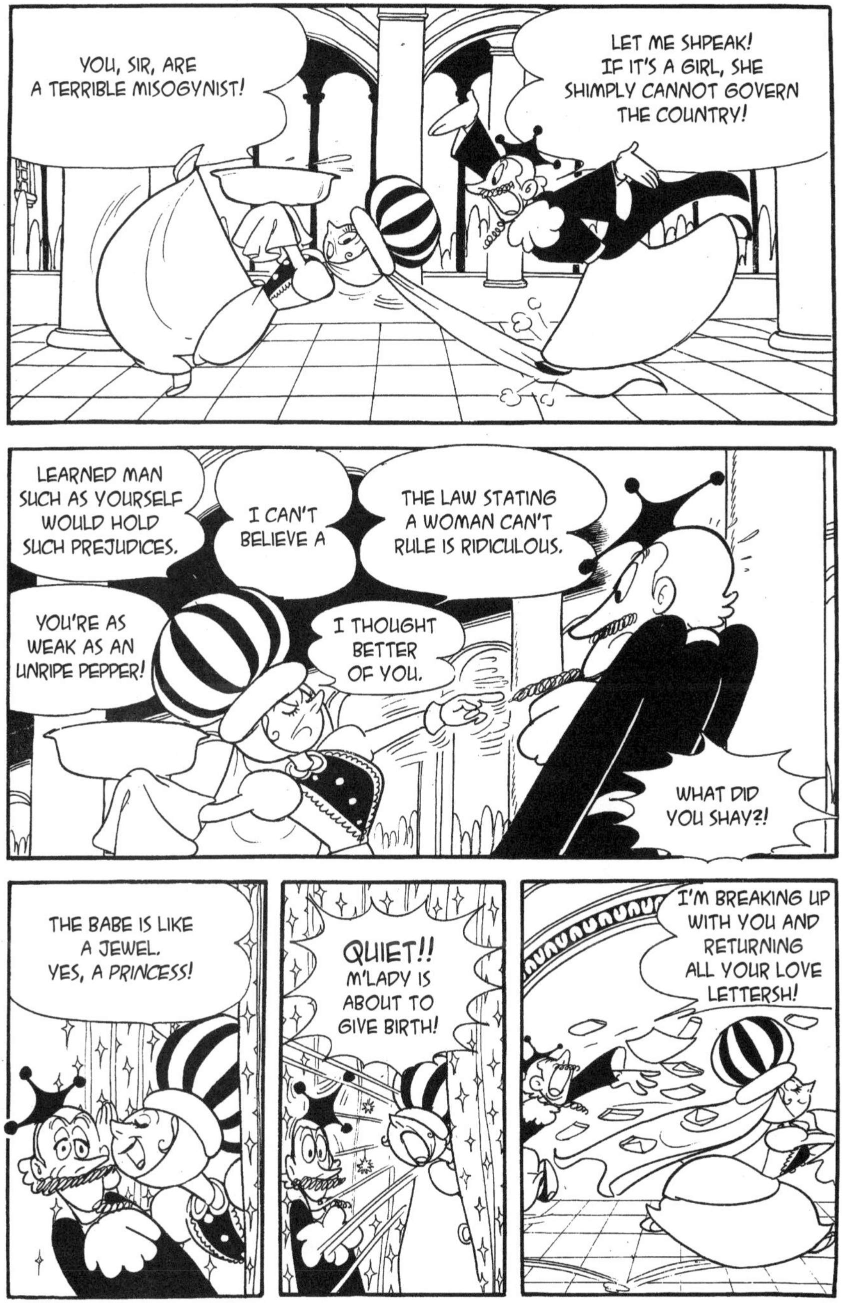
LET ME SHPEAK! IF IT'S A GIRL, SHE SHIMPLY CANNOT GOVERN THE COUNTRY!
YOU, SIR, ARE A TERRIBLE MISOGYNIST!
THE LAW STATING A WOMAN CAN'T RULE IS RIDICULOUS.
I CAN'T BELIEVE A
LEARNED MAN SUCH AS YOURSELF WOULD HOLD SUCH PREJUDICES.
I THOUGHT BETTER OF YOU.
YOU'RE AS WEAK AS AN UNRIPE PEPPER!
WHAT DID YOU SHAY?!
I'M BREAKING UP WITH YOU AND RETURNING ALL YOUR LOVE LETTERSH!
QUIET!! M'LADY IS ABOUT TO GIVE BIRTH!
THE BABE IS LIKE A JEWEL. YES, A *PRINCESS*!

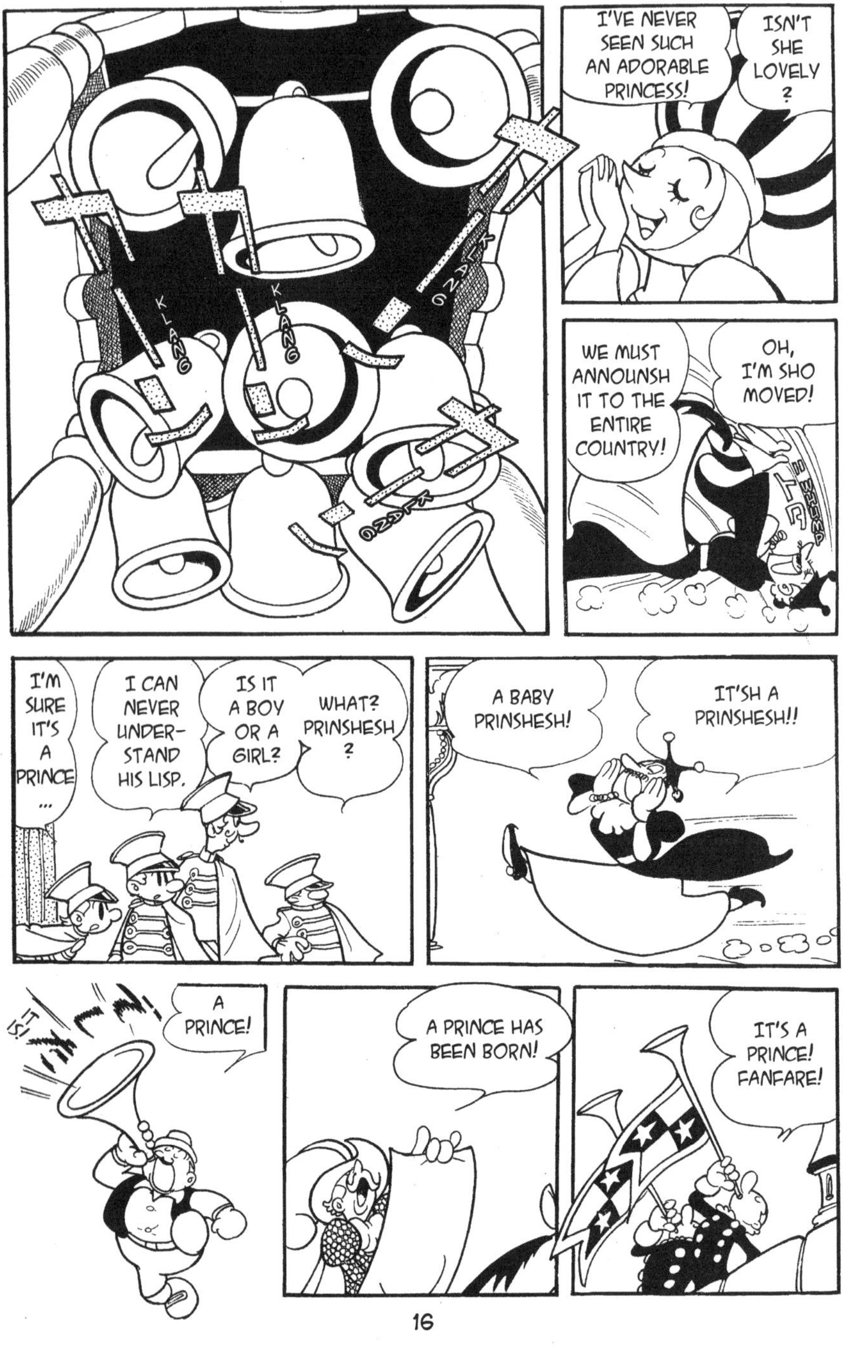
ISN'T SHE LOVELY?
I'VE NEVER SEEN SUCH AN ADORABLE PRINCESS!
OH, I'M SHO MOVED!
WE MUST ANNOUNSH IT TO THE ENTIRE COUNTRY!
KLANG
KLANG
KLANG
KLANG
IT'SH A PRINSHESH!!
A BABY PRINSHESH!
WHAT? PRINSHESH?
IS IT A BOY OR A GIRL?
I CAN NEVER UNDERSTAND HIS LISP.
I'M SURE IT'S A PRINCE...
IT'S A PRINCE! FANFARE!
A PRINCE HAS BEEN BORN!
A PRINCE!
IT'S!

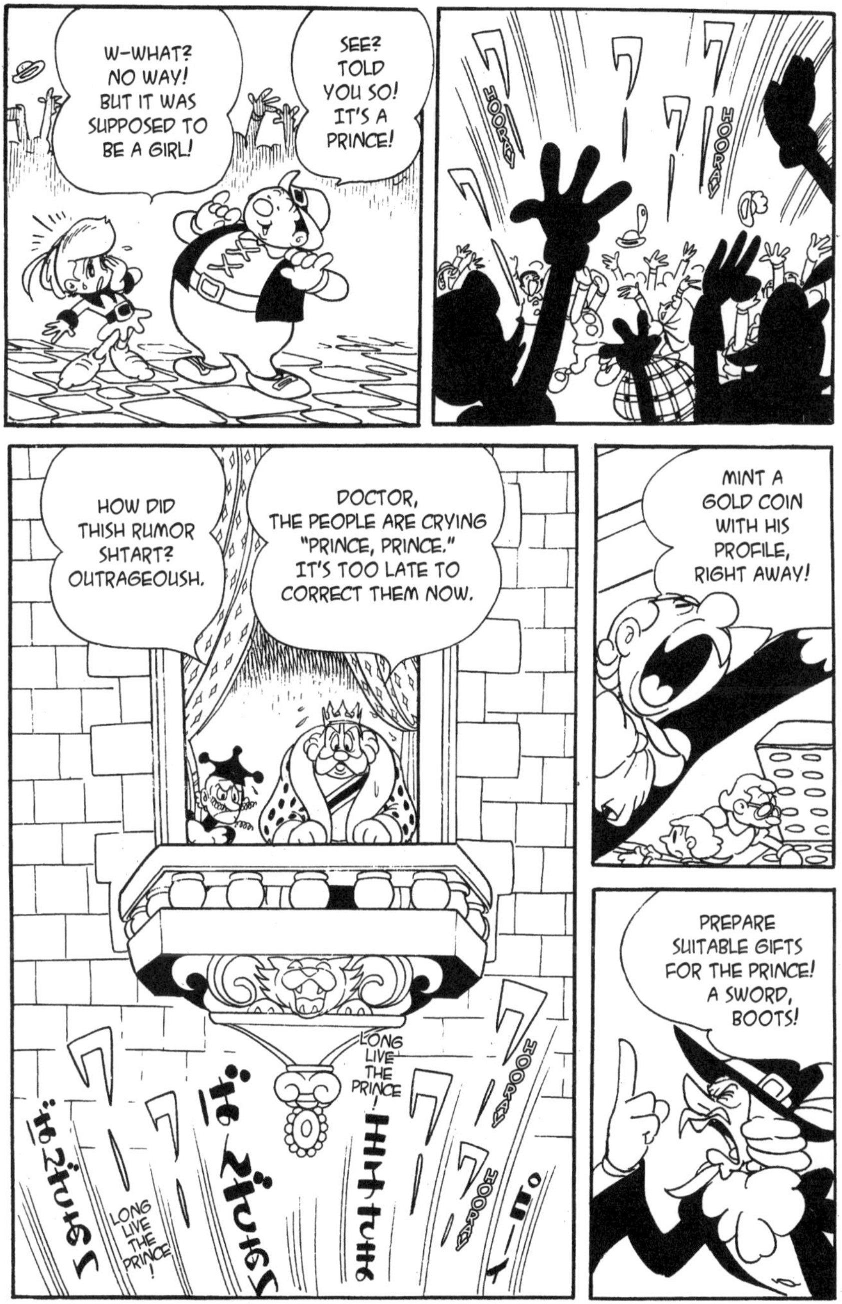
HOORAY
HOORAY
SEE? TOLD YOU SO! IT'S A PRINCE!
W-WHAT? NO WAY! BUT IT WAS SUPPOSED TO BE A GIRL!
MINT A GOLD COIN WITH HIS PROFILE, RIGHT AWAY!
PREPARE SUITABLE GIFTS FOR THE PRINCE! A SWORD, BOOTS!
DOCTOR, THE PEOPLE ARE CRYING "PRINCE, PRINCE." IT'S TOO LATE TO CORRECT THEM NOW.
HOW DID THISH RUMOR SHTART? OUTRAGEOUSH.
HOORAY
LONG LIVE THE PRINCE!
HOORAY
LONG LIVE THE PRINCE!

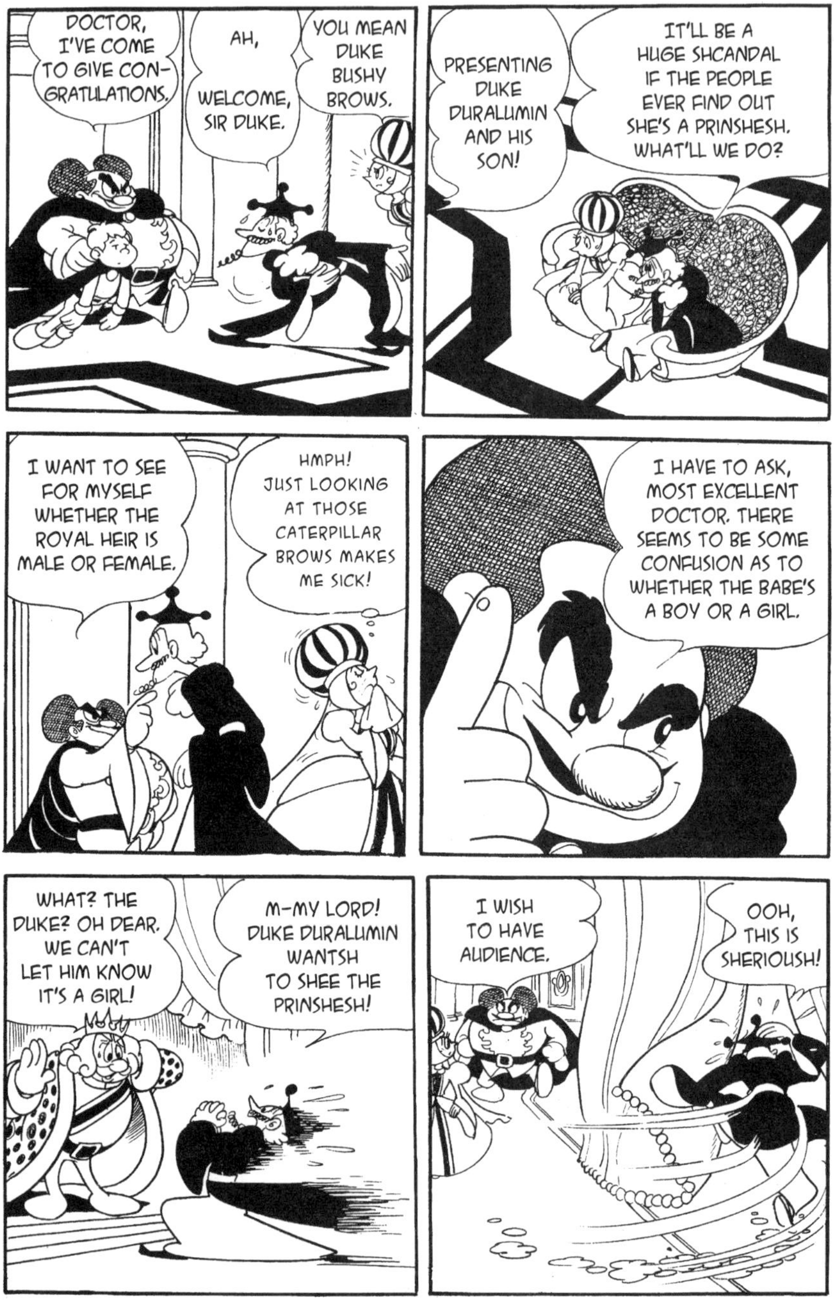

IT'LL BE A HUGE SHCANDAL IF THE PEOPLE EVER FIND OUT SHE'S A PRINSHESH. WHAT'LL WE DO?
PRESENTING DUKE DURALUMIN AND HIS SON!
YOU MEAN DUKE BUSHY BROWS.
AH, WELCOME, SIR DUKE.
DOCTOR, I'VE COME TO GIVE CON-GRATULATIONS.
I HAVE TO ASK, MOST EXCELLENT DOCTOR. THERE SEEMS TO BE SOME CONFUSION AS TO WHETHER THE BABE'S A BOY OR A GIRL.
HMPH! JUST LOOKING AT THOSE CATERPILLAR BROWS MAKES ME SICK!
I WANT TO SEE FOR MYSELF WHETHER THE ROYAL HEIR IS MALE OR FEMALE.
OOH, THIS IS SHERIOUSH!
I WISH TO HAVE AUDIENCE.
M-MY LORD! DUKE DURALUMIN WANTSH TO SHEE THE PRINSHESH!
WHAT? THE DUKE? OH DEAR. WE CAN'T LET HIM KNOW IT'S A GIRL!

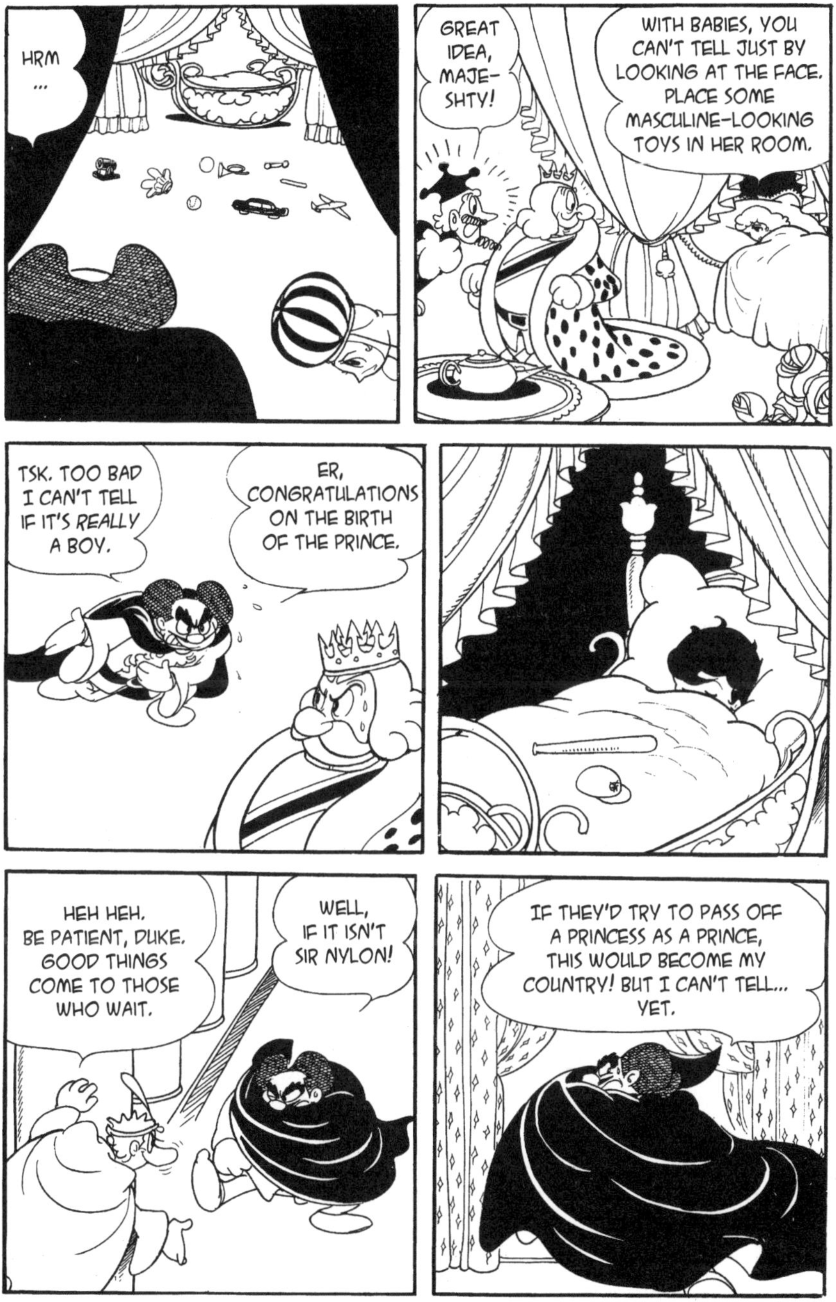
WITH BABIES, YOU CAN'T TELL JUST BY LOOKING AT THE FACE. PLACE SOME MASCULINE-LOOKING TOYS IN HER ROOM.
GREAT IDEA, MAJE-SHTY!
HRM ...
ER, CONGRATULATIONS ON THE BIRTH OF THE PRINCE.
TSK. TOO BAD I CAN'T TELL IF IT'S *REALLY* A BOY.
IF THEY'D TRY TO PASS OFF A PRINCESS AS A PRINCE, THIS WOULD BECOME MY COUNTRY! BUT I CAN'T TELL... YET.
WELL, IF IT ISN'T SIR NYLON!
HEH HEH. BE PATIENT, DUKE. GOOD THINGS COME TO THOSE WHO WAIT.

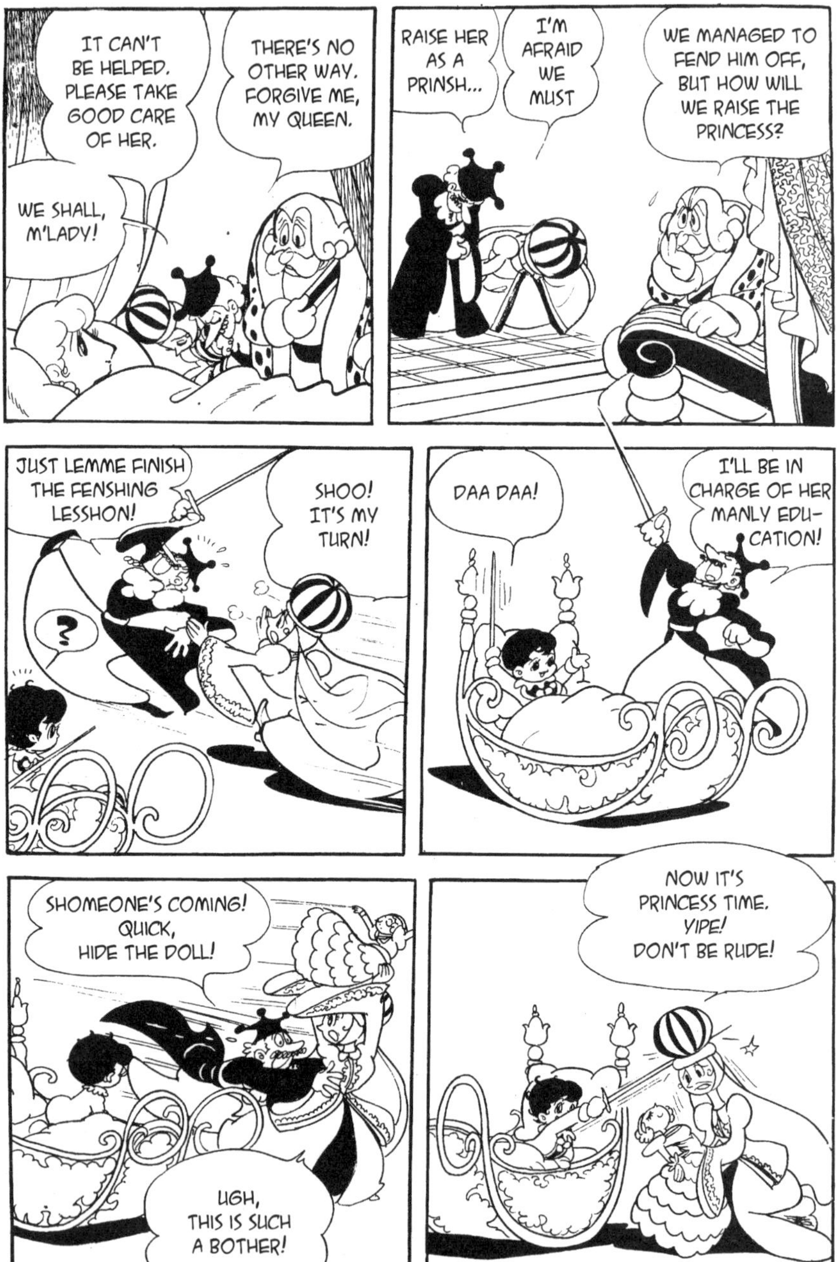
WE MANAGED TO FEND HIM OFF, BUT HOW WILL WE RAISE THE PRINCESS?
I'M AFRAID WE MUST
RAISE HER AS A PRINSH...
THERE'S NO OTHER WAY. FORGIVE ME, MY QUEEN.
IT CAN'T BE HELPED. PLEASE TAKE GOOD CARE OF HER.
WE SHALL, M'LADY!
I'LL BE IN CHARGE OF HER MANLY EDUCATION!
DAA DAA!
SHOO! IT'S MY TURN!
JUST LEMME FINISH THE FENSHING LESSHON!
?
NOW IT'S PRINCESS TIME. YIPE! DON'T BE RUDE!
SHOMEONE'S COMING! QUICK, HIDE THE DOLL!
UGH, THIS IS SUCH A BOTHER!

Chapter 2

Flowers and Parades

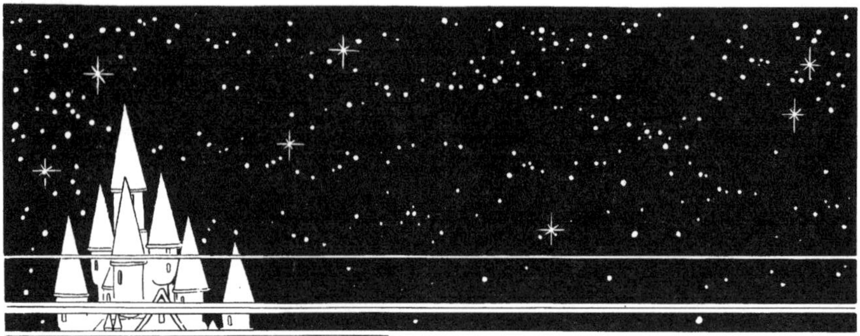

THUS DID
FIFTEEN YEARS
PASS.
THE PRINCE TURNED
FIFTEEN YEARS OLD.
HOWEVER, TINK,
BEING AN ANGEL,
LOOKED
THE SAME AS
THE DAY
HE FELL TO
EARTH.

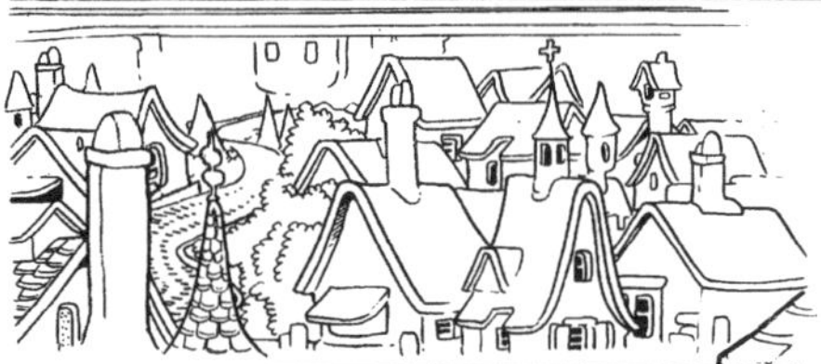

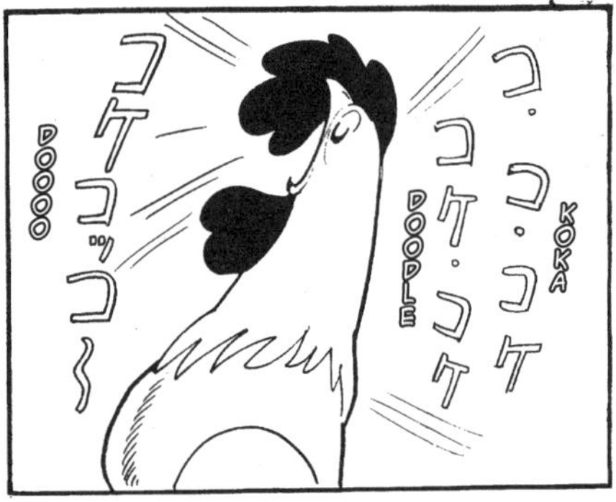
コ・コ・コケ・コケ
KOKA
DOODLE
コケコッコ～
DOOOO

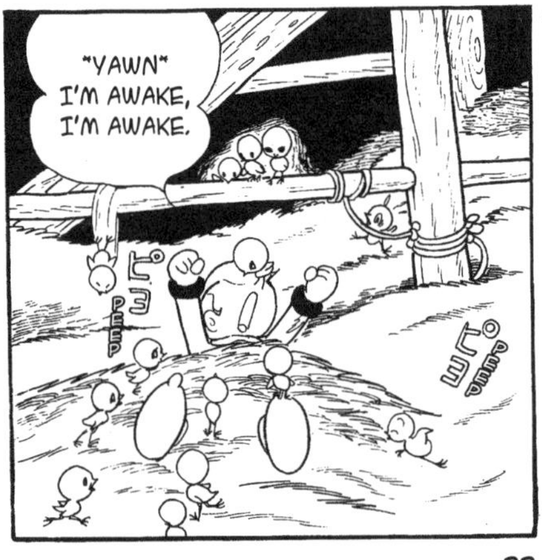
"YAWN" I'M AWAKE, I'M AWAKE.
ピヨ
PEEP
ピヨ
PEEP

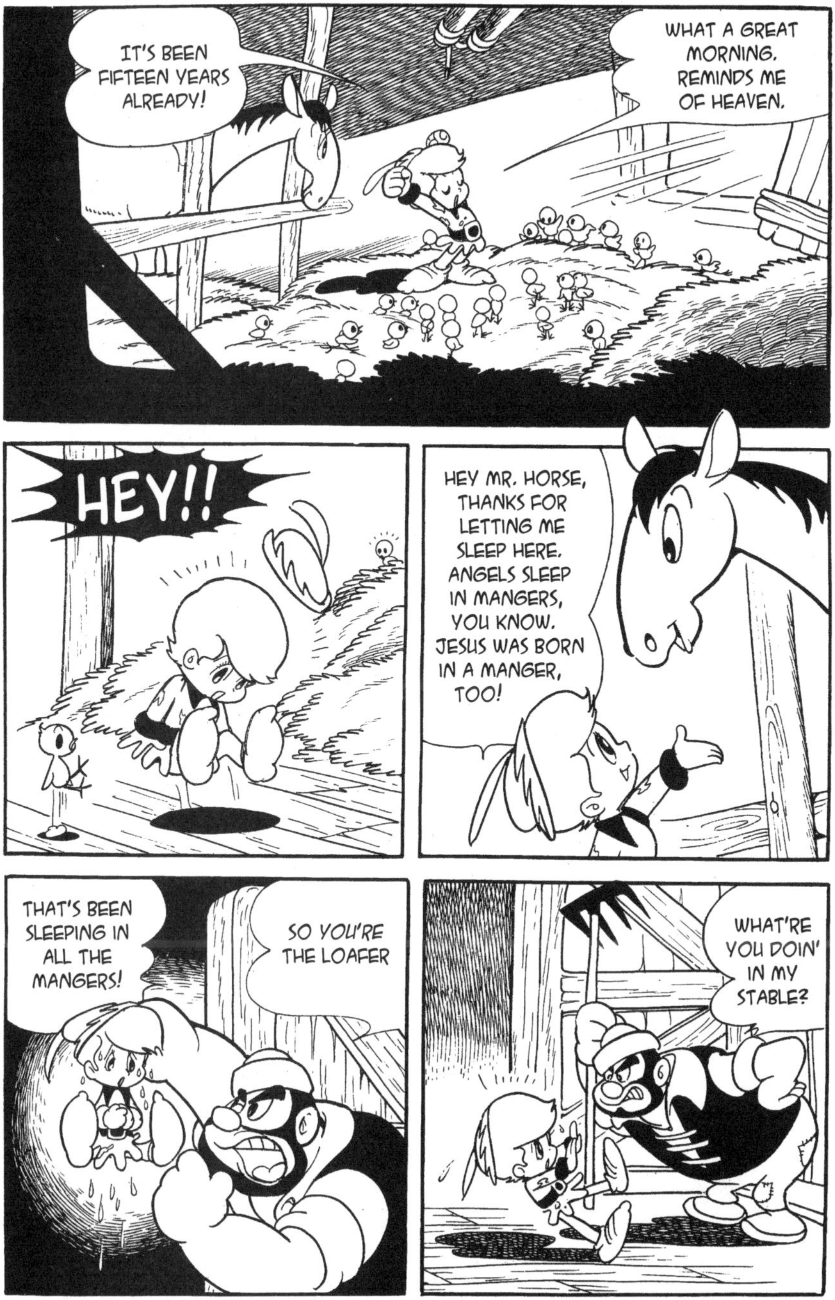
WHAT A GREAT MORNING. REMINDS ME OF HEAVEN.
IT'S BEEN FIFTEEN YEARS ALREADY!
HEY MR. HORSE, THANKS FOR LETTING ME SLEEP HERE. ANGELS SLEEP IN MANGERS, YOU KNOW. JESUS WAS BORN IN A MANGER, TOO!
HEY!!
WHAT'RE YOU DOIN' IN MY STABLE?
SO YOU'RE THE LOAFER
THAT'S BEEN SLEEPING IN ALL THE MANGERS!

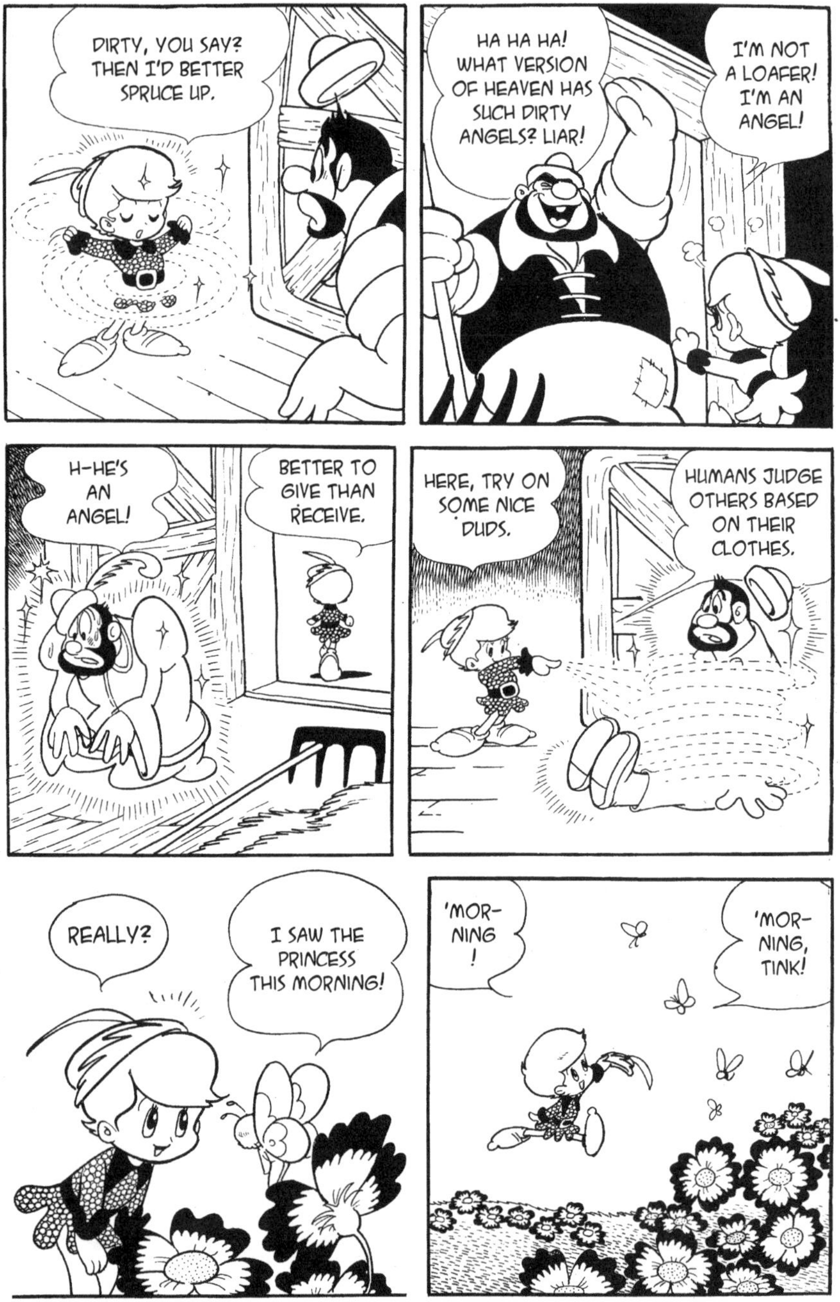
I'M NOT A LOAFER! I'M AN ANGEL!
HA HA HA! WHAT VERSION OF HEAVEN HAS SUCH DIRTY ANGELS? LIAR!
DIRTY, YOU SAY? THEN I'D BETTER SPRUCE UP.
HUMANS JUDGE OTHERS BASED ON THEIR CLOTHES.
HERE, TRY ON SOME NICE DUDS.
BETTER TO GIVE THAN RECEIVE.
H-HE'S AN ANGEL!
'MOR-NING, TINK!
'MOR-NING!
I SAW THE PRINCESS THIS MORNING!
REALLY?

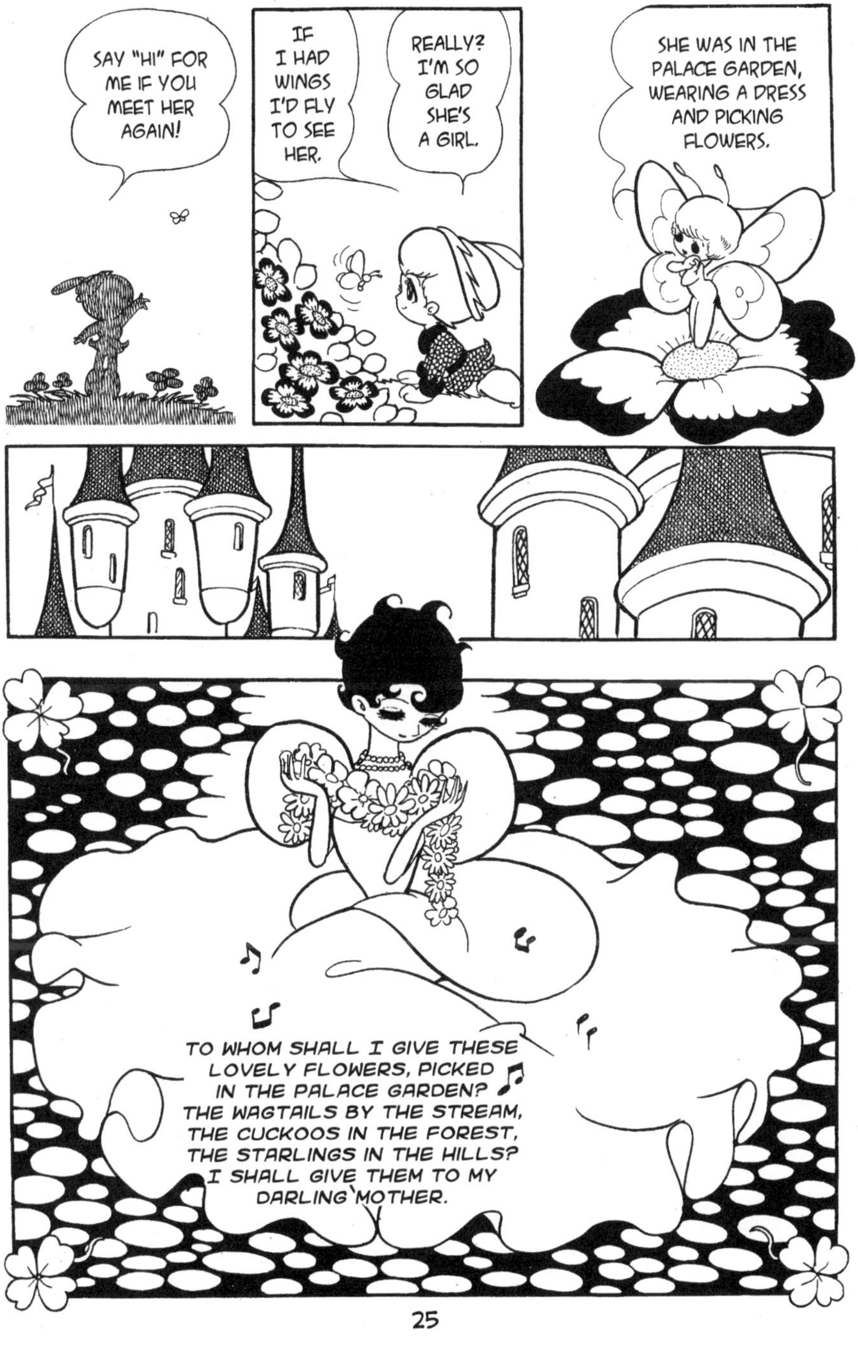
SHE WAS IN THE PALACE GARDEN, WEARING A DRESS AND PICKING FLOWERS.
REALLY? I'M SO GLAD SHE'S A GIRL.
IF I HAD WINGS I'D FLY TO SEE HER.
SAY "HI" FOR ME IF YOU MEET HER AGAIN!
TO WHOM SHALL I GIVE THESE LOVELY FLOWERS, PICKED IN THE PALACE GARDEN? THE WAGTAILS BY THE STREAM, THE CUCKOOS IN THE FOREST, THE STARLINGS IN THE HILLS? I SHALL GIVE THEM TO MY DARLING MOTHER.

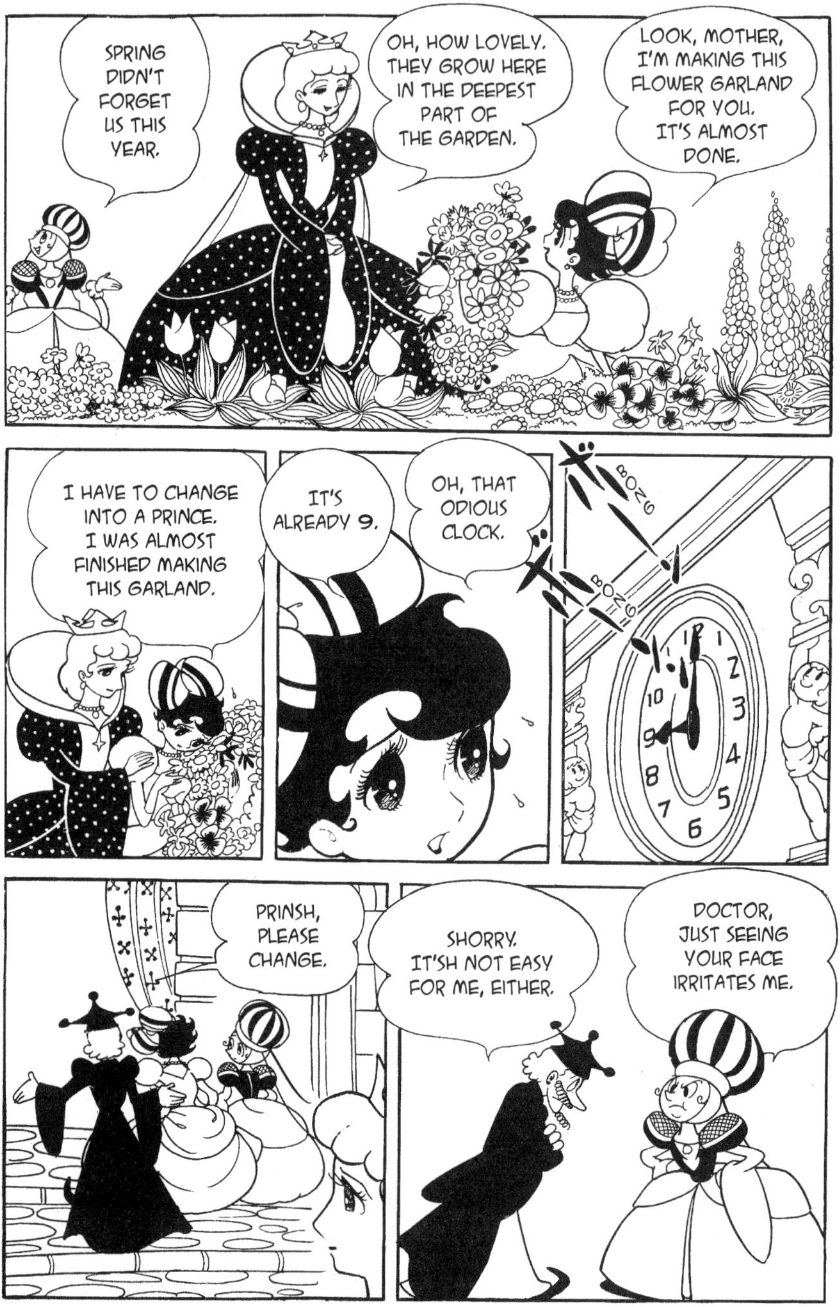

LOOK, MOTHER, I'M MAKING THIS FLOWER GARLAND FOR YOU. IT'S ALMOST DONE.
OH, HOW LOVELY. THEY GROW HERE IN THE DEEPEST PART OF THE GARDEN.
SPRING DIDN'T FORGET US THIS YEAR.
BONG
BONG
OH, THAT ODIOUS CLOCK.
IT'S ALREADY 9.
I HAVE TO CHANGE INTO A PRINCE. I WAS ALMOST FINISHED MAKING THIS GARLAND.
DOCTOR, JUST SEEING YOUR FACE IRRITATES ME.
SHORRY. IT'SH NOT EASY FOR ME, EITHER.
PRINSH, PLEASE CHANGE.

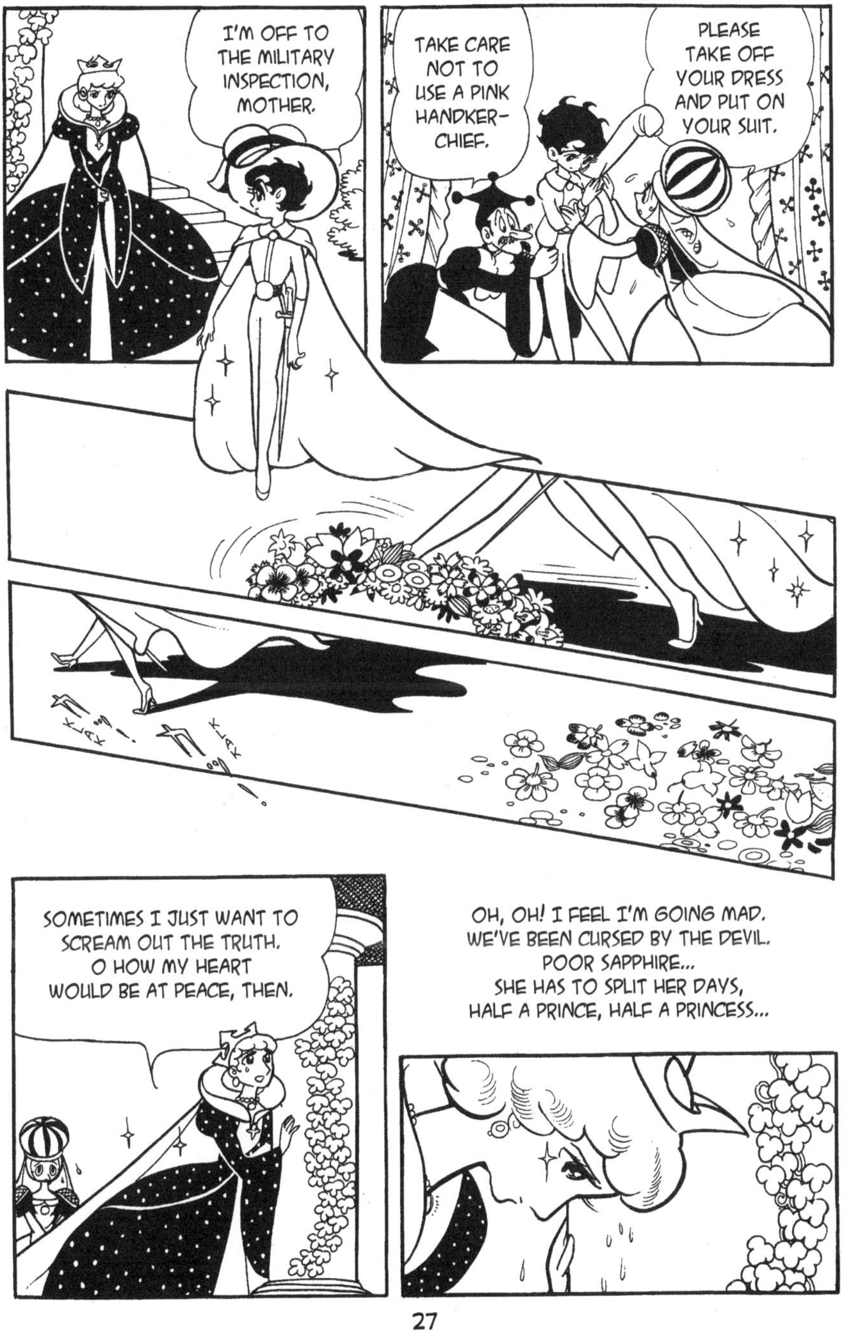

PLEASE TAKE OFF YOUR DRESS AND PUT ON YOUR SUIT.
TAKE CARE NOT TO USE A PINK HANDKER-CHIEF.
I'M OFF TO THE MILITARY INSPECTION, MOTHER.
OH, OH! I FEEL I'M GOING MAD. WE'VE BEEN CURSED BY THE DEVIL. POOR SAPPHIRE... SHE HAS TO SPLIT HER DAYS, HALF A PRINCE, HALF A PRINCESS...
SOMETIMES I JUST WANT TO SCREAM OUT THE TRUTH. O HOW MY HEART WOULD BE AT PEACE, THEN.

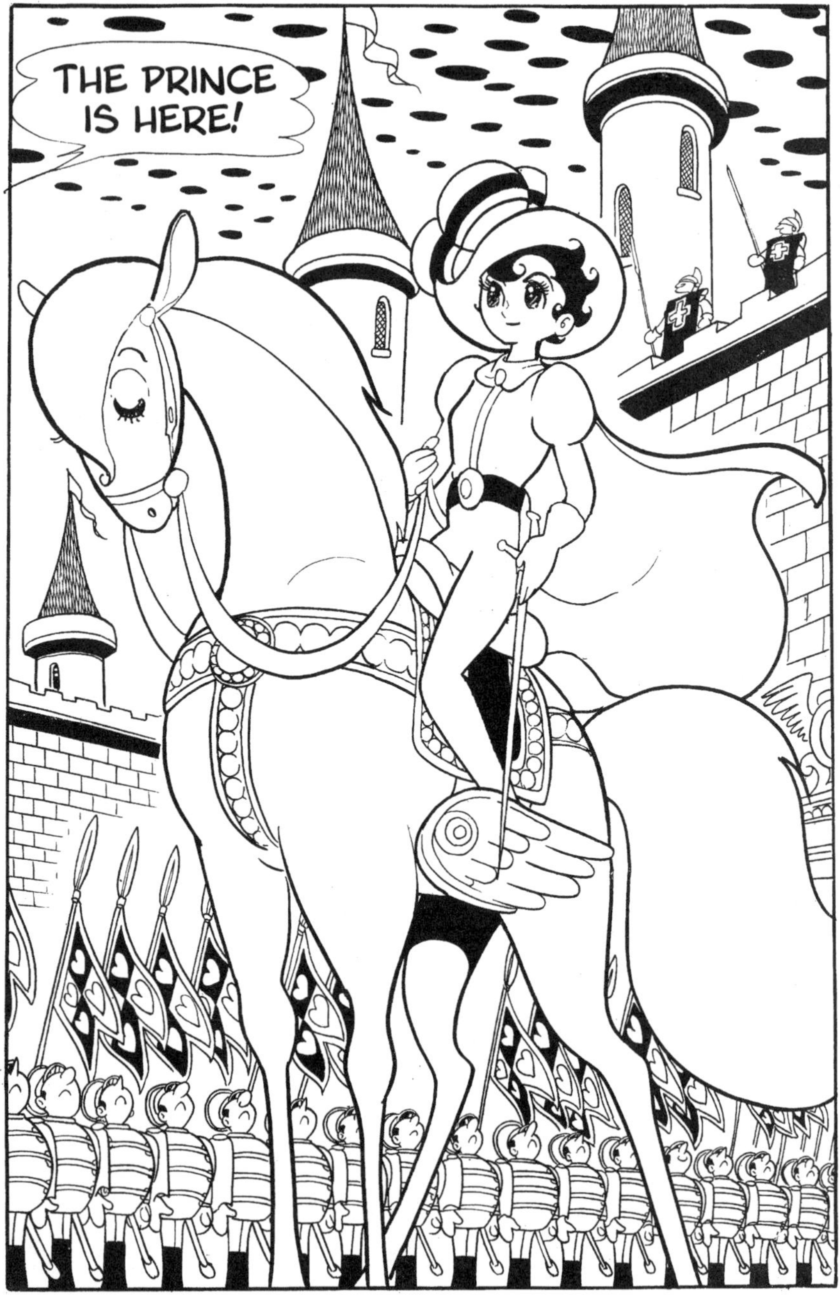
THE PRINCE IS HERE!

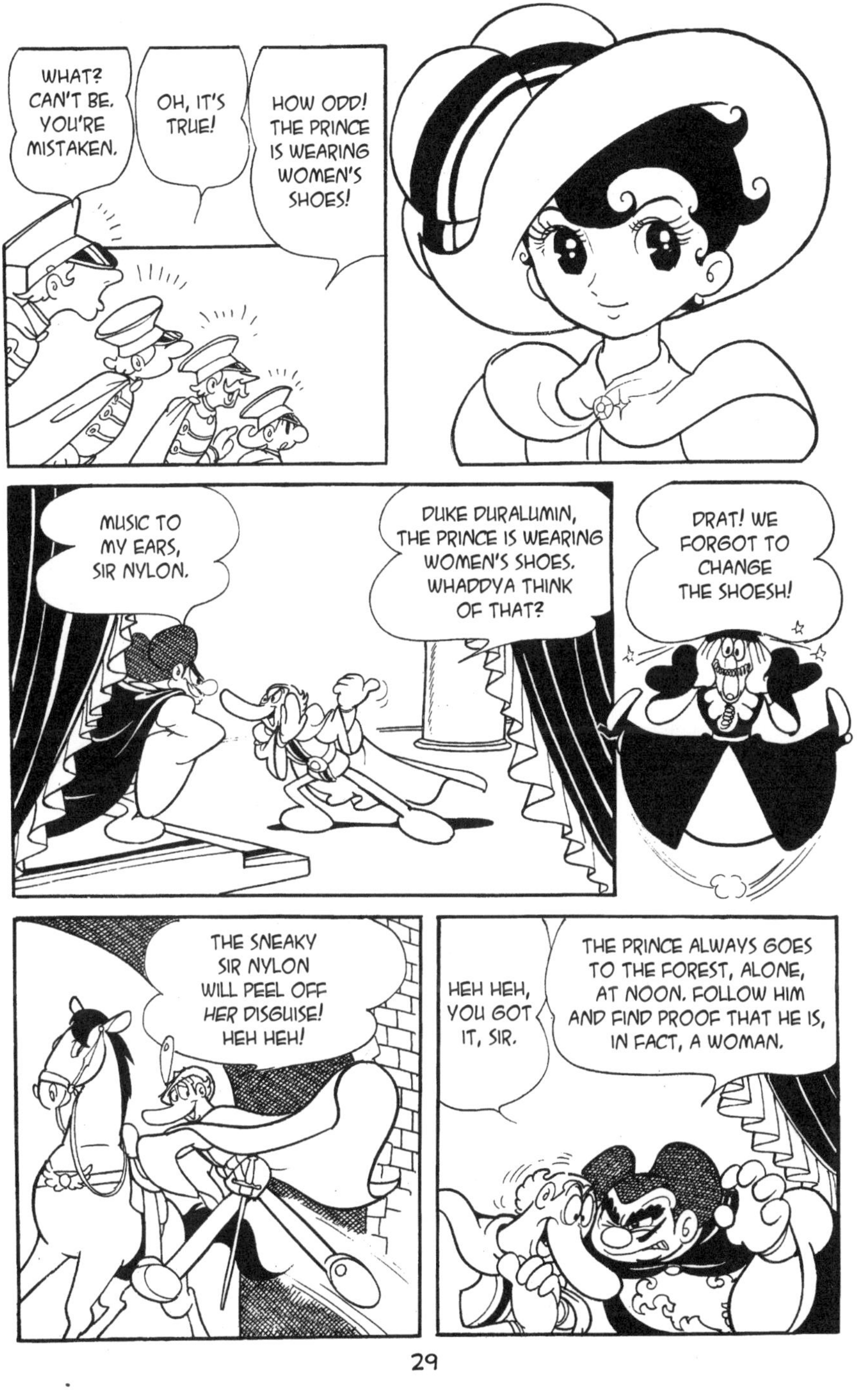
HOW ODD! THE PRINCE IS WEARING WOMEN'S SHOES!
OH, IT'S TRUE!
WHAT? CAN'T BE. YOU'RE MISTAKEN.
DRAT! WE FORGOT TO CHANGE THE SHOESH!
DUKE DURALUMIN, THE PRINCE IS WEARING WOMEN'S SHOES. WHADDYA THINK OF THAT?
MUSIC TO MY EARS, SIR NYLON.
THE PRINCE ALWAYS GOES TO THE FOREST, ALONE, AT NOON. FOLLOW HIM AND FIND PROOF THAT HE IS, IN FACT, A WOMAN.
HEH HEH, YOU GOT IT, SIR.
THE SNEAKY SIR NYLON WILL PEEL OFF HER DISGUISE! HEH HEH!

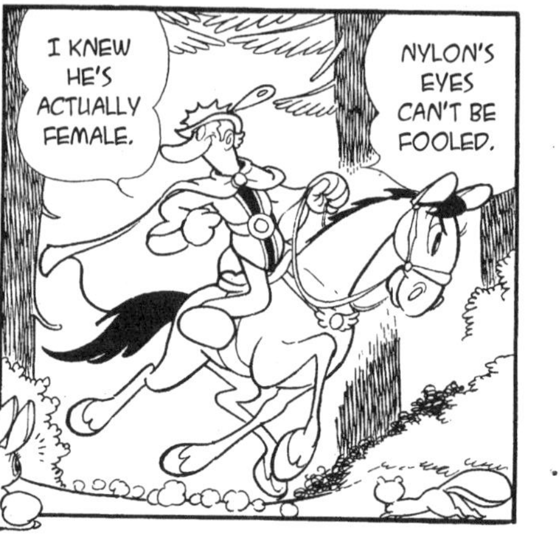
NYLON'S EYES CAN'T BE FOOLED.
I KNEW HE'S ACTUALLY FEMALE.
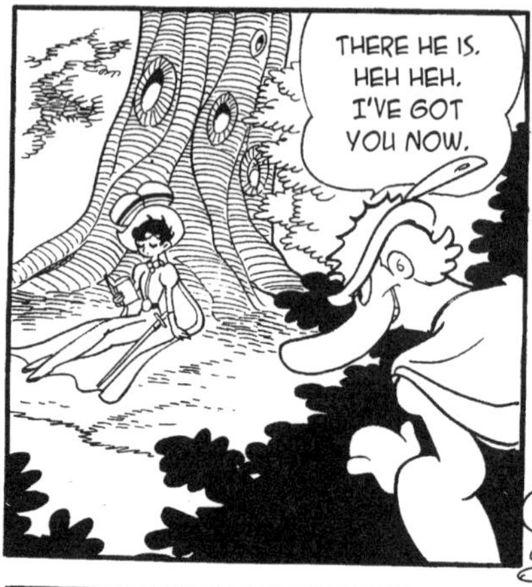
THERE HE IS. HEH HEH. I'VE GOT YOU NOW.
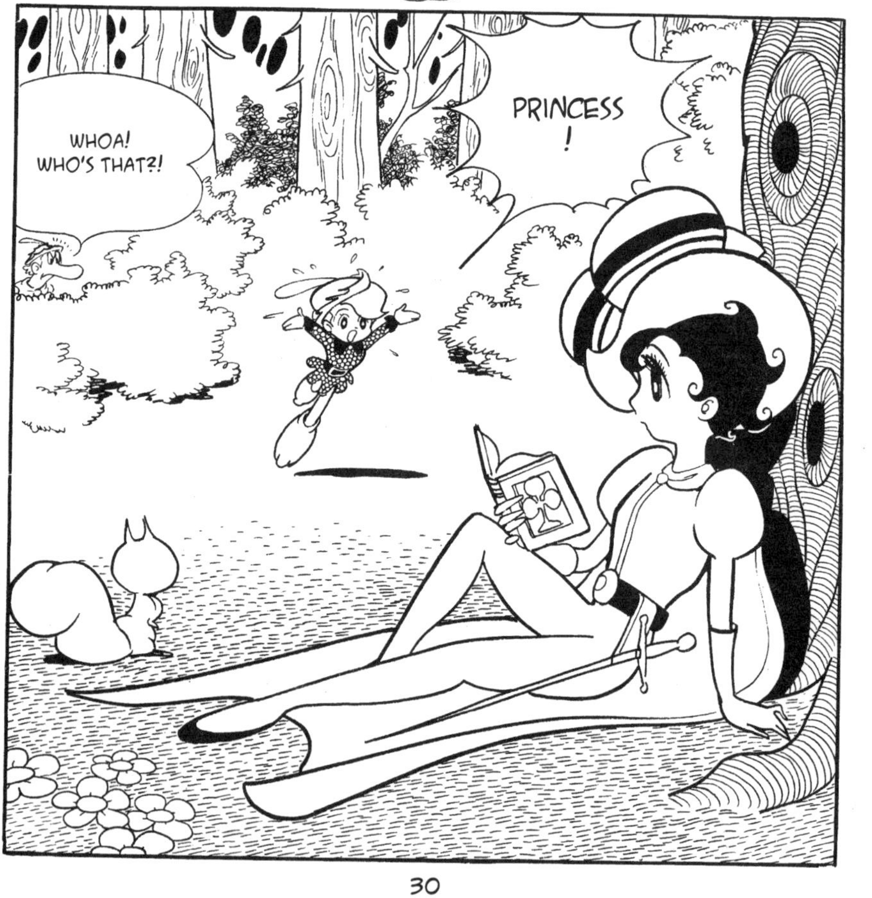
PRINCESS !
WHOA! WHO'S THAT?!

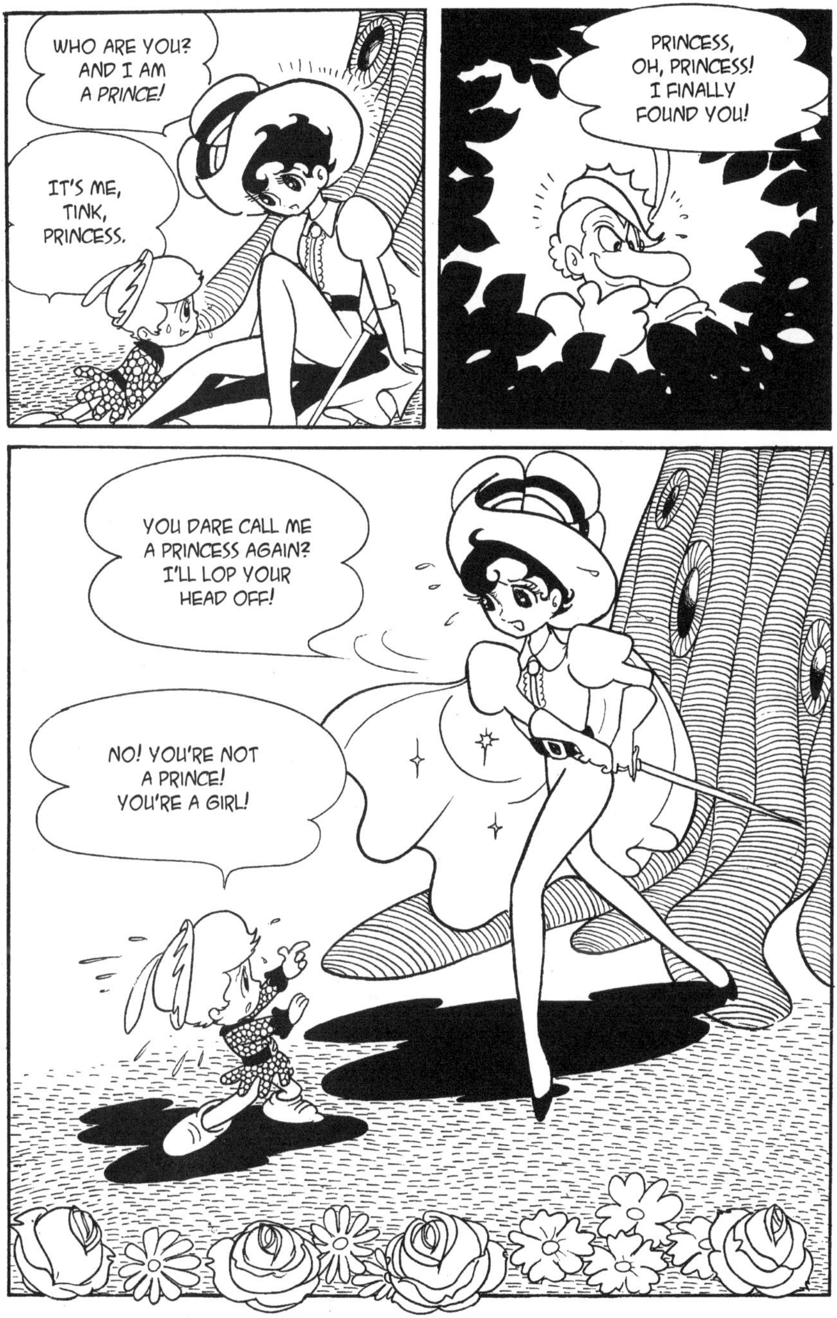
PRINCESS, OH, PRINCESS! I FINALLY FOUND YOU!
WHO ARE YOU? AND I AM A PRINCE!
IT'S ME, TINK, PRINCESS.
YOU DARE CALL ME A PRINCESS AGAIN? I'LL LOP YOUR HEAD OFF!
NO! YOU'RE NOT A PRINCE! YOU'RE A GIRL!

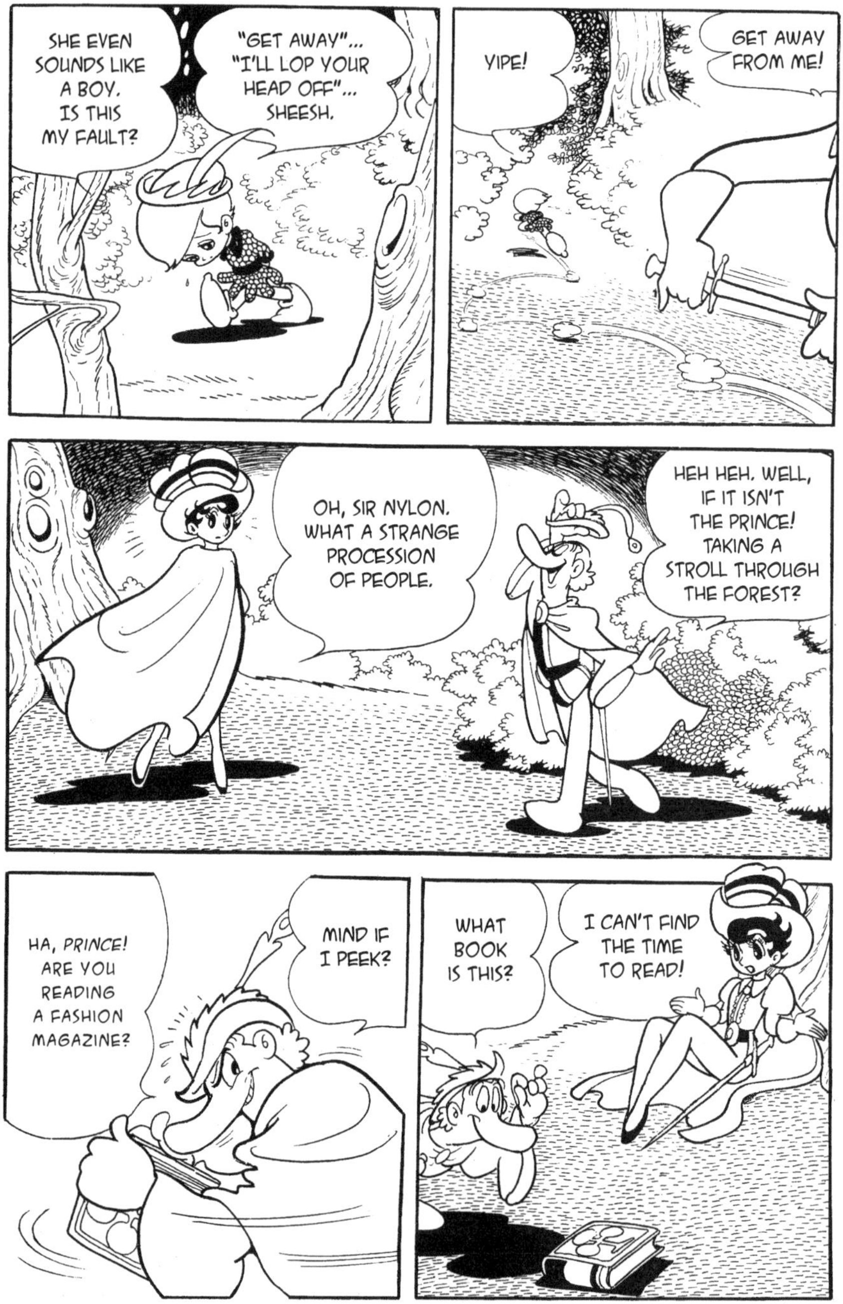
GET AWAY FROM ME!
YIPE!
"GET AWAY"... "I'LL LOP YOUR HEAD OFF"... SHEESH.
SHE EVEN SOUNDS LIKE A BOY. IS THIS MY FAULT?
HEH HEH. WELL, IF IT ISN'T THE PRINCE! TAKING A STROLL THROUGH THE FOREST?
OH, SIR NYLON. WHAT A STRANGE PROCESSION OF PEOPLE.
I CAN'T FIND THE TIME TO READ!
WHAT BOOK IS THIS?
MIND IF I PEEK?
HA, *PRINCE!* ARE YOU READING A FASHION MAGAZINE?

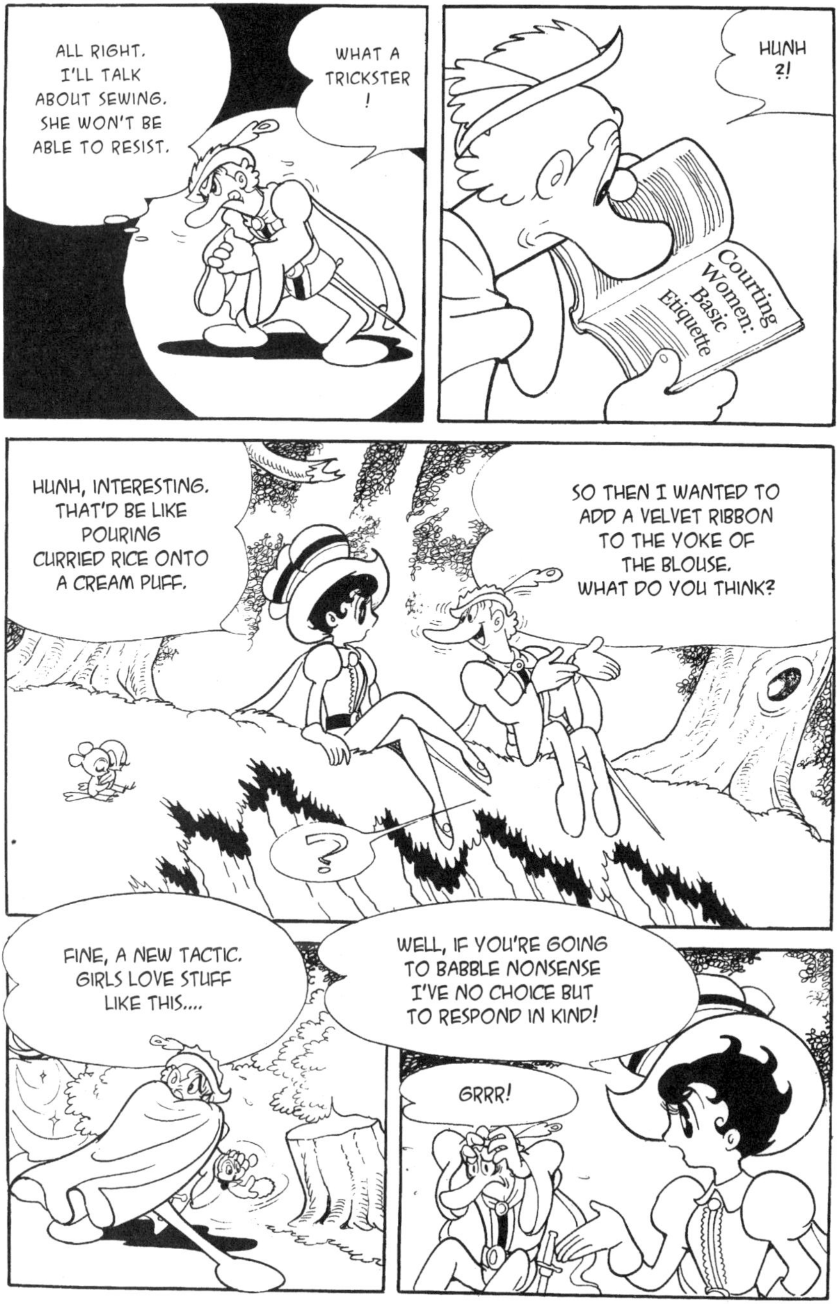
HUNH ?!
Courting Women: Basic Etiquette
WHAT A TRICKSTER !
ALL RIGHT. I'LL TALK ABOUT SEWING. SHE WON'T BE ABLE TO RESIST.
SO THEN I WANTED TO ADD A VELVET RIBBON TO THE YOKE OF THE BLOUSE. WHAT DO YOU THINK?
HUNH, INTERESTING. THAT'D BE LIKE POURING CURRIED RICE ONTO A CREAM PUFF.
?
WELL, IF YOU'RE GOING TO BABBLE NONSENSE I'VE NO CHOICE BUT TO RESPOND IN KIND!
GRRR!
FINE, A NEW TACTIC. GIRLS LOVE STUFF LIKE THIS....

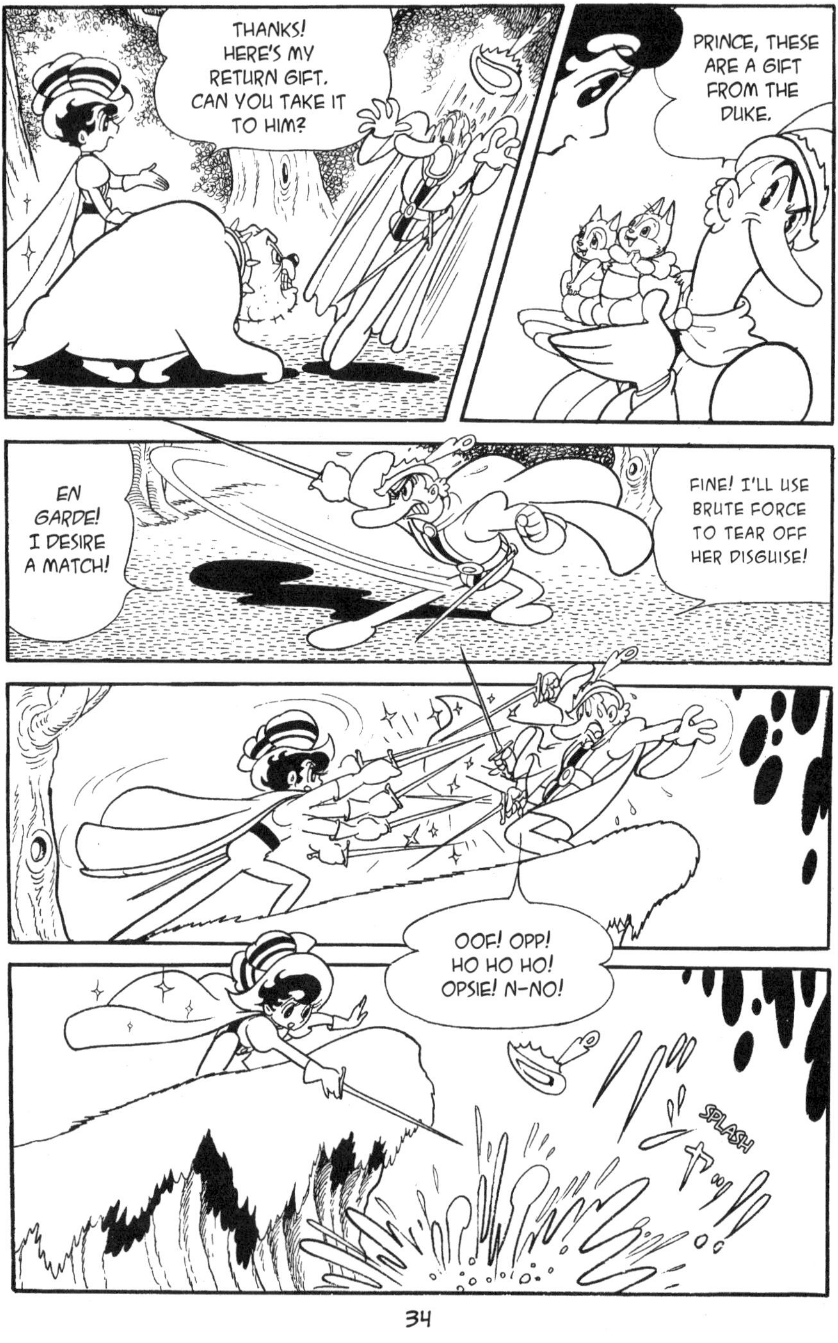
PRINCE, THESE ARE A GIFT FROM THE DUKE.
THANKS! HERE'S MY RETURN GIFT. CAN YOU TAKE IT TO HIM?
FINE! I'LL USE BRUTE FORCE TO TEAR OFF HER DISGUISE!
EN GARDE! I DESIRE A MATCH!
OOF! OPP! HO HO HO! OPSIE! N-NO!
SPLASH

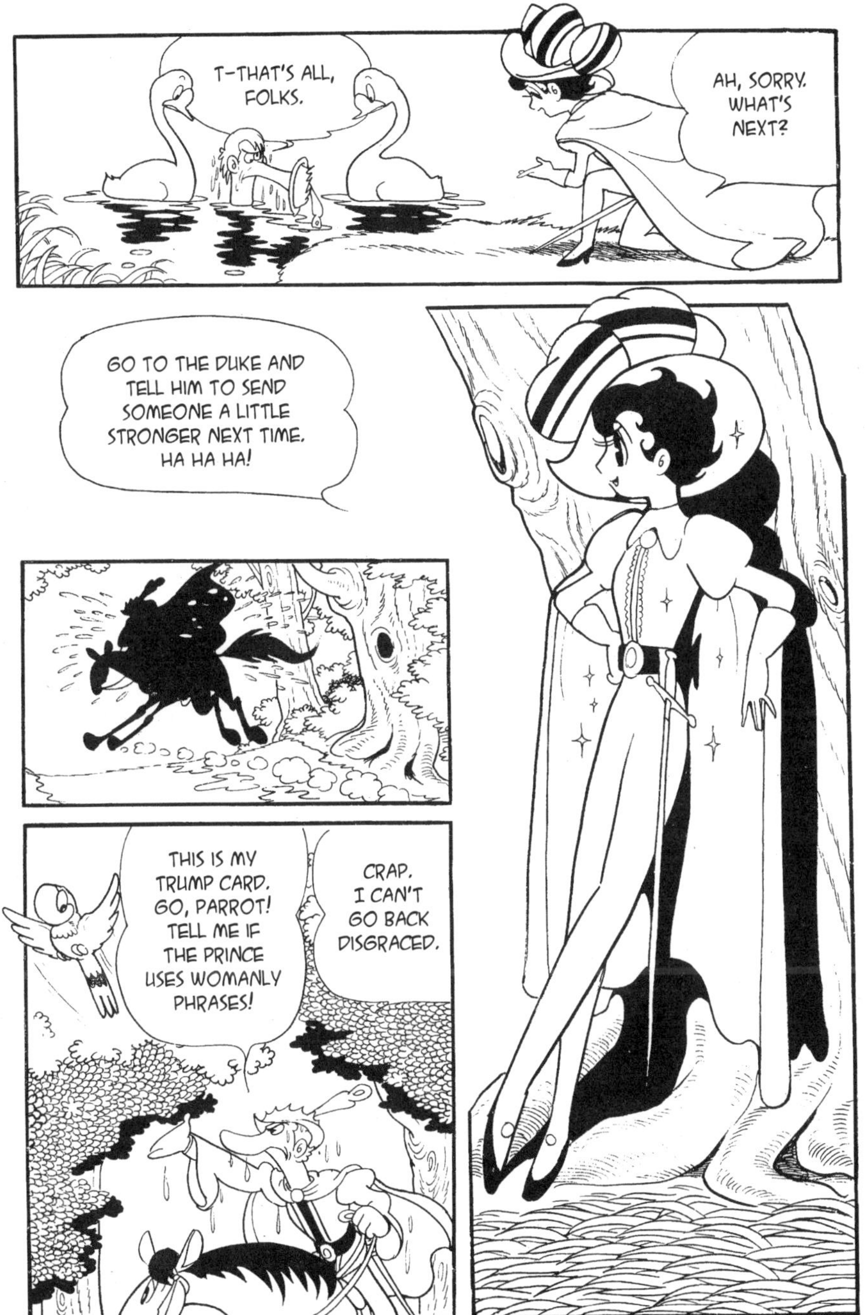
AH, SORRY. WHAT'S NEXT?
T-THAT'S ALL, FOLKS.
GO TO THE DUKE AND TELL HIM TO SEND SOMEONE A LITTLE STRONGER NEXT TIME. HA HA HA!
CRAP. I CAN'T GO BACK DISGRACED.
THIS IS MY TRUMP CARD. GO, PARROT! TELL ME IF THE PRINCE USES WOMANLY PHRASES!

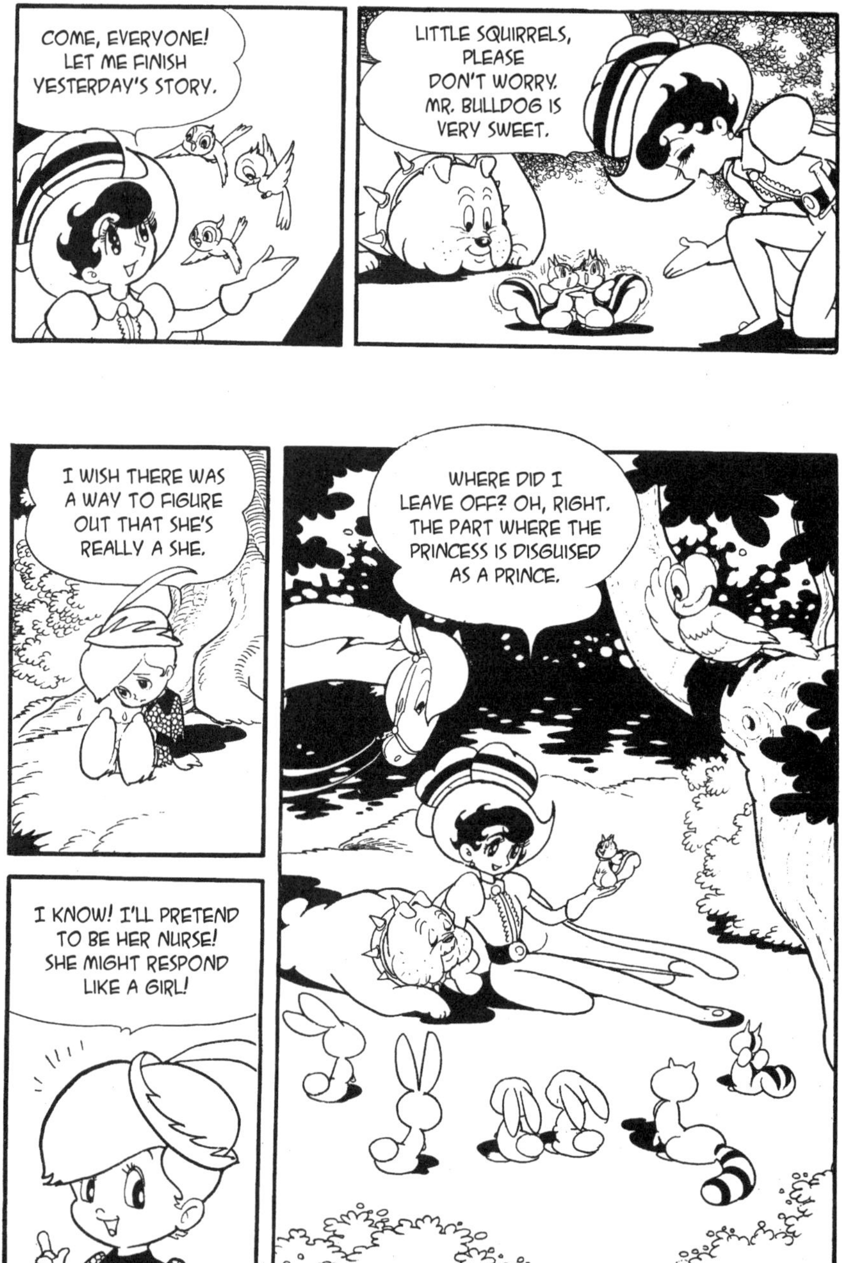
LITTLE SQUIRRELS, PLEASE DON'T WORRY. MR. BULLDOG IS VERY SWEET.
COME, EVERYONE! LET ME FINISH YESTERDAY'S STORY.
WHERE DID I LEAVE OFF? OH, RIGHT. THE PART WHERE THE PRINCESS IS DISGUISED AS A PRINCE.
I WISH THERE WAS A WAY TO FIGURE OUT THAT SHE'S REALLY A SHE.
I KNOW! I'LL PRETEND TO BE HER NURSE! SHE MIGHT RESPOND LIKE A GIRL!

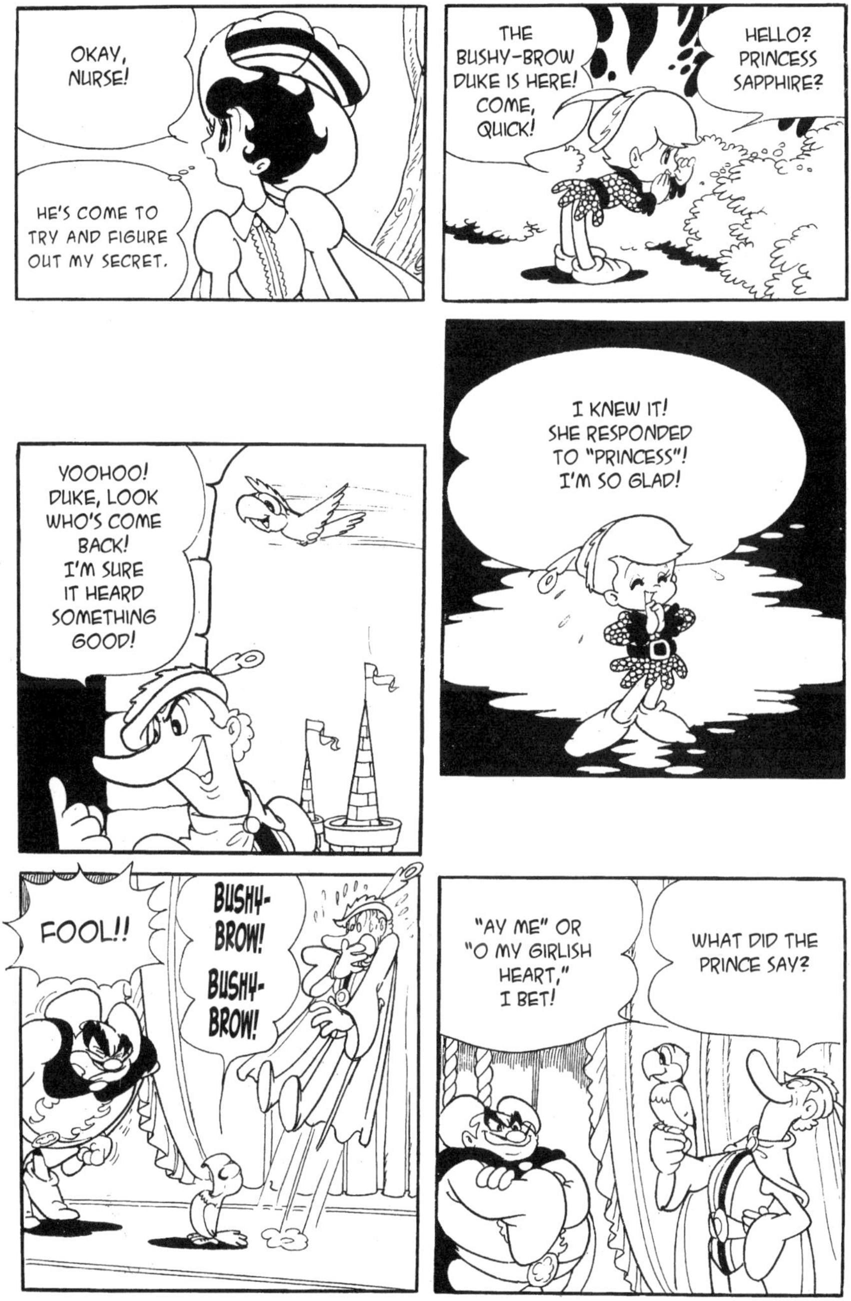
HELLO? PRINCESS SAPPHIRE?
THE BUSHY-BROW DUKE IS HERE! COME, QUICK!
OKAY, NURSE!
HE'S COME TO TRY AND FIGURE OUT MY SECRET.
I KNEW IT! SHE RESPONDED TO "PRINCESS"! I'M SO GLAD!
YOOHOO! DUKE, LOOK WHO'S COME BACK! I'M SURE IT HEARD SOMETHING GOOD!
WHAT DID THE PRINCE SAY?
"AY ME" OR "O MY GIRLISH HEART," I BET!
BUSHY-BROW! BUSHY-BROW!
FOOL!!

Chapter 3

The Carnival

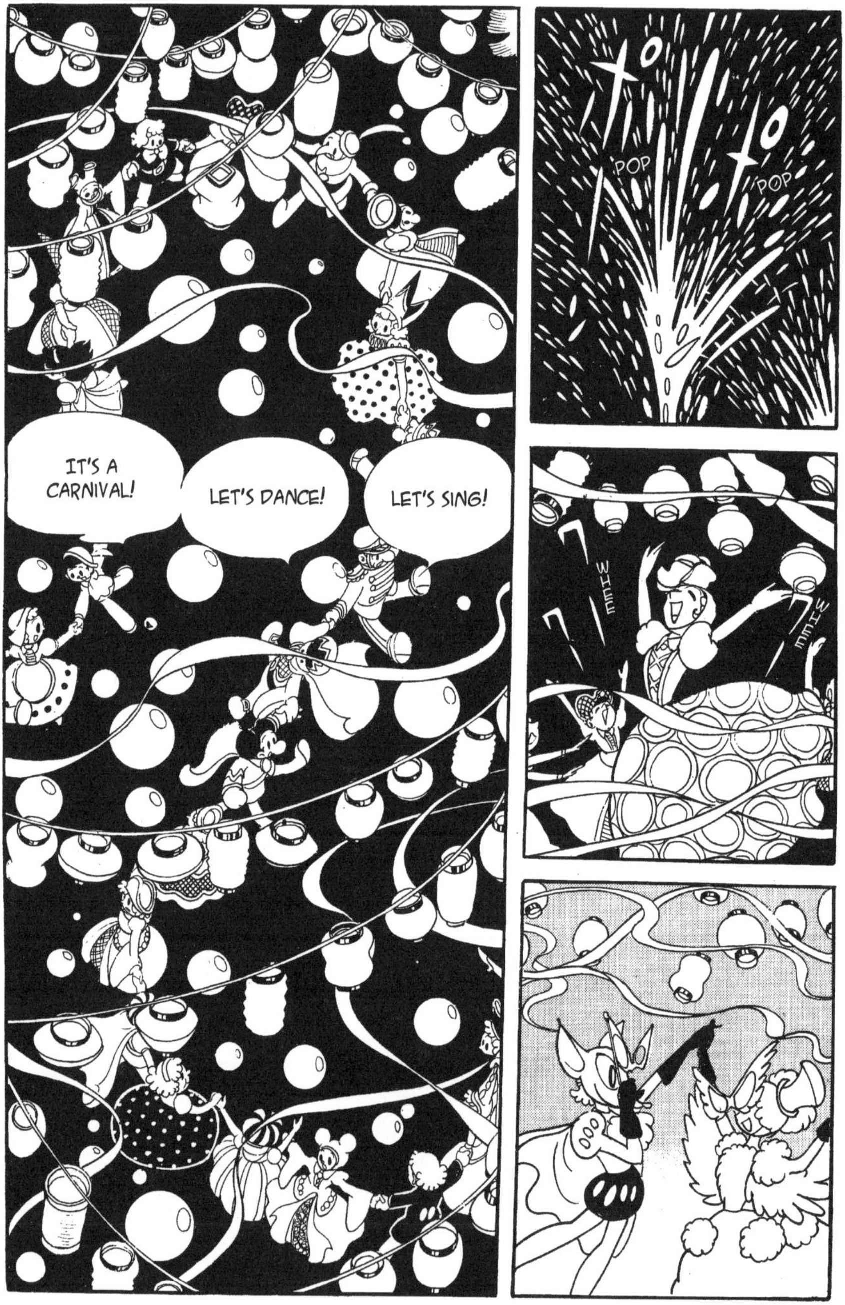
POP
POP
WHEE
WHEE
LET'S SING!
LET'S DANCE!
IT'S A CARNIVAL!

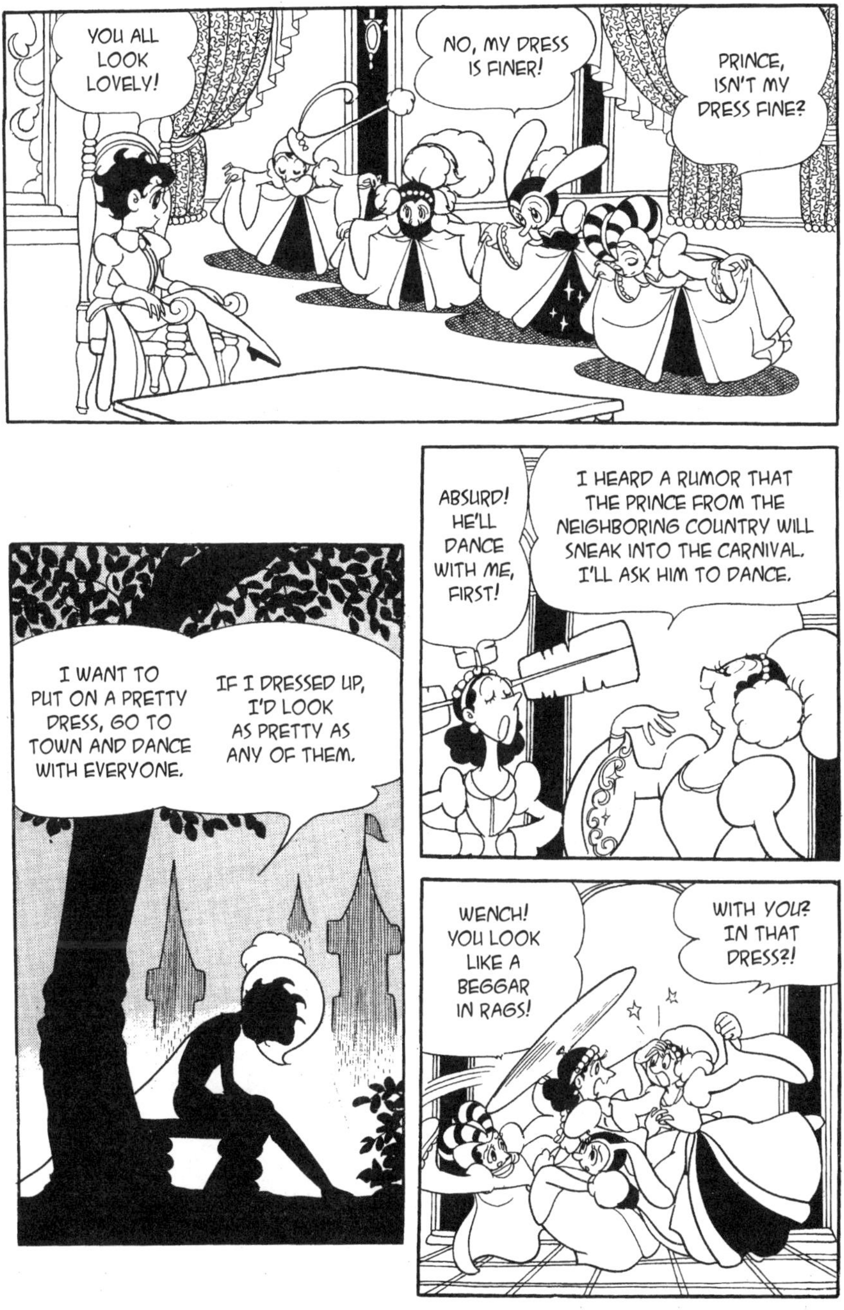
PRINCE, ISN'T MY DRESS FINE?
NO, MY DRESS IS FINER!
YOU ALL LOOK LOVELY!
I HEARD A RUMOR THAT THE PRINCE FROM THE NEIGHBORING COUNTRY WILL SNEAK INTO THE CARNIVAL. I'LL ASK HIM TO DANCE.
ABSURD! HE'LL DANCE WITH ME, FIRST!
WITH YOU? IN THAT DRESS?!
WENCH! YOU LOOK LIKE A BEGGAR IN RAGS!
I WANT TO PUT ON A PRETTY DRESS, GO TO TOWN AND DANCE WITH EVERYONE.
IF I DRESSED UP, I'D LOOK AS PRETTY AS ANY OF THEM.

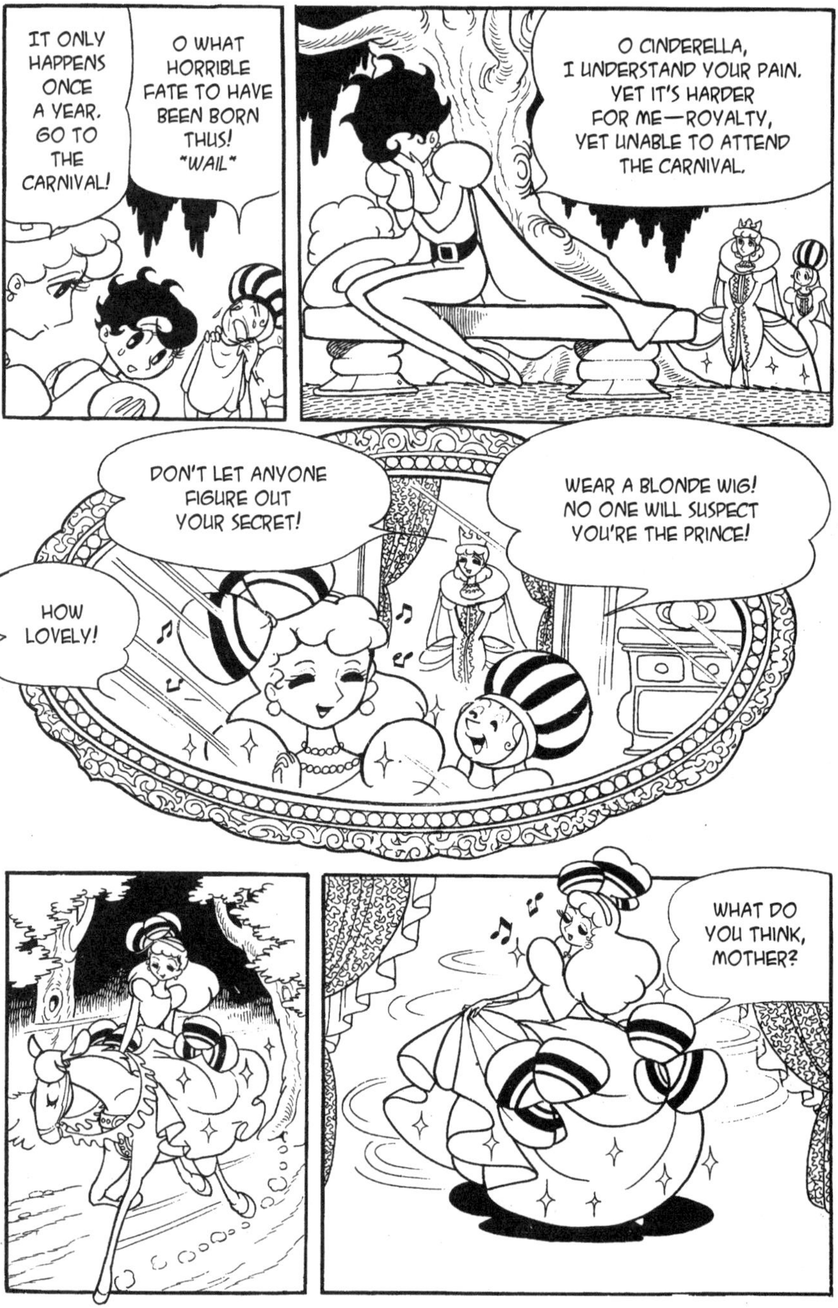
O CINDERELLA, I UNDERSTAND YOUR PAIN. YET IT'S HARDER FOR ME—ROYALTY, YET UNABLE TO ATTEND THE CARNIVAL.
O WHAT HORRIBLE FATE TO HAVE BEEN BORN THUS! *WAIL*
IT ONLY HAPPENS ONCE A YEAR. GO TO THE CARNIVAL!
WEAR A BLONDE WIG! NO ONE WILL SUSPECT YOU'RE THE PRINCE!
DON'T LET ANYONE FIGURE OUT YOUR SECRET!
HOW LOVELY!
WHAT DO YOU THINK, MOTHER?

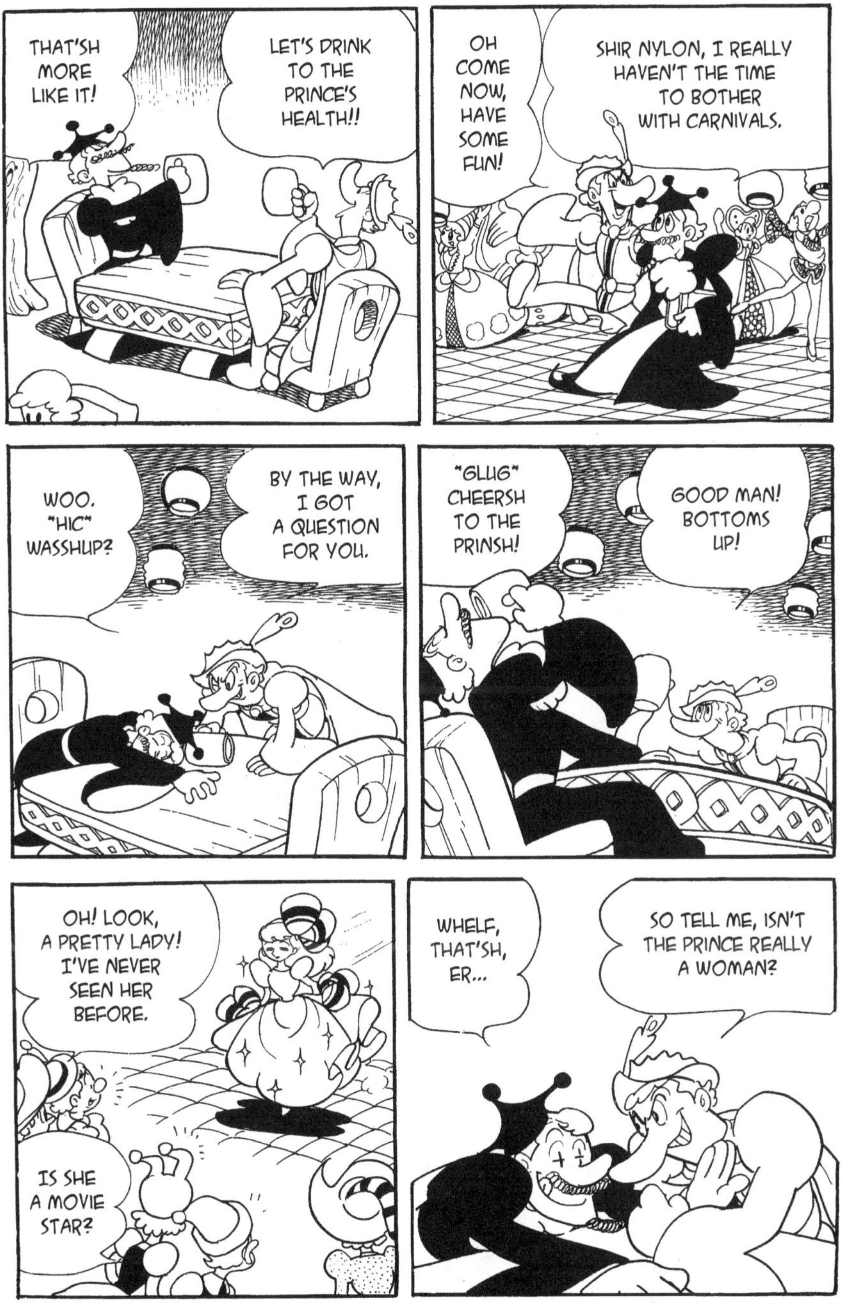
SHIR NYLON, I REALLY HAVEN'T THE TIME TO BOTHER WITH CARNIVALS.
OH COME NOW, HAVE SOME FUN!
LET'S DRINK TO THE PRINCE'S HEALTH!!
THAT'SH MORE LIKE IT!
GOOD MAN! BOTTOMS UP!
GLUG CHEERSH TO THE PRINSH!
BY THE WAY, I GOT A QUESTION FOR YOU.
WOO. *HIC* WASSHUP?
SO TELL ME, ISN'T THE PRINCE REALLY A WOMAN?
WHELF, THAT'SH, ER...
OH! LOOK, A PRETTY LADY! I'VE NEVER SEEN HER BEFORE.
IS SHE A MOVIE STAR?

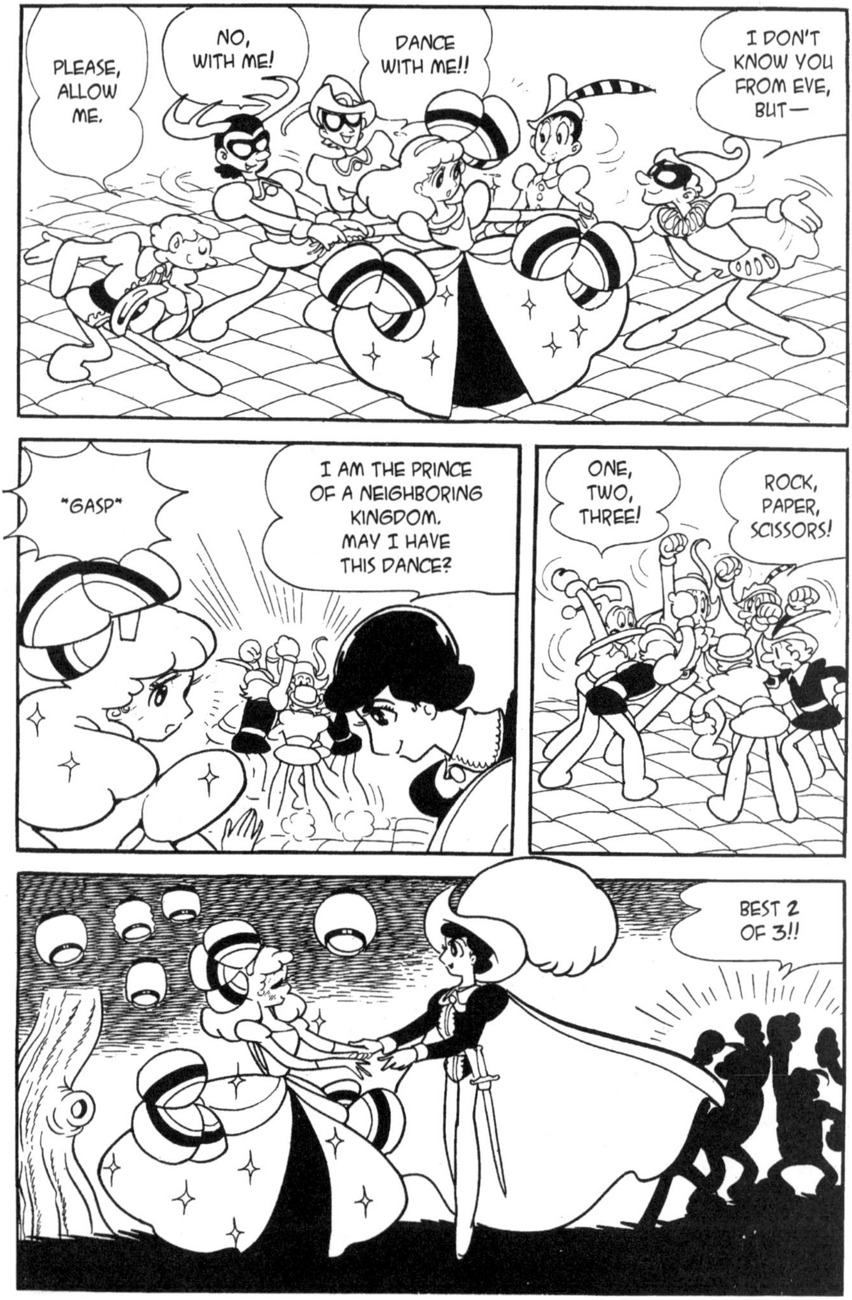

I DON'T KNOW YOU FROM EVE, BUT—
DANCE WITH ME!!
NO, WITH ME!
PLEASE, ALLOW ME.
ROCK, PAPER, SCISSORS!
ONE, TWO, THREE!
I AM THE PRINCE OF A NEIGHBORING KINGDOM. MAY I HAVE THIS DANCE?
GASP
BEST 2 OF 3!!

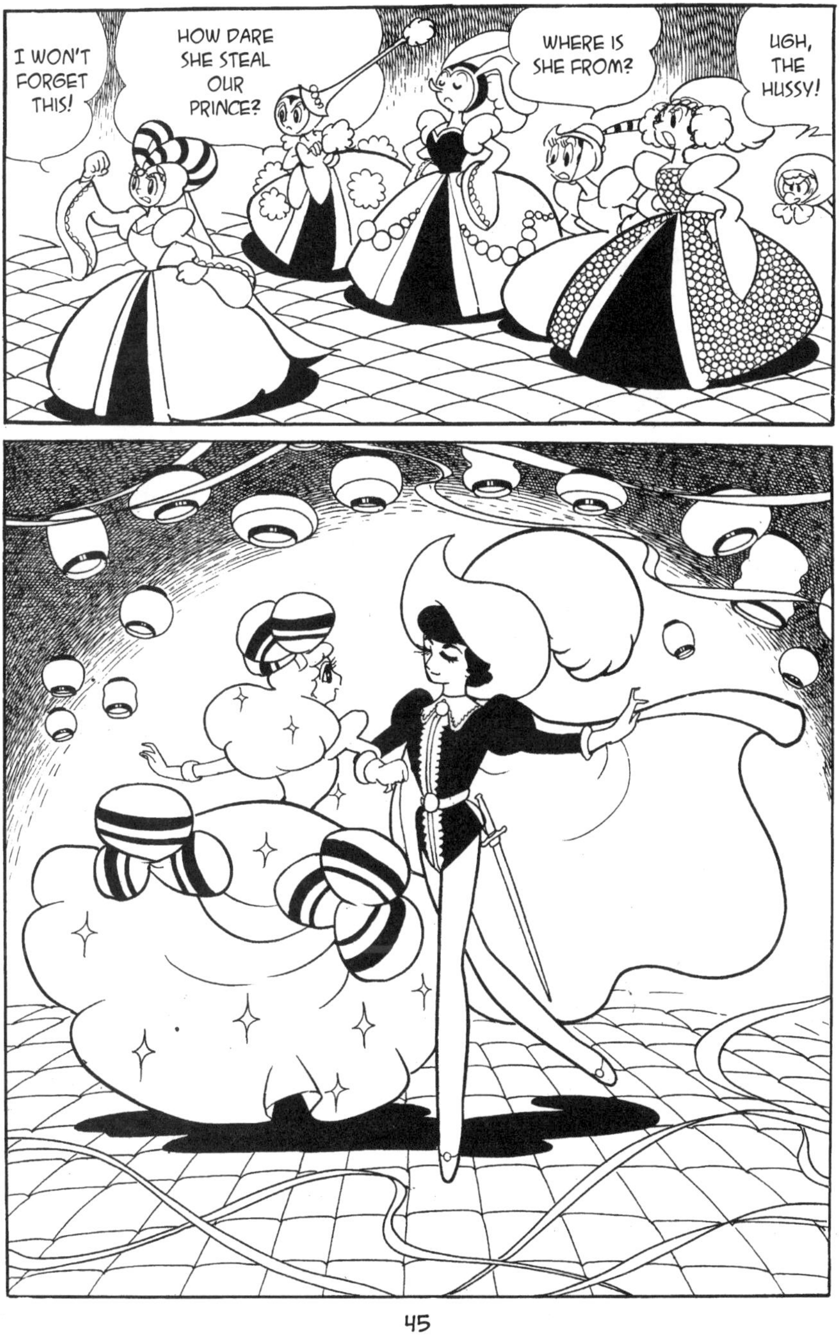
UGH, THE HUSSY!
WHERE IS SHE FROM?
HOW DARE SHE STEAL OUR PRINCE?
I WON'T FORGET THIS!

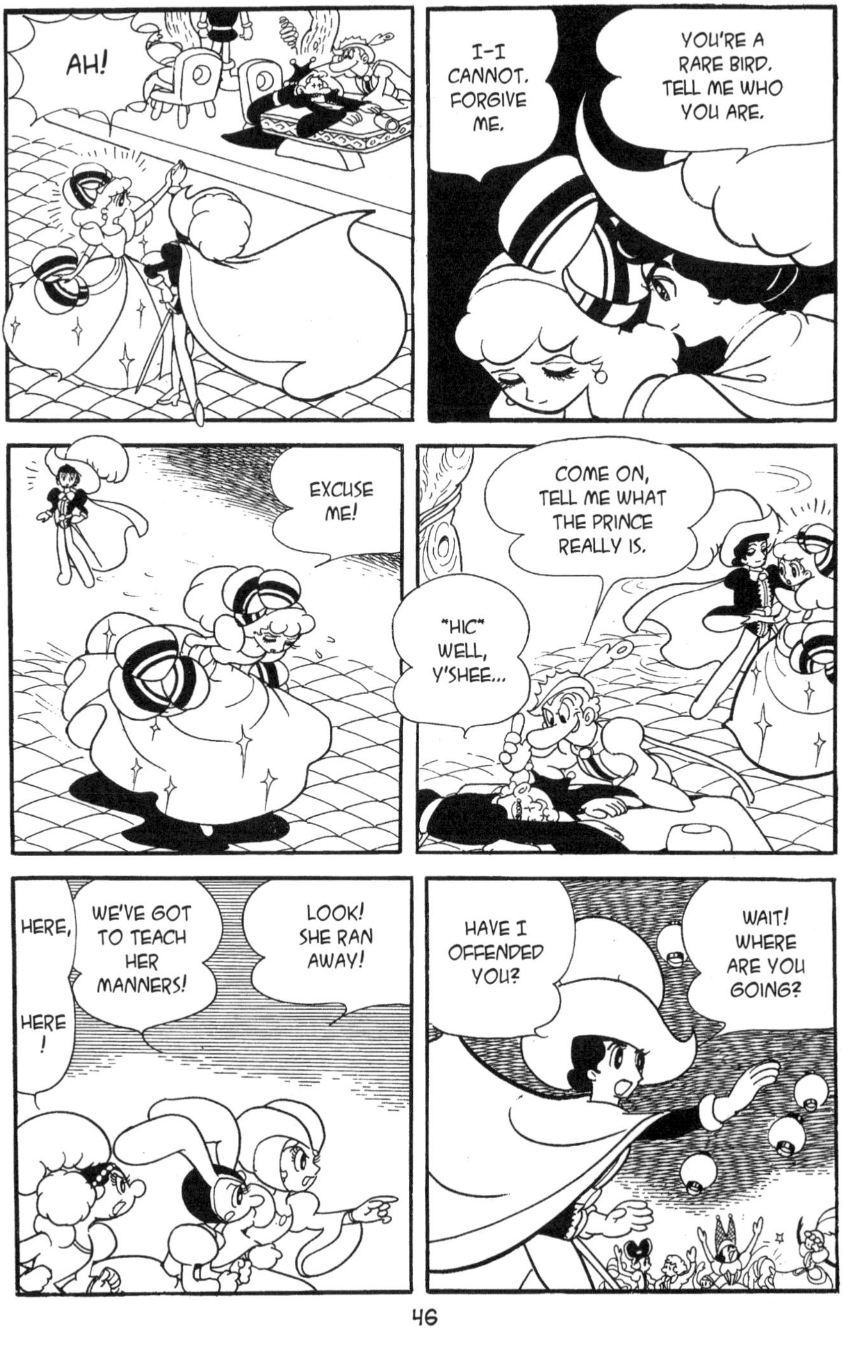
YOU'RE A RARE BIRD. TELL ME WHO YOU ARE.
I-I CANNOT. FORGIVE ME.
AH!
COME ON, TELL ME WHAT THE PRINCE REALLY IS.
HIC WELL, Y'SHEE...
EXCUSE ME!
WAIT! WHERE ARE YOU GOING?
HAVE I OFFENDED YOU?
LOOK! SHE RAN AWAY!
WE'VE GOT TO TEACH HER MANNERS!
HERE,
HERE !

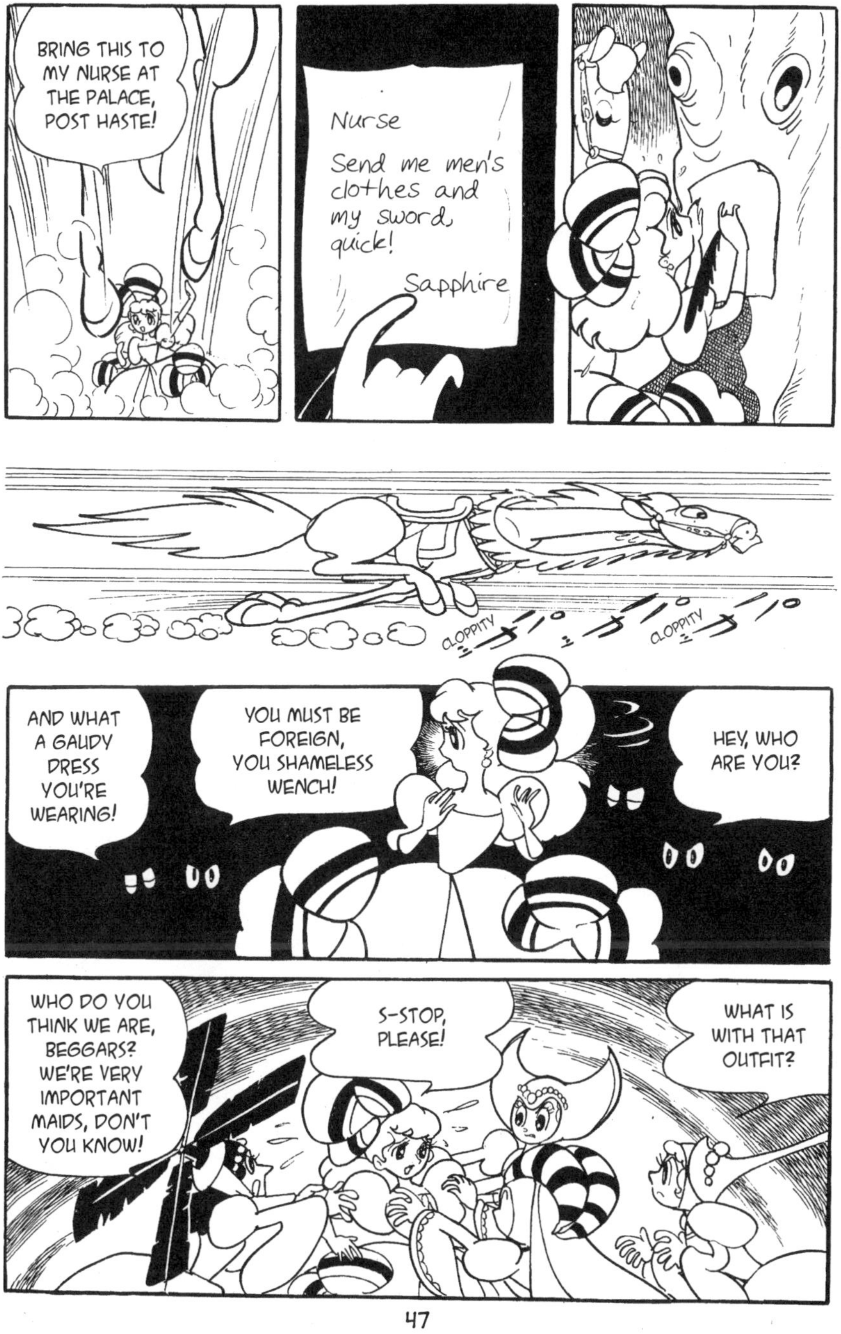
Nurse
Send me men's clothes and my sword, quick!
Sapphire
BRING THIS TO MY NURSE AT THE PALACE, POST HASTE!
CLOPPITY
CLOPPITY
HEY, WHO ARE YOU?
YOU MUST BE FOREIGN, YOU SHAMELESS WENCH!
AND WHAT A GAUDY DRESS YOU'RE WEARING!
WHAT IS WITH THAT OUTFIT?
S-STOP, PLEASE!
WHO DO YOU THINK WE ARE, BEGGARS? WE'RE VERY IMPORTANT MAIDS, DON'T YOU KNOW!

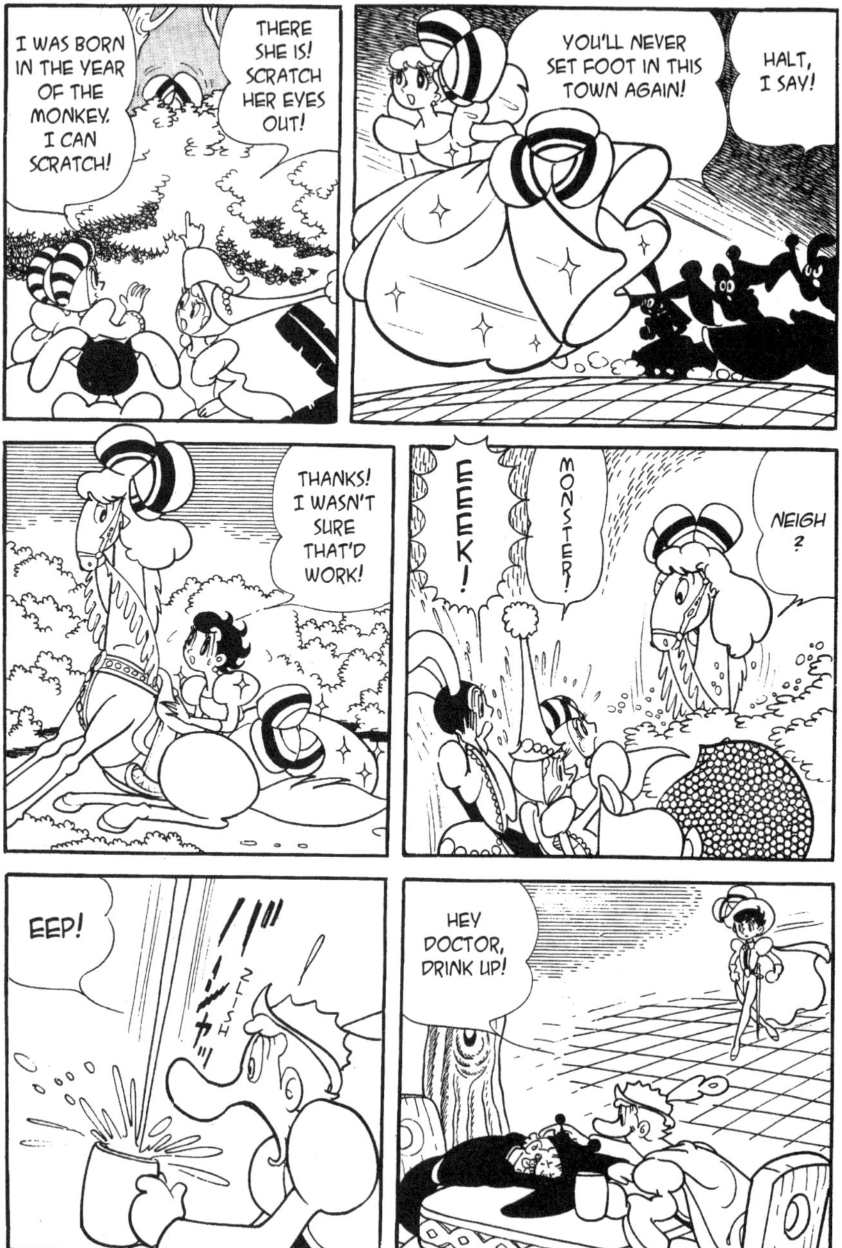
HALT, I SAY!
YOU'LL NEVER SET FOOT IN THIS TOWN AGAIN!
THERE SHE IS! SCRATCH HER EYES OUT!
I WAS BORN IN THE YEAR OF THE MONKEY. I CAN SCRATCH!
NEIGH ?
MONSTER!
EEEK!
THANKS! I WASN'T SURE THAT'D WORK!
HEY DOCTOR, DRINK UP!
EEP!

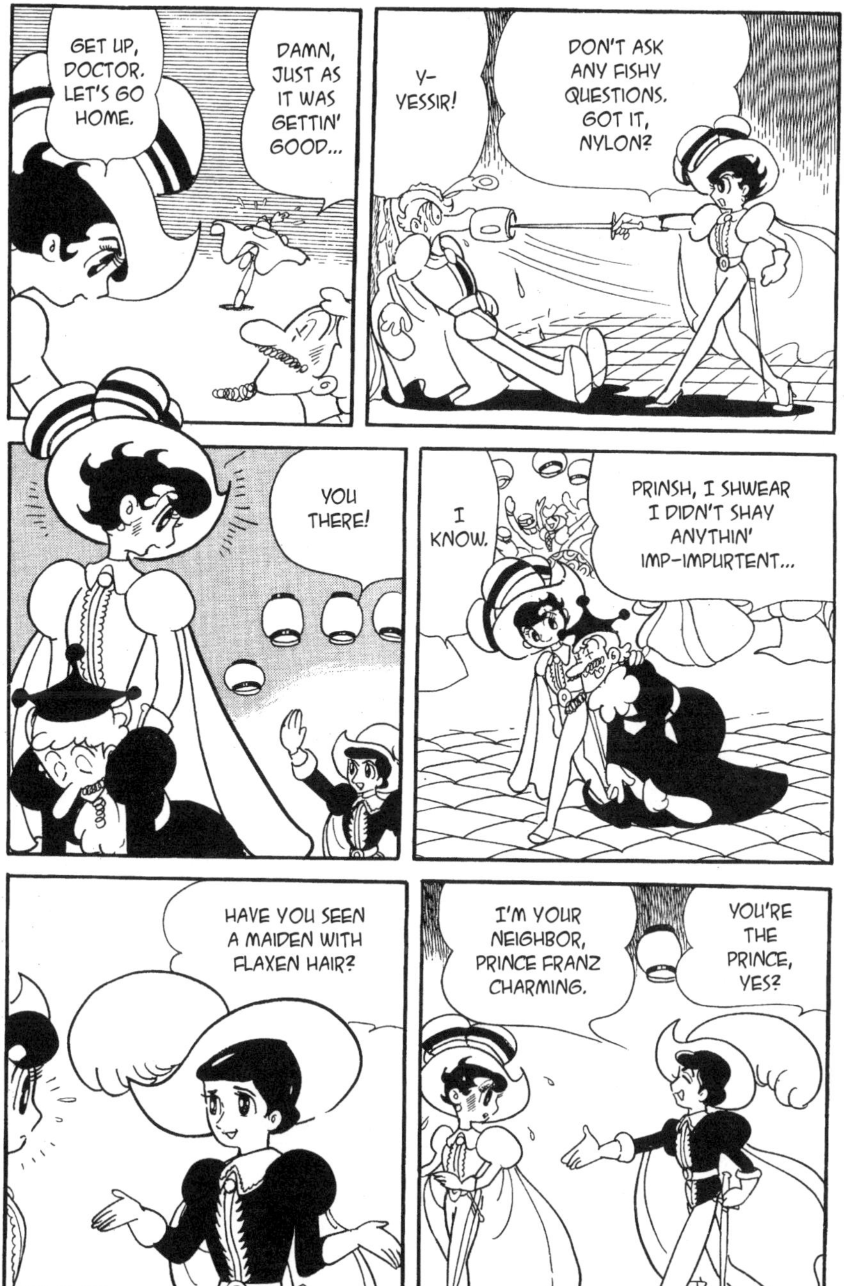
DON'T ASK ANY FISHY QUESTIONS. GOT IT, NYLON?
Y-YESSIR!
DAMN, JUST AS IT WAS GETTIN' GOOD...
GET UP, DOCTOR. LET'S GO HOME.
PRINSH, I SHWEAR I DIDN'T SHAY ANYTHIN' IMP-IMPURTENT...
I KNOW.
YOU THERE!
YOU'RE THE PRINCE, YES?
I'M YOUR NEIGHBOR, PRINCE FRANZ CHARMING.
HAVE YOU SEEN A MAIDEN WITH FLAXEN HAIR?

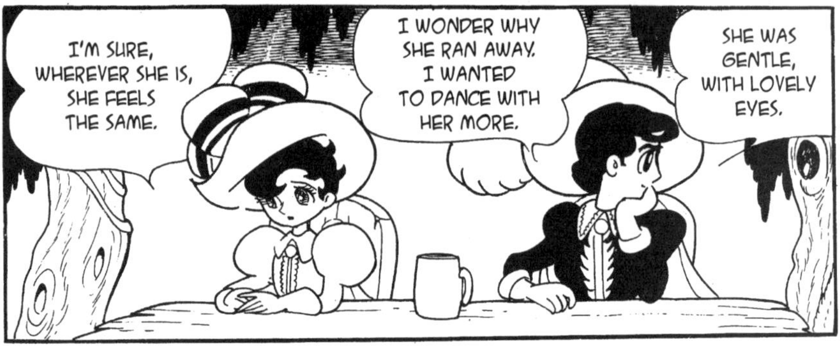
SHE WAS GENTLE, WITH LOVELY EYES.
I WONDER WHY SHE RAN AWAY. I WANTED TO DANCE WITH HER MORE.
I'M SURE, WHEREVER SHE IS, SHE FEELS THE SAME.

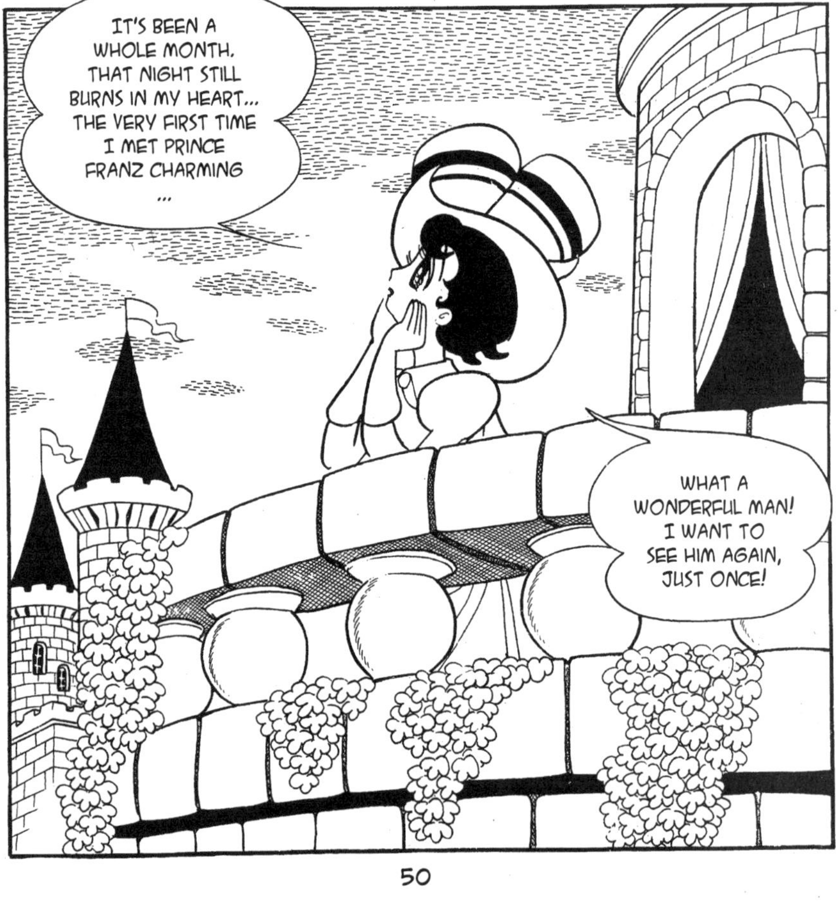
IT'S BEEN A WHOLE MONTH. THAT NIGHT STILL BURNS IN MY HEART... THE VERY FIRST TIME I MET PRINCE FRANZ CHARMING ...
WHAT A WONDERFUL MAN! I WANT TO SEE HIM AGAIN, JUST ONCE!

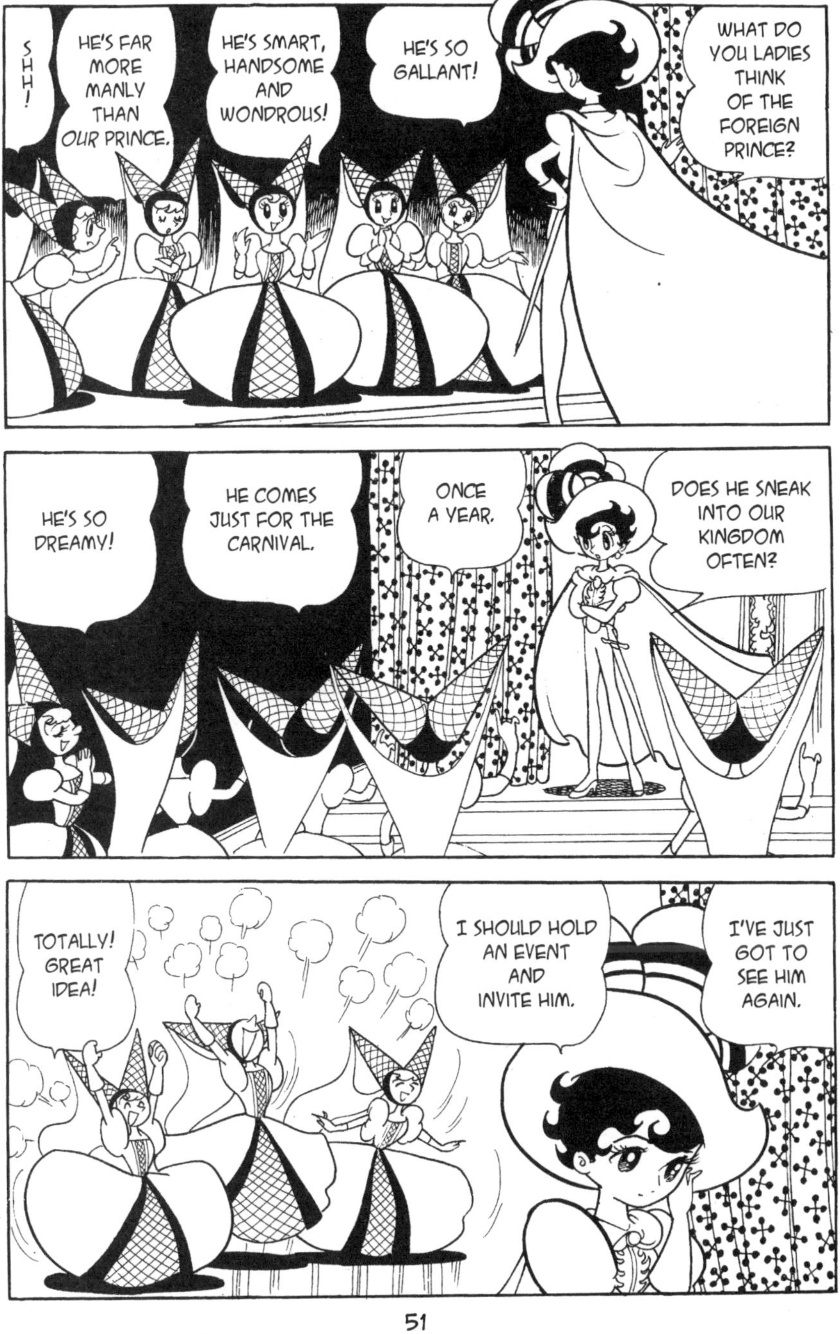
WHAT DO YOU LADIES THINK OF THE FOREIGN PRINCE?
HE'S SO GALLANT!
HE'S SMART, HANDSOME AND WONDROUS!
HE'S FAR MORE MANLY THAN OUR PRINCE.
SHH!
DOES HE SNEAK INTO OUR KINGDOM OFTEN?
ONCE A YEAR.
HE COMES JUST FOR THE CARNIVAL.
HE'S SO DREAMY!
I'VE JUST GOT TO SEE HIM AGAIN.
I SHOULD HOLD AN EVENT AND INVITE HIM.
TOTALLY! GREAT IDEA!

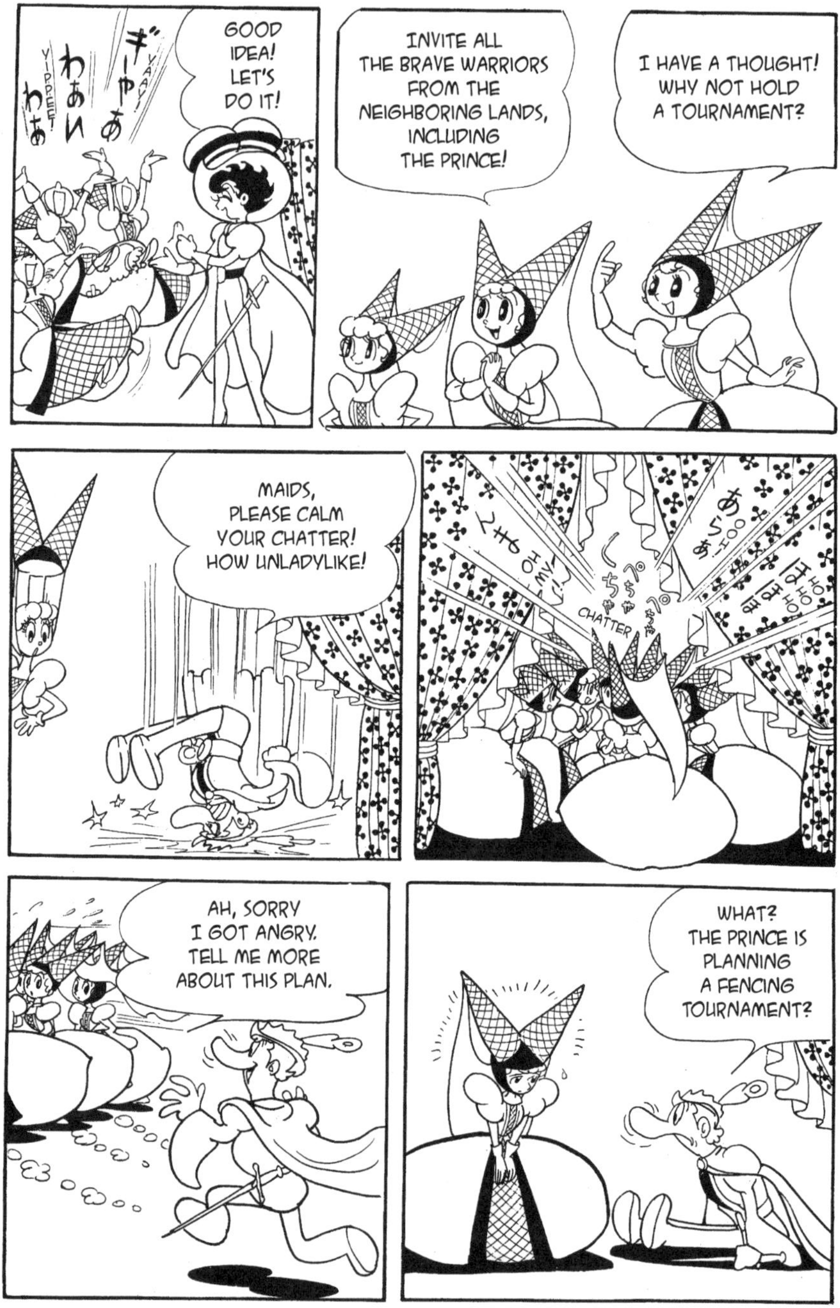
I HAVE A THOUGHT! WHY NOT HOLD A TOURNAMENT?
INVITE ALL THE BRAVE WARRIORS FROM THE NEIGHBORING LANDS, INCLUDING THE PRINCE!
GOOD IDEA! LET'S DO IT!
ギーゃあ
YAAY!
わあい
わあ
YIPPEE!
あらあ
OOOH
ほほほ
HO HO HO!
くちゃくちゃぺちゃぺちゃ
CHATTER
まあ
OH MY!
MAIDS, PLEASE CALM YOUR CHATTER! HOW UNLADYLIKE!
WHAT? THE PRINCE IS PLANNING A FENCING TOURNAMENT?
AH, SORRY I GOT ANGRY. TELL ME MORE ABOUT THIS PLAN.

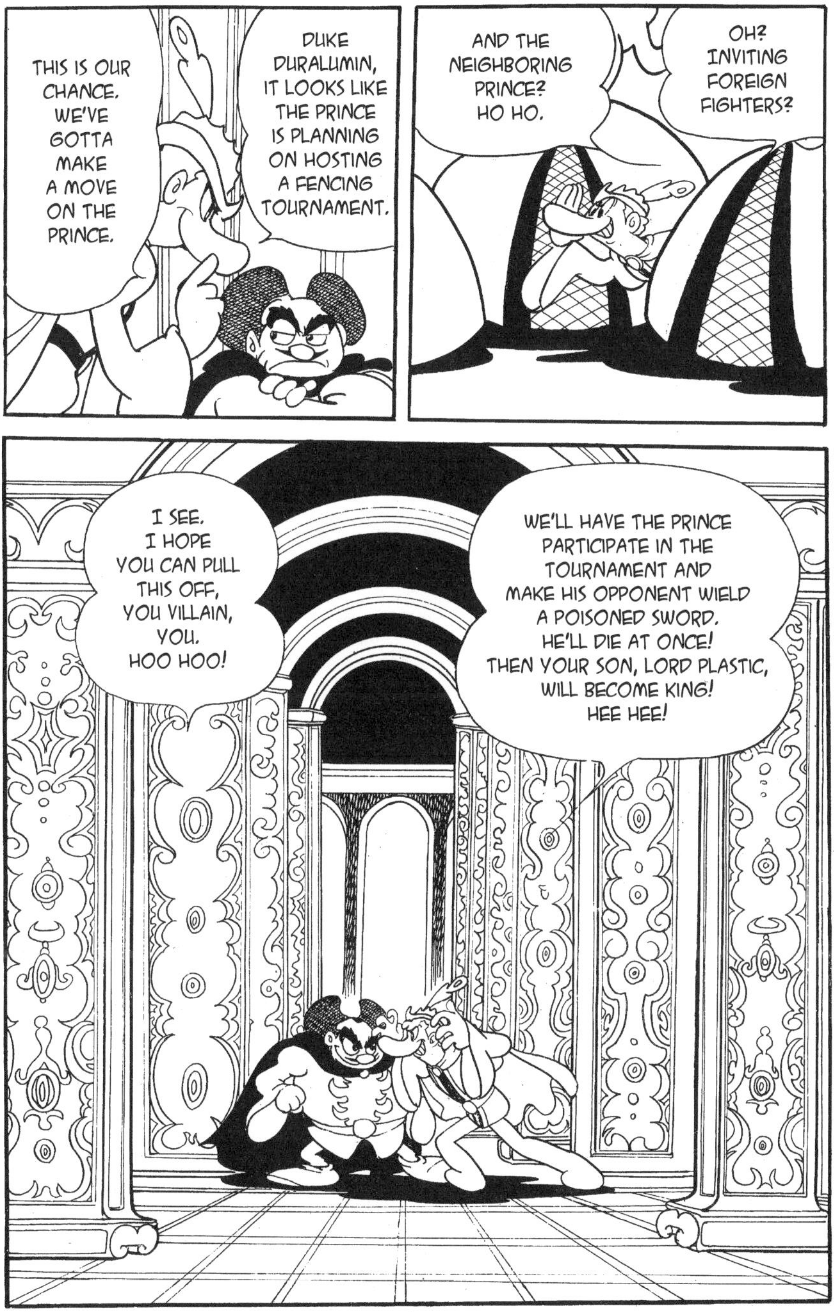
OH? INVITING FOREIGN FIGHTERS?
AND THE NEIGHBORING PRINCE? HO HO.
DUKE DURALUMIN, IT LOOKS LIKE THE PRINCE IS PLANNING ON HOSTING A FENCING TOURNAMENT.
THIS IS OUR CHANCE. WE'VE GOTTA MAKE A MOVE ON THE PRINCE.
WE'LL HAVE THE PRINCE PARTICIPATE IN THE TOURNAMENT AND MAKE HIS OPPONENT WIELD A POISONED SWORD. HE'LL DIE AT ONCE! THEN YOUR SON, LORD PLASTIC, WILL BECOME KING! HEE HEE!
I SEE. I HOPE YOU CAN PULL THIS OFF, YOU VILLAIN, YOU. HOO HOO!

Chapter 4

The Tournament

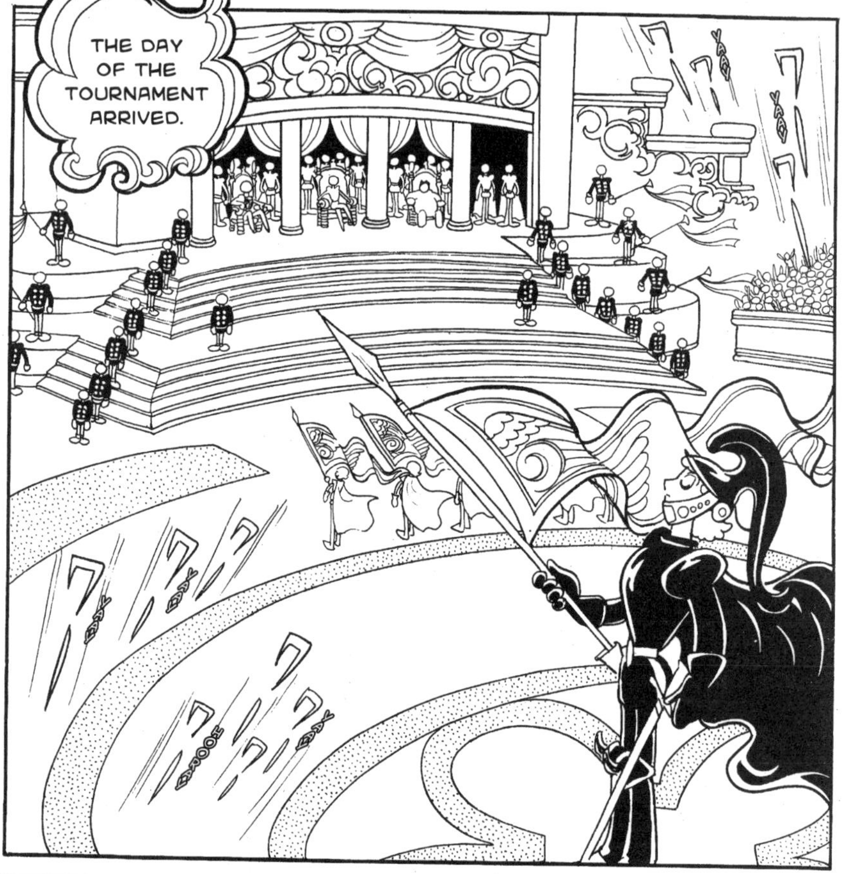
THE DAY OF THE TOURNAMENT ARRIVED.
YAAY
YAAY
YAAY
YAAY
YAAY
HOORAY

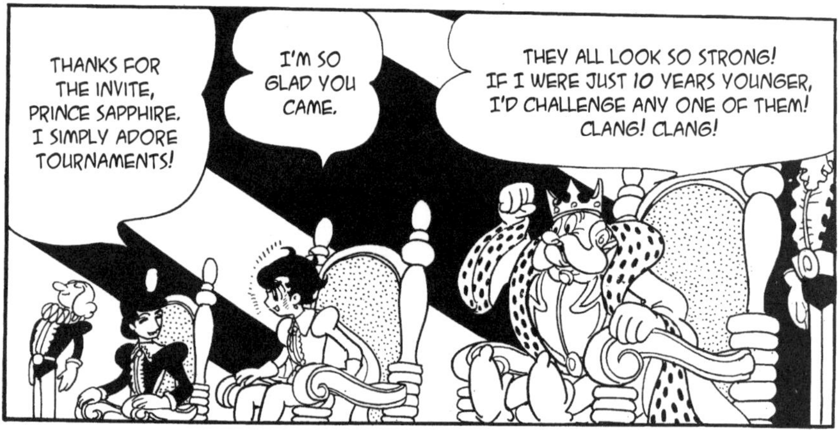
THEY ALL LOOK SO STRONG! IF I WERE JUST 10 YEARS YOUNGER, I'D CHALLENGE ANY ONE OF THEM! CLANG! CLANG!
I'M SO GLAD YOU CAME.
THANKS FOR THE INVITE, PRINCE SAPPHIRE. I SIMPLY ADORE TOURNAMENTS!

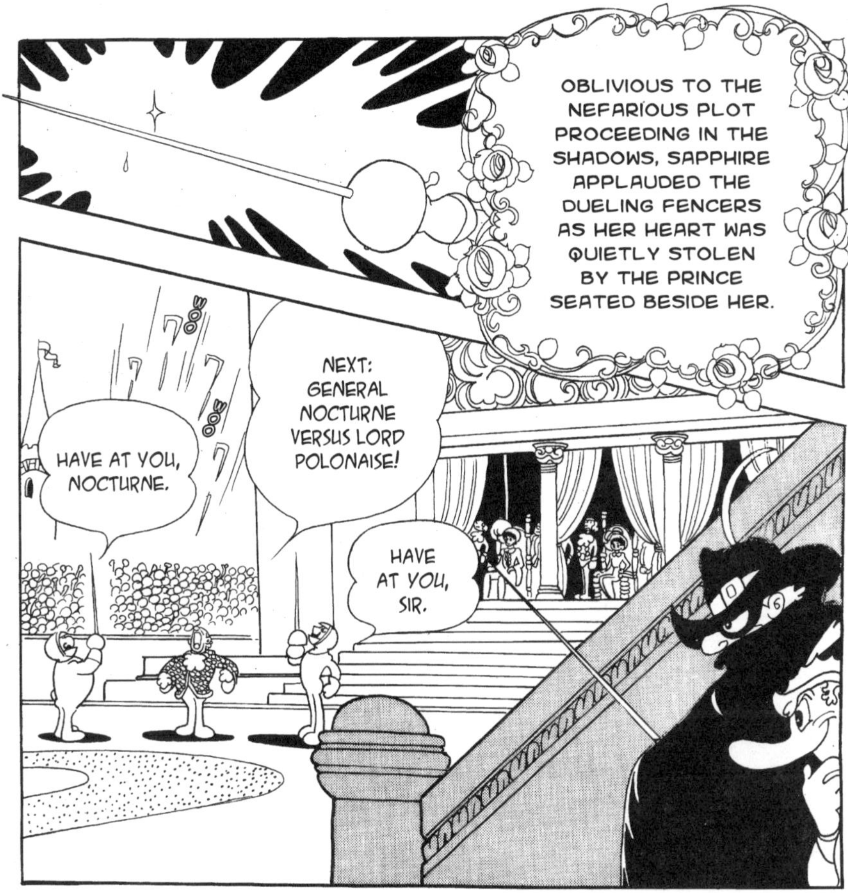
OBLIVIOUS TO THE NEFARIOUS PLOT PROCEEDING IN THE SHADOWS, SAPPHIRE APPLAUDED THE DUELING FENCERS AS HER HEART WAS QUIETLY STOLEN BY THE PRINCE SEATED BESIDE HER.
NEXT: GENERAL NOCTURNE VERSUS LORD POLONAISE!
WOO
WOO
HAVE AT YOU, SIR.
HAVE AT YOU, NOCTURNE.

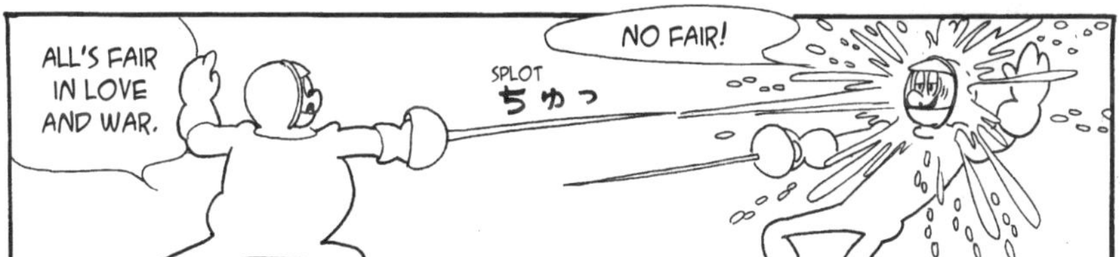
NO FAIR!
SPLOT
ちゅっ
ALL'S FAIR IN LOVE AND WAR.

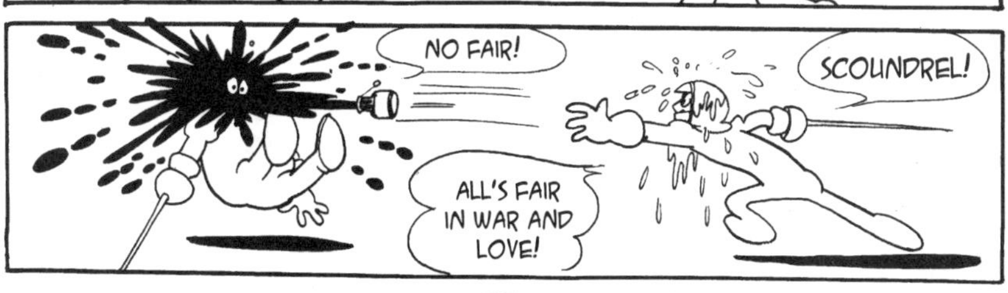
SCOUNDREL!
NO FAIR!
ALL'S FAIR IN WAR AND LOVE!

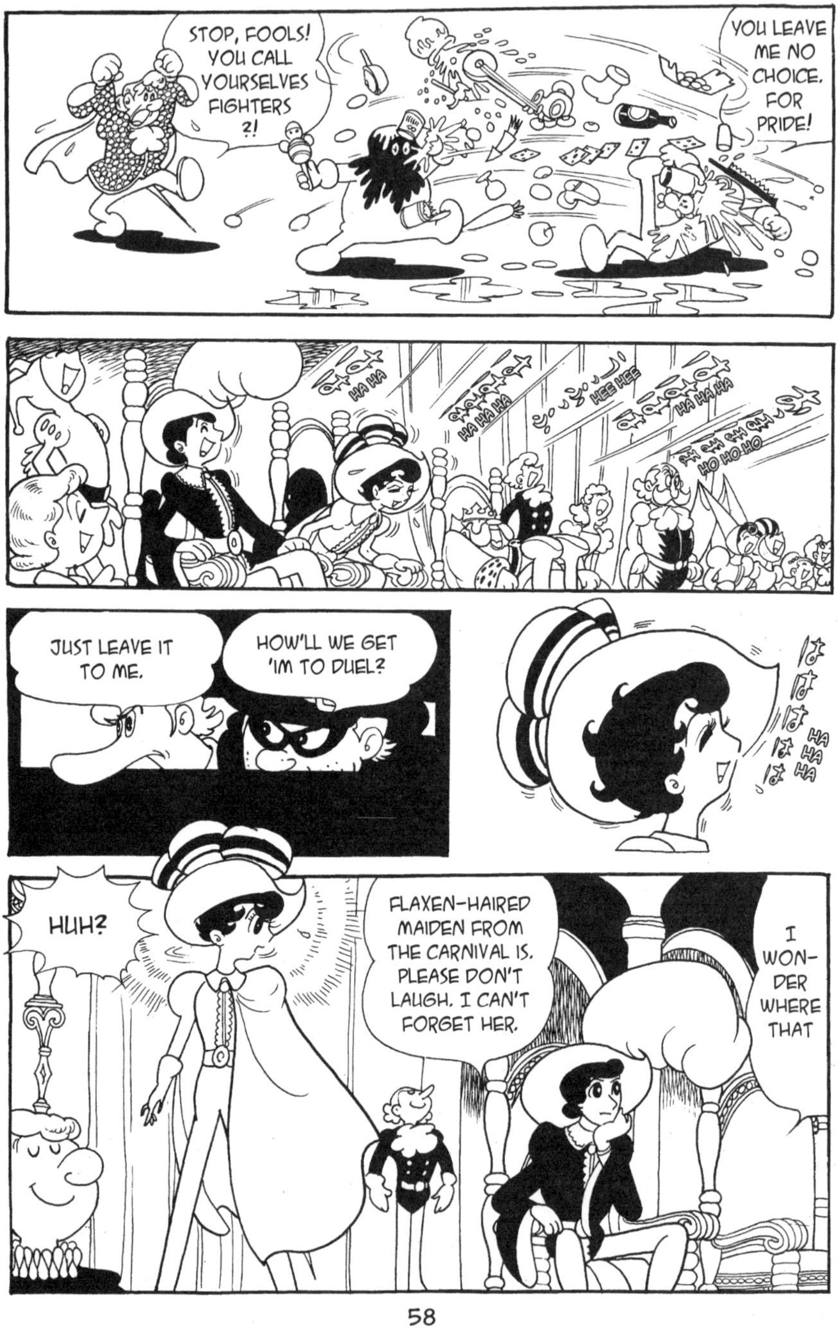

YOU LEAVE ME NO CHOICE. FOR PRIDE!
STOP, FOOLS! YOU CALL YOURSELVES FIGHTERS ?!
HO HO HO
HA HA HA
HEE HEE
HA HA HA
HA HA
ははははは!
HA HA HA
HOW'LL WE GET 'IM TO DUEL?
JUST LEAVE IT TO ME.
I WON-DER WHERE THAT
FLAXEN-HAIRED MAIDEN FROM THE CARNIVAL IS. PLEASE DON'T LAUGH. I CAN'T FORGET HER.
HUH?

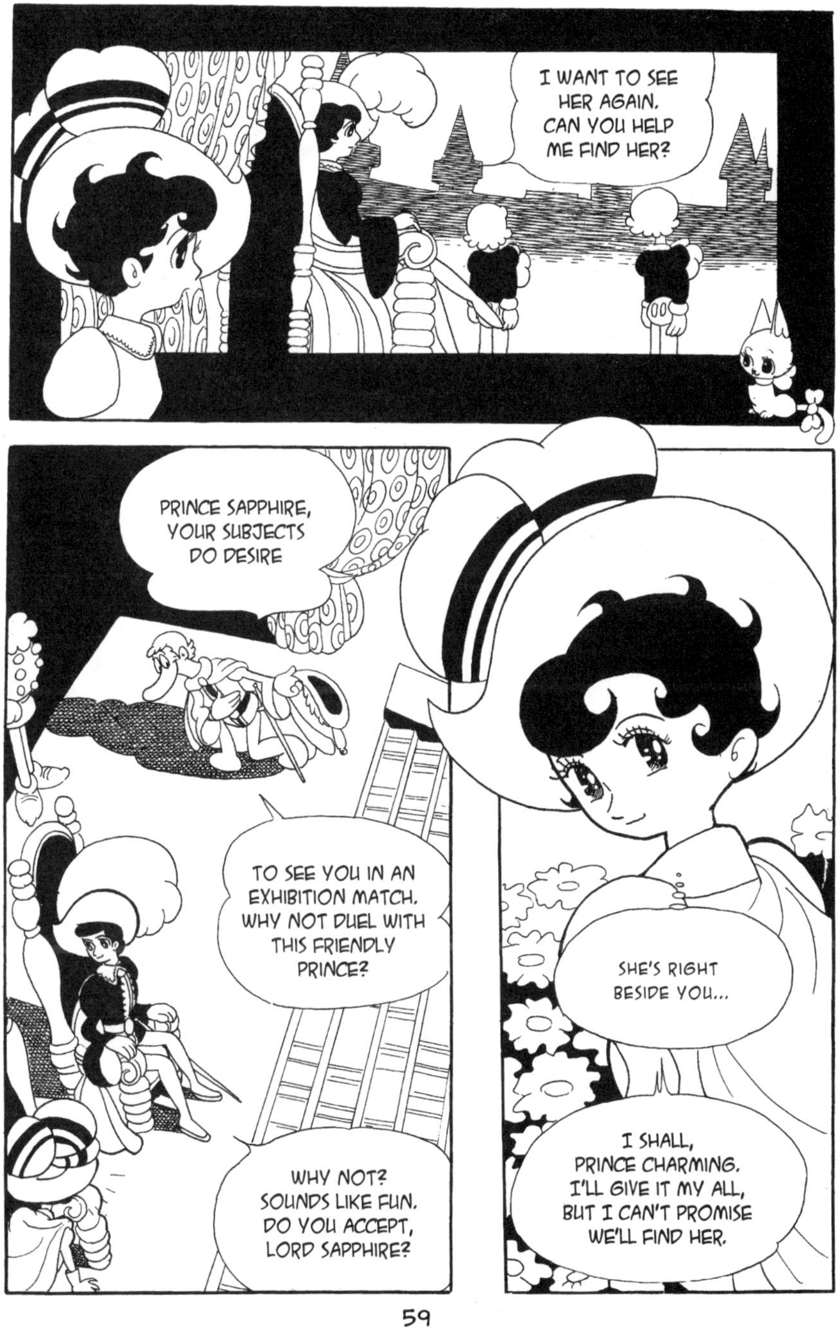
I WANT TO SEE HER AGAIN. CAN YOU HELP ME FIND HER?
SHE'S RIGHT BESIDE YOU...
I SHALL, PRINCE CHARMING. I'LL GIVE IT MY ALL, BUT I CAN'T PROMISE WE'LL FIND HER.
PRINCE SAPPHIRE, YOUR SUBJECTS DO DESIRE
TO SEE YOU IN AN EXHIBITION MATCH. WHY NOT DUEL WITH THIS FRIENDLY PRINCE?
WHY NOT? SOUNDS LIKE FUN. DO YOU ACCEPT, LORD SAPPHIRE?

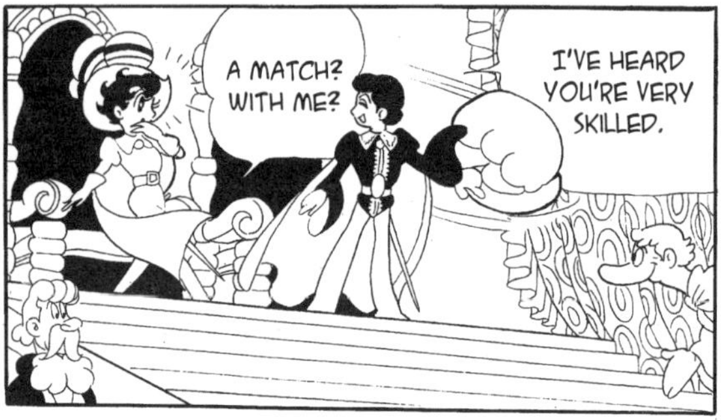
I'VE HEARD YOU'RE VERY SKILLED.
A MATCH? WITH ME?

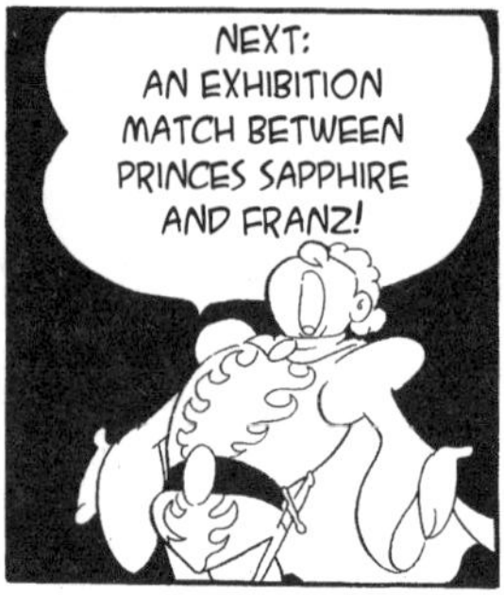
NEXT: AN EXHIBITION MATCH BETWEEN PRINCES SAPPHIRE AND FRANZ!

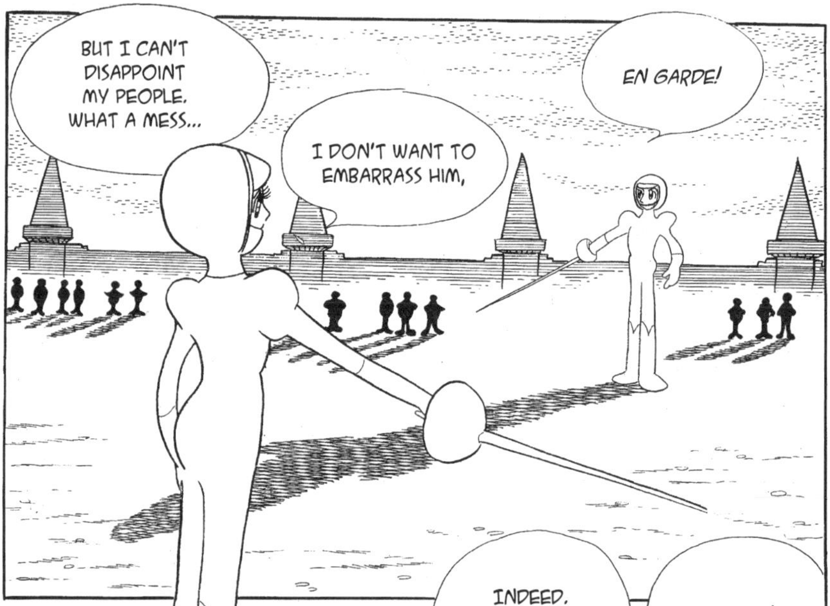
EN GARDE!
I DON'T WANT TO EMBARRASS HIM,
BUT I CAN'T DISAPPOINT MY PEOPLE. WHAT A MESS...

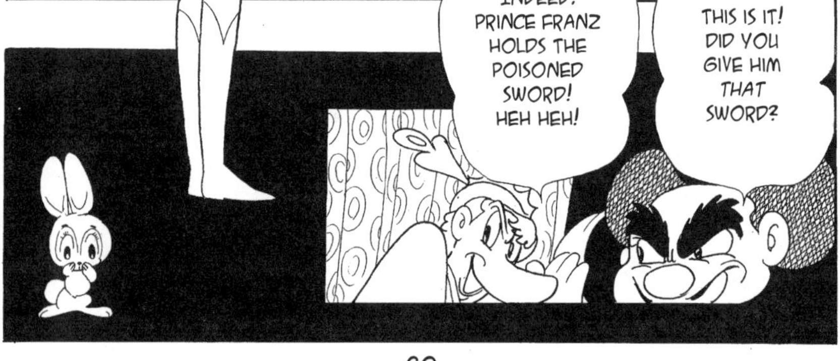
THIS IS IT! DID YOU GIVE HIM THAT SWORD?
INDEED. PRINCE FRANZ HOLDS THE POISONED SWORD! HEH HEH!

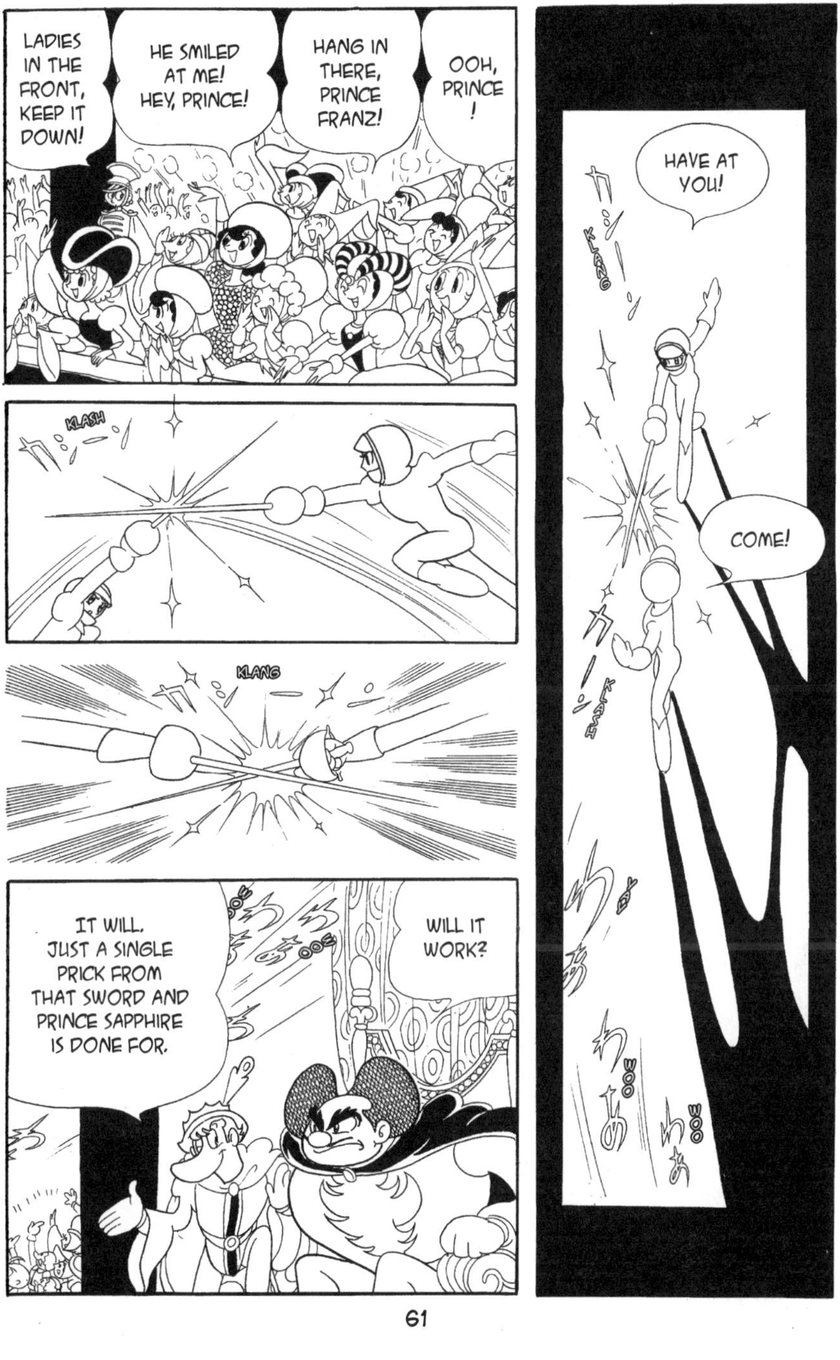
HAVE AT YOU!
KLANG
COME!
KLASH
WOO
WOO
OOH, PRINCE!
HANG IN THERE, PRINCE FRANZ!
HE SMILED AT ME! HEY, PRINCE!
LADIES IN THE FRONT, KEEP IT DOWN!
KLASH
KLANG
WILL IT WORK?
IT WILL. JUST A SINGLE PRICK FROM THAT SWORD AND PRINCE SAPPHIRE IS DONE FOR.

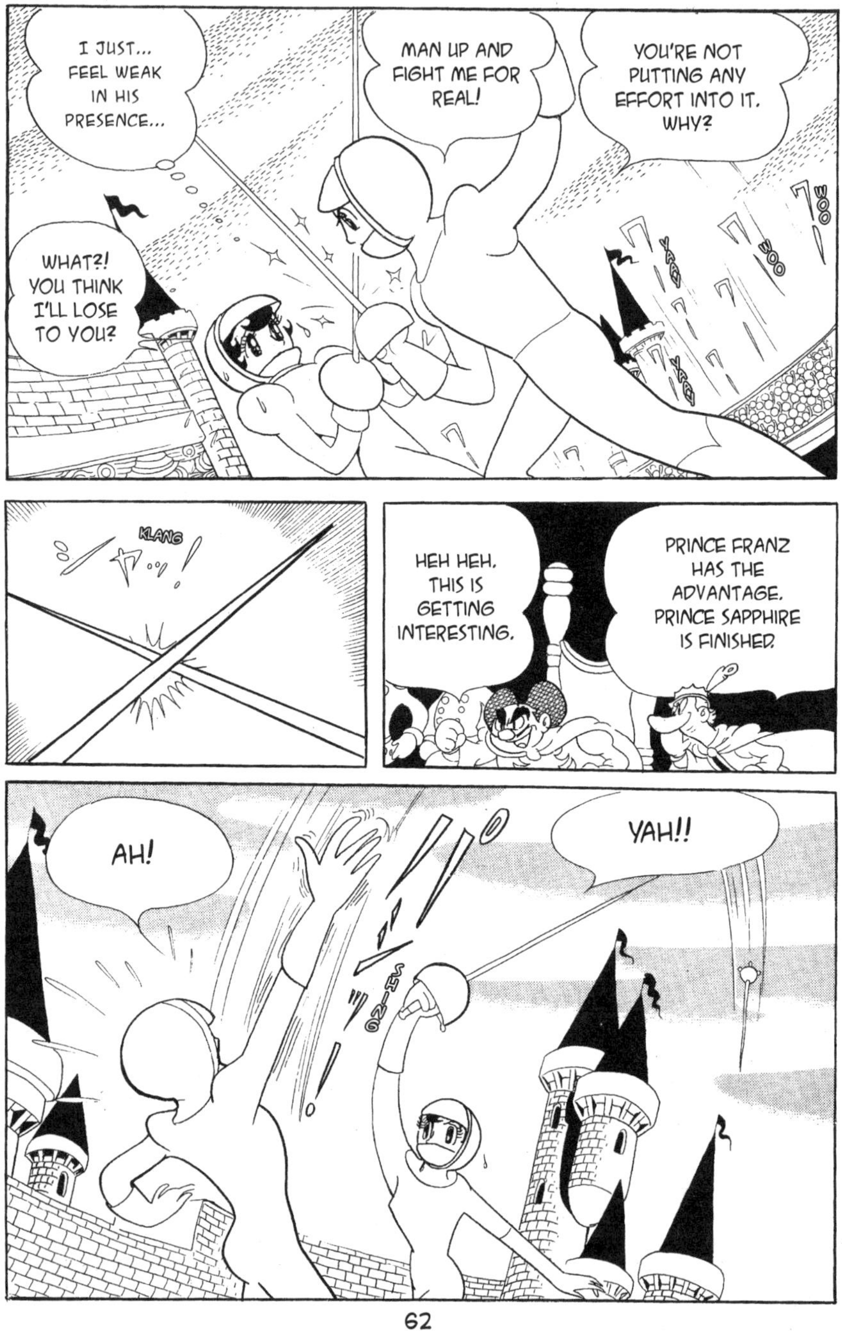
YOU'RE NOT PUTTING ANY EFFORT INTO IT. WHY?
MAN UP AND FIGHT ME FOR REAL!
WOO
WOO
YAAY
YAAY
I JUST... FEEL WEAK IN HIS PRESENCE...
WHAT?! YOU THINK I'LL LOSE TO YOU?
PRINCE FRANZ HAS THE ADVANTAGE. PRINCE SAPPHIRE IS FINISHED.
HEH HEH. THIS IS GETTING INTERESTING.
KLANG
YAH!!
SHI-NG
AH!

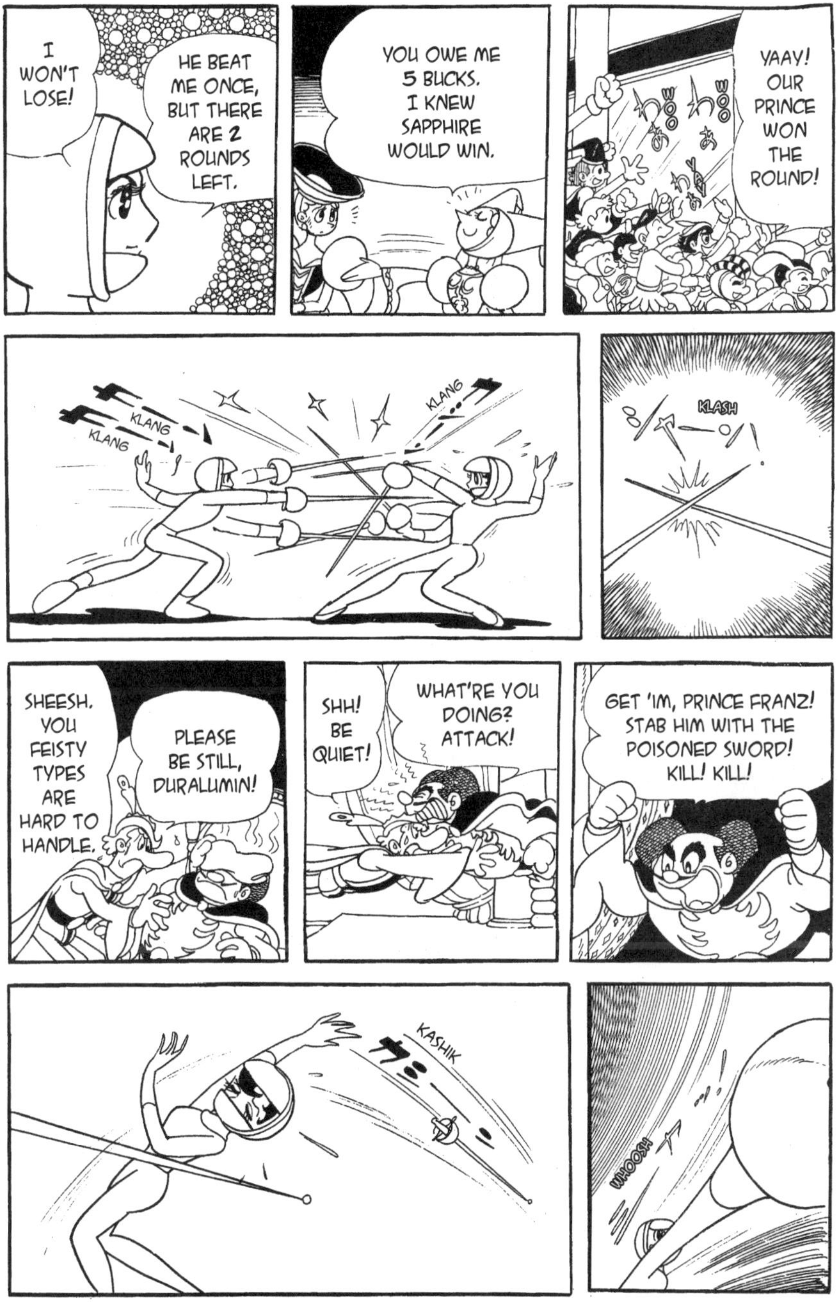
YAAY! OUR PRINCE WON THE ROUND!
WOO
WOO
YOU OWE ME 5 BUCKS. I KNEW SAPPHIRE WOULD WIN.
HE BEAT ME ONCE, BUT THERE ARE 2 ROUNDS LEFT.
I WON'T LOSE!
KLASH
KLANG
KLANG
KLANG
GET 'IM, PRINCE FRANZ! STAB HIM WITH THE POISONED SWORD! KILL! KILL!
WHAT'RE YOU DOING? ATTACK!
SHH! BE QUIET!
PLEASE BE STILL, DURALUMIN!
SHEESH. YOU FEISTY TYPES ARE HARD TO HANDLE.
WHOOSH
KASHIK

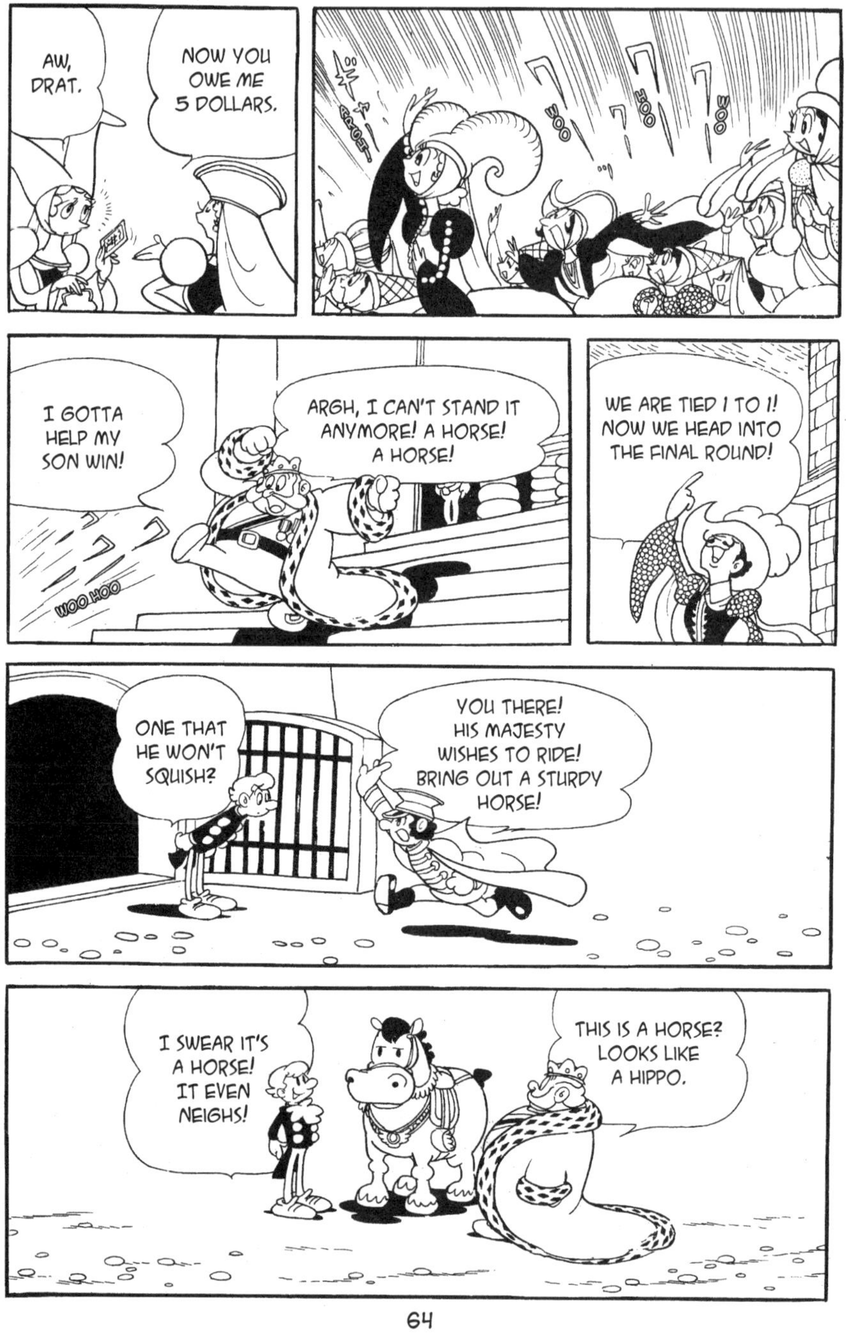

WOO
HOO
WOO
ARGH!
NOW YOU OWE ME 5 DOLLARS.
AW, DRAT.
WE ARE TIED 1 TO 1! NOW WE HEAD INTO THE FINAL ROUND!
ARGH, I CAN'T STAND IT ANYMORE! A HORSE! A HORSE!
I GOTTA HELP MY SON WIN!
WOO HOO
YOU THERE! HIS MAJESTY WISHES TO RIDE! BRING OUT A STURDY HORSE!
ONE THAT HE WON'T SQUISH?
THIS IS A HORSE? LOOKS LIKE A HIPPO.
I SWEAR IT'S A HORSE! IT EVEN NEIGHS!

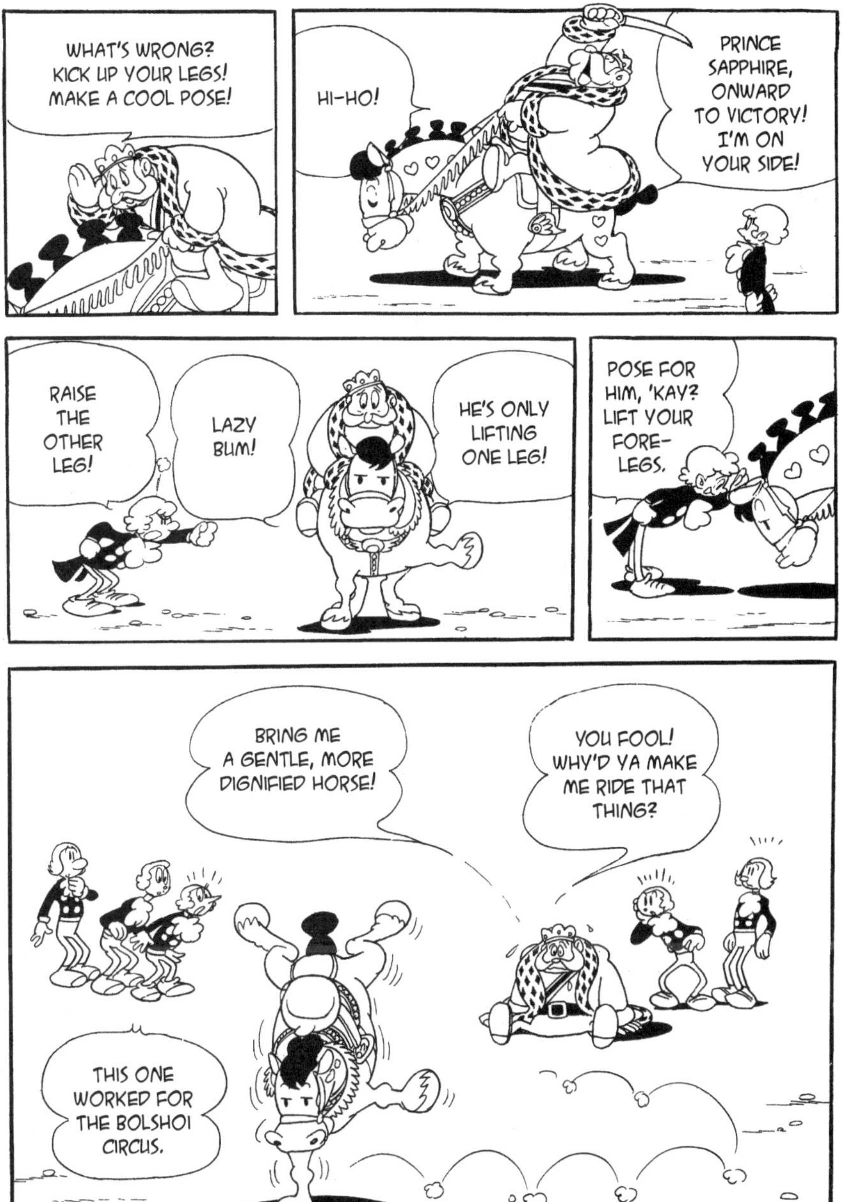
PRINCE SAPPHIRE, ONWARD TO VICTORY! I'M ON YOUR SIDE!
HI-HO!
WHAT'S WRONG? KICK UP YOUR LEGS! MAKE A COOL POSE!
POSE FOR HIM, 'KAY? LIFT YOUR FORE-LEGS.
HE'S ONLY LIFTING ONE LEG!
LAZY BUM!
RAISE THE OTHER LEG!
YOU FOOL! WHY'D YA MAKE ME RIDE THAT THING?
BRING ME A GENTLE, MORE DIGNIFIED HORSE!
THIS ONE WORKED FOR THE BOLSHOI CIRCUS.

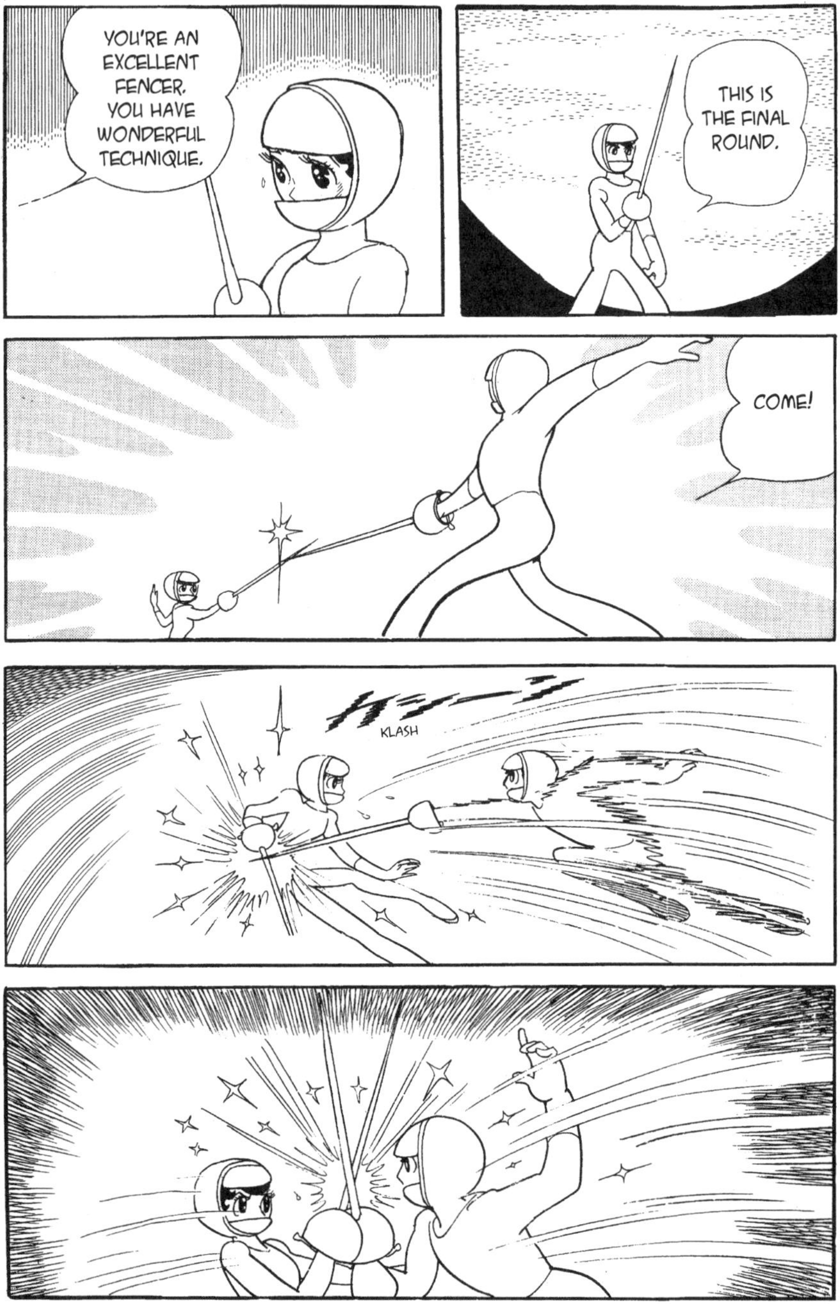
THIS IS THE FINAL ROUND.
YOU'RE AN EXCELLENT FENCER. YOU HAVE WONDERFUL TECHNIQUE.
COME!
KLASH

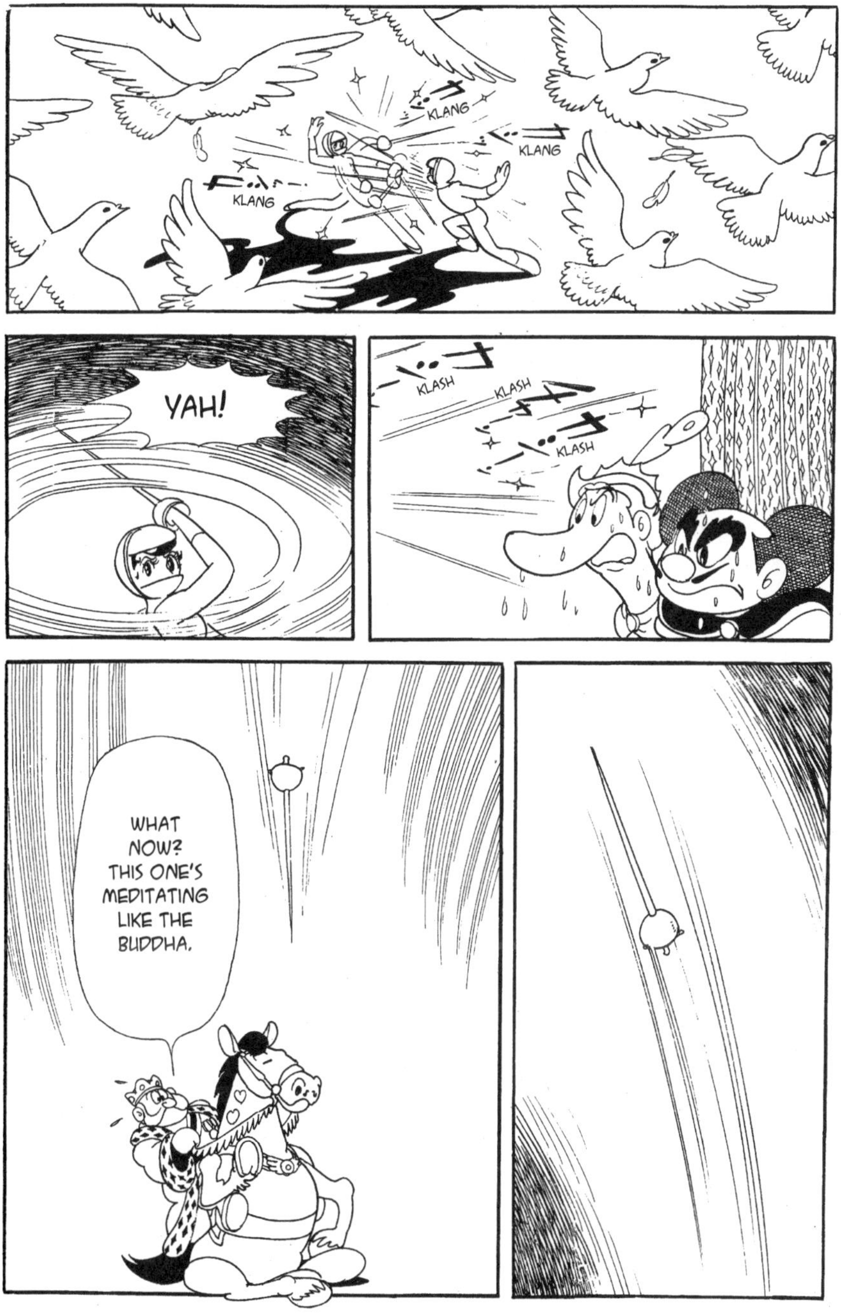
KLANG
KLANG
KLANG
KLASH
KLASH
KLASH
YAH!
WHAT NOW? THIS ONE'S MEDITATING LIKE THE BUDDHA.

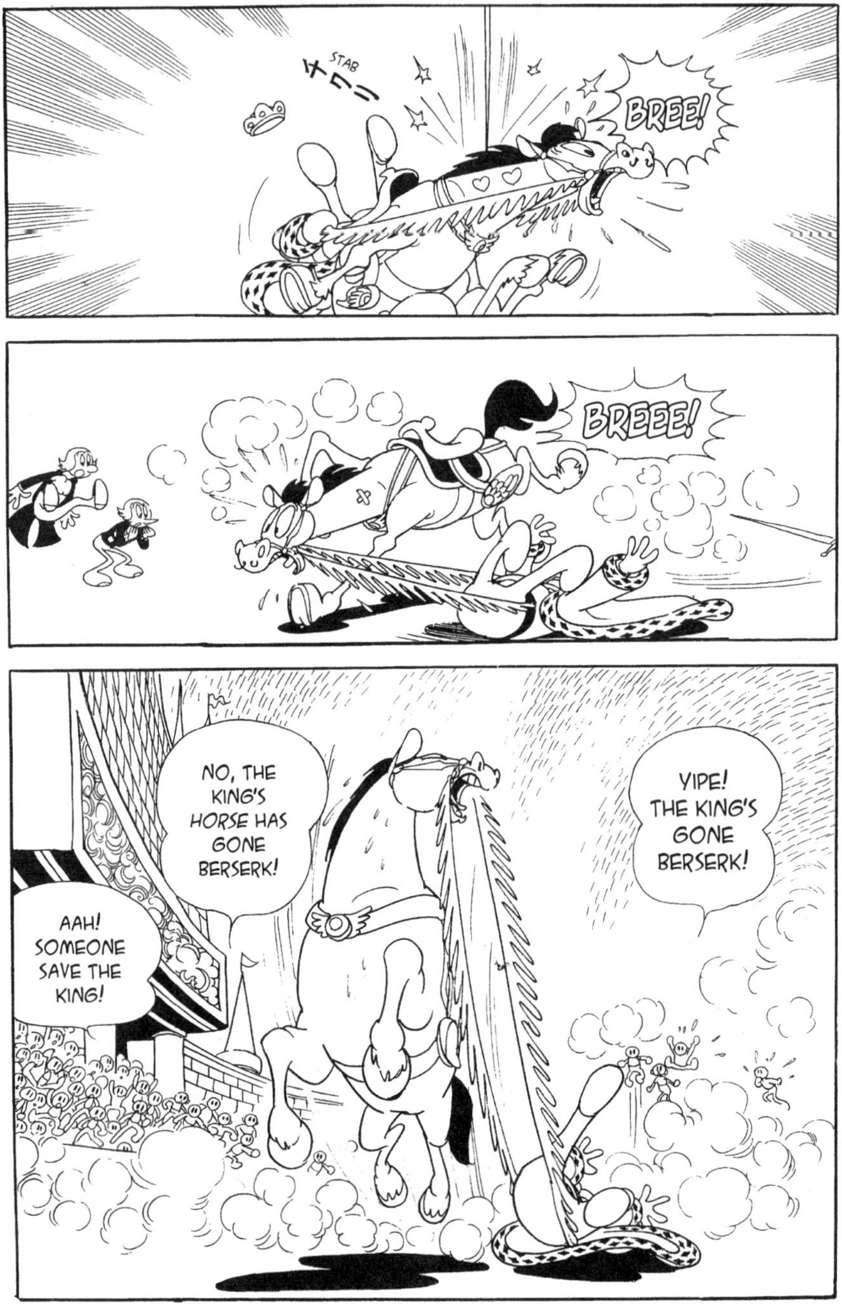
BREE!
チクリ
STAB
BREEE!
YIPE! THE KING'S GONE BERSERK!
NO, THE KING'S HORSE HAS GONE BERSERK!
AAH! SOMEONE SAVE THE KING!

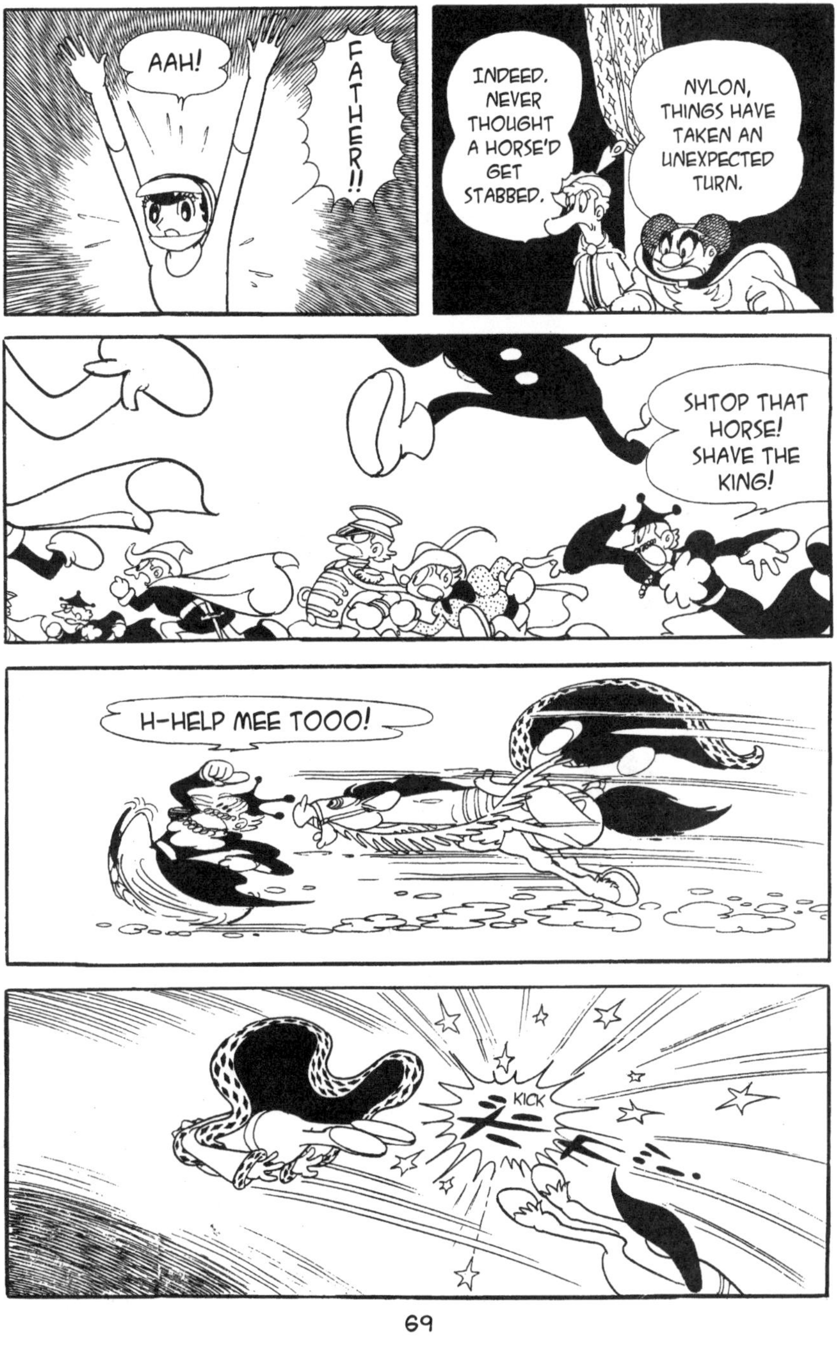
NYLON, THINGS HAVE TAKEN AN UNEXPECTED TURN.
INDEED. NEVER THOUGHT A HORSE'D GET STABBED.
FATHER!!
AAH!
SHTOP THAT HORSE! SHAVE THE KING!
H-HELP MEE TOOO!
KICK

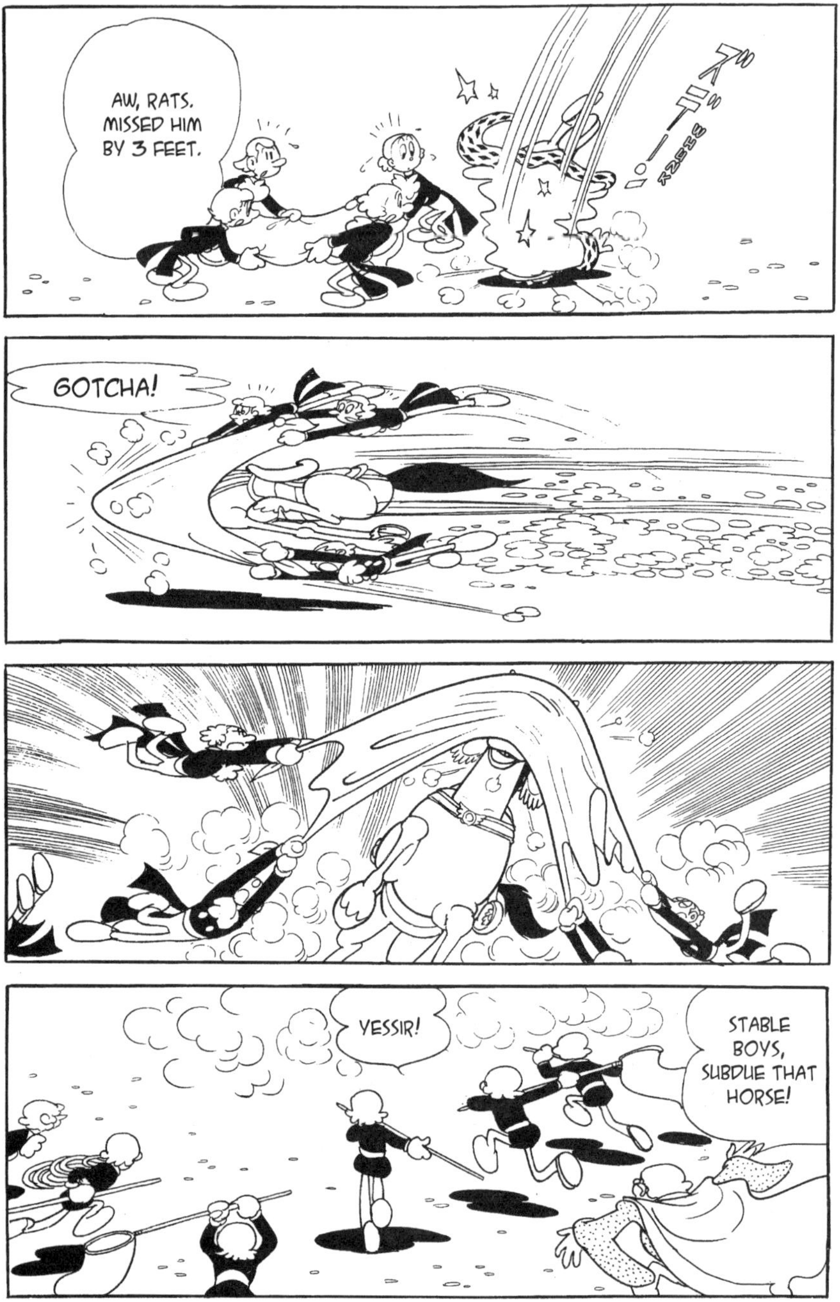
AW, RATS. MISSED HIM BY 3 FEET.
GOTCHA!
STABLE BOYS, SUBDUE THAT HORSE!
YESSIR!

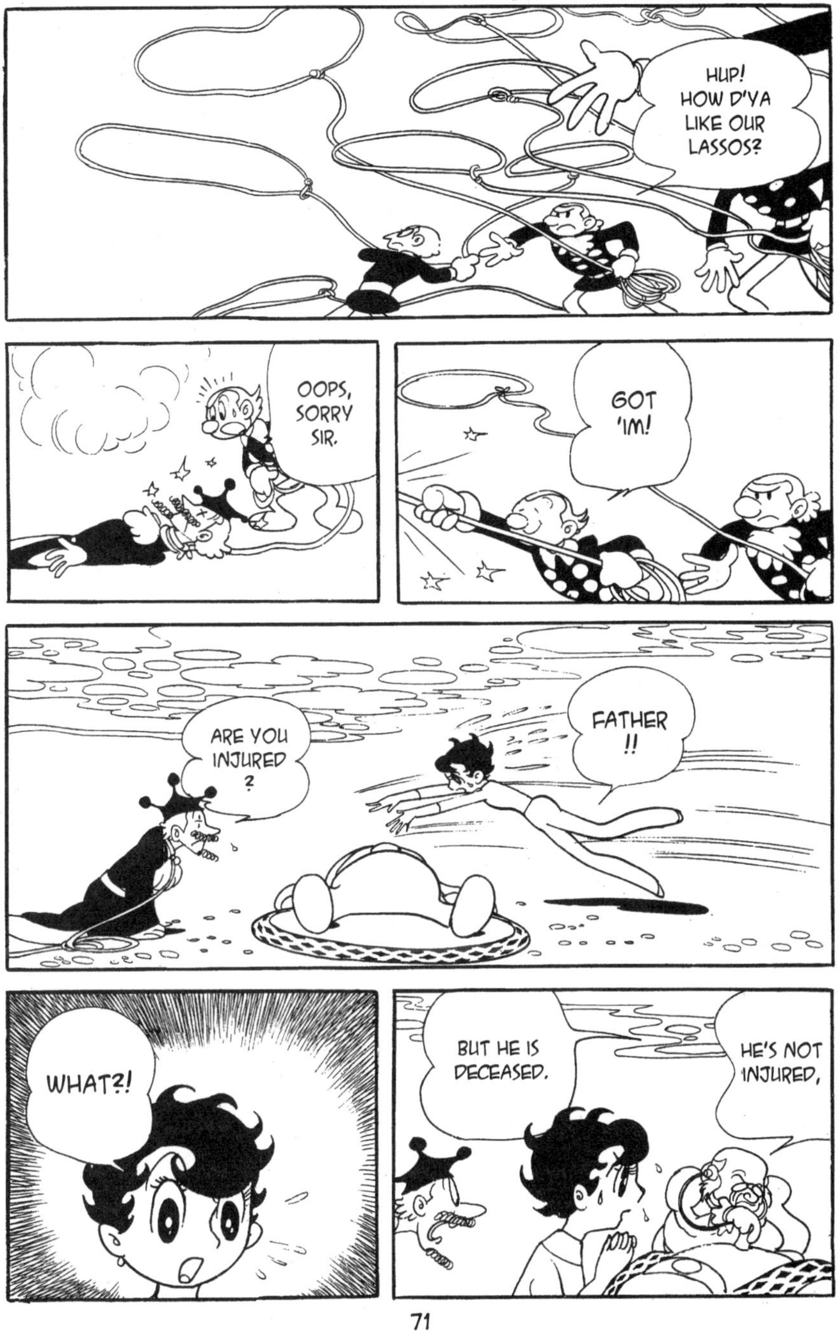
HUP! HOW D'YA LIKE OUR LASSOS?
GOT 'IM!
OOPS, SORRY SIR.
FATHER !!
ARE YOU INJURED ?
HE'S NOT INJURED,
BUT HE IS DECEASED.
WHAT?!

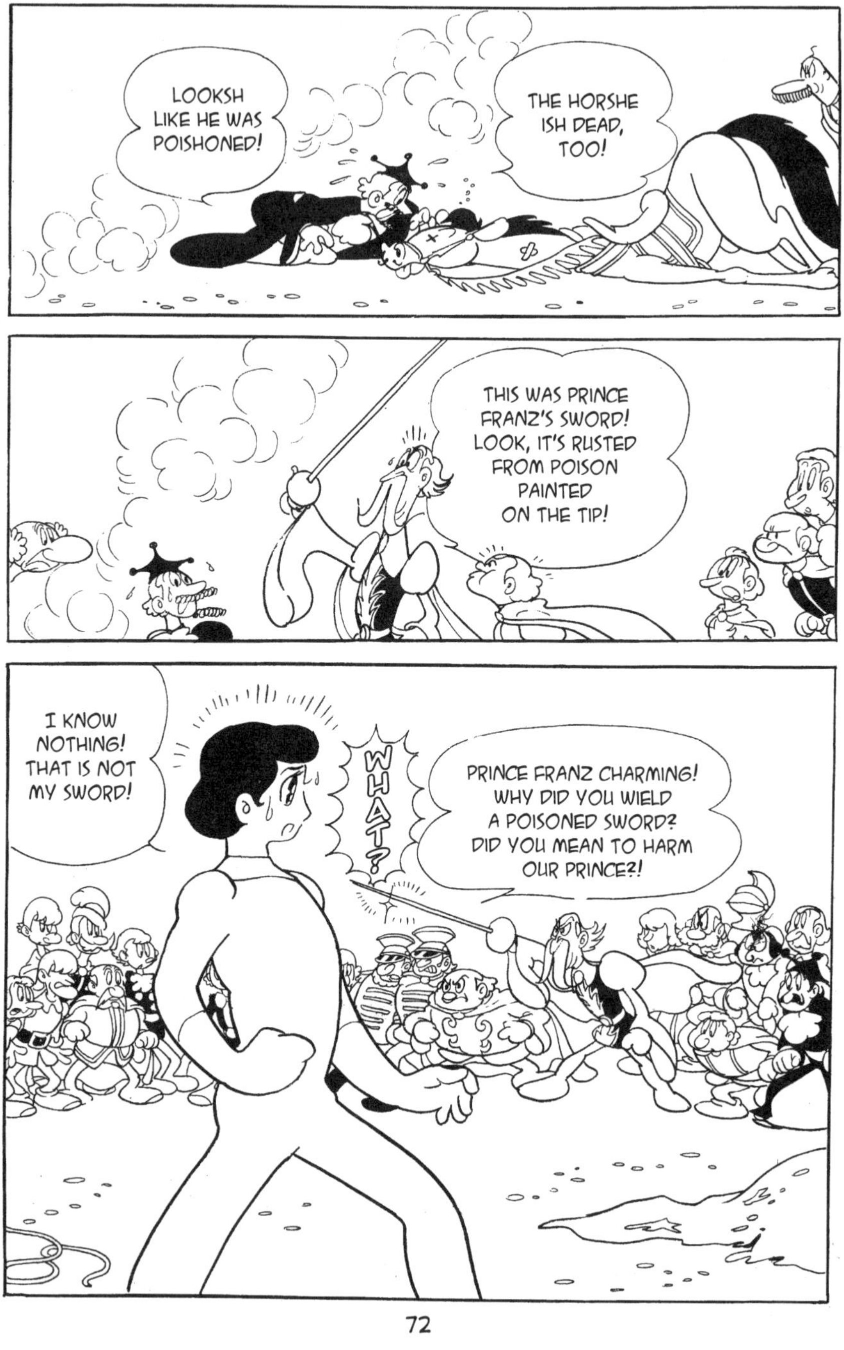
THE HORSHE ISH DEAD, TOO!
LOOKSH LIKE HE WAS POISHONED!
THIS WAS PRINCE FRANZ'S SWORD! LOOK, IT'S RUSTED FROM POISON PAINTED ON THE TIP!
PRINCE FRANZ CHARMING! WHY DID YOU WIELD A POISONED SWORD? DID YOU MEAN TO HARM OUR PRINCE?!
WHAT?
I KNOW NOTHING! THAT IS NOT MY SWORD!

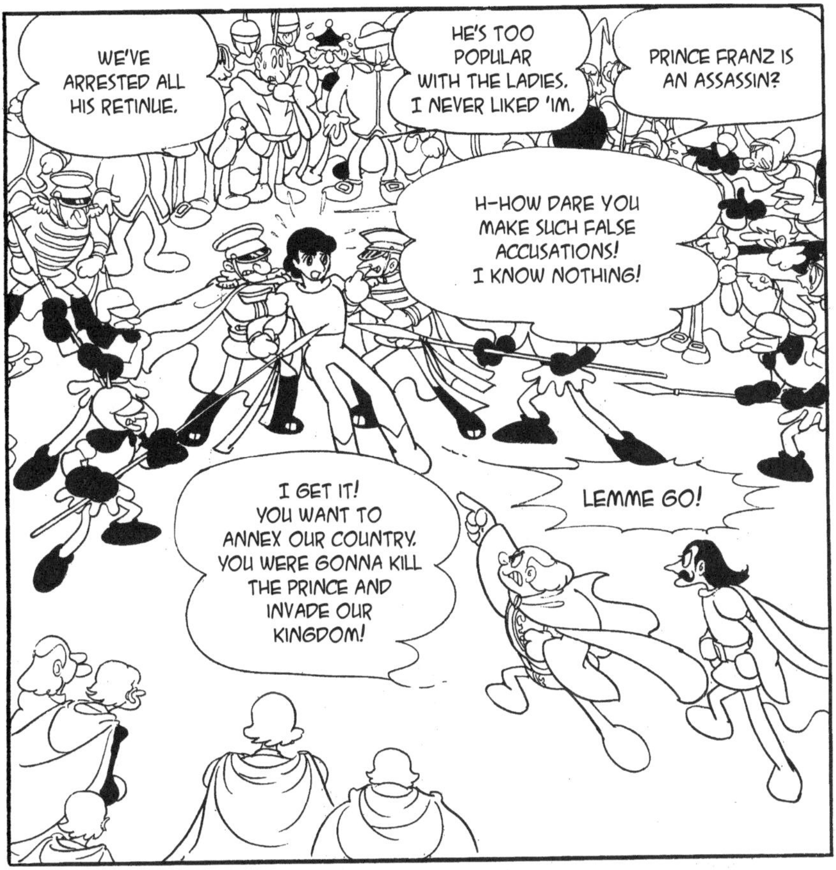
PRINCE FRANZ IS AN ASSASSIN?
HE'S TOO POPULAR WITH THE LADIES. I NEVER LIKED 'IM.
WE'VE ARRESTED ALL HIS RETINUE.
H-HOW DARE YOU MAKE SUCH FALSE ACCUSATIONS! I KNOW NOTHING!
LEMME GO!
I GET IT! YOU WANT TO ANNEX OUR COUNTRY. YOU WERE GONNA KILL THE PRINCE AND INVADE OUR KINGDOM!

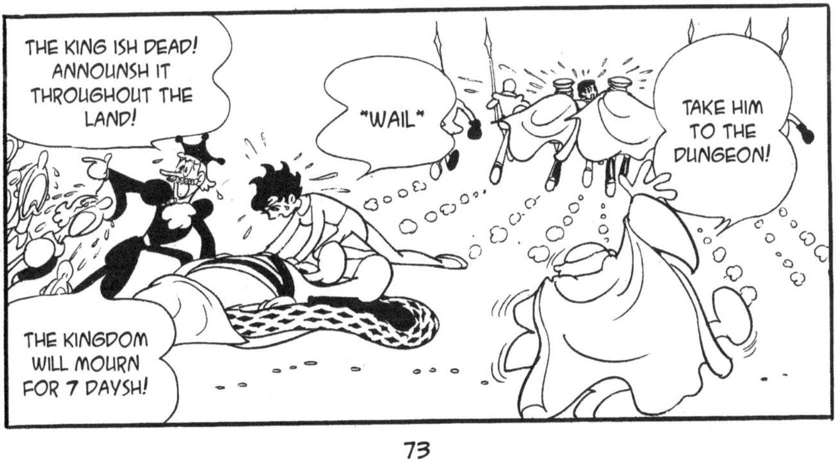
TAKE HIM TO THE DUNGEON!
WAIL
THE KING ISH DEAD! ANNOUNSH IT THROUGHOUT THE LAND!
THE KINGDOM WILL MOURN FOR 7 DAYSH!

Chapter 5

Prisoner Prince

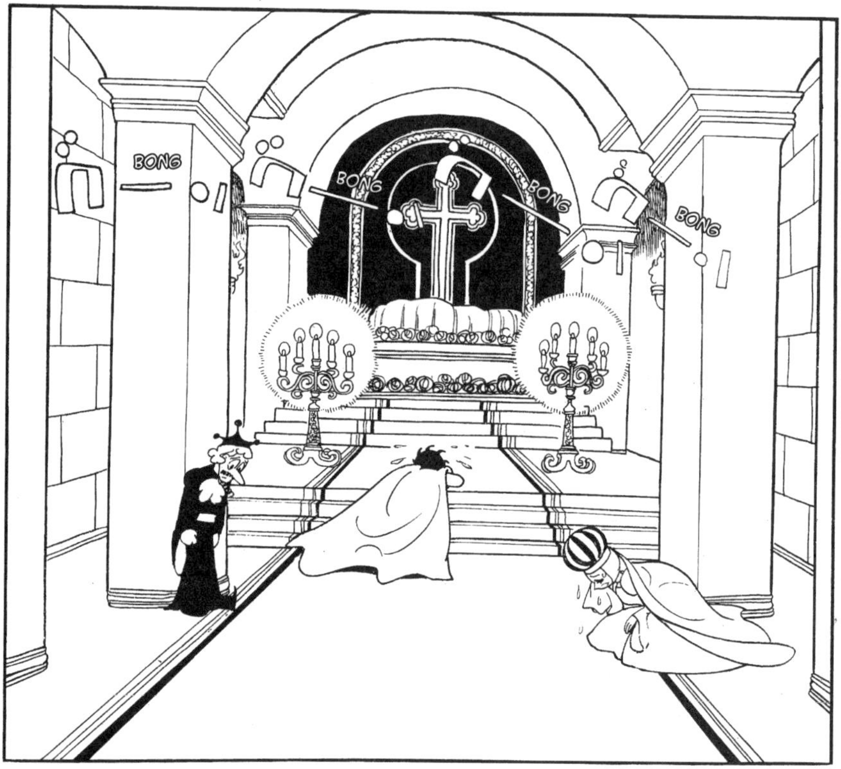
ゴーン
BONG
ゴーン
BONG
ゴーン
BONG
ゴーン
BONG

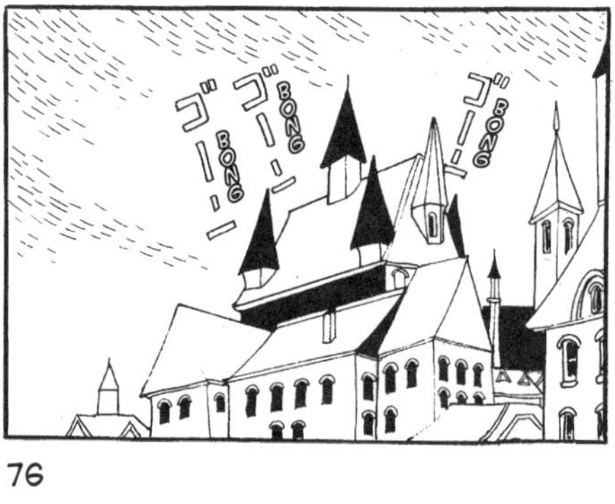
ゴーン
BONG
ゴーン
BONG
ゴーン
BONG

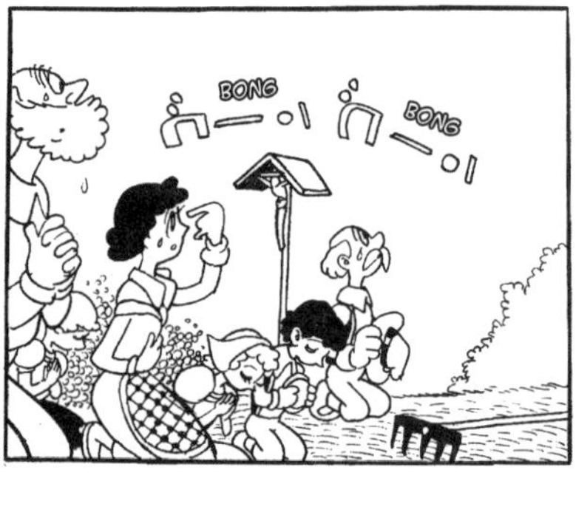
ゴーン
BONG
ゴーン
BONG

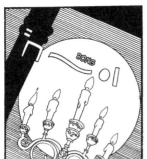

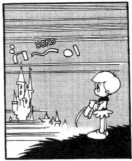

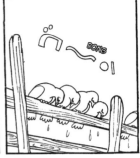

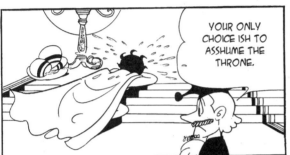

BONG
BONG
BONG
PRINSH, GRIEVING WON'T BRING HIM BACK TO LIFE.
YOUR ONLY CHOICE ISH TO ASSHUME THE THRONE.
IF YOU DON'T, DUKE DURALUMIN WILL MAKE A MOVE FOR THE CROWN.
PLEASE BE STRONG. YOU CAN'T JUST FALL TO PIECES.
THANKS, NURSE.

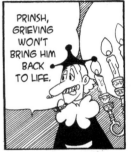

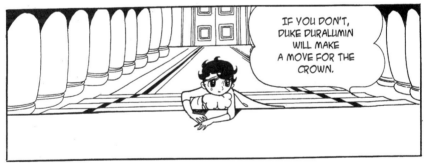

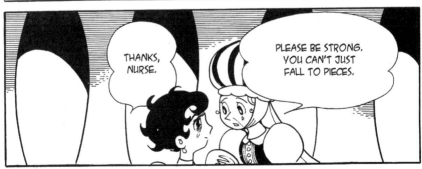

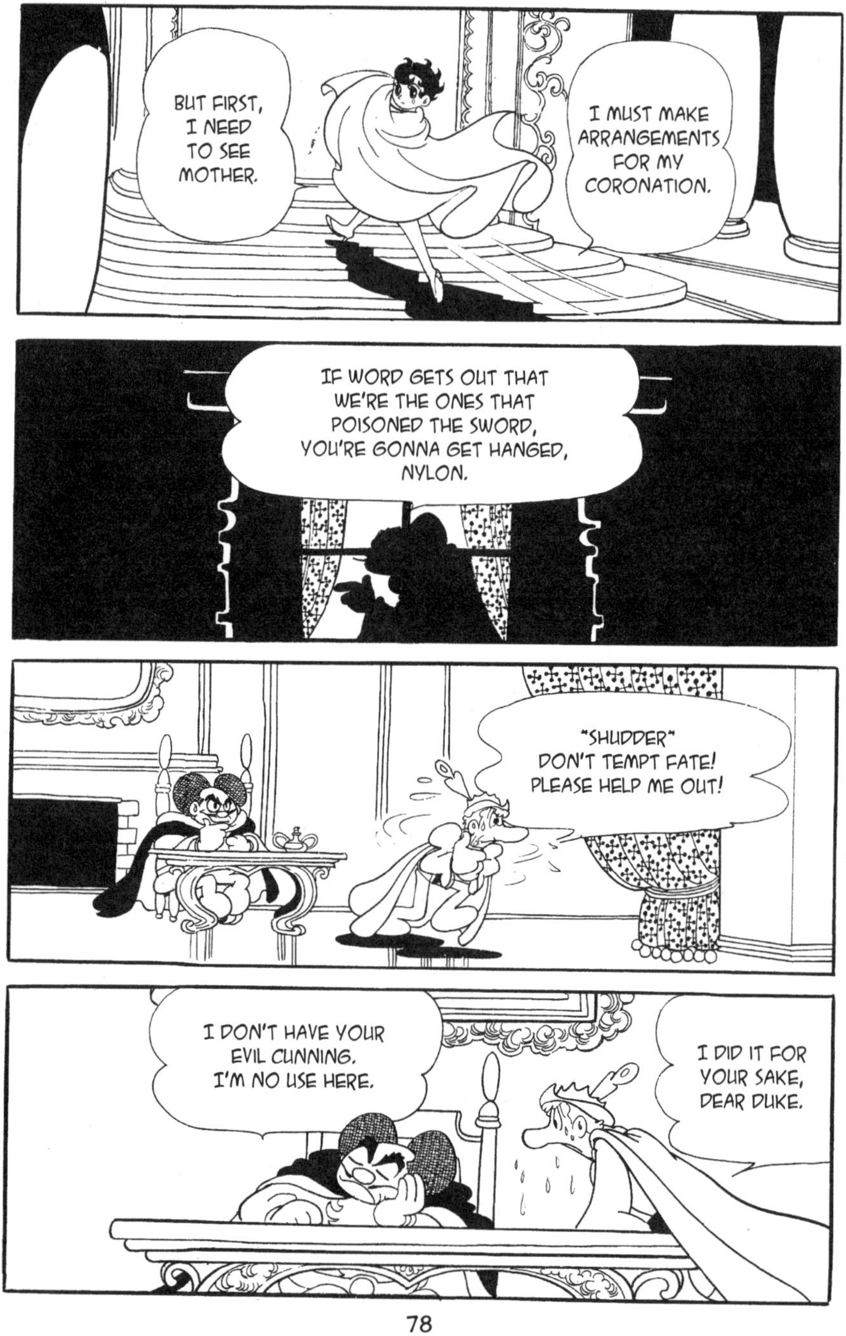
I MUST MAKE ARRANGEMENTS FOR MY CORONATION.
BUT FIRST, I NEED TO SEE MOTHER.
IF WORD GETS OUT THAT WE'RE THE ONES THAT POISONED THE SWORD, YOU'RE GONNA GET HANGED, NYLON.
"SHUDDER" DON'T TEMPT FATE! PLEASE HELP ME OUT!
I DID IT FOR YOUR SAKE, DEAR DUKE.
I DON'T HAVE YOUR EVIL CUNNING. I'M NO USE HERE.

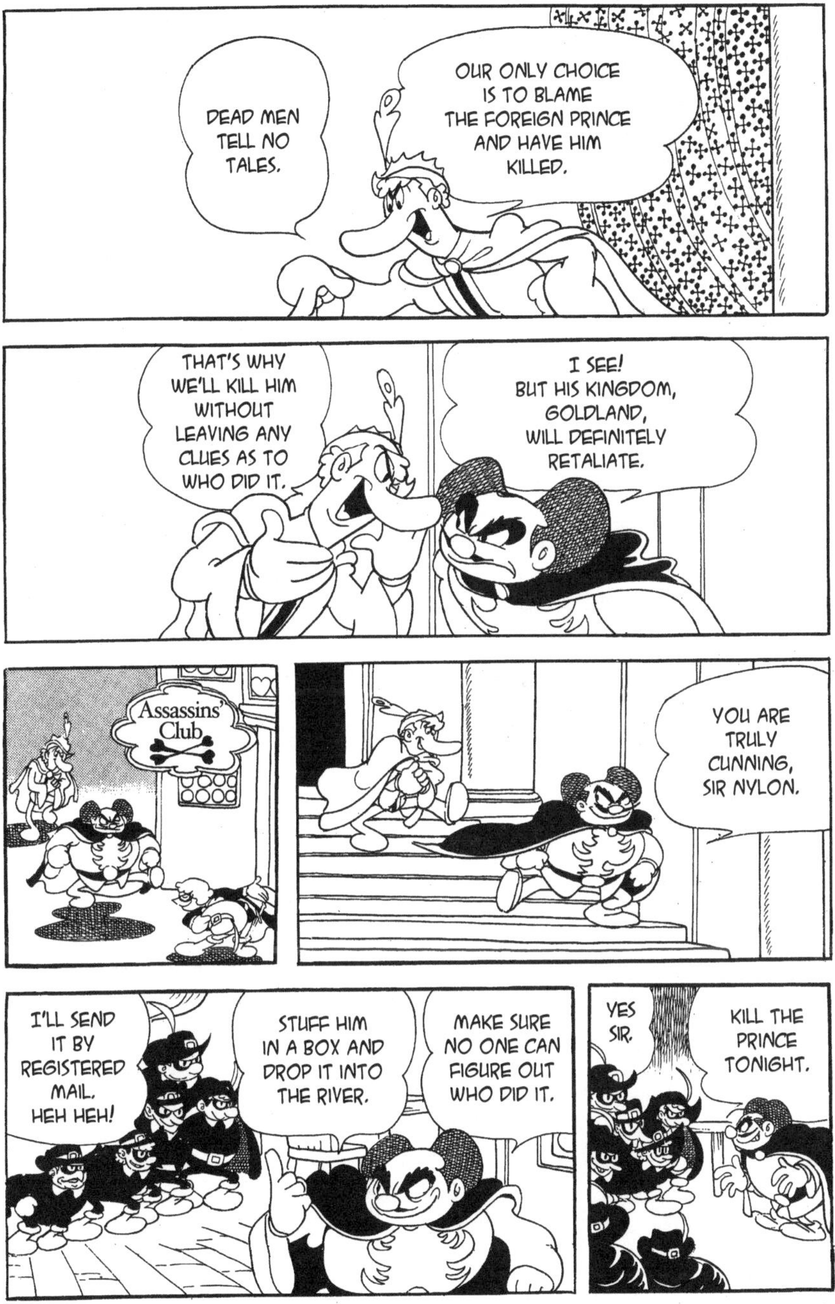
OUR ONLY CHOICE IS TO BLAME THE FOREIGN PRINCE AND HAVE HIM KILLED.
DEAD MEN TELL NO TALES.
I SEE! BUT HIS KINGDOM, GOLDLAND, WILL DEFINITELY RETALIATE.
THAT'S WHY WE'LL KILL HIM WITHOUT LEAVING ANY CLUES AS TO WHO DID IT.
YOU ARE TRULY CUNNING, SIR NYLON.
Assassins' Club
KILL THE PRINCE TONIGHT.
YES SIR.
MAKE SURE NO ONE CAN FIGURE OUT WHO DID IT.
STUFF HIM IN A BOX AND DROP IT INTO THE RIVER.
I'LL SEND IT BY REGISTERED MAIL. HEH HEH!

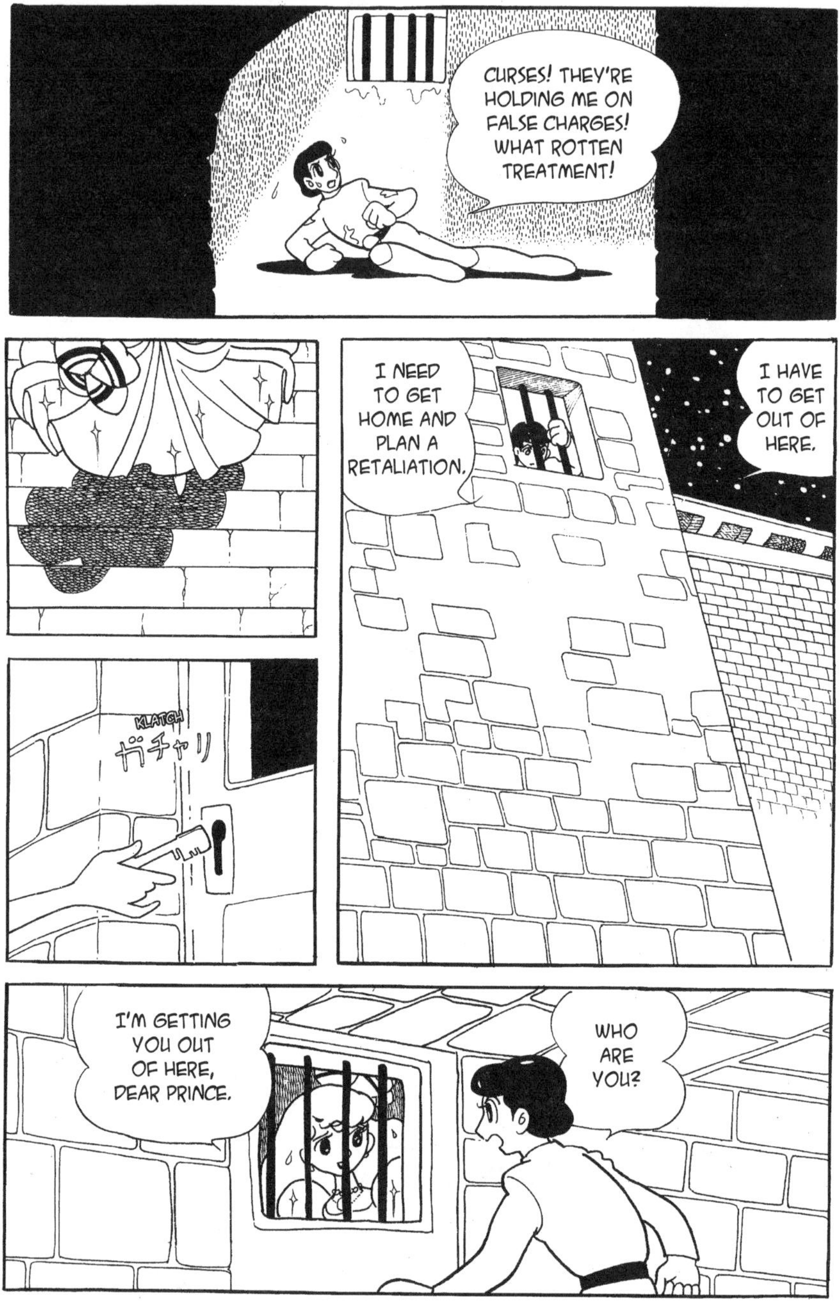
CURSES! THEY'RE HOLDING ME ON FALSE CHARGES! WHAT ROTTEN TREATMENT!
I HAVE TO GET OUT OF HERE.
I NEED TO GET HOME AND PLAN A RETALIATION.
KLATCH
ガチャリ
WHO ARE YOU?
I'M GETTING YOU OUT OF HERE, DEAR PRINCE.

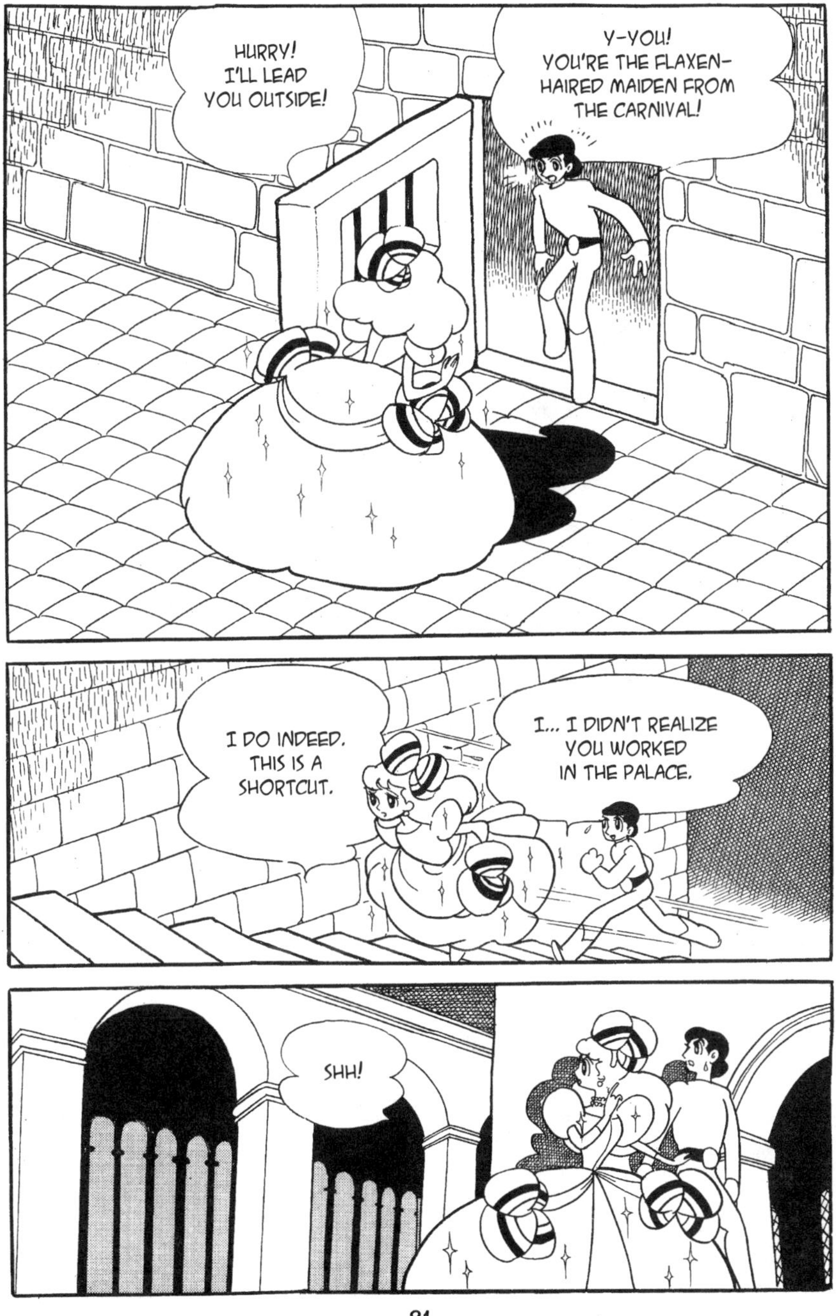
Y-YOU! YOU'RE THE FLAXEN-HAIRED MAIDEN FROM THE CARNIVAL!
HURRY! I'LL LEAD YOU OUTSIDE!
I... I DIDN'T REALIZE YOU WORKED IN THE PALACE.
I DO INDEED. THIS IS A SHORTCUT.
SHH!

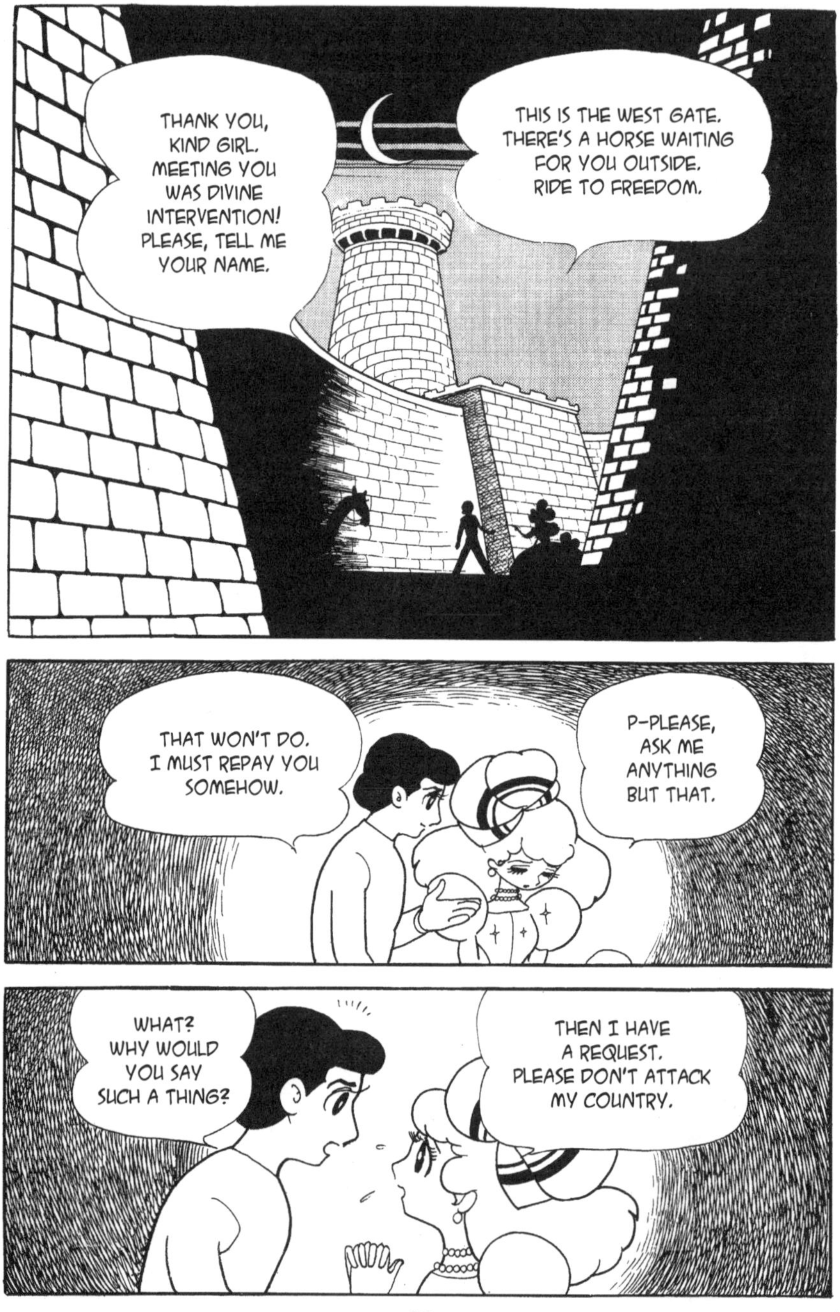
THIS IS THE WEST GATE. THERE'S A HORSE WAITING FOR YOU OUTSIDE. RIDE TO FREEDOM.
THANK YOU, KIND GIRL. MEETING YOU WAS DIVINE INTERVENTION! PLEASE, TELL ME YOUR NAME.
P-PLEASE, ASK ME ANYTHING BUT THAT.
THAT WON'T DO. I MUST REPAY YOU SOMEHOW.
THEN I HAVE A REQUEST. PLEASE DON'T ATTACK MY COUNTRY.
WHAT? WHY WOULD YOU SAY SUCH A THING?

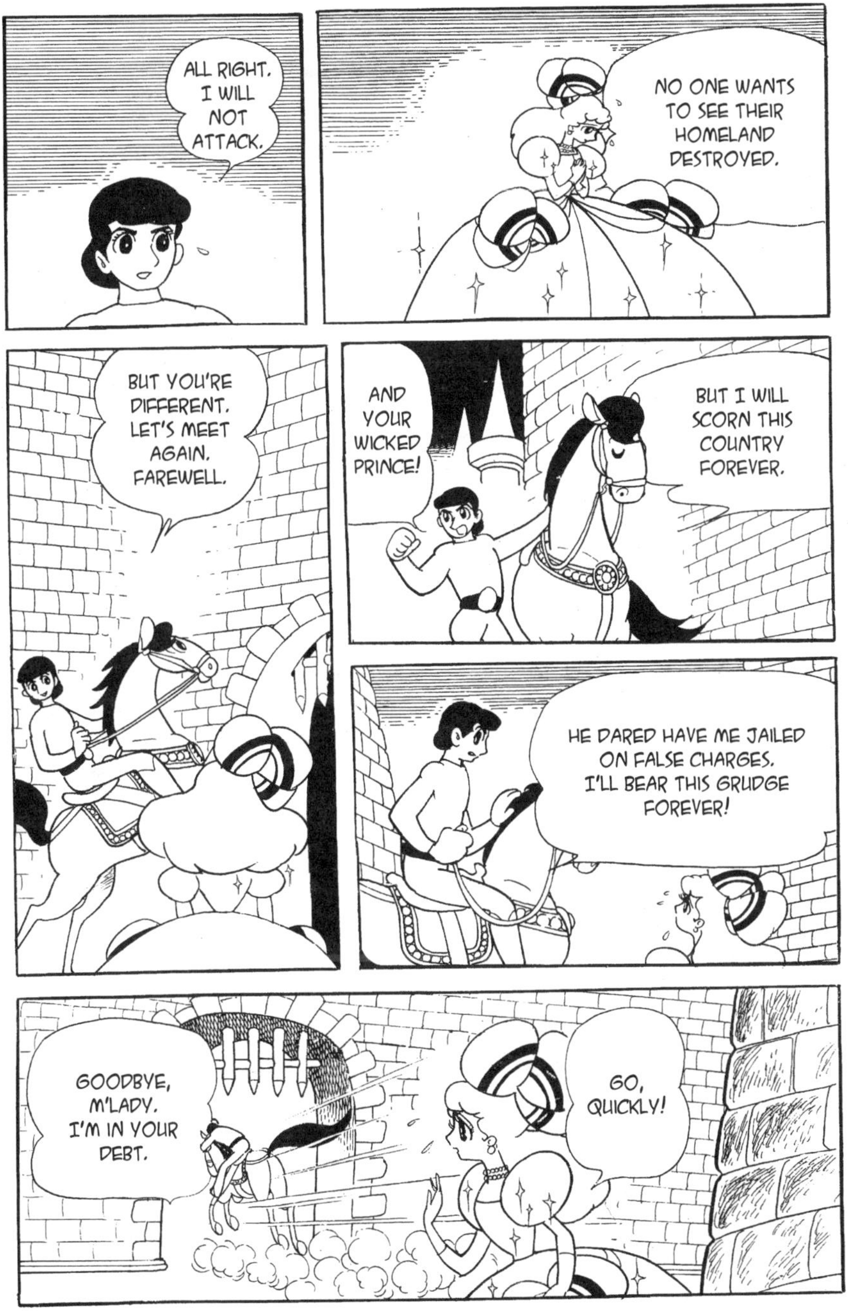
NO ONE WANTS TO SEE THEIR HOMELAND DESTROYED.
ALL RIGHT. I WILL NOT ATTACK.
BUT I WILL SCORN THIS COUNTRY FOREVER.
AND YOUR WICKED PRINCE!
HE DARED HAVE ME JAILED ON FALSE CHARGES. I'LL BEAR THIS GRUDGE FOREVER!
BUT YOU'RE DIFFERENT. LET'S MEET AGAIN. FAREWELL.
GO, QUICKLY!
GOODBYE, M'LADY. I'M IN YOUR DEBT.

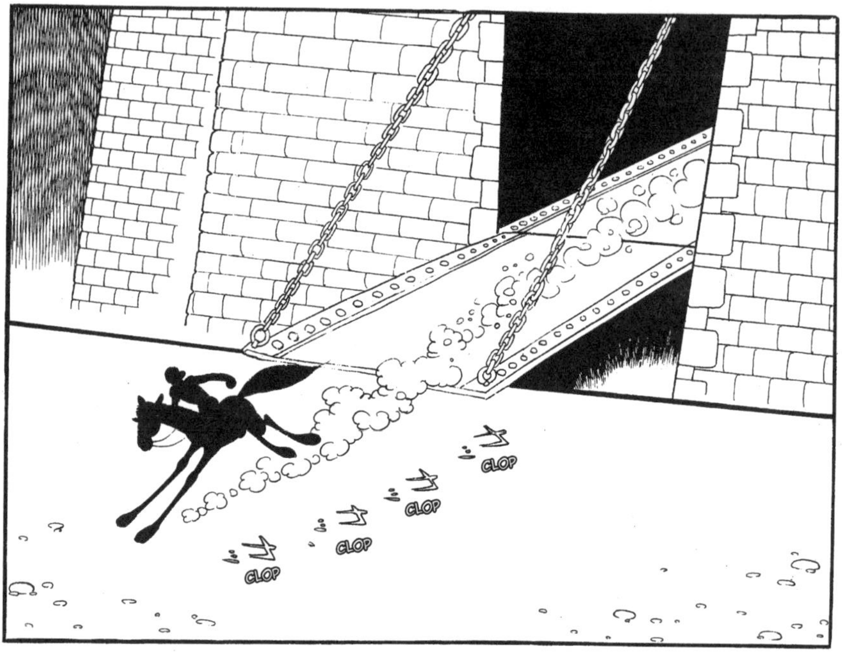
CLOP
CLOP
CLOP
CLOP

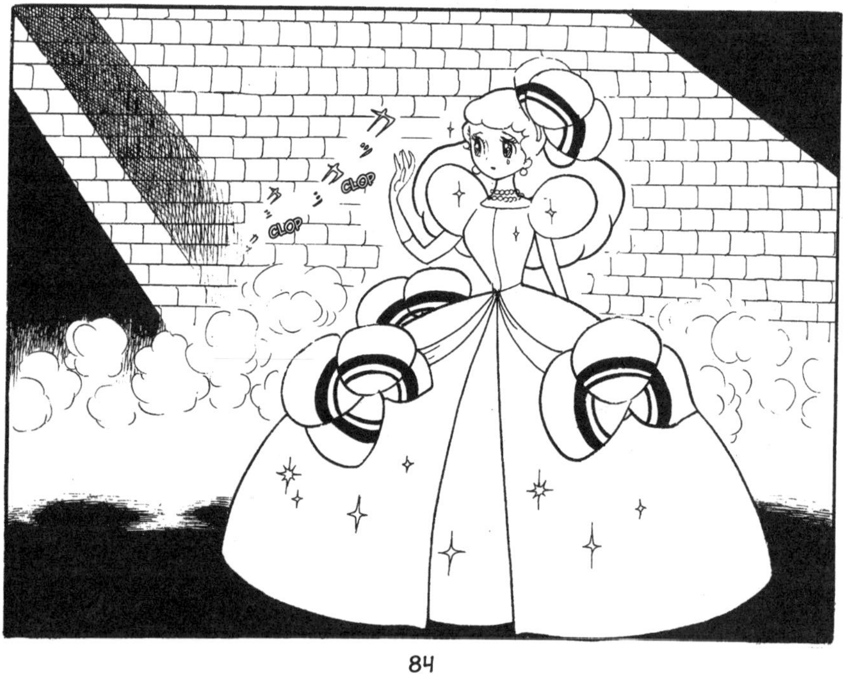
CLOP
CLOP

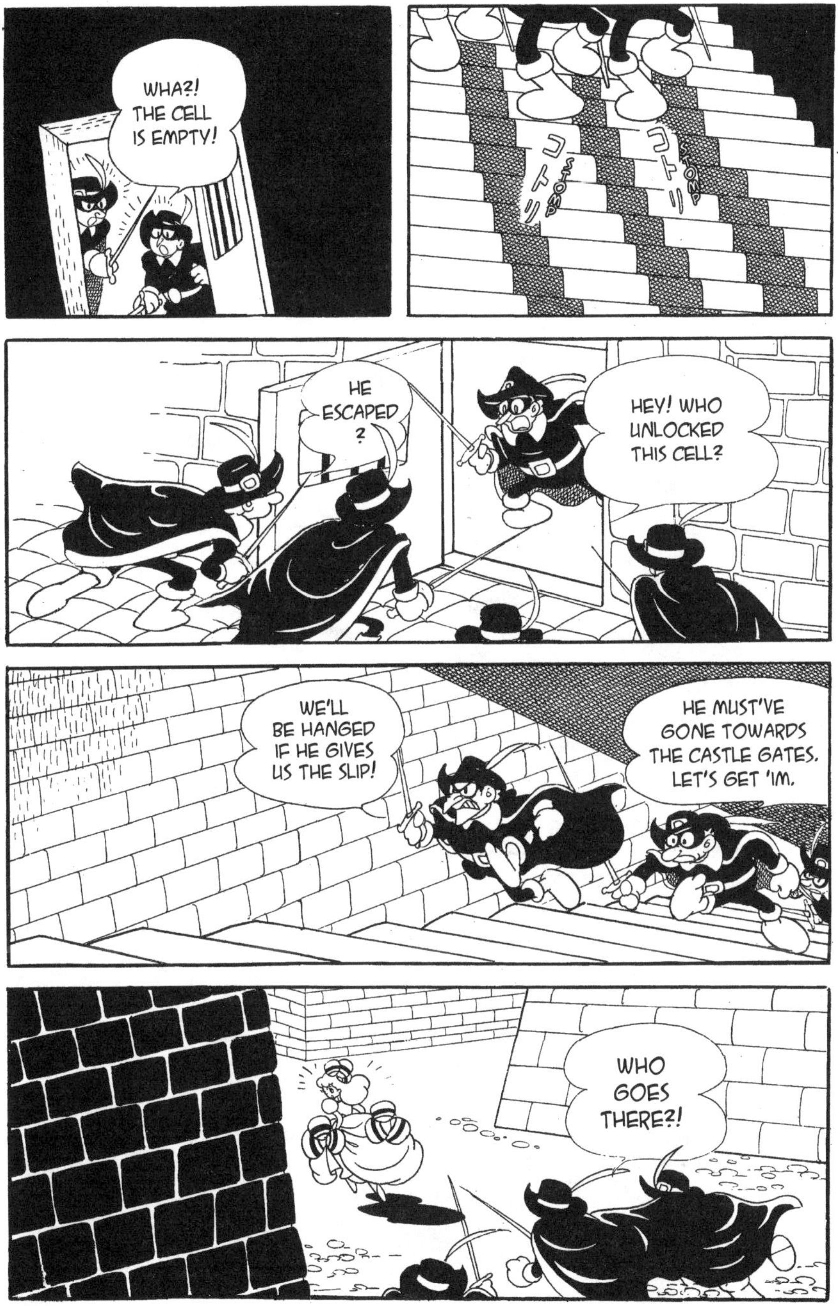
コトリ STOMP
コトリ STOMP
WHA?! THE CELL IS EMPTY!
HEY! WHO UNLOCKED THIS CELL?
HE ESCAPED?
HE MUST'VE GONE TOWARDS THE CASTLE GATES. LET'S GET 'IM.
WE'LL BE HANGED IF HE GIVES US THE SLIP!
WHO GOES THERE?!

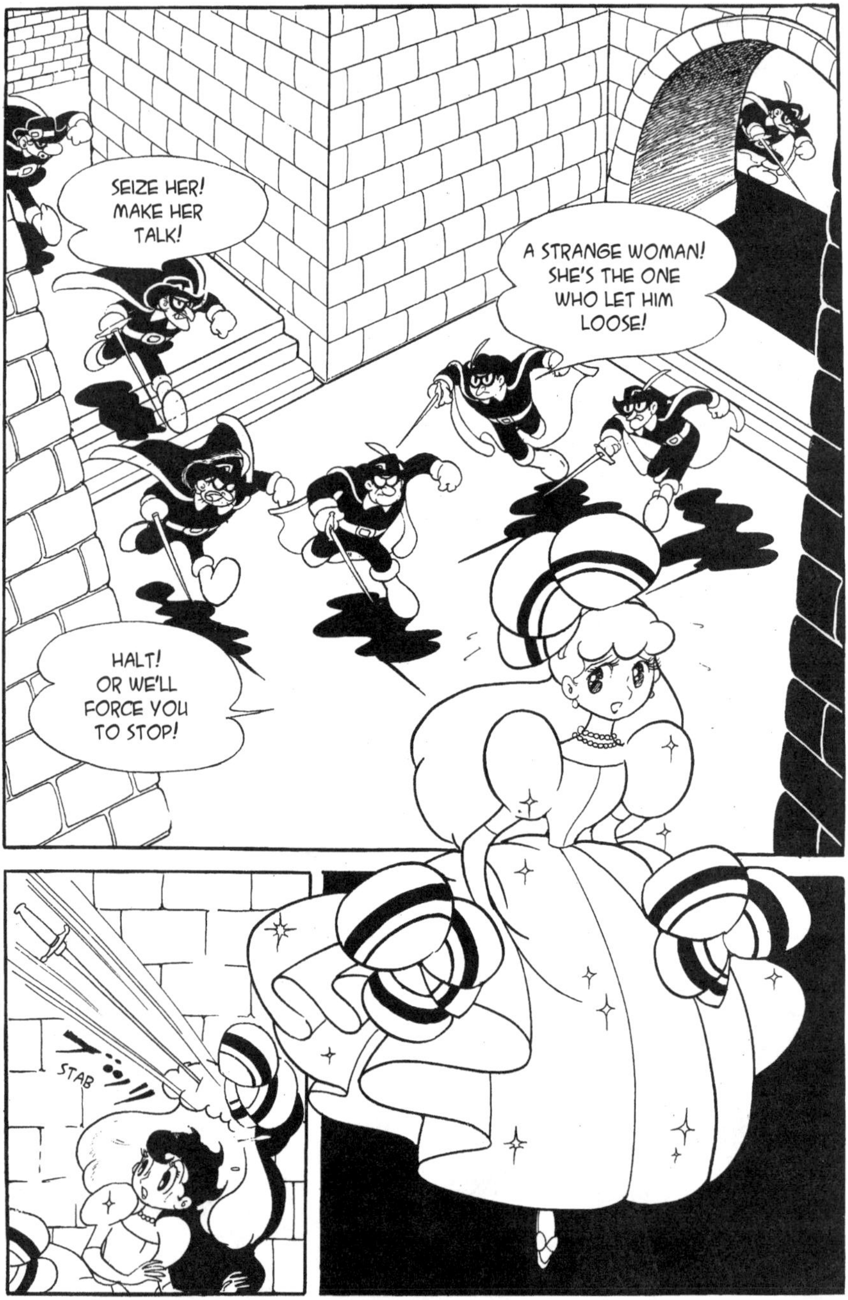
A STRANGE WOMAN! SHE'S THE ONE WHO LET HIM LOOSE!
SEIZE HER! MAKE HER TALK!
HALT! OR WE'LL FORCE YOU TO STOP!
STAB

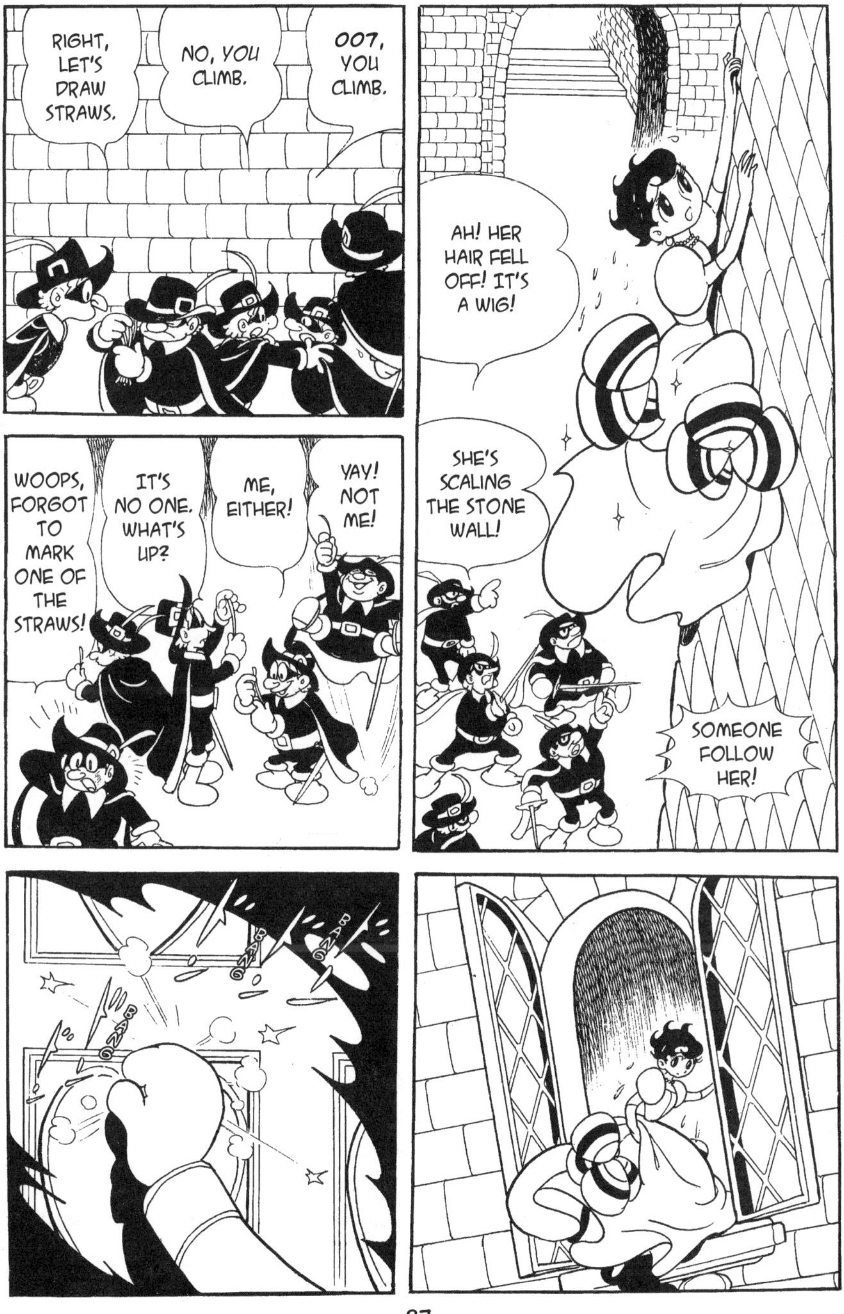
AH! HER HAIR FELL OFF! IT'S A WIG!
SHE'S SCALING THE STONE WALL!
SOMEONE FOLLOW HER!
007, YOU CLIMB.
NO, YOU CLIMB.
RIGHT, LET'S DRAW STRAWS.
YAY! NOT ME!
ME, EITHER!
IT'S NO ONE. WHAT'S UP?
WOOPS, FORGOT TO MARK ONE OF THE STRAWS!
BANG
BANG
BANG

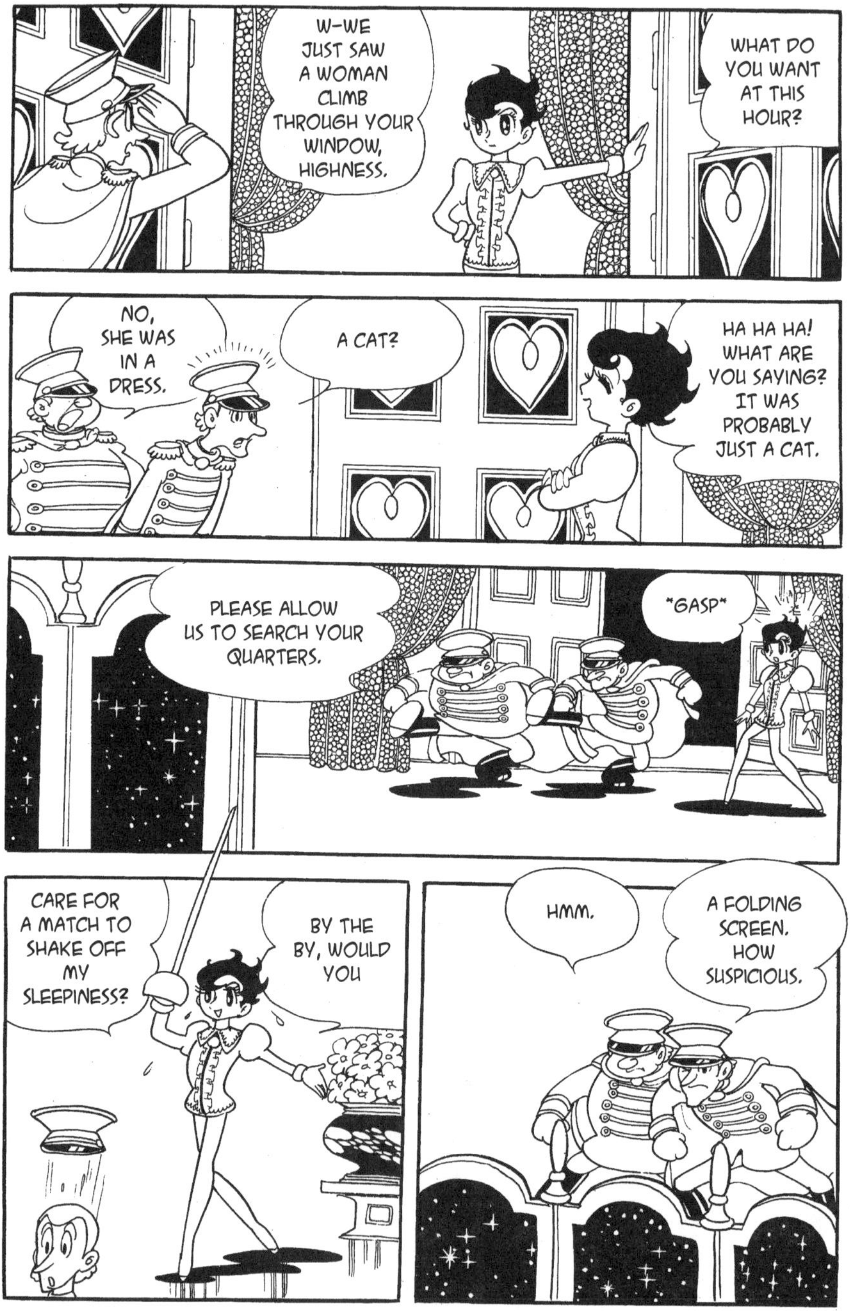
WHAT DO YOU WANT AT THIS HOUR?
W-WE JUST SAW A WOMAN CLIMB THROUGH YOUR WINDOW, HIGHNESS.
HA HA HA! WHAT ARE YOU SAYING? IT WAS PROBABLY JUST A CAT.
A CAT?
NO, SHE WAS IN A DRESS.
GASP
PLEASE ALLOW US TO SEARCH YOUR QUARTERS.
A FOLDING SCREEN. HOW SUSPICIOUS.
HMM.
BY THE BY, WOULD YOU
CARE FOR A MATCH TO SHAKE OFF MY SLEEPINESS?

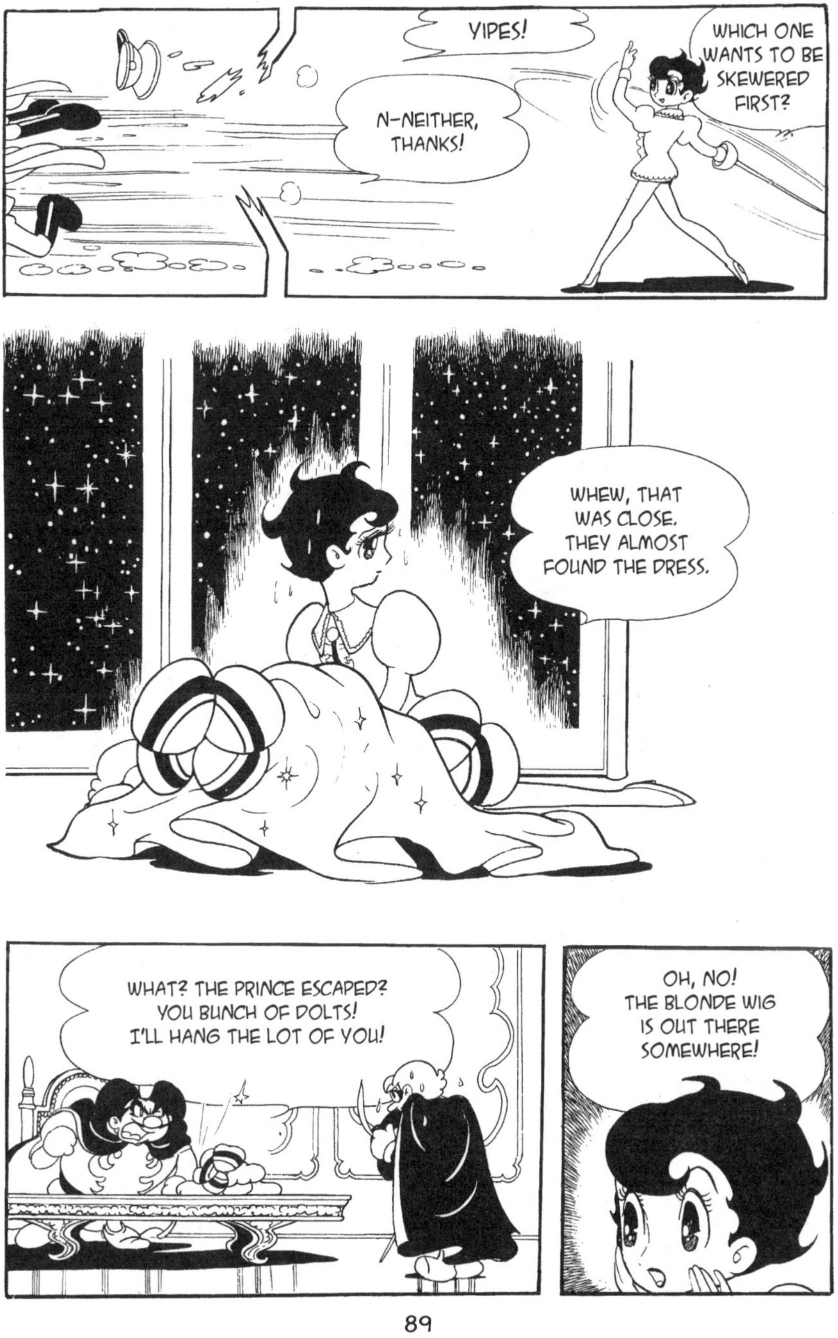
WHICH ONE WANTS TO BE SKEWERED FIRST?
YIPES!
N-NEITHER, THANKS!
WHEW, THAT WAS CLOSE. THEY ALMOST FOUND THE DRESS.
OH, NO! THE BLONDE WIG IS OUT THERE SOMEWHERE!
WHAT? THE PRINCE ESCAPED? YOU BUNCH OF DOLTS! I'LL HANG THE LOT OF YOU!

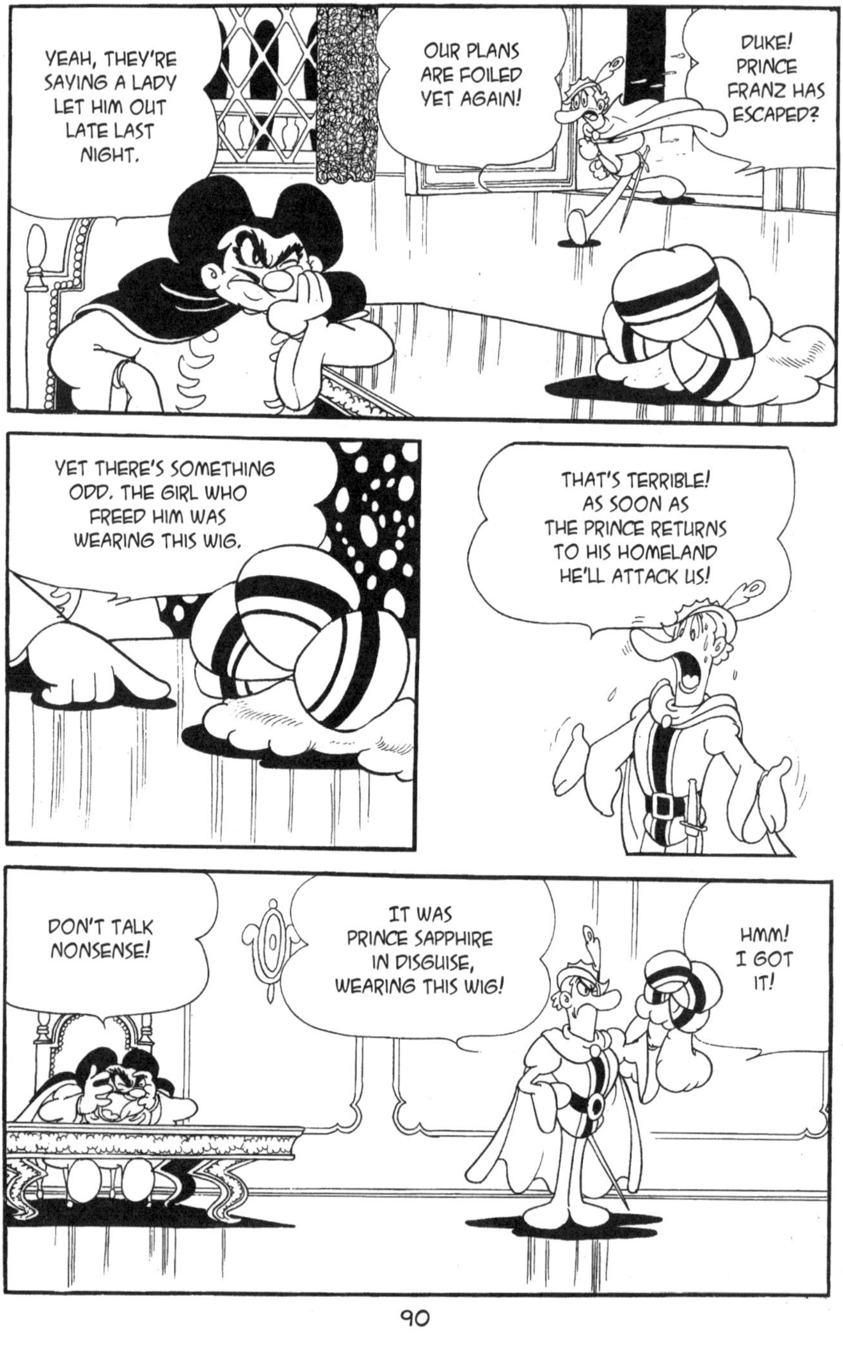
DUKE! PRINCE FRANZ HAS ESCAPED?
OUR PLANS ARE FOILED YET AGAIN!
YEAH, THEY'RE SAYING A LADY LET HIM OUT LATE LAST NIGHT.
THAT'S TERRIBLE! AS SOON AS THE PRINCE RETURNS TO HIS HOMELAND HE'LL ATTACK US!
YET THERE'S SOMETHING ODD. THE GIRL WHO FREED HIM WAS WEARING THIS WIG.
HMM! I GOT IT!
IT WAS PRINCE SAPPHIRE IN DISGUISE, WEARING THIS WIG!
DON'T TALK NONSENSE!

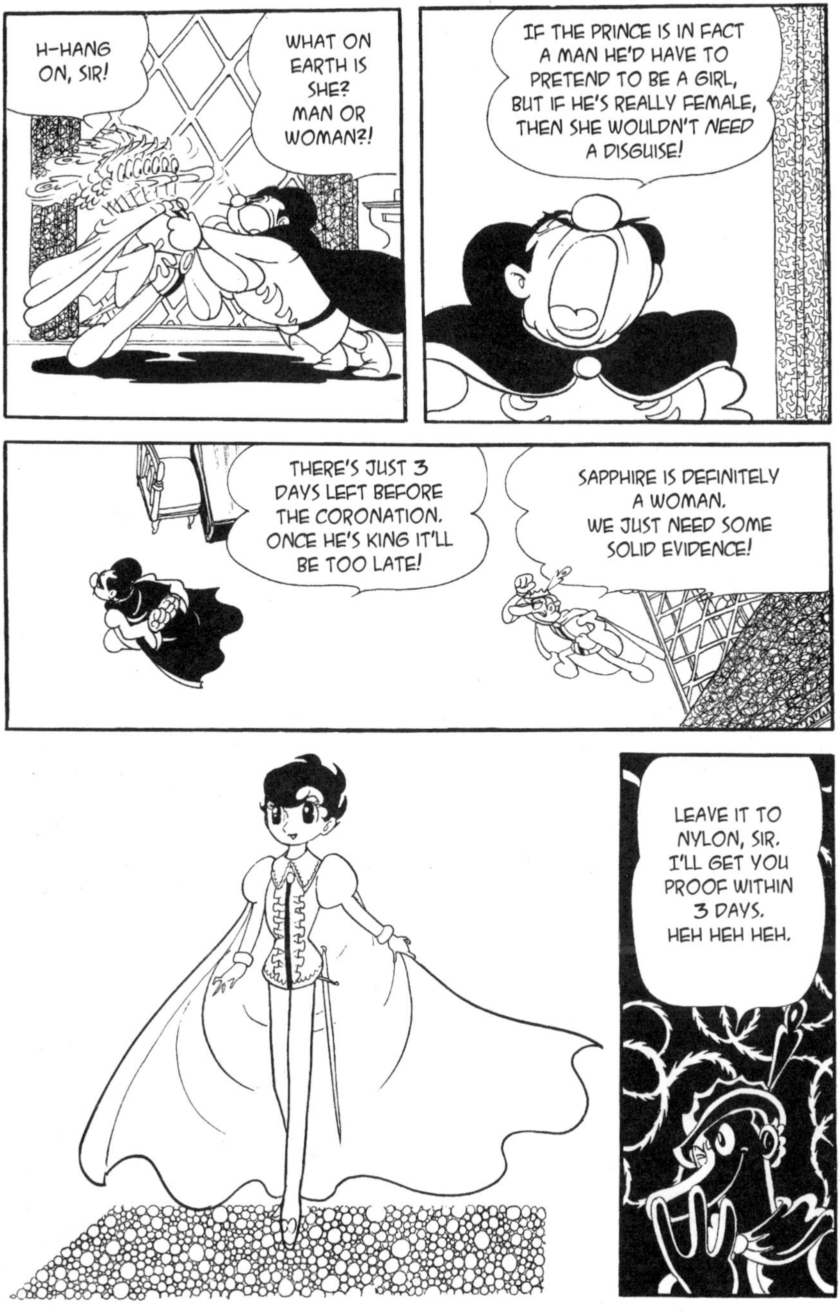
IF THE PRINCE IS IN FACT A MAN HE'D HAVE TO PRETEND TO BE A GIRL, BUT IF HE'S REALLY FEMALE, THEN SHE WOULDN'T NEED A DISGUISE!
WHAT ON EARTH IS SHE? MAN OR WOMAN?!
H-HANG ON, SIR!
SAPPHIRE IS DEFINITELY A WOMAN. WE JUST NEED SOME SOLID EVIDENCE!
THERE'S JUST 3 DAYS LEFT BEFORE THE CORONATION. ONCE HE'S KING IT'LL BE TOO LATE!
LEAVE IT TO NYLON, SIR. I'LL GET YOU PROOF WITHIN 3 DAYS. HEH HEH HEH.

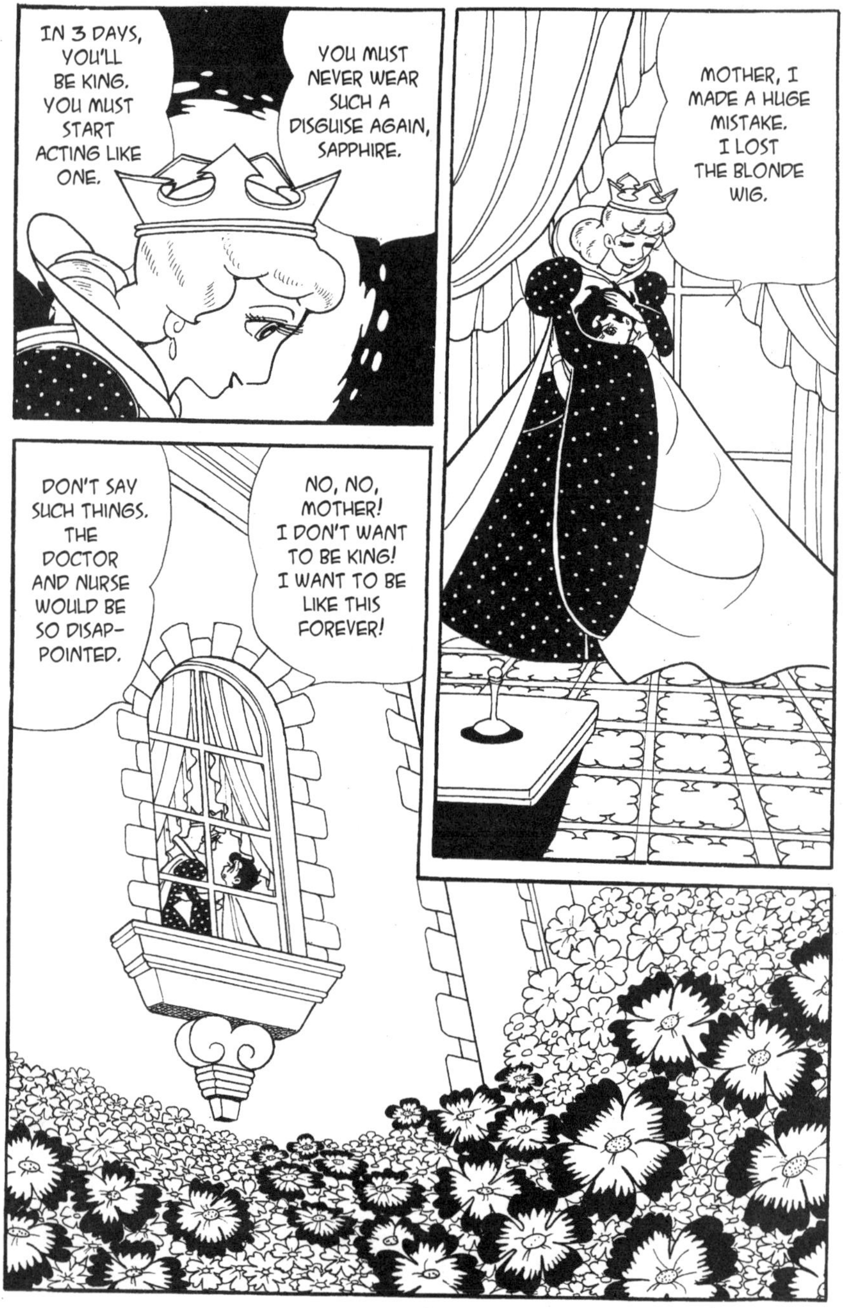
MOTHER, I MADE A HUGE MISTAKE. I LOST THE BLONDE WIG.
YOU MUST NEVER WEAR SUCH A DISGUISE AGAIN, SAPPHIRE.
IN 3 DAYS, YOU'LL BE KING. YOU MUST START ACTING LIKE ONE.
NO, NO, MOTHER! I DON'T WANT TO BE KING! I WANT TO BE LIKE THIS FOREVER!
DON'T SAY SUCH THINGS. THE DOCTOR AND NURSE WOULD BE SO DISAP-POINTED.

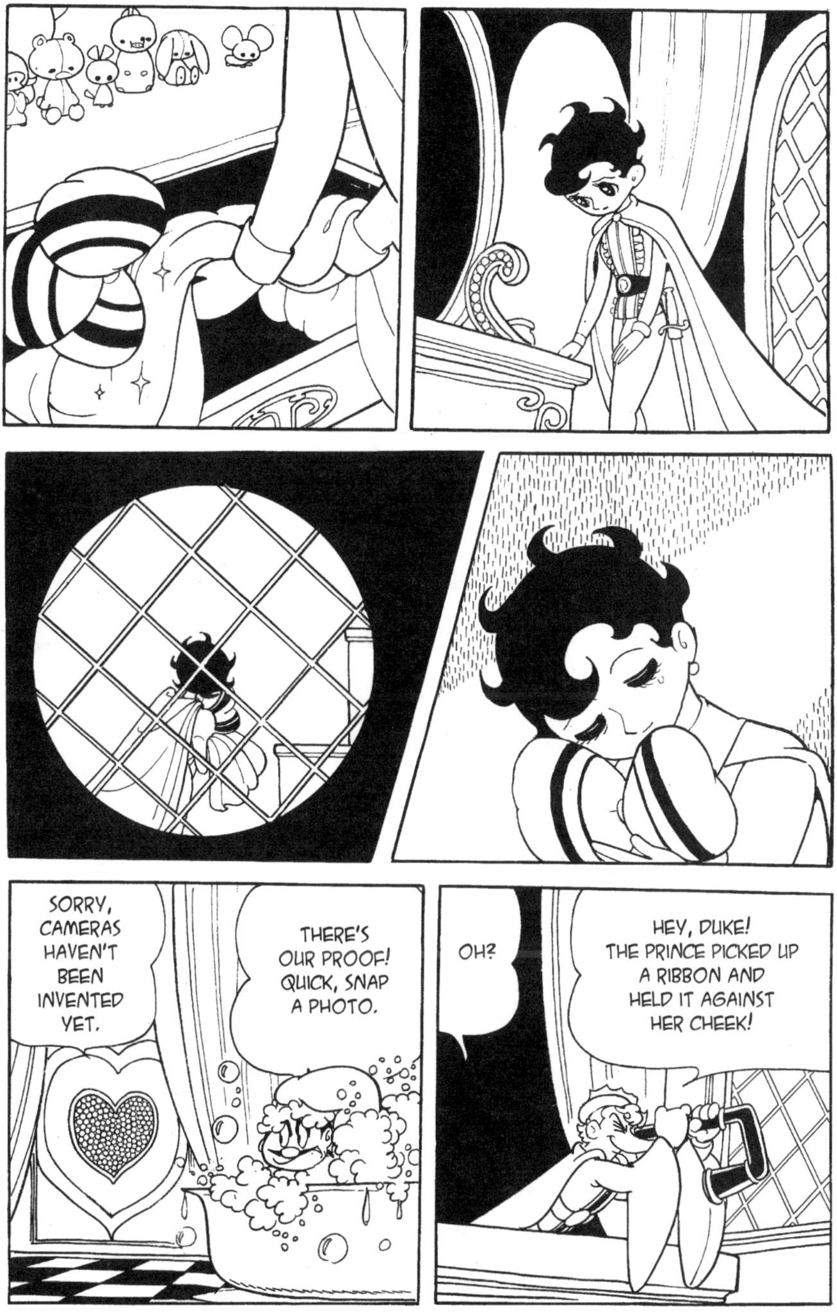
HEY, DUKE!
THE PRINCE PICKED UP A RIBBON AND HELD IT AGAINST HER CHEEK!
OH?
THERE'S OUR PROOF! QUICK, SNAP A PHOTO.
SORRY, CAMERAS HAVEN'T BEEN INVENTED YET.

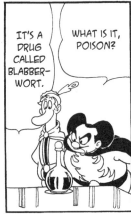

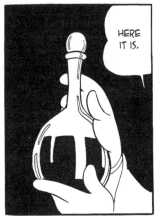

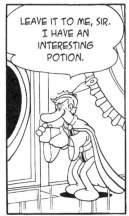

LEAVE IT TO ME, SIR. I HAVE AN INTERESTING POTION.
HERE IT IS.
WHAT IS IT, POISON?
IT'S A DRUG CALLED BLABBER-WORT.
ANYONE WHO DRINKS IT WILL BE INSTANTLY INTOXICATED AND TELL THE TRUTH ABOUT ANYTHING.
SO WHO'LL WE GET TO DRINK IT?
THE DOWAGER QUEEN, OF COURSE!
SHH!
DURING THE TOAST FOR THE CORONATION, I'LL SLIP THIS INTO THE QUEEN'S WINE GOBLET.
SHE'LL INSTANTLY GIVE UP ANY SECRETS REGARDING THE PRINCE'S IDENTITY.

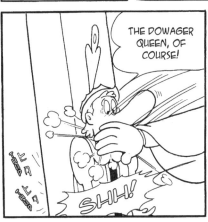

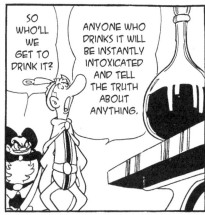

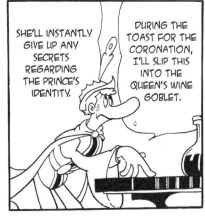

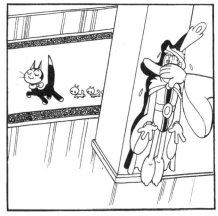

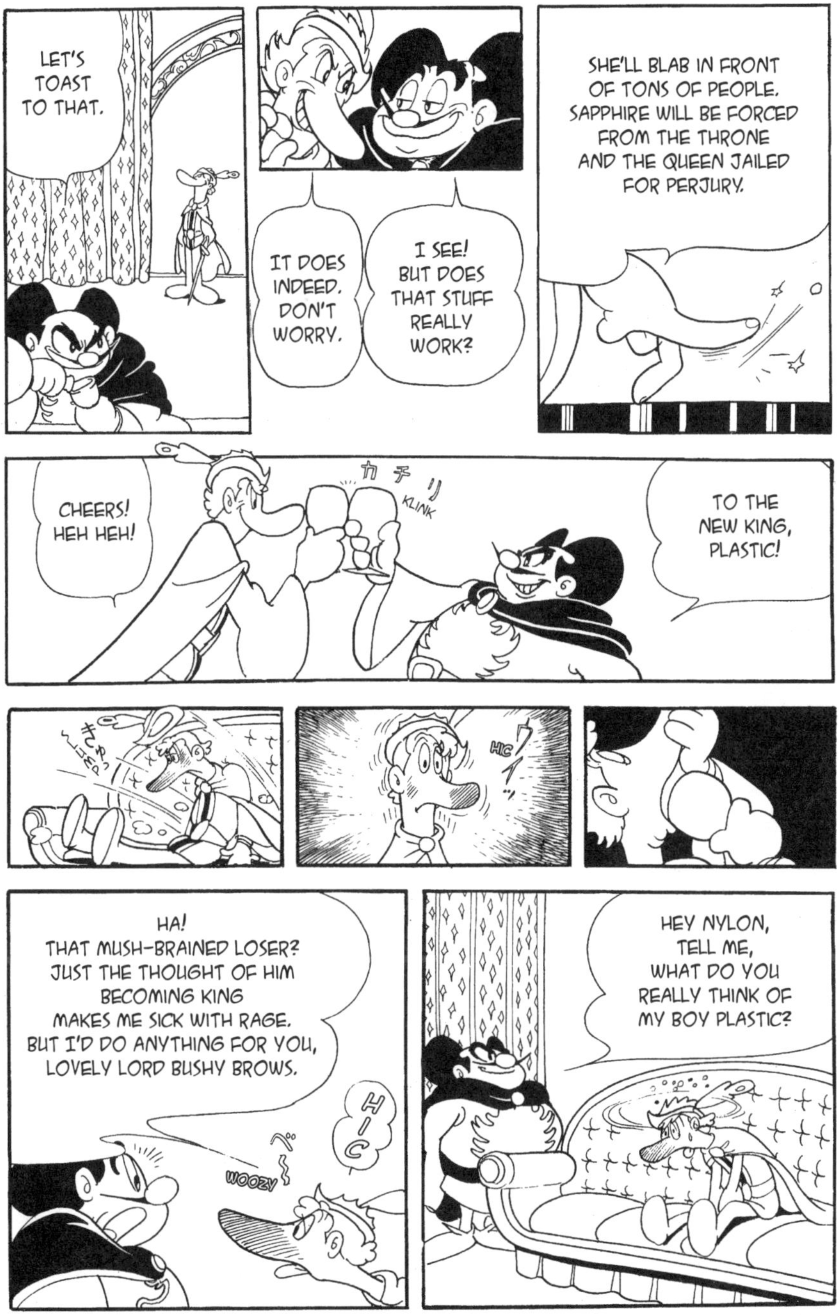
SHE'LL BLAB IN FRONT OF TONS OF PEOPLE. SAPPHIRE WILL BE FORCED FROM THE THRONE AND THE QUEEN JAILED FOR PERJURY.
I SEE! BUT DOES THAT STUFF REALLY WORK?
IT DOES INDEED. DON'T WORRY.
LET'S TOAST TO THAT.
TO THE NEW KING, PLASTIC!
カチリ
KLINK
CHEERS! HEH HEH!
ウィ
HIC
HEY NYLON, TELL ME, WHAT DO YOU REALLY THINK OF MY BOY PLASTIC?
HA! THAT MUSH-BRAINED LOSER? JUST THE THOUGHT OF HIM BECOMING KING MAKES ME SICK WITH RAGE. BUT I'D DO ANYTHING FOR YOU, LOVELY LORD BUSHY BROWS.
HIC
べ～
WOOZY

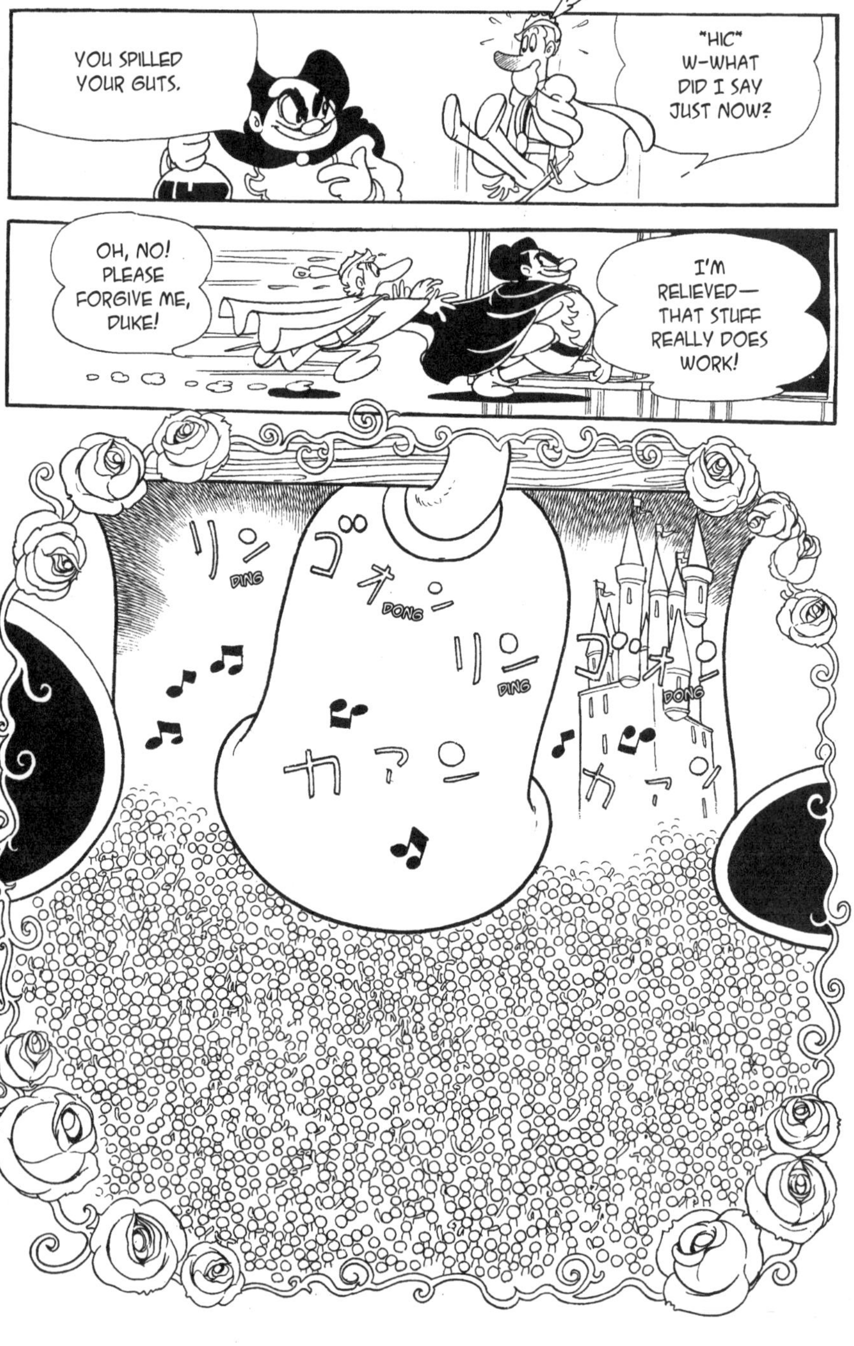
HIC
W-WHAT
DID I SAY
JUST NOW?
YOU SPILLED
YOUR GUTS.
I'M
RELIEVED—
THAT STUFF
REALLY DOES
WORK!
OH, NO!
PLEASE
FORGIVE ME,
DUKE!
リン
DING
ゴォーン
DONG
リン
DING
ゴォー
DONG
カァーン
カァーン

Chapter 6

Coronation

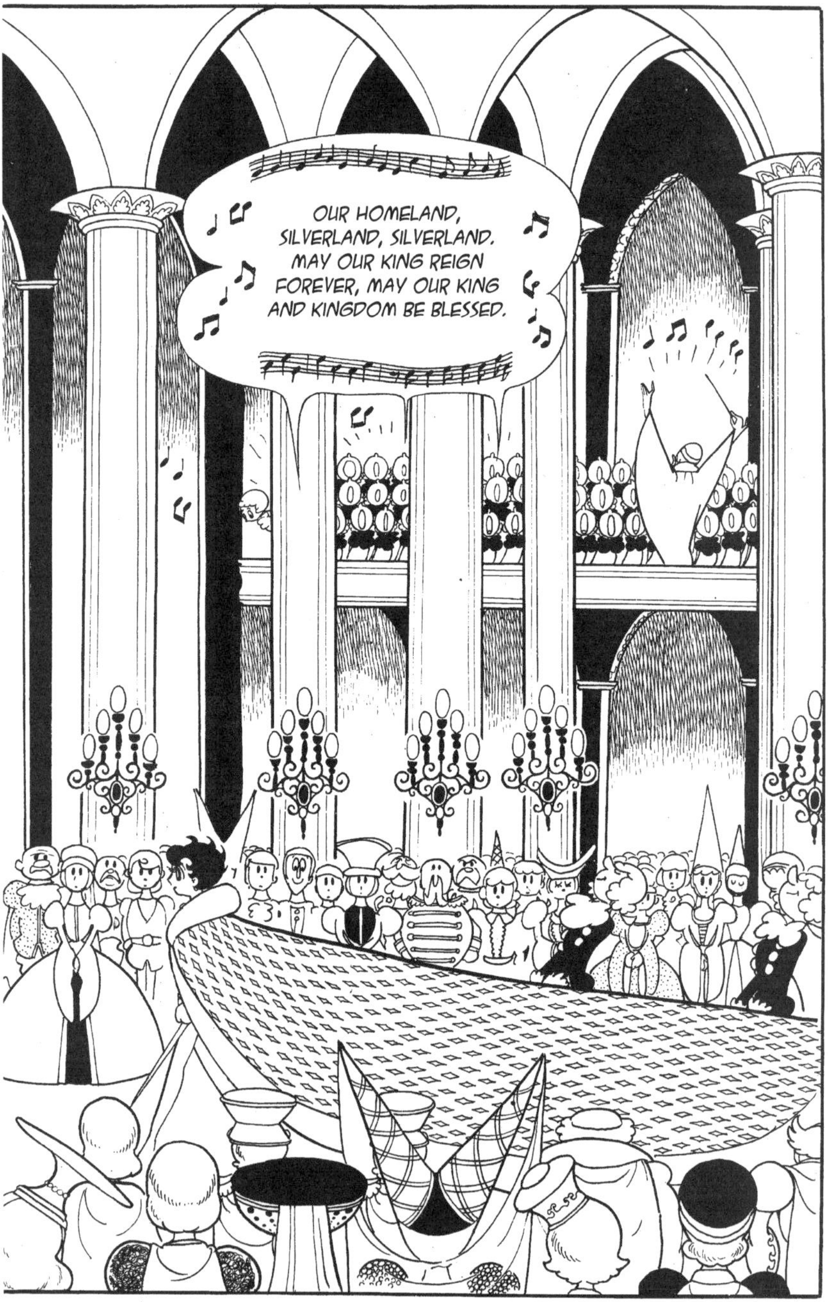
OUR HOMELAND, SILVERLAND, SILVERLAND. MAY OUR KING REIGN FOREVER, MAY OUR KING AND KINGDOM BE BLESSED.

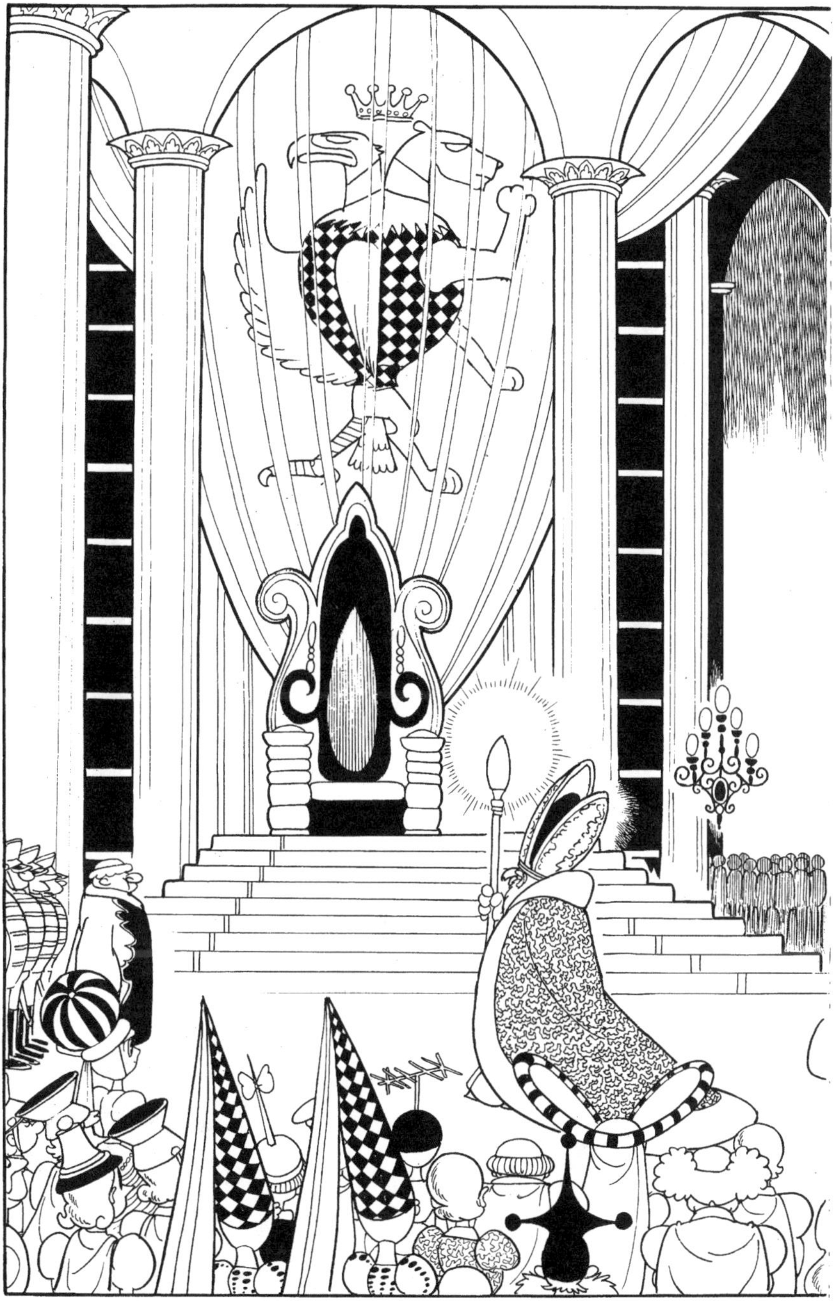

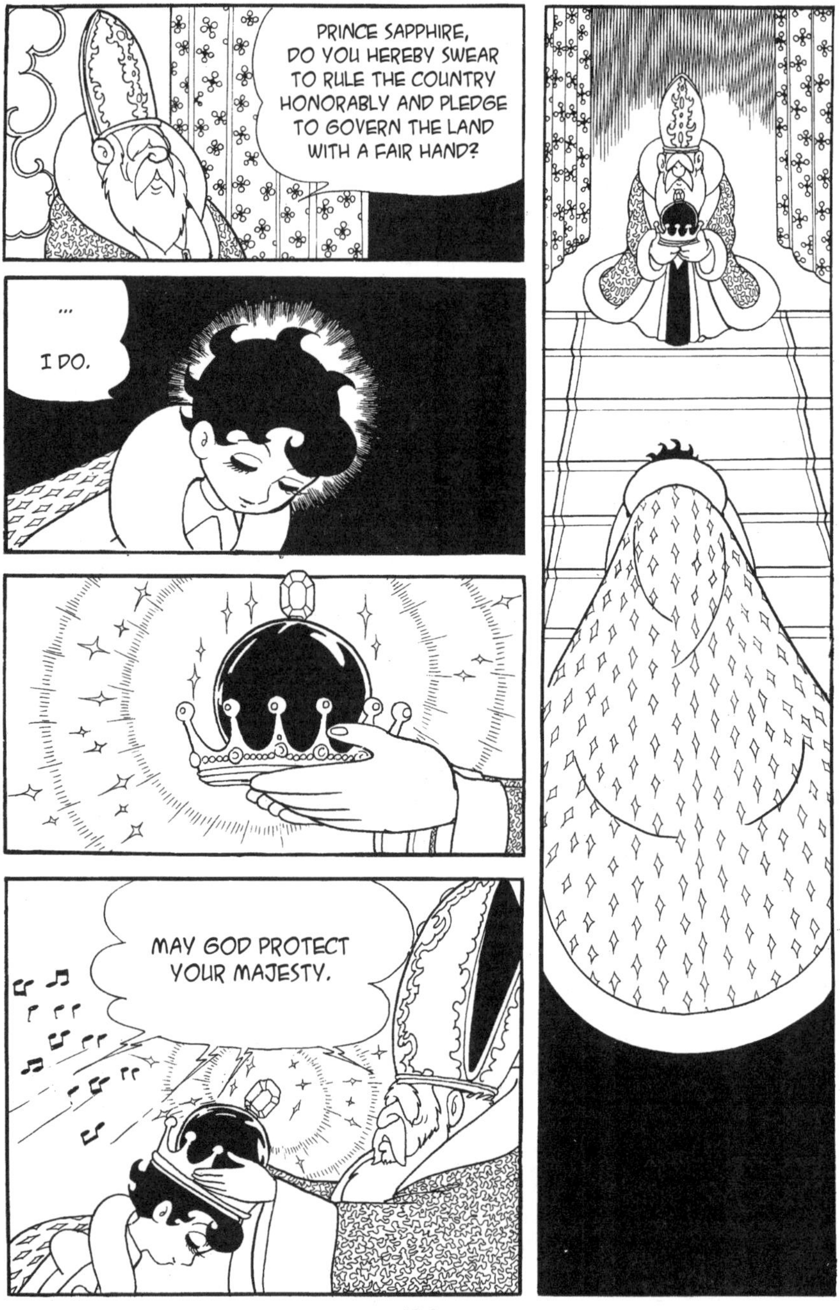
PRINCE SAPPHIRE, DO YOU HEREBY SWEAR TO RULE THE COUNTRY HONORABLY AND PLEDGE TO GOVERN THE LAND WITH A FAIR HAND?
...
I DO.
MAY GOD PROTECT YOUR MAJESTY.

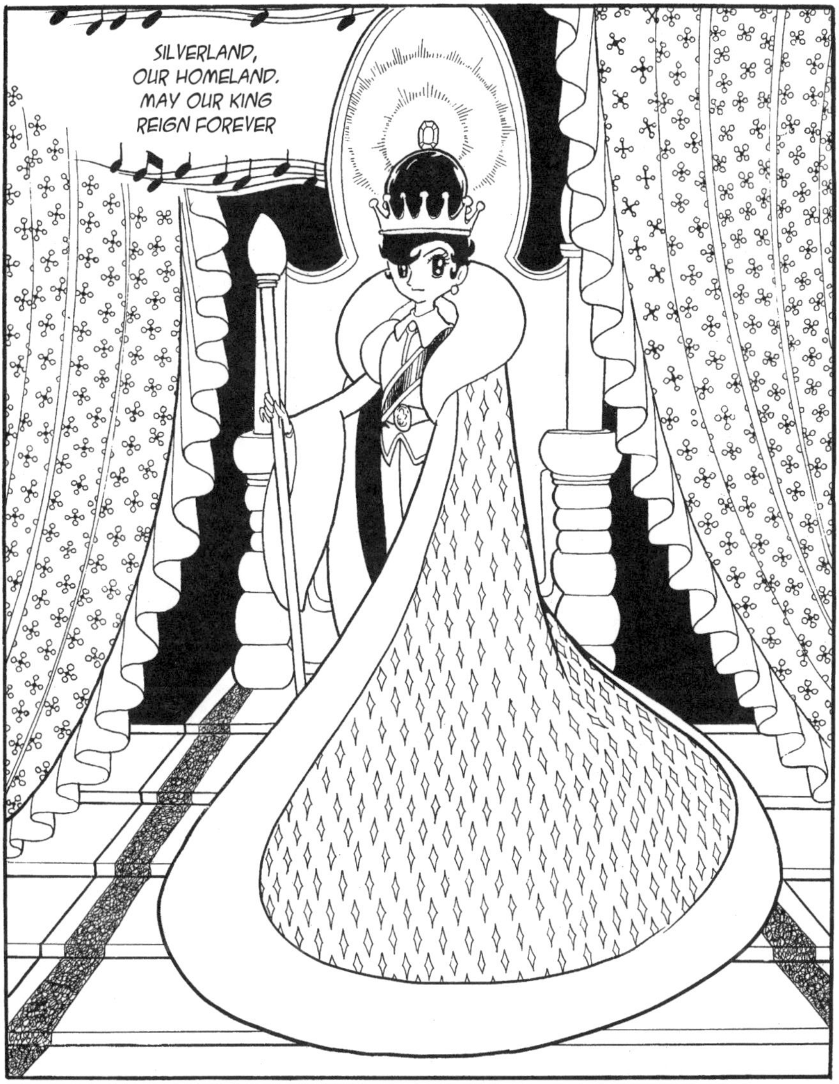
SILVERLAND, OUR HOMELAND. MAY OUR KING REIGN FOREVER

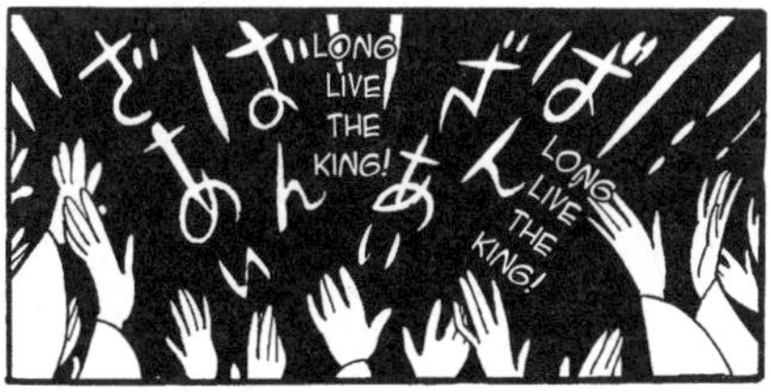
LONG LIVE THE KING!
LONG LIVE THE KING!

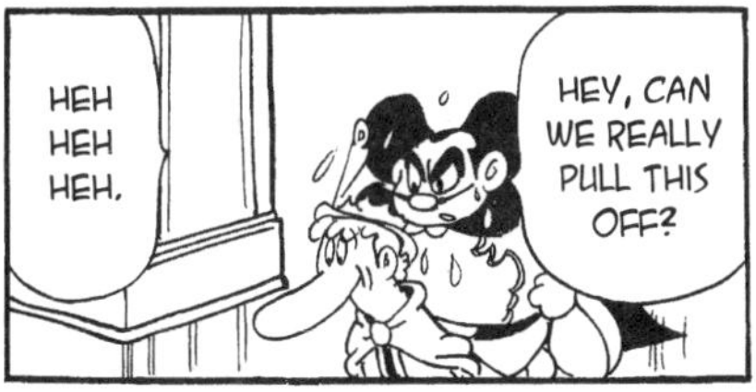
HEY, CAN WE REALLY PULL THIS OFF?
HEH HEH HEH.

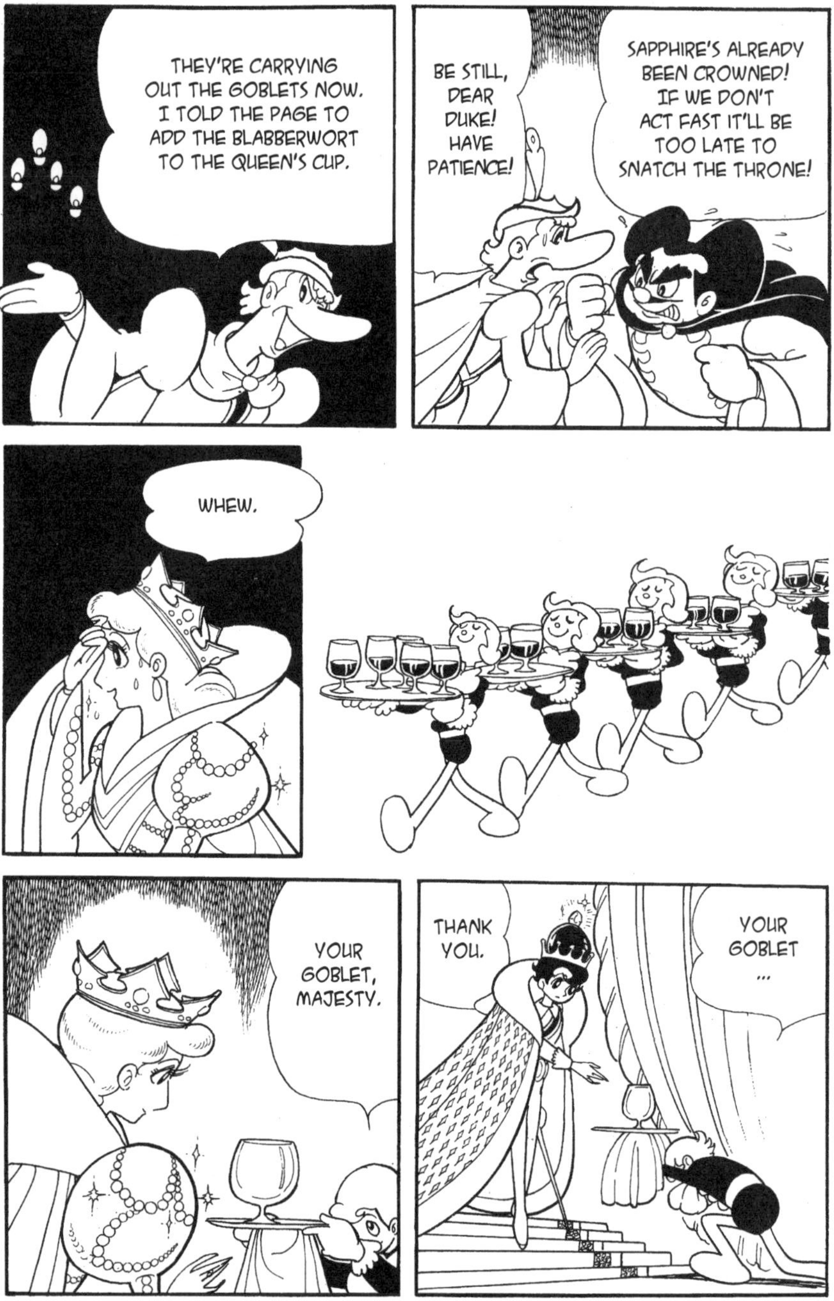
SAPPHIRE'S ALREADY BEEN CROWNED! IF WE DON'T ACT FAST IT'LL BE TOO LATE TO SNATCH THE THRONE!
BE STILL, DEAR DUKE! HAVE PATIENCE!
THEY'RE CARRYING OUT THE GOBLETS NOW. I TOLD THE PAGE TO ADD THE BLABBERWORT TO THE QUEEN'S CUP.
WHEW.
YOUR GOBLET ...
THANK YOU.
YOUR GOBLET, MAJESTY.

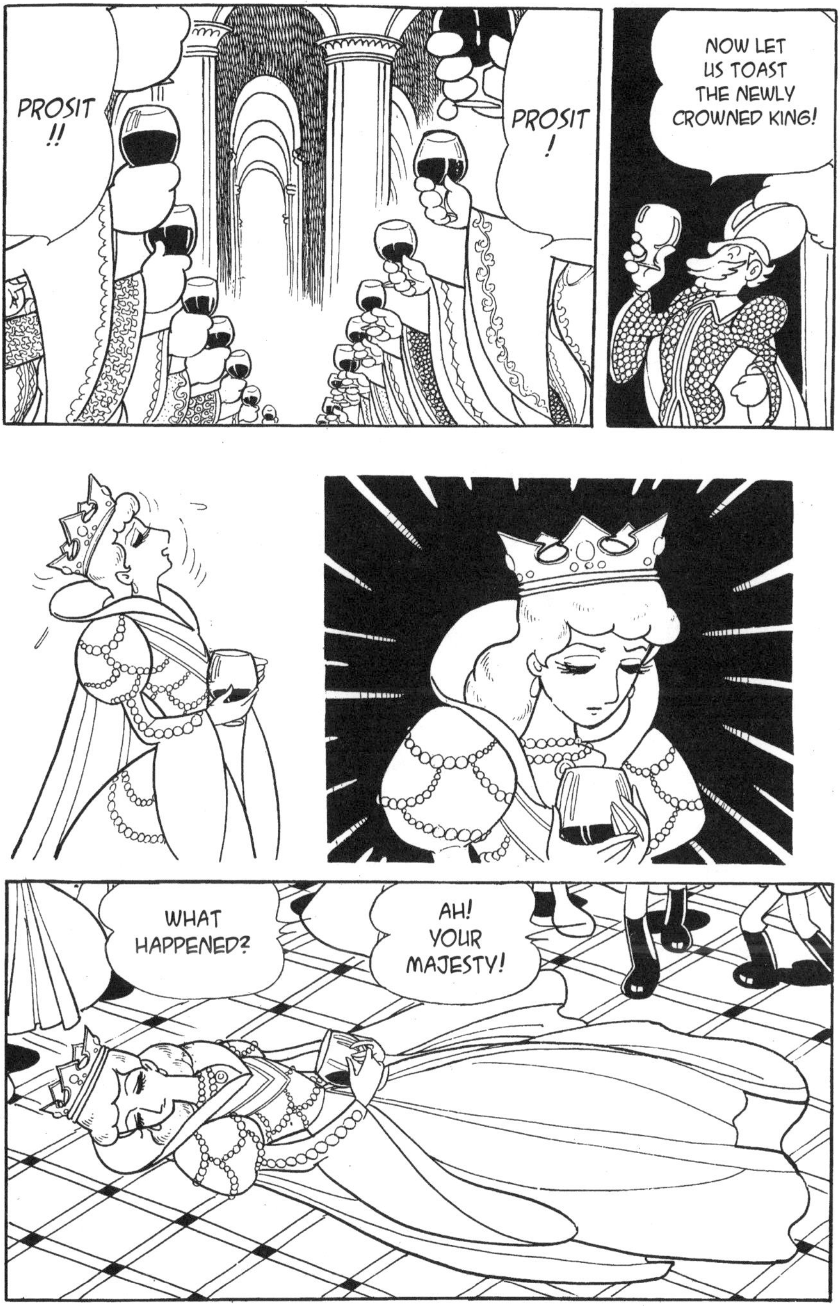
NOW LET US TOAST THE NEWLY CROWNED KING!
PROSIT !
PROSIT !!
AH! YOUR MAJESTY!
WHAT HAPPENED?

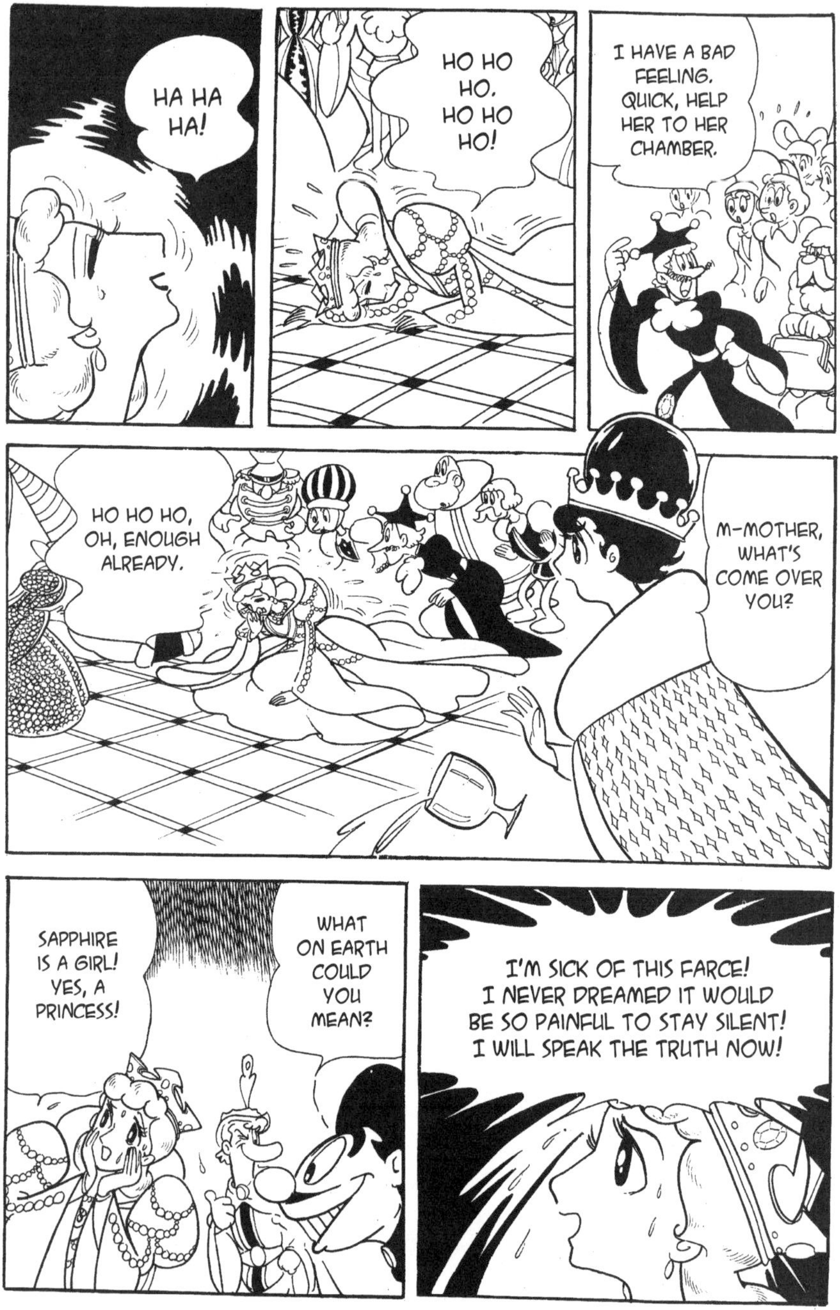
I HAVE A BAD FEELING. QUICK, HELP HER TO HER CHAMBER.
HO HO HO. HO HO HO!
HA HA HA!
M-MOTHER, WHAT'S COME OVER YOU?
HO HO HO, OH, ENOUGH ALREADY.
I'M SICK OF THIS FARCE! I NEVER DREAMED IT WOULD BE SO PAINFUL TO STAY SILENT! I WILL SPEAK THE TRUTH NOW!
WHAT ON EARTH COULD YOU MEAN?
SAPPHIRE IS A GIRL! YES, A PRINCESS!

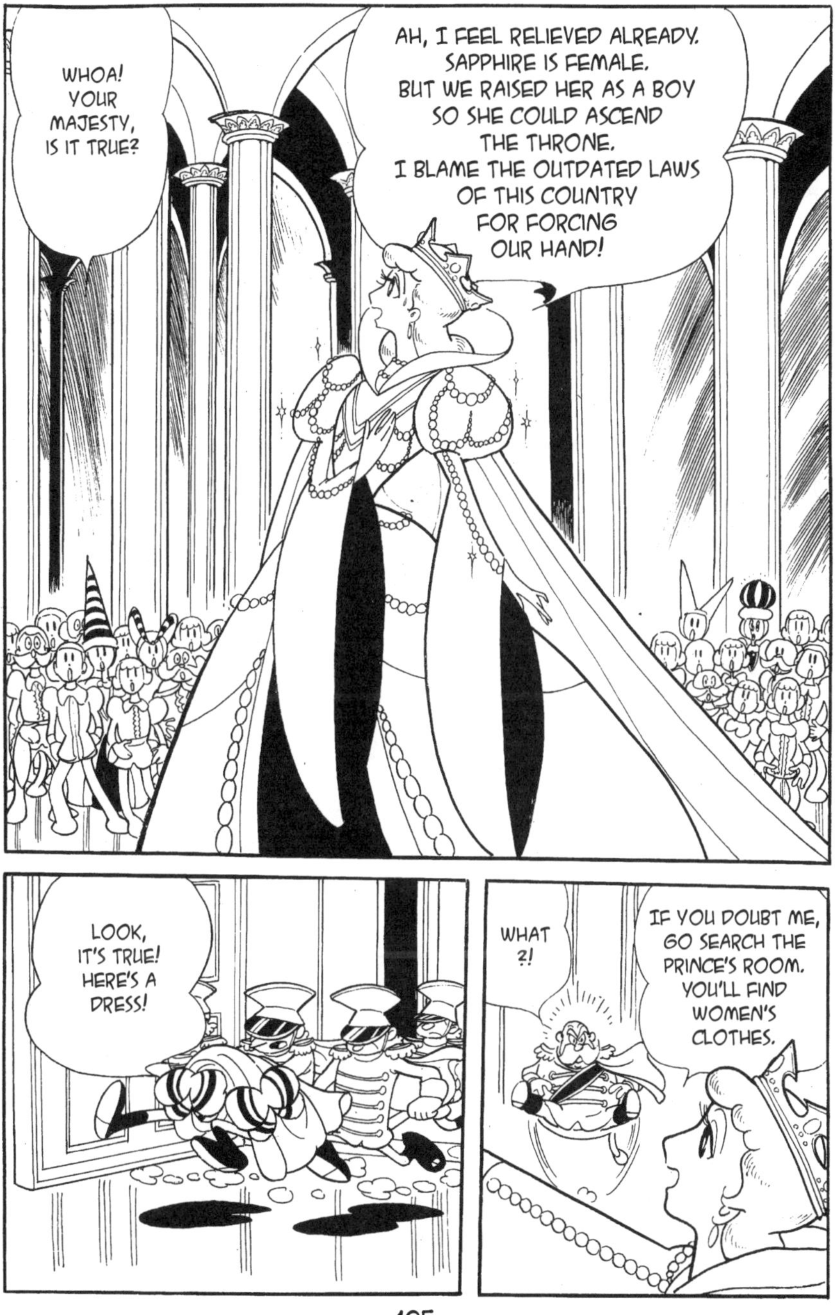
AH, I FEEL RELIEVED ALREADY. SAPPHIRE IS FEMALE. BUT WE RAISED HER AS A BOY SO SHE COULD ASCEND THE THRONE. I BLAME THE OUTDATED LAWS OF THIS COUNTRY FOR FORCING OUR HAND!
WHOA! YOUR MAJESTY, IS IT TRUE?
IF YOU DOUBT ME, GO SEARCH THE PRINCE'S ROOM. YOU'LL FIND WOMEN'S CLOTHES.
WHAT?!
LOOK, IT'S TRUE! HERE'S A DRESS!

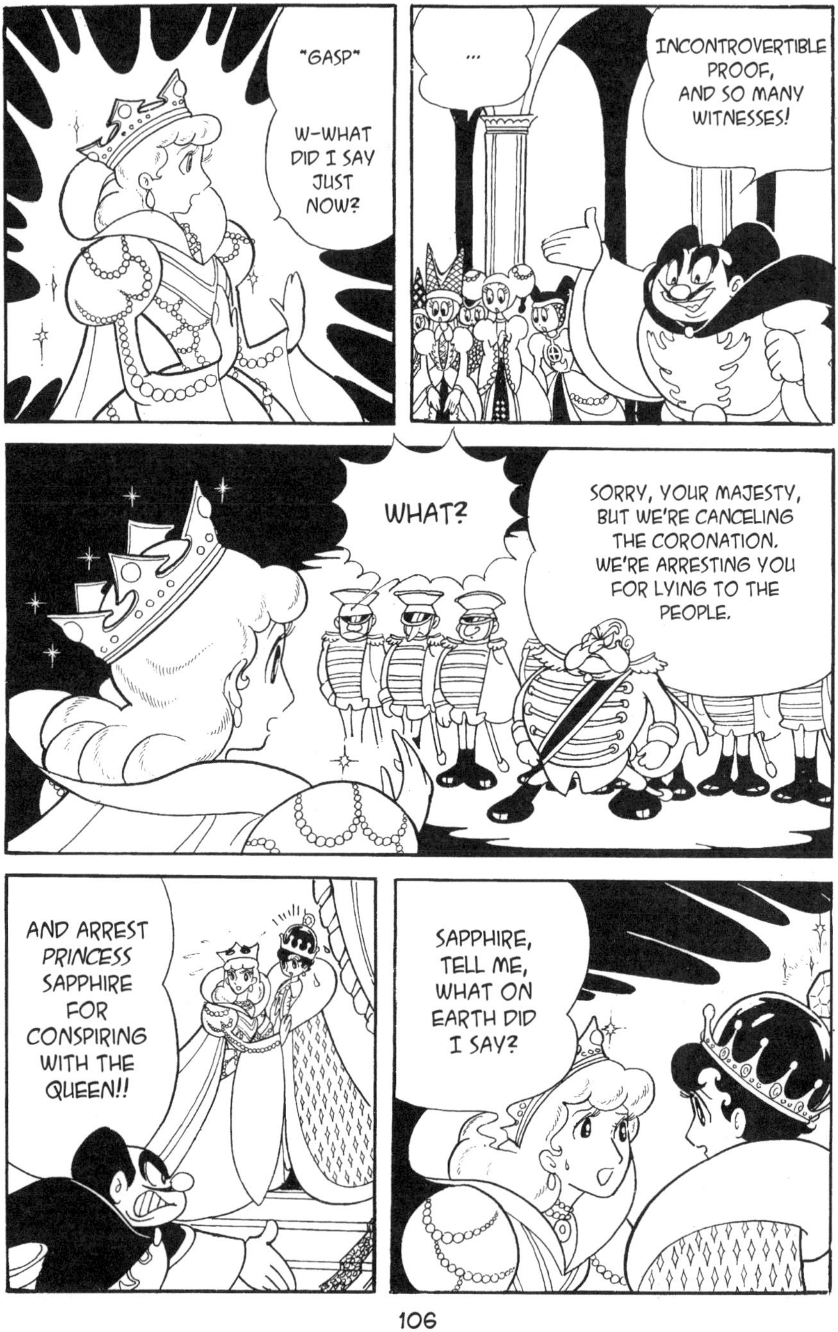
INCONTROVERTIBLE PROOF, AND SO MANY WITNESSES!
...
"GASP"
W-WHAT DID I SAY JUST NOW?
SORRY, YOUR MAJESTY, BUT WE'RE CANCELING THE CORONATION. WE'RE ARRESTING YOU FOR LYING TO THE PEOPLE.
WHAT?
SAPPHIRE, TELL ME, WHAT ON EARTH DID I SAY?
AND ARREST PRINCESS SAPPHIRE FOR CONSPIRING WITH THE QUEEN!!

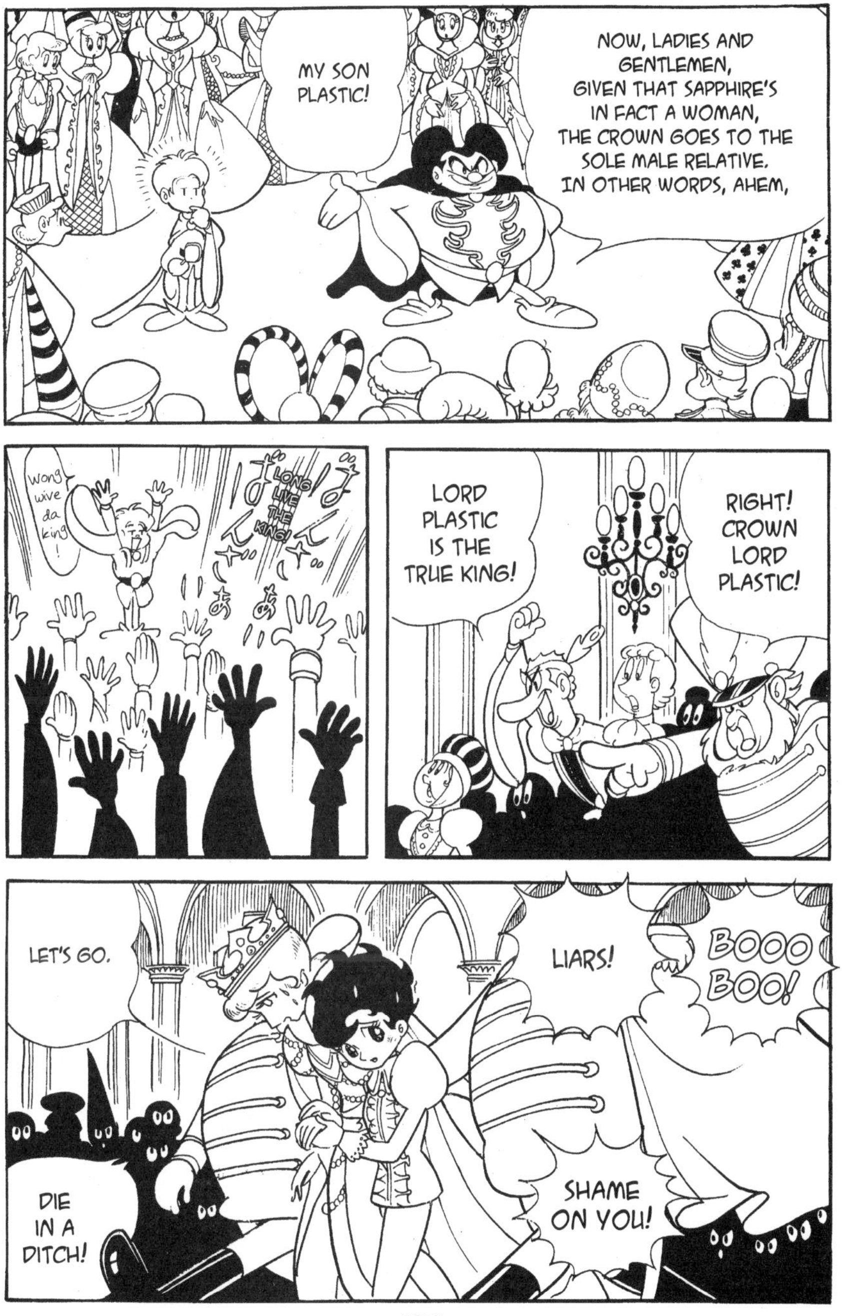
NOW, LADIES AND GENTLEMEN, GIVEN THAT SAPPHIRE'S IN FACT A WOMAN, THE CROWN GOES TO THE SOLE MALE RELATIVE. IN OTHER WORDS, AHEM,
MY SON PLASTIC!
RIGHT! CROWN LORD PLASTIC!
LORD PLASTIC IS THE TRUE KING!
LONG LIVE THE KING!
wong wive da king!
BOOO BOO!
LIARS!
SHAME ON YOU!
LET'S GO.
DIE IN A DITCH!

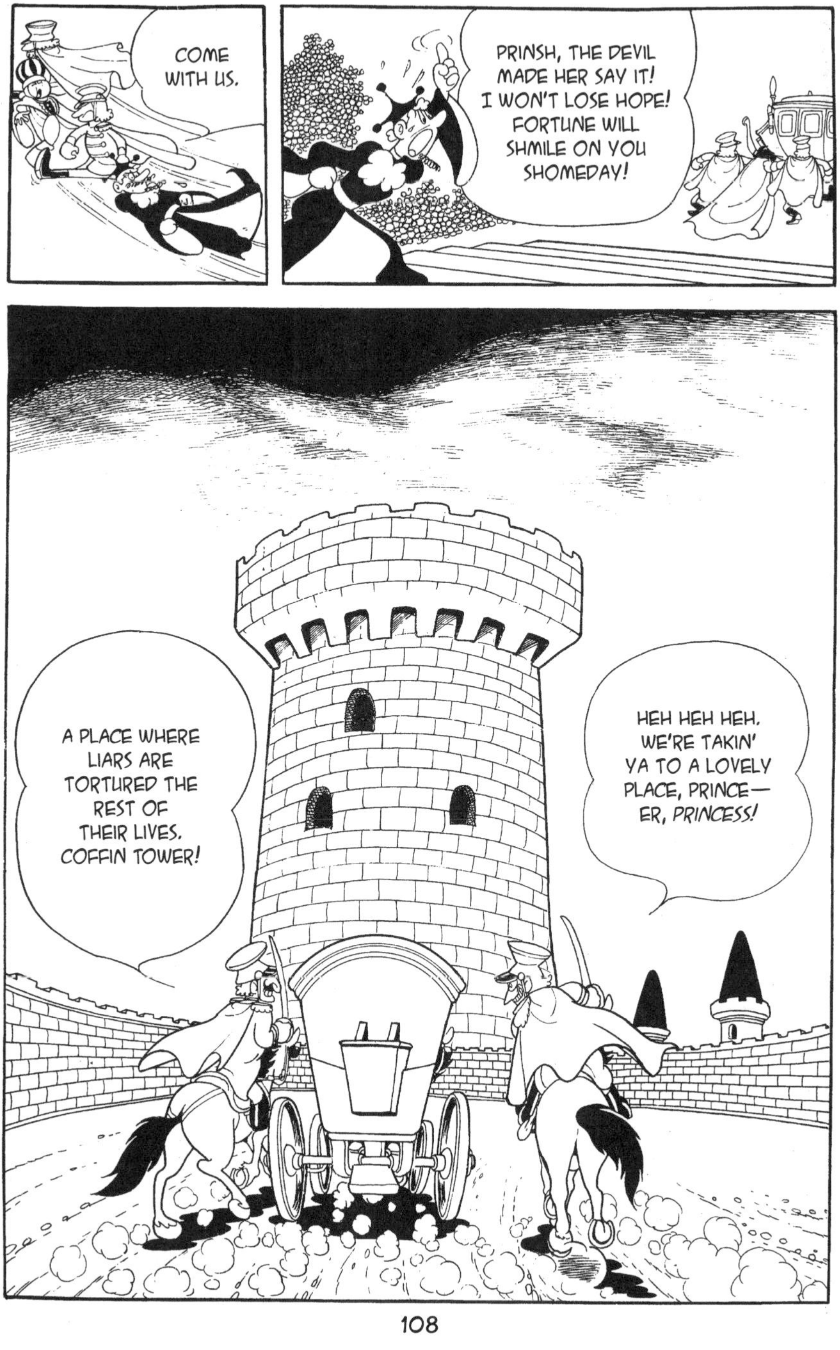
PRINSH, THE DEVIL MADE HER SAY IT! I WON'T LOSE HOPE! FORTUNE WILL SHMILE ON YOU SHOMEDAY!
COME WITH US.
HEH HEH HEH. WE'RE TAKIN' YA TO A LOVELY PLACE, PRINCE— ER, *PRINCESS!*
A PLACE WHERE LIARS ARE TORTURED THE REST OF THEIR LIVES. COFFIN TOWER!

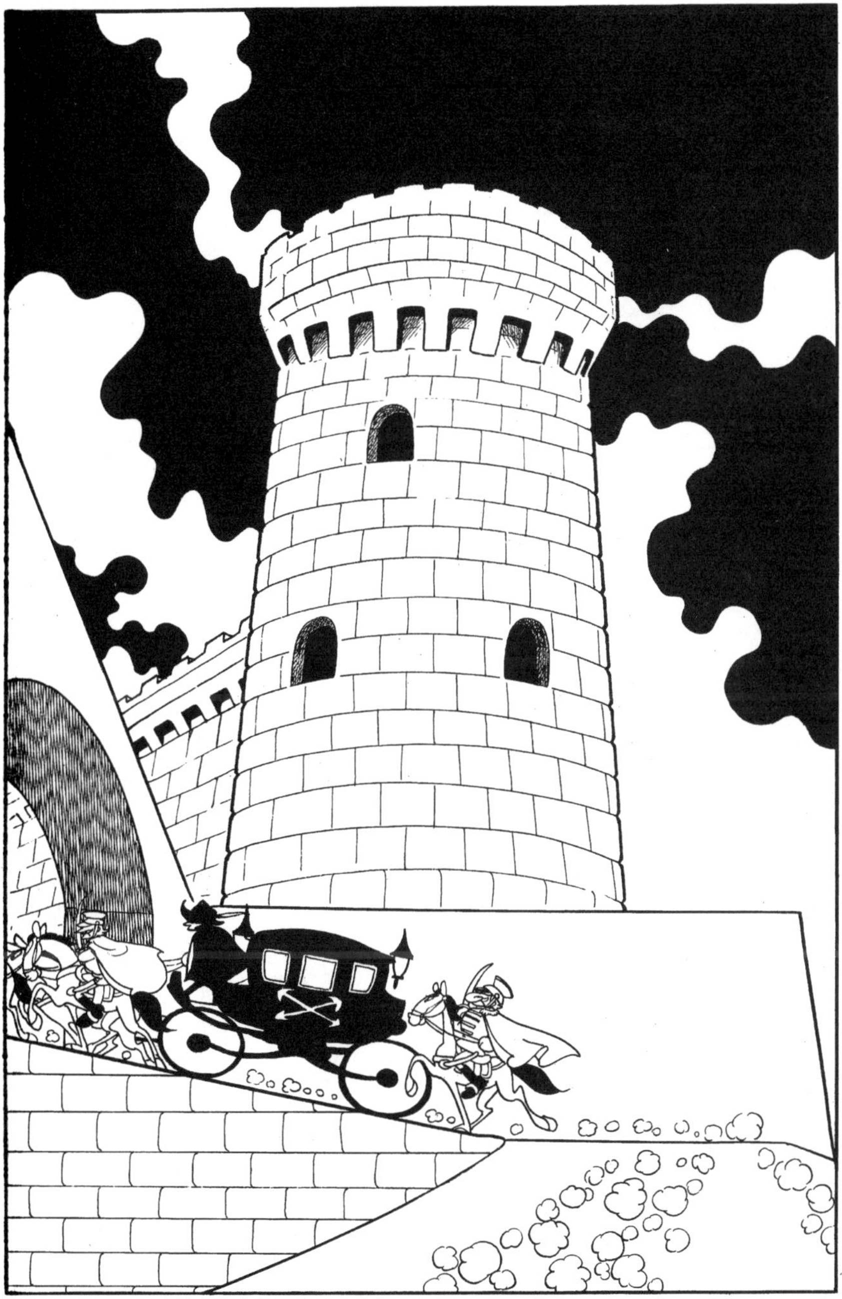

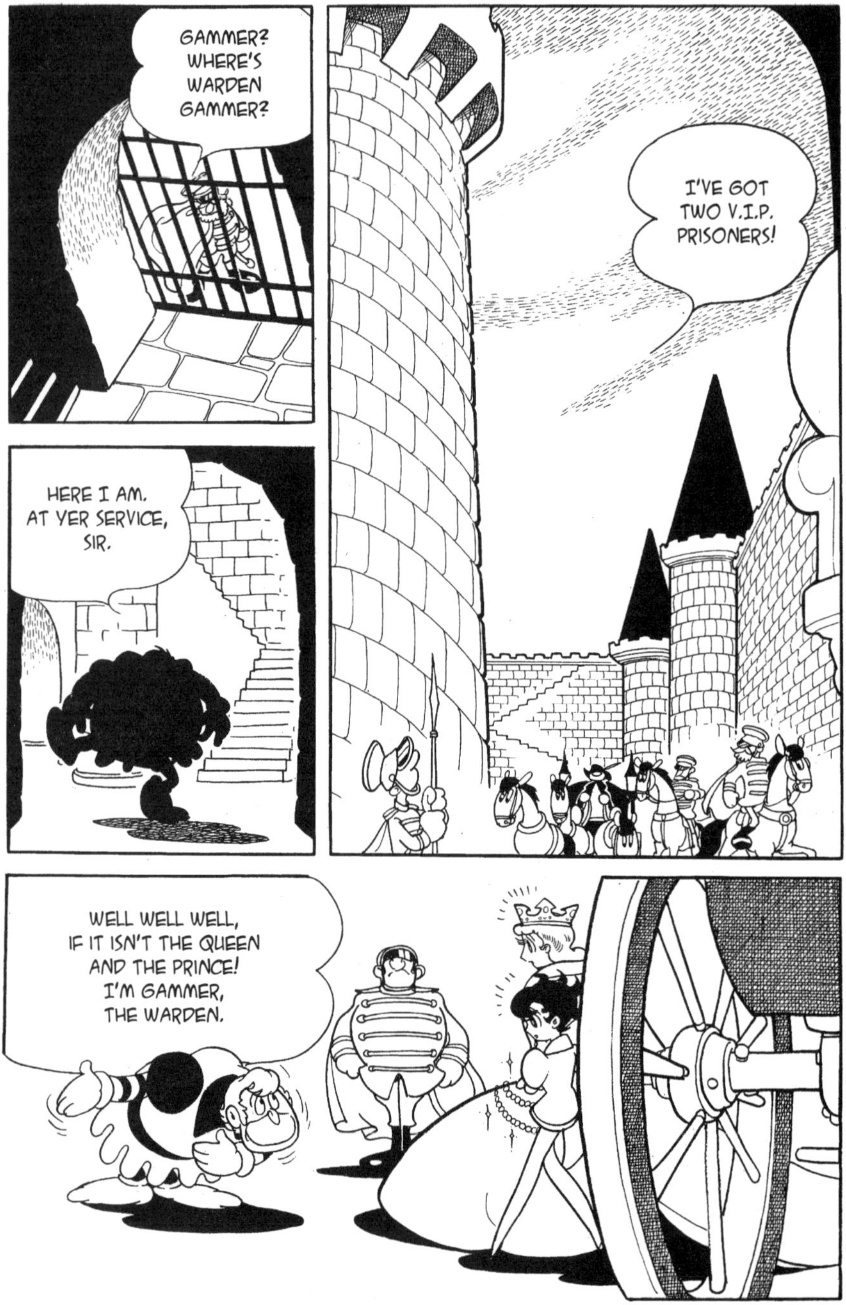
I'VE GOT TWO V.I.P. PRISONERS!
GAMMER? WHERE'S WARDEN GAMMER?
HERE I AM. AT YER SERVICE, SIR.
WELL WELL WELL, IF IT ISN'T THE QUEEN AND THE PRINCE! I'M GAMMER, THE WARDEN.

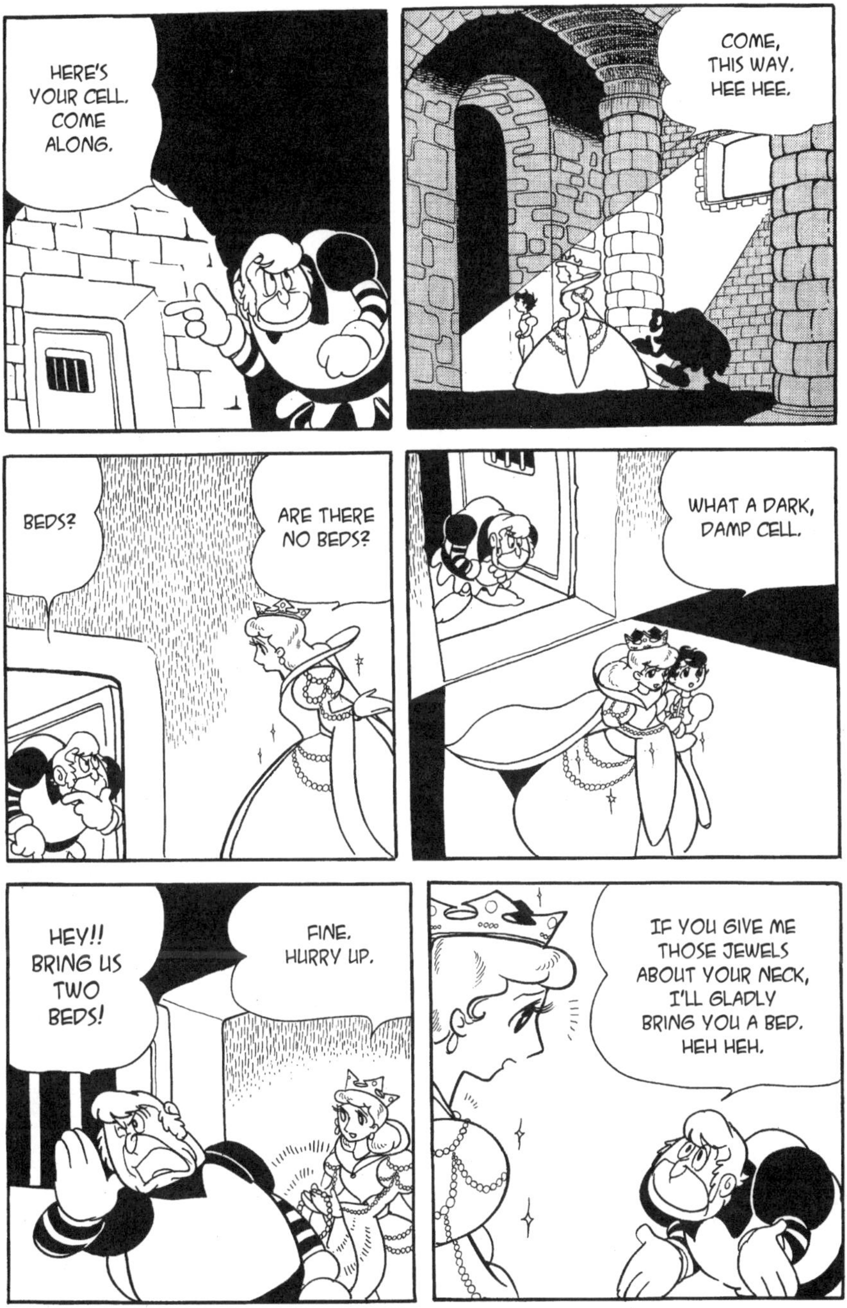
COME, THIS WAY. HEE HEE.
HERE'S YOUR CELL. COME ALONG.
WHAT A DARK, DAMP CELL.
ARE THERE NO BEDS?
BEDS?
IF YOU GIVE ME THOSE JEWELS ABOUT YOUR NECK, I'LL GLADLY BRING YOU A BED. HEH HEH.
FINE. HURRY UP.
HEY!! BRING US TWO BEDS!

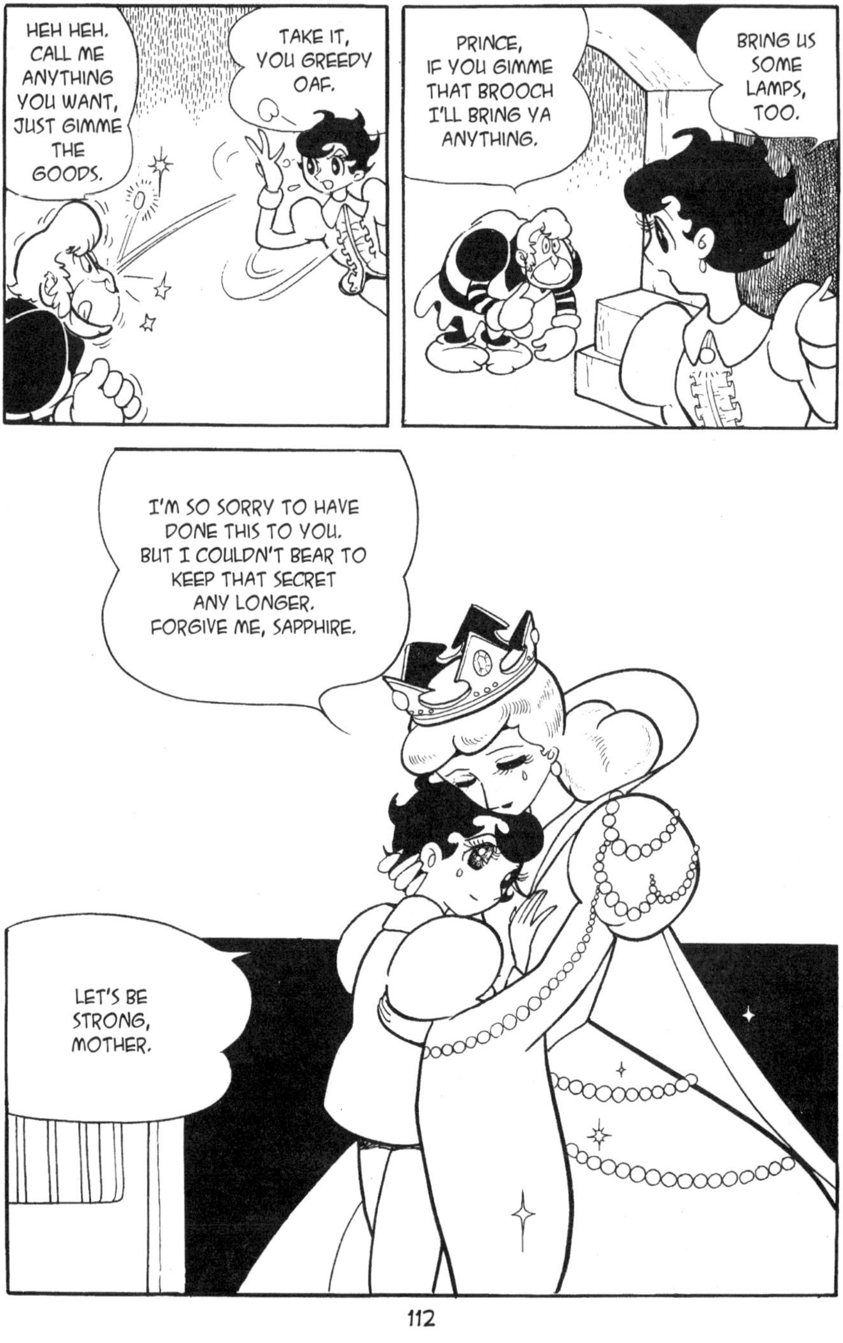
BRING US SOME LAMPS, TOO.
PRINCE, IF YOU GIMME THAT BROOCH I'LL BRING YA ANYTHING.
TAKE IT, YOU GREEDY OAF.
HEH HEH. CALL ME ANYTHING YOU WANT, JUST GIMME THE GOODS.
I'M SO SORRY TO HAVE DONE THIS TO YOU. BUT I COULDN'T BEAR TO KEEP THAT SECRET ANY LONGER. FORGIVE ME, SAPPHIRE.
LET'S BE STRONG, MOTHER.

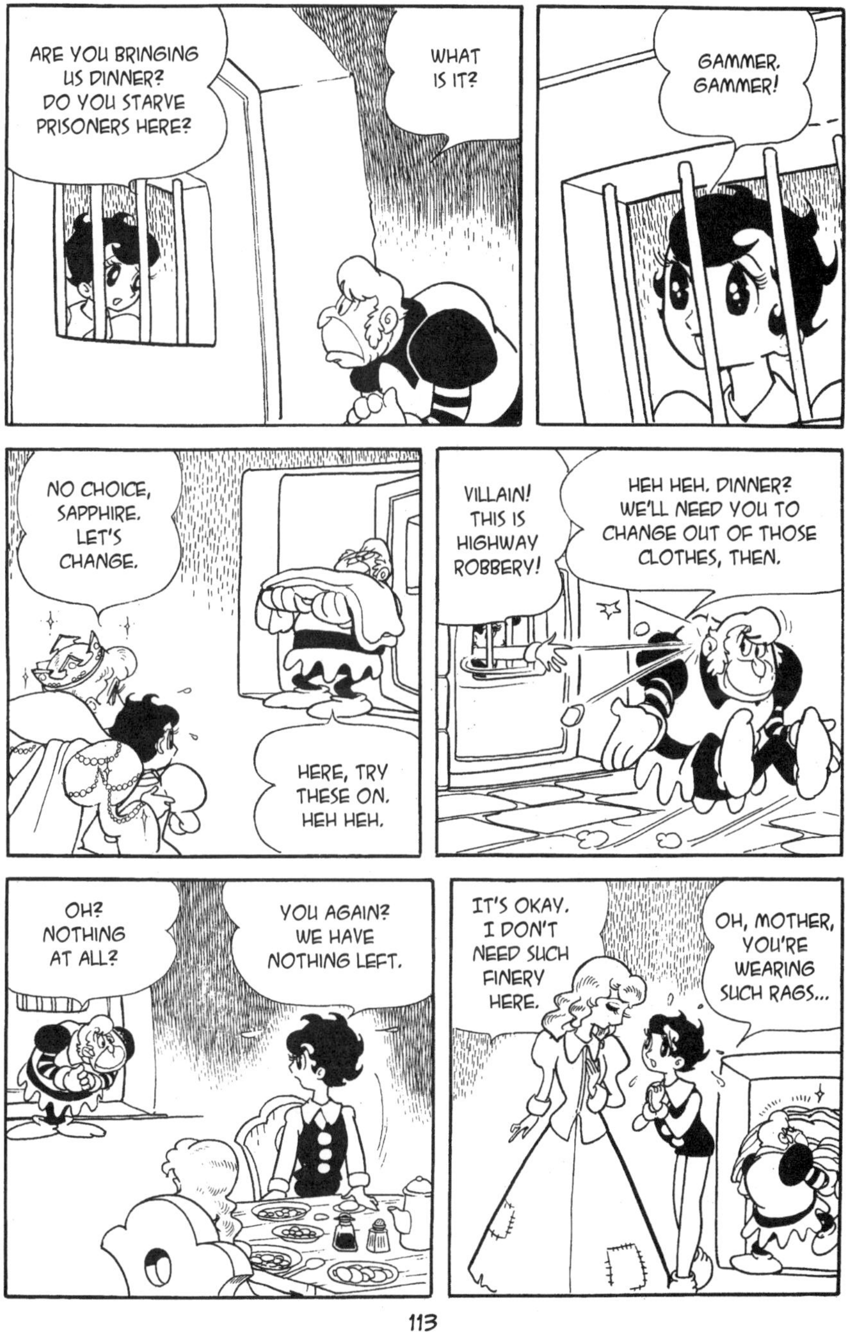
GAMMER. GAMMER!
WHAT IS IT?
ARE YOU BRINGING US DINNER? DO YOU STARVE PRISONERS HERE?
HEH HEH. DINNER? WE'LL NEED YOU TO CHANGE OUT OF THOSE CLOTHES, THEN.
VILLAIN! THIS IS HIGHWAY ROBBERY!
HERE, TRY THESE ON. HEH HEH.
NO CHOICE, SAPPHIRE. LET'S CHANGE.
OH, MOTHER, YOU'RE WEARING SUCH RAGS...
IT'S OKAY. I DON'T NEED SUCH FINERY HERE.
YOU AGAIN? WE HAVE NOTHING LEFT.
OH? NOTHING AT ALL?

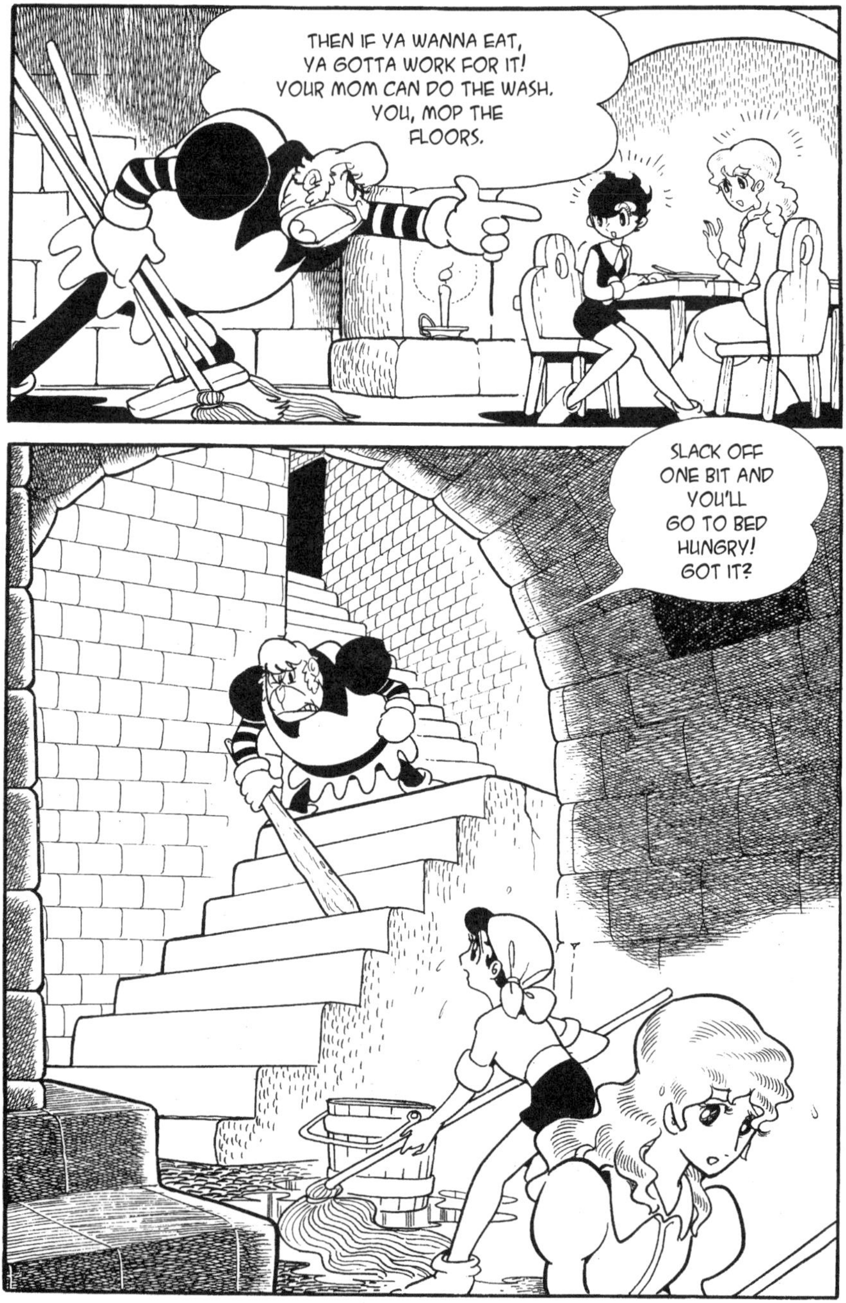
THEN IF YA WANNA EAT, YA GOTTA WORK FOR IT! YOUR MOM CAN DO THE WASH. YOU, MOP THE FLOORS.
SLACK OFF ONE BIT AND YOU'LL GO TO BED HUNGRY! GOT IT?

Chapter 7

Sapphire in Coffin Tower

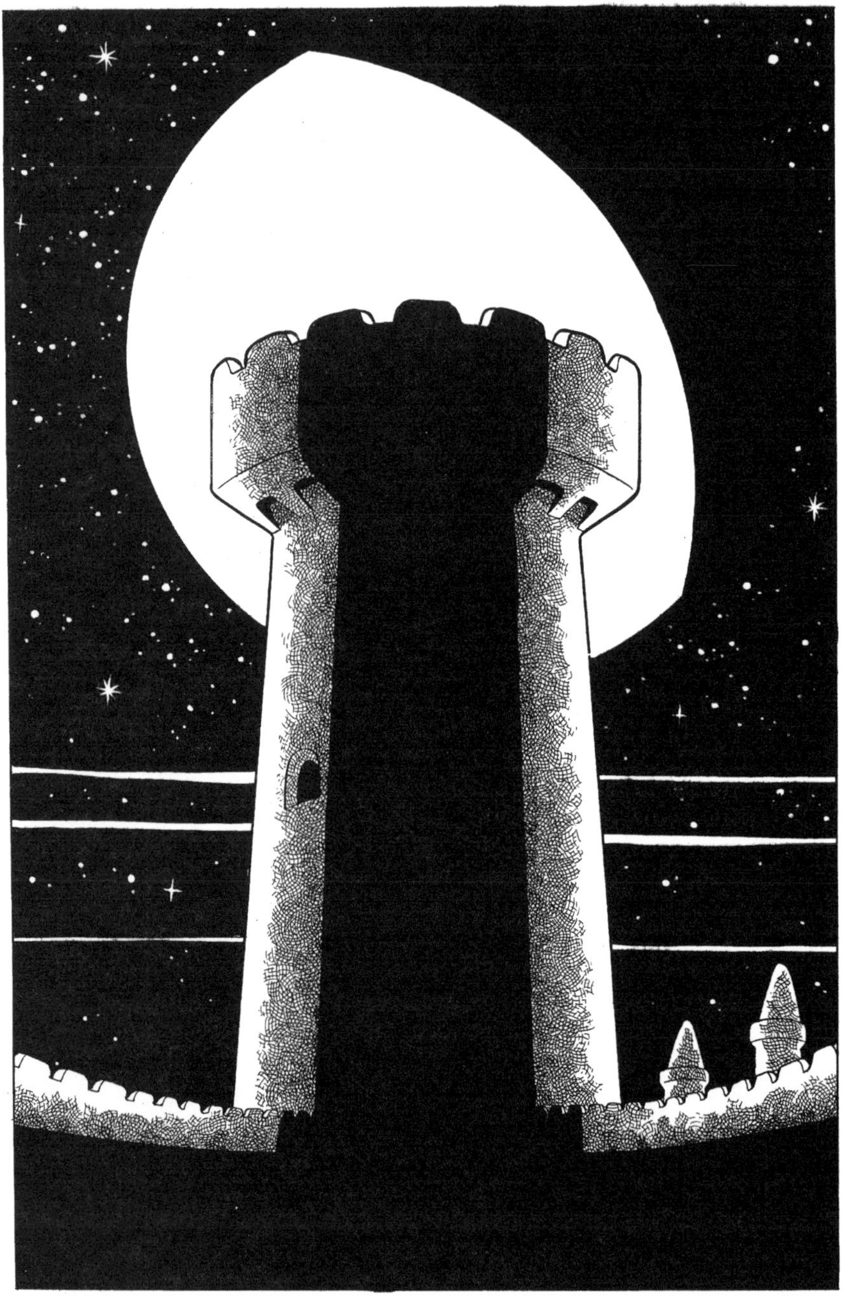

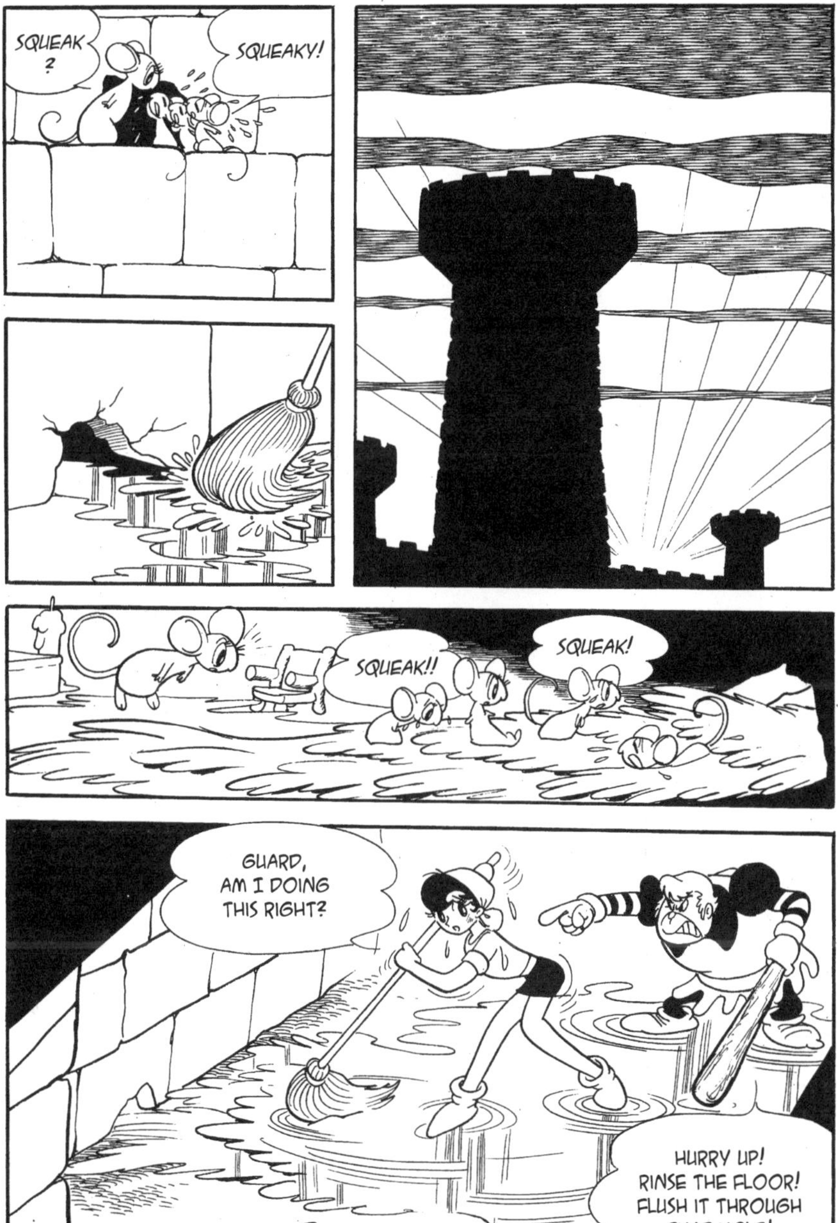
SQUEAKY!
SQUEAK ?
SQUEAK!
SQUEAK!!
GUARD, AM I DOING THIS RIGHT?
HURRY UP! RINSE THE FLOOR! FLUSH IT THROUGH THAT HOLE!

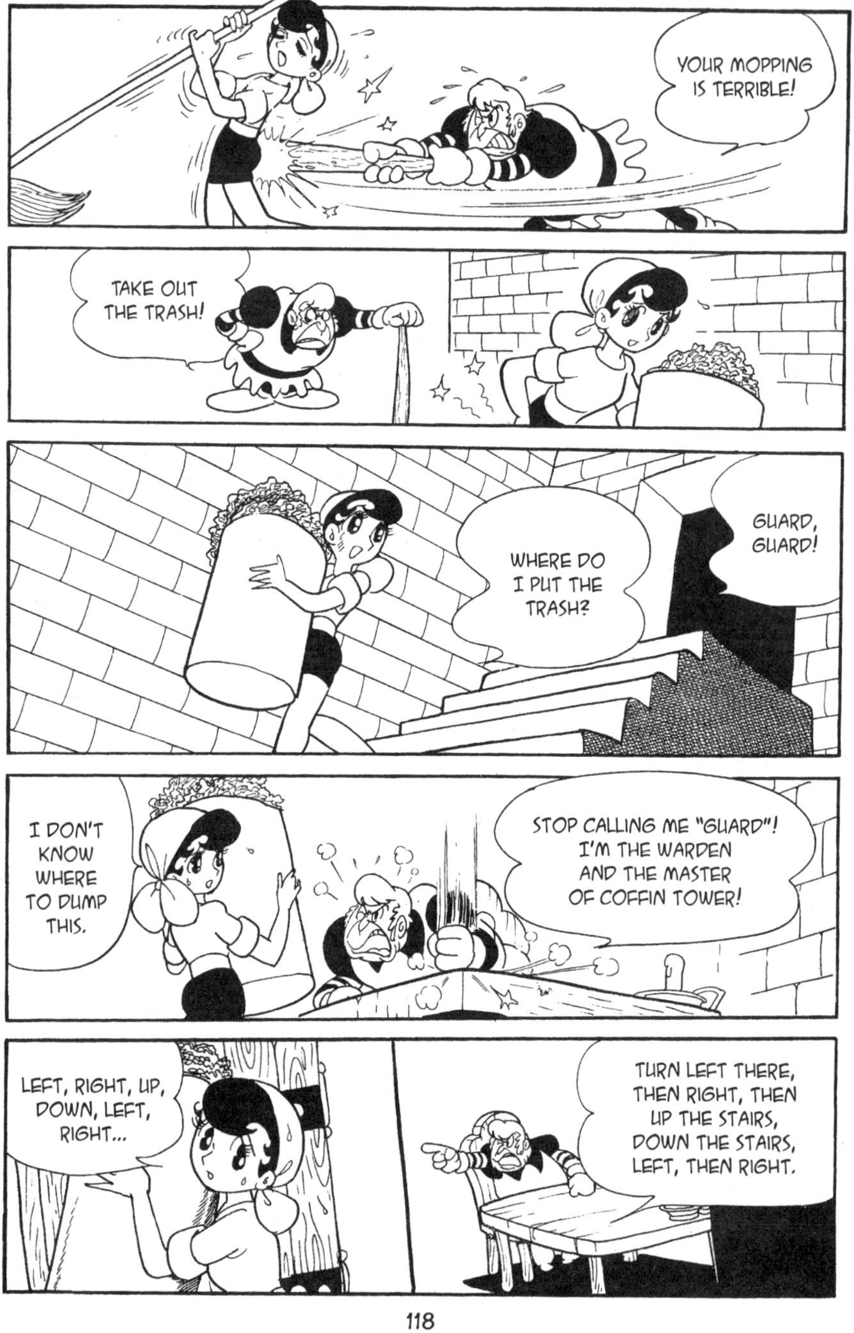
YOUR MOPPING IS TERRIBLE!
TAKE OUT THE TRASH!
GUARD, GUARD!
WHERE DO I PUT THE TRASH?
STOP CALLING ME "GUARD"! I'M THE WARDEN AND THE MASTER OF COFFIN TOWER!
I DON'T KNOW WHERE TO DUMP THIS.
TURN LEFT THERE, THEN RIGHT, THEN UP THE STAIRS, DOWN THE STAIRS, LEFT, THEN RIGHT.
LEFT, RIGHT, UP, DOWN, LEFT, RIGHT...

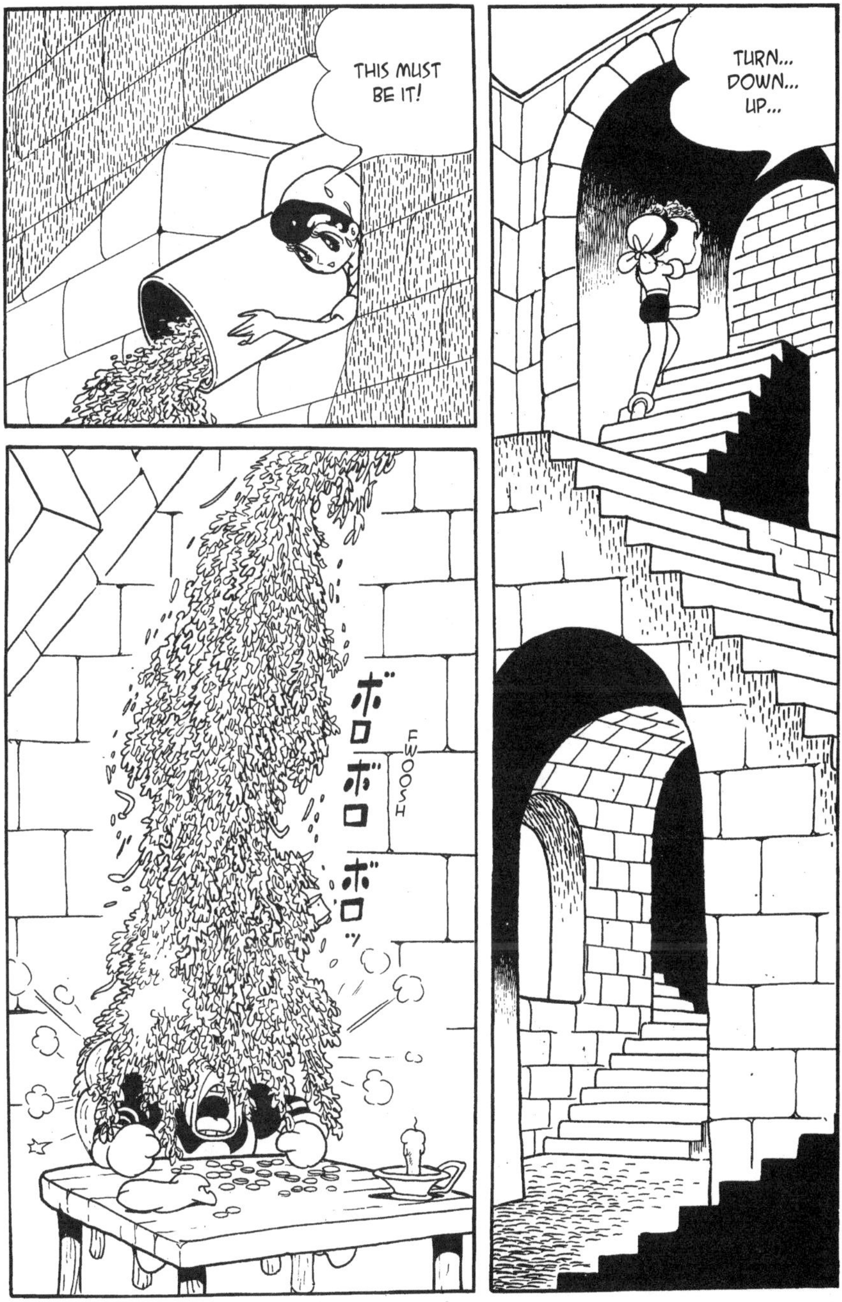
TURN... DOWN... UP...
THIS MUST BE IT!
ボロボロ ボロッ
FWOOSH

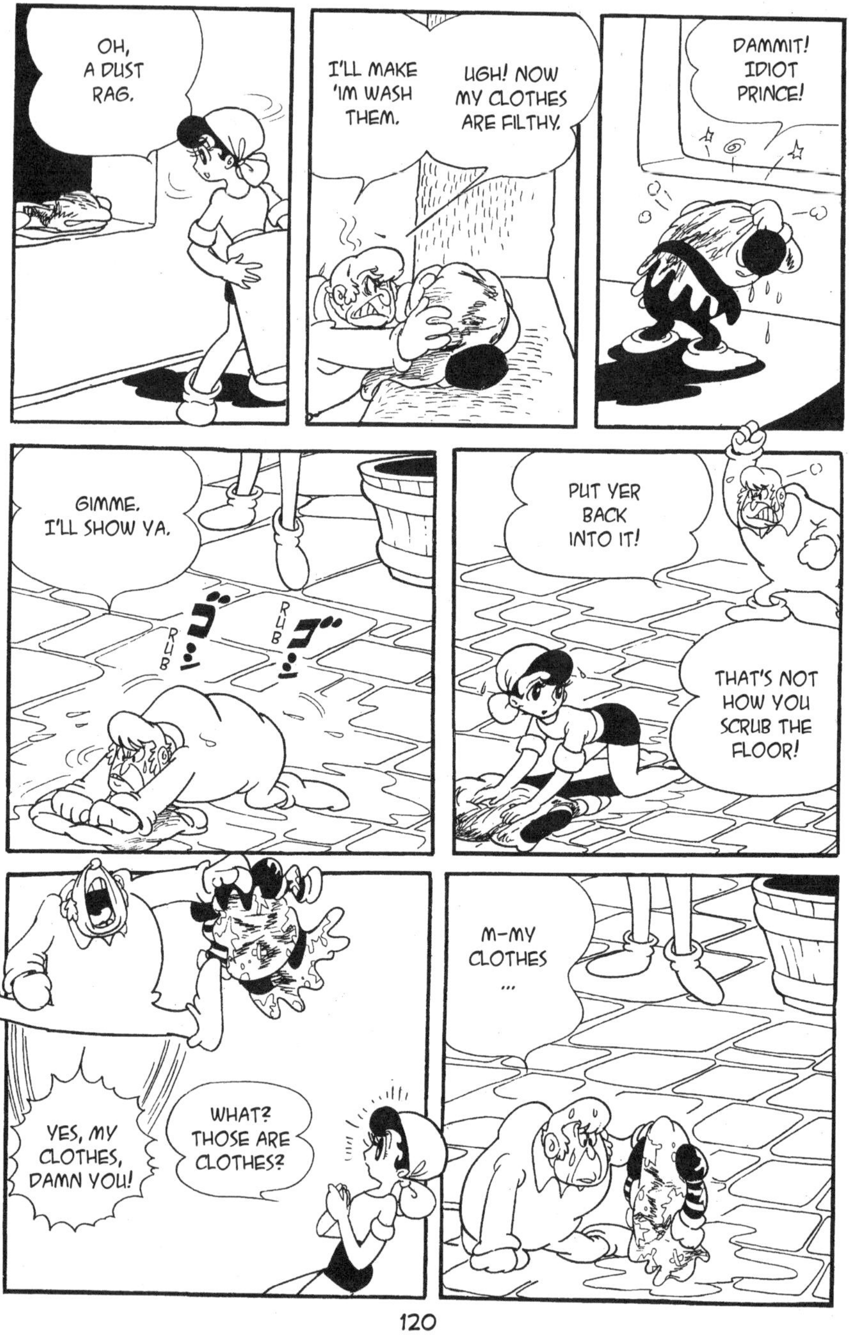
DAMMIT! IDIOT PRINCE!
UGH! NOW MY CLOTHES ARE FILTHY.
I'LL MAKE 'IM WASH THEM.
OH, A DUST RAG.
PUT YER BACK INTO IT!
THAT'S NOT HOW YOU SCRUB THE FLOOR!
GIMME. I'LL SHOW YA.
RUB ゴシ
RUB ゴシ
M-MY CLOTHES ...
WHAT? THOSE ARE CLOTHES?
YES, MY CLOTHES, DAMN YOU!

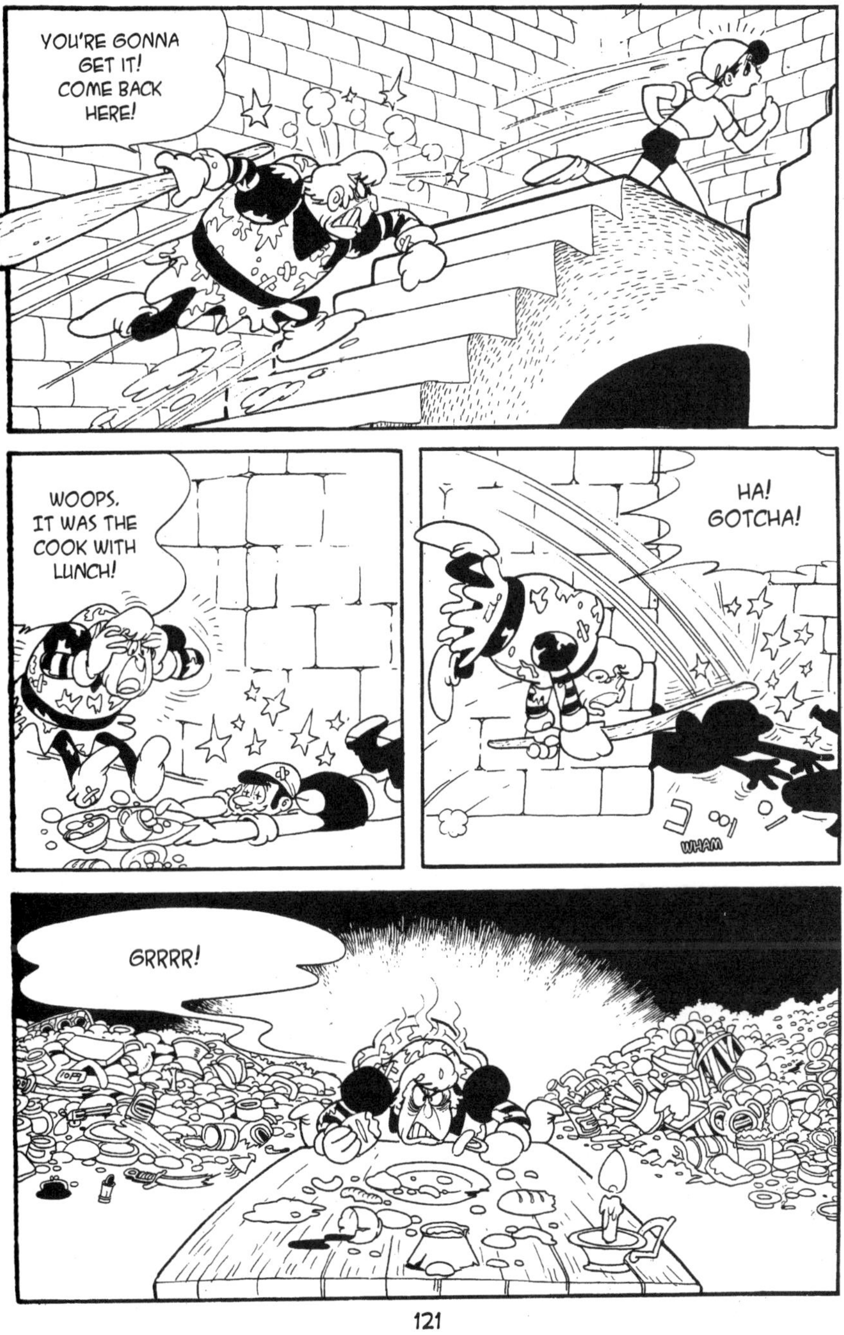
YOU'RE GONNA GET IT! COME BACK HERE!
HA! GOTCHA!
WHAM
WOOPS. IT WAS THE COOK WITH LUNCH!
GRRRR!

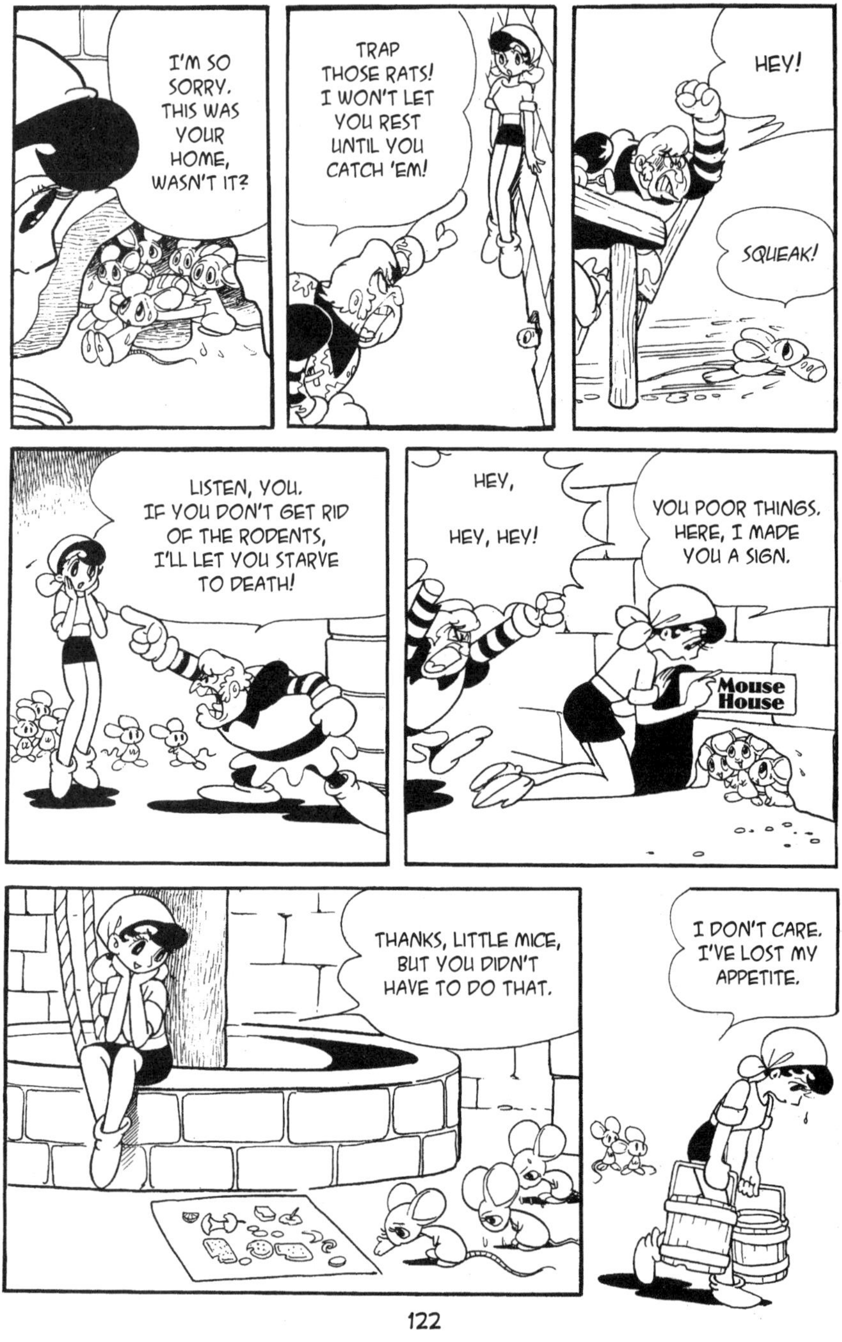
HEY!
SQUEAK!
TRAP THOSE RATS! I WON'T LET YOU REST UNTIL YOU CATCH 'EM!
I'M SO SORRY. THIS WAS YOUR HOME, WASN'T IT?
YOU POOR THINGS. HERE, I MADE YOU A SIGN.
HEY, HEY, HEY!
Mouse House
LISTEN, YOU. IF YOU DON'T GET RID OF THE RODENTS, I'LL LET YOU STARVE TO DEATH!
I DON'T CARE. I'VE LOST MY APPETITE.
THANKS, LITTLE MICE, BUT YOU DIDN'T HAVE TO DO THAT.

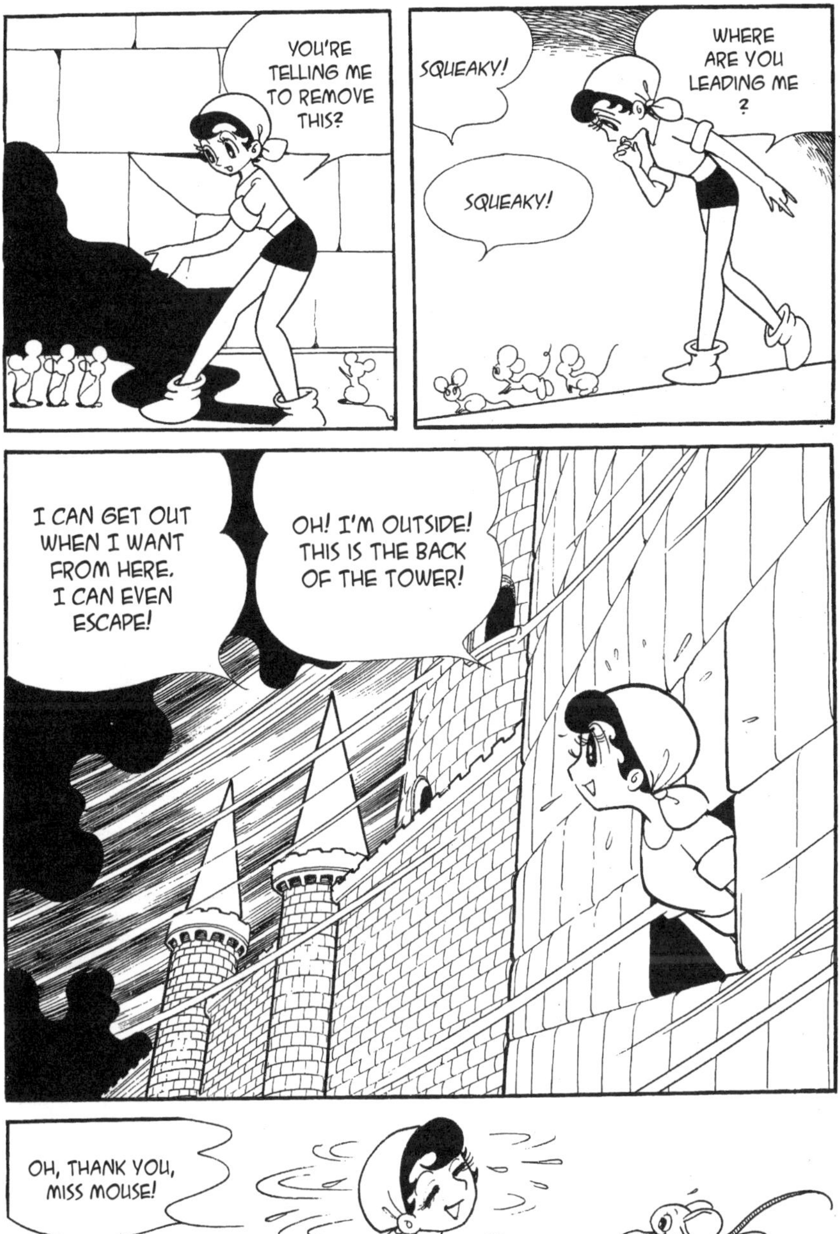
WHERE ARE YOU LEADING ME?
SQUEAKY!
SQUEAKY!
YOU'RE TELLING ME TO REMOVE THIS?
OH! I'M OUTSIDE! THIS IS THE BACK OF THE TOWER!
I CAN GET OUT WHEN I WANT FROM HERE. I CAN EVEN ESCAPE!
OH, THANK YOU, MISS MOUSE!

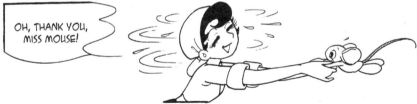

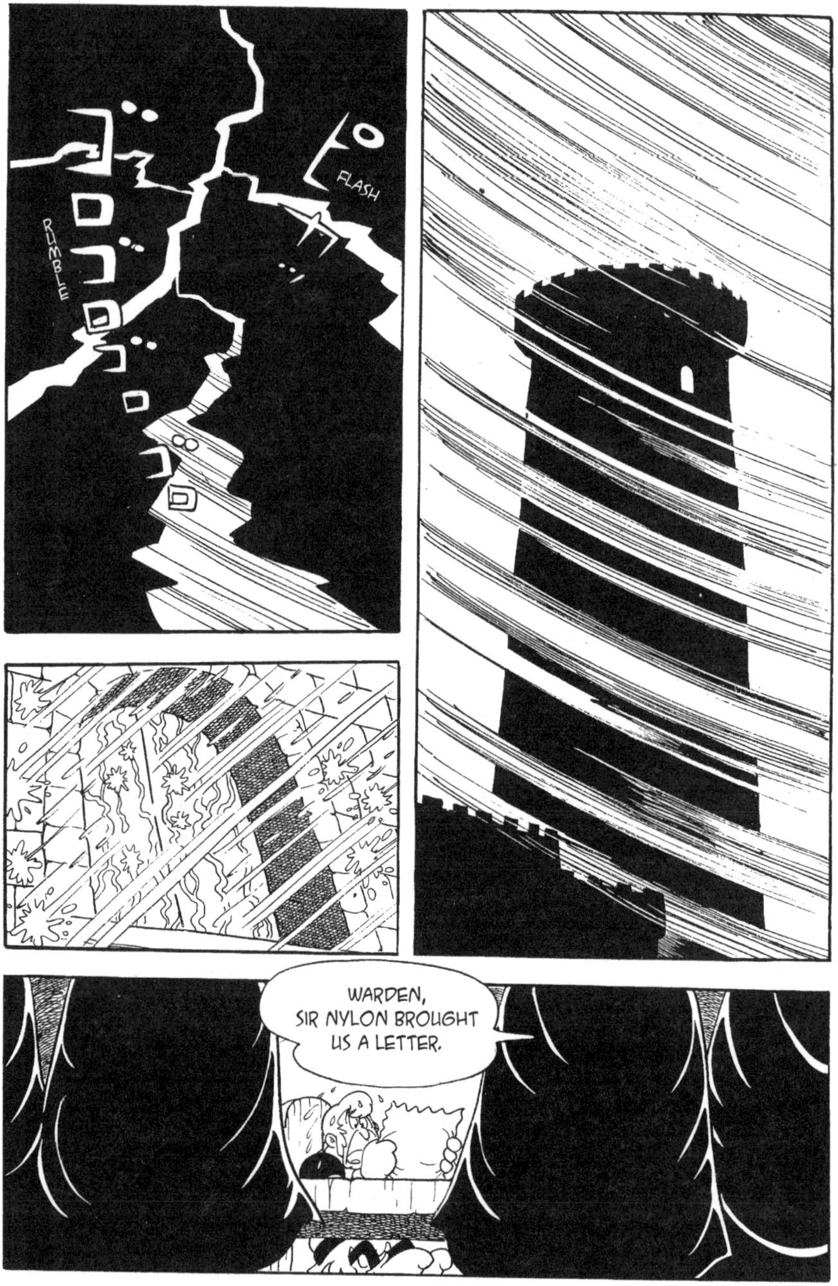
ピ
FLASH
ゴロゴロゴロゴロ
RUMBLE
WARDEN, SIR NYLON BROUGHT US A LETTER.

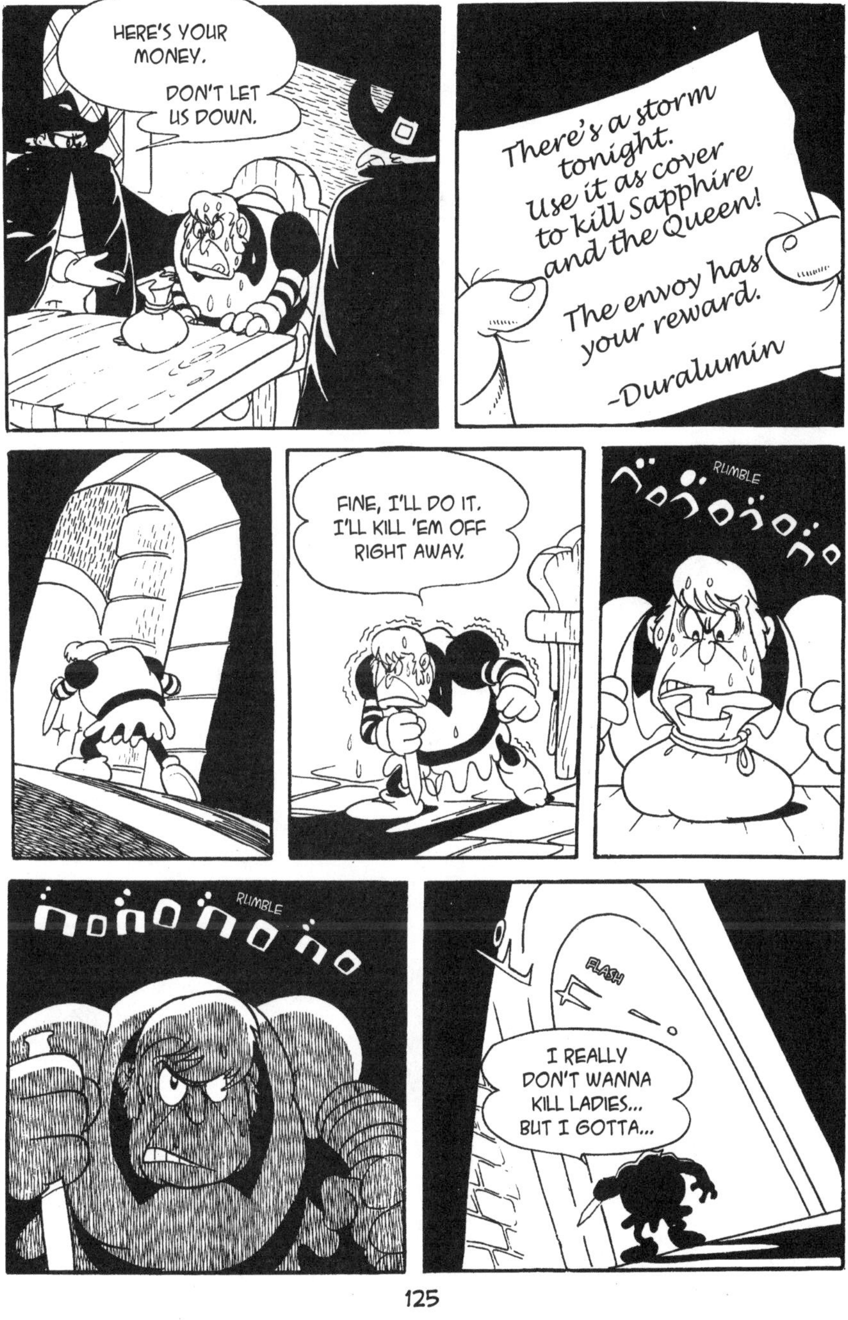
There's a storm tonight. Use it as cover to kill Sapphire and the Queen!
The envoy has your reward.
-Duralumin
HERE'S YOUR MONEY.
DON'T LET US DOWN.
RUMBLE
FINE, I'LL DO IT. I'LL KILL 'EM OFF RIGHT AWAY.
FLASH
I REALLY DON'T WANNA KILL LADIES... BUT I GOTTA...
RUMBLE

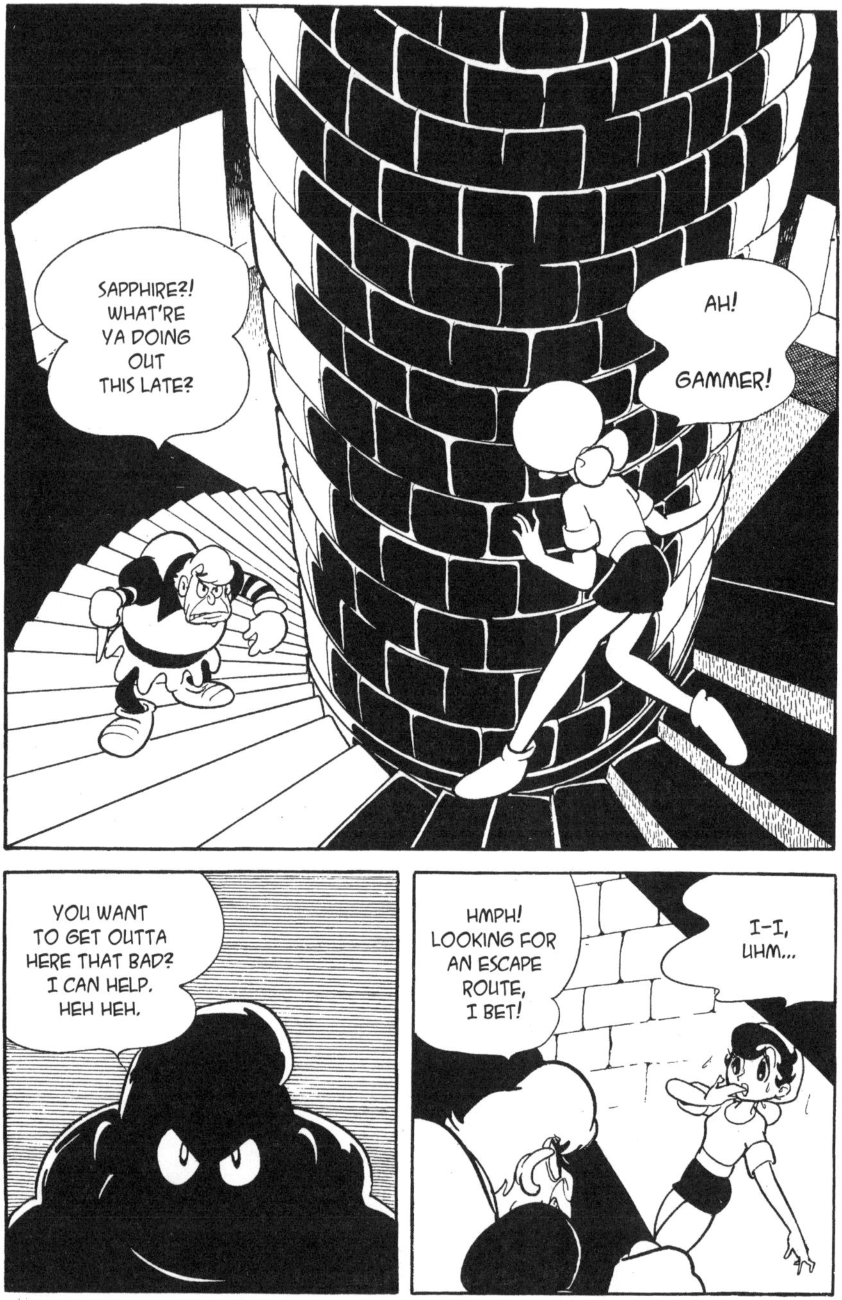
AH! GAMMER!
SAPPHIRE?! WHAT'RE YA DOING OUT THIS LATE?
I-I, UHM...
HMPH! LOOKING FOR AN ESCAPE ROUTE, I BET!
YOU WANT TO GET OUTTA HERE THAT BAD? I CAN HELP. HEH HEH.

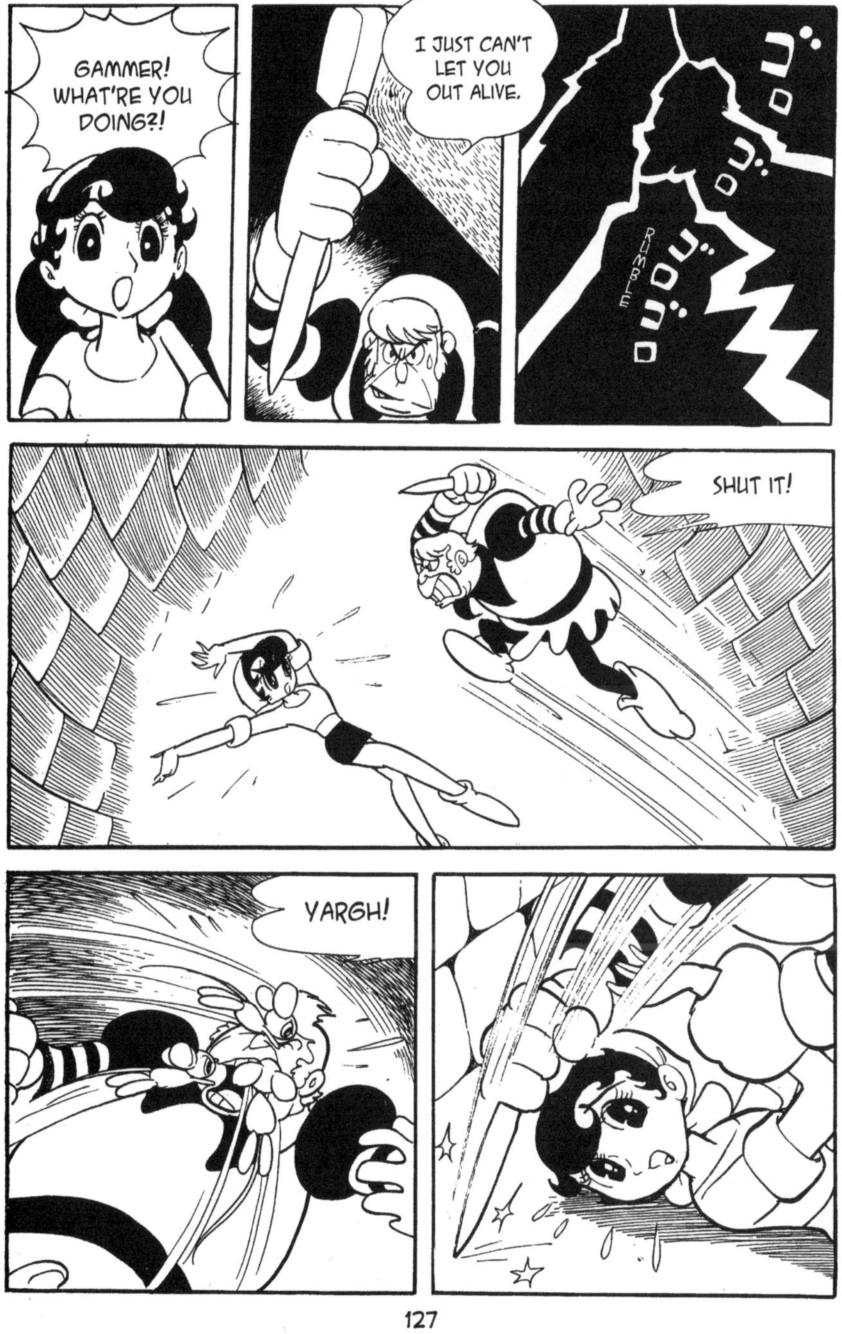
ゴロゴロゴロゴロ
RUMBLE
I JUST CAN'T LET YOU OUT ALIVE.
GAMMER! WHAT'RE YOU DOING?!
SHUT IT!
YARGH!

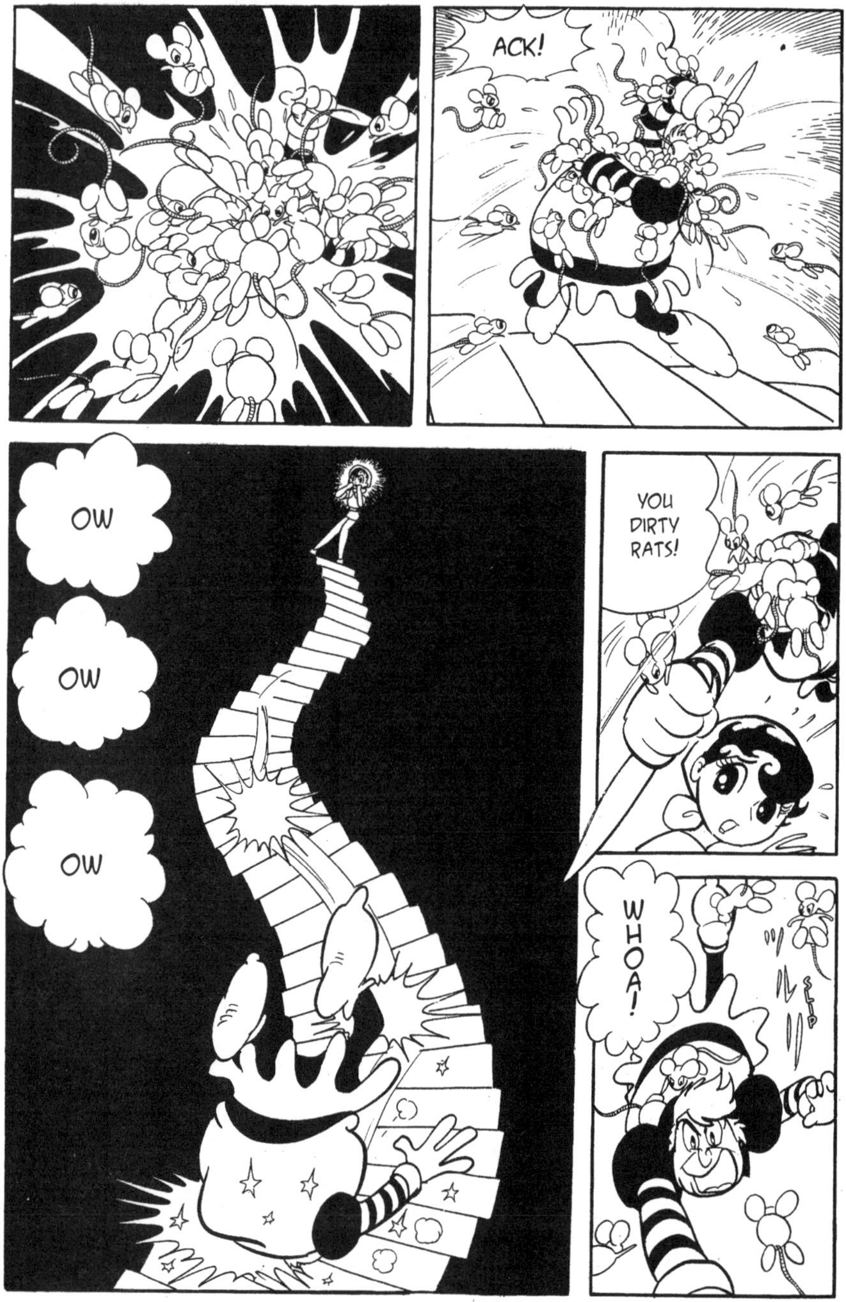
ACK!
YOU DIRTY RATS!
WHOA!
SLIP
OW
OW
OW

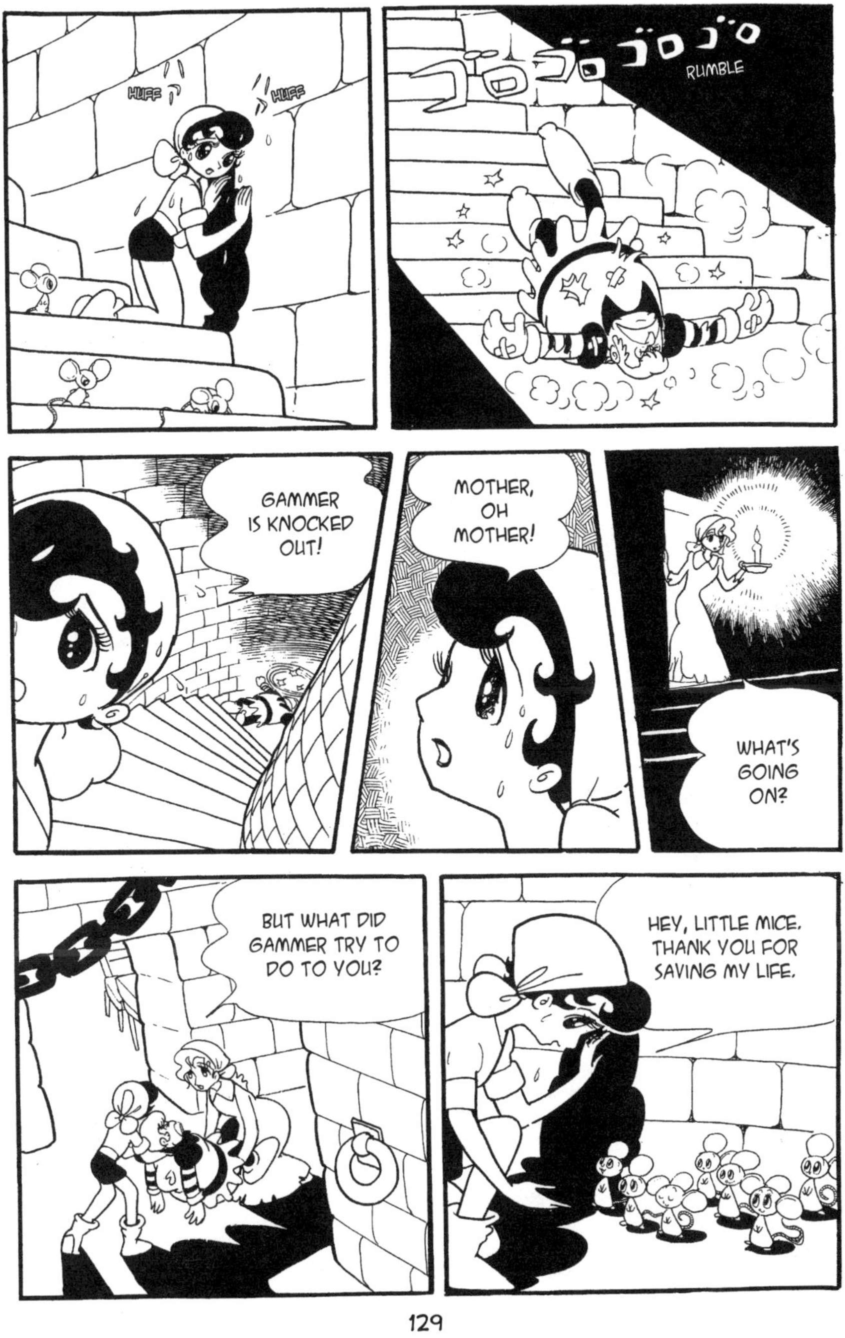
ゴロゴロゴロ
RUMBLE
HUFF
HUFF
WHAT'S GOING ON?
MOTHER, OH MOTHER!
GAMMER IS KNOCKED OUT!
HEY, LITTLE MICE. THANK YOU FOR SAVING MY LIFE.
BUT WHAT DID GAMMER TRY TO DO TO YOU?

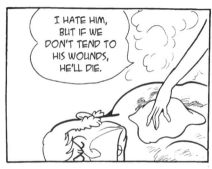

I HATE HIM, BUT IF WE DON'T TEND TO HIS WOUNDS, HE'LL DIE.

N– NOTHING ...

THUP

THUP

ISN'T THAT GAMMER?

GASP

130

UR... URR...
I WASHED YOUR WOUNDS AND APPLIED MEDICINE.
WHISK
UNH...
HUP!

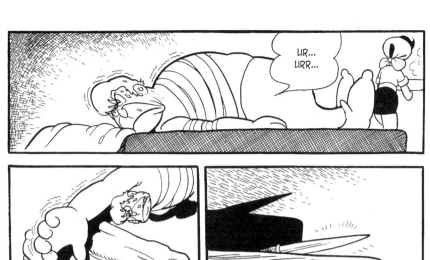

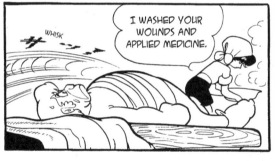

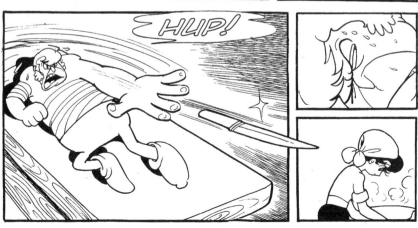

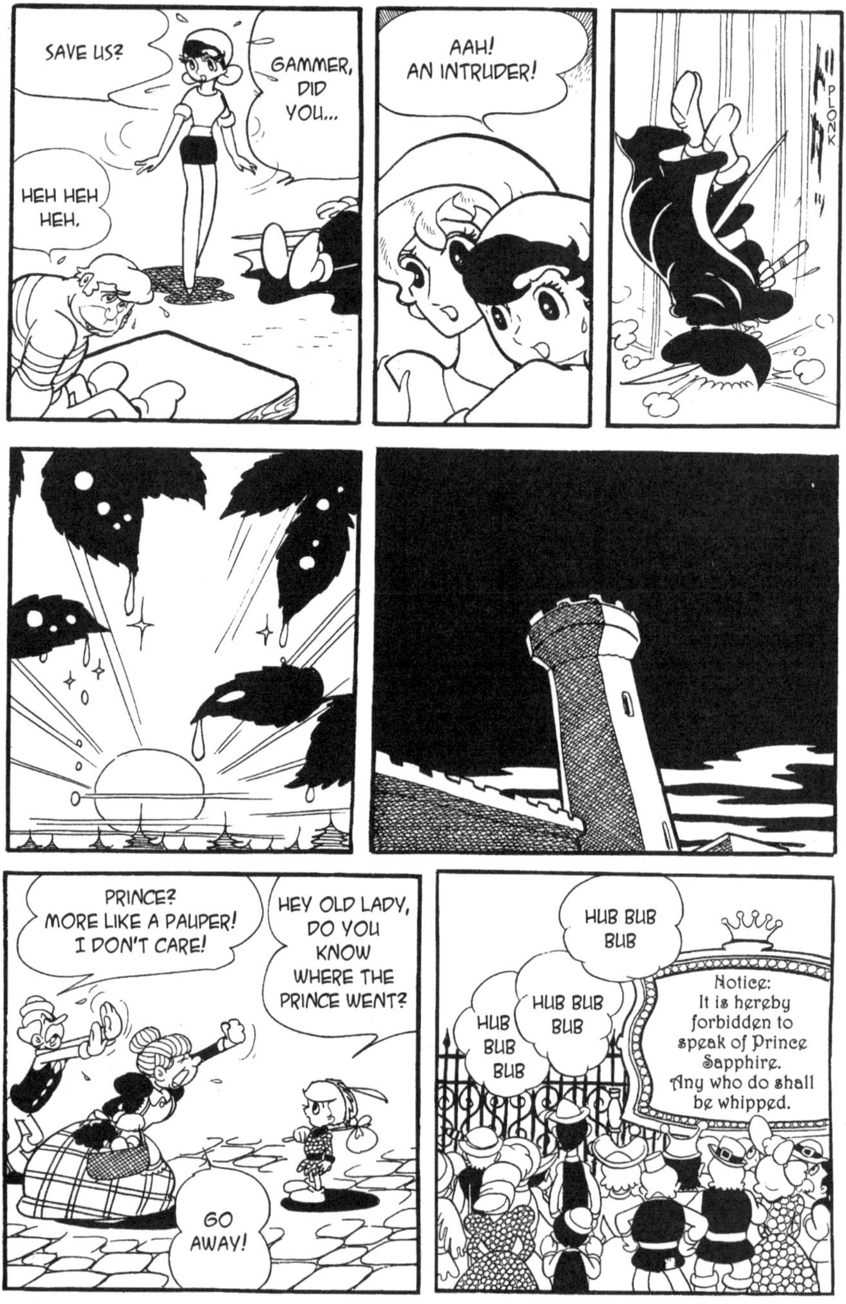
PLONK
AAH! AN INTRUDER!
GAMMER, DID YOU...
SAVE US?
HEH HEH HEH.
HUB BUB BUB
Notice: It is hereby forbidden to speak of Prince Sapphire. Any who do shall be whipped.
HUB BUB BUB
HUB BUB BUB
HEY OLD LADY, DO YOU KNOW WHERE THE PRINCE WENT?
PRINCE? MORE LIKE A PAUPER! I DON'T CARE!
GO AWAY!

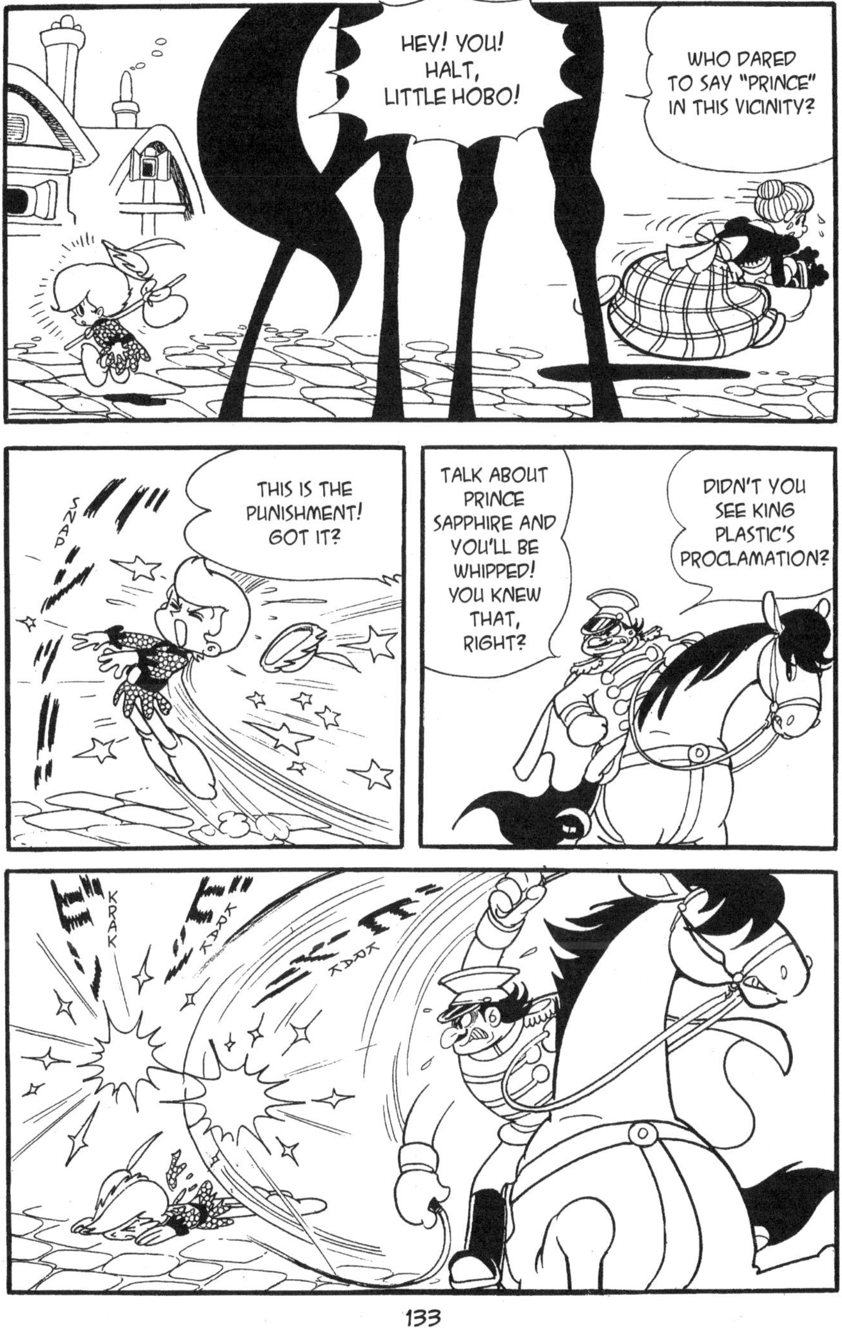
WHO DARED TO SAY "PRINCE" IN THIS VICINITY?
HEY! YOU! HALT, LITTLE HOBO!
DIDN'T YOU SEE KING PLASTIC'S PROCLAMATION?
TALK ABOUT PRINCE SAPPHIRE AND YOU'LL BE WHIPPED! YOU KNEW THAT, RIGHT?
THIS IS THE PUNISHMENT! GOT IT?
SNAP
KRAK
KRAK
KRAK

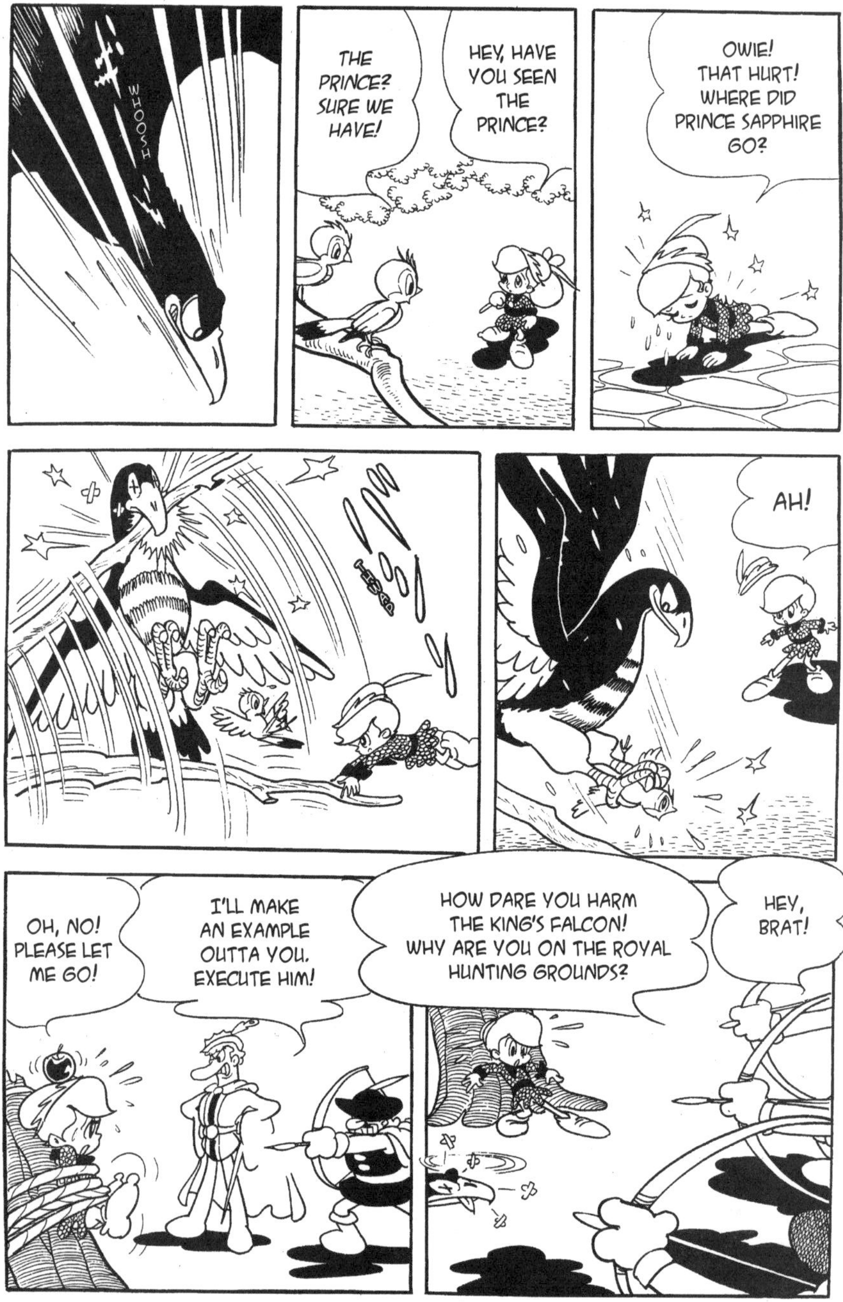
OWIE! THAT HURT! WHERE DID PRINCE SAPPHIRE GO?
HEY, HAVE YOU SEEN THE PRINCE?
THE PRINCE? SURE WE HAVE!
WHOOSH
AH!
HEY, BRAT!
HOW DARE YOU HARM THE KING'S FALCON! WHY ARE YOU ON THE ROYAL HUNTING GROUNDS?
I'LL MAKE AN EXAMPLE OUTTA YOU. EXECUTE HIM!
OH, NO! PLEASE LET ME GO!

Chapter 8

Phantom Knight's Debut

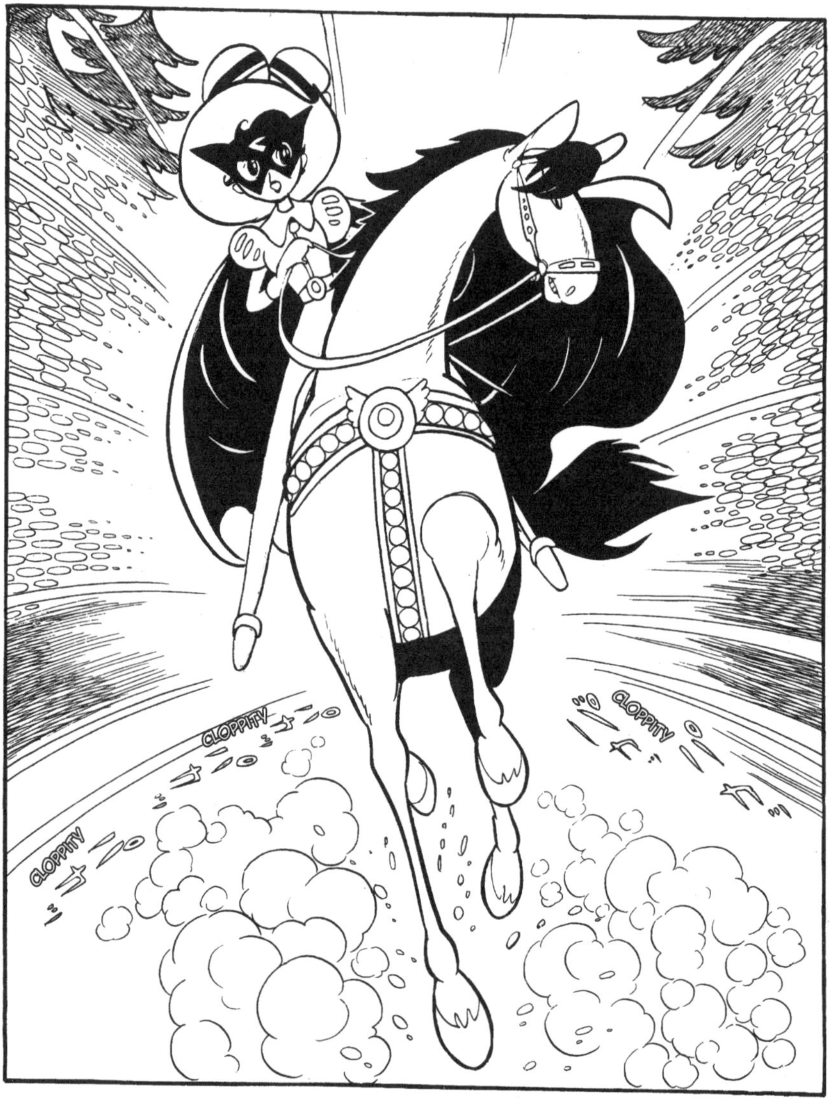
CLOPPITY
CLOPPITY
CLOPPITY

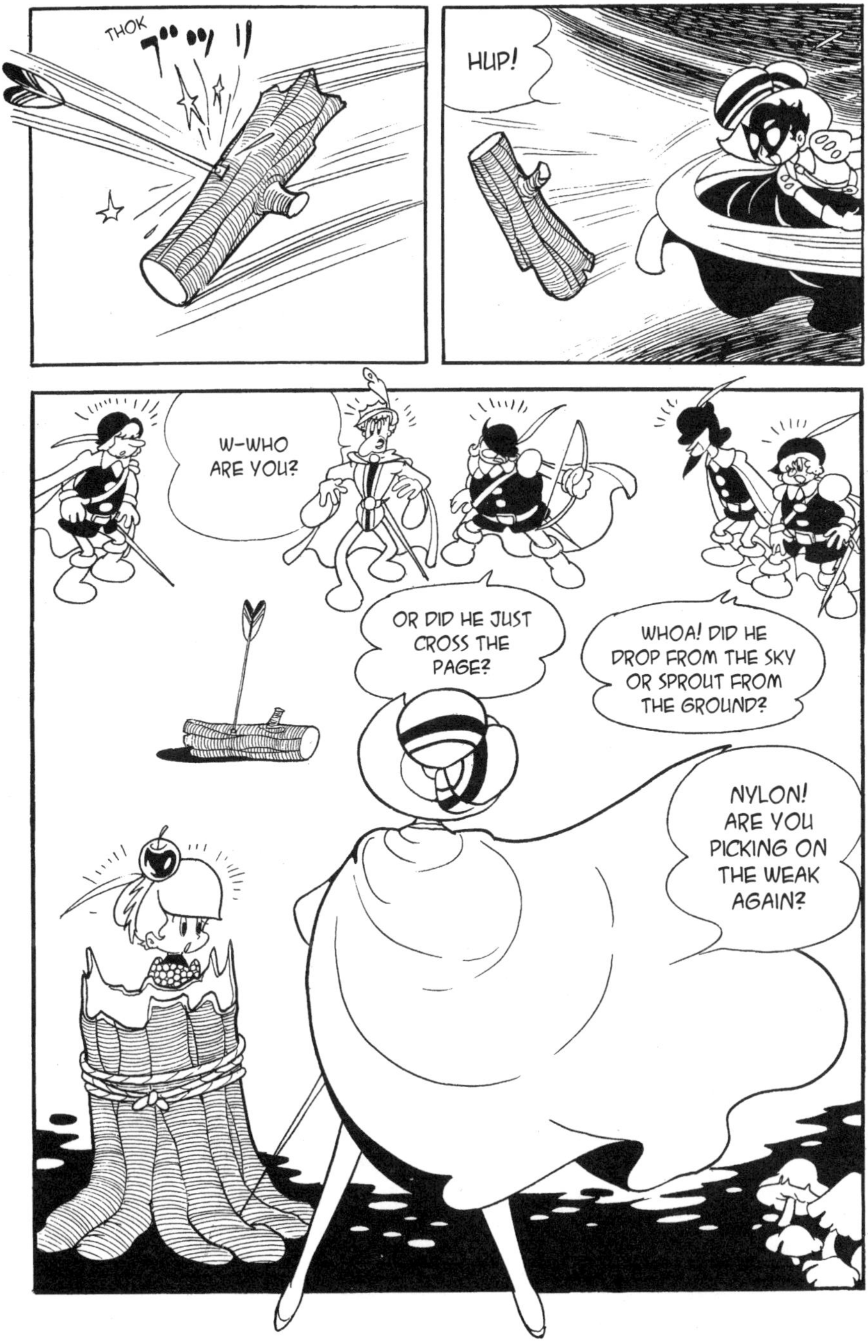

HUP!
THOK
W-WHO ARE YOU?
WHOA! DID HE DROP FROM THE SKY OR SPROUT FROM THE GROUND?
OR DID HE JUST CROSS THE PAGE?
NYLON! ARE YOU PICKING ON THE WEAK AGAIN?

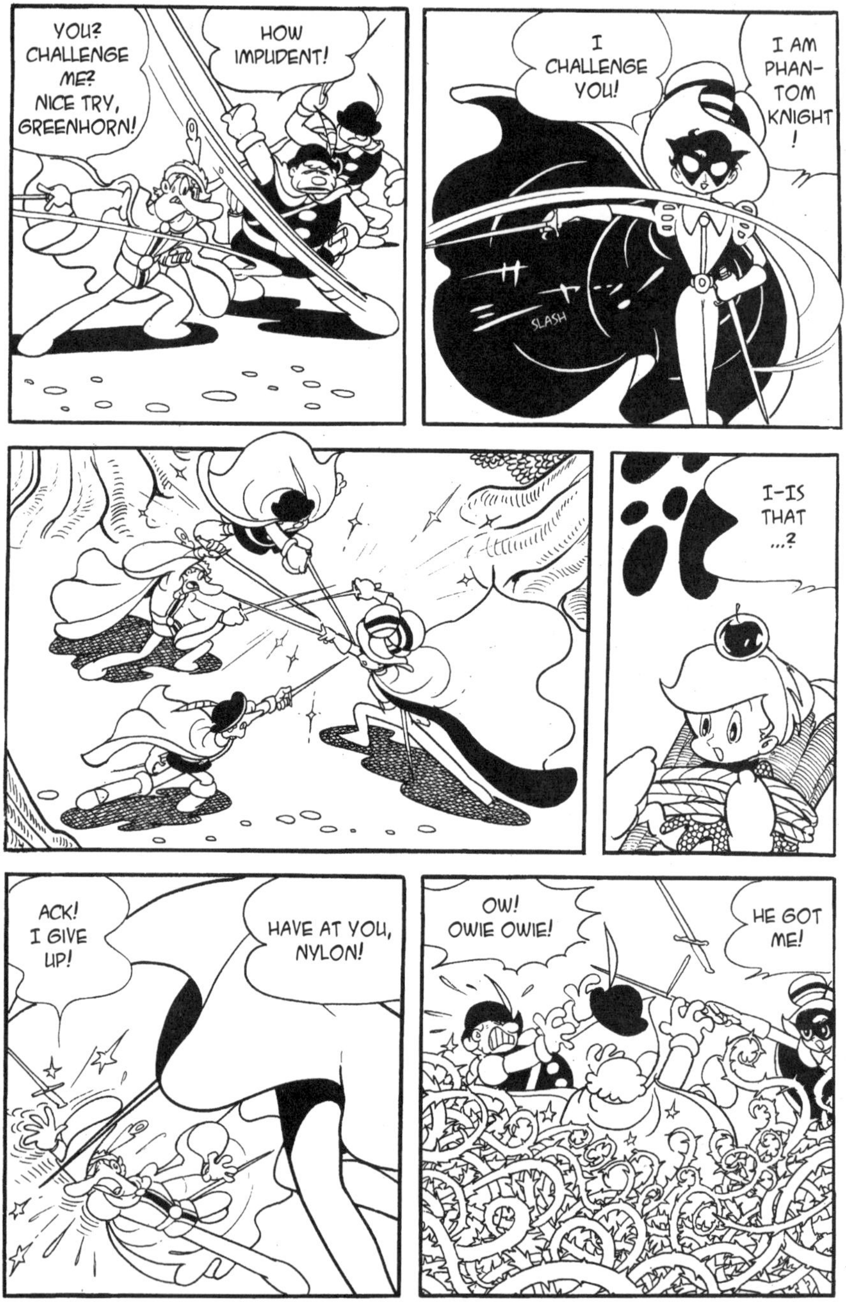
I AM PHAN-TOM KNIGHT!
I CHALLENGE YOU!
SLASH
HOW IMPUDENT!
YOU? CHALLENGE ME? NICE TRY, GREENHORN!
I-IS THAT ...?
HE GOT ME!
OW! OWIE OWIE!
HAVE AT YOU, NYLON!
ACK! I GIVE UP!

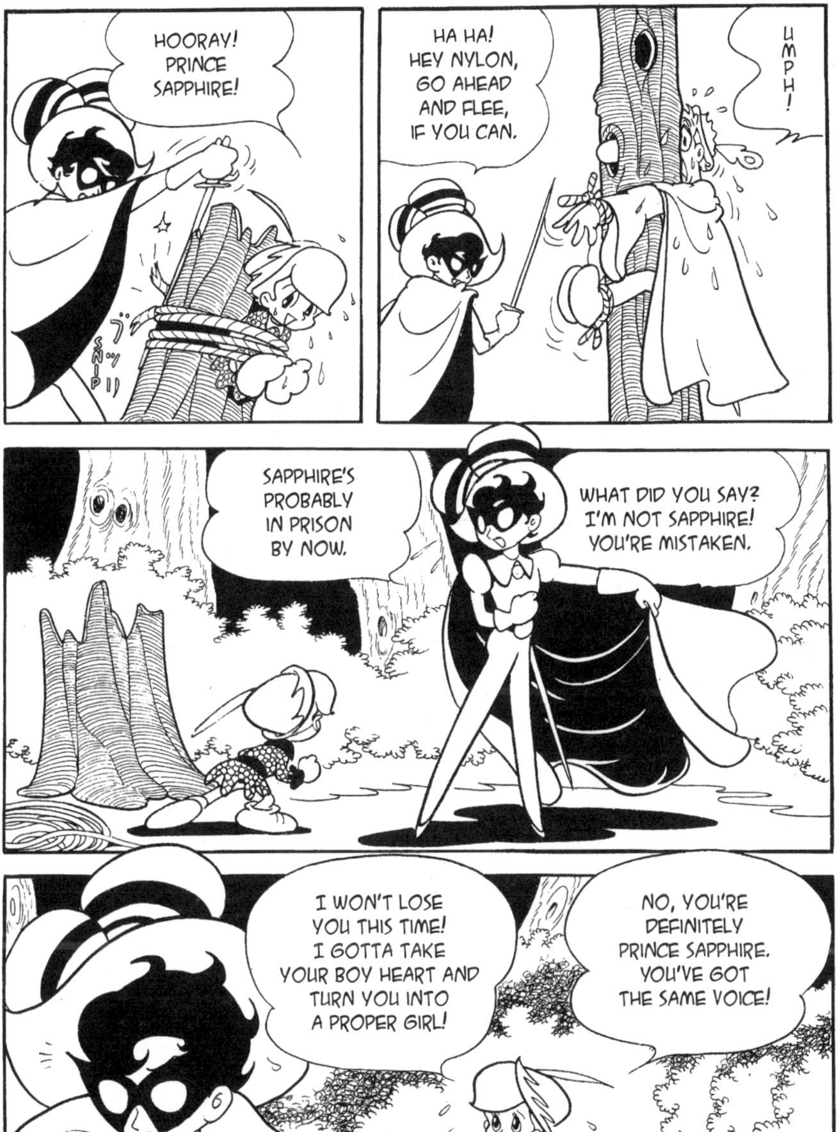
UMPH!
HA HA! HEY NYLON, GO AHEAD AND FLEE, IF YOU CAN.
HOORAY! PRINCE SAPPHIRE!
SNIP
WHAT DID YOU SAY? I'M NOT SAPPHIRE! YOU'RE MISTAKEN.
SAPPHIRE'S PROBABLY IN PRISON BY NOW.
NO, YOU'RE DEFINITELY PRINCE SAPPHIRE. YOU'VE GOT THE SAME VOICE!
I WON'T LOSE YOU THIS TIME! I GOTTA TAKE YOUR BOY HEART AND TURN YOU INTO A PROPER GIRL!
NO, YOU'RE WRONG, I SAY!

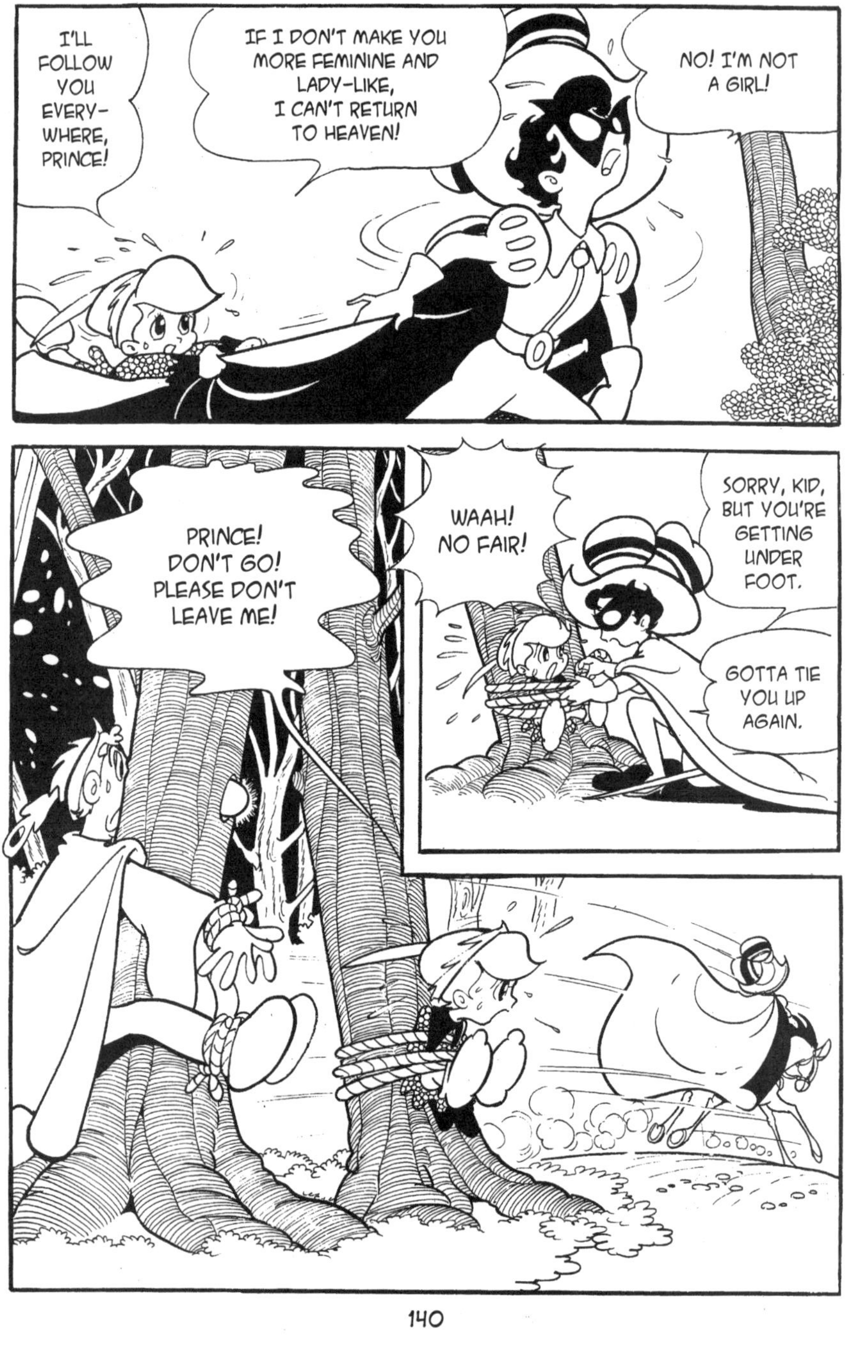
NO! I'M NOT A GIRL!
IF I DON'T MAKE YOU MORE FEMININE AND LADY-LIKE, I CAN'T RETURN TO HEAVEN!
I'LL FOLLOW YOU EVERY-WHERE, PRINCE!
SORRY, KID, BUT YOU'RE GETTING UNDER FOOT.
GOTTA TIE YOU UP AGAIN.
WAAH! NO FAIR!
PRINCE! DON'T GO! PLEASE DON'T LEAVE ME!

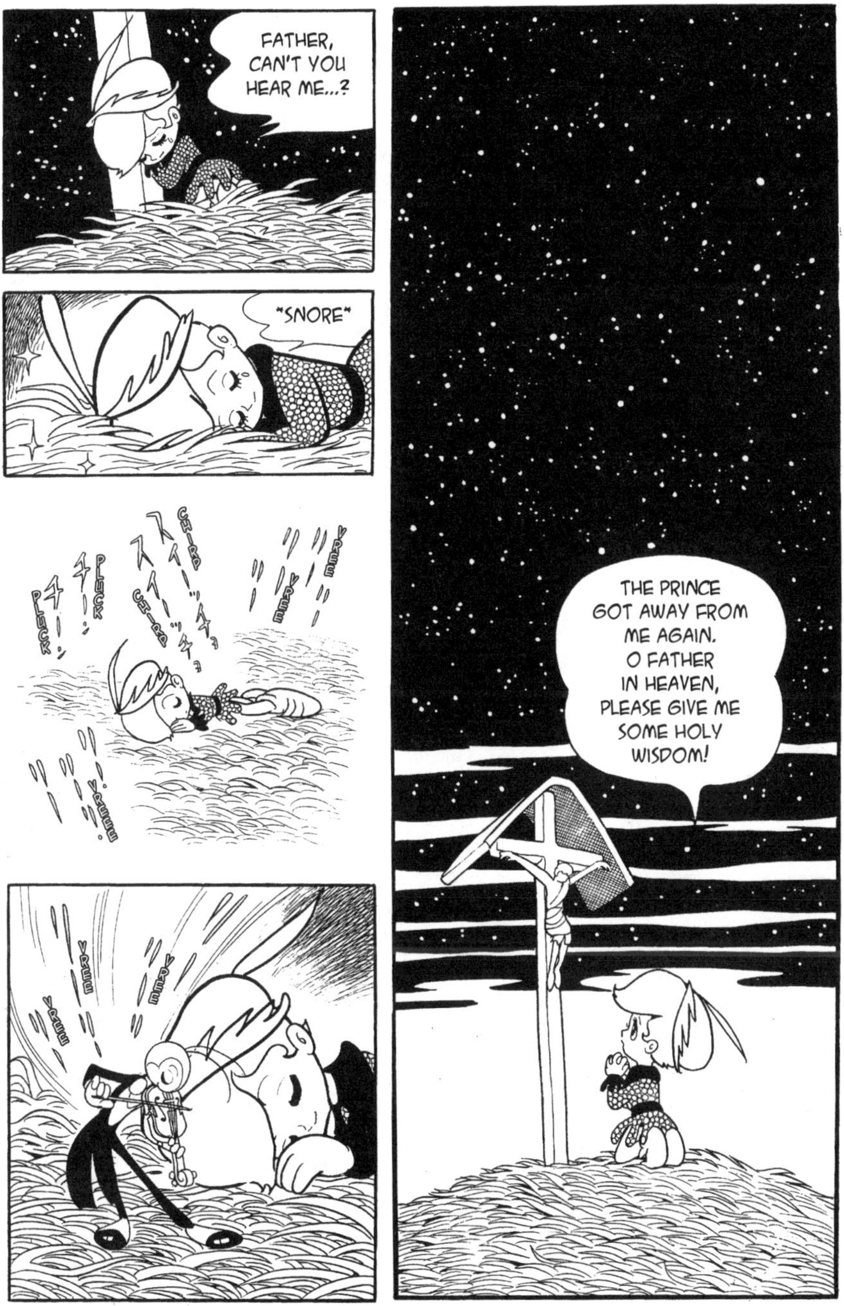
THE PRINCE GOT AWAY FROM ME AGAIN. O FATHER IN HEAVEN, PLEASE GIVE ME SOME HOLY WISDOM!
FATHER, CAN'T YOU HEAR ME...?
SNORE
VREE
VREE
CHIRP
CHIRP
PLUCK
PLUCK
VREEE
VREE
VREE
VREEE

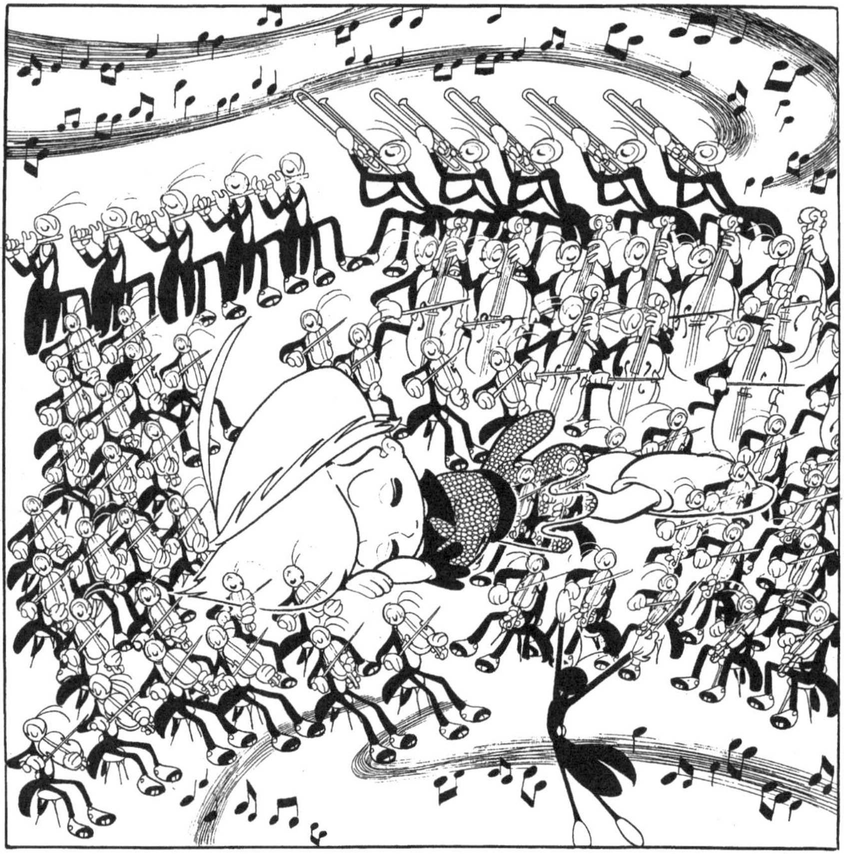

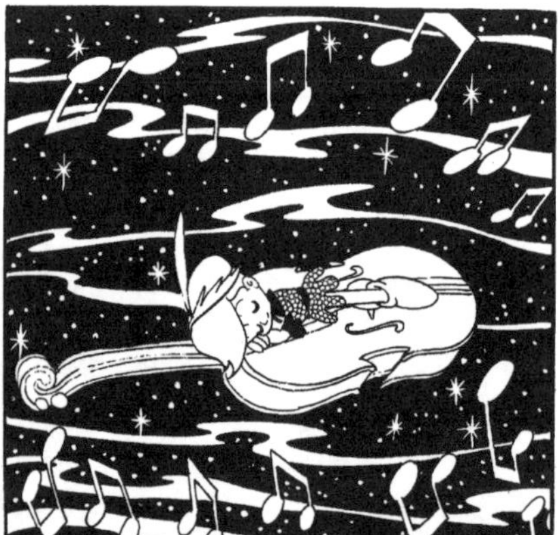

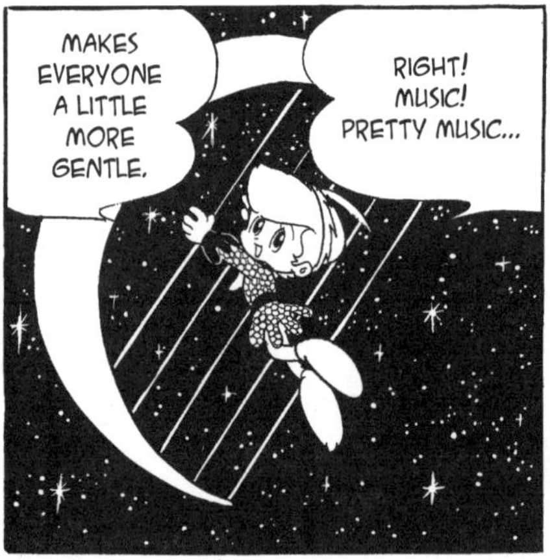
RIGHT! MUSIC! PRETTY MUSIC...
MAKES EVERYONE A LITTLE MORE GENTLE.

AH! I WAS DREAMING? THANK YOU, FATHER! I GET IT.

I'LL MAKE A FLUTE FROM A BEECH TWIG!

LET'S SEE HOW IT SOUNDS.

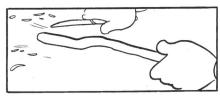

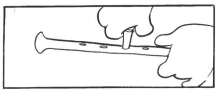

FINISHED!

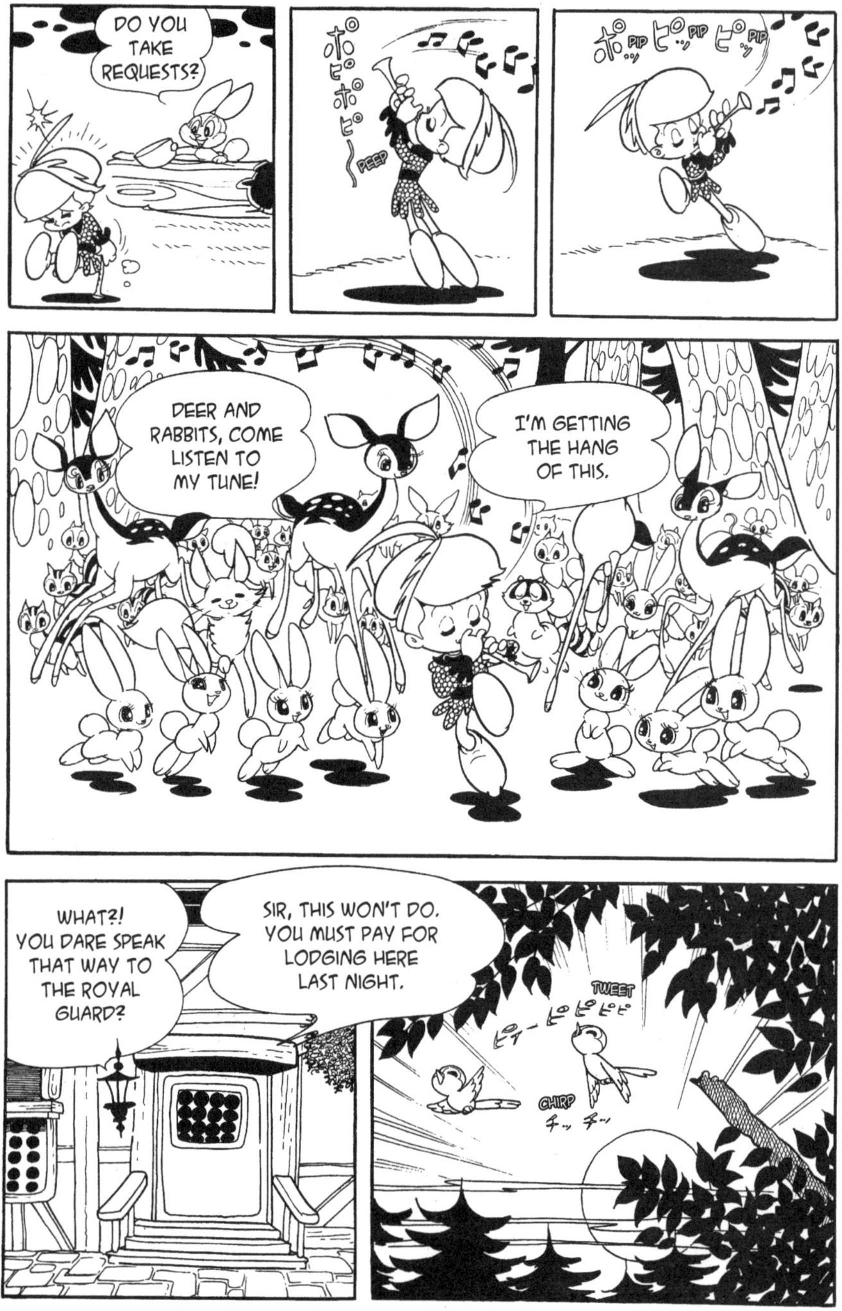
PIP
PIP
PIP
PEEP
DO YOU TAKE REQUESTS?
I'M GETTING THE HANG OF THIS.
DEER AND RABBITS, COME LISTEN TO MY TUNE!
TWEET
CHIRP
SIR, THIS WON'T DO. YOU MUST PAY FOR LODGING HERE LAST NIGHT.
WHAT?! YOU DARE SPEAK THAT WAY TO THE ROYAL GUARD?

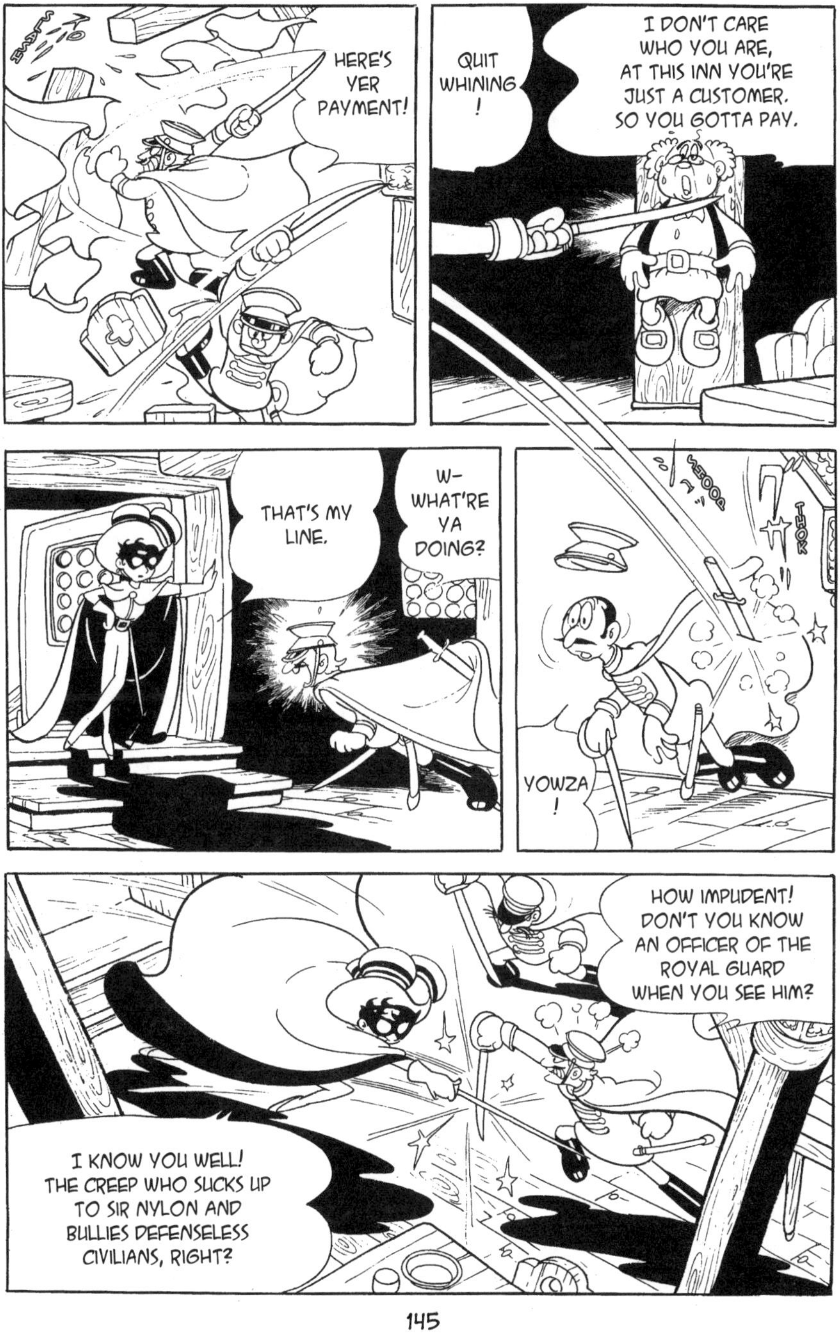
I DON'T CARE WHO YOU ARE, AT THIS INN YOU'RE JUST A CUSTOMER. SO YOU GOTTA PAY.
QUIT WHINING!
HERE'S YER PAYMENT!
THOK
YOWZA!
W- WHAT'RE YA DOING?
THAT'S MY LINE.
HOW IMPUDENT! DON'T YOU KNOW AN OFFICER OF THE ROYAL GUARD WHEN YOU SEE HIM?
I KNOW YOU WELL! THE CREEP WHO SUCKS UP TO SIR NYLON AND BULLIES DEFENSELESS CIVILIANS, RIGHT?

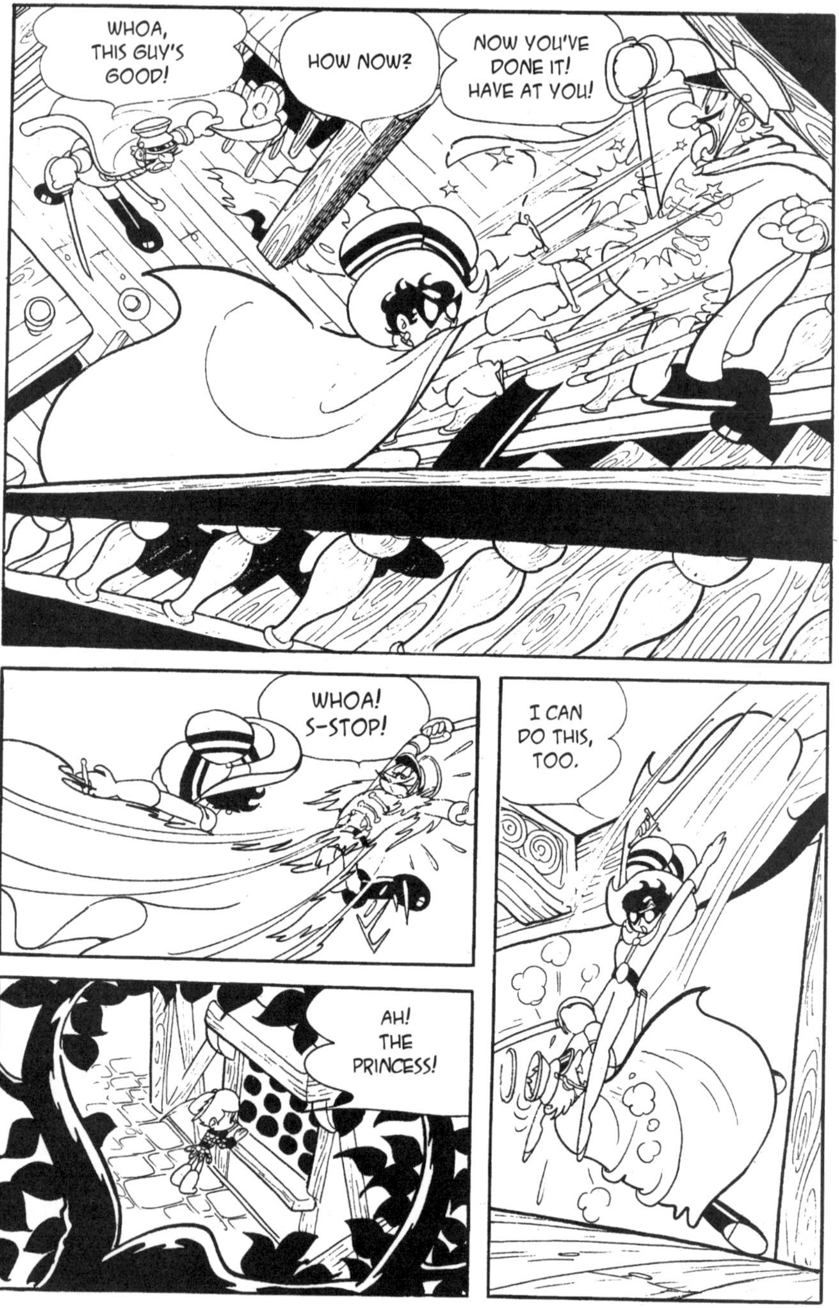
NOW YOU'VE DONE IT! HAVE AT YOU!
HOW NOW?
WHOA, THIS GUY'S GOOD!
I CAN DO THIS, TOO.
WHOA! S-STOP!
AH! THE PRINCESS!

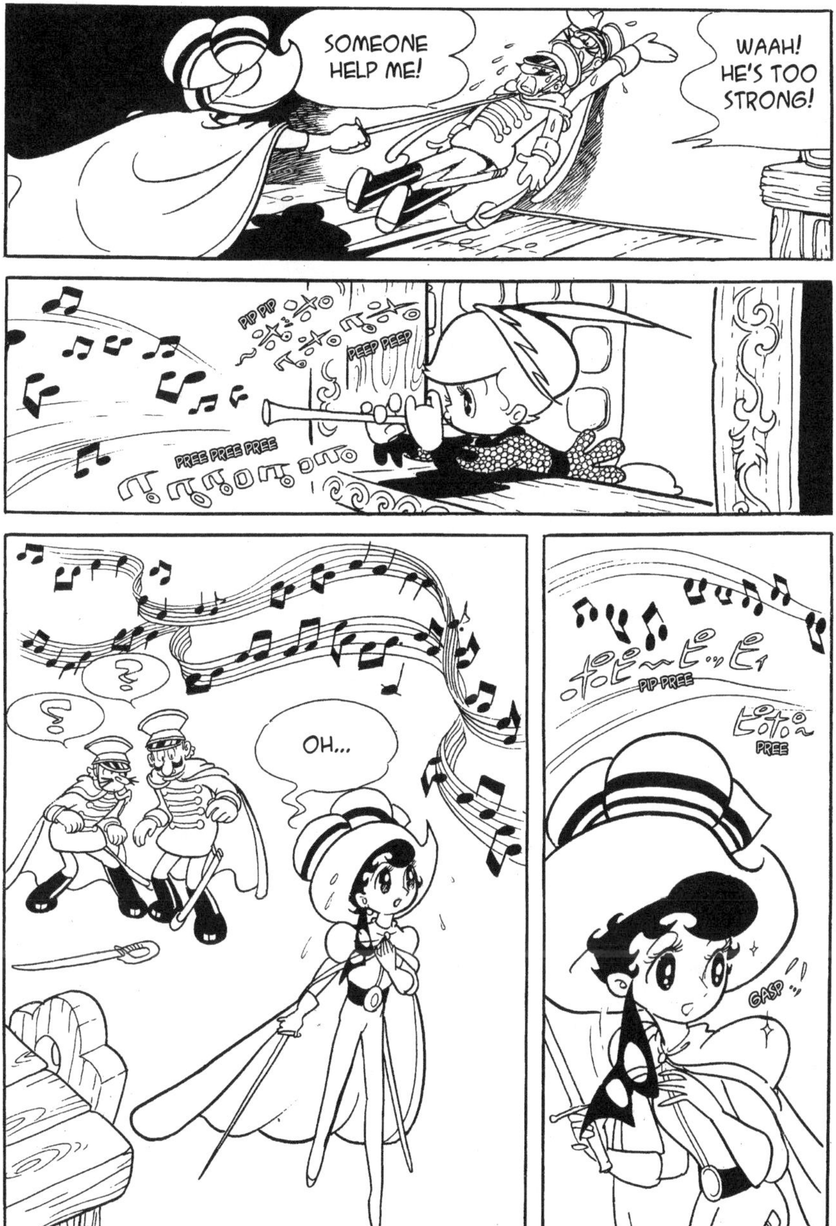
WAAH! HE'S TOO STRONG!
SOMEONE HELP ME!
PIP PIP
PEEP PEEP
PREE PREE PREE
PIP PREE
PREE
GASP
?
?
OH...

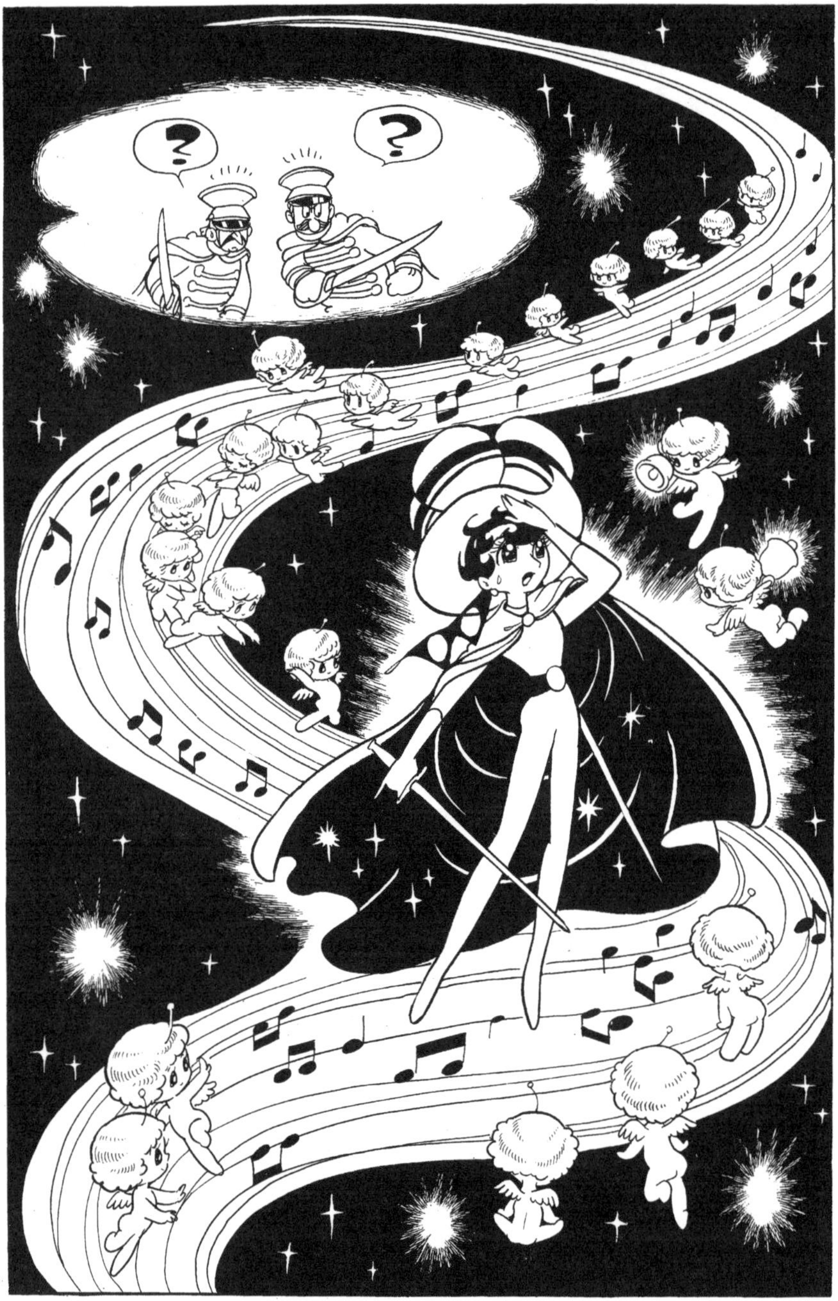
?
?

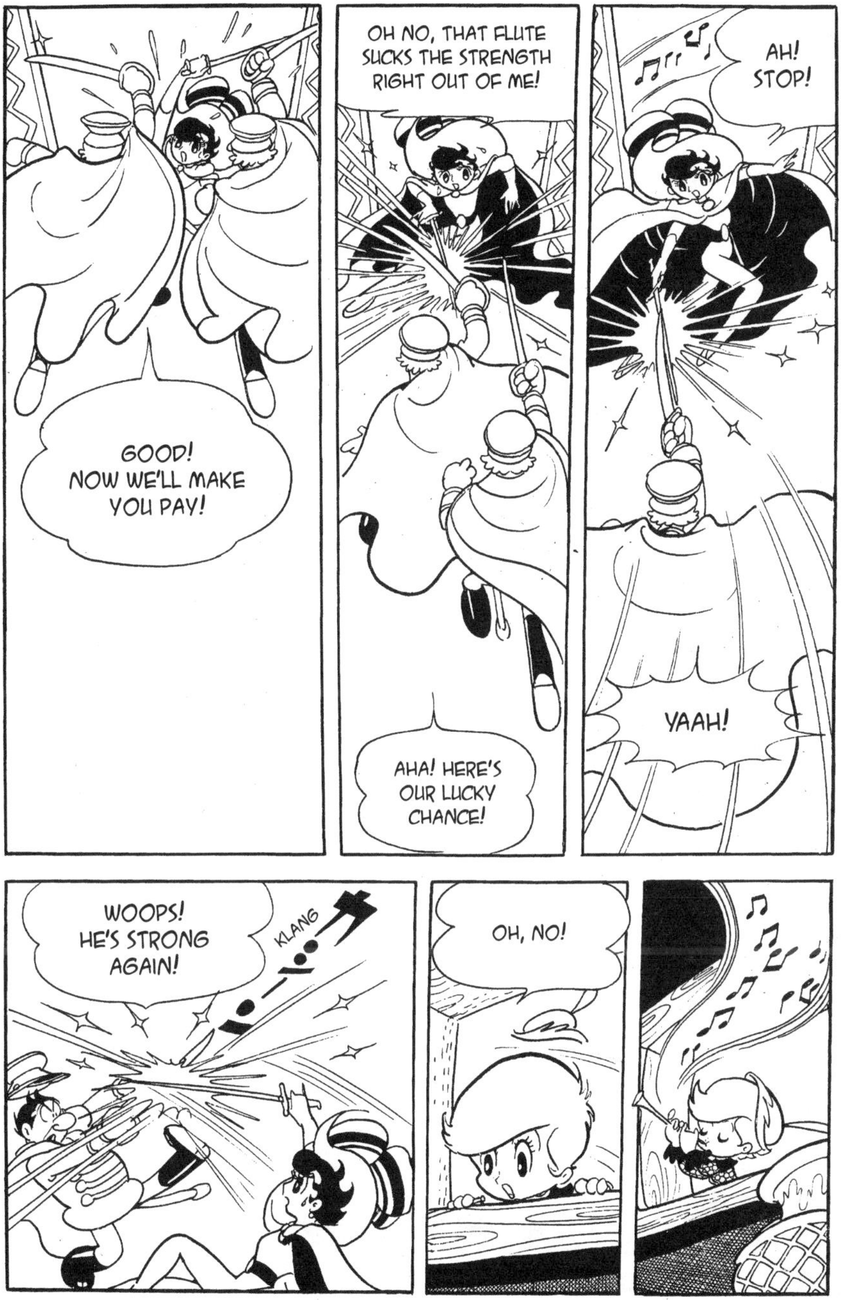
AH! STOP!
YAAH!
OH NO, THAT FLUTE SUCKS THE STRENGTH RIGHT OUT OF ME!
AHA! HERE'S OUR LUCKY CHANCE!
GOOD! NOW WE'LL MAKE YOU PAY!
OH, NO!
WOOPS! HE'S STRONG AGAIN!
KLANG

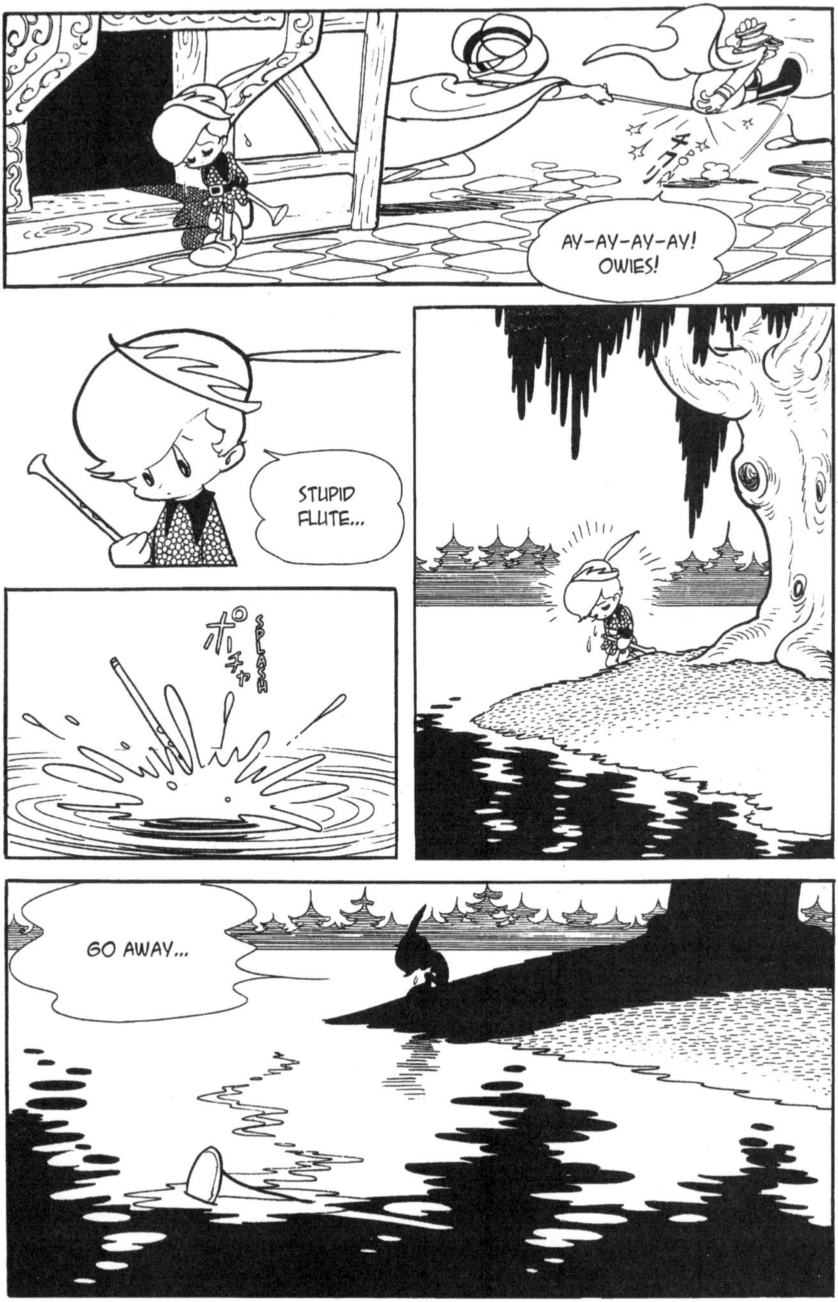
チクリ
AY-AY-AY-AY! OWIES!
STUPID FLUTE...
ポチャ
SPLASH
GO AWAY...

Chapter 9

The Idiot King's Bride

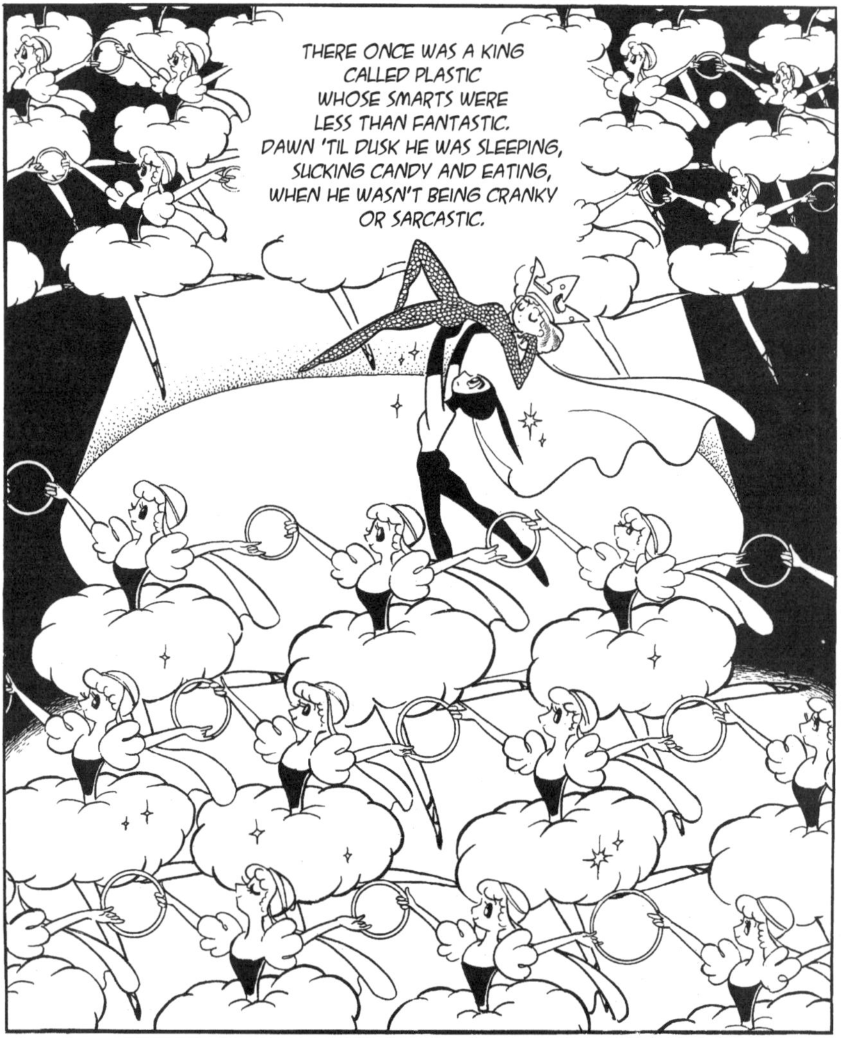
THERE ONCE WAS A KING CALLED PLASTIC WHOSE SMARTS WERE LESS THAN FANTASTIC. DAWN 'TIL DUSK HE WAS SLEEPING, SUCKING CANDY AND EATING, WHEN HE WASN'T BEING CRANKY OR SARCASTIC.

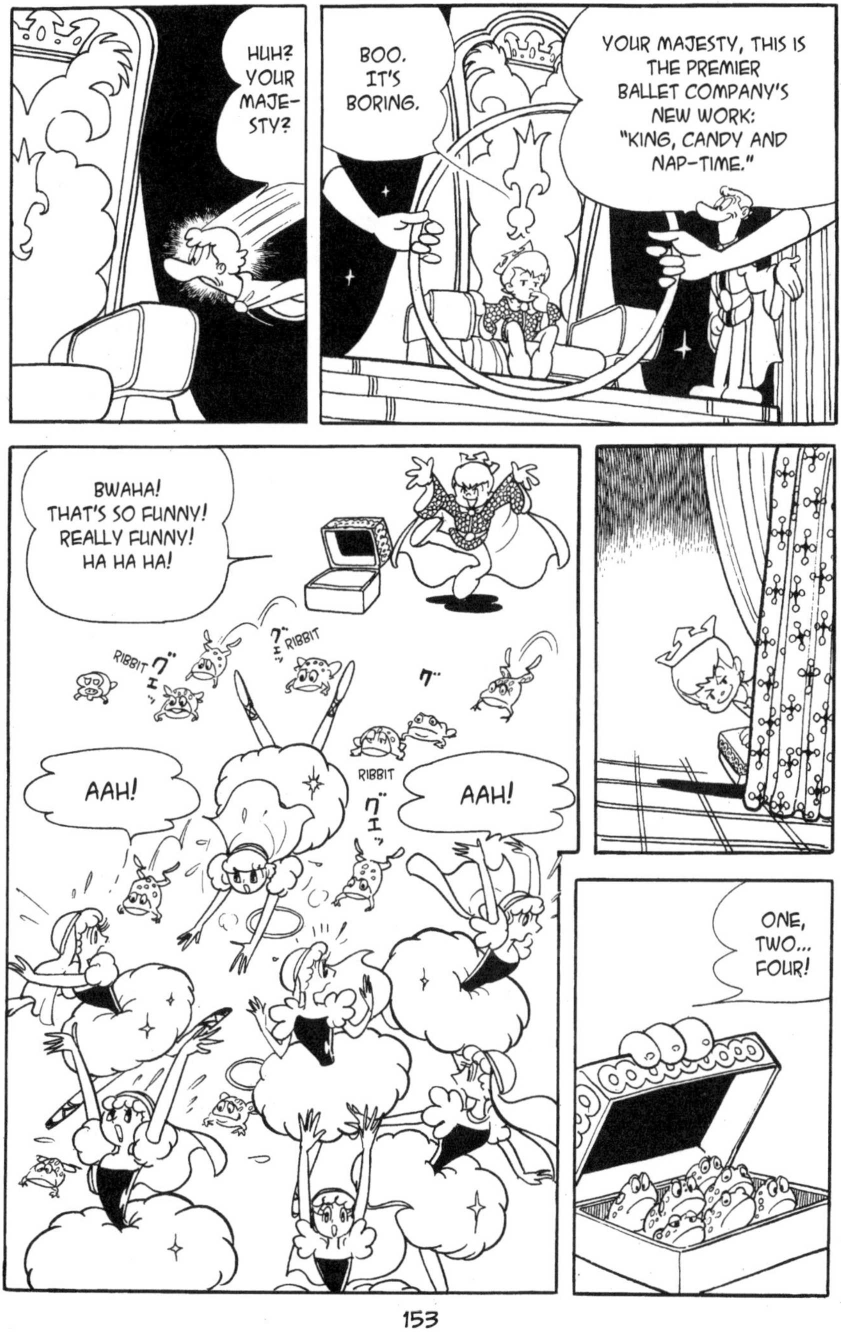
YOUR MAJESTY, THIS IS THE PREMIER BALLET COMPANY'S NEW WORK: "KING, CANDY AND NAP-TIME."
BOO. IT'S BORING.
HUH? YOUR MAJE- STY?
ONE, TWO... FOUR!
BWAHA! THAT'S SO FUNNY! REALLY FUNNY! HA HA HA!
RIBBIT
グエッ
RIBBIT
グェッ
グ
RIBBIT
グエッ
RIBBIT
グエッ
AAH!
AAH!

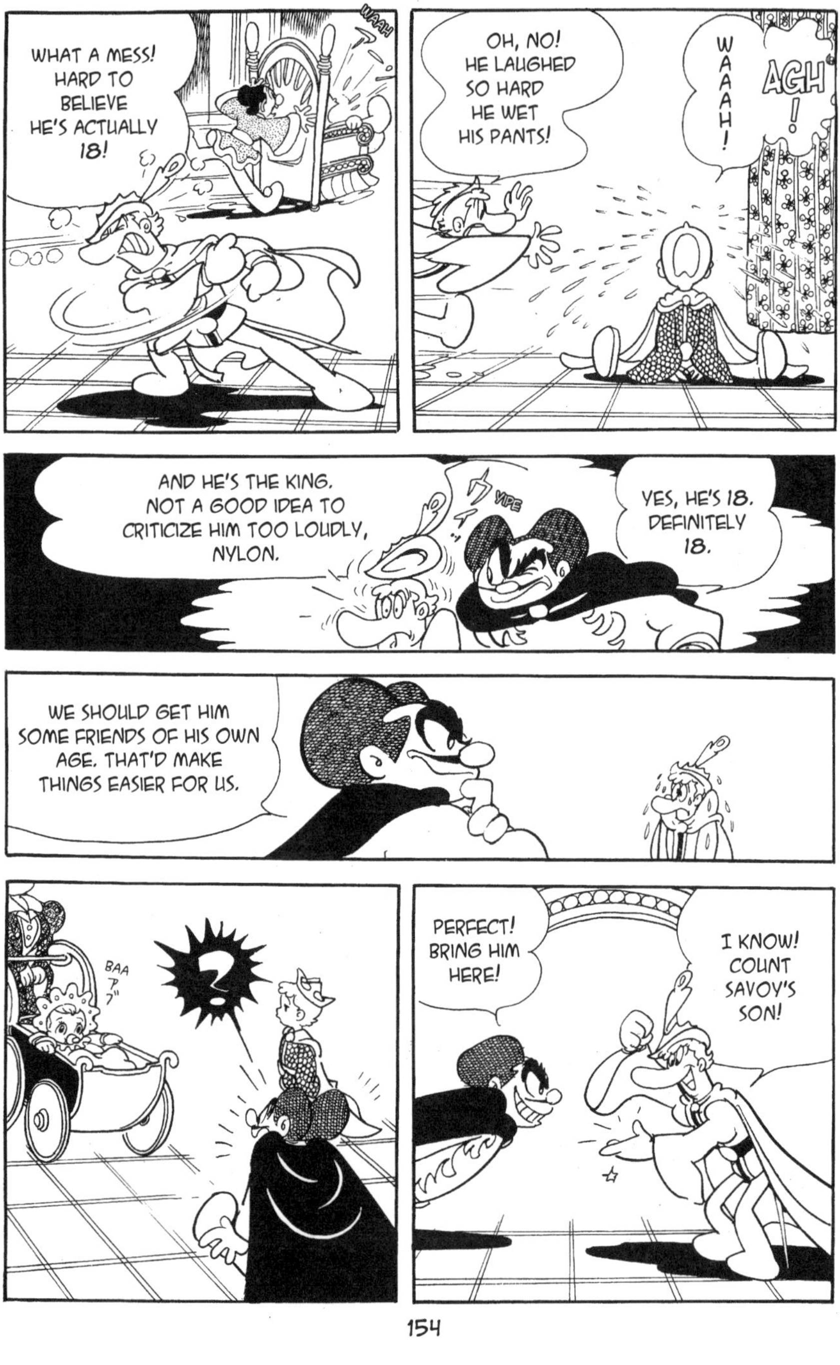
AGH!
WAAAH!
OH, NO! HE LAUGHED SO HARD HE WET HIS PANTS!
WAAH
WHAT A MESS! HARD TO BELIEVE HE'S ACTUALLY 18!
YES, HE'S 18. DEFINITELY 18.
YIPE
AND HE'S THE KING. NOT A GOOD IDEA TO CRITICIZE HIM TOO LOUDLY, NYLON.
WE SHOULD GET HIM SOME FRIENDS OF HIS OWN AGE. THAT'D MAKE THINGS EASIER FOR US.
I KNOW! COUNT SAVOY'S SON!
PERFECT! BRING HIM HERE!
?
BAA

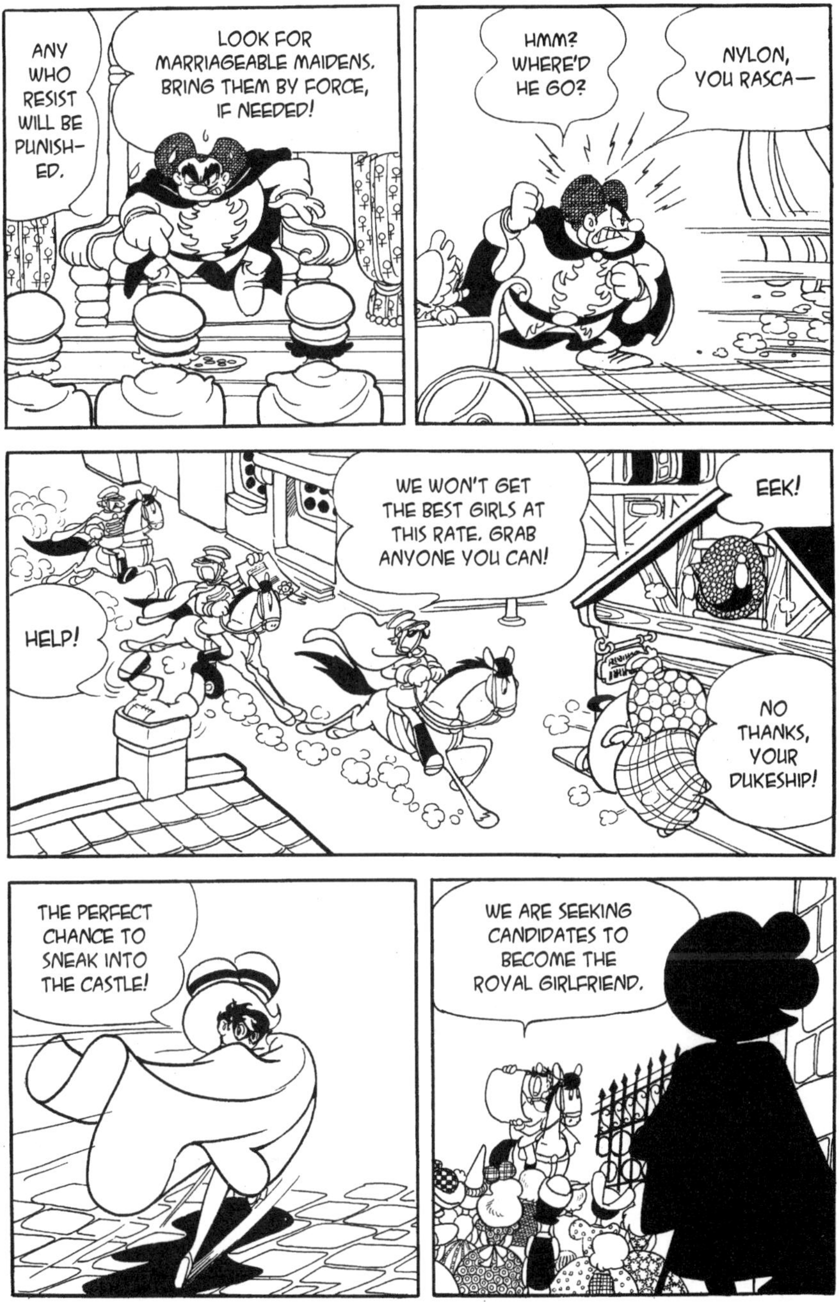

NYLON, YOU RASCA—
HMM? WHERE'D HE GO?
LOOK FOR MARRIAGEABLE MAIDENS. BRING THEM BY FORCE, IF NEEDED!
ANY WHO RESIST WILL BE PUNISH-ED.
EEK!
WE WON'T GET THE BEST GIRLS AT THIS RATE. GRAB ANYONE YOU CAN!
NO THANKS, YOUR DUKESHIP!
HELP!
WE ARE SEEKING CANDIDATES TO BECOME THE ROYAL GIRLFRIEND.
THE PERFECT CHANCE TO SNEAK INTO THE CASTLE!

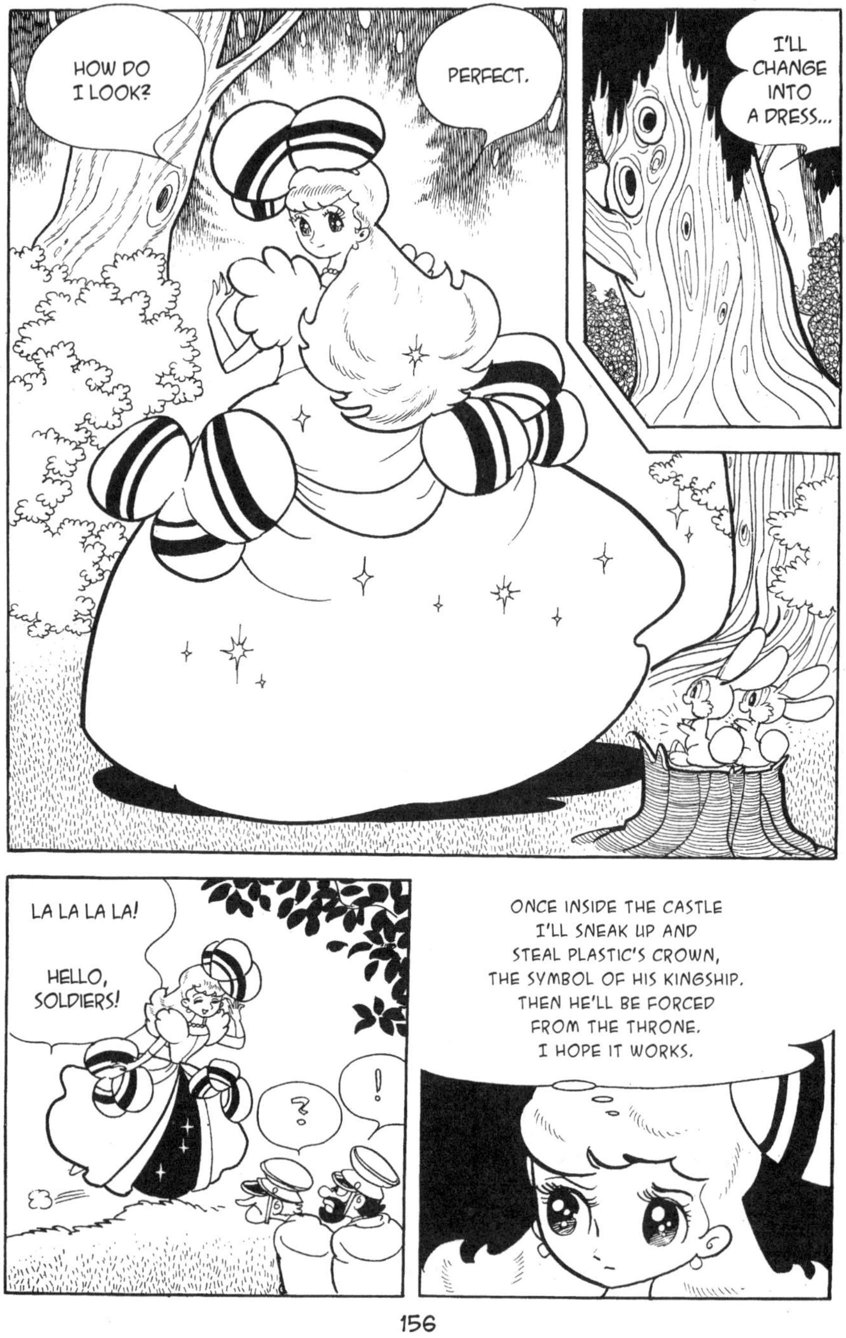
I'LL CHANGE INTO A DRESS...
PERFECT.
HOW DO I LOOK?
ONCE INSIDE THE CASTLE I'LL SNEAK UP AND STEAL PLASTIC'S CROWN, THE SYMBOL OF HIS KINGSHIP. THEN HE'LL BE FORCED FROM THE THRONE. I HOPE IT WORKS.
LA LA LA LA!
HELLO, SOLDIERS!
!
?

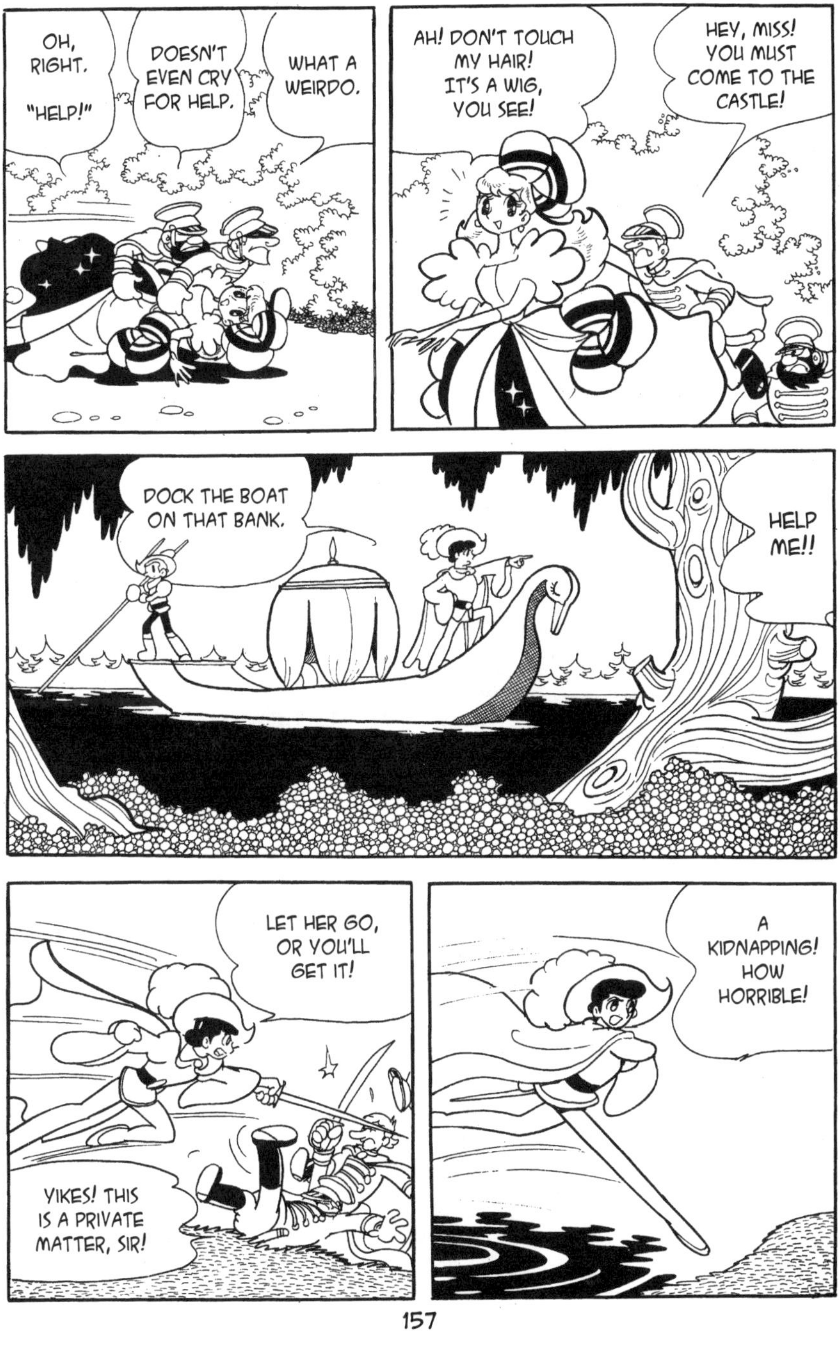
HEY, MISS! YOU MUST COME TO THE CASTLE!
AH! DON'T TOUCH MY HAIR! IT'S A WIG, YOU SEE!
WHAT A WEIRDO.
DOESN'T EVEN CRY FOR HELP.
OH, RIGHT. "HELP!"
HELP ME!!
DOCK THE BOAT ON THAT BANK.
A KIDNAPPING! HOW HORRIBLE!
LET HER GO, OR YOU'LL GET IT!
YIKES! THIS IS A PRIVATE MATTER, SIR!

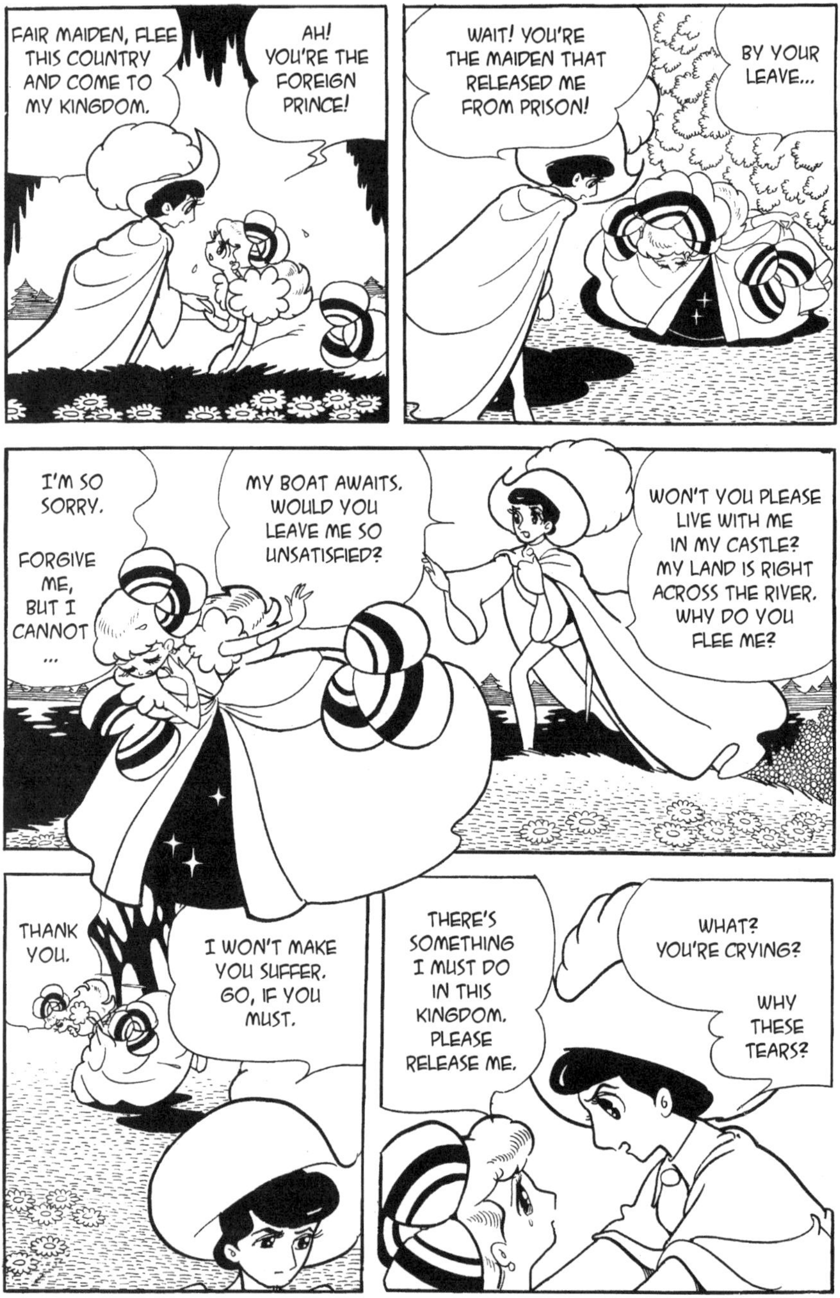

BY YOUR LEAVE...
WAIT! YOU'RE THE MAIDEN THAT RELEASED ME FROM PRISON!
AH! YOU'RE THE FOREIGN PRINCE!
FAIR MAIDEN, FLEE THIS COUNTRY AND COME TO MY KINGDOM.
WON'T YOU PLEASE LIVE WITH ME IN MY CASTLE? MY LAND IS RIGHT ACROSS THE RIVER. WHY DO YOU FLEE ME?
MY BOAT AWAITS. WOULD YOU LEAVE ME SO UNSATISFIED?
I'M SO SORRY.
FORGIVE ME, BUT I CANNOT ...
WHAT? YOU'RE CRYING?
WHY THESE TEARS?
THERE'S SOMETHING I MUST DO IN THIS KINGDOM. PLEASE RELEASE ME.
I WON'T MAKE YOU SUFFER. GO, IF YOU MUST.
THANK YOU.

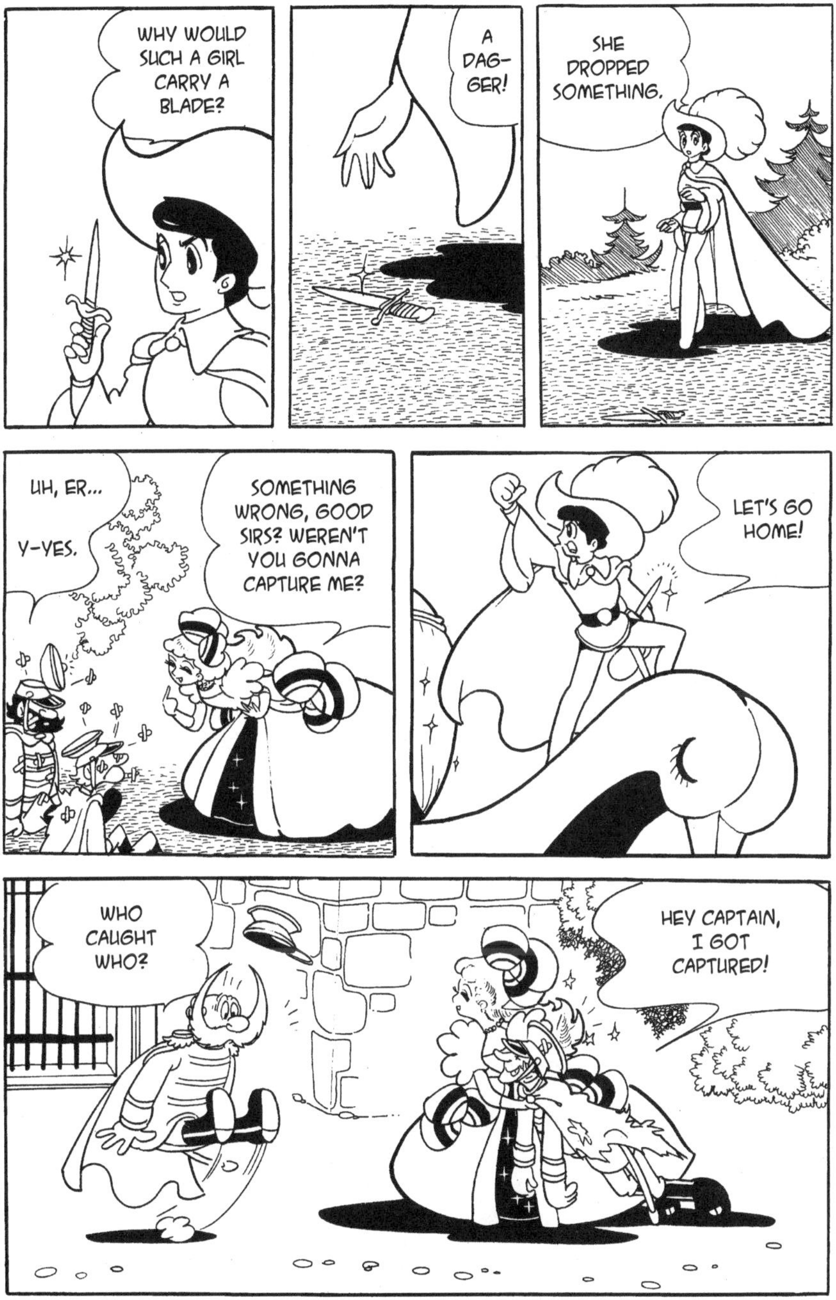

SHE DROPPED SOMETHING.
A DAG-GER!
WHY WOULD SUCH A GIRL CARRY A BLADE?
LET'S GO HOME!
SOMETHING WRONG, GOOD SIRS? WEREN'T YOU GONNA CAPTURE ME?
UH, ER...
Y-YES.
HEY CAPTAIN, I GOT CAPTURED!
WHO CAUGHT WHO?

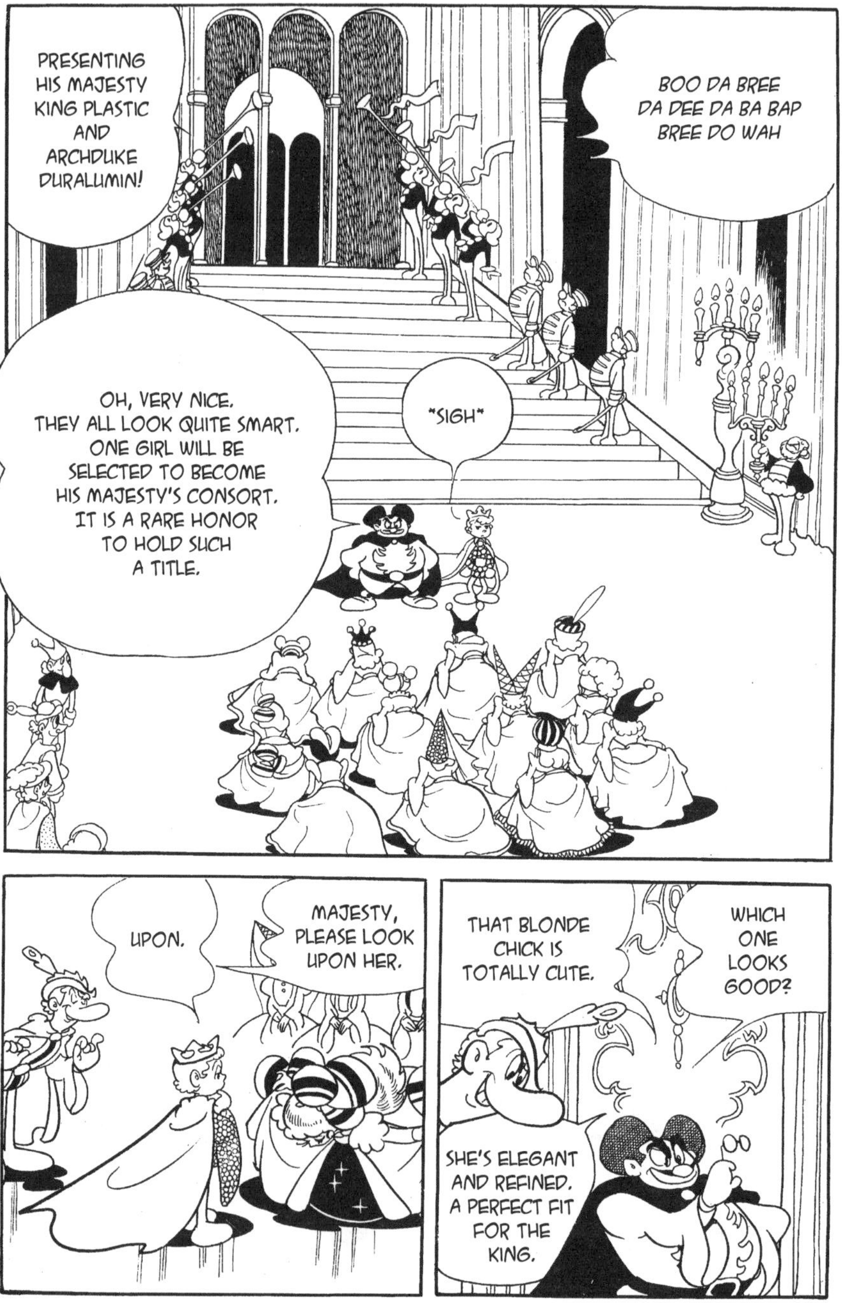
BOO DA BREE DA DEE DA BA BAP BREE DO WAH
PRESENTING HIS MAJESTY KING PLASTIC AND ARCHDUKE DURALUMIN!
SIGH
OH, VERY NICE. THEY ALL LOOK QUITE SMART. ONE GIRL WILL BE SELECTED TO BECOME HIS MAJESTY'S CONSORT. IT IS A RARE HONOR TO HOLD SUCH A TITLE.
WHICH ONE LOOKS GOOD?
THAT BLONDE CHICK IS TOTALLY CUTE.
SHE'S ELEGANT AND REFINED. A PERFECT FIT FOR THE KING.
MAJESTY, PLEASE LOOK UPON HER.
UPON.

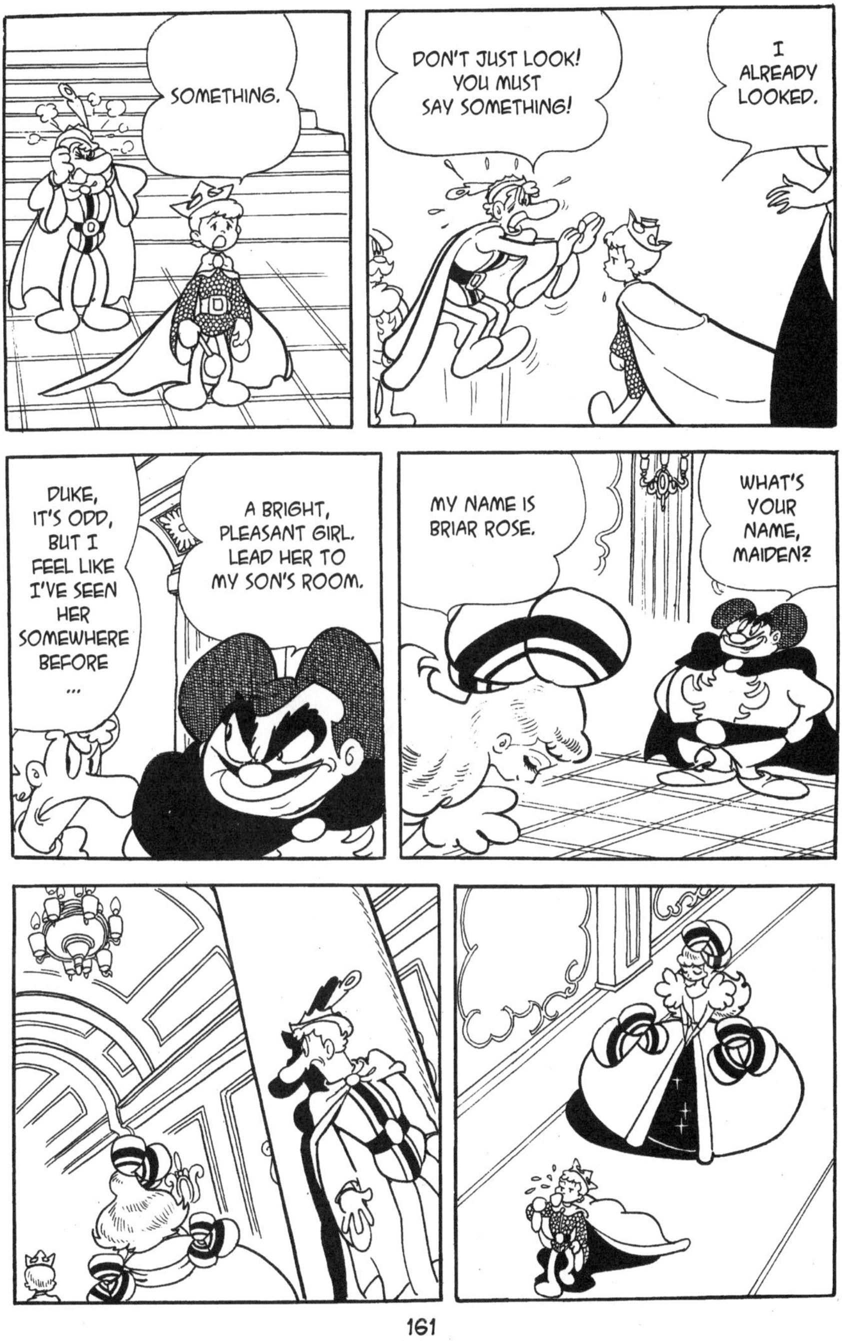
I ALREADY LOOKED.
DON'T JUST LOOK! YOU MUST SAY SOMETHING!
SOMETHING.
WHAT'S YOUR NAME, MAIDEN?
MY NAME IS BRIAR ROSE.
A BRIGHT, PLEASANT GIRL. LEAD HER TO MY SON'S ROOM.
DUKE, IT'S ODD, BUT I FEEL LIKE I'VE SEEN HER SOMEWHERE BEFORE ...

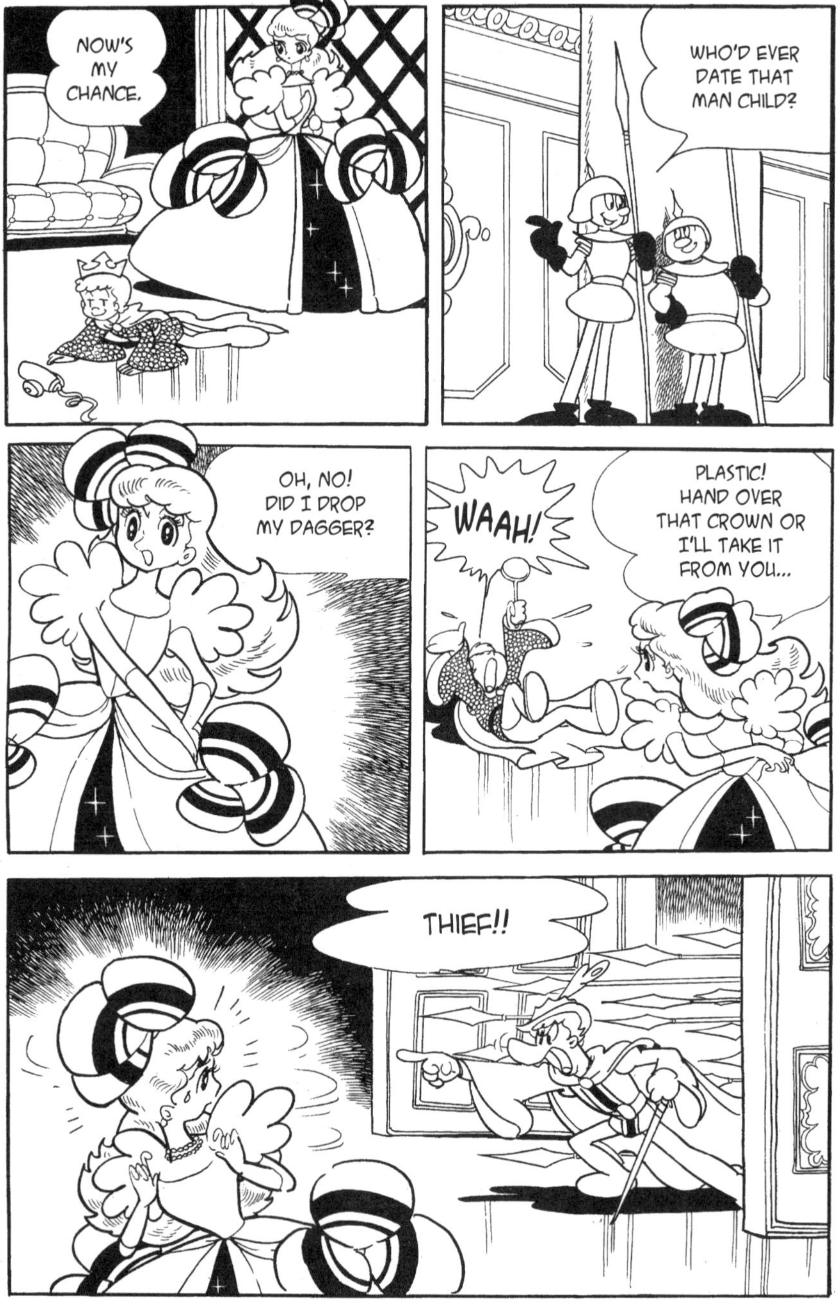
WHO'D EVER DATE THAT MAN CHILD?
NOW'S MY CHANCE.
PLASTIC! HAND OVER THAT CROWN OR I'LL TAKE IT FROM YOU...
WAAH!
OH, NO! DID I DROP MY DAGGER?
THIEF!!

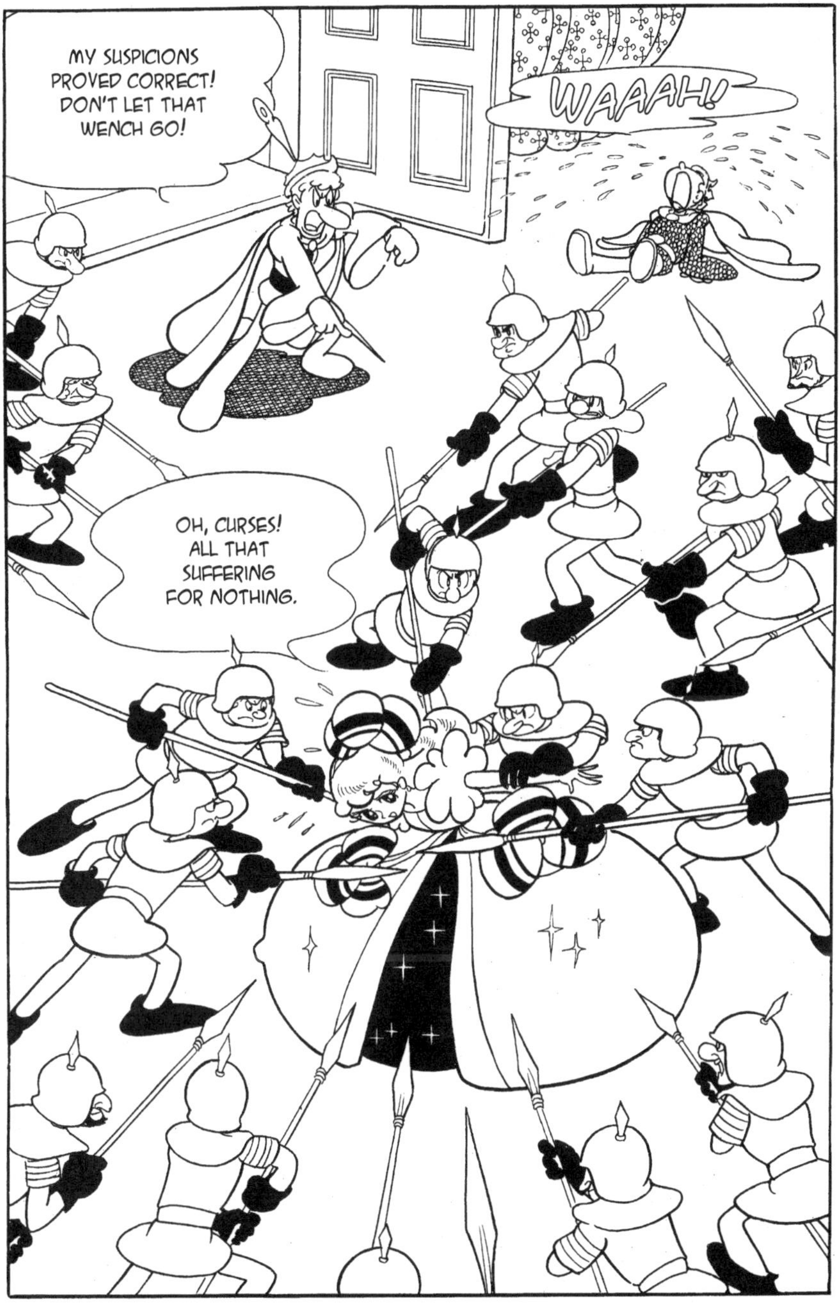
WAAAH!
MY SUSPICIONS PROVED CORRECT! DON'T LET THAT WENCH GO!
OH, CURSES! ALL THAT SUFFERING FOR NOTHING.

Chapter 10

Devil's Whisper

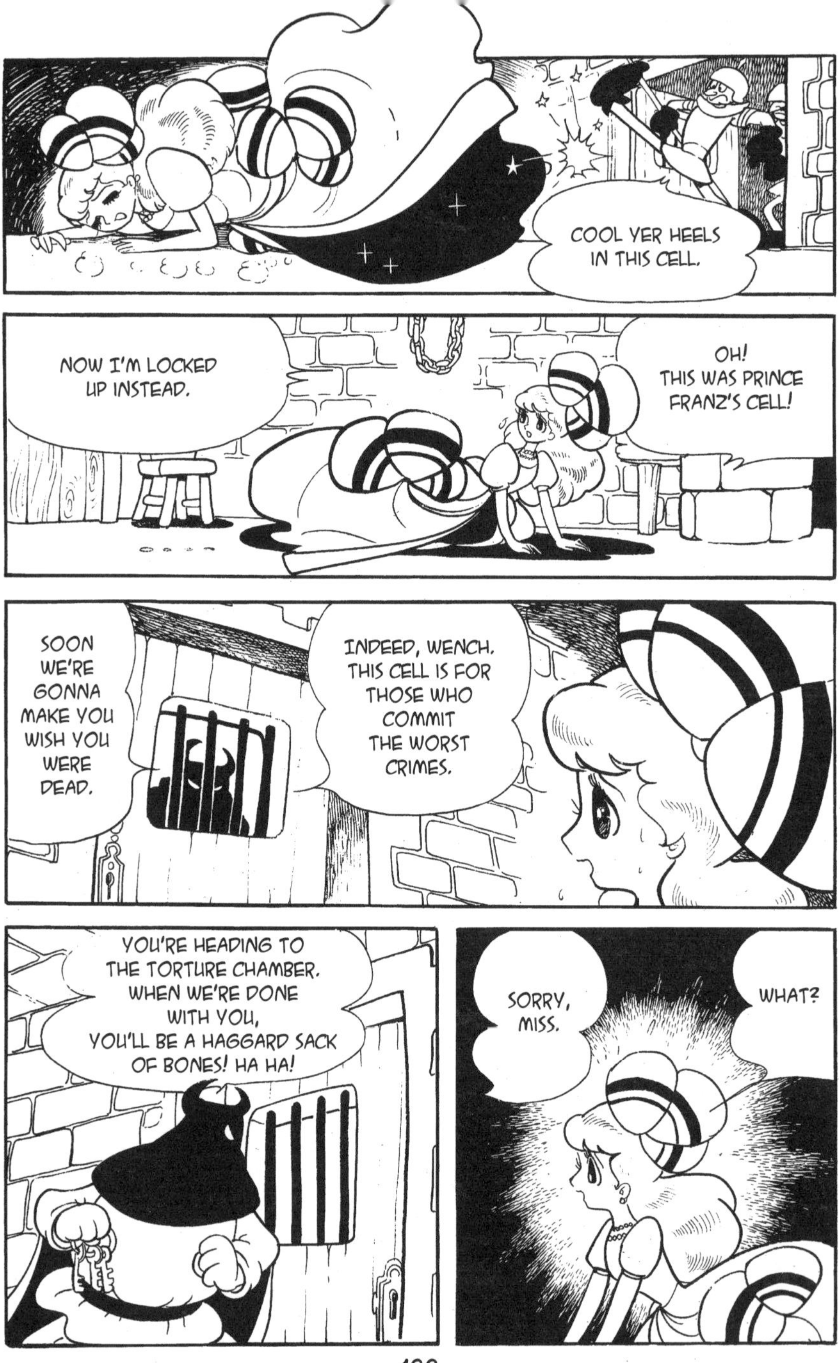
COOL YER HEELS IN THIS CELL.
OH! THIS WAS PRINCE FRANZ'S CELL!
NOW I'M LOCKED UP INSTEAD.
INDEED, WENCH. THIS CELL IS FOR THOSE WHO COMMIT THE WORST CRIMES.
SOON WE'RE GONNA MAKE YOU WISH YOU WERE DEAD.
WHAT?
SORRY, MISS.
YOU'RE HEADING TO THE TORTURE CHAMBER. WHEN WE'RE DONE WITH YOU, YOU'LL BE A HAGGARD SACK OF BONES! HA HA!

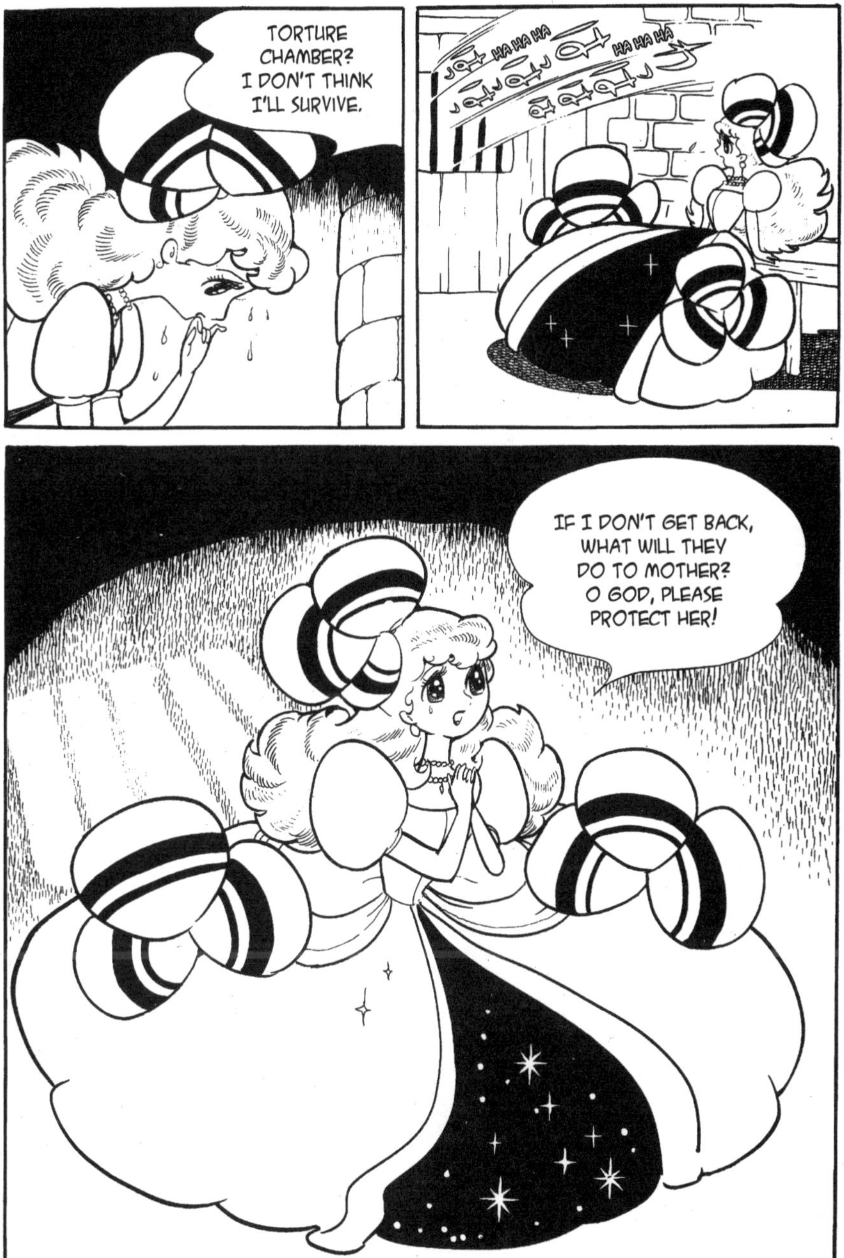
HA HA HA
HA HA HA
TORTURE CHAMBER? I DON'T THINK I'LL SURVIVE.
IF I DON'T GET BACK, WHAT WILL THEY DO TO MOTHER? O GOD, PLEASE PROTECT HER!

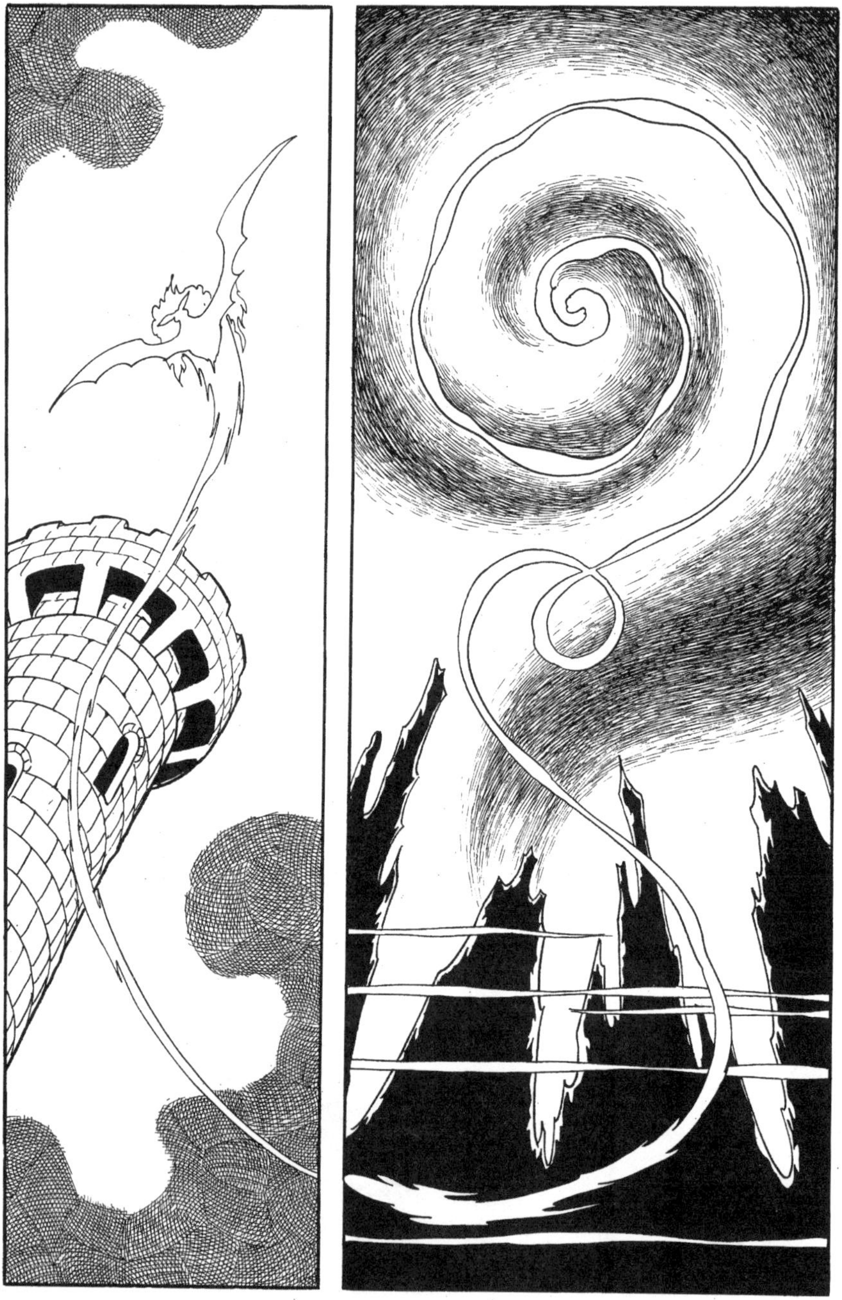

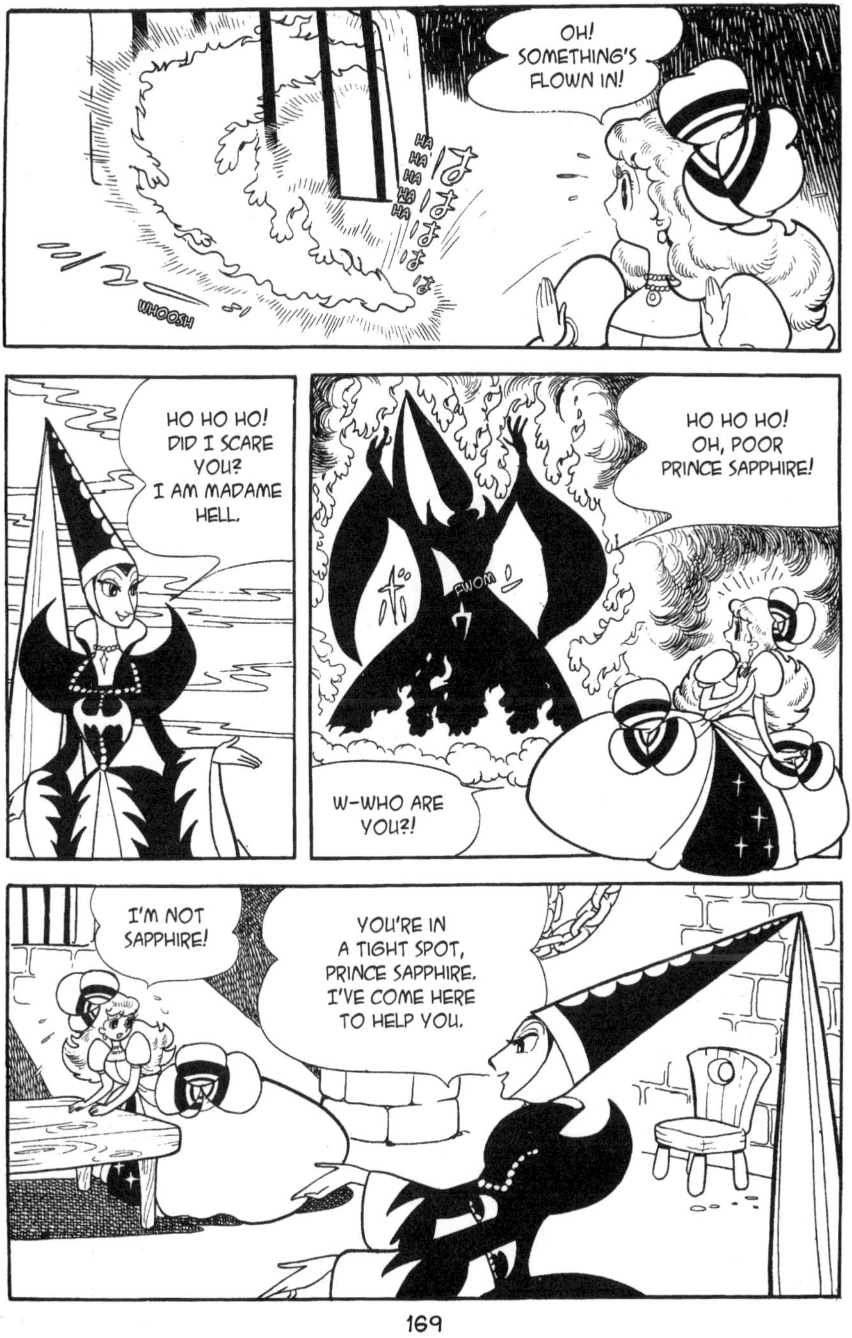
OH! SOMETHING'S FLOWN IN!
HA HA HA HA HA
WHOOSH
HO HO HO! OH, POOR PRINCE SAPPHIRE!
FWOM
W-WHO ARE YOU?!
HO HO HO! DID I SCARE YOU? I AM MADAME HELL.
YOU'RE IN A TIGHT SPOT, PRINCE SAPPHIRE. I'VE COME HERE TO HELP YOU.
I'M NOT SAPPHIRE!

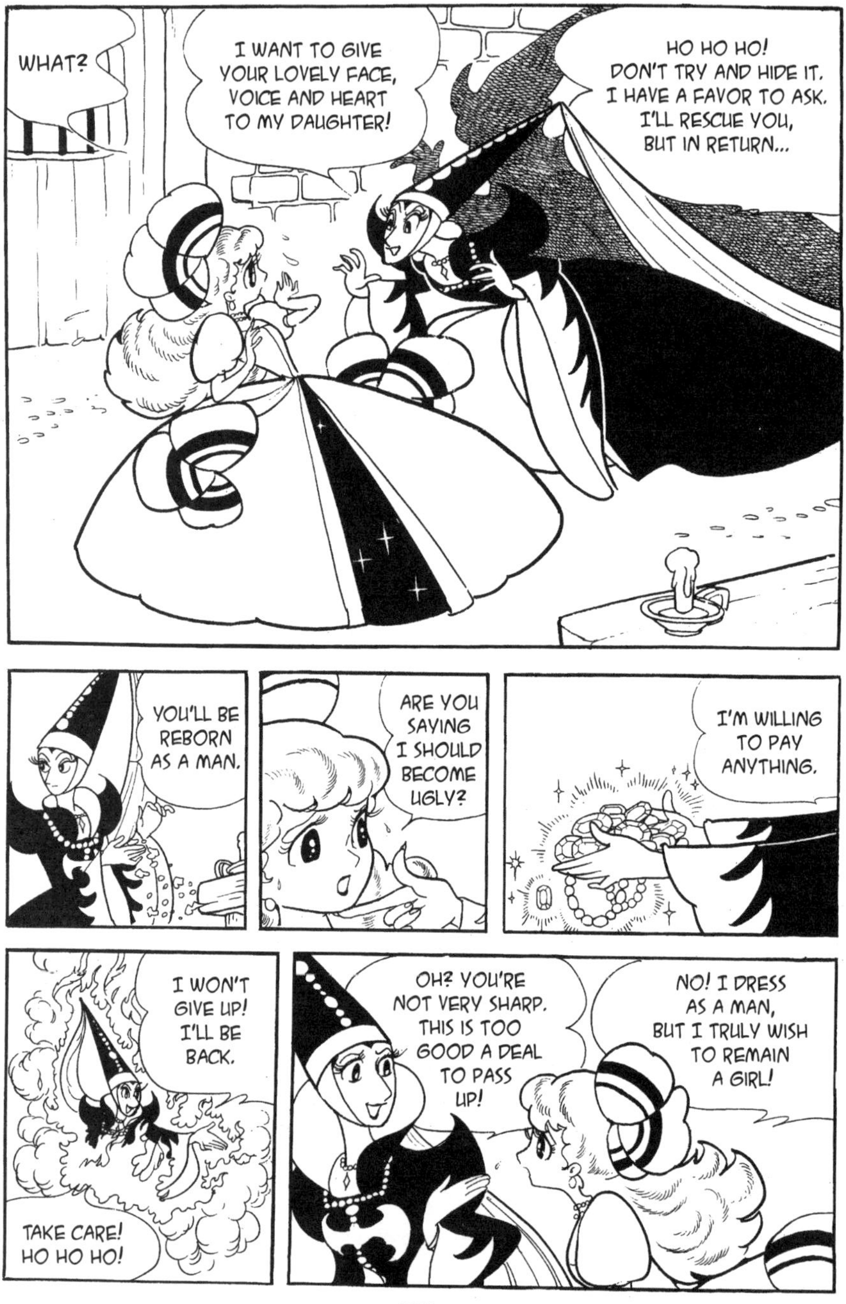
HO HO HO! DON'T TRY AND HIDE IT. I HAVE A FAVOR TO ASK. I'LL RESCUE YOU, BUT IN RETURN...
I WANT TO GIVE YOUR LOVELY FACE, VOICE AND HEART TO MY DAUGHTER!
WHAT?
I'M WILLING TO PAY ANYTHING.
ARE YOU SAYING I SHOULD BECOME UGLY?
YOU'LL BE REBORN AS A MAN.
NO! I DRESS AS A MAN, BUT I TRULY WISH TO REMAIN A GIRL!
OH? YOU'RE NOT VERY SHARP. THIS IS TOO GOOD A DEAL TO PASS UP!
I WON'T GIVE UP! I'LL BE BACK.
TAKE CARE! HO HO HO!

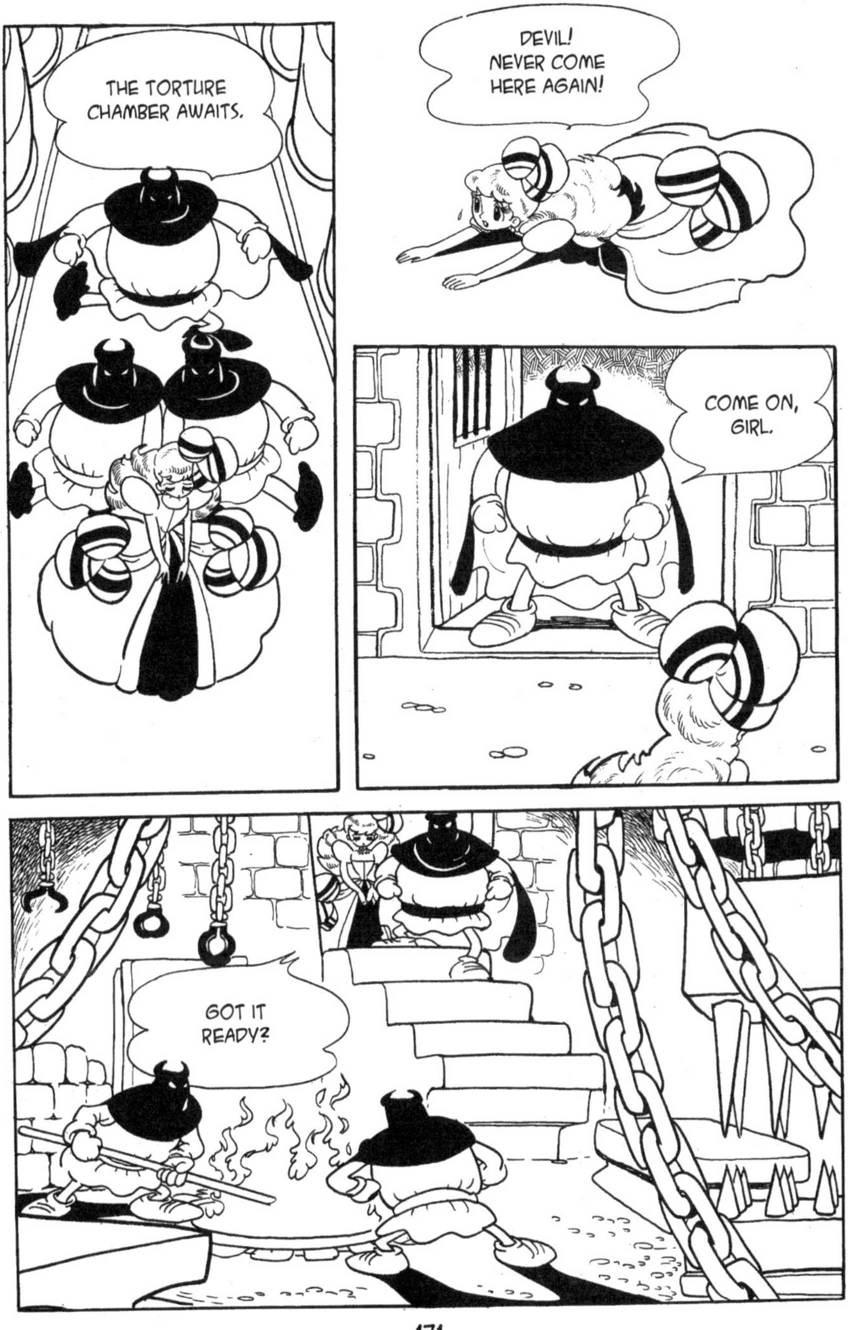
DEVIL! NEVER COME HERE AGAIN!
COME ON, GIRL.
THE TORTURE CHAMBER AWAITS.
GOT IT READY?

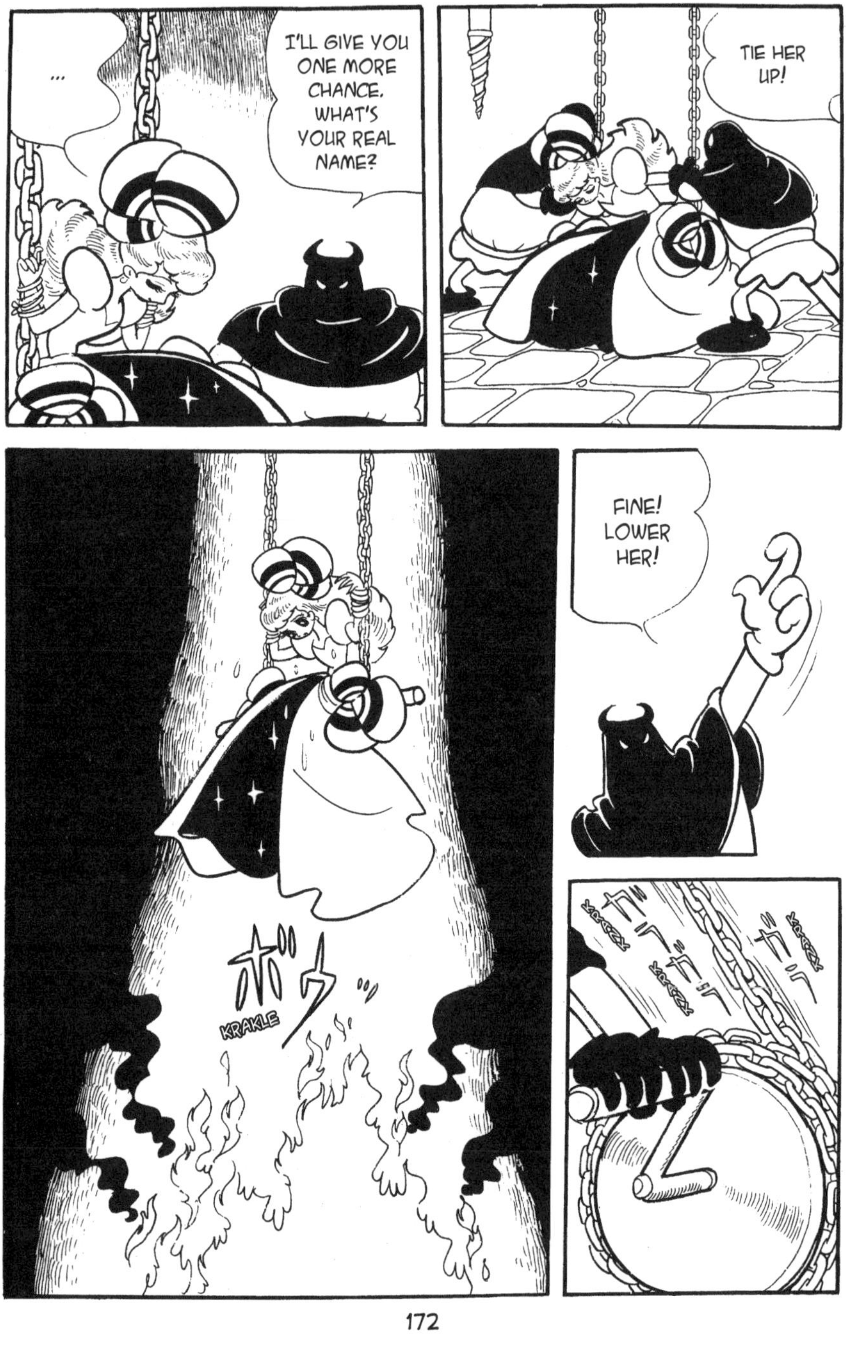
TIE HER UP!
I'LL GIVE YOU ONE MORE CHANCE. WHAT'S YOUR REAL NAME?
...
FINE! LOWER HER!
ボッ
KRAKLE

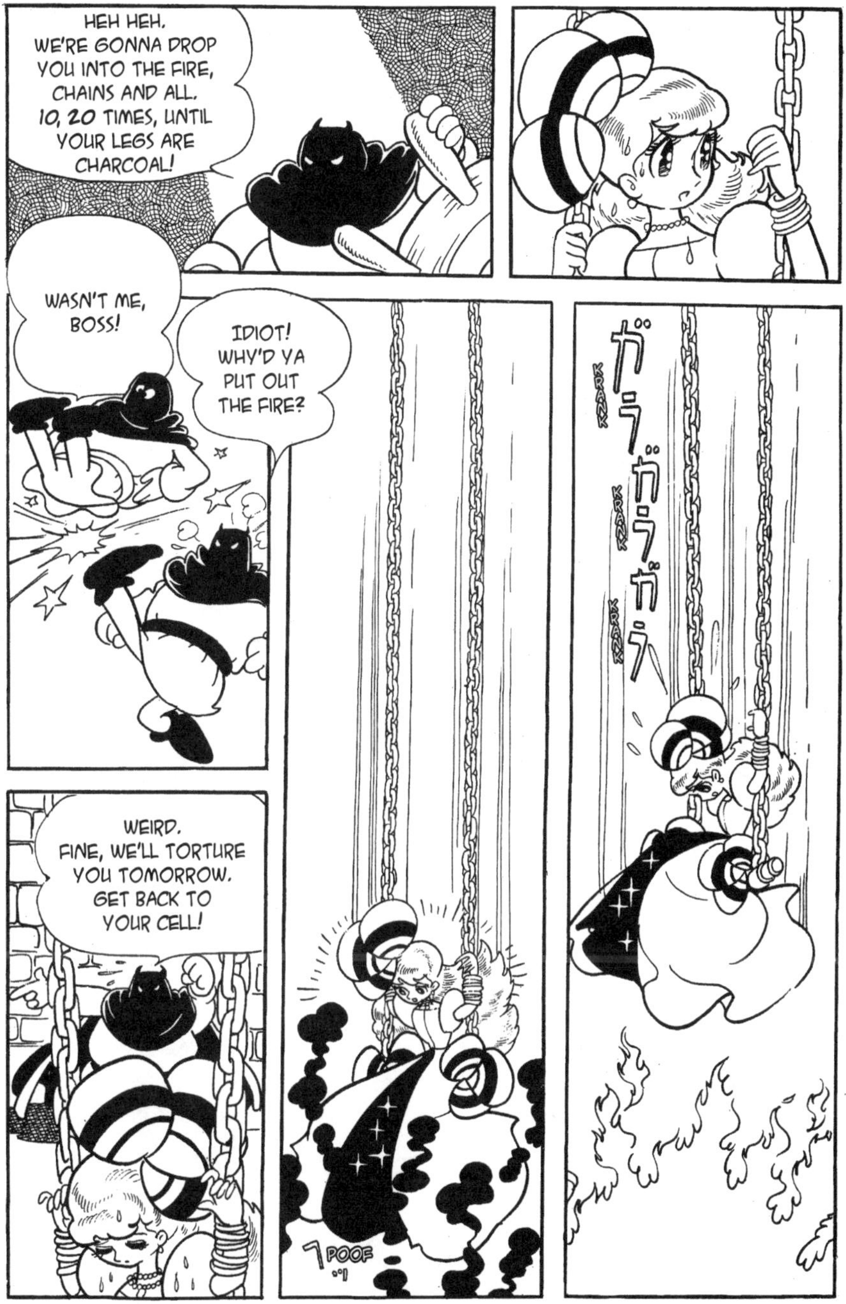
HEH HEH.
WE'RE GONNA DROP YOU INTO THE FIRE, CHAINS AND ALL. 10, 20 TIMES, UNTIL YOUR LEGS ARE CHARCOAL!
ガラガラガラ
KRANK
KRANK
KRANK
POOF
IDIOT! WHY'D YA PUT OUT THE FIRE?
WASN'T ME, BOSS!
WEIRD.
FINE, WE'LL TORTURE YOU TOMORROW. GET BACK TO YOUR CELL!

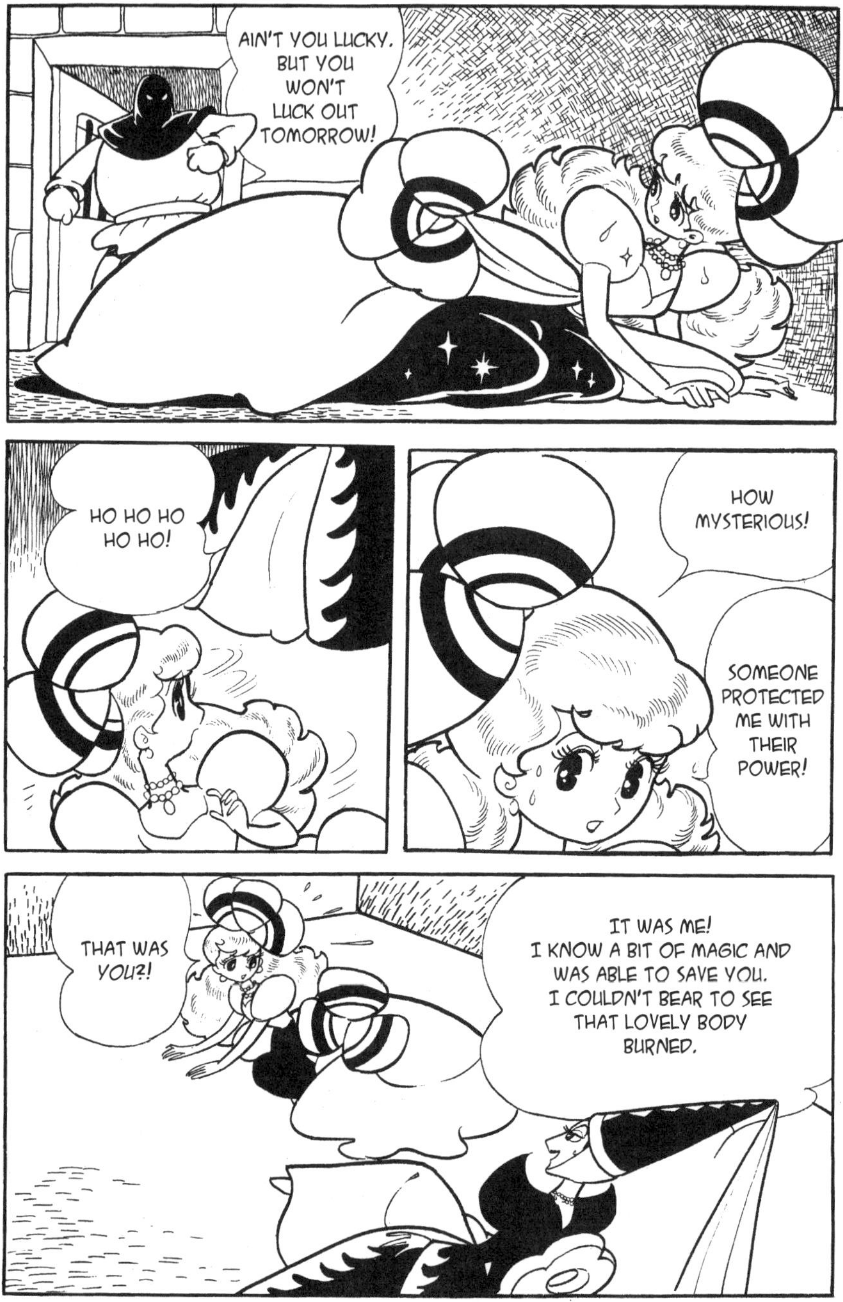
AIN'T YOU LUCKY. BUT YOU WON'T LUCK OUT TOMORROW!
HOW MYSTERIOUS!
SOMEONE PROTECTED ME WITH THEIR POWER!
HO HO HO HO HO!
IT WAS ME! I KNOW A BIT OF MAGIC AND WAS ABLE TO SAVE YOU. I COULDN'T BEAR TO SEE THAT LOVELY BODY BURNED.
THAT WAS YOU?!

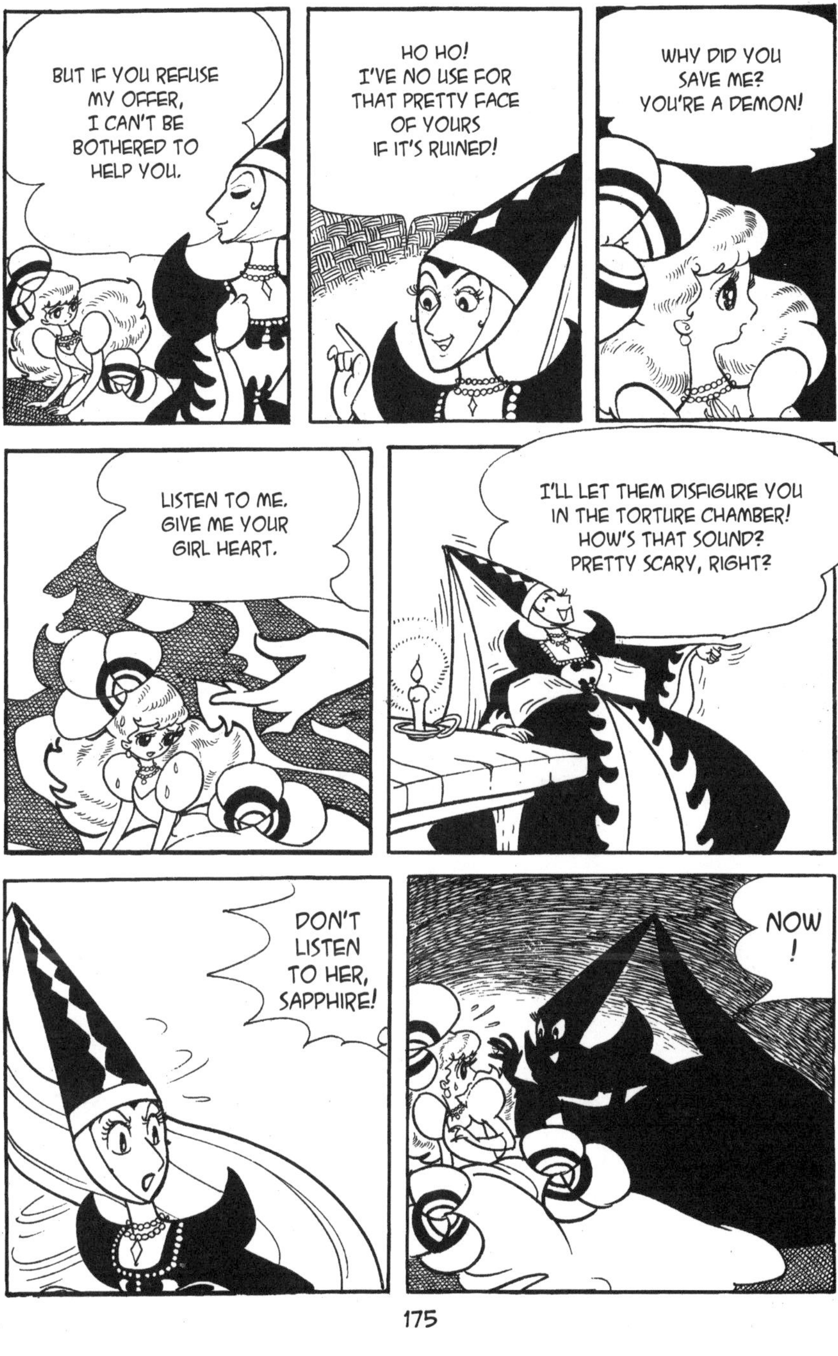
WHY DID YOU SAVE ME? YOU'RE A DEMON!
HO HO! I'VE NO USE FOR THAT PRETTY FACE OF YOURS IF IT'S RUINED!
BUT IF YOU REFUSE MY OFFER, I CAN'T BE BOTHERED TO HELP YOU.
I'LL LET THEM DISFIGURE YOU IN THE TORTURE CHAMBER! HOW'S THAT SOUND? PRETTY SCARY, RIGHT?
LISTEN TO ME. GIVE ME YOUR GIRL HEART.
NOW!
DON'T LISTEN TO HER, SAPPHIRE!

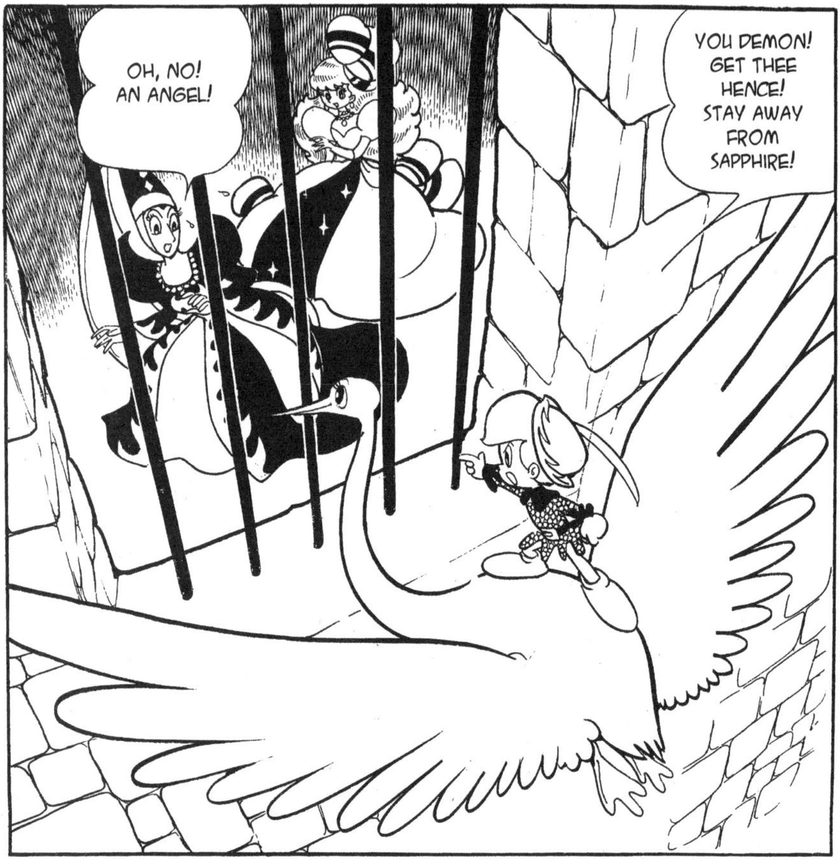
YOU DEMON! GET THEE HENCE! STAY AWAY FROM SAPPHIRE!
OH, NO! AN ANGEL!

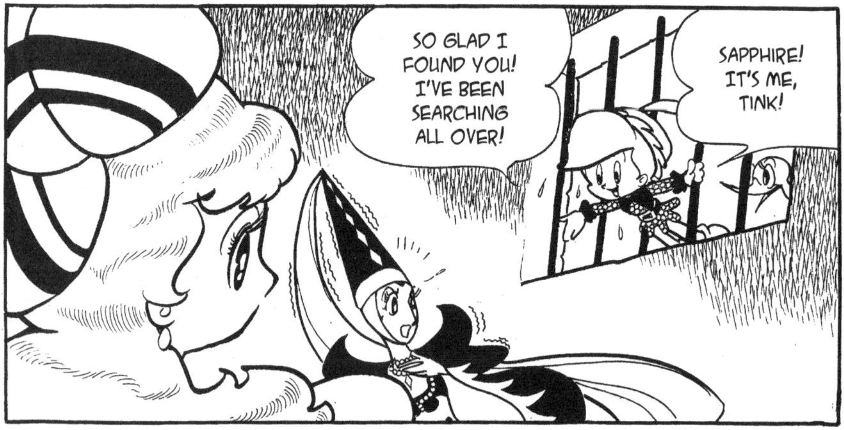
SAPPHIRE! IT'S ME, TINK!
SO GLAD I FOUND YOU! I'VE BEEN SEARCHING ALL OVER!

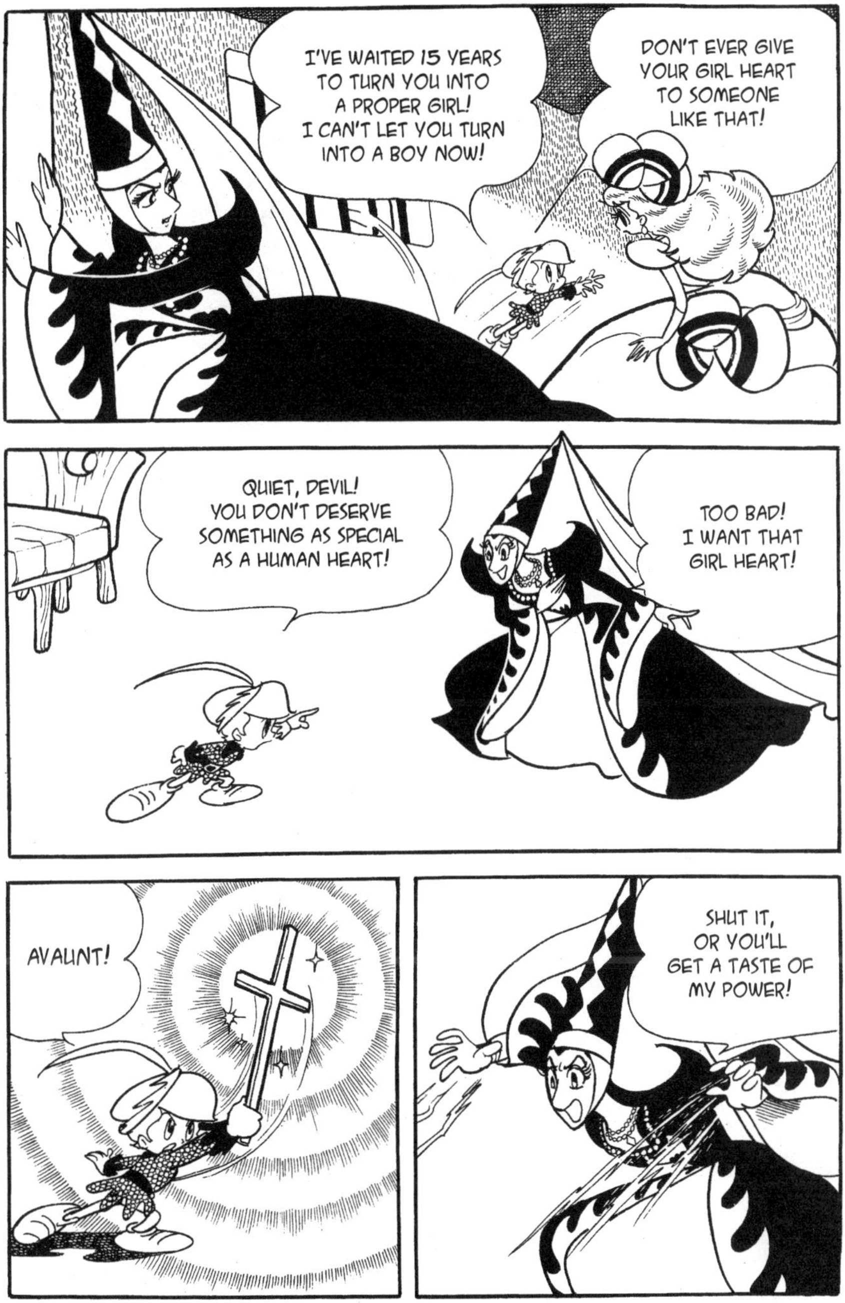
DON'T EVER GIVE YOUR GIRL HEART TO SOMEONE LIKE THAT!
I'VE WAITED 15 YEARS TO TURN YOU INTO A PROPER GIRL! I CAN'T LET YOU TURN INTO A BOY NOW!
TOO BAD! I WANT THAT GIRL HEART!
QUIET, DEVIL! YOU DON'T DESERVE SOMETHING AS SPECIAL AS A HUMAN HEART!
SHUT IT, OR YOU'LL GET A TASTE OF MY POWER!
AVAUNT!

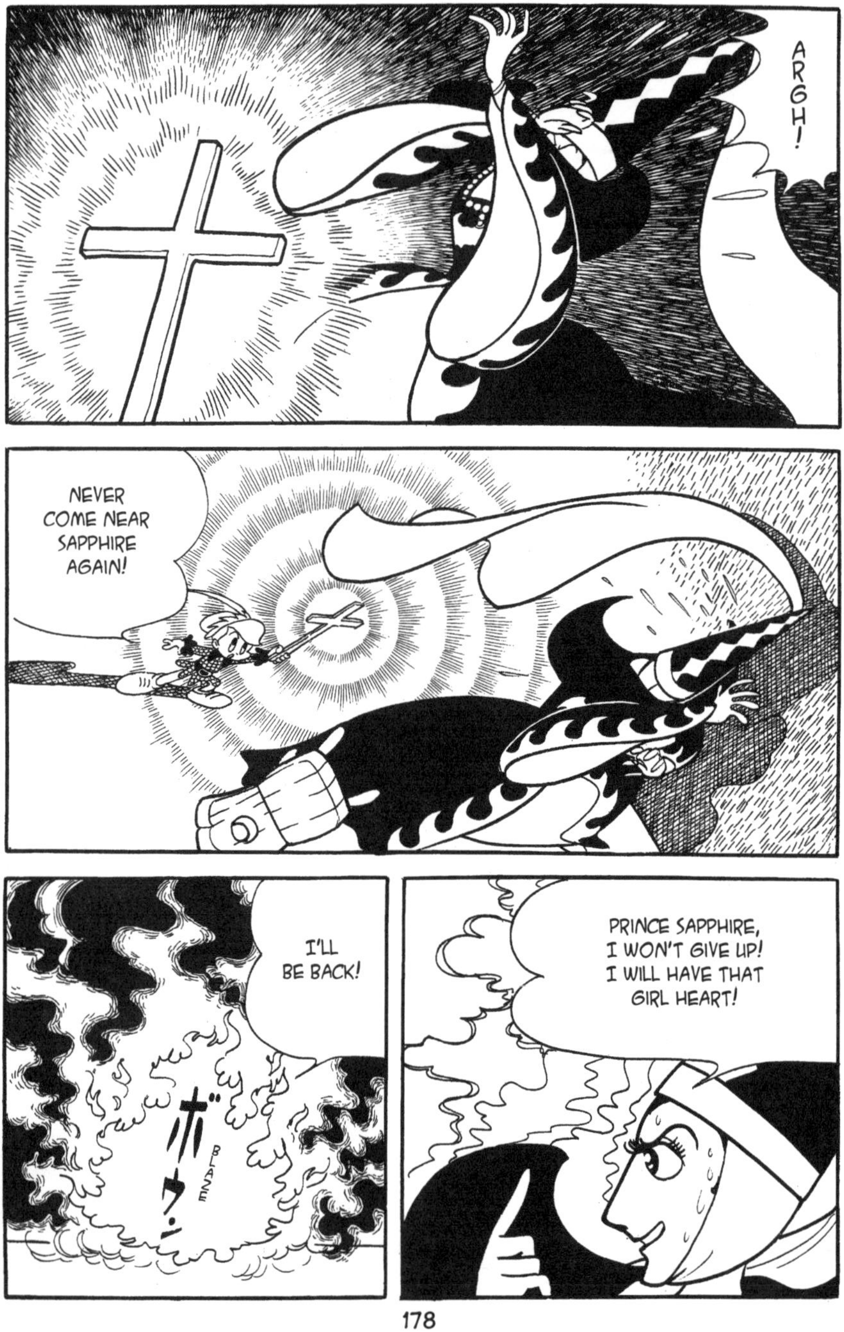
ARGH!
NEVER COME NEAR SAPPHIRE AGAIN!
PRINCE SAPPHIRE, I WON'T GIVE UP! I WILL HAVE THAT GIRL HEART!
I'LL BE BACK!
ボウッ
BLAZE

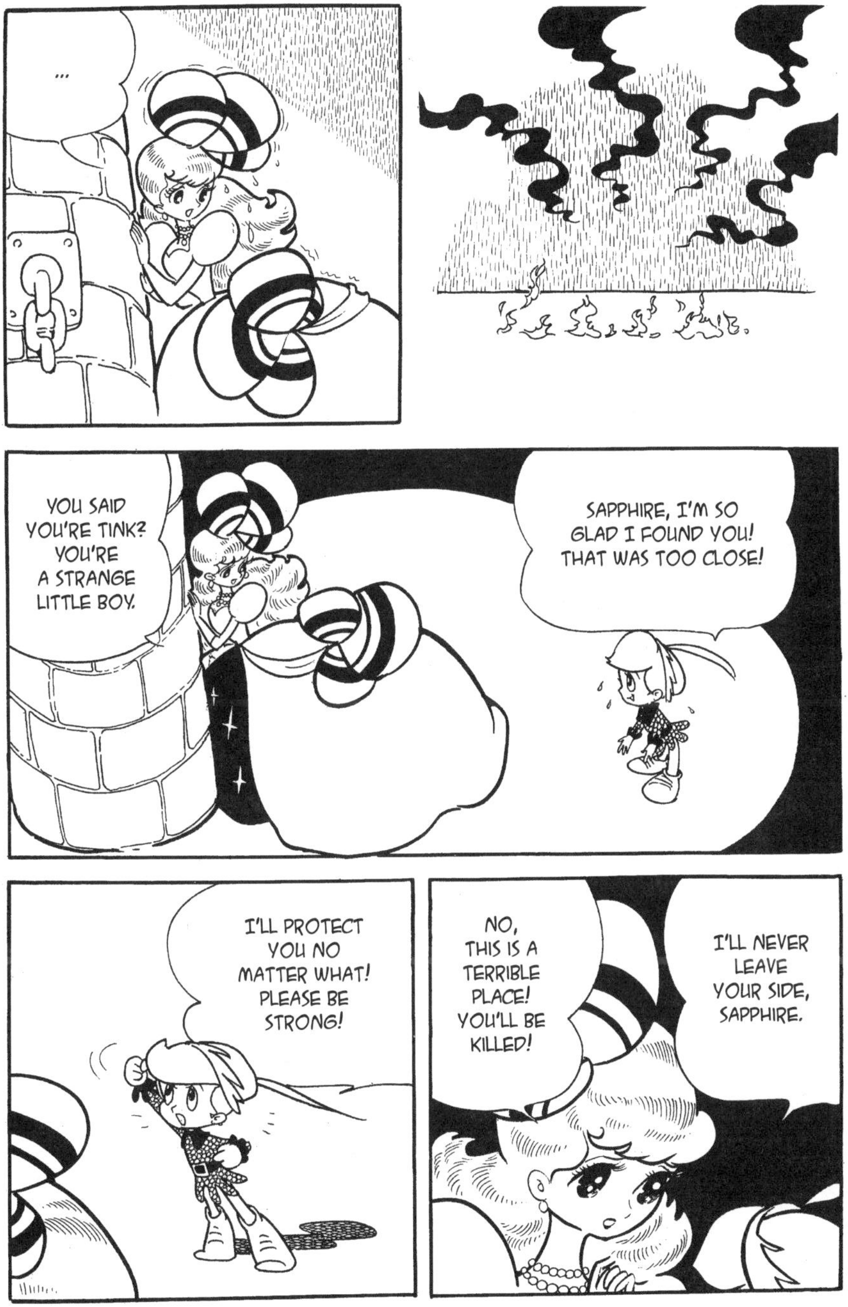
...
SAPPHIRE, I'M SO GLAD I FOUND YOU! THAT WAS TOO CLOSE!
YOU SAID YOU'RE TINK? YOU'RE A STRANGE LITTLE BOY.
I'LL NEVER LEAVE YOUR SIDE, SAPPHIRE.
NO, THIS IS A TERRIBLE PLACE! YOU'LL BE KILLED!
I'LL PROTECT YOU NO MATTER WHAT! PLEASE BE STRONG!

Chapter 11

Two By the Quarry

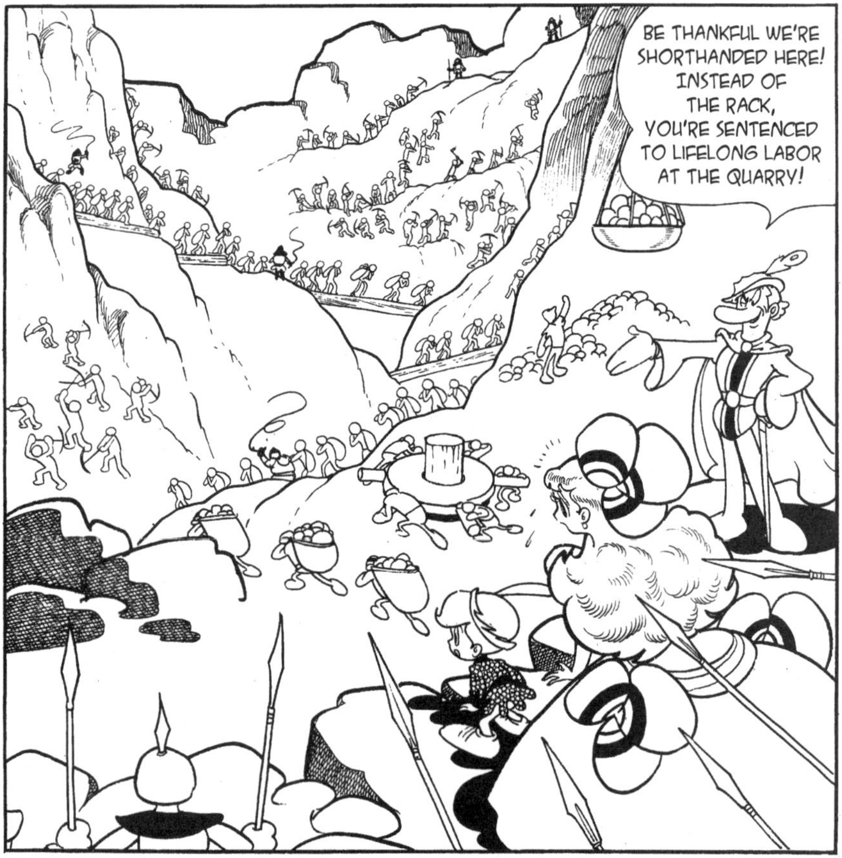
BE THANKFUL WE'RE SHORTHANDED HERE! INSTEAD OF THE RACK, YOU'RE SENTENCED TO LIFELONG LABOR AT THE QUARRY!

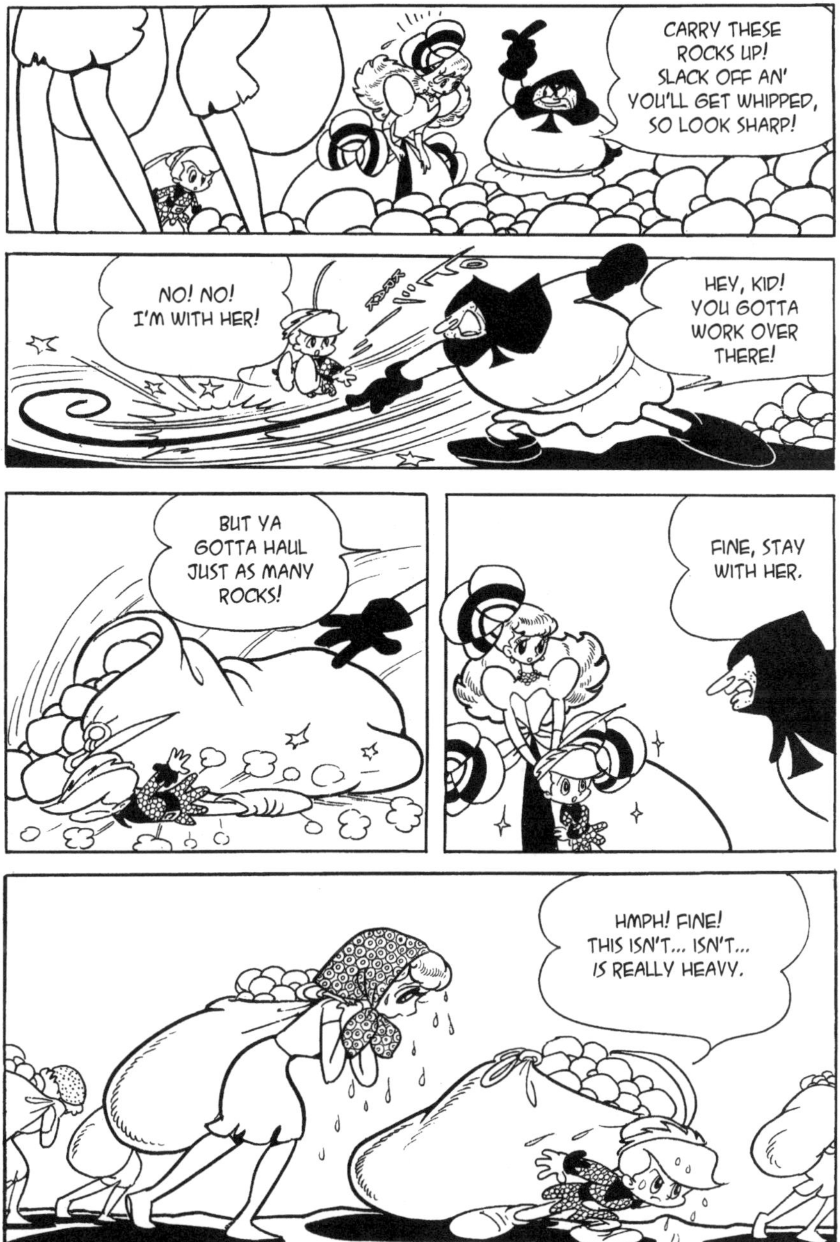
CARRY THESE ROCKS UP! SLACK OFF AN' YOU'LL GET WHIPPED, SO LOOK SHARP!
HEY, KID! YOU GOTTA WORK OVER THERE!
NO! NO! I'M WITH HER!
FINE, STAY WITH HER.
BUT YA GOTTA HAUL JUST AS MANY ROCKS!
HMPH! FINE! THIS ISN'T... ISN'T... IS REALLY HEAVY.

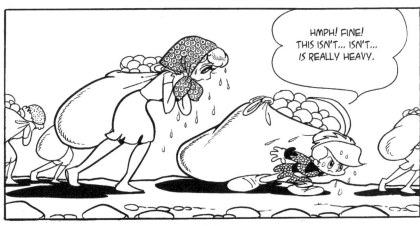

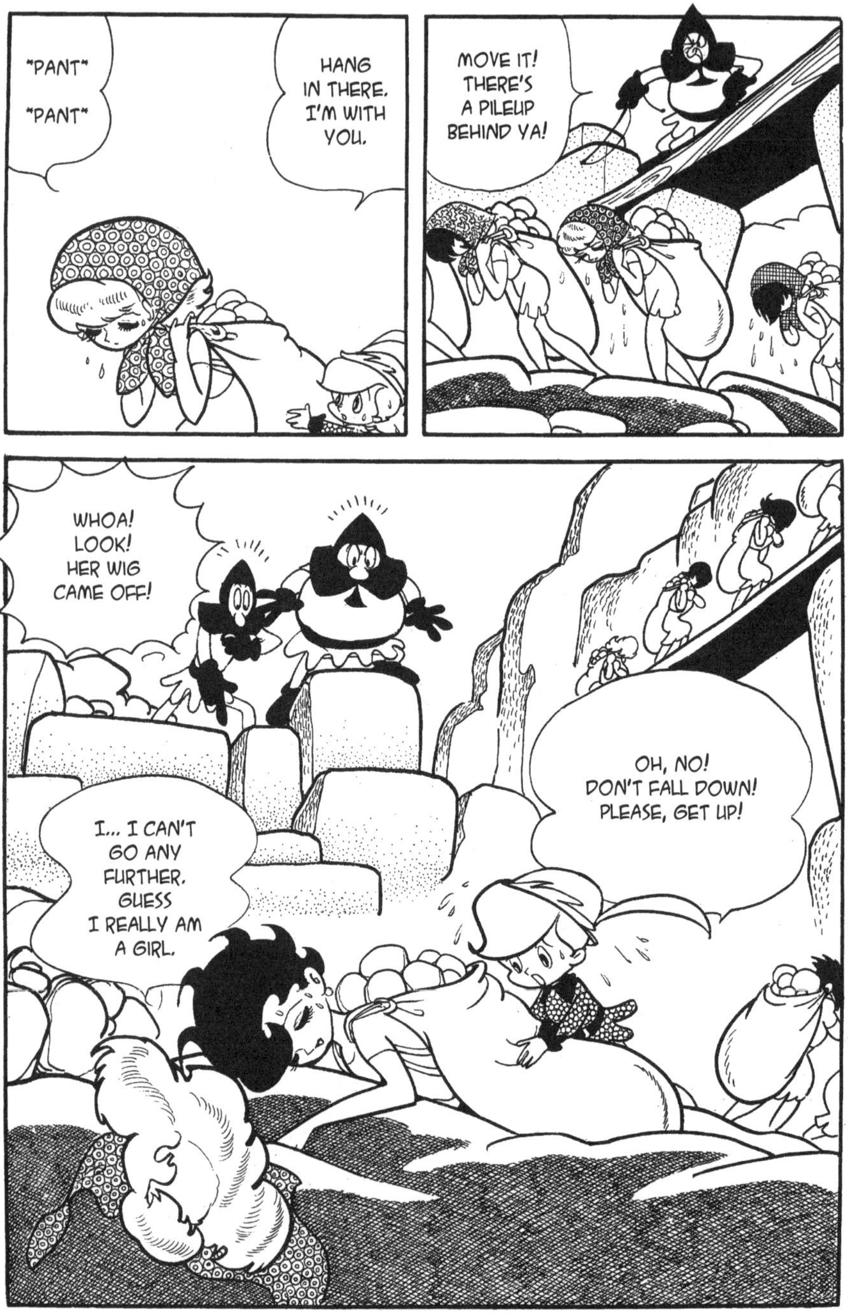
MOVE IT! THERE'S A PILEUP BEHIND YA!
HANG IN THERE. I'M WITH YOU.
PANT *PANT*
WHOA! LOOK! HER WIG CAME OFF!
OH, NO! DON'T FALL DOWN! PLEASE, GET UP!
I... I CAN'T GO ANY FURTHER. GUESS I REALLY AM A GIRL.

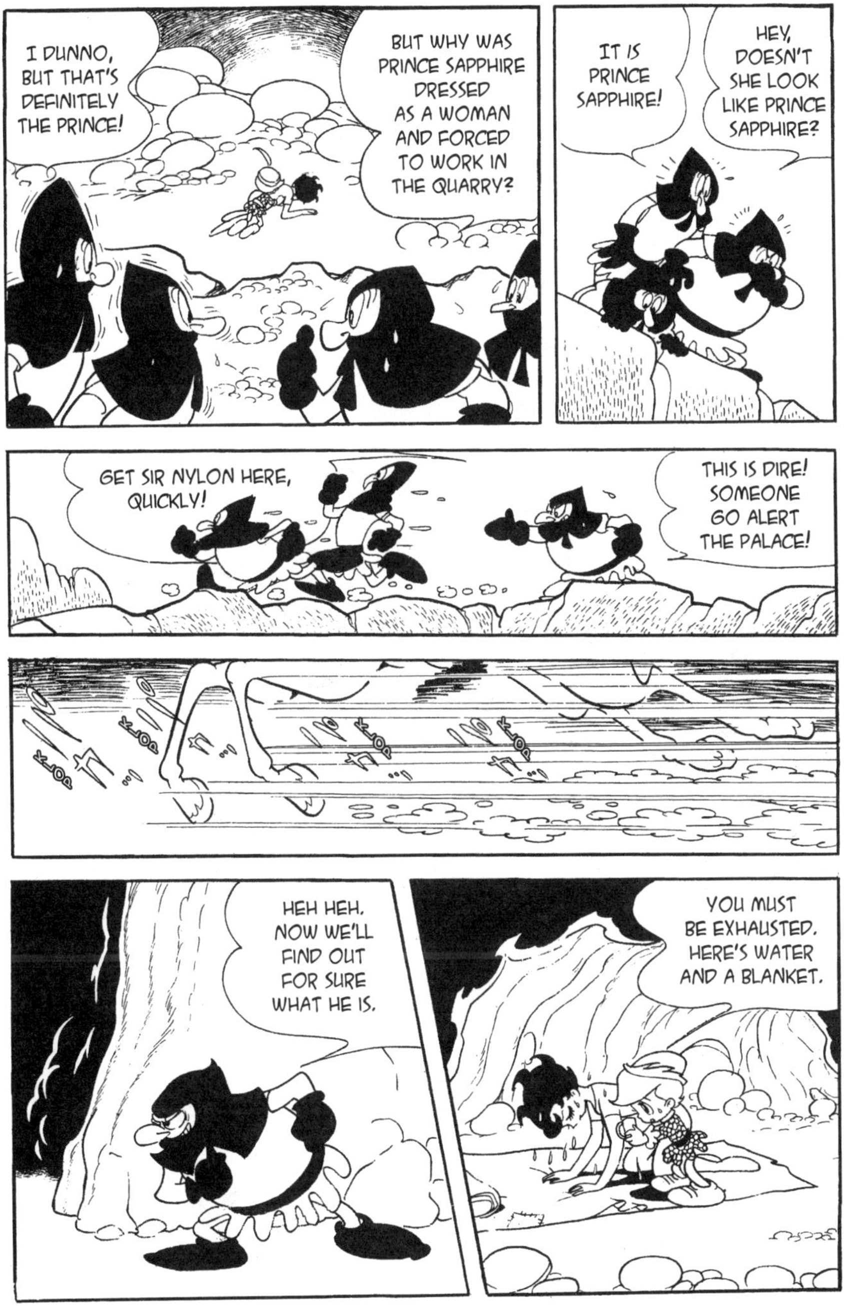
HEY, DOESN'T SHE LOOK LIKE PRINCE SAPPHIRE?
IT IS PRINCE SAPPHIRE!
BUT WHY WAS PRINCE SAPPHIRE DRESSED AS A WOMAN AND FORCED TO WORK IN THE QUARRY?
I DUNNO, BUT THAT'S DEFINITELY THE PRINCE!
THIS IS DIRE! SOMEONE GO ALERT THE PALACE!
GET SIR NYLON HERE, QUICKLY!
KLOP
KLOP
KLOP
KLOP
YOU MUST BE EXHAUSTED. HERE'S WATER AND A BLANKET.
HEH HEH. NOW WE'LL FIND OUT FOR SURE WHAT HE IS.

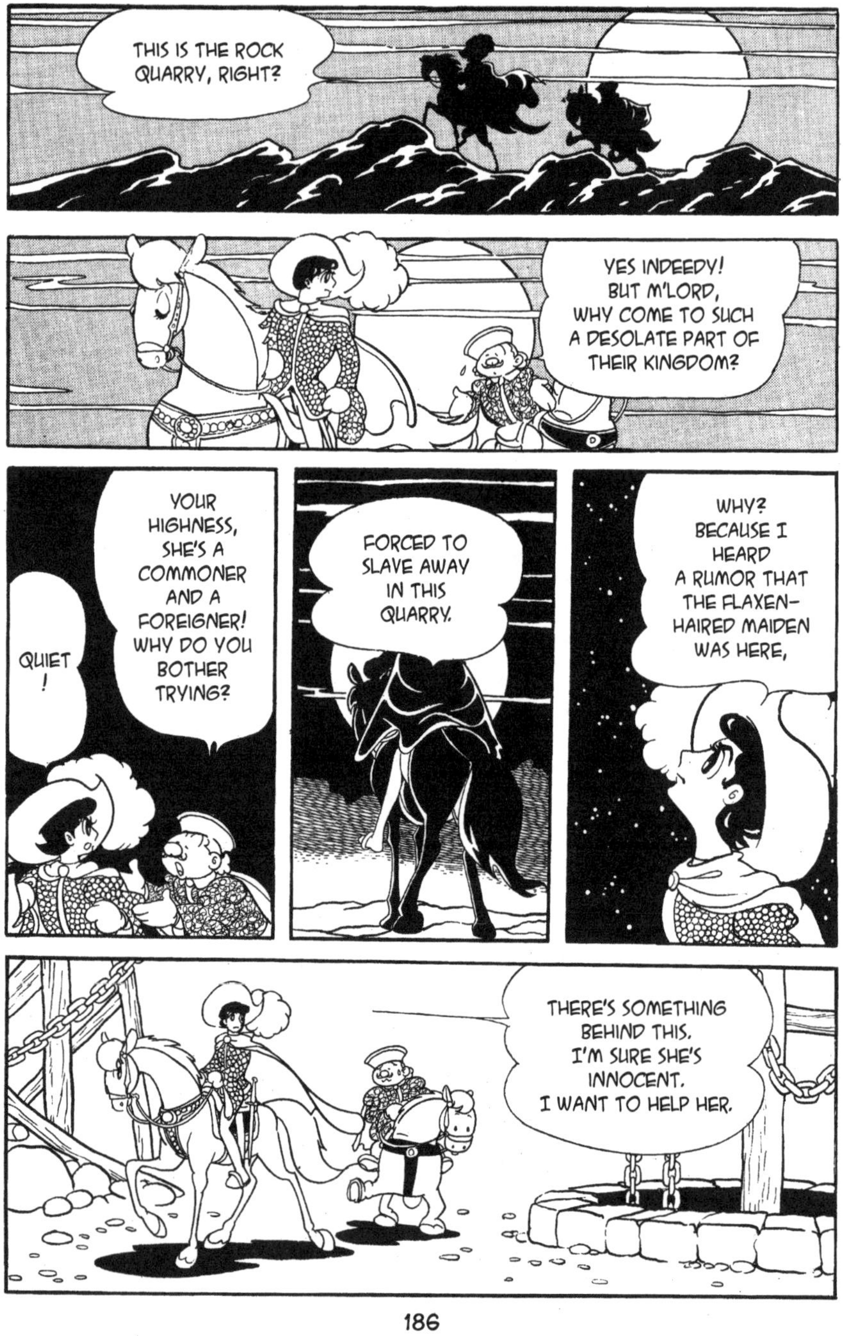
THIS IS THE ROCK QUARRY, RIGHT?
YES INDEEDY! BUT M'LORD, WHY COME TO SUCH A DESOLATE PART OF THEIR KINGDOM?
WHY? BECAUSE I HEARD A RUMOR THAT THE FLAXEN-HAIRED MAIDEN WAS HERE,
FORCED TO SLAVE AWAY IN THIS QUARRY.
YOUR HIGHNESS, SHE'S A COMMONER AND A FOREIGNER! WHY DO YOU BOTHER TRYING?
QUIET!
THERE'S SOMETHING BEHIND THIS. I'M SURE SHE'S INNOCENT. I WANT TO HELP HER.

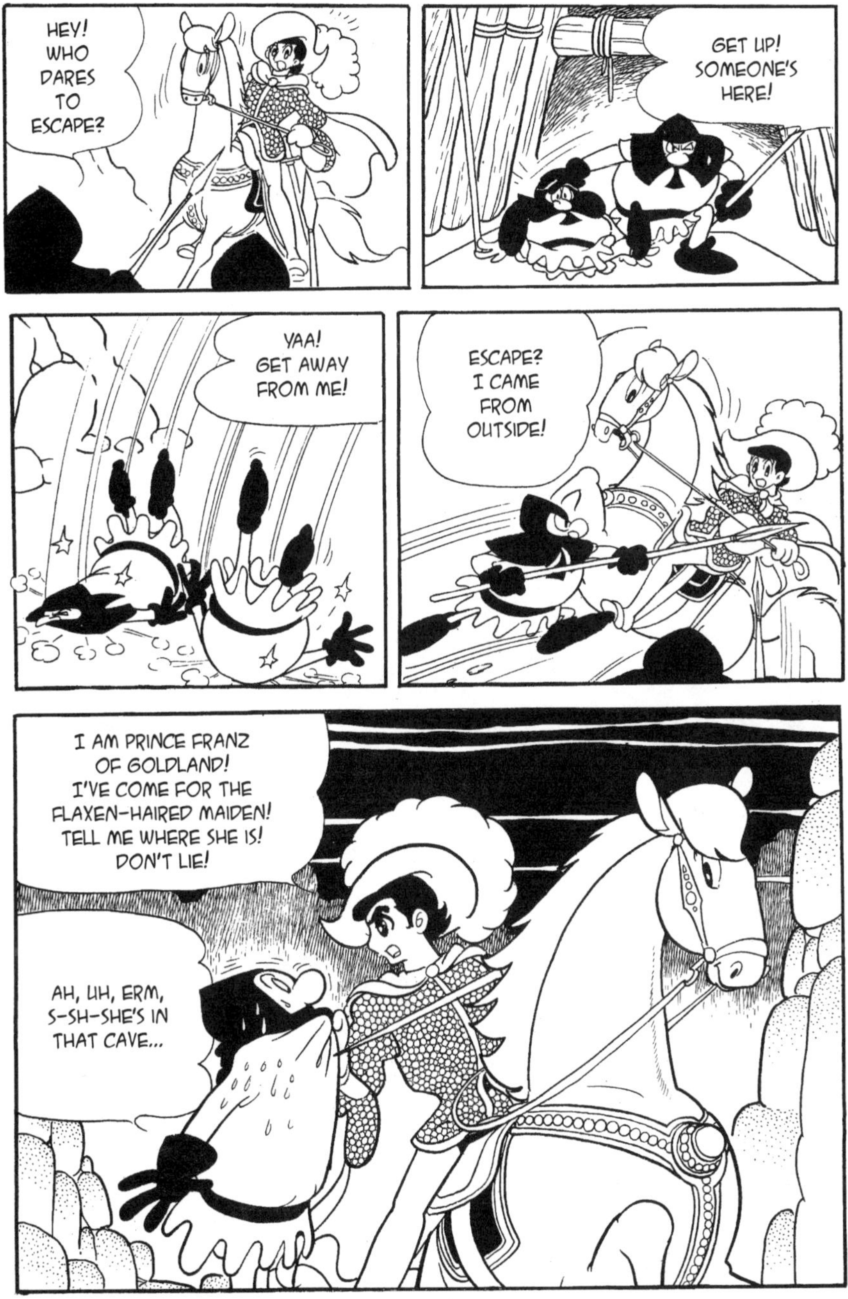
GET UP! SOMEONE'S HERE!
HEY! WHO DARES TO ESCAPE?
ESCAPE? I CAME FROM OUTSIDE!
YAA! GET AWAY FROM ME!
I AM PRINCE FRANZ OF GOLDLAND! I'VE COME FOR THE FLAXEN-HAIRED MAIDEN! TELL ME WHERE SHE IS! DON'T LIE!
AH, UH, ERM, S-SH-SHE'S IN THAT CAVE...

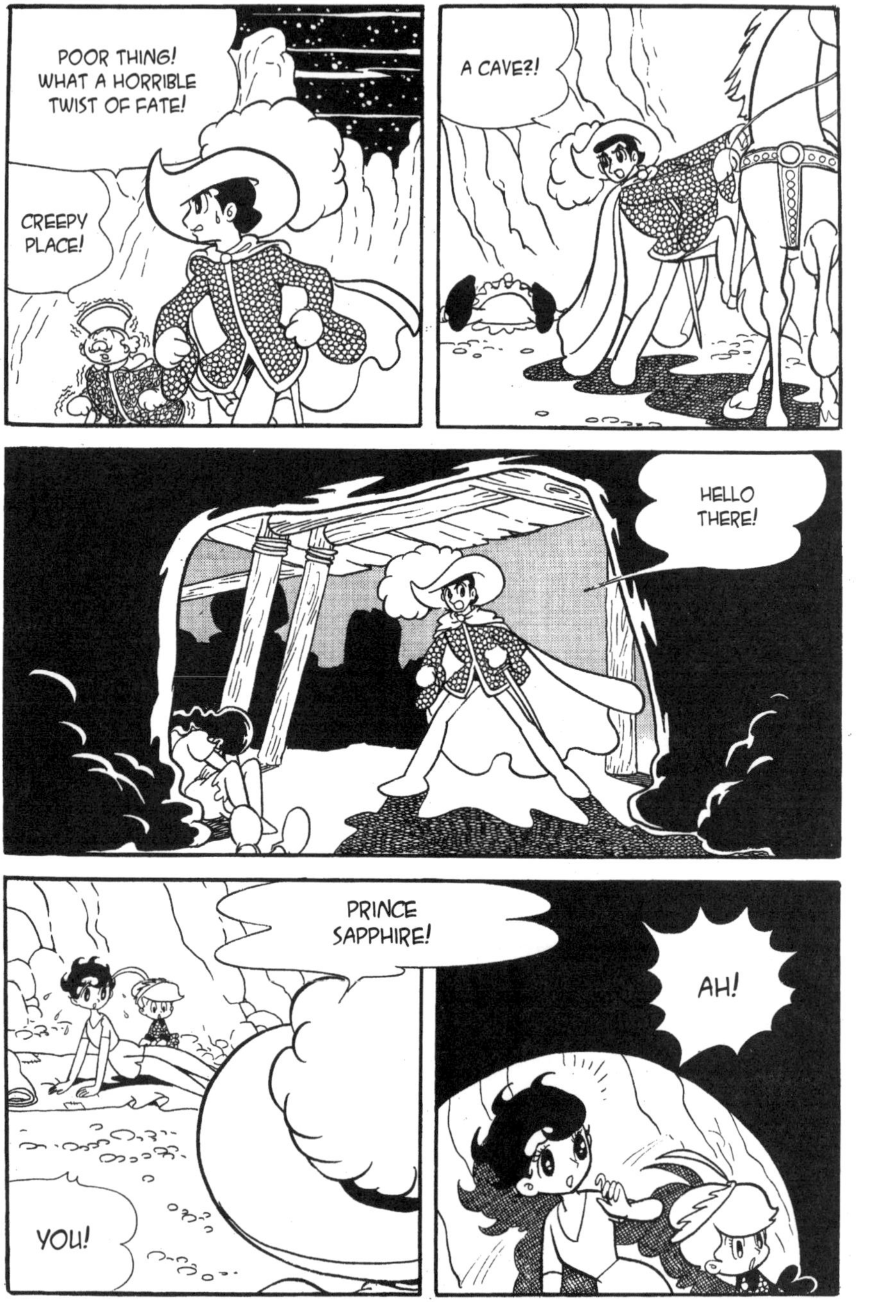
A CAVE?!
POOR THING! WHAT A HORRIBLE TWIST OF FATE!
CREEPY PLACE!
HELLO THERE!
AH!
PRINCE SAPPHIRE!
YOU!

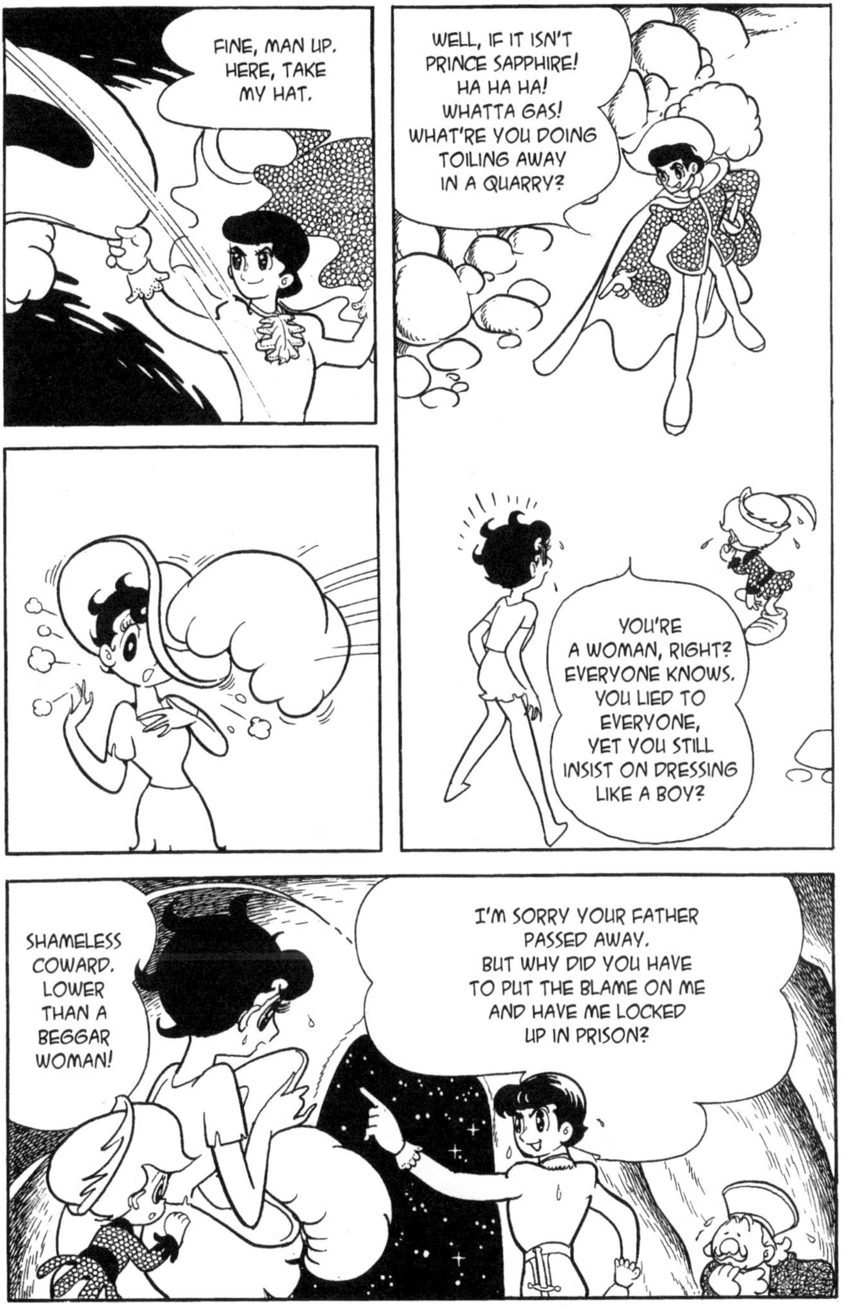
WELL, IF IT ISN'T PRINCE SAPPHIRE! HA HA HA! WHATTA GAS! WHAT'RE YOU DOING TOILING AWAY IN A QUARRY?
FINE, MAN UP. HERE, TAKE MY HAT.
YOU'RE A WOMAN, RIGHT? EVERYONE KNOWS. YOU LIED TO EVERYONE, YET YOU STILL INSIST ON DRESSING LIKE A BOY?
I'M SORRY YOUR FATHER PASSED AWAY. BUT WHY DID YOU HAVE TO PUT THE BLAME ON ME AND HAVE ME LOCKED UP IN PRISON?
SHAMELESS COWARD. LOWER THAN A BEGGAR WOMAN!

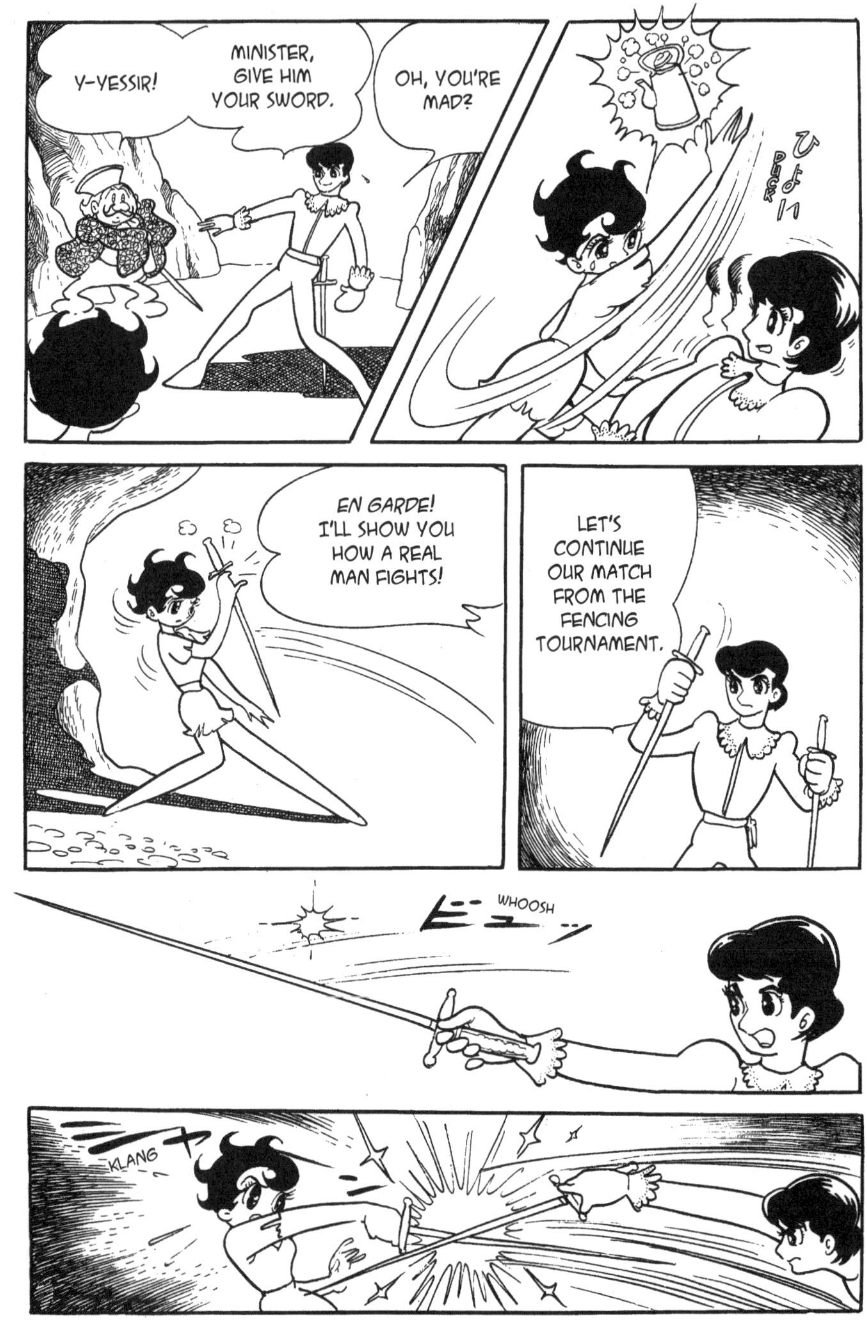
ひょい
DUCK
OH, YOU'RE MAD?
MINISTER, GIVE HIM YOUR SWORD.
Y-YESSIR!
LET'S CONTINUE OUR MATCH FROM THE FENCING TOURNAMENT.
EN GARDE! I'LL SHOW YOU HOW A REAL MAN FIGHTS!
WHOOSH
KLANG

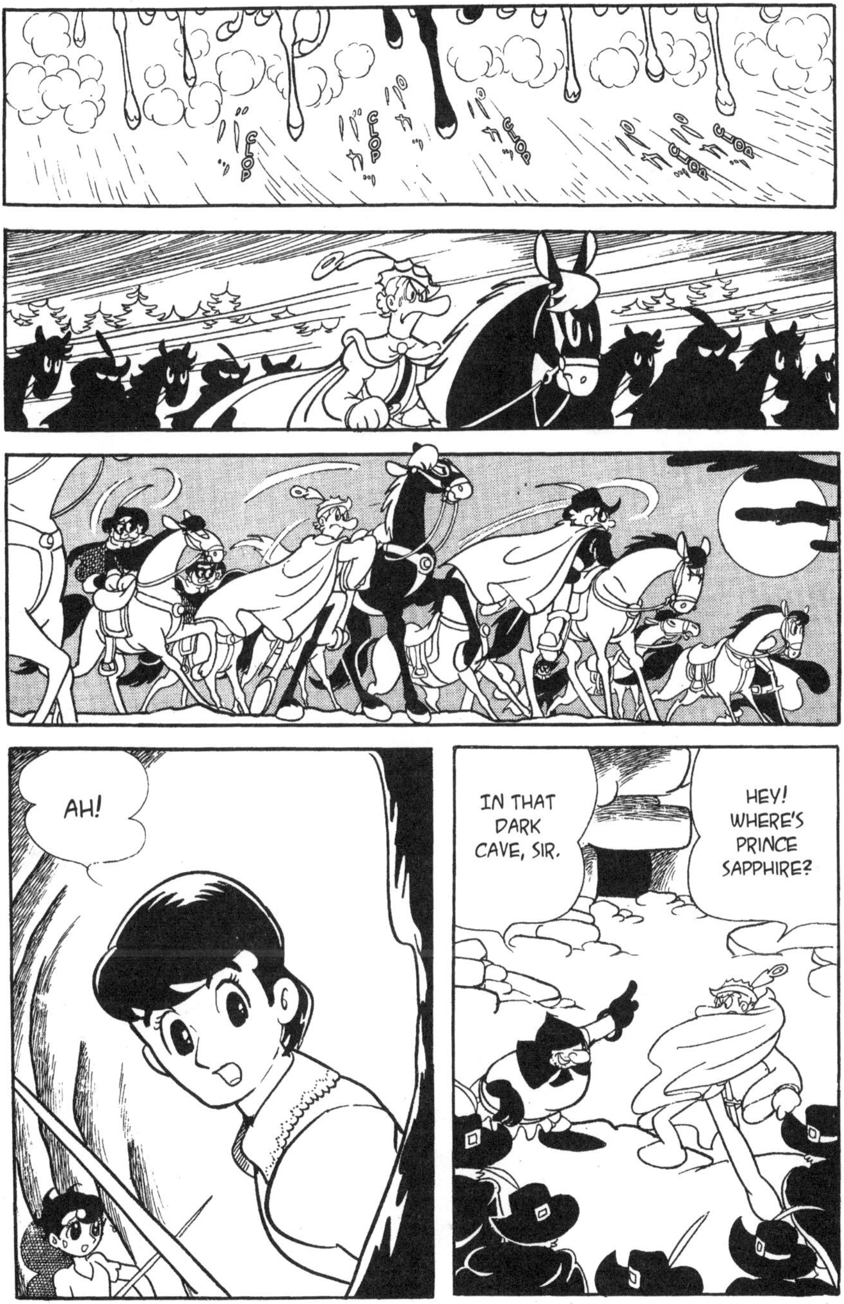
CLOP
CLOP
CLOP
CLOP
CLOP
HEY! WHERE'S PRINCE SAPPHIRE?
IN THAT DARK CAVE, SIR.
AH!

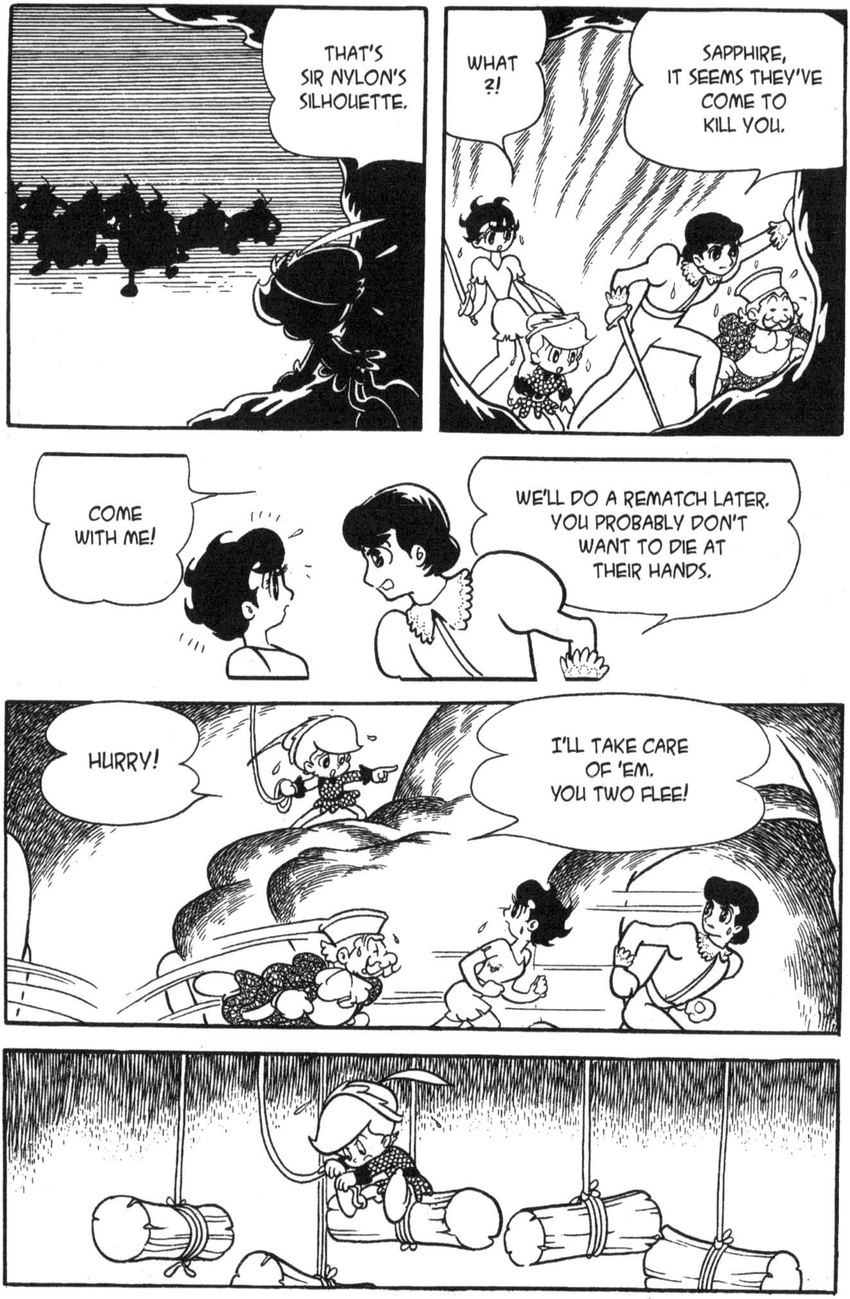
SAPPHIRE, IT SEEMS THEY'VE COME TO KILL YOU.
WHAT ?!
THAT'S SIR NYLON'S SILHOUETTE.
WE'LL DO A REMATCH LATER. YOU PROBABLY DON'T WANT TO DIE AT THEIR HANDS.
COME WITH ME!
I'LL TAKE CARE OF 'EM. YOU TWO FLEE!
HURRY!

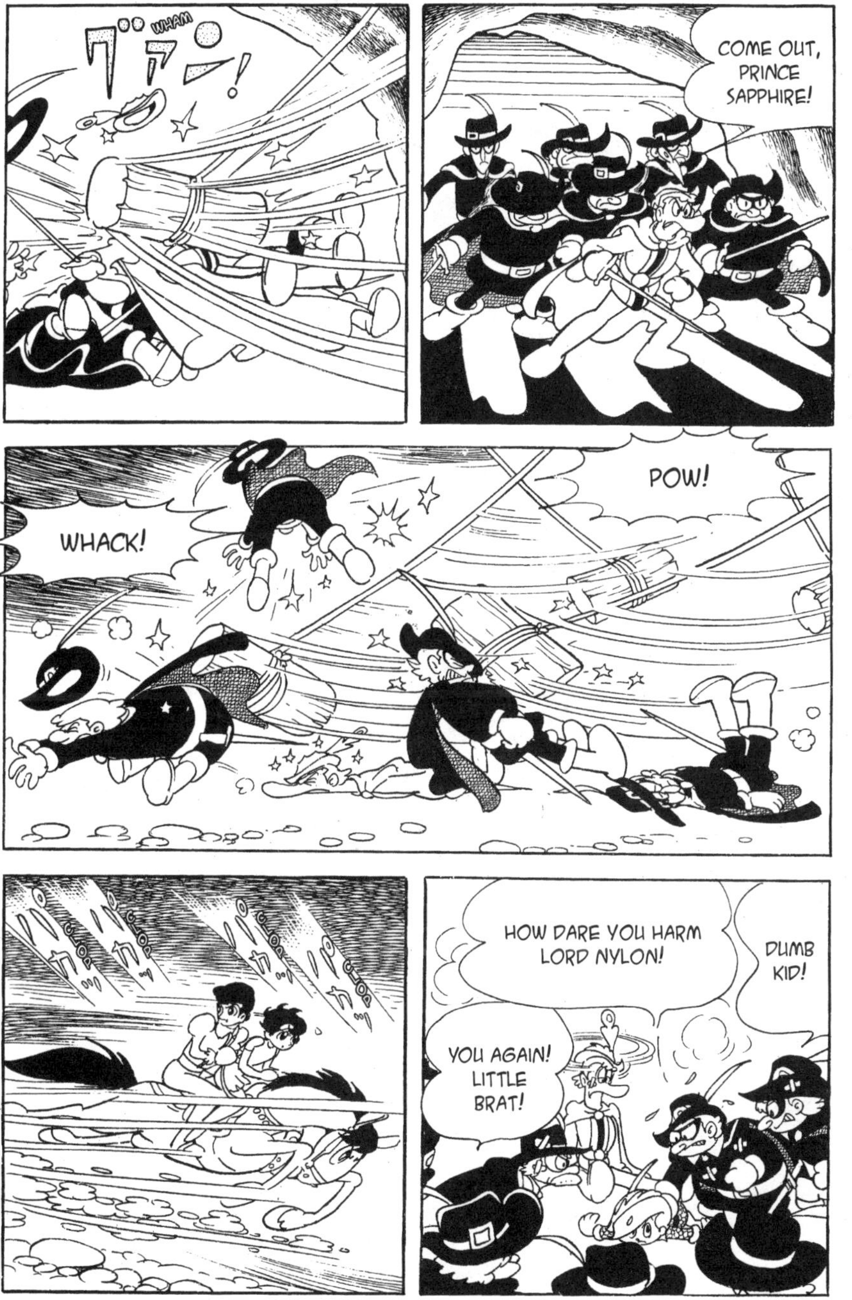
COME OUT, PRINCE SAPPHIRE!
WHAM
POW!
WHACK!
DUMB KID!
HOW DARE YOU HARM LORD NYLON!
YOU AGAIN! LITTLE BRAT!
CLOP
CLOP
CLOP
CLOP

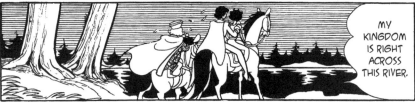

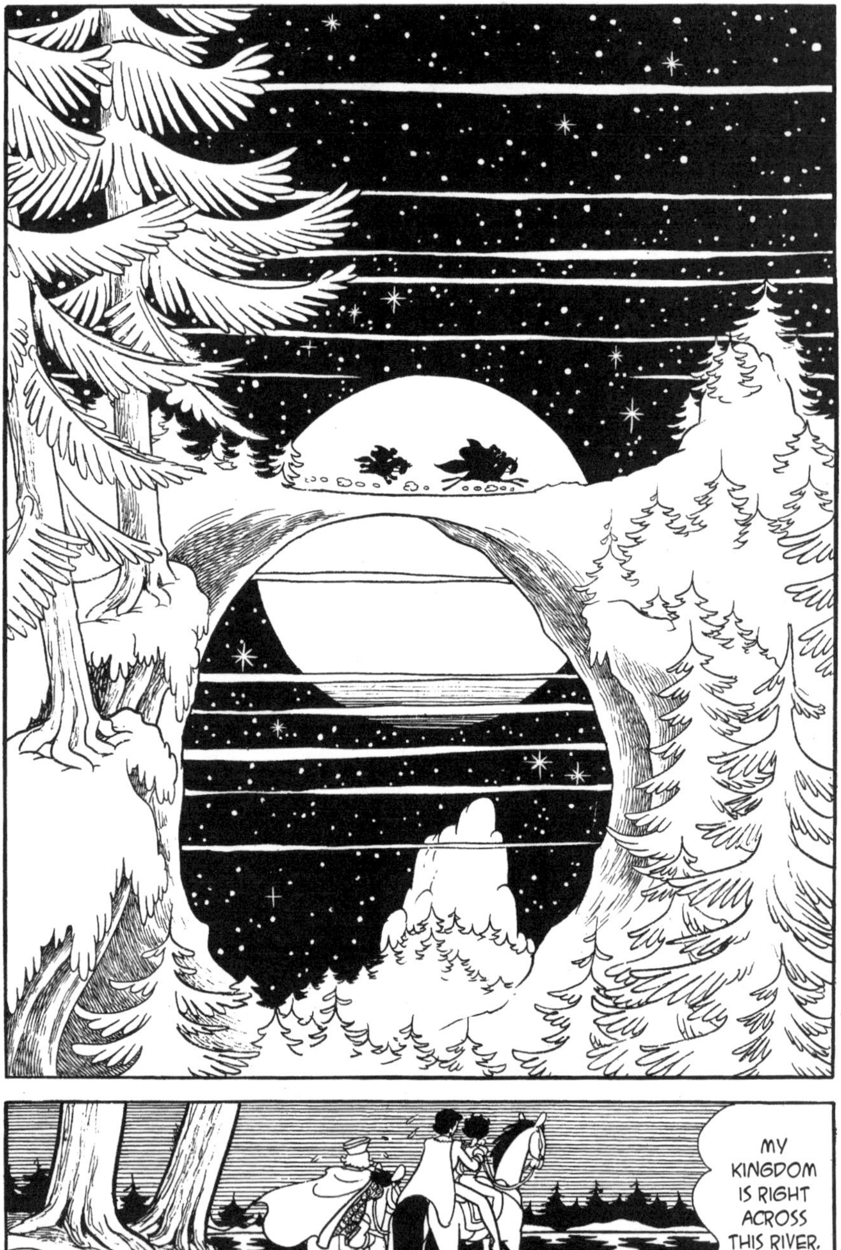
MY KINGDOM IS RIGHT ACROSS THIS RIVER.

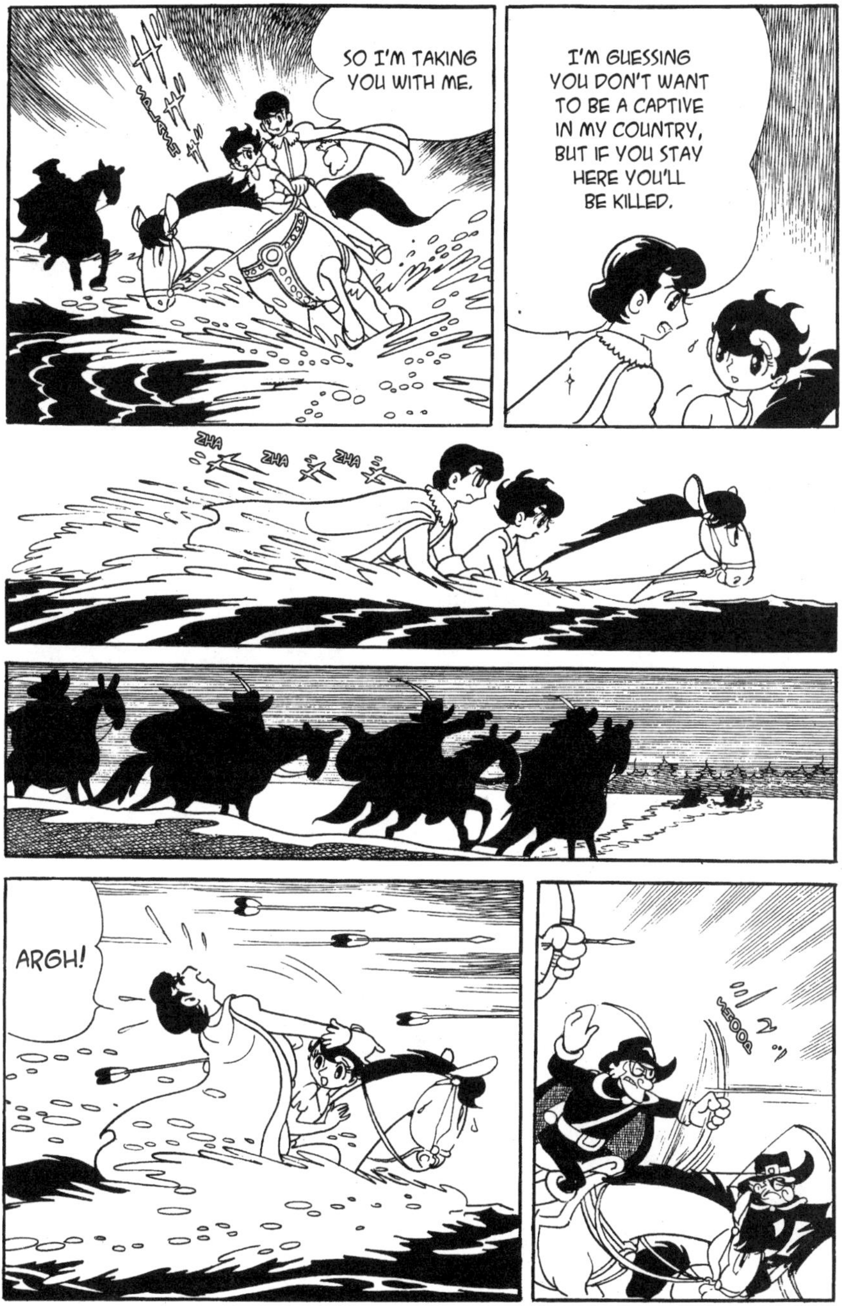
I'M GUESSING YOU DON'T WANT TO BE A CAPTIVE IN MY COUNTRY, BUT IF YOU STAY HERE YOU'LL BE KILLED.
SO I'M TAKING YOU WITH ME.
ZHA
ZHA
ZHA
ARGH!

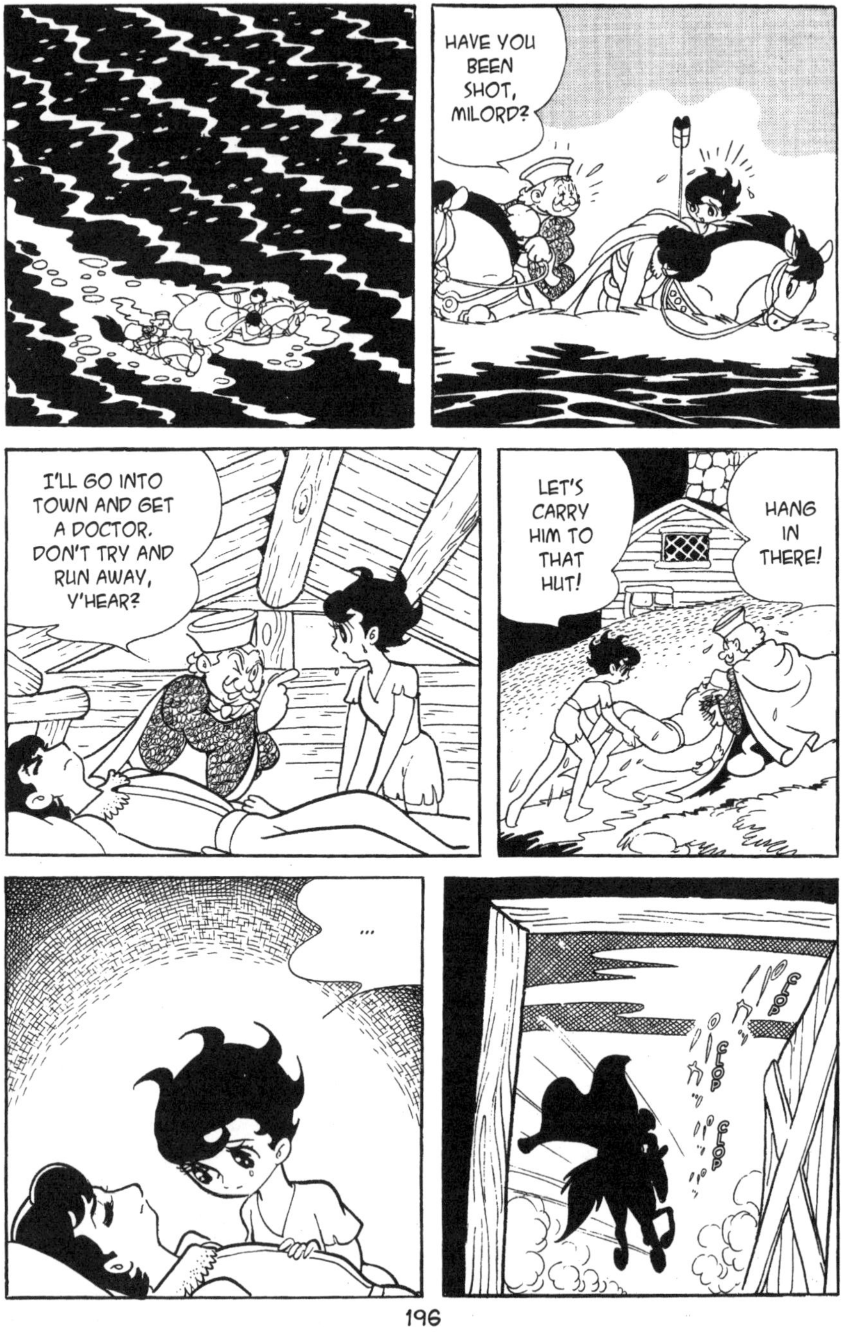
HAVE YOU BEEN SHOT, MILORD?
HANG IN THERE!
LET'S CARRY HIM TO THAT HUT!
I'LL GO INTO TOWN AND GET A DOCTOR. DON'T TRY AND RUN AWAY, Y'HEAR?
CLOP
CLOP
CLOP
...

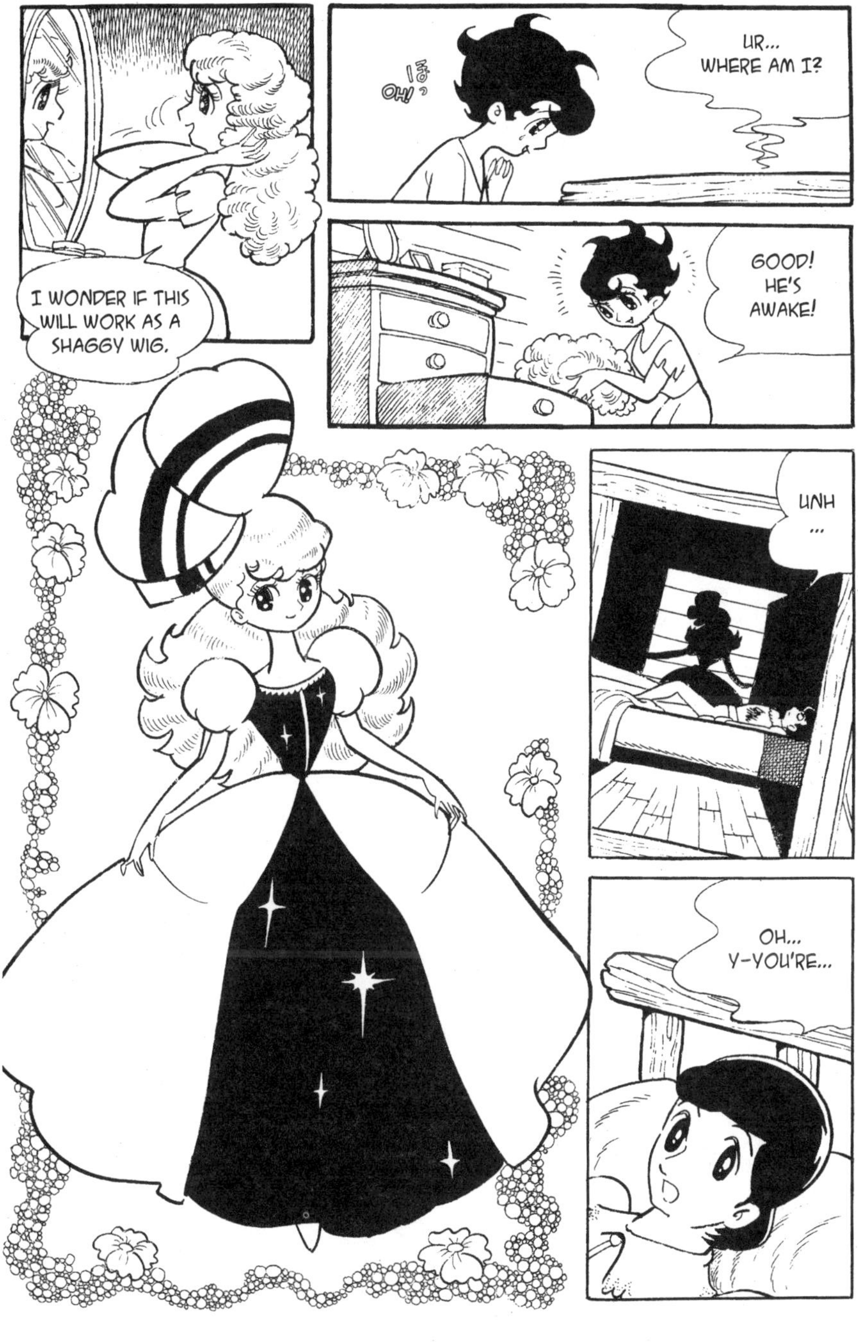
UR... WHERE AM I?
OH!
GOOD! HE'S AWAKE!
I WONDER IF THIS WILL WORK AS A SHAGGY WIG.
UNH ...
OH... Y-YOU'RE...

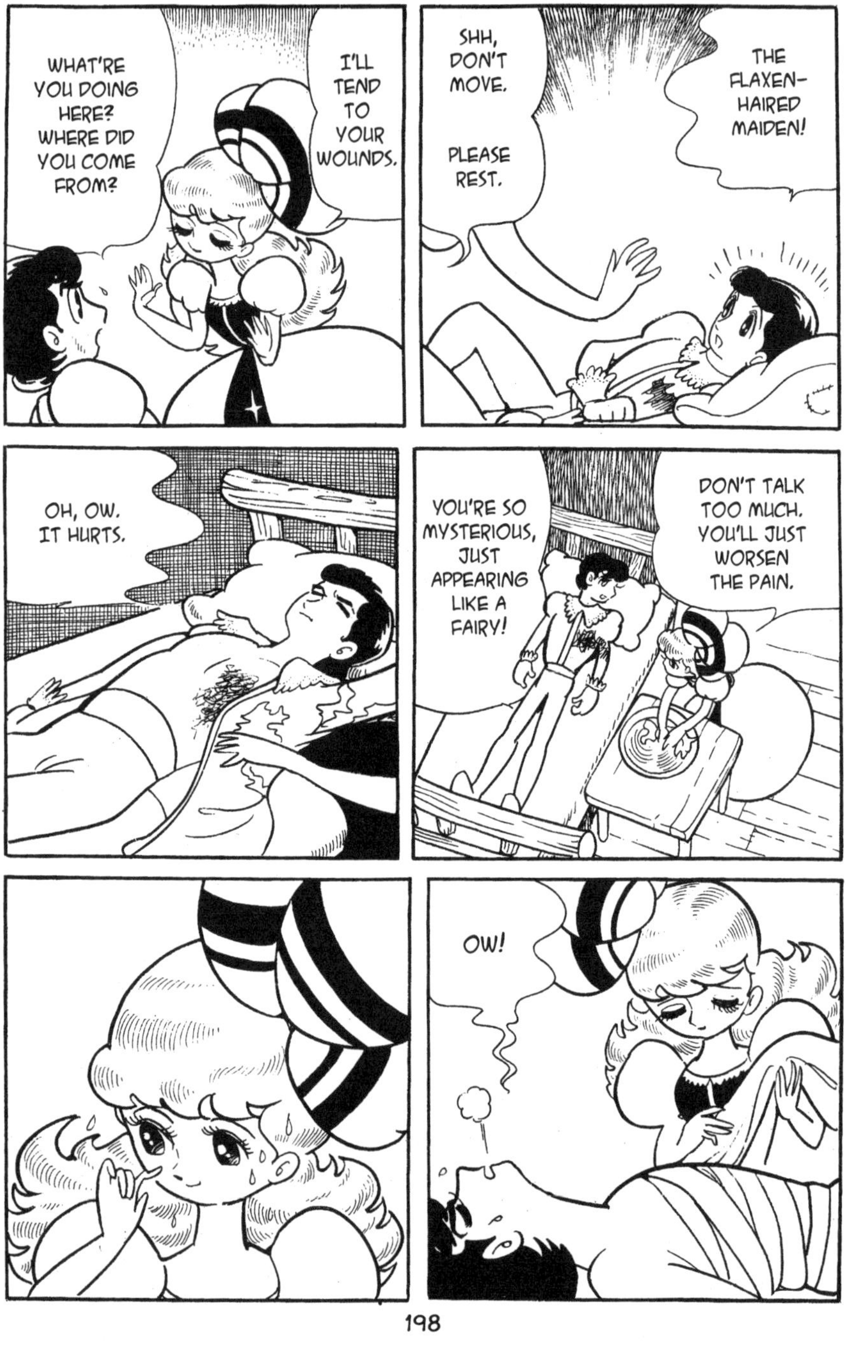
THE FLAXEN-HAIRED MAIDEN!
SHH, DON'T MOVE.
PLEASE REST.
I'LL TEND TO YOUR WOUNDS.
WHAT'RE YOU DOING HERE? WHERE DID YOU COME FROM?
DON'T TALK TOO MUCH. YOU'LL JUST WORSEN THE PAIN.
YOU'RE SO MYSTERIOUS, JUST APPEARING LIKE A FAIRY!
OH, OW. IT HURTS.
OW!

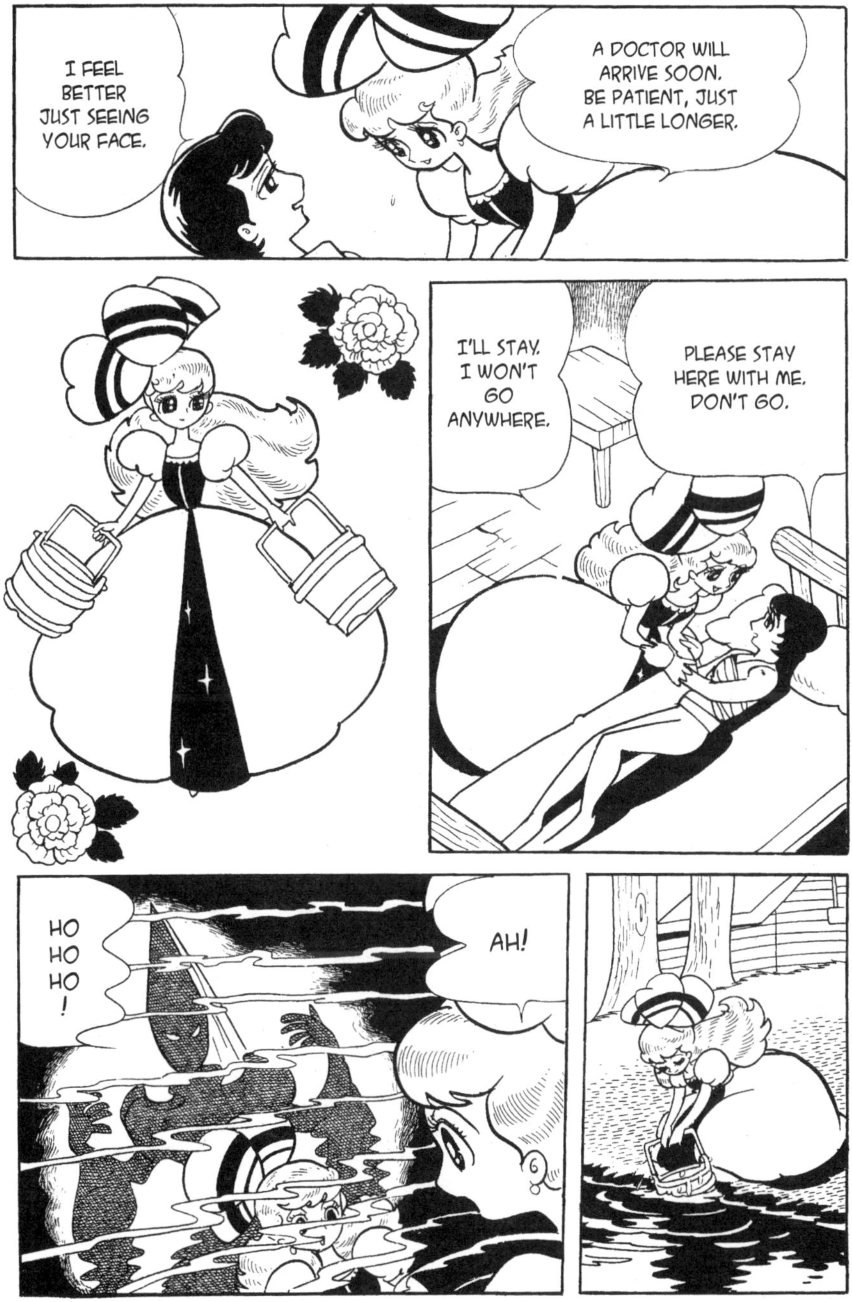
A DOCTOR WILL ARRIVE SOON. BE PATIENT, JUST A LITTLE LONGER.
I FEEL BETTER JUST SEEING YOUR FACE.
PLEASE STAY HERE WITH ME. DON'T GO.
I'LL STAY. I WON'T GO ANYWHERE.
AH!
HO HO HO!

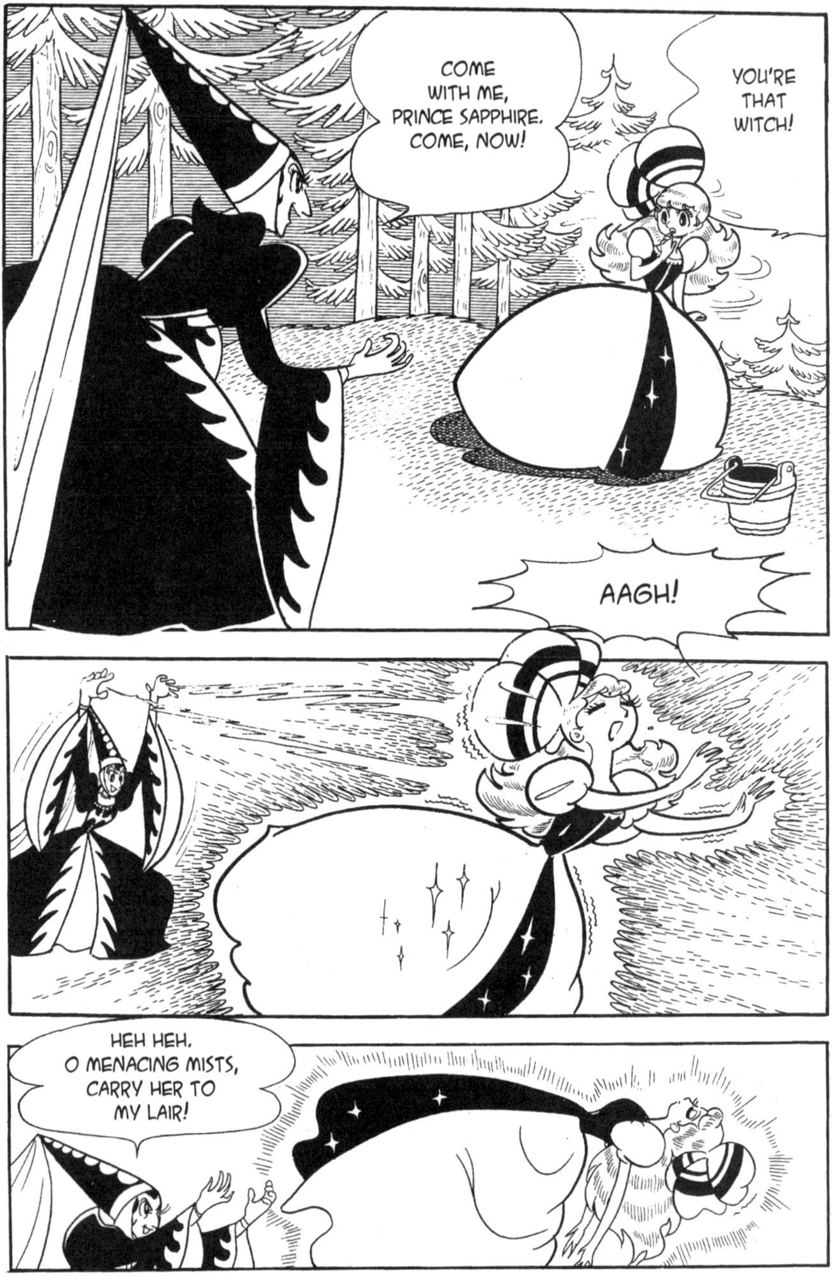
YOU'RE THAT WITCH!
COME WITH ME, PRINCE SAPPHIRE. COME, NOW!
AAGH!
HEH HEH. O MENACING MISTS, CARRY HER TO MY LAIR!

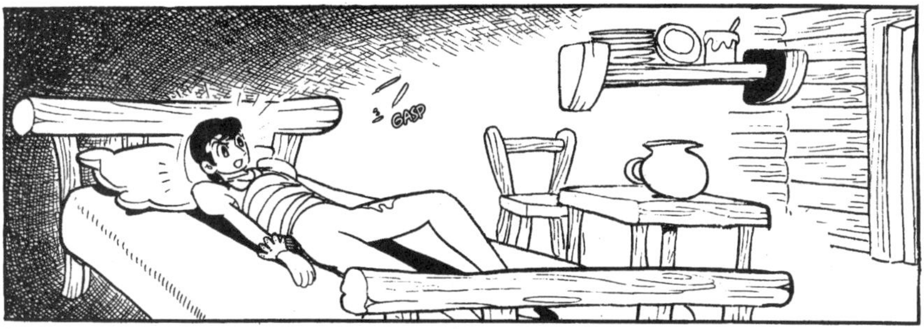
GASP
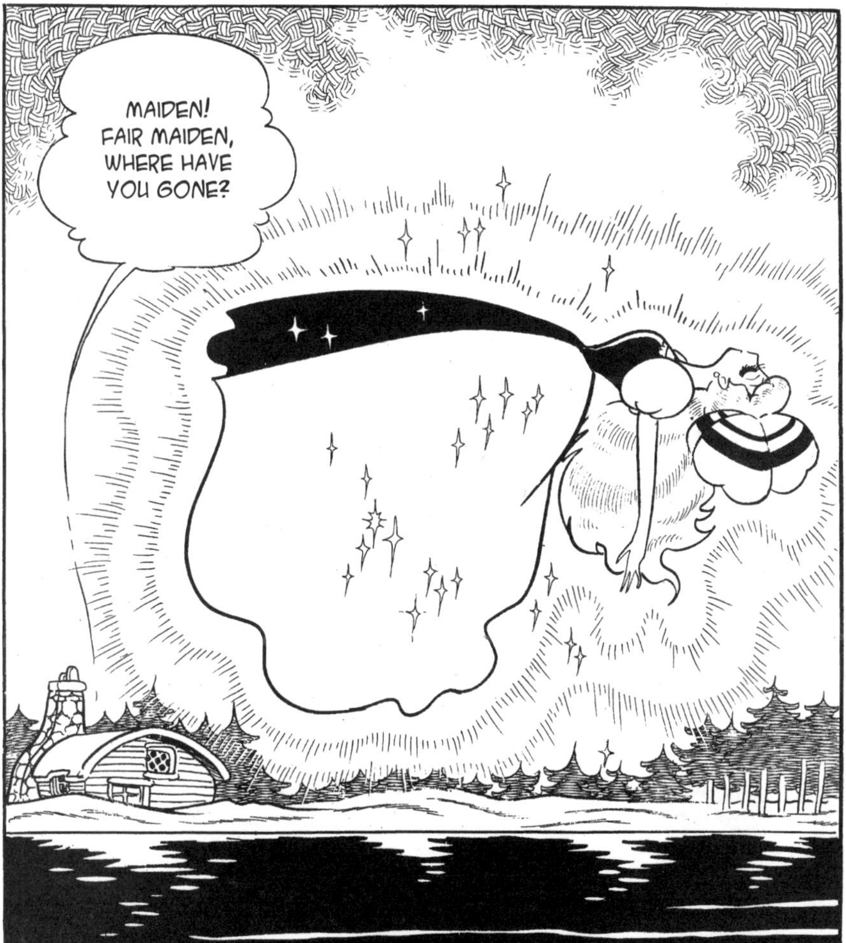
MAIDEN! FAIR MAIDEN, WHERE HAVE YOU GONE?

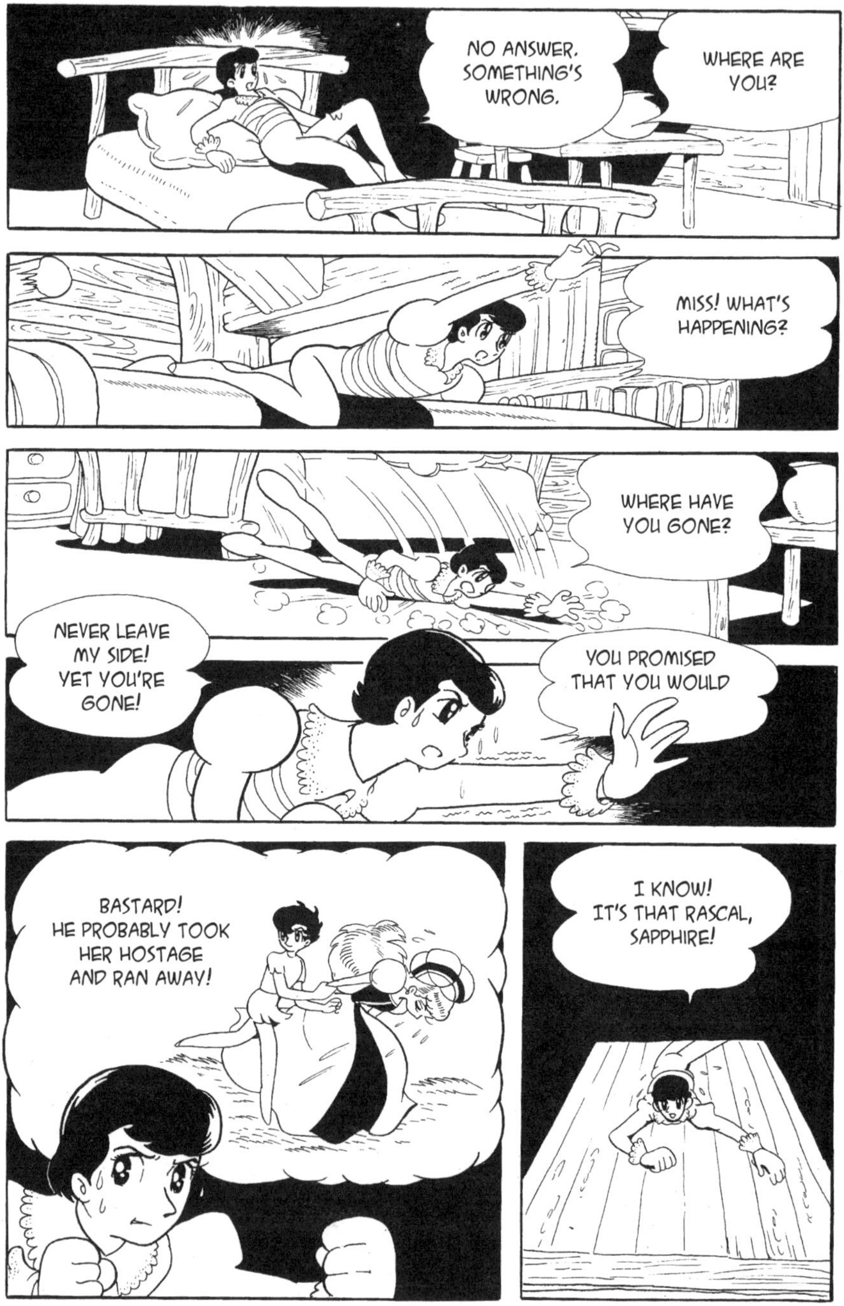
WHERE ARE YOU?
NO ANSWER. SOMETHING'S WRONG.
MISS! WHAT'S HAPPENING?
WHERE HAVE YOU GONE?
YOU PROMISED THAT YOU WOULD
NEVER LEAVE MY SIDE! YET YOU'RE GONE!
I KNOW! IT'S THAT RASCAL, SAPPHIRE!
BASTARD! HE PROBABLY TOOK HER HOSTAGE AND RAN AWAY!

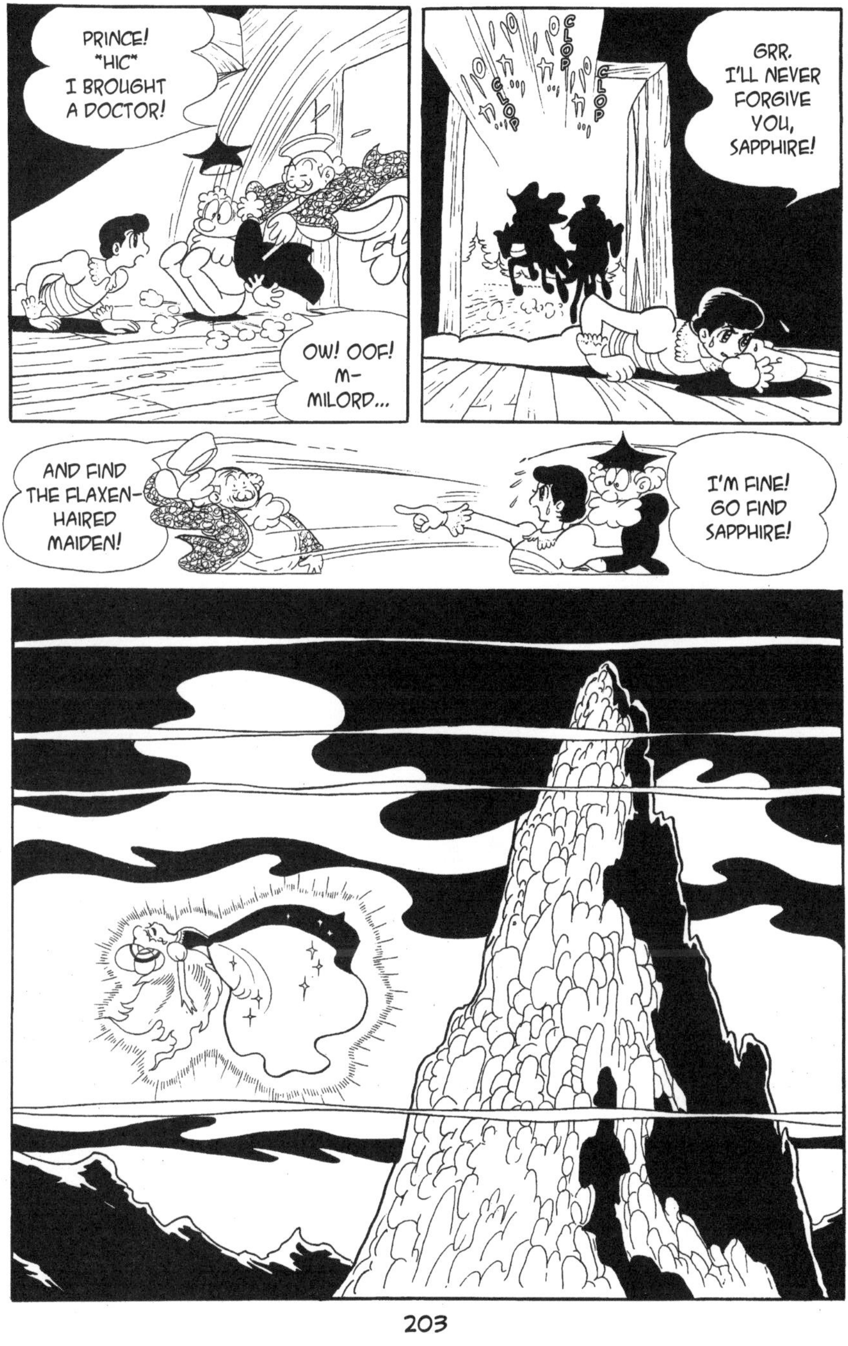
CLOP
CLOP
CLOP
GRR. I'LL NEVER FORGIVE YOU, SAPPHIRE!
PRINCE! *HIC* I BROUGHT A DOCTOR!
OW! OOF! M-MILORD...
I'M FINE! GO FIND SAPPHIRE!
AND FIND THE FLAXEN-HAIRED MAIDEN!

Chapter 12

The Witch's Lair

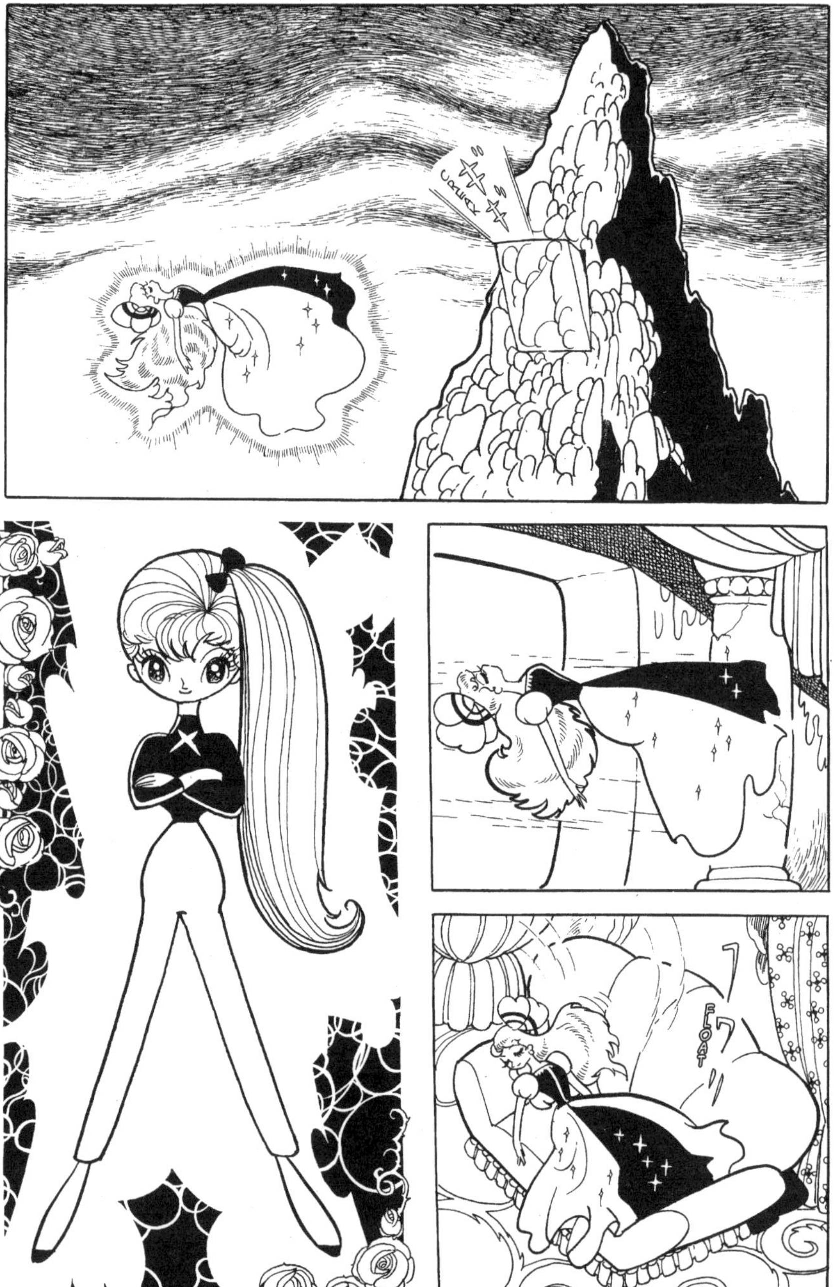
FLOAT

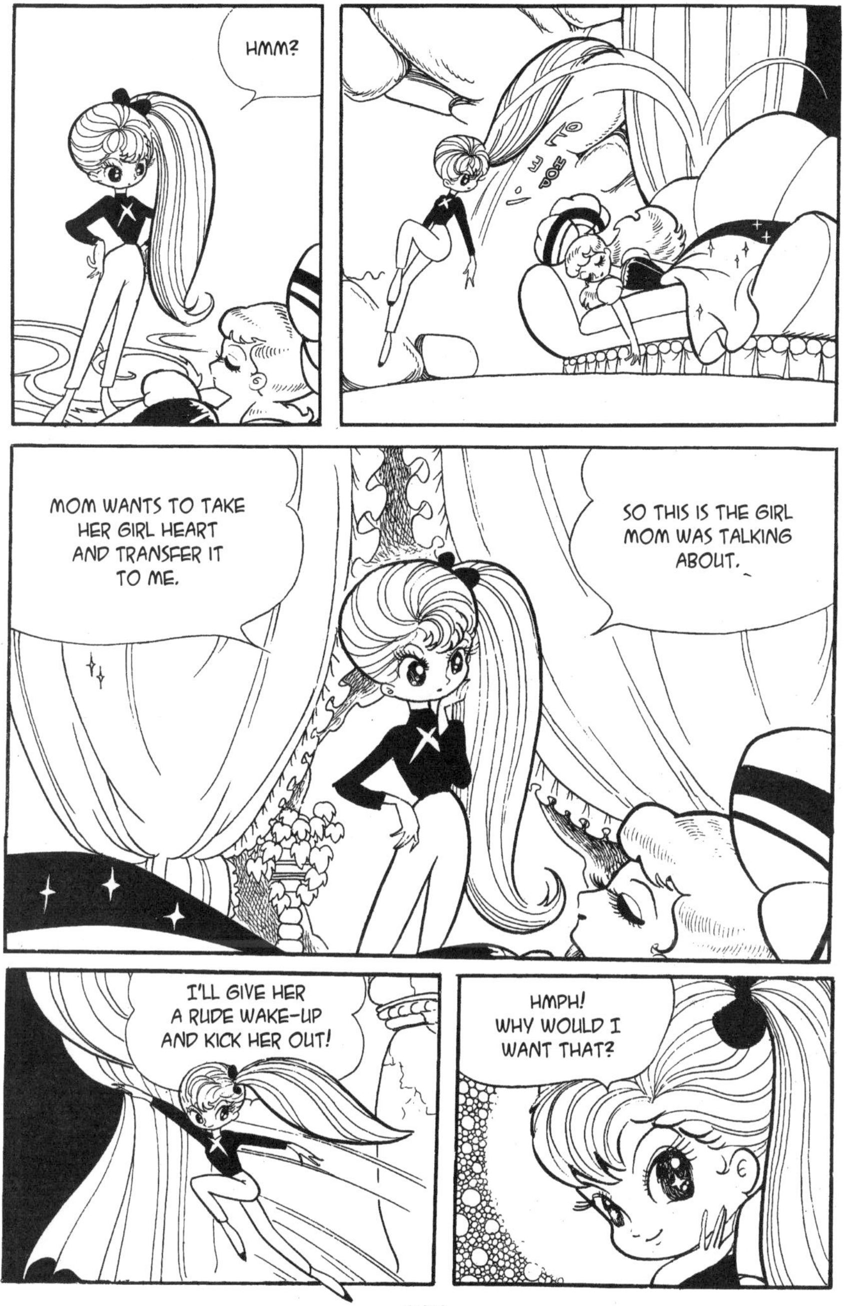
HMM?
SO THIS IS THE GIRL MOM WAS TALKING ABOUT.
MOM WANTS TO TAKE HER GIRL HEART AND TRANSFER IT TO ME.
HMPH! WHY WOULD I WANT THAT?
I'LL GIVE HER A RUDE WAKE-UP AND KICK HER OUT!

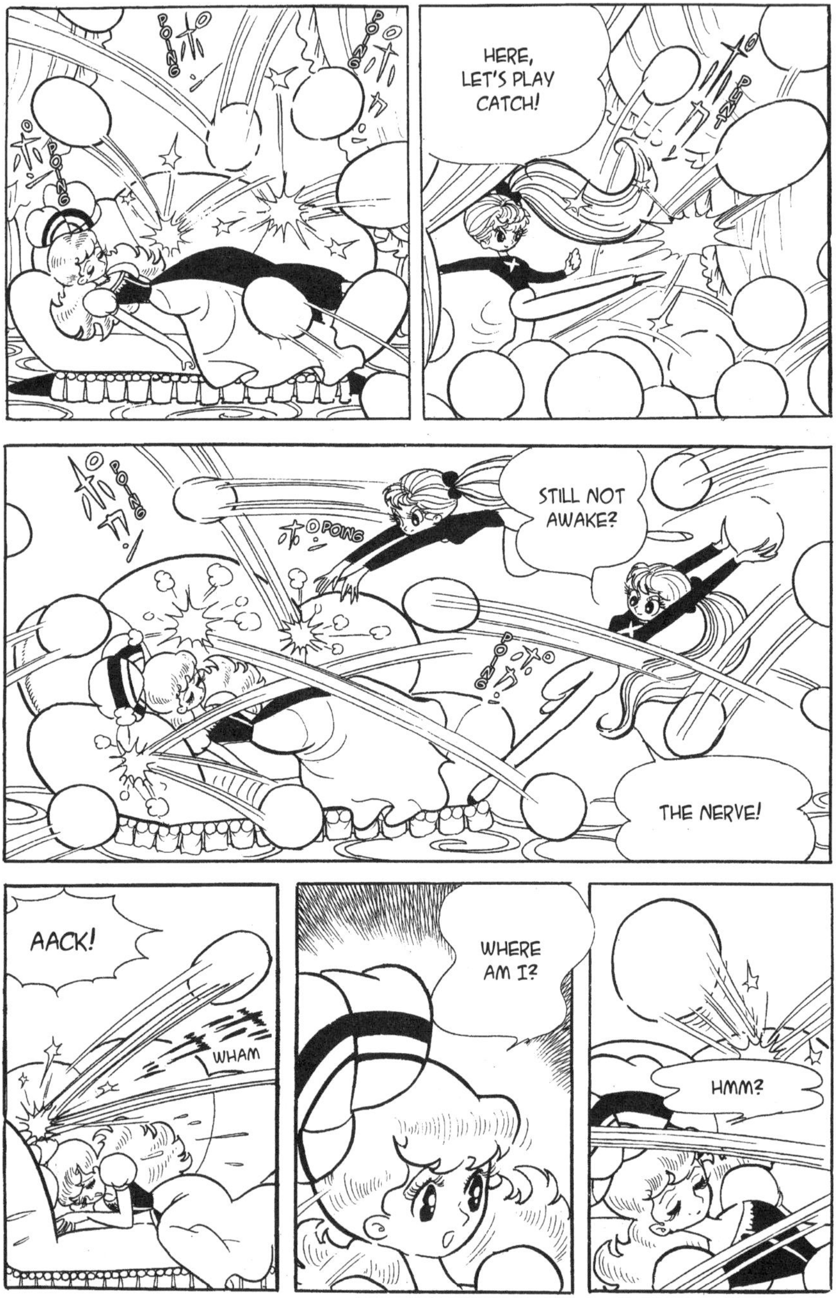
HERE, LET'S PLAY CATCH!
POING
POING
POING
STILL NOT AWAKE?
POING
POING
POING
THE NERVE!
HMM?
WHERE AM I?
AACK!
WHAM

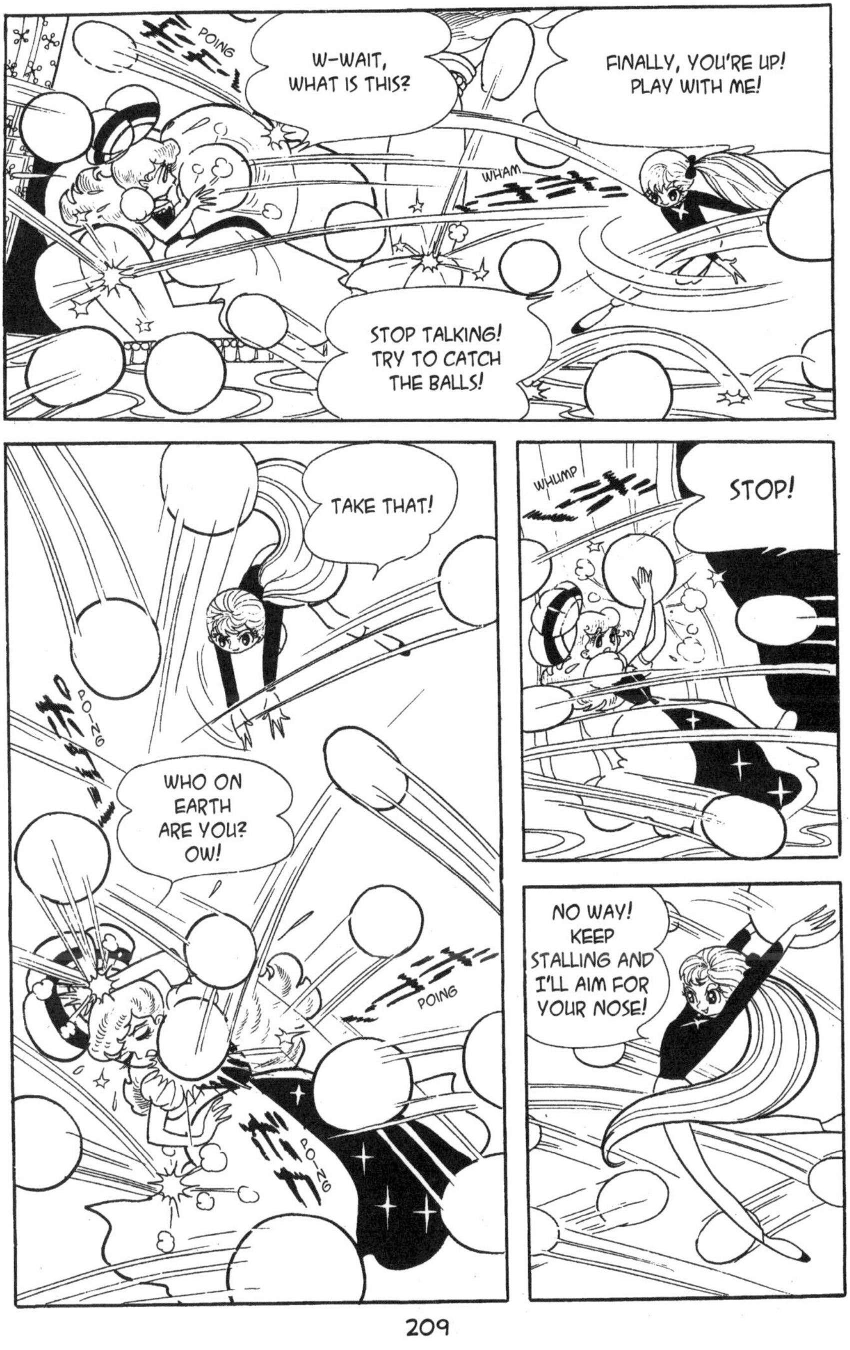

FINALLY, YOU'RE UP! PLAY WITH ME!
W-WAIT, WHAT IS THIS?
POING
WHAM
STOP TALKING! TRY TO CATCH THE BALLS!
WHUMP
STOP!
NO WAY! KEEP STALLING AND I'LL AIM FOR YOUR NOSE!
TAKE THAT!
POING
WHO ON EARTH ARE YOU? OW!
POING
POING

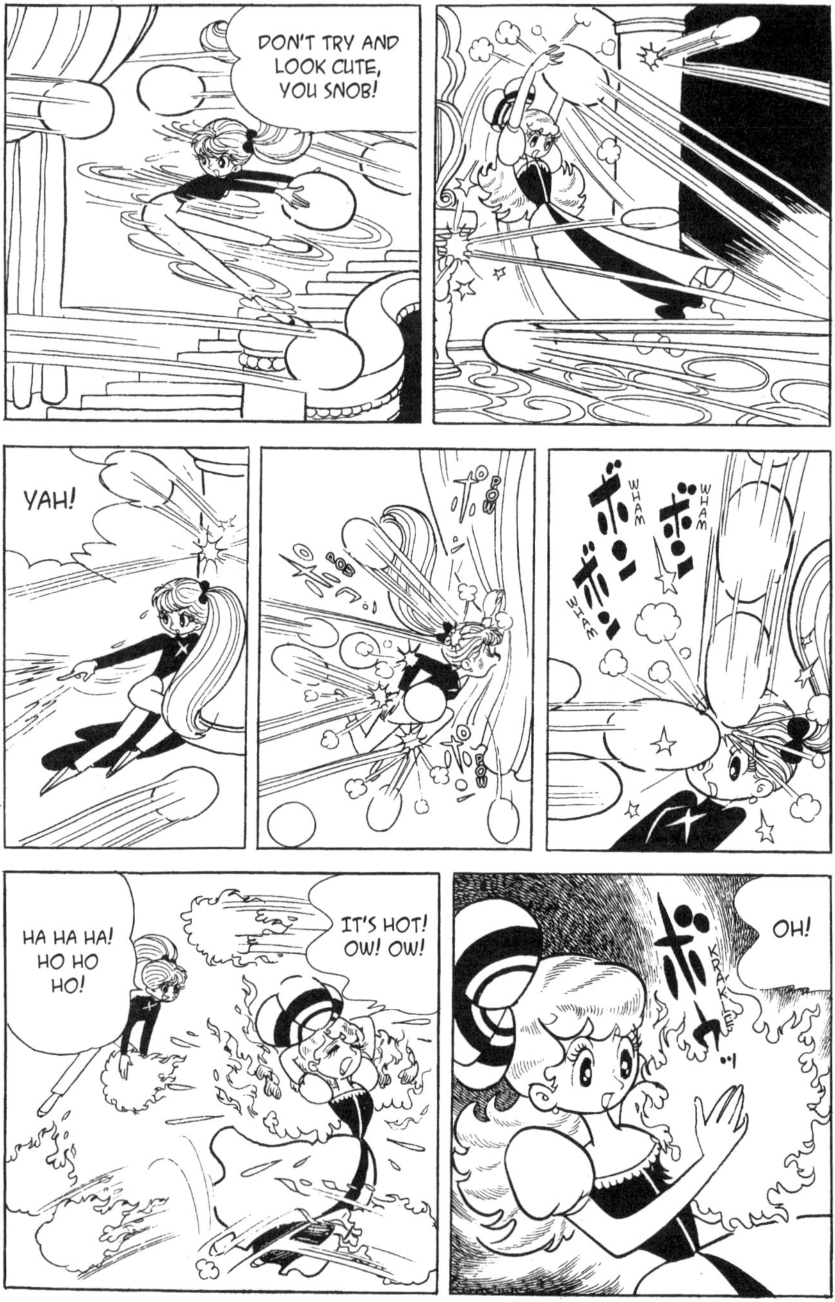
DON'T TRY AND LOOK CUTE, YOU SNOB!
WHAM
WHAM
WHAM
POW
POB
POW
YAH!
OH!
KRAKLE
IT'S HOT! OW! OW!
HA HA HA! HO HO HO!

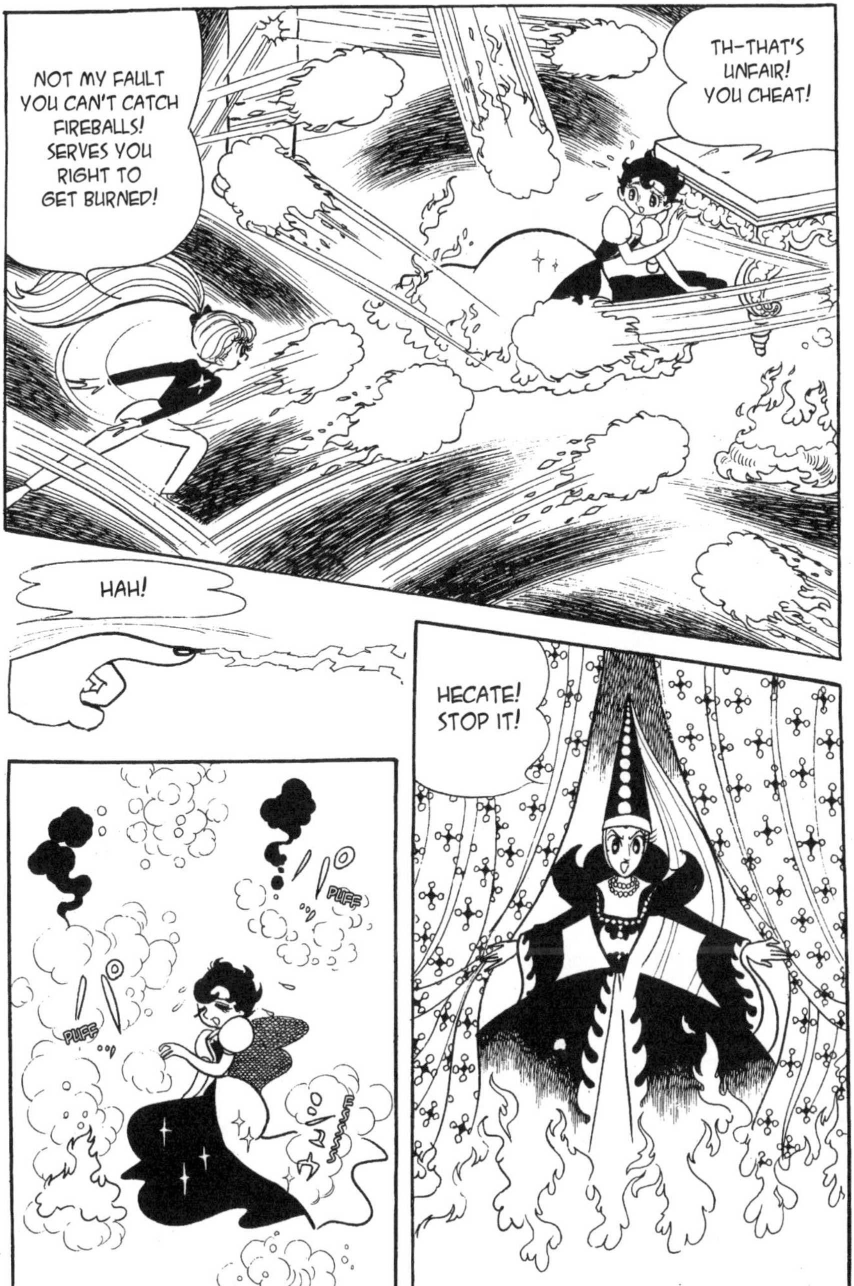
TH-THAT'S UNFAIR! YOU CHEAT!
NOT MY FAULT YOU CAN'T CATCH FIREBALLS! SERVES YOU RIGHT TO GET BURNED!
HECATE! STOP IT!
HAH!
PUFF
PUFF

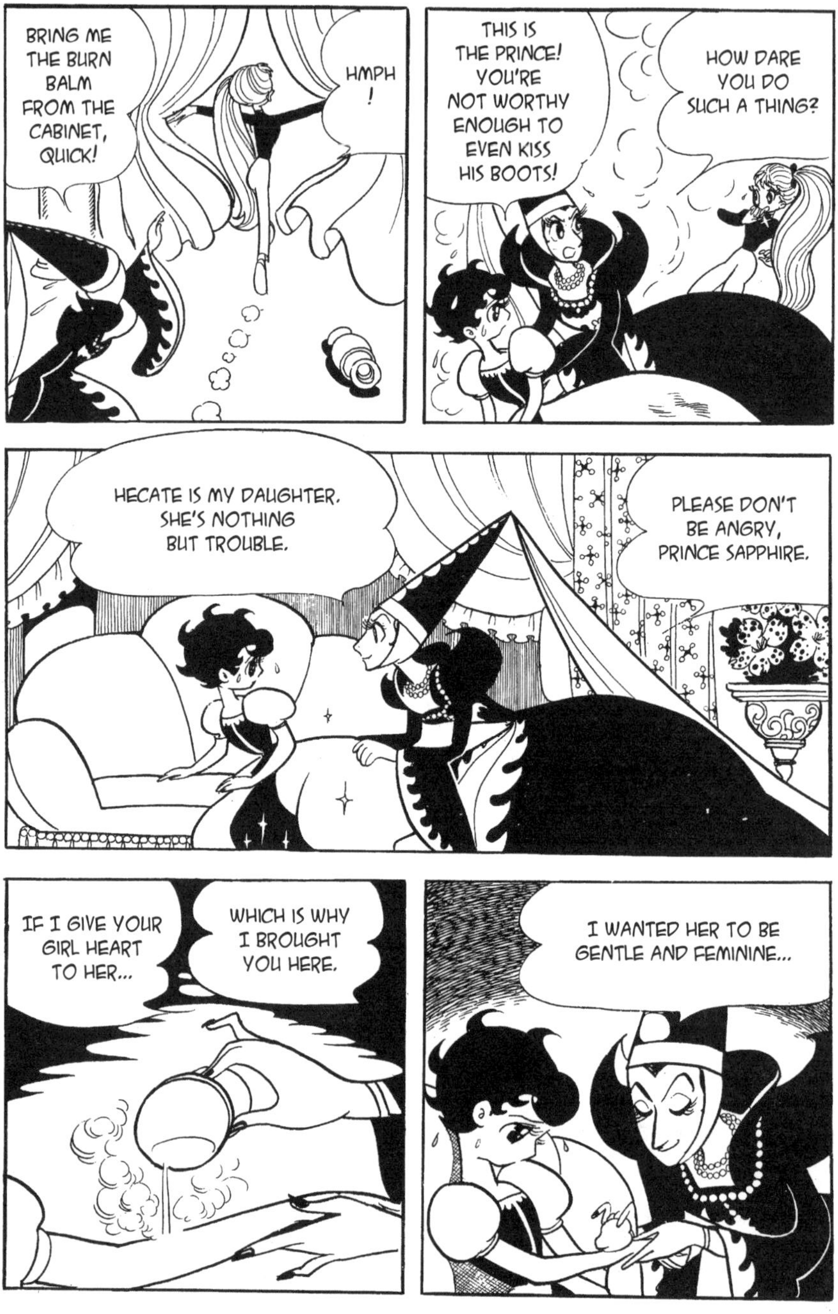
HOW DARE YOU DO SUCH A THING?
THIS IS THE PRINCE! YOU'RE NOT WORTHY ENOUGH TO EVEN KISS HIS BOOTS!
HMPH!
BRING ME THE BURN BALM FROM THE CABINET, QUICK!
PLEASE DON'T BE ANGRY, PRINCE SAPPHIRE.
HECATE IS MY DAUGHTER. SHE'S NOTHING BUT TROUBLE.
I WANTED HER TO BE GENTLE AND FEMININE...
WHICH IS WHY I BROUGHT YOU HERE.
IF I GIVE YOUR GIRL HEART TO HER...

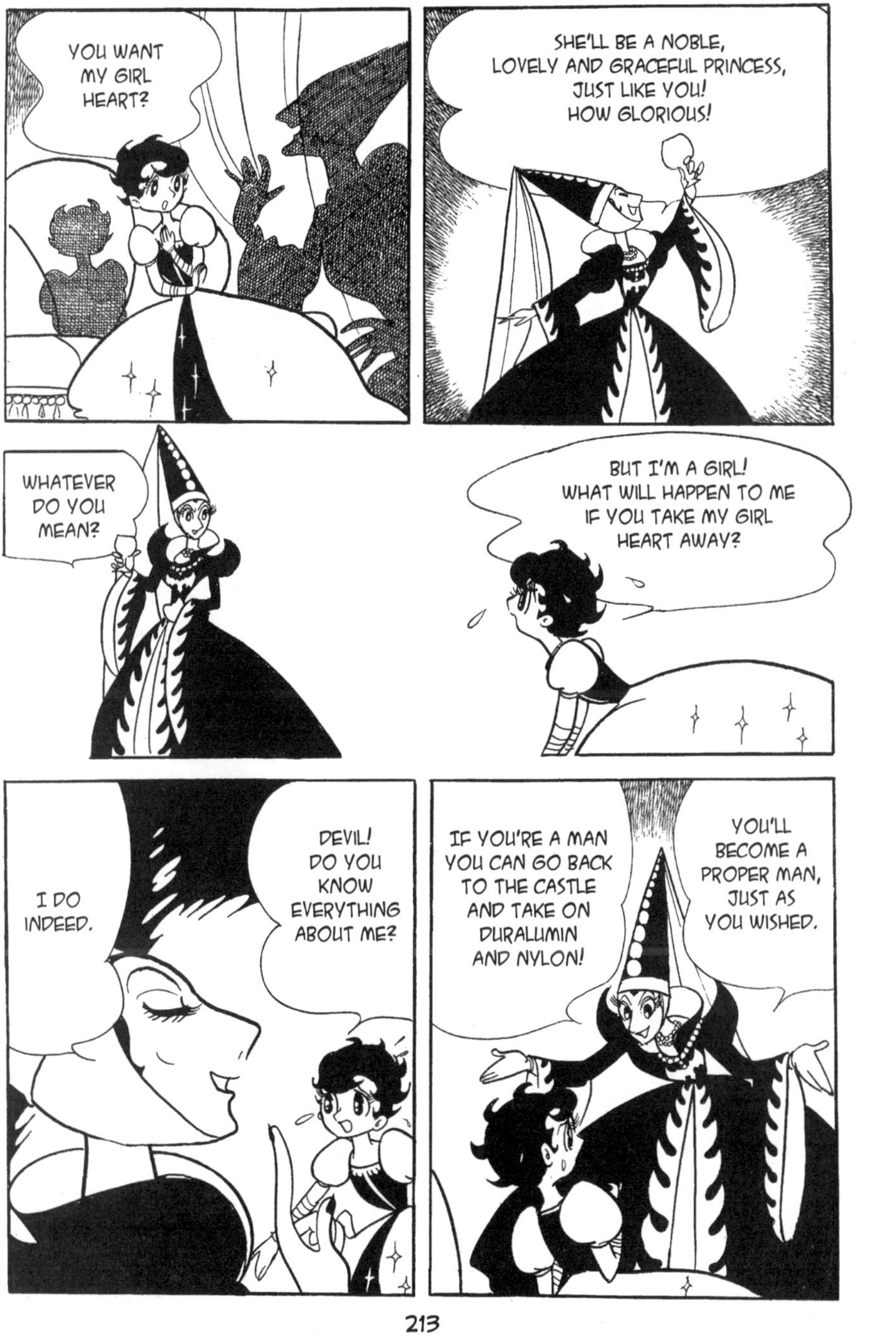

SHE'LL BE A NOBLE, LOVELY AND GRACEFUL PRINCESS, JUST LIKE YOU! HOW GLORIOUS!
YOU WANT MY GIRL HEART?
BUT I'M A GIRL! WHAT WILL HAPPEN TO ME IF YOU TAKE MY GIRL HEART AWAY?
WHATEVER DO YOU MEAN?
YOU'LL BECOME A PROPER MAN, JUST AS YOU WISHED.
IF YOU'RE A MAN YOU CAN GO BACK TO THE CASTLE AND TAKE ON DURALUMIN AND NYLON!
DEVIL! DO YOU KNOW EVERYTHING ABOUT ME?
I DO INDEED.

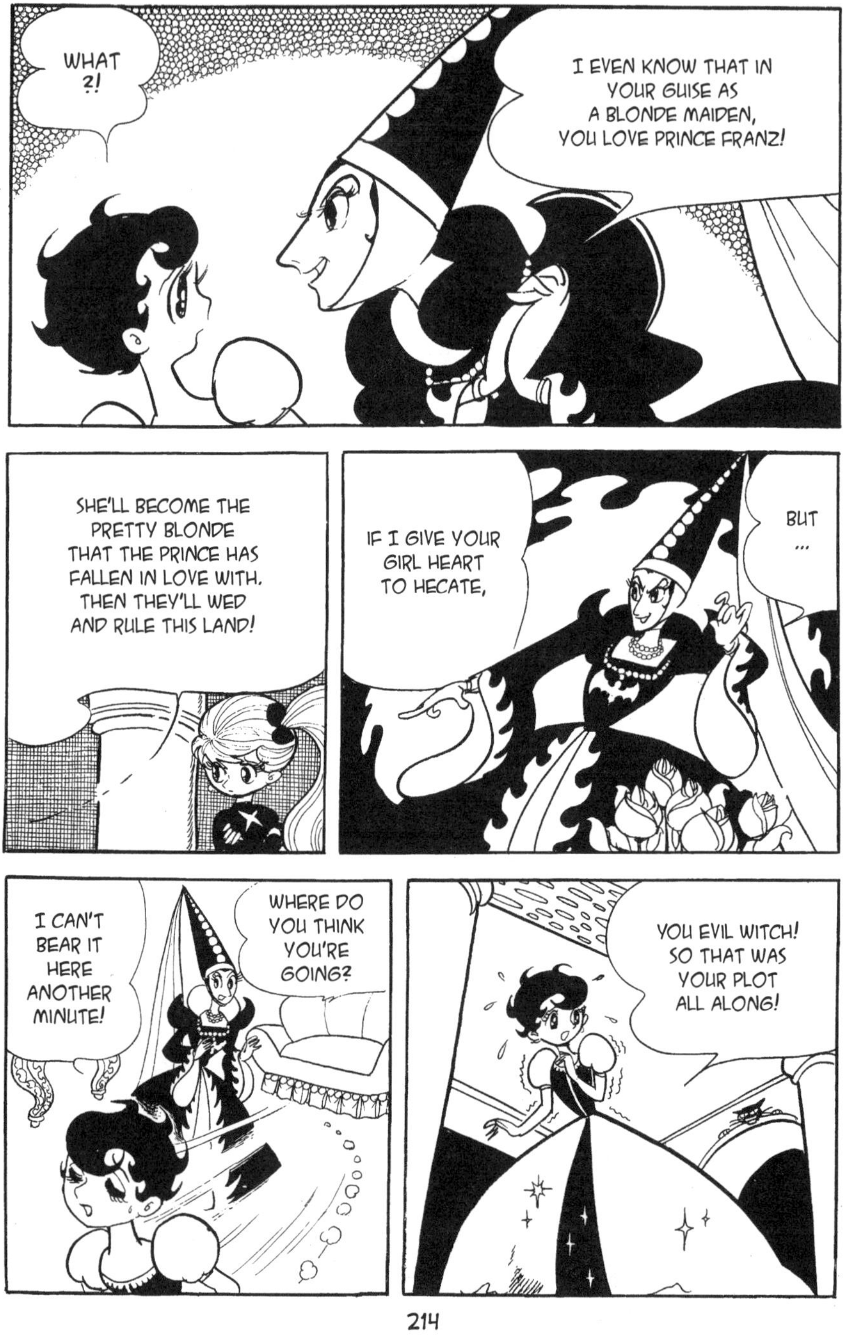
I EVEN KNOW THAT IN YOUR GUISE AS A BLONDE MAIDEN, YOU LOVE PRINCE FRANZ!
WHAT ?!
BUT ...
IF I GIVE YOUR GIRL HEART TO HECATE,
SHE'LL BECOME THE PRETTY BLONDE THAT THE PRINCE HAS FALLEN IN LOVE WITH. THEN THEY'LL WED AND RULE THIS LAND!
YOU EVIL WITCH! SO THAT WAS YOUR PLOT ALL ALONG!
WHERE DO YOU THINK YOU'RE GOING?
I CAN'T BEAR IT HERE ANOTHER MINUTE!

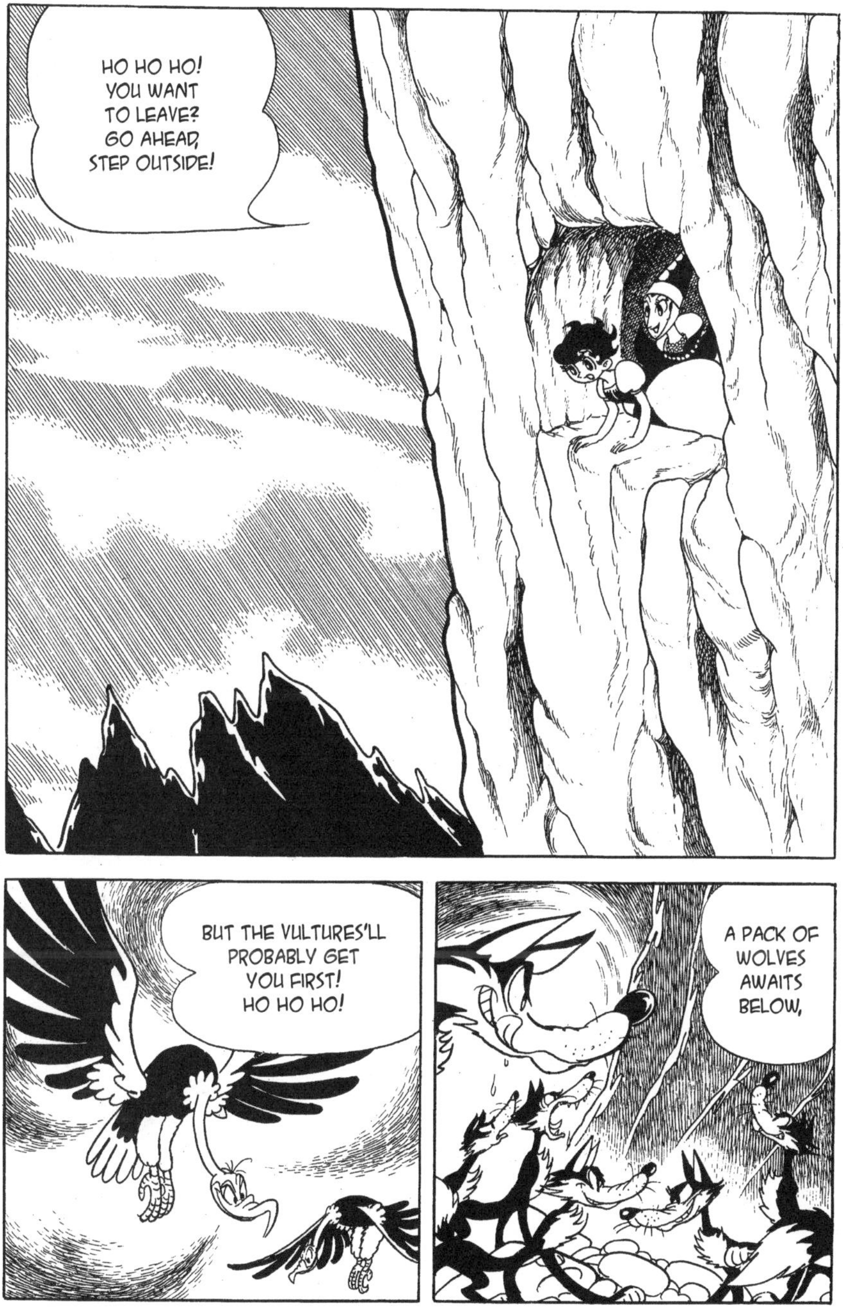
HO HO HO! YOU WANT TO LEAVE? GO AHEAD, STEP OUTSIDE!
A PACK OF WOLVES AWAITS BELOW,
BUT THE VULTURES'LL PROBABLY GET YOU FIRST! HO HO HO!

TOOT
TOOT
CLOP CLOP CLOP
CLOP CLOP
MY WOUNDS... STILL ACHE...

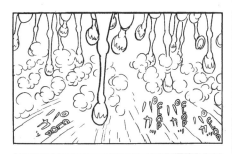

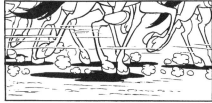

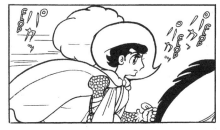

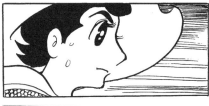

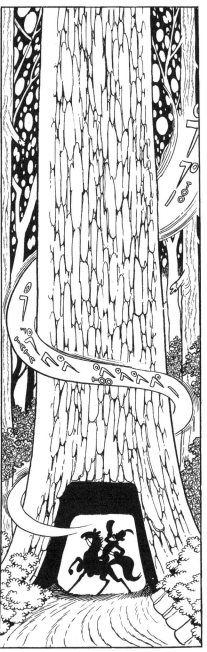

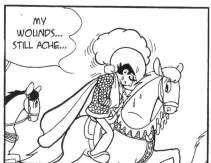

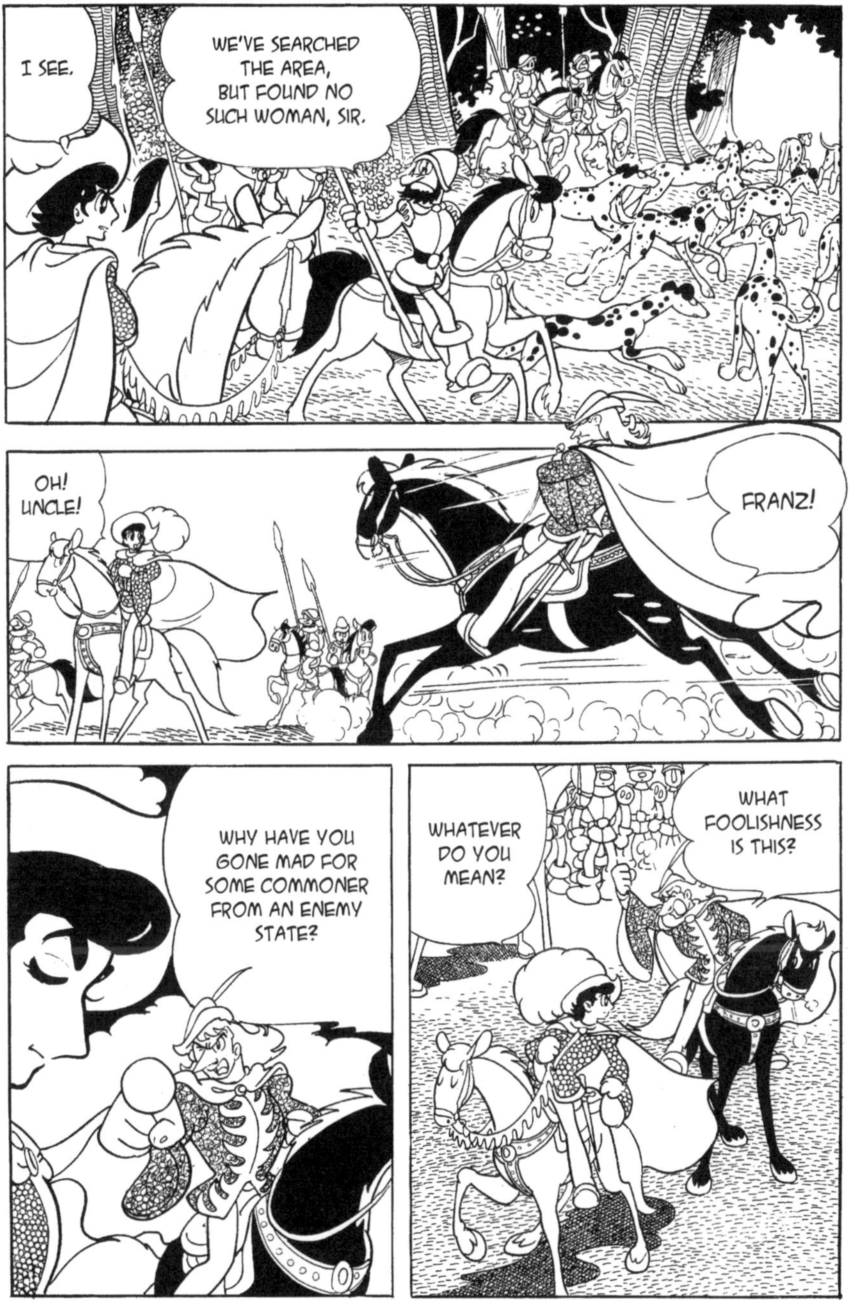
WE'VE SEARCHED THE AREA, BUT FOUND NO SUCH WOMAN, SIR.
I SEE.
FRANZ!
OH! UNCLE!
WHAT FOOLISHNESS IS THIS?
WHATEVER DO YOU MEAN?
WHY HAVE YOU GONE MAD FOR SOME COMMONER FROM AN ENEMY STATE?

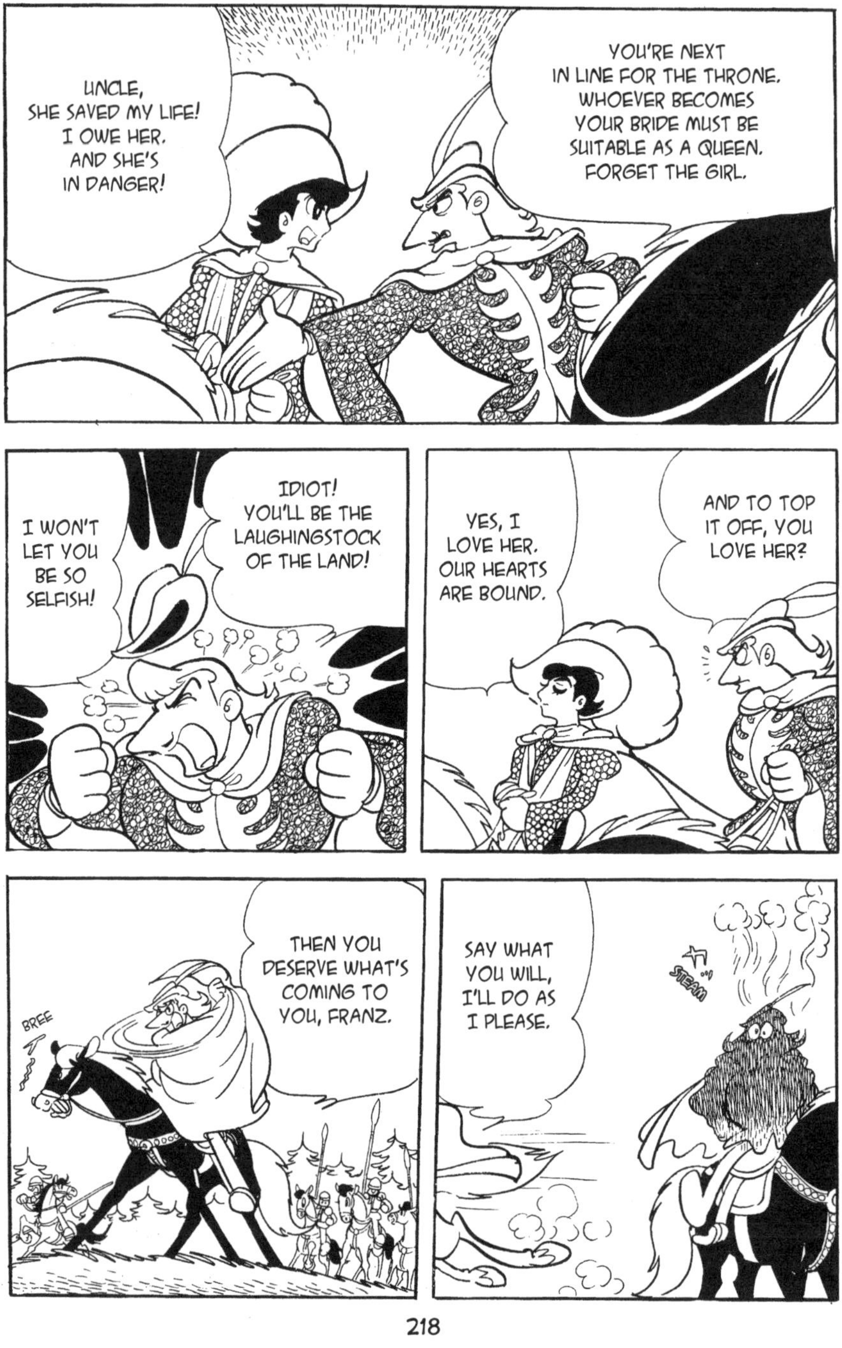
YOU'RE NEXT IN LINE FOR THE THRONE. WHOEVER BECOMES YOUR BRIDE MUST BE SUITABLE AS A QUEEN. FORGET THE GIRL.
UNCLE, SHE SAVED MY LIFE! I OWE HER. AND SHE'S IN DANGER!
AND TO TOP IT OFF, YOU LOVE HER?
YES, I LOVE HER. OUR HEARTS ARE BOUND.
IDIOT! YOU'LL BE THE LAUGHINGSTOCK OF THE LAND!
I WON'T LET YOU BE SO SELFISH!
STEAM
SAY WHAT YOU WILL, I'LL DO AS I PLEASE.
THEN YOU DESERVE WHAT'S COMING TO YOU, FRANZ.
BREE

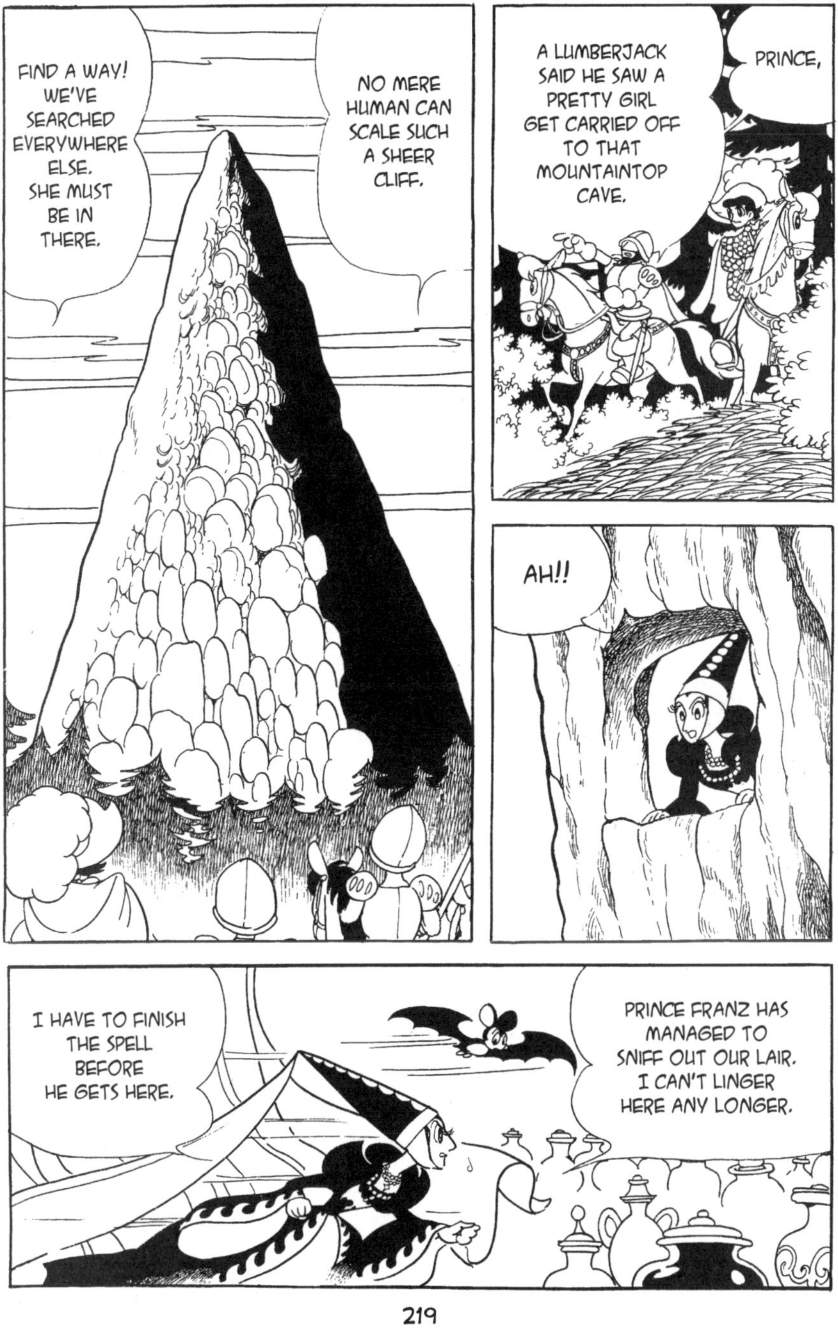
PRINCE,
A LUMBERJACK SAID HE SAW A PRETTY GIRL GET CARRIED OFF TO THAT MOUNTAINTOP CAVE.
AH!!
NO MERE HUMAN CAN SCALE SUCH A SHEER CLIFF.
FIND A WAY! WE'VE SEARCHED EVERYWHERE ELSE. SHE MUST BE IN THERE.
PRINCE FRANZ HAS MANAGED TO SNIFF OUT OUR LAIR. I CAN'T LINGER HERE ANY LONGER.
I HAVE TO FINISH THE SPELL BEFORE HE GETS HERE.

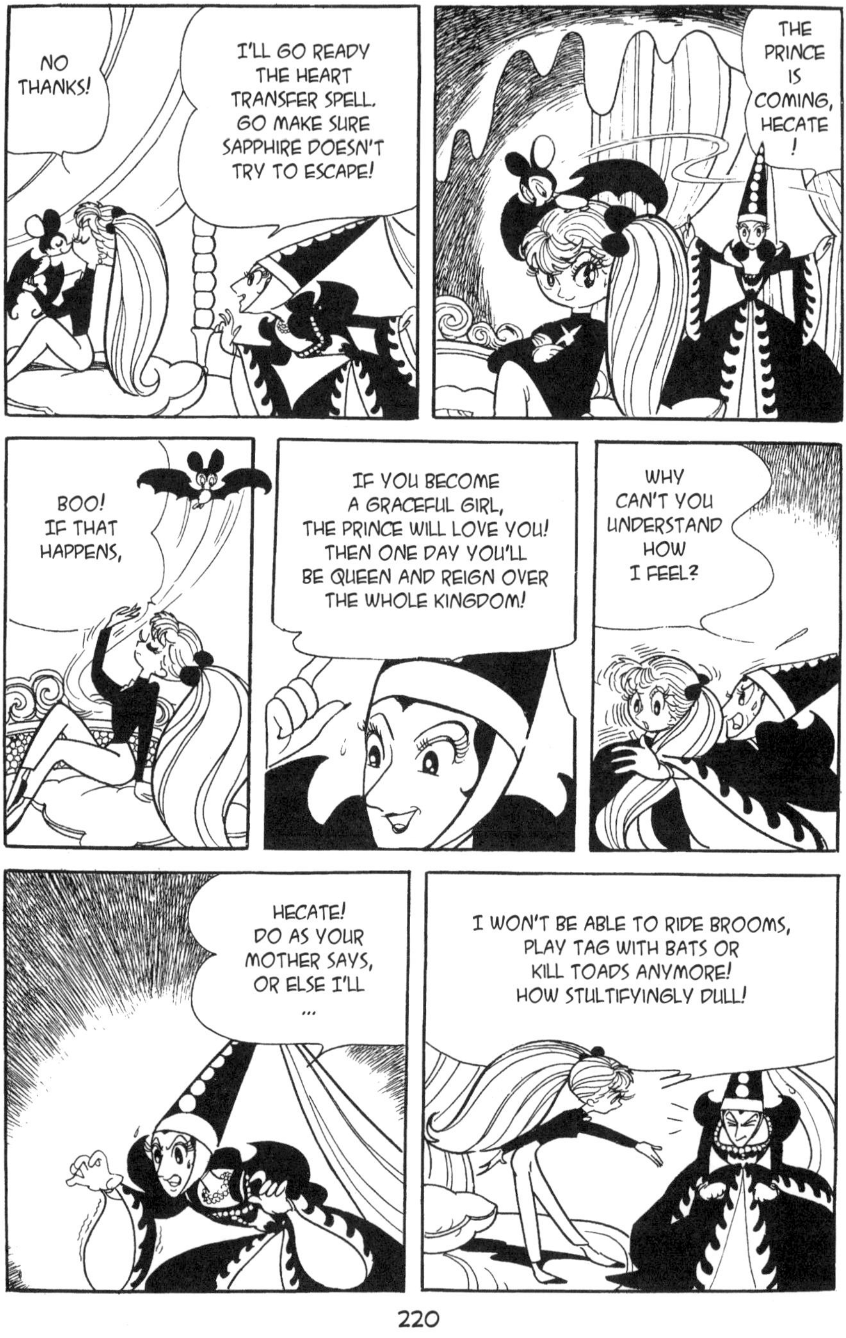
THE PRINCE IS COMING, HECATE!
I'LL GO READY THE HEART TRANSFER SPELL. GO MAKE SURE SAPPHIRE DOESN'T TRY TO ESCAPE!
NO THANKS!
WHY CAN'T YOU UNDERSTAND HOW I FEEL?
IF YOU BECOME A GRACEFUL GIRL, THE PRINCE WILL LOVE YOU! THEN ONE DAY YOU'LL BE QUEEN AND REIGN OVER THE WHOLE KINGDOM!
BOO! IF THAT HAPPENS,
I WON'T BE ABLE TO RIDE BROOMS, PLAY TAG WITH BATS OR KILL TOADS ANYMORE! HOW STULTIFYINGLY DULL!
HECATE! DO AS YOUR MOTHER SAYS, OR ELSE I'LL ...

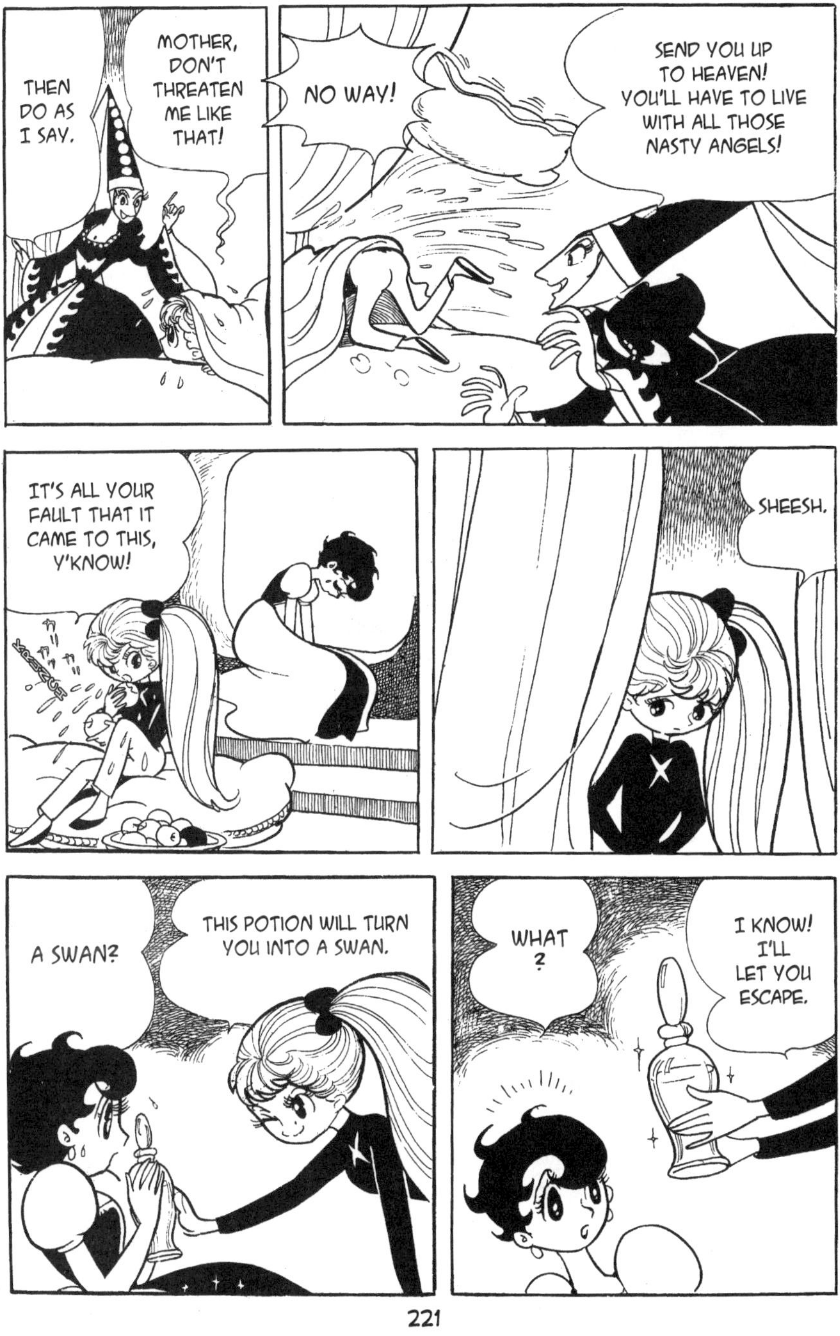
SEND YOU UP TO HEAVEN! YOU'LL HAVE TO LIVE WITH ALL THOSE NASTY ANGELS!
NO WAY!
MOTHER, DON'T THREATEN ME LIKE THAT!
THEN DO AS I SAY.
SHEESH.
IT'S ALL YOUR FAULT THAT IT CAME TO THIS, Y'KNOW!
I KNOW! I'LL LET YOU ESCAPE.
WHAT?
THIS POTION WILL TURN YOU INTO A SWAN.
A SWAN?

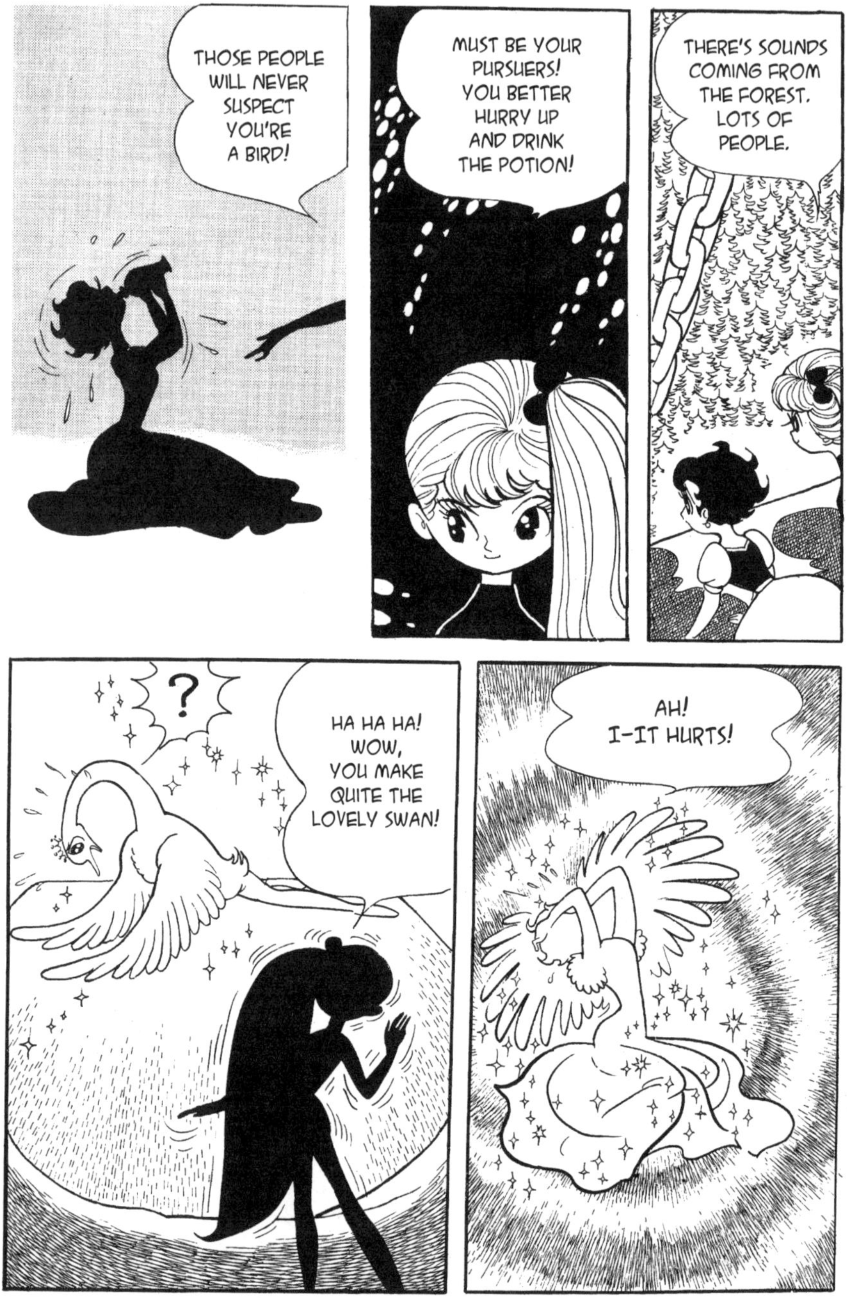
THERE'S SOUNDS COMING FROM THE FOREST. LOTS OF PEOPLE.
MUST BE YOUR PURSUERS! YOU BETTER HURRY UP AND DRINK THE POTION!
THOSE PEOPLE WILL NEVER SUSPECT YOU'RE A BIRD!
AH! I-IT HURTS!
?
HA HA HA! WOW, YOU MAKE QUITE THE LOVELY SWAN!

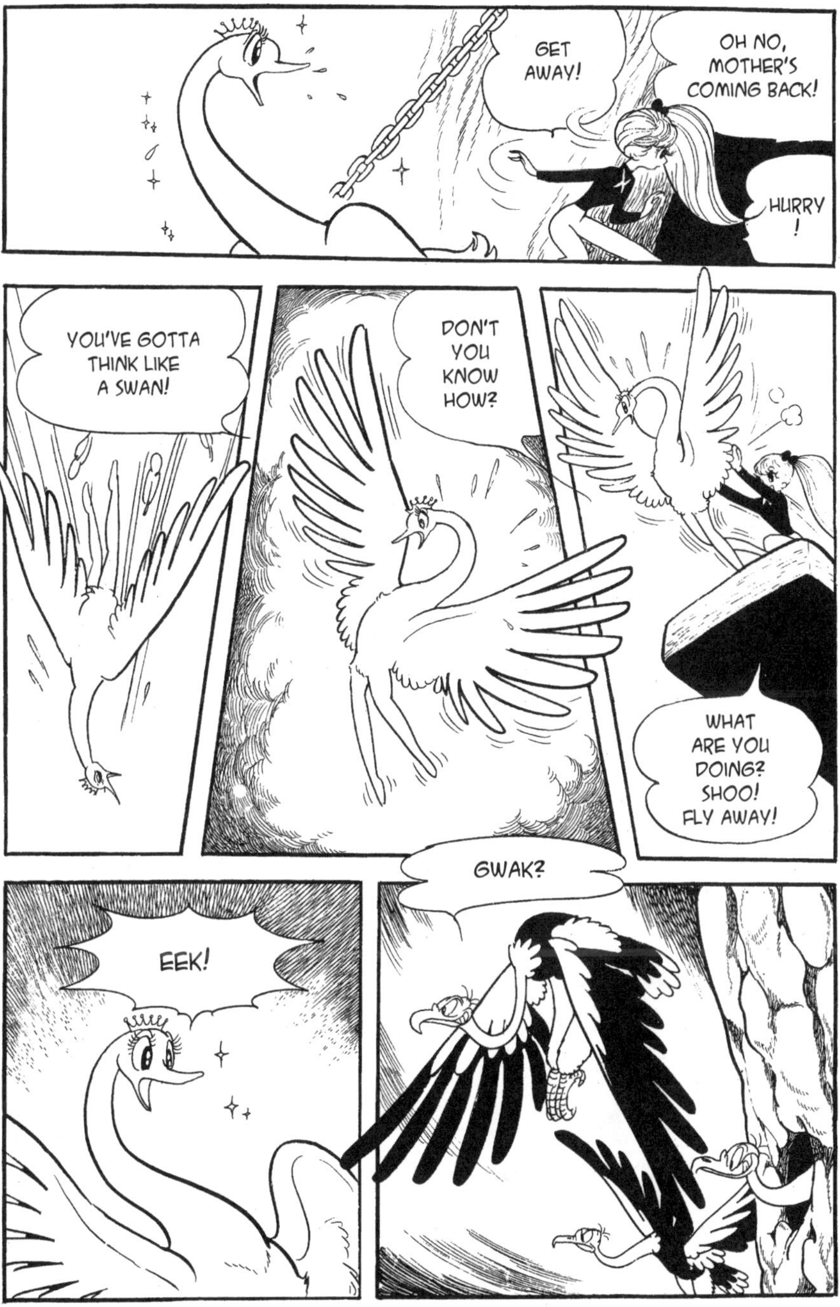
OH NO, MOTHER'S COMING BACK!
GET AWAY!
HURRY!
WHAT ARE YOU DOING? SHOO! FLY AWAY!
DON'T YOU KNOW HOW?
YOU'VE GOTTA THINK LIKE A SWAN!
GWAK?
EEK!

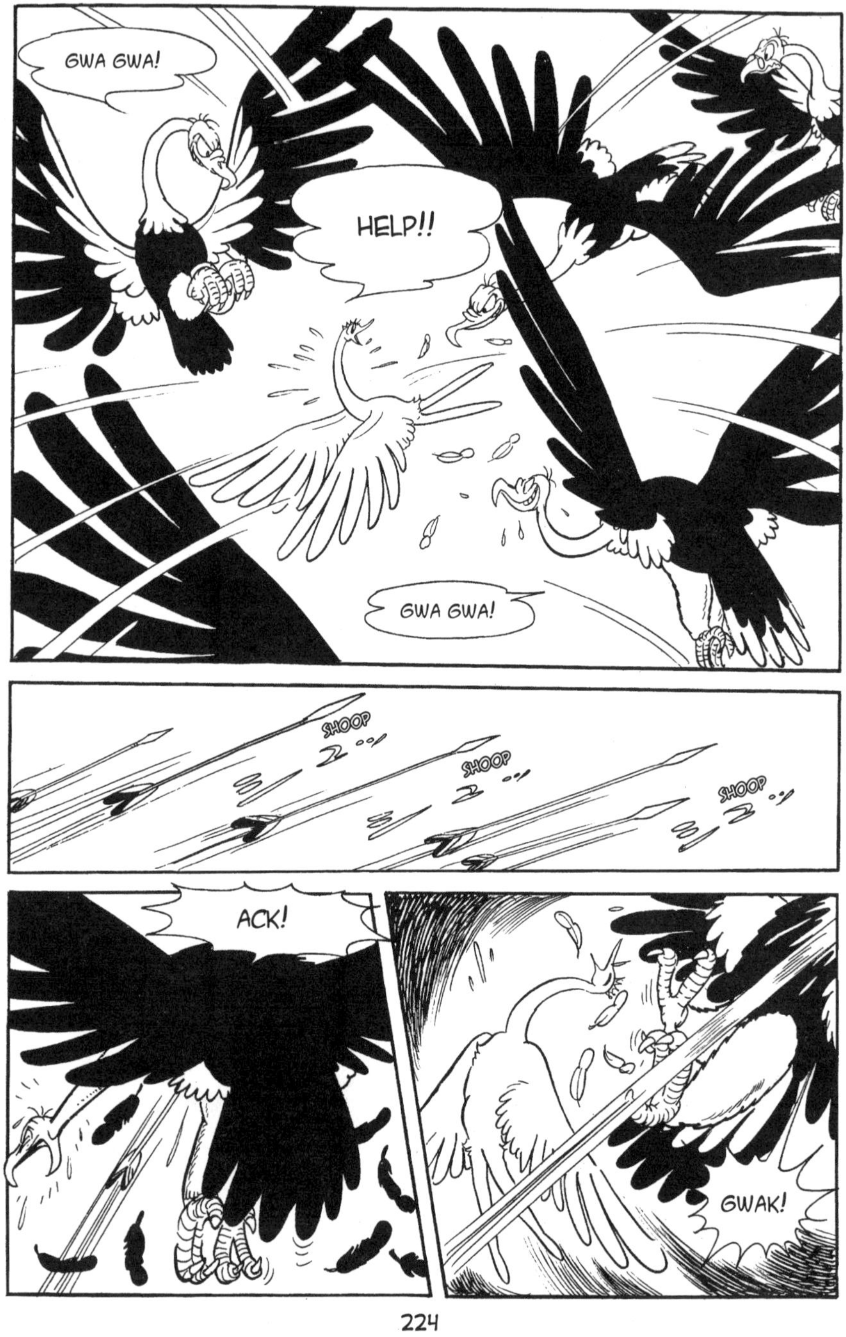
GWA GWA!
HELP!!
GWA GWA!
SHOOP
SHOOP
SHOOP
GWAK!
ACK!

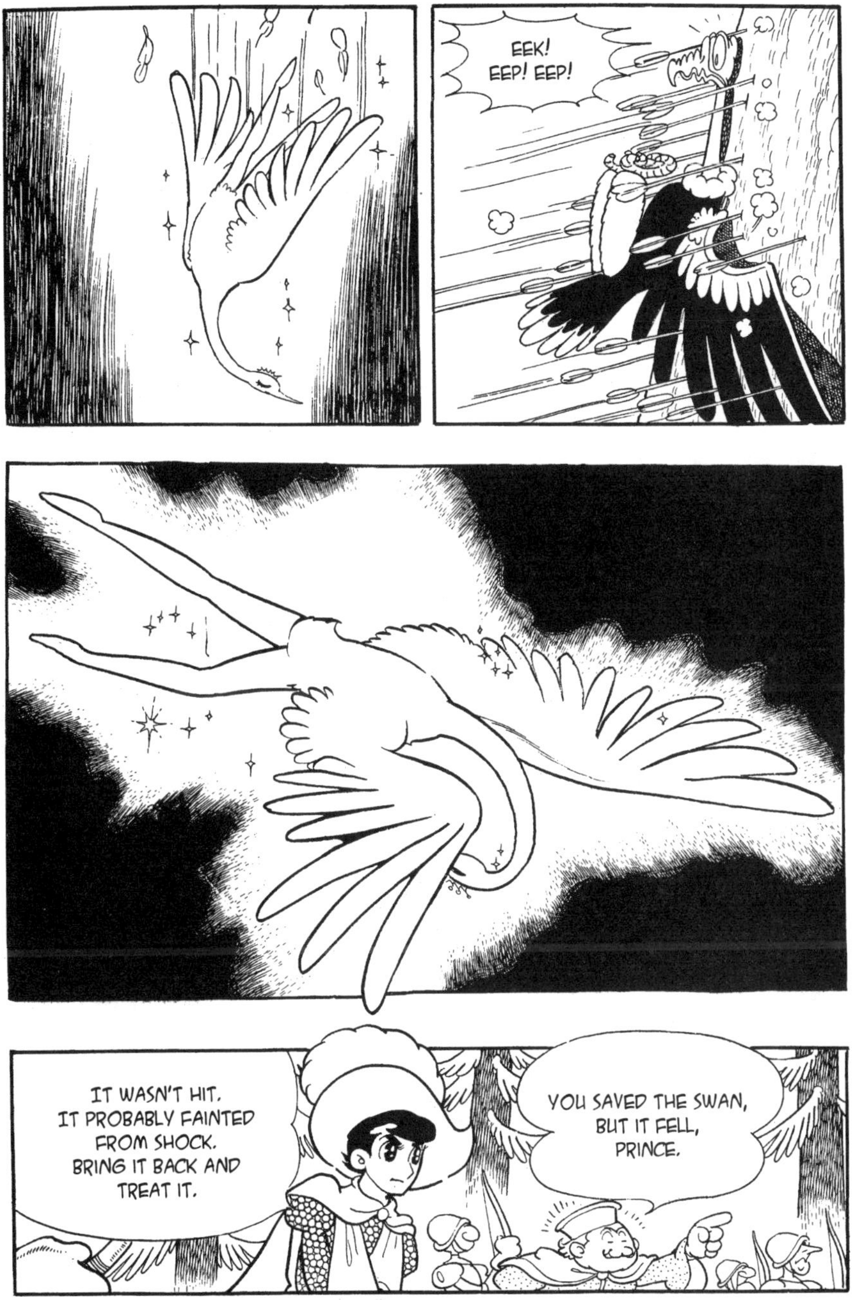
EEK! EEP! EEP!
YOU SAVED THE SWAN, BUT IT FELL, PRINCE.
IT WASN'T HIT. IT PROBABLY FAINTED FROM SHOCK. BRING IT BACK AND TREAT IT.

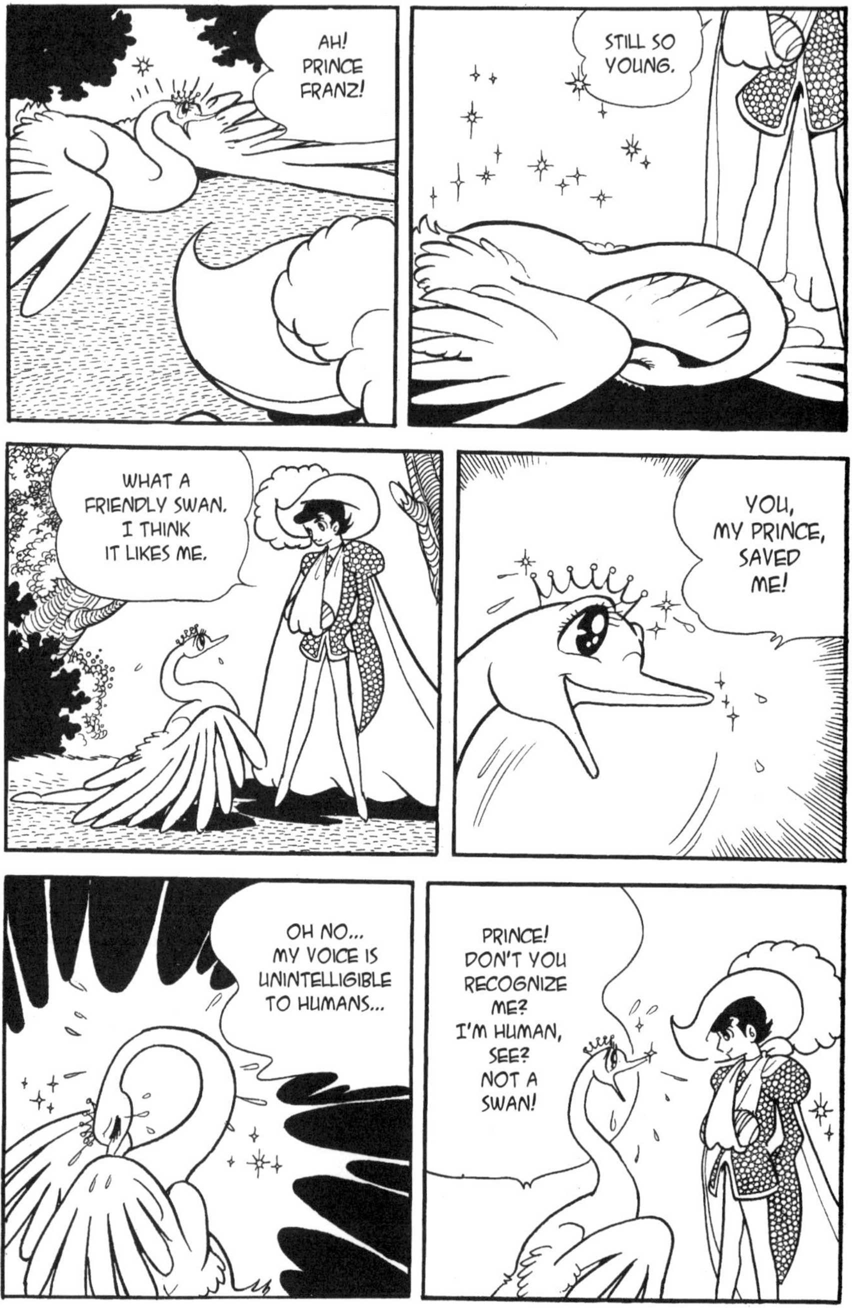
STILL SO YOUNG.
AH! PRINCE FRANZ!
YOU, MY PRINCE, SAVED ME!
WHAT A FRIENDLY SWAN. I THINK IT LIKES ME.
PRINCE! DON'T YOU RECOGNIZE ME? I'M HUMAN, SEE? NOT A SWAN!
OH NO... MY VOICE IS UNINTELLIGIBLE TO HUMANS...

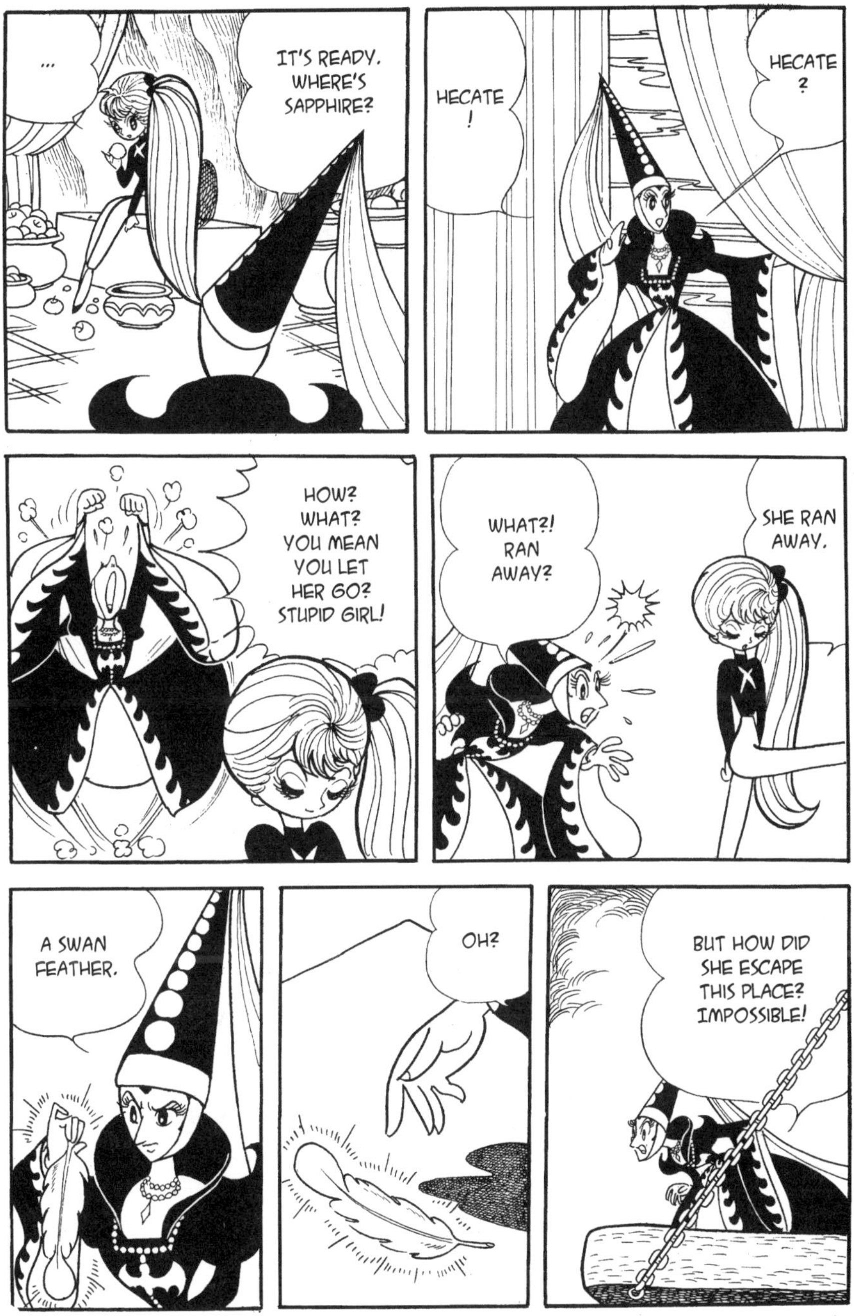
HECATE ?
HECATE !
IT'S READY. WHERE'S SAPPHIRE?
...
SHE RAN AWAY.
WHAT?! RAN AWAY?
HOW? WHAT? YOU MEAN YOU LET HER GO? STUPID GIRL!
BUT HOW DID SHE ESCAPE THIS PLACE? IMPOSSIBLE!
OH?
A SWAN FEATHER.

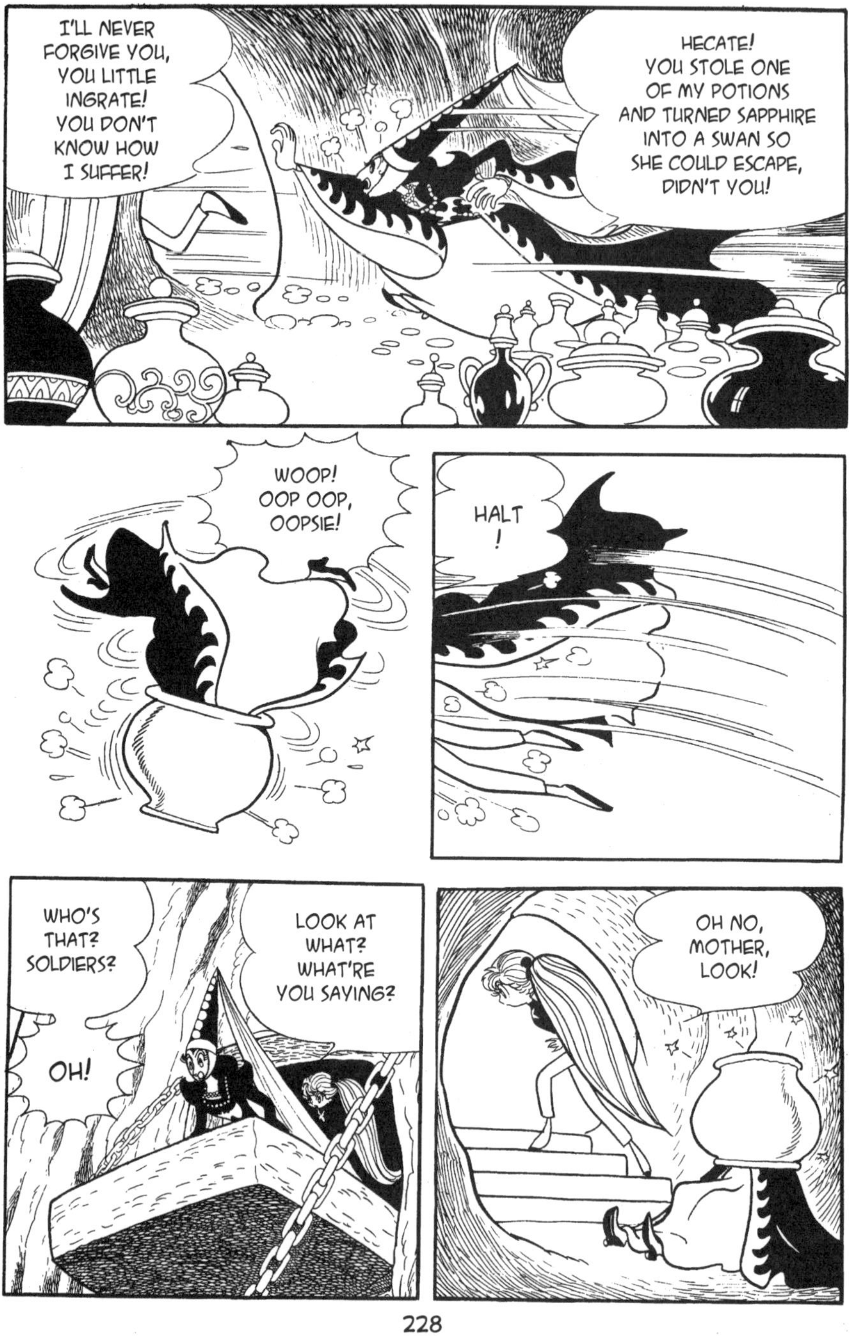
HECATE! YOU STOLE ONE OF MY POTIONS AND TURNED SAPPHIRE INTO A SWAN SO SHE COULD ESCAPE, DIDN'T YOU!
I'LL NEVER FORGIVE YOU, YOU LITTLE INGRATE! YOU DON'T KNOW HOW I SUFFER!
HALT!
WOOP! OOP OOP, OOPSIE!
OH NO, MOTHER, LOOK!
LOOK AT WHAT? WHAT'RE YOU SAYING?
WHO'S THAT? SOLDIERS?
OH!

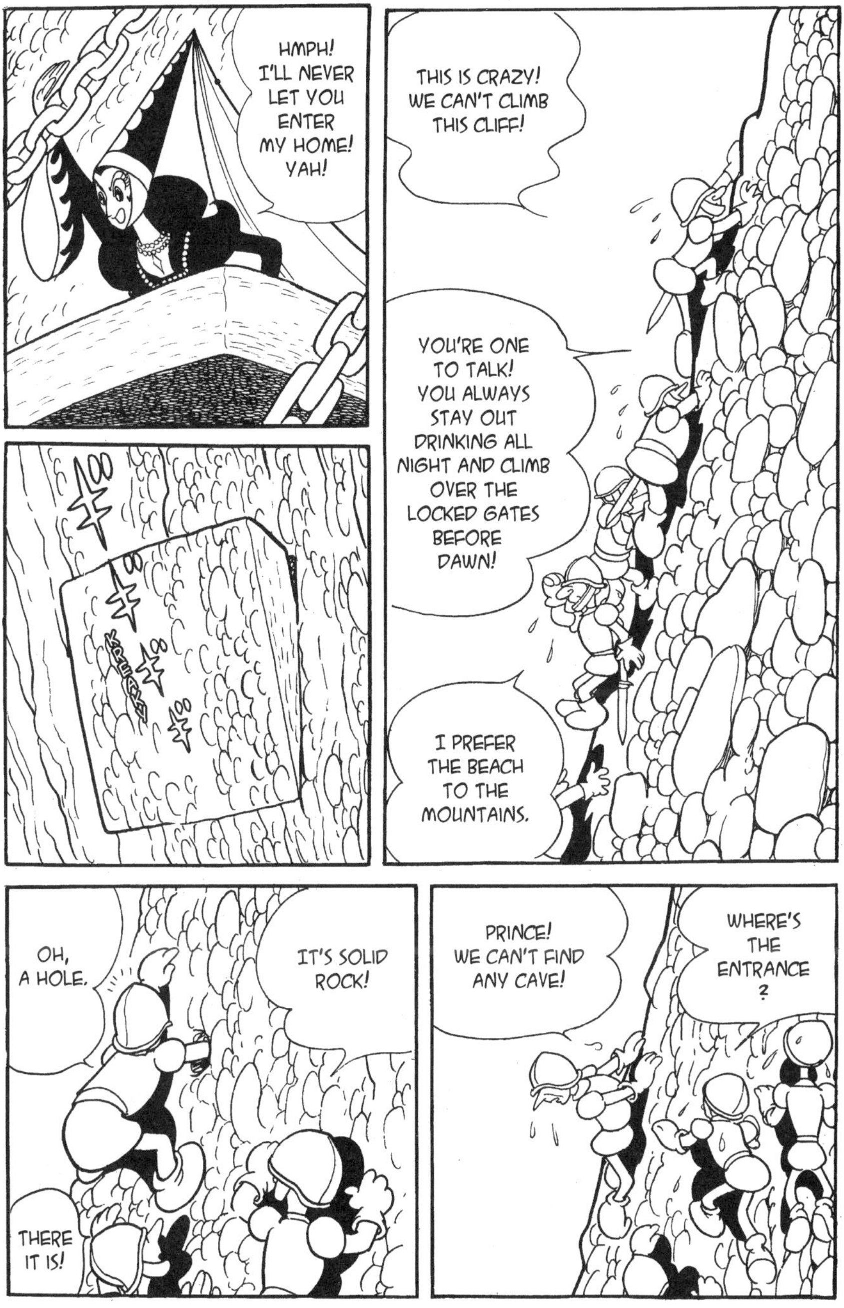
THIS IS CRAZY! WE CAN'T CLIMB THIS CLIFF!
YOU'RE ONE TO TALK! YOU ALWAYS STAY OUT DRINKING ALL NIGHT AND CLIMB OVER THE LOCKED GATES BEFORE DAWN!
I PREFER THE BEACH TO THE MOUNTAINS.
HMPH! I'LL NEVER LET YOU ENTER MY HOME! YAH!
KREAK
WHERE'S THE ENTRANCE ?
PRINCE! WE CAN'T FIND ANY CAVE!
IT'S SOLID ROCK!
OH, A HOLE.
THERE IT IS!

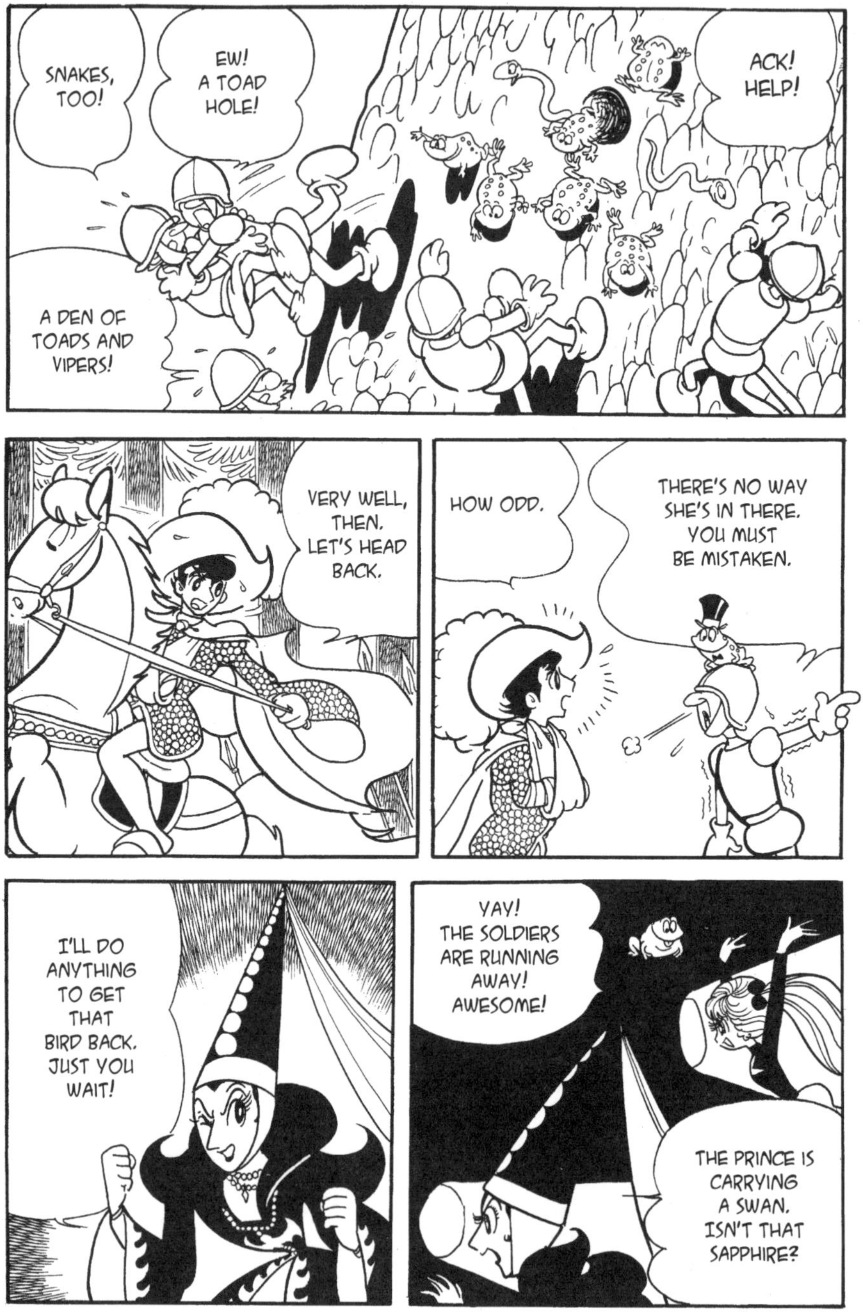
ACK! HELP!
EW! A TOAD HOLE!
SNAKES, TOO!
A DEN OF TOADS AND VIPERS!
THERE'S NO WAY SHE'S IN THERE. YOU MUST BE MISTAKEN.
HOW ODD.
VERY WELL, THEN. LET'S HEAD BACK.
YAY! THE SOLDIERS ARE RUNNING AWAY! AWESOME!
THE PRINCE IS CARRYING A SWAN. ISN'T THAT SAPPHIRE?
I'LL DO ANYTHING TO GET THAT BIRD BACK. JUST YOU WAIT!

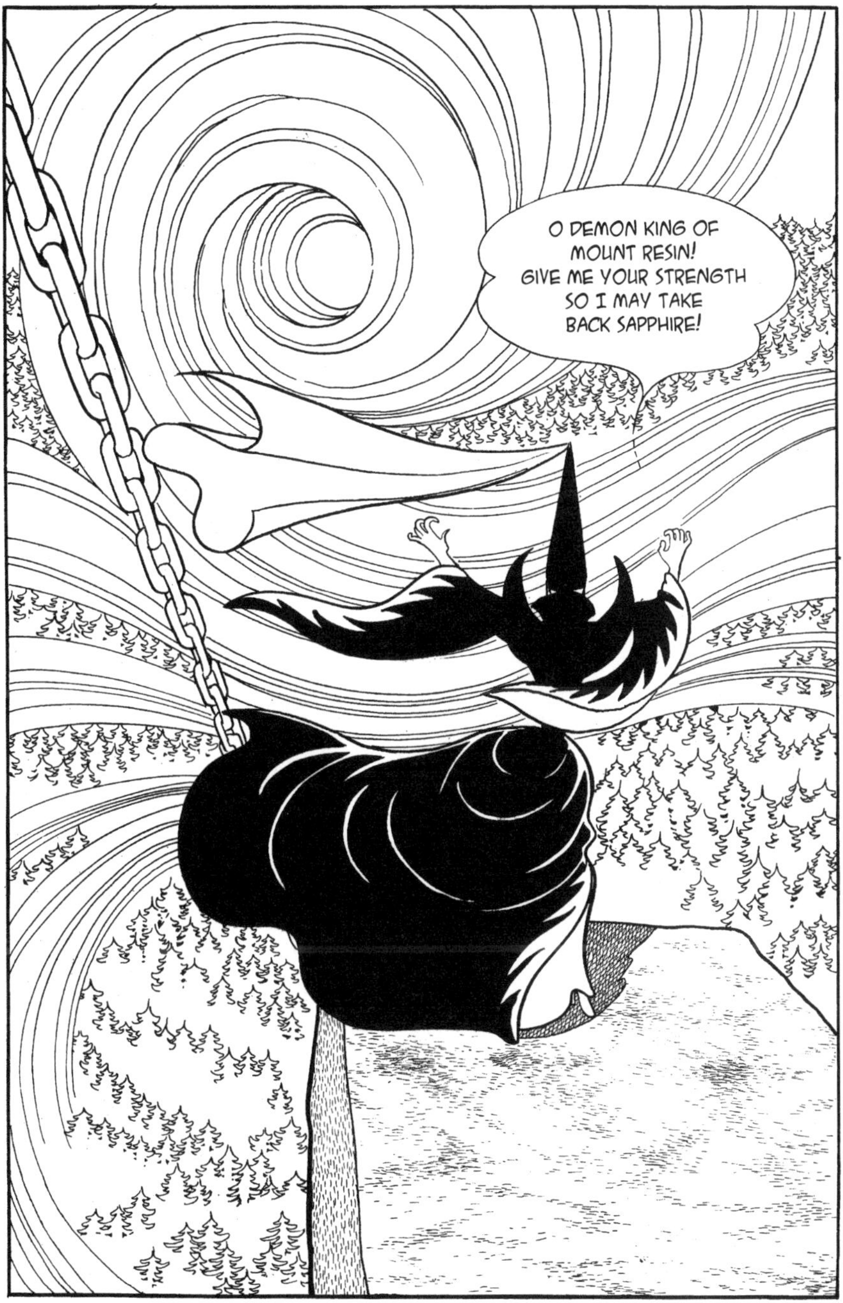
O DEMON KING OF MOUNT RESIN! GIVE ME YOUR STRENGTH SO I MAY TAKE BACK SAPPHIRE!

Chapter 13

Grieving Swan

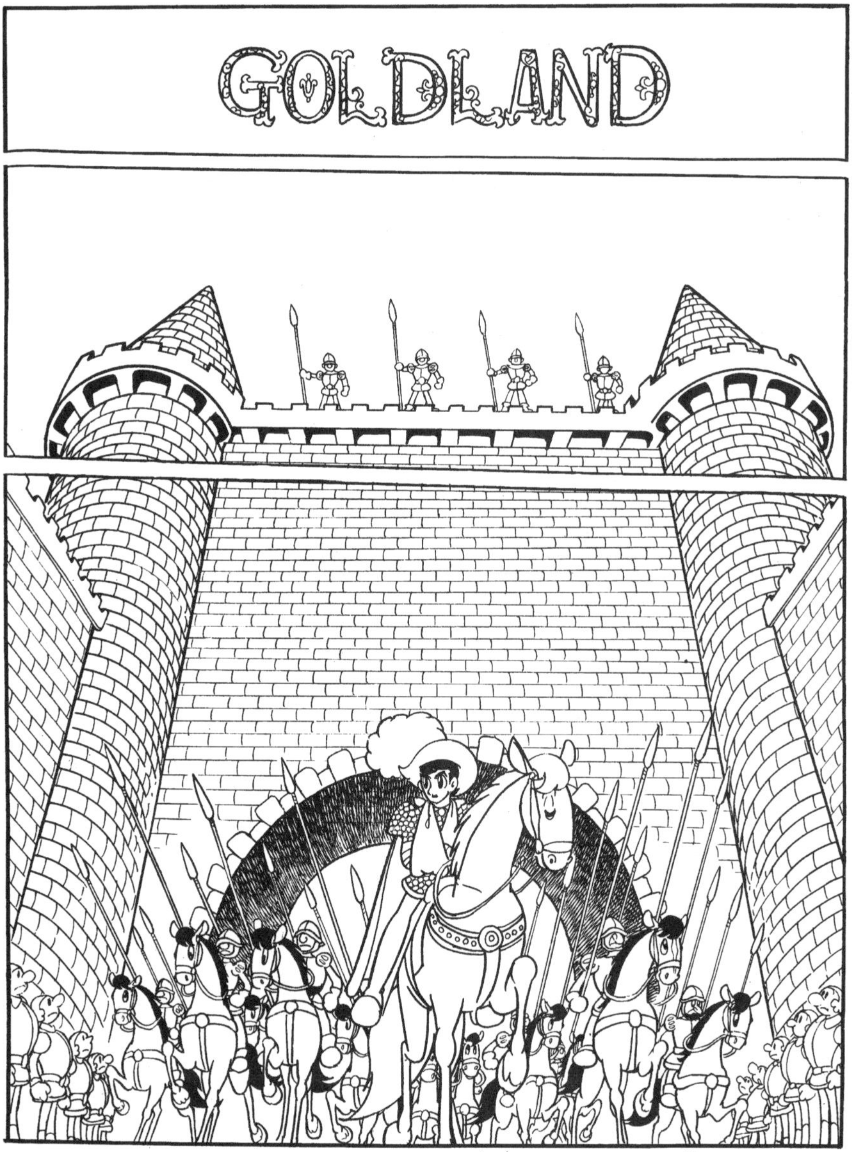
GOLDLAND

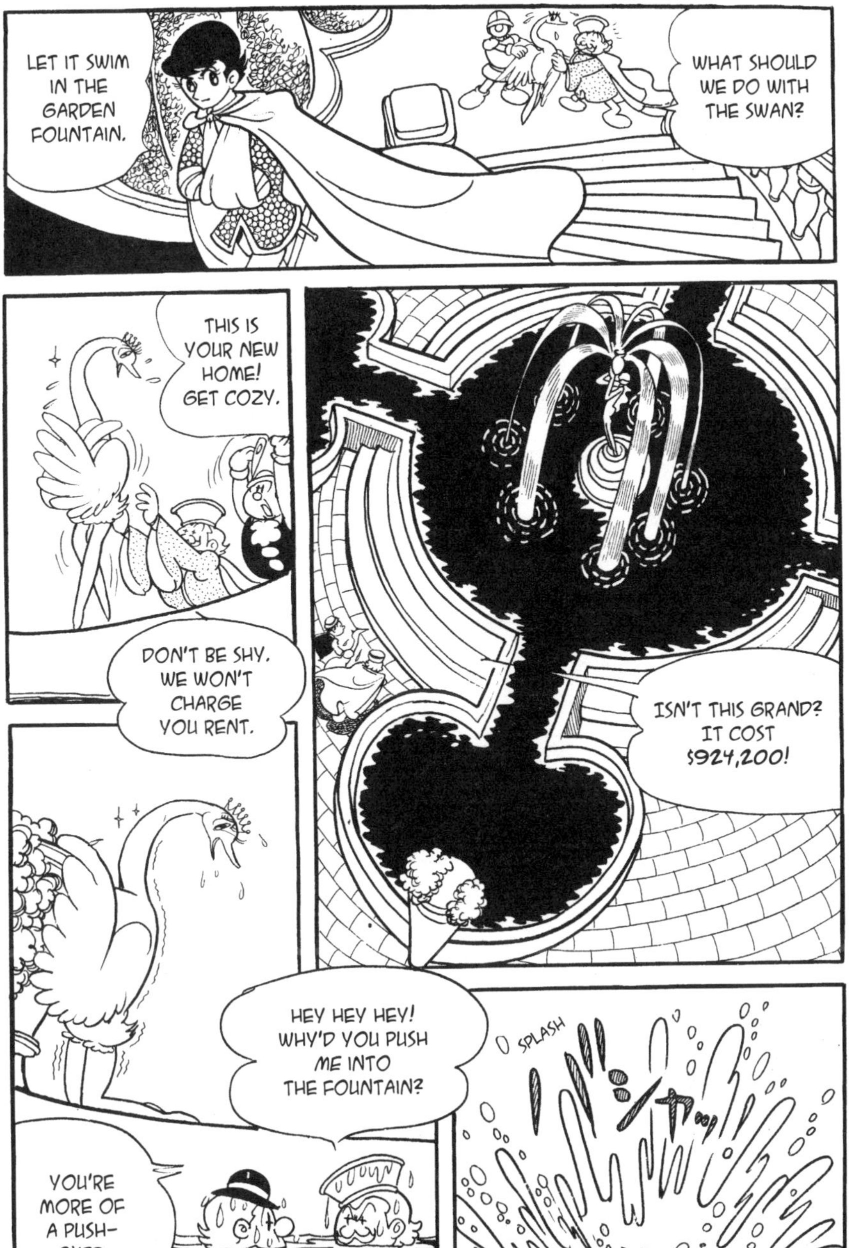

WHAT SHOULD WE DO WITH THE SWAN?
LET IT SWIM IN THE GARDEN FOUNTAIN.
ISN'T THIS GRAND? IT COST $924,200!
THIS IS YOUR NEW HOME! GET COZY.
DON'T BE SHY. WE WON'T CHARGE YOU RENT.
SPLASH
HEY HEY HEY! WHY'D YOU PUSH ME INTO THE FOUNTAIN?
YOU'RE MORE OF A PUSH-OVER.

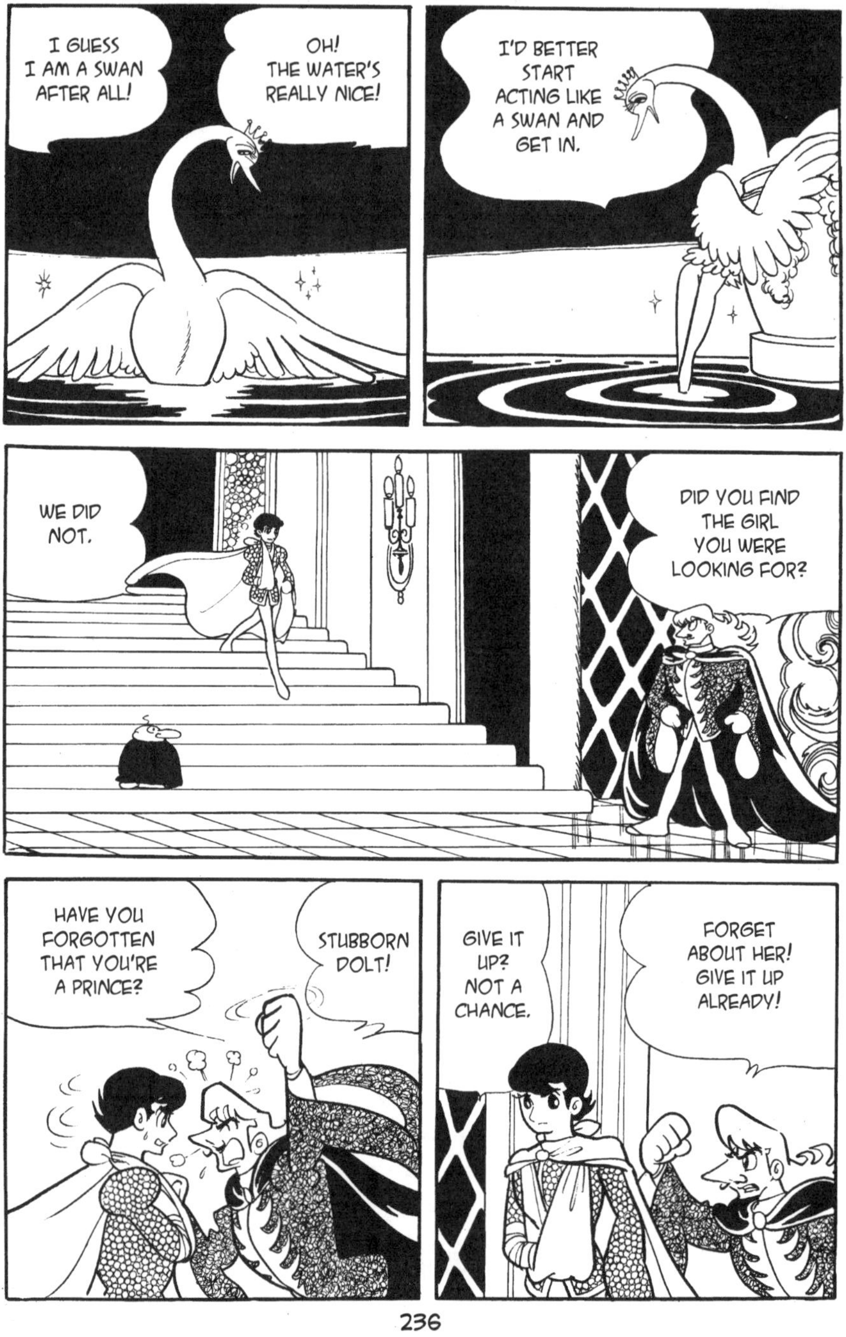
I'D BETTER START ACTING LIKE A SWAN AND GET IN.
OH! THE WATER'S REALLY NICE!
I GUESS I AM A SWAN AFTER ALL!
DID YOU FIND THE GIRL YOU WERE LOOKING FOR?
WE DID NOT.
FORGET ABOUT HER! GIVE IT UP ALREADY!
GIVE IT UP? NOT A CHANCE.
STUBBORN DOLT!
HAVE YOU FORGOTTEN THAT YOU'RE A PRINCE?

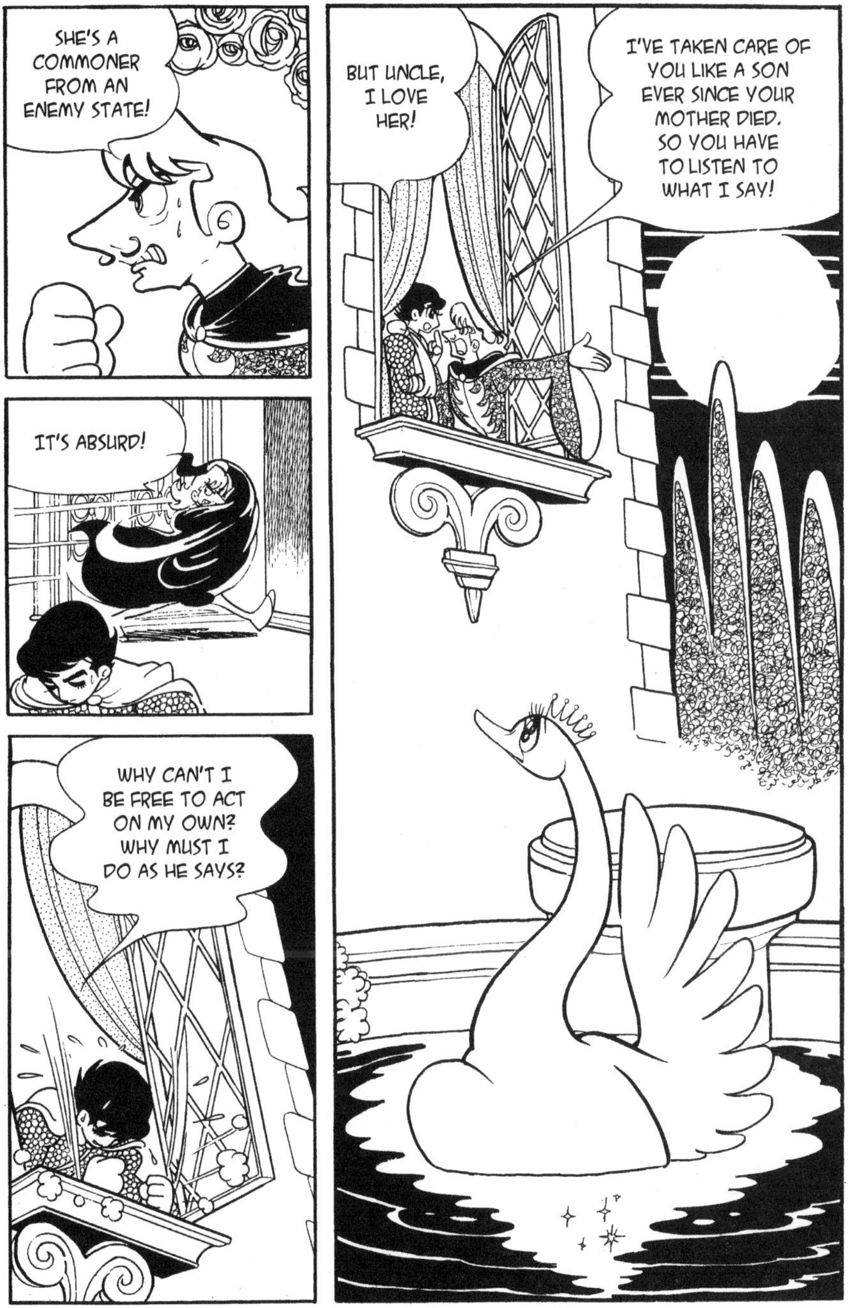
SHE'S A COMMONER FROM AN ENEMY STATE!
IT'S ABSURD!
WHY CAN'T I BE FREE TO ACT ON MY OWN? WHY MUST I DO AS HE SAYS?
BUT UNCLE, I LOVE HER!
I'VE TAKEN CARE OF YOU LIKE A SON EVER SINCE YOUR MOTHER DIED. SO YOU HAVE TO LISTEN TO WHAT I SAY!

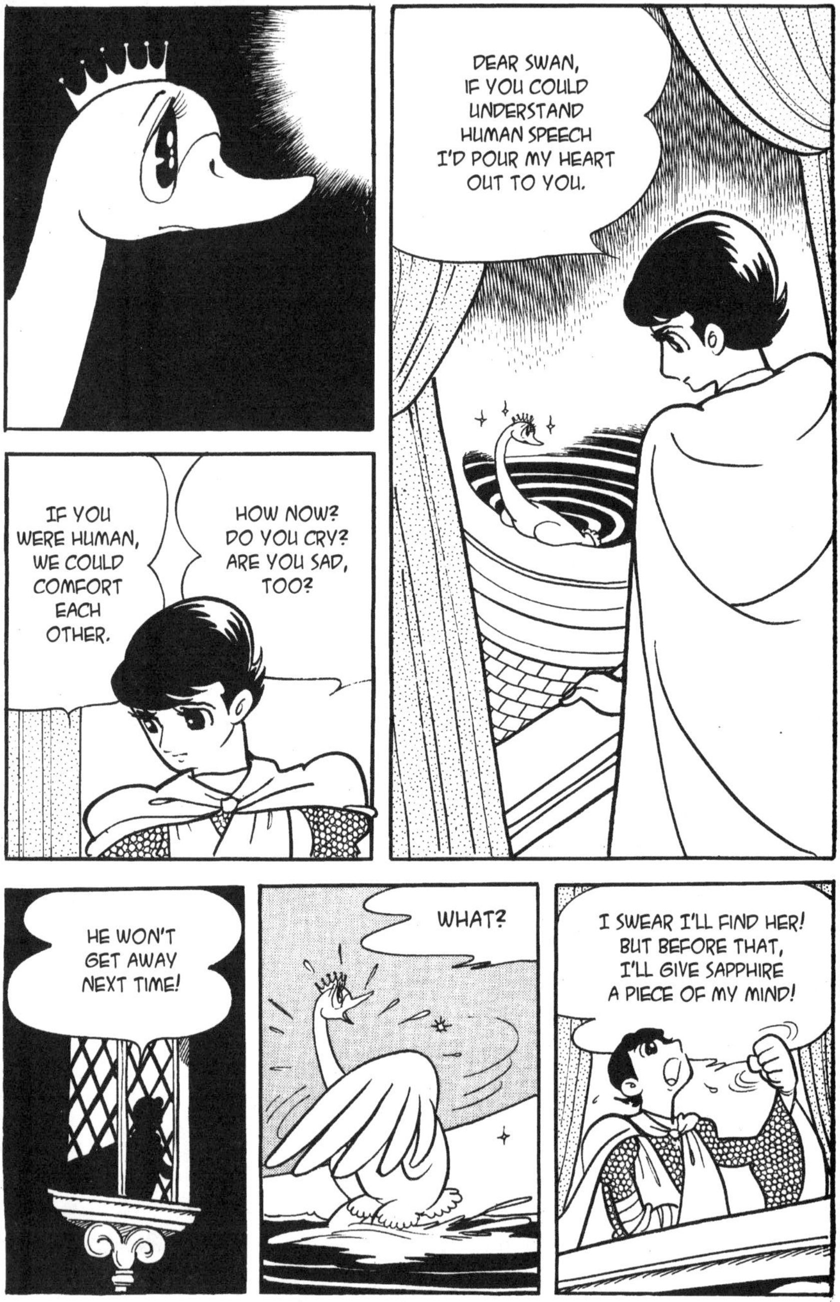
DEAR SWAN, IF YOU COULD UNDERSTAND HUMAN SPEECH I'D POUR MY HEART OUT TO YOU.
HOW NOW? DO YOU CRY? ARE YOU SAD, TOO?
IF YOU WERE HUMAN, WE COULD COMFORT EACH OTHER.
I SWEAR I'LL FIND HER! BUT BEFORE THAT, I'LL GIVE SAPPHIRE A PIECE OF MY MIND!
WHAT?
HE WON'T GET AWAY NEXT TIME!

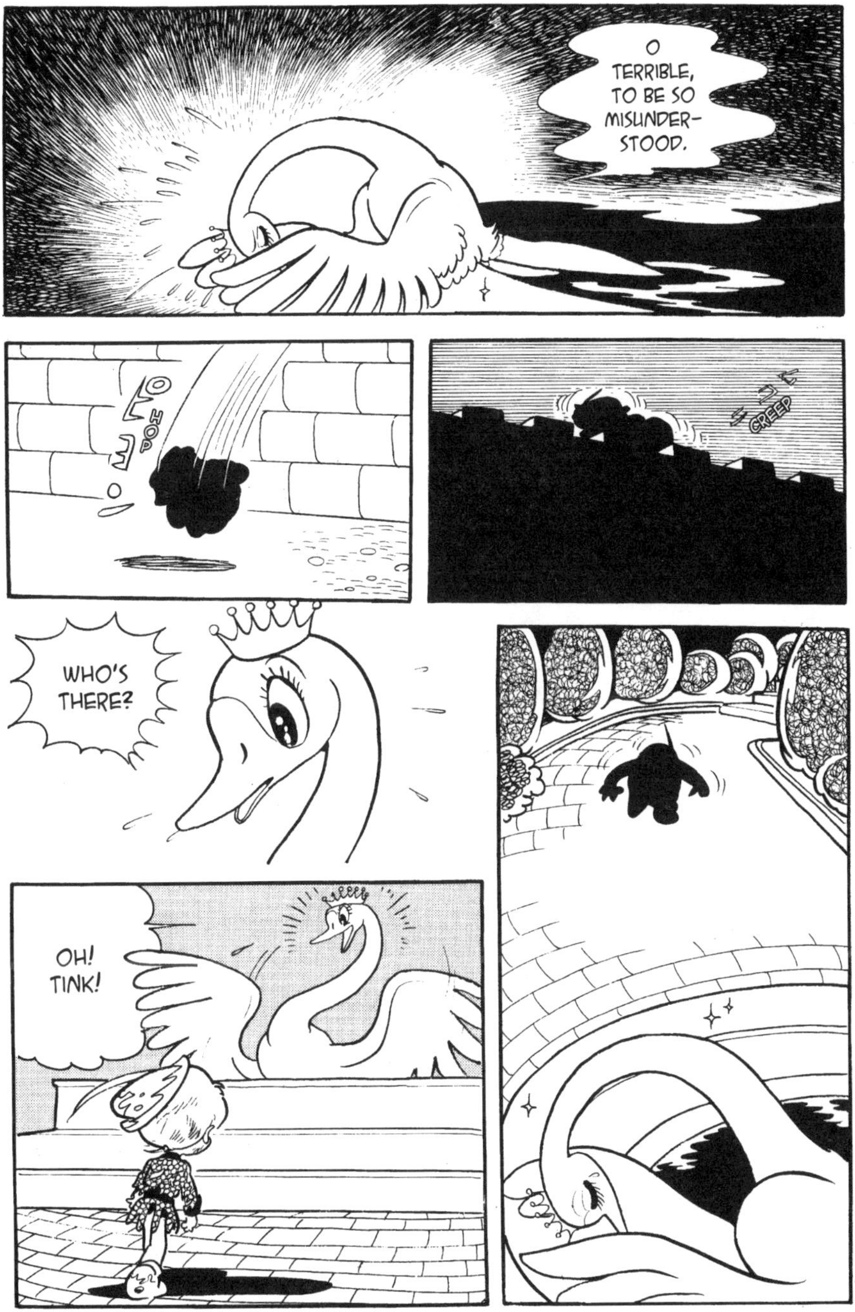
O TERRIBLE, TO BE SO MISUNDERSTOOD.
CREEP
HOP
WHO'S THERE?
OH! TINK!

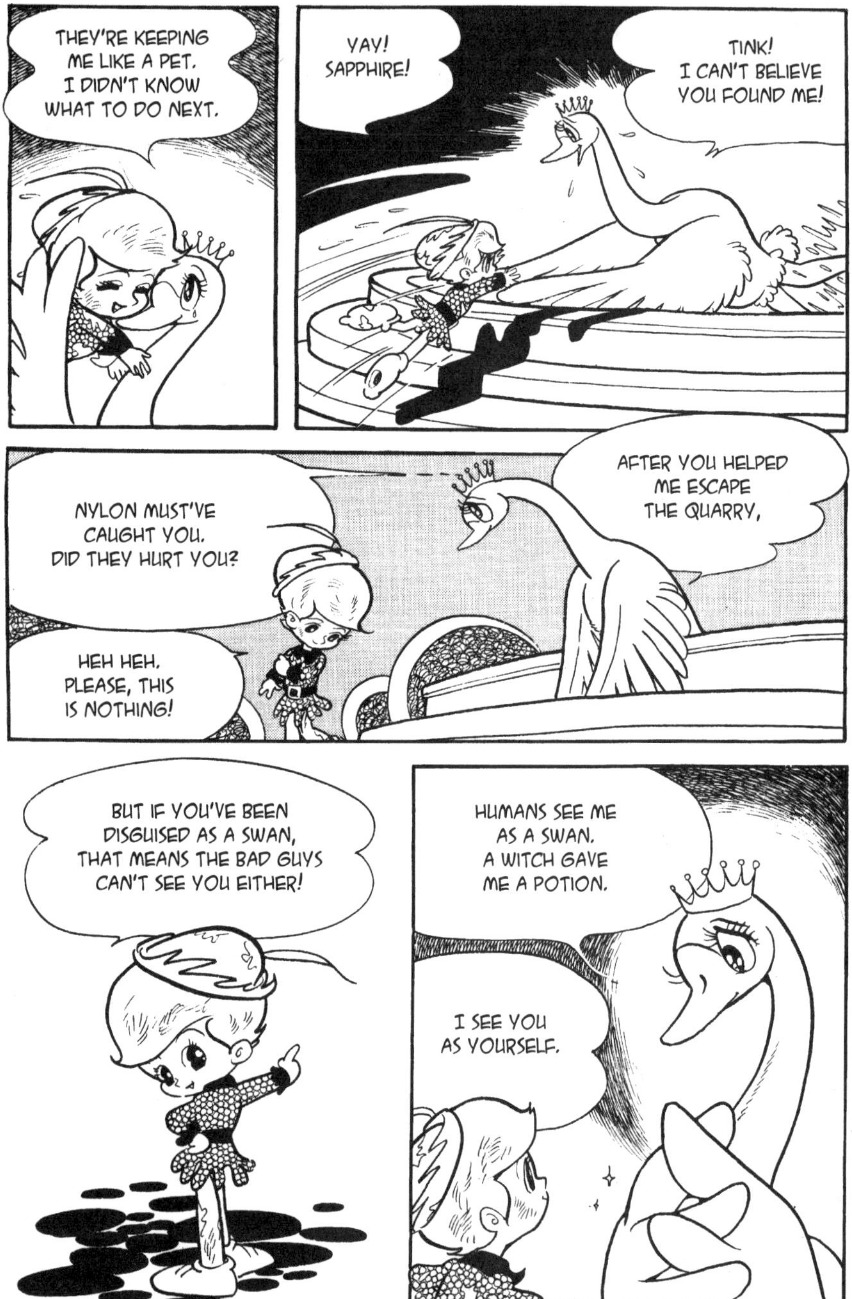
TINK! I CAN'T BELIEVE YOU FOUND ME!
YAY! SAPPHIRE!
THEY'RE KEEPING ME LIKE A PET. I DIDN'T KNOW WHAT TO DO NEXT.
AFTER YOU HELPED ME ESCAPE THE QUARRY,
NYLON MUST'VE CAUGHT YOU. DID THEY HURT YOU?
HEH HEH. PLEASE, THIS IS NOTHING!
HUMANS SEE ME AS A SWAN. A WITCH GAVE ME A POTION.
I SEE YOU AS YOURSELF.
BUT IF YOU'VE BEEN DISGUISED AS A SWAN, THAT MEANS THE BAD GUYS CAN'T SEE YOU EITHER!

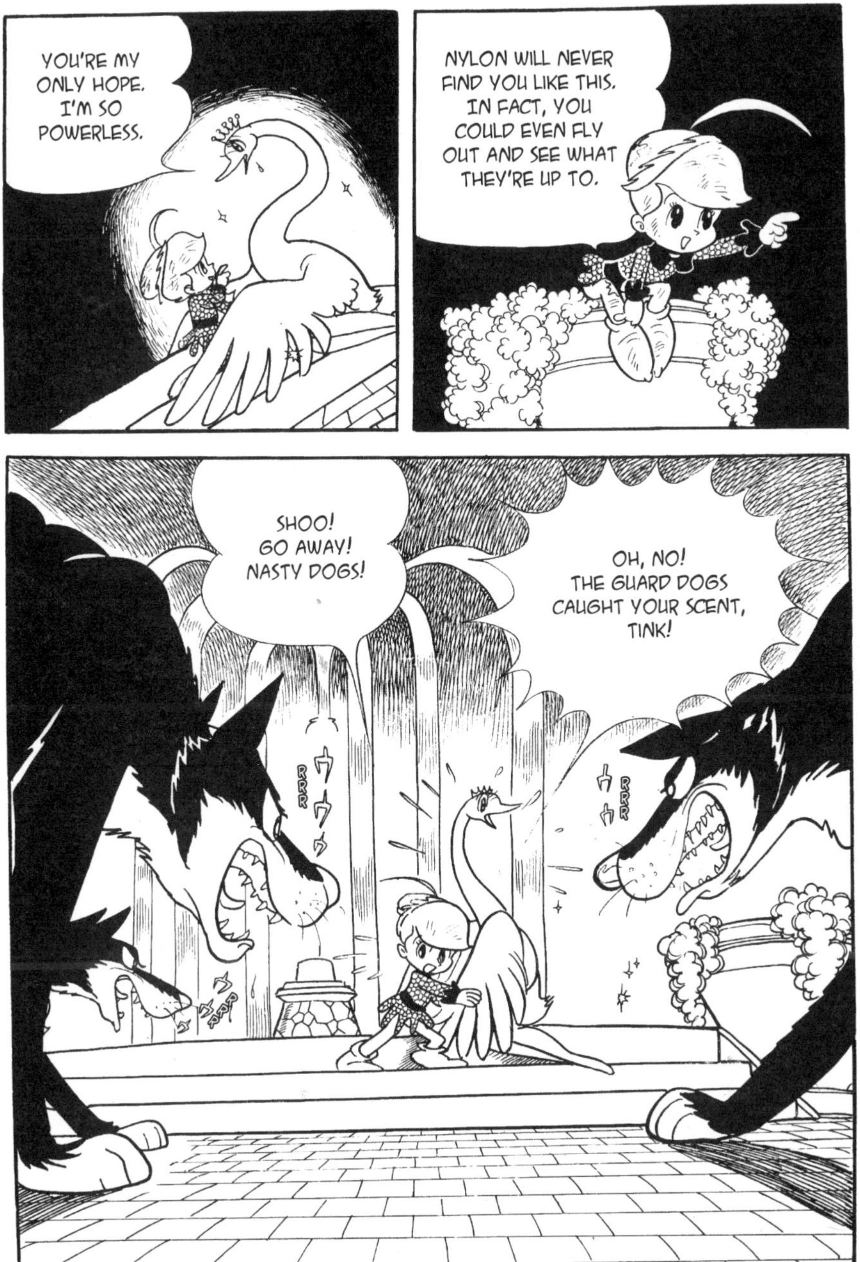
NYLON WILL NEVER FIND YOU LIKE THIS. IN FACT, YOU COULD EVEN FLY OUT AND SEE WHAT THEY'RE UP TO.
YOU'RE MY ONLY HOPE. I'M SO POWERLESS.
OH, NO! THE GUARD DOGS CAUGHT YOUR SCENT, TINK!
RRR
SHOO! GO AWAY! NASTY DOGS!
RRR
RRR

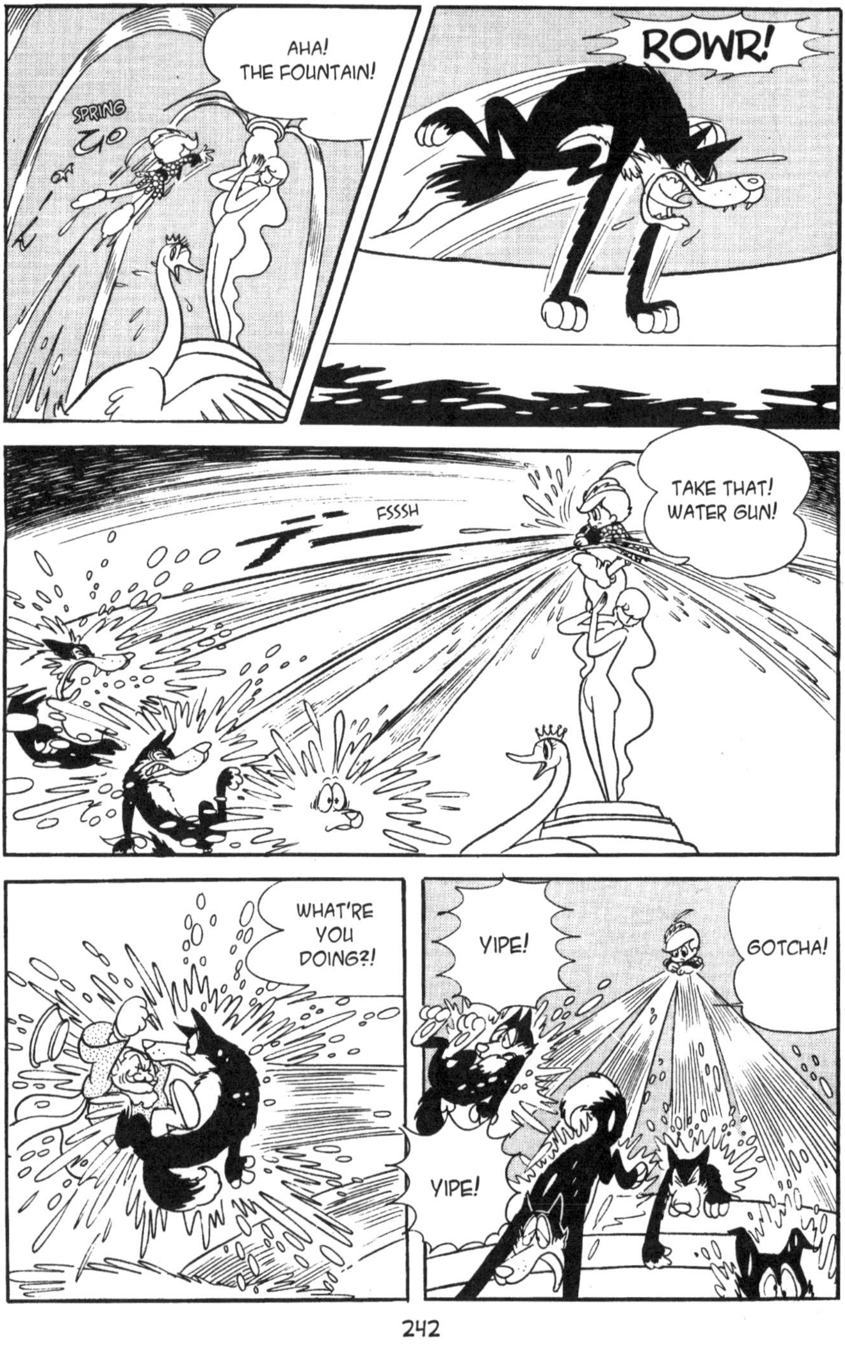
ROWR!
AHA! THE FOUNTAIN!
SPRING
TAKE THAT! WATER GUN!
FSSSH
GOTCHA!
YIPE!
YIPE!
WHAT'RE YOU DOING?!

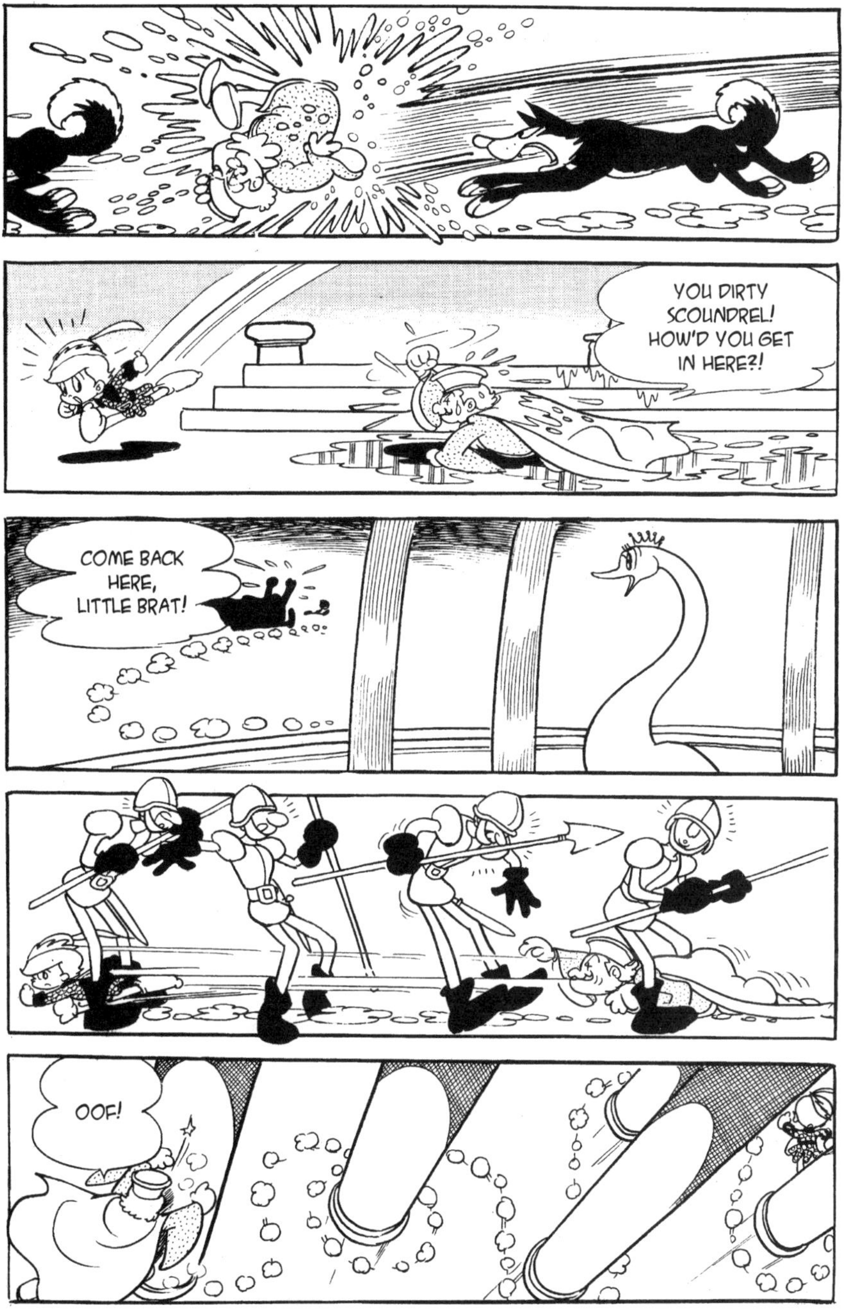
YOU DIRTY SCOUNDREL! HOW'D YOU GET IN HERE?!
COME BACK HERE, LITTLE BRAT!
OOF!

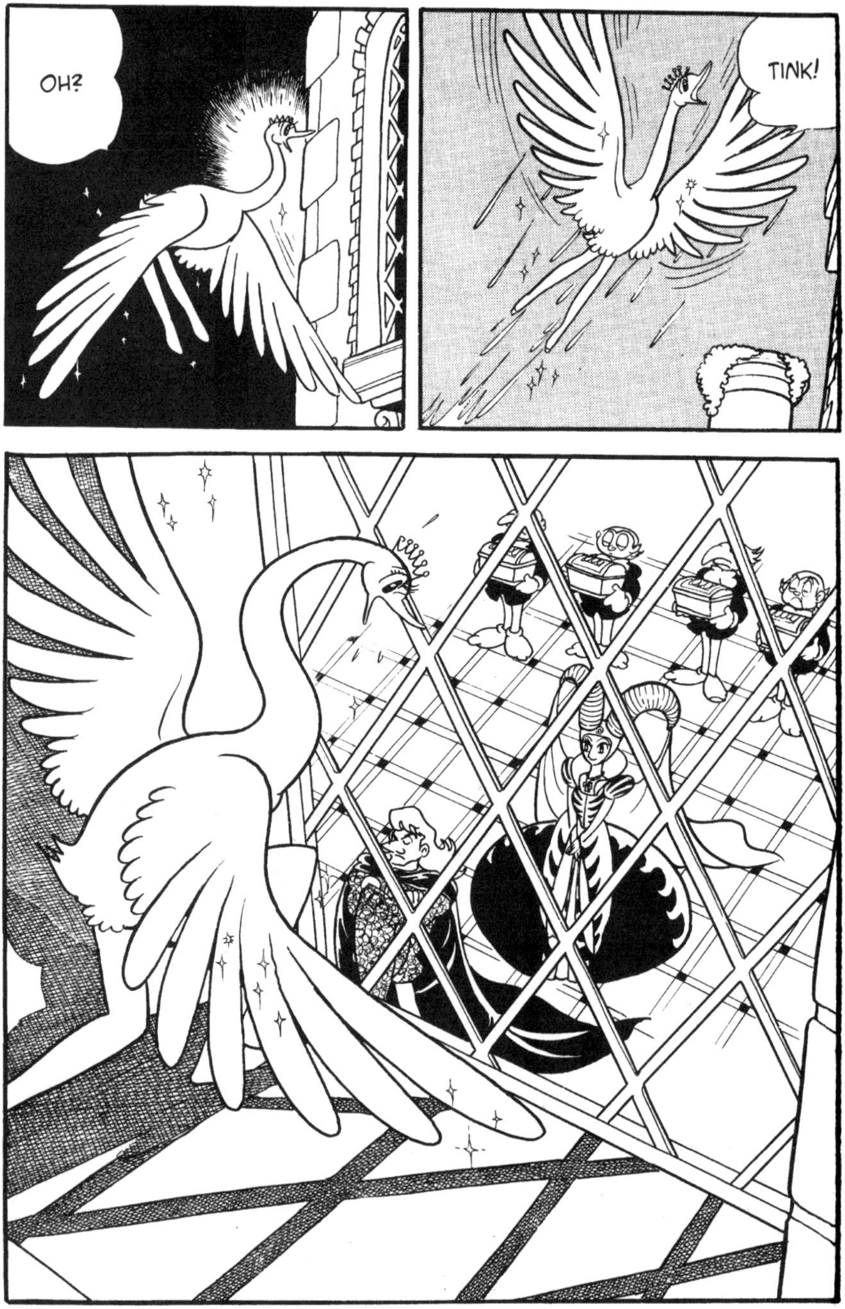
TINK!
OH?

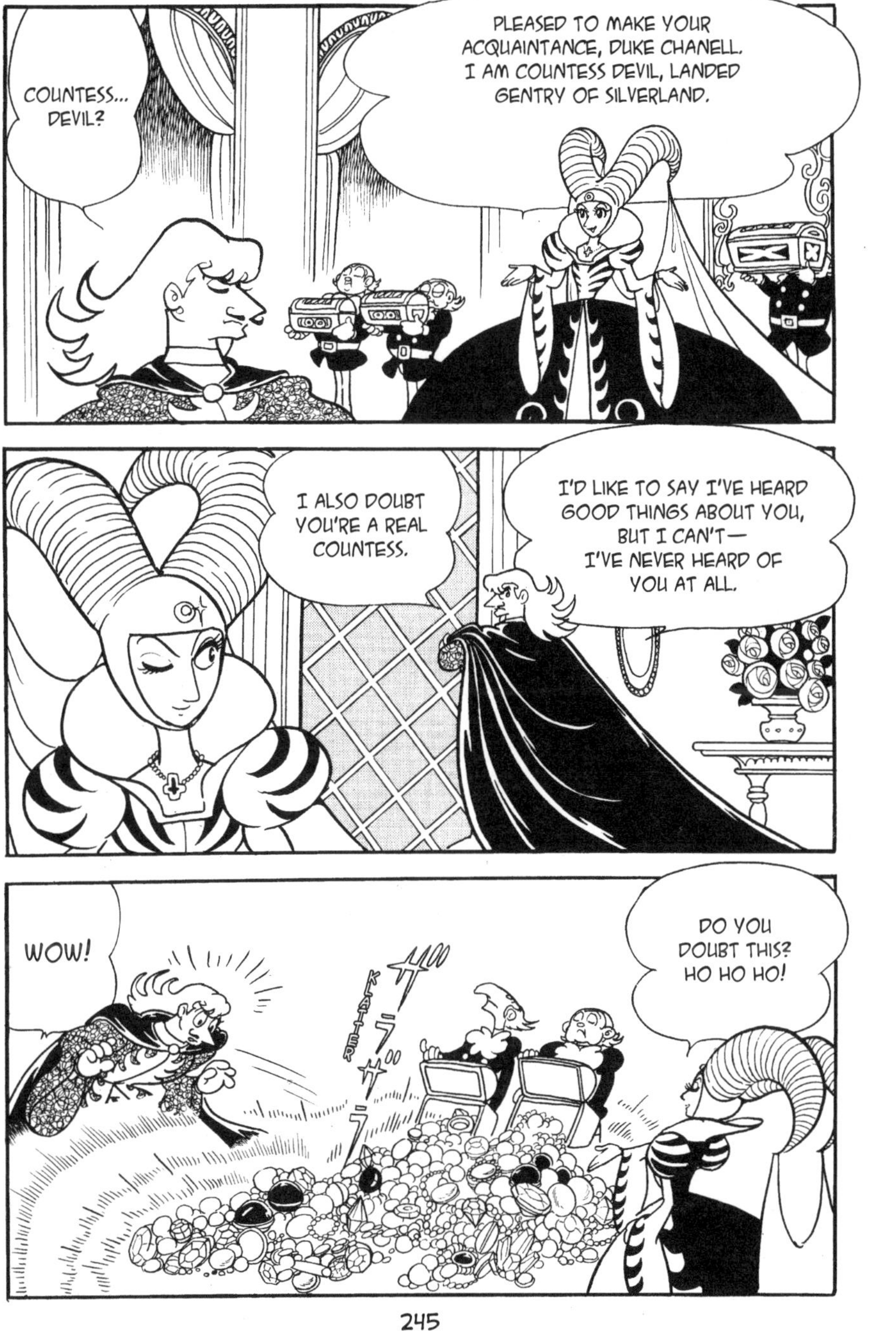
PLEASED TO MAKE YOUR ACQUAINTANCE, DUKE CHANELL. I AM COUNTESS DEVIL, LANDED GENTRY OF SILVERLAND.
COUNTESS... DEVIL?
I'D LIKE TO SAY I'VE HEARD GOOD THINGS ABOUT YOU, BUT I CAN'T— I'VE NEVER HEARD OF YOU AT ALL.
I ALSO DOUBT YOU'RE A REAL COUNTESS.
DO YOU DOUBT THIS? HO HO HO!
KLATTER
WOW!

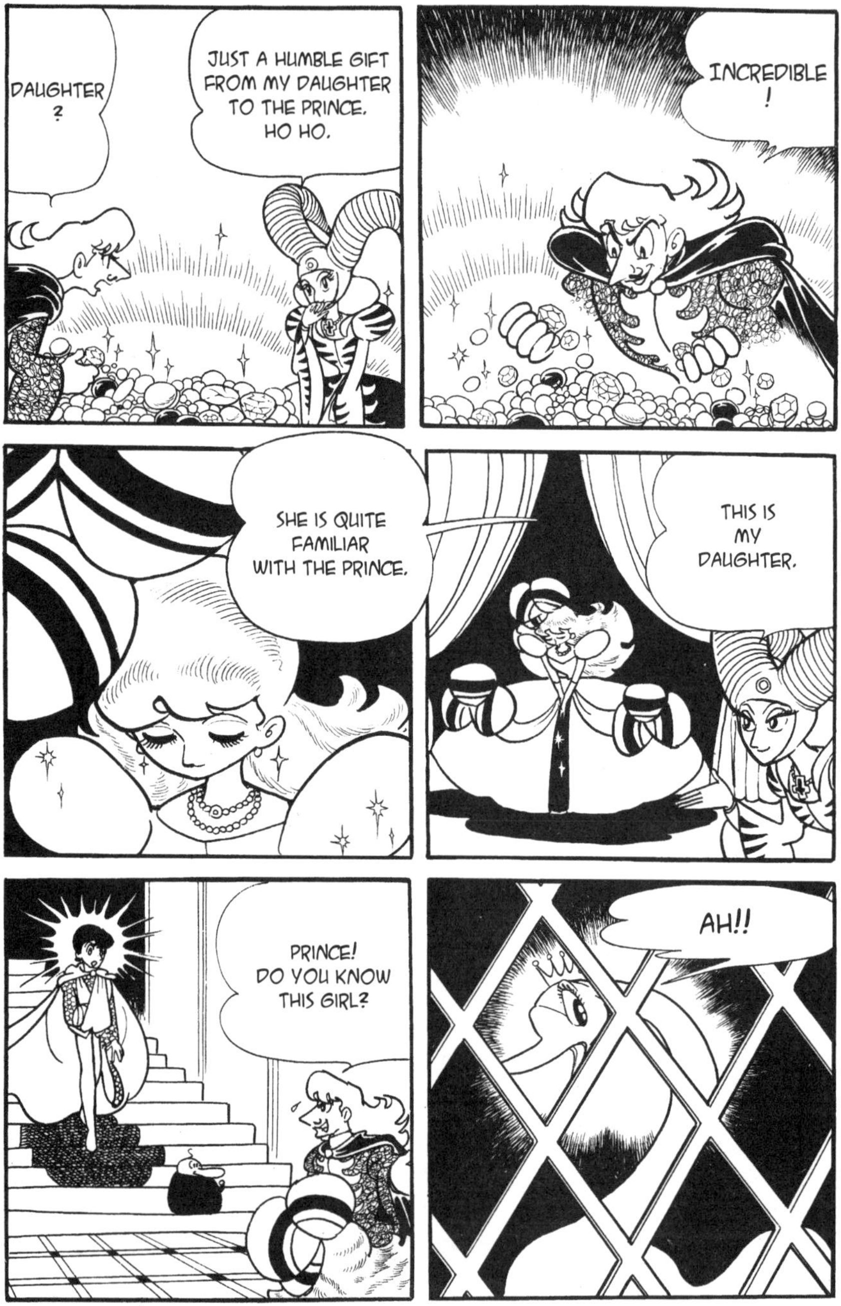
INCREDIBLE!
JUST A HUMBLE GIFT FROM MY DAUGHTER TO THE PRINCE. HO HO.
DAUGHTER?
THIS IS MY DAUGHTER.
SHE IS QUITE FAMILIAR WITH THE PRINCE.
AH!!
PRINCE! DO YOU KNOW THIS GIRL?

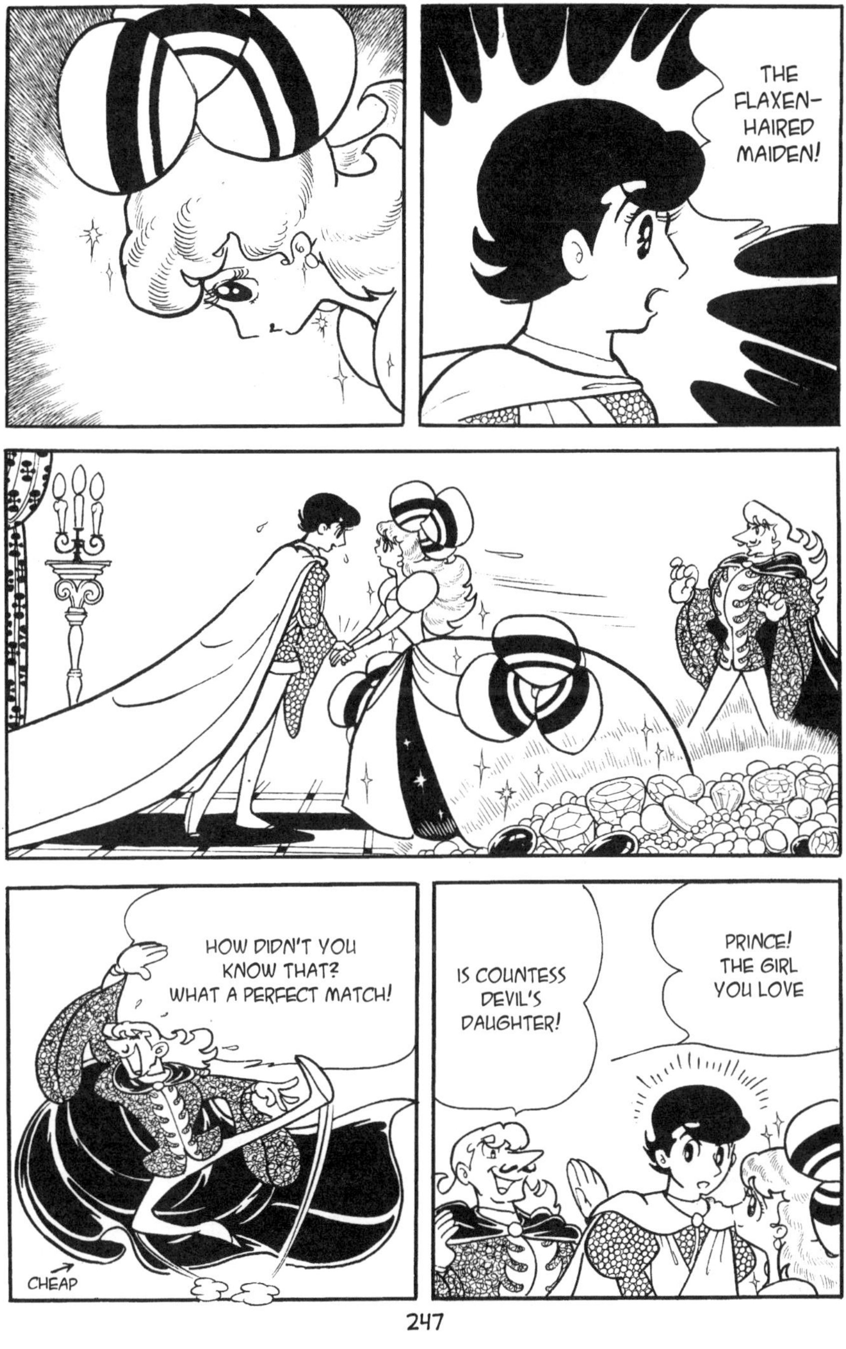
THE FLAXEN-HAIRED MAIDEN!
PRINCE! THE GIRL YOU LOVE
IS COUNTESS DEVIL'S DAUGHTER!
HOW DIDN'T YOU KNOW THAT? WHAT A PERFECT MATCH!
CHEAP

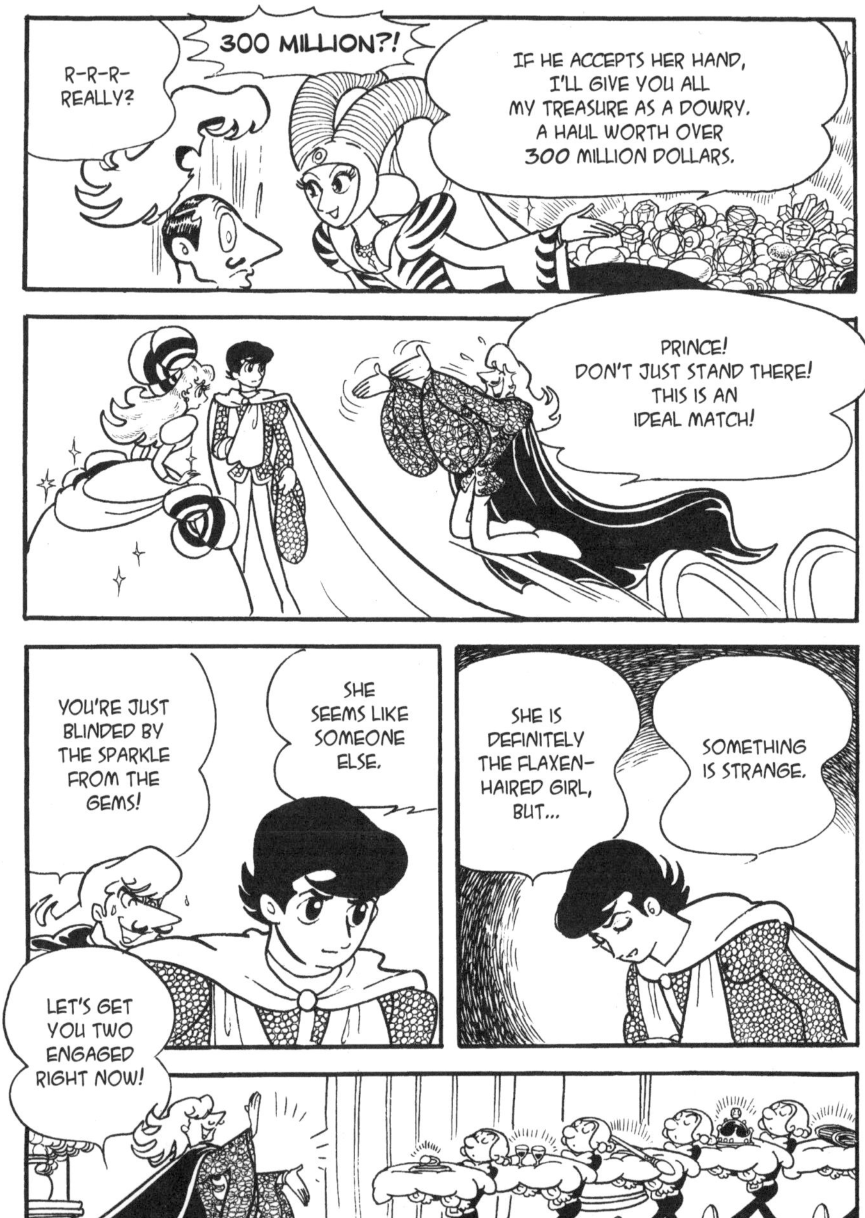
IF HE ACCEPTS HER HAND, I'LL GIVE YOU ALL MY TREASURE AS A DOWRY. A HAUL WORTH OVER 300 MILLION DOLLARS.
300 MILLION?!
R-R-R- REALLY?
PRINCE! DON'T JUST STAND THERE! THIS IS AN IDEAL MATCH!
SOMETHING IS STRANGE.
SHE IS DEFINITELY THE FLAXEN-HAIRED GIRL, BUT...
SHE SEEMS LIKE SOMEONE ELSE.
YOU'RE JUST BLINDED BY THE SPARKLE FROM THE GEMS!
LET'S GET YOU TWO ENGAGED RIGHT NOW!

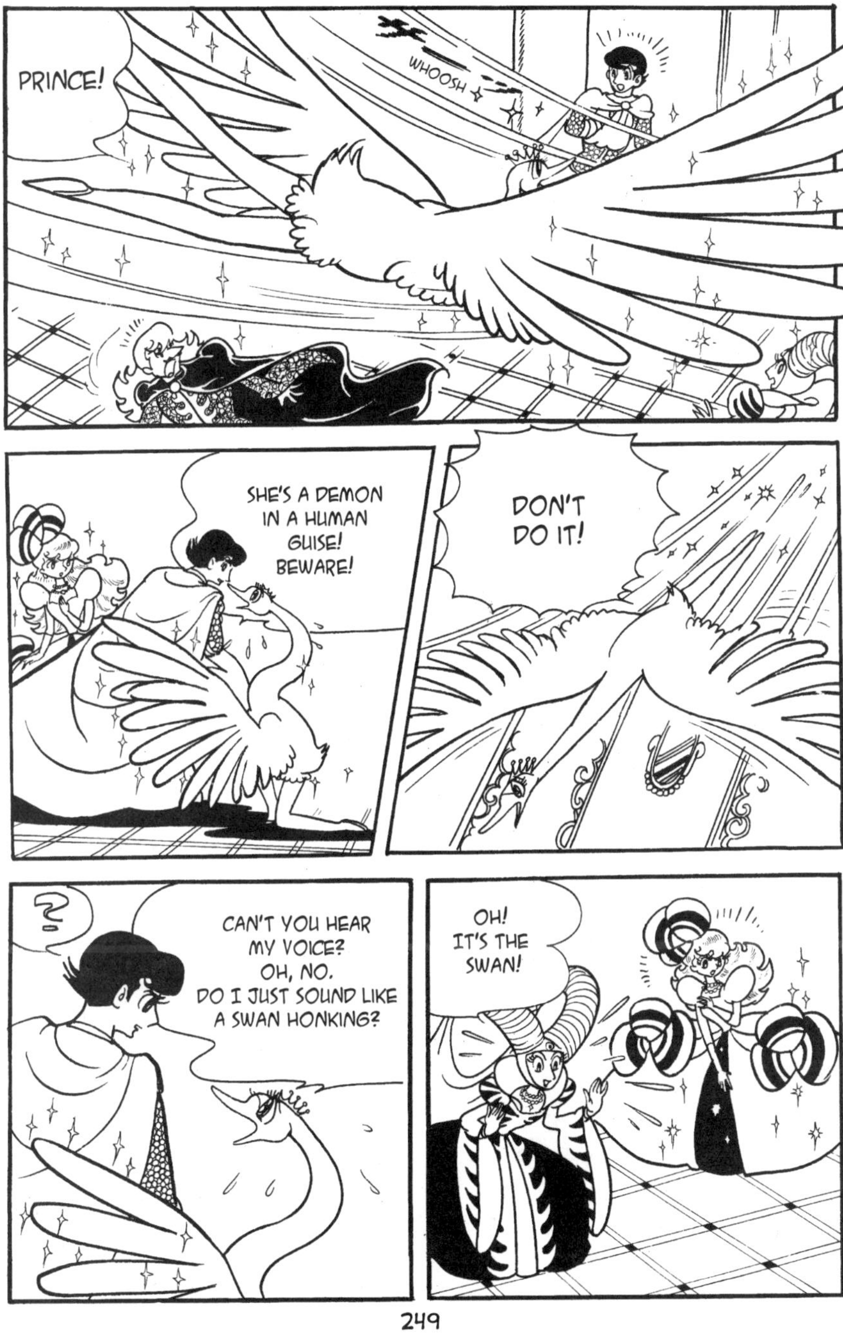
WHOOSH
PRINCE!
DON'T DO IT!
SHE'S A DEMON IN A HUMAN GUISE! BEWARE!
OH! IT'S THE SWAN!
CAN'T YOU HEAR MY VOICE? OH, NO. DO I JUST SOUND LIKE A SWAN HONKING?
?

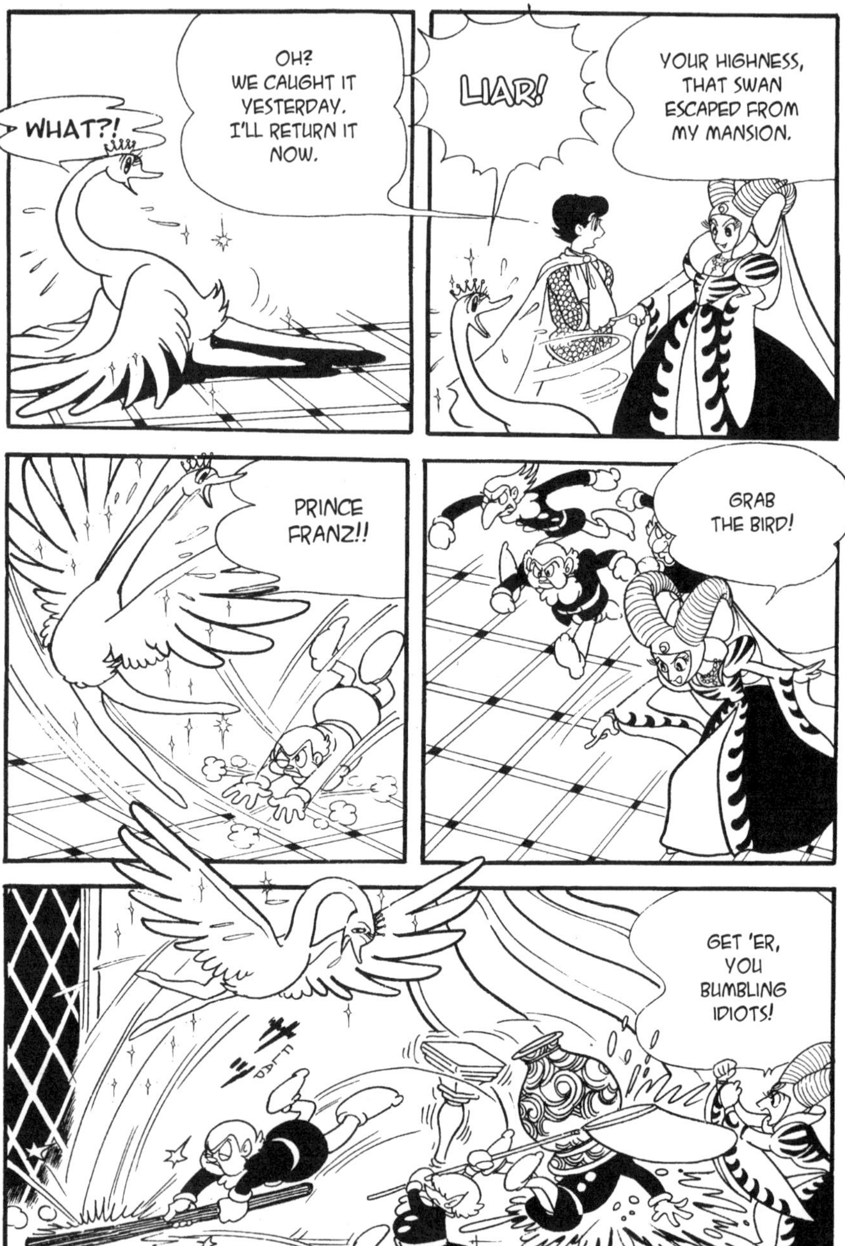
YOUR HIGHNESS, THAT SWAN ESCAPED FROM MY MANSION.
LIAR!
OH? WE CAUGHT IT YESTERDAY. I'LL RETURN IT NOW.
WHAT?!
GRAB THE BIRD!
PRINCE FRANZ!!
GET 'ER, YOU BUMBLING IDIOTS!

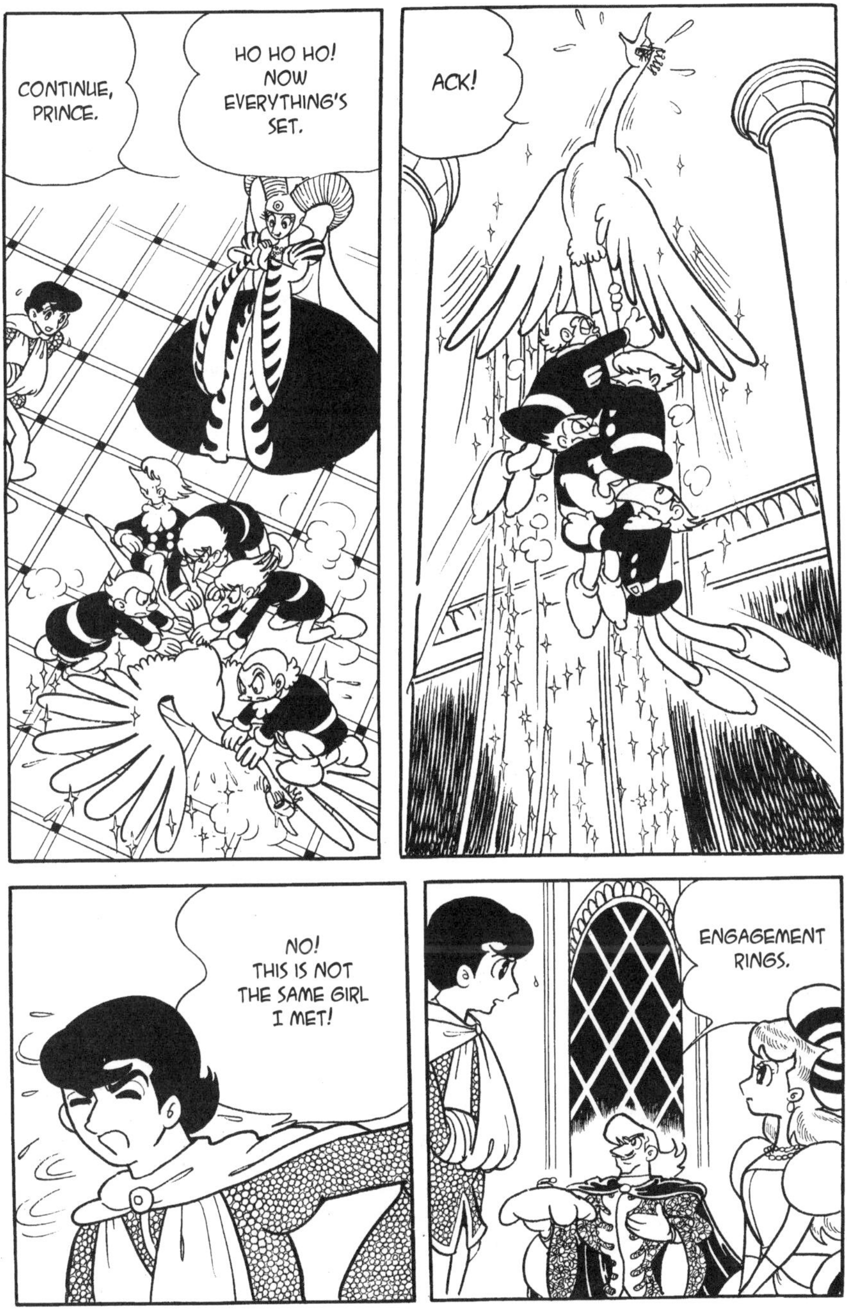
ACK!
HO HO HO! NOW EVERYTHING'S SET.
CONTINUE, PRINCE.
ENGAGEMENT RINGS.
NO! THIS IS NOT THE SAME GIRL I MET!

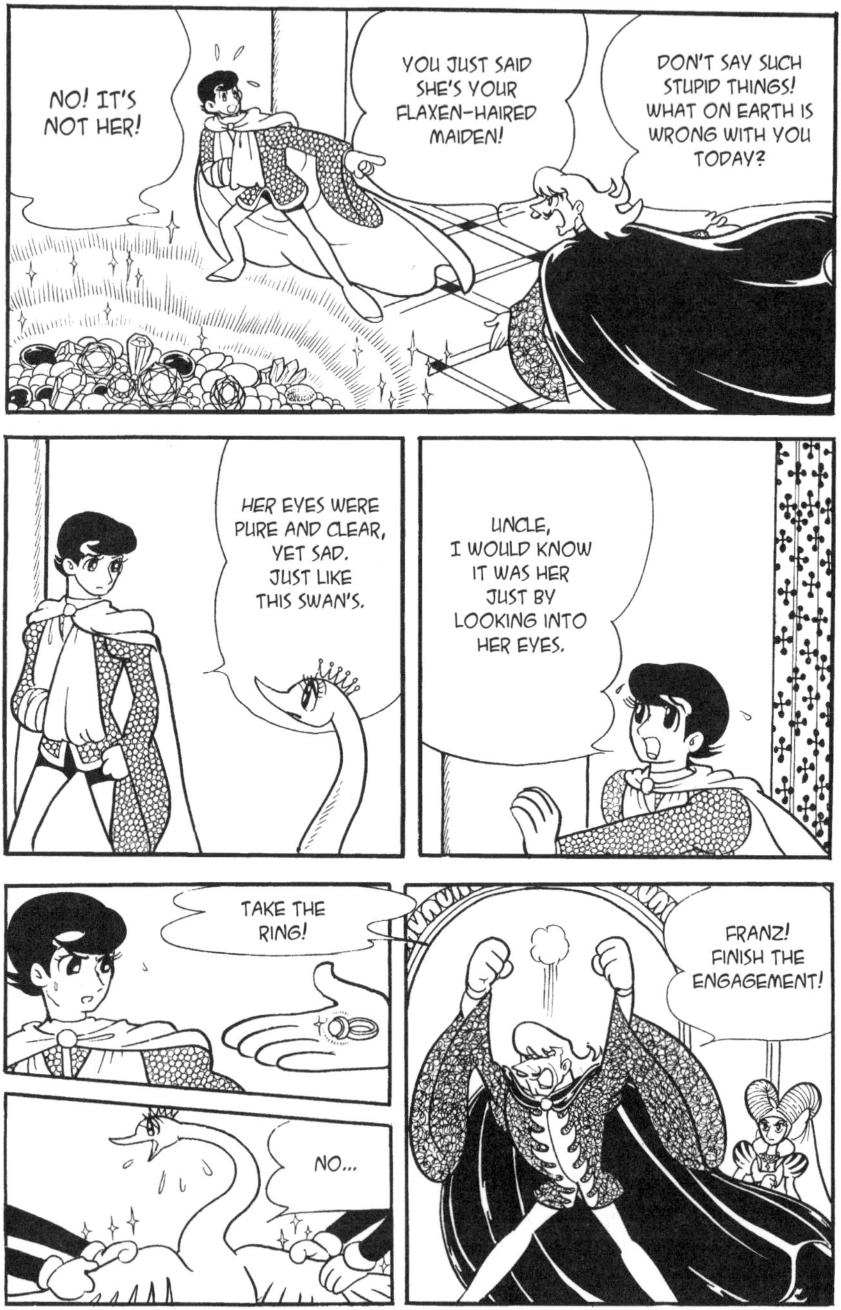
DON'T SAY SUCH STUPID THINGS! WHAT ON EARTH IS WRONG WITH YOU TODAY?
YOU JUST SAID SHE'S YOUR FLAXEN-HAIRED MAIDEN!
NO! IT'S NOT HER!
UNCLE, I WOULD KNOW IT WAS HER JUST BY LOOKING INTO HER EYES.
HER EYES WERE PURE AND CLEAR, YET SAD. JUST LIKE THIS SWAN'S.
FRANZ! FINISH THE ENGAGEMENT!
TAKE THE RING!
NO...

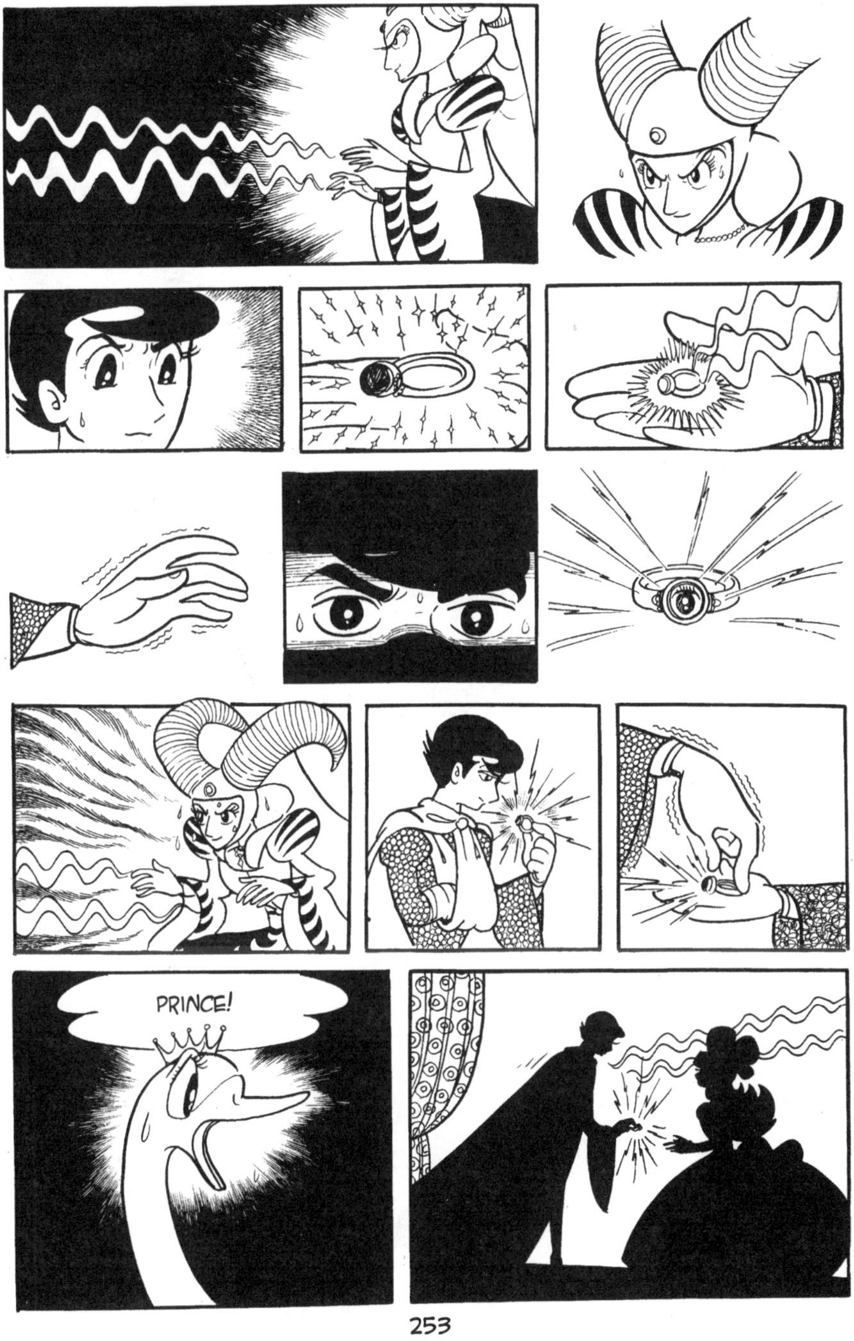
PRINCE!

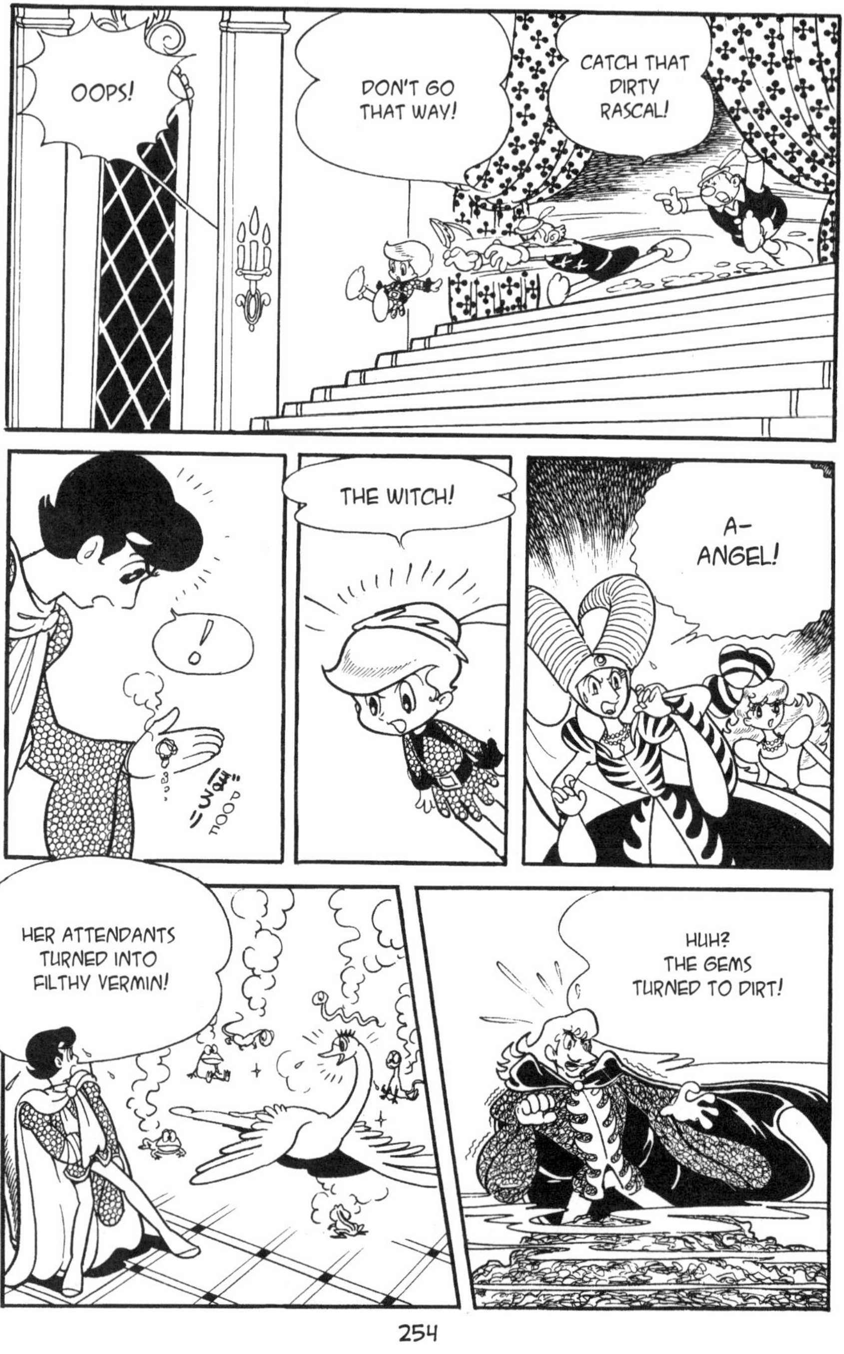
CATCH THAT DIRTY RASCAL!
DON'T GO THAT WAY!
OOPS!
A- ANGEL!
THE WITCH!
!
HUH? THE GEMS TURNED TO DIRT!
HER ATTENDANTS TURNED INTO FILTHY VERMIN!

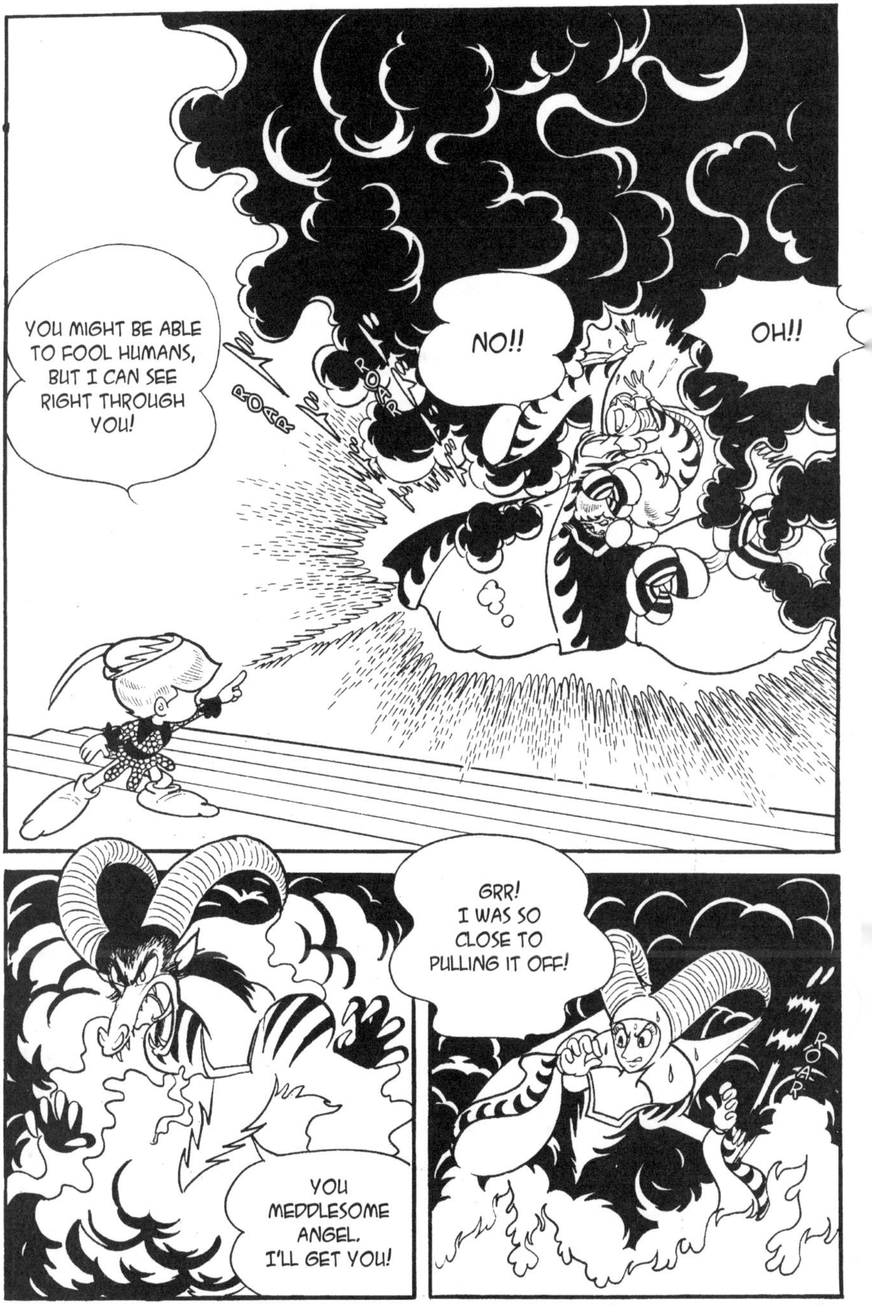
OH!!
NO!!
ROAR
ROAR
YOU MIGHT BE ABLE TO FOOL HUMANS, BUT I CAN SEE RIGHT THROUGH YOU!
ROAR
GRR! I WAS SO CLOSE TO PULLING IT OFF!
YOU MEDDLESOME ANGEL. I'LL GET YOU!

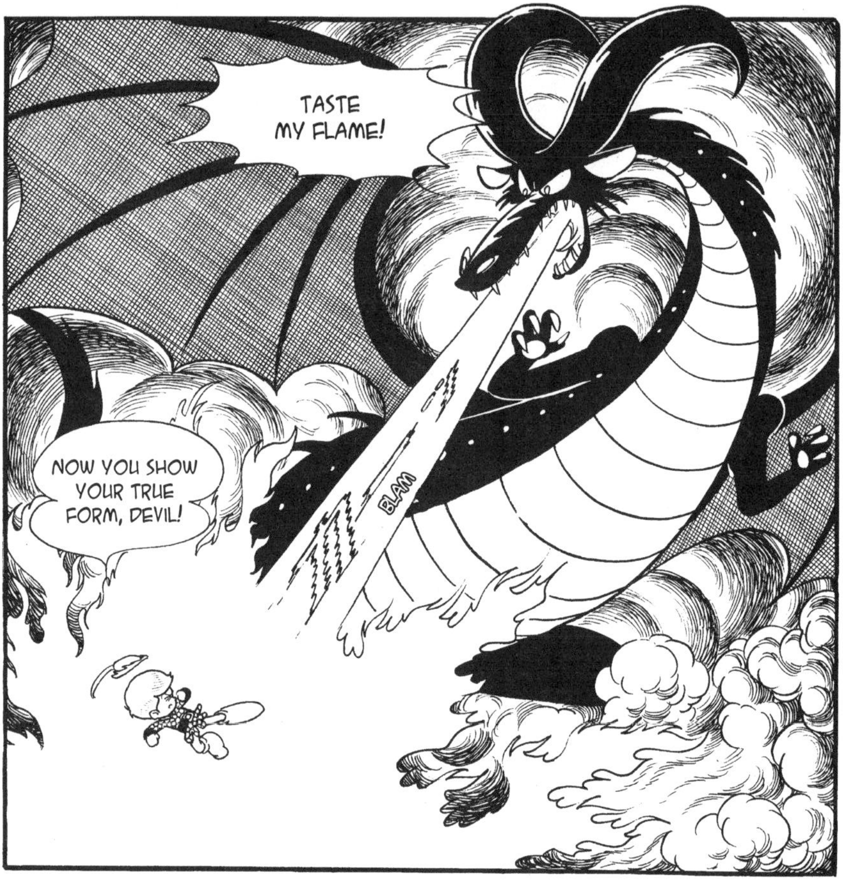
TASTE MY FLAME!
BLAM
NOW YOU SHOW YOUR TRUE FORM, DEVIL!

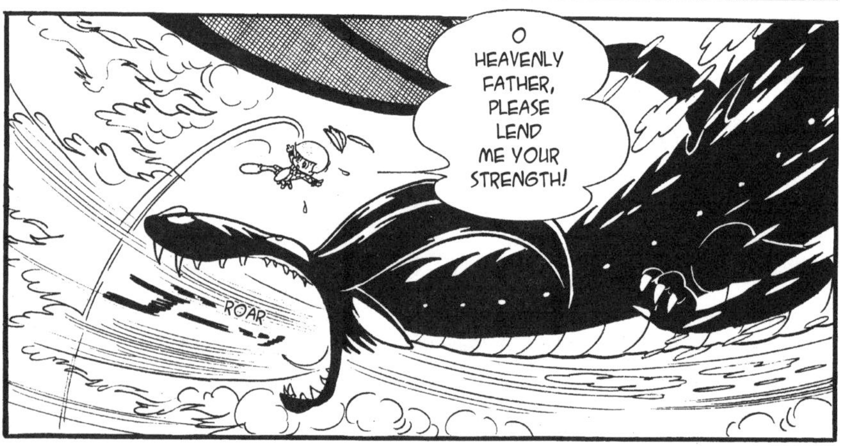
O HEAVENLY FATHER, PLEASE LEND ME YOUR STRENGTH!
ROAR

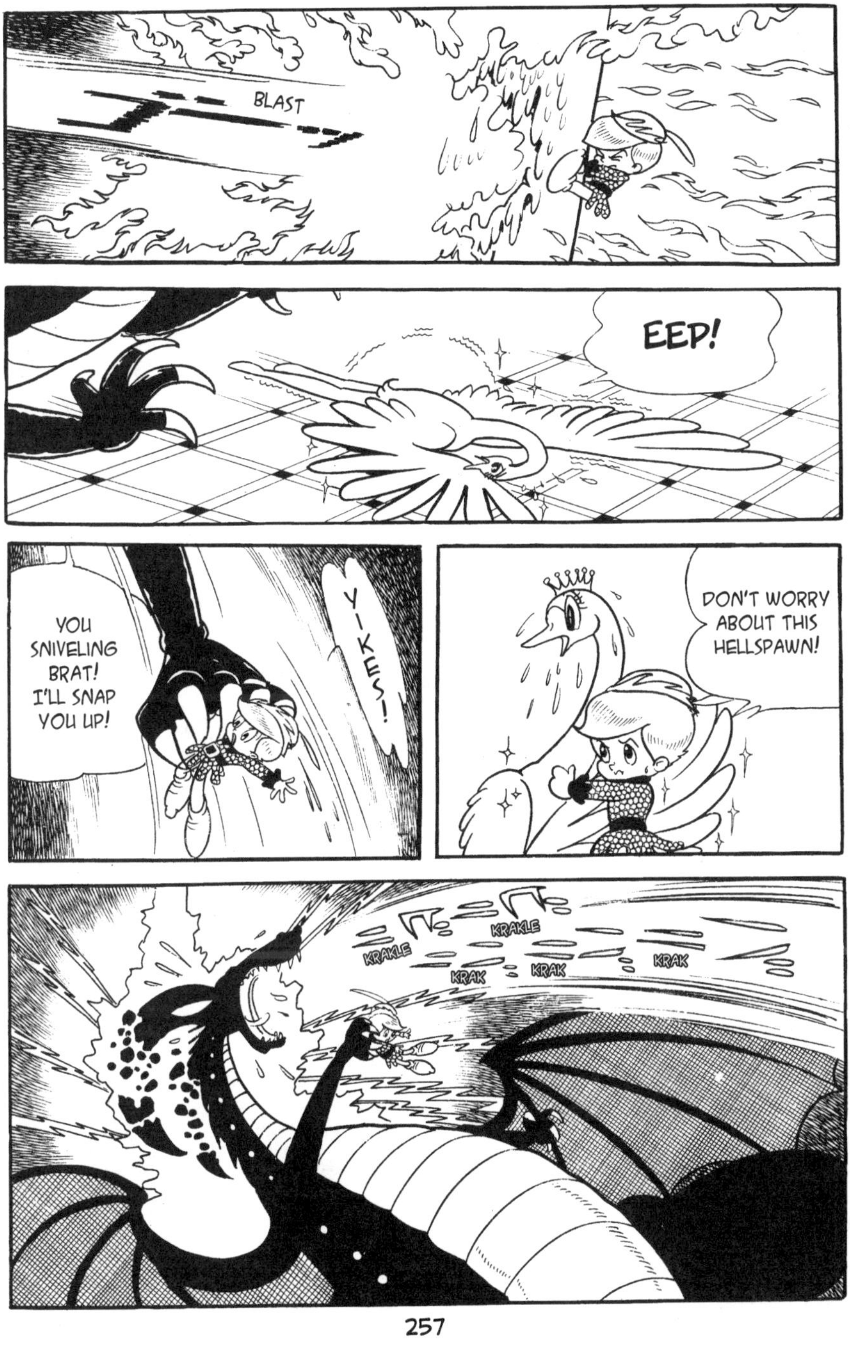
BLAST
EEP!
DON'T WORRY ABOUT THIS HELLSPAWN!
YIKES!
YOU SNIVELING BRAT! I'LL SNAP YOU UP!
KRAKLE
KRAKLE
KRAK
KRAK
KRAK

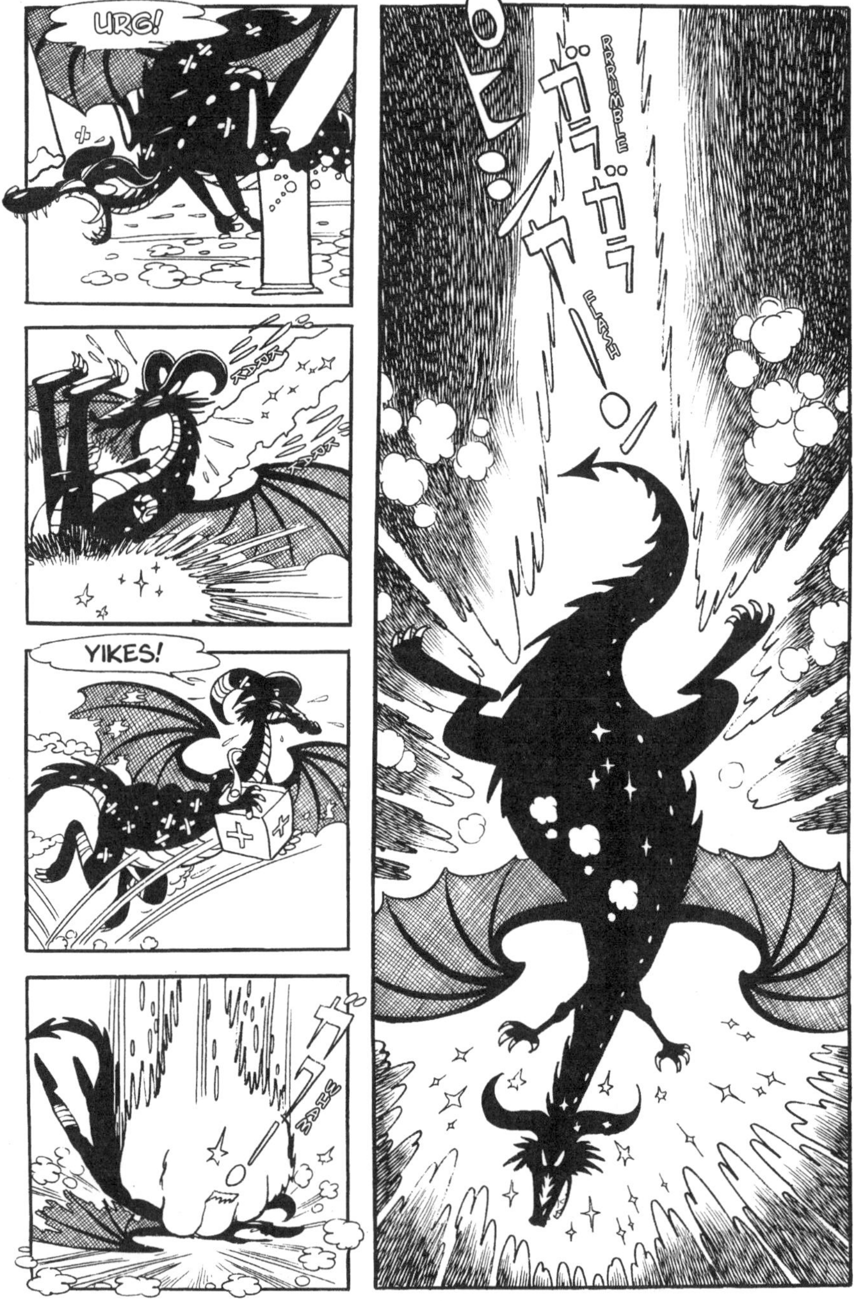
RRRUMBLE
ガラガラ
FLASH
URG!
YIKES!

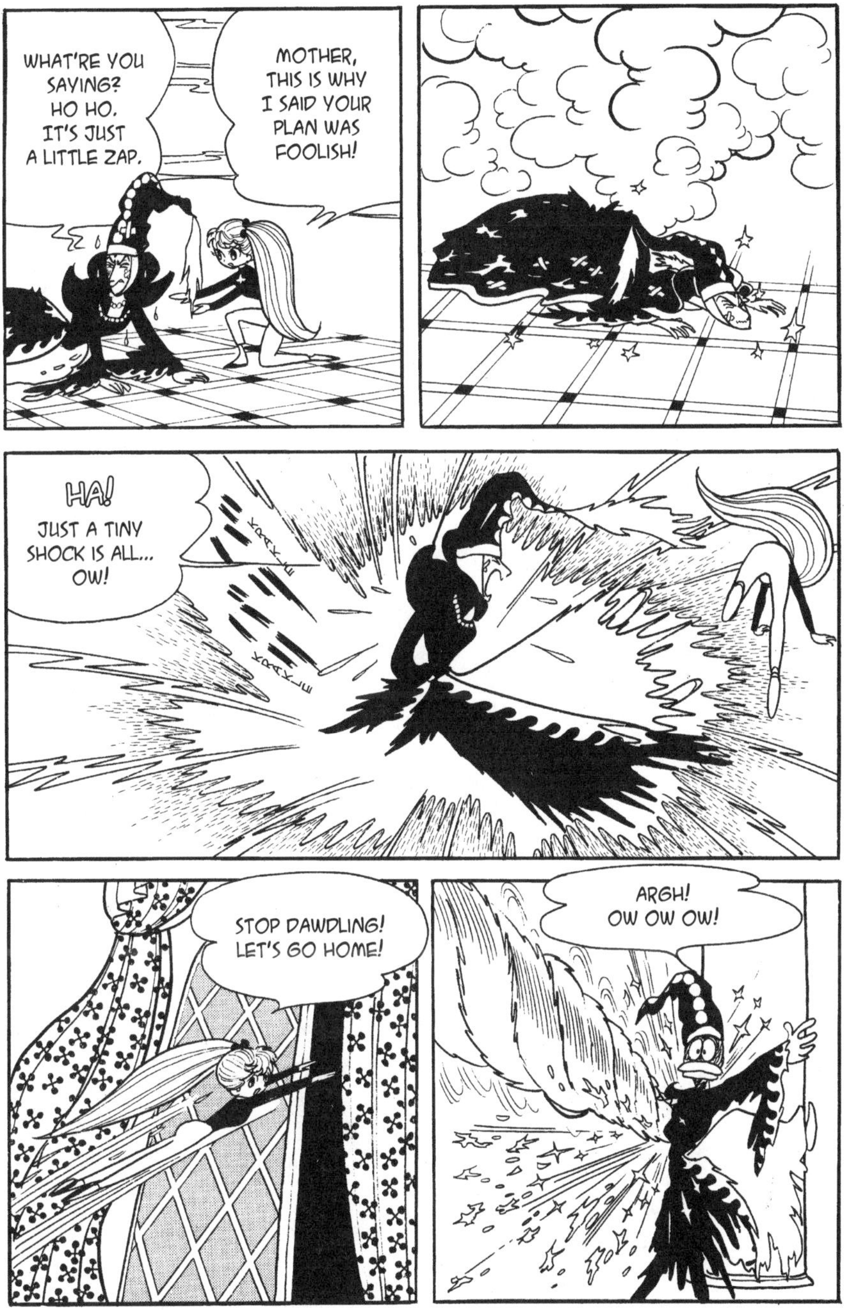
MOTHER, THIS IS WHY I SAID YOUR PLAN WAS FOOLISH!
WHAT'RE YOU SAYING? HO HO. IT'S JUST A LITTLE ZAP.
HA! JUST A TINY SHOCK IS ALL... OW!
ARGH! OW OW OW!
STOP DAWDLING! LET'S GO HOME!

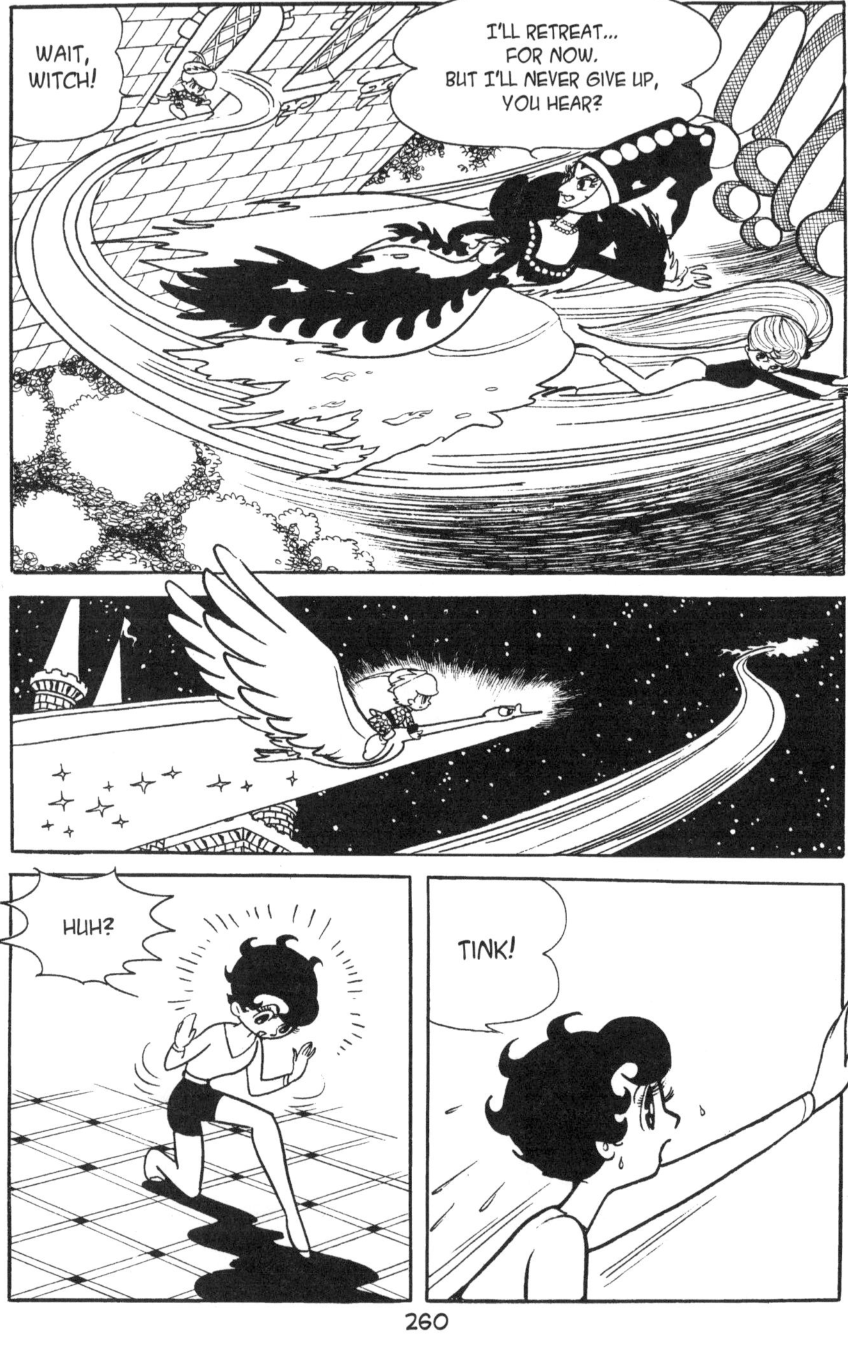
I'LL RETREAT... FOR NOW. BUT I'LL NEVER GIVE UP, YOU HEAR?
WAIT, WITCH!
TINK!
HUH?

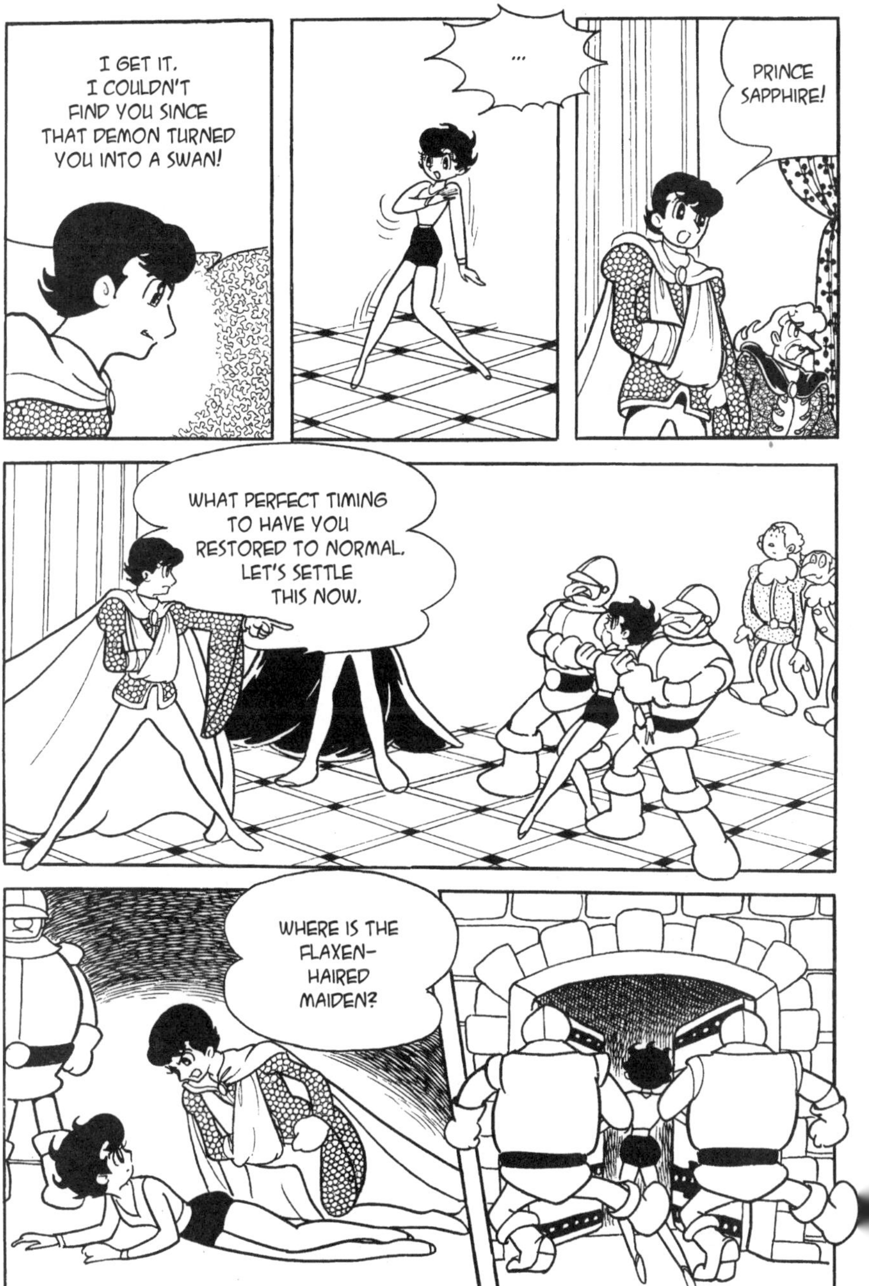
PRINCE SAPPHIRE!
...
I GET IT. I COULDN'T FIND YOU SINCE THAT DEMON TURNED YOU INTO A SWAN!
WHAT PERFECT TIMING TO HAVE YOU RESTORED TO NORMAL. LET'S SETTLE THIS NOW.
WHERE IS THE FLAXEN-HAIRED MAIDEN?

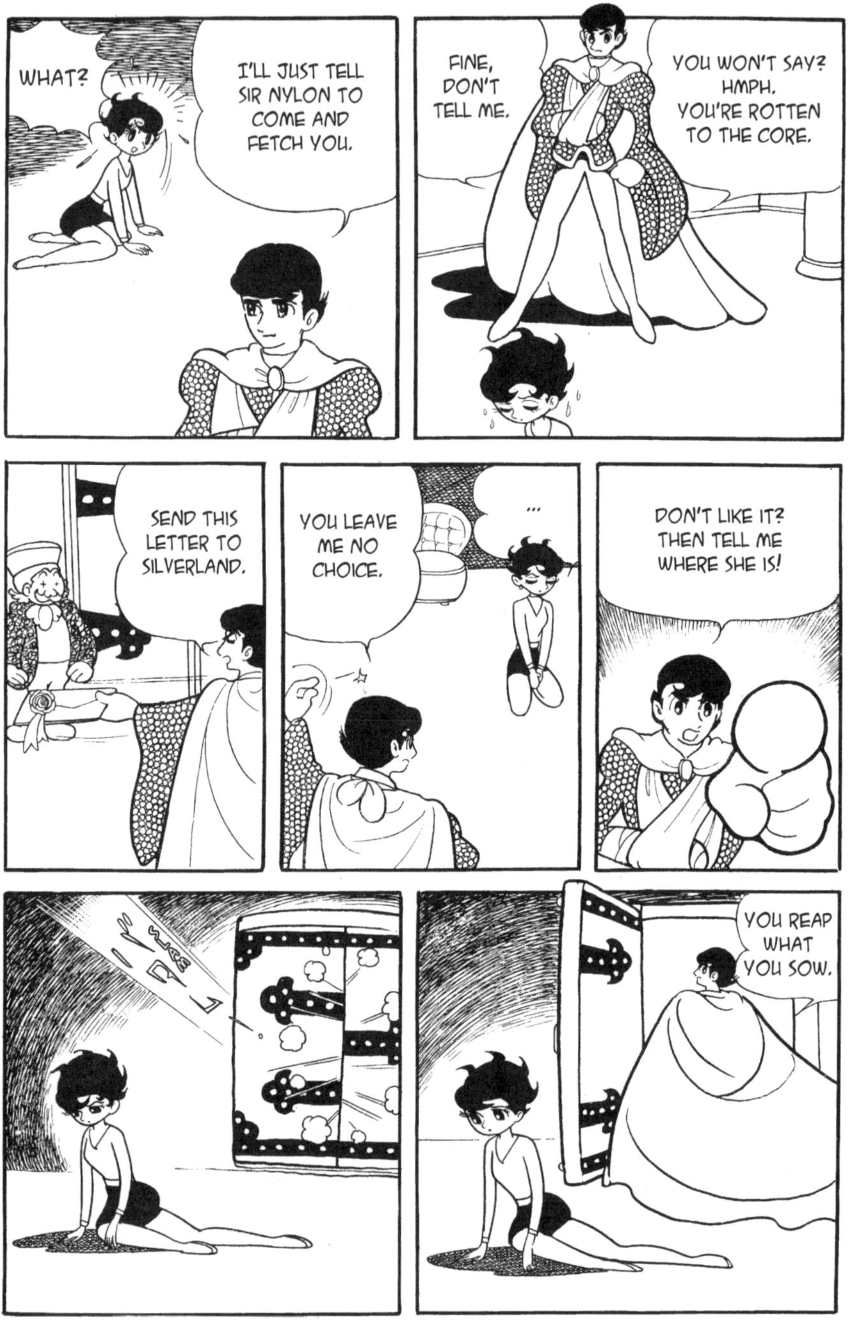
YOU WON'T SAY? HMPH. YOU'RE ROTTEN TO THE CORE.
FINE, DON'T TELL ME.
I'LL JUST TELL SIR NYLON TO COME AND FETCH YOU.
WHAT?
DON'T LIKE IT? THEN TELL ME WHERE SHE IS!
...
YOU LEAVE ME NO CHOICE.
SEND THIS LETTER TO SILVERLAND.
YOU REAP WHAT YOU SOW.

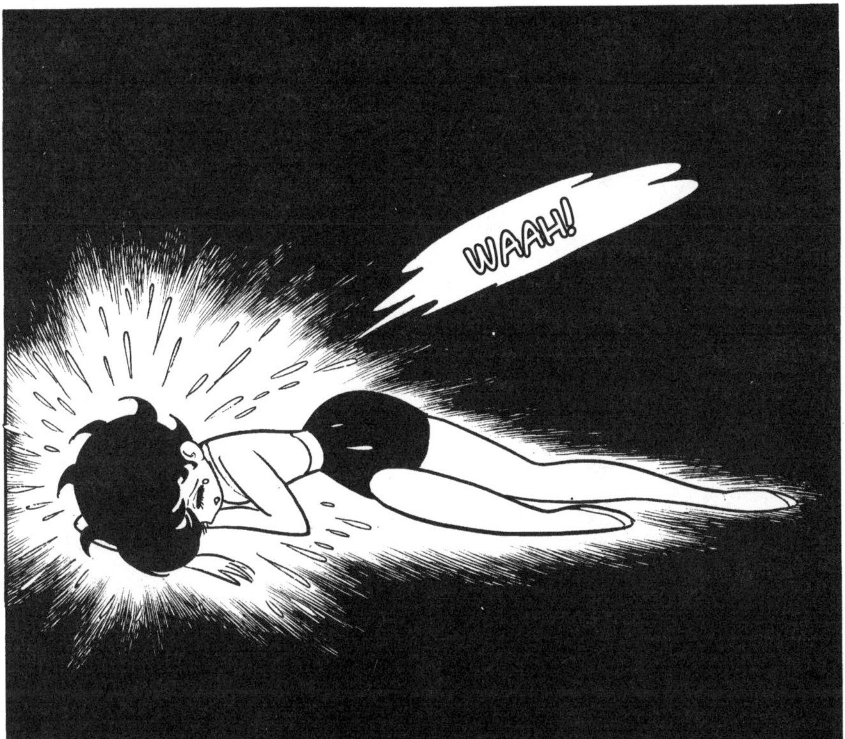
WAAH!

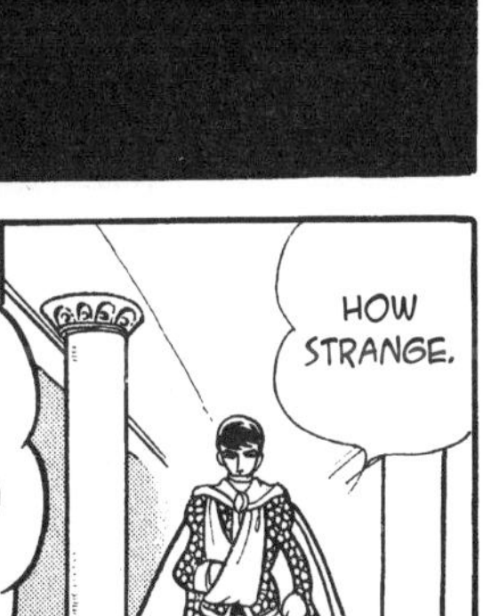
HOW STRANGE.

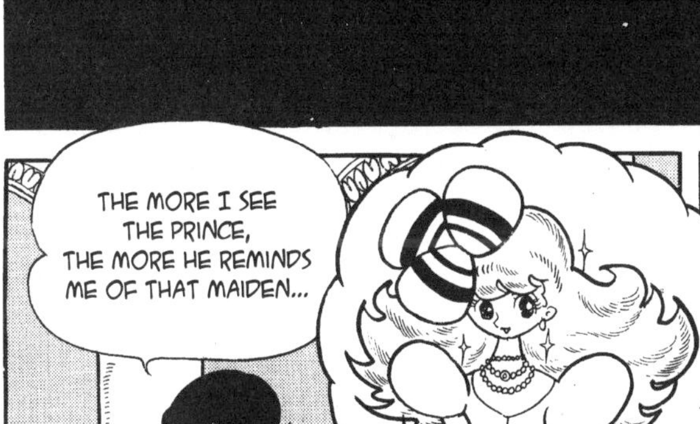
THE MORE I SEE THE PRINCE, THE MORE HE REMINDS ME OF THAT MAIDEN...

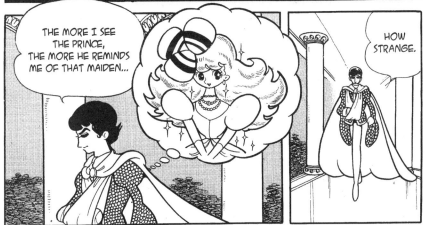

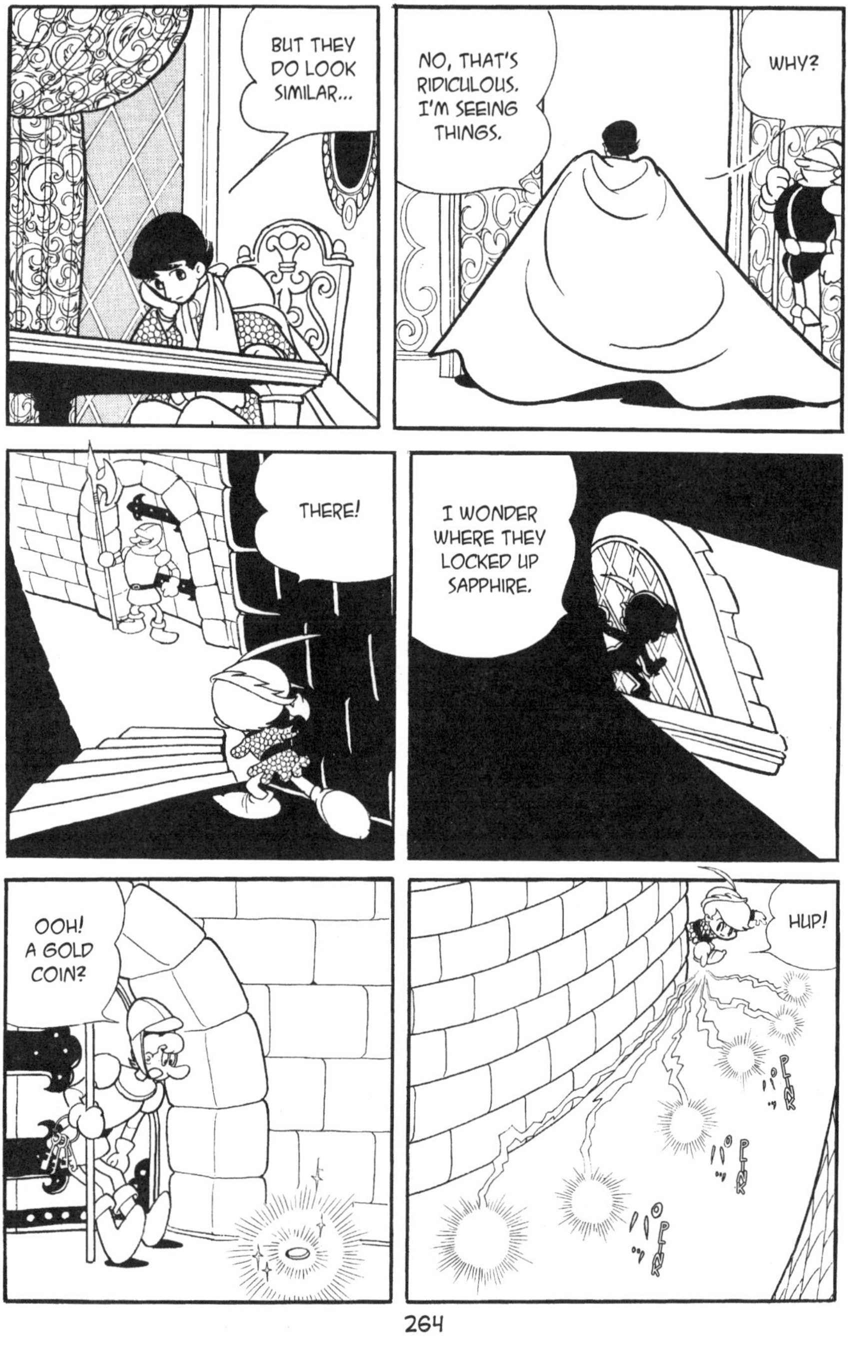
WHY?
NO, THAT'S RIDICULOUS. I'M SEEING THINGS.
BUT THEY DO LOOK SIMILAR...
I WONDER WHERE THEY LOCKED UP SAPPHIRE.
THERE!
HUP!
PLINK
PLINK
PLINK
OOH! A GOLD COIN?

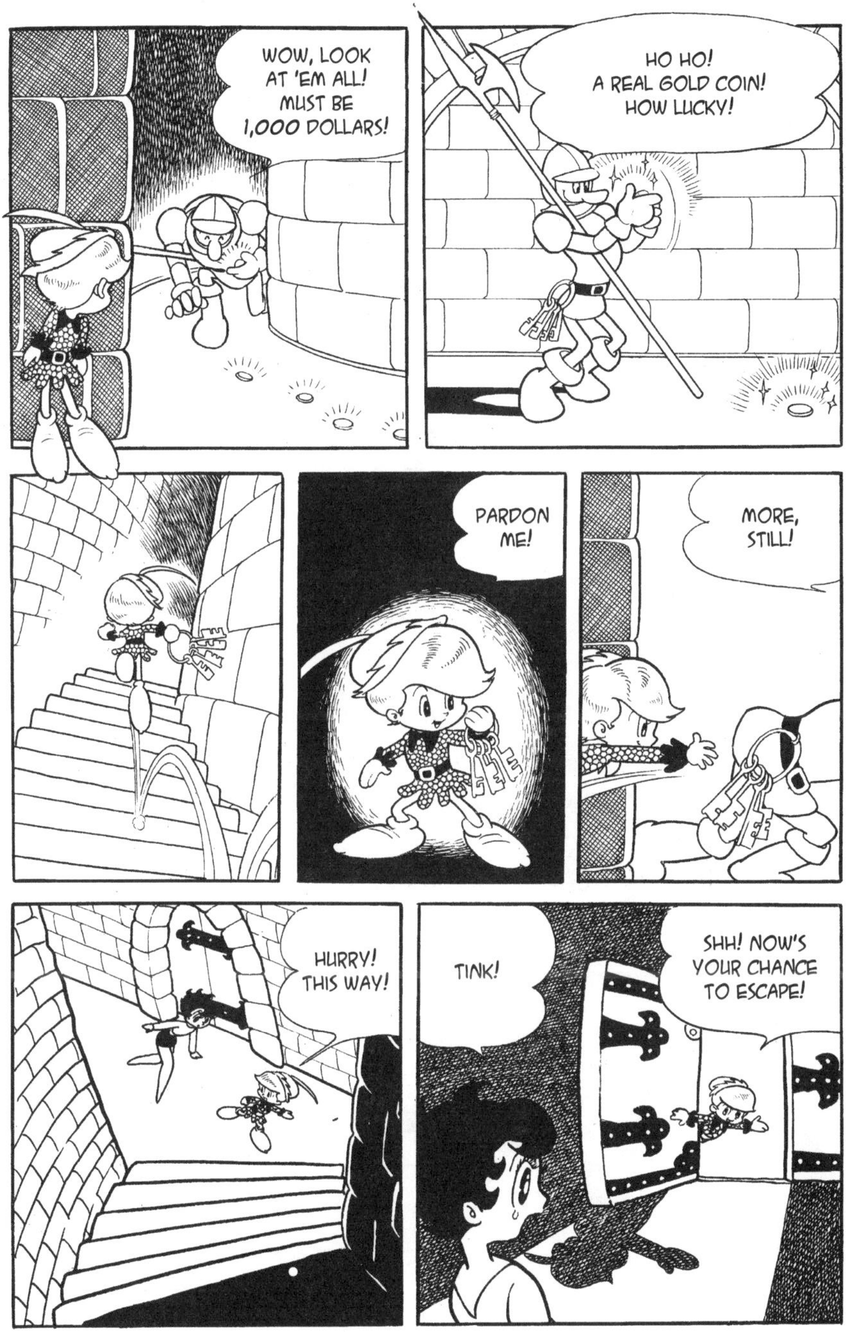

HO HO! A REAL GOLD COIN! HOW LUCKY!
WOW, LOOK AT 'EM ALL! MUST BE 1,000 DOLLARS!
MORE, STILL!
PARDON ME!
SHH! NOW'S YOUR CHANCE TO ESCAPE!
TINK!
HURRY! THIS WAY!

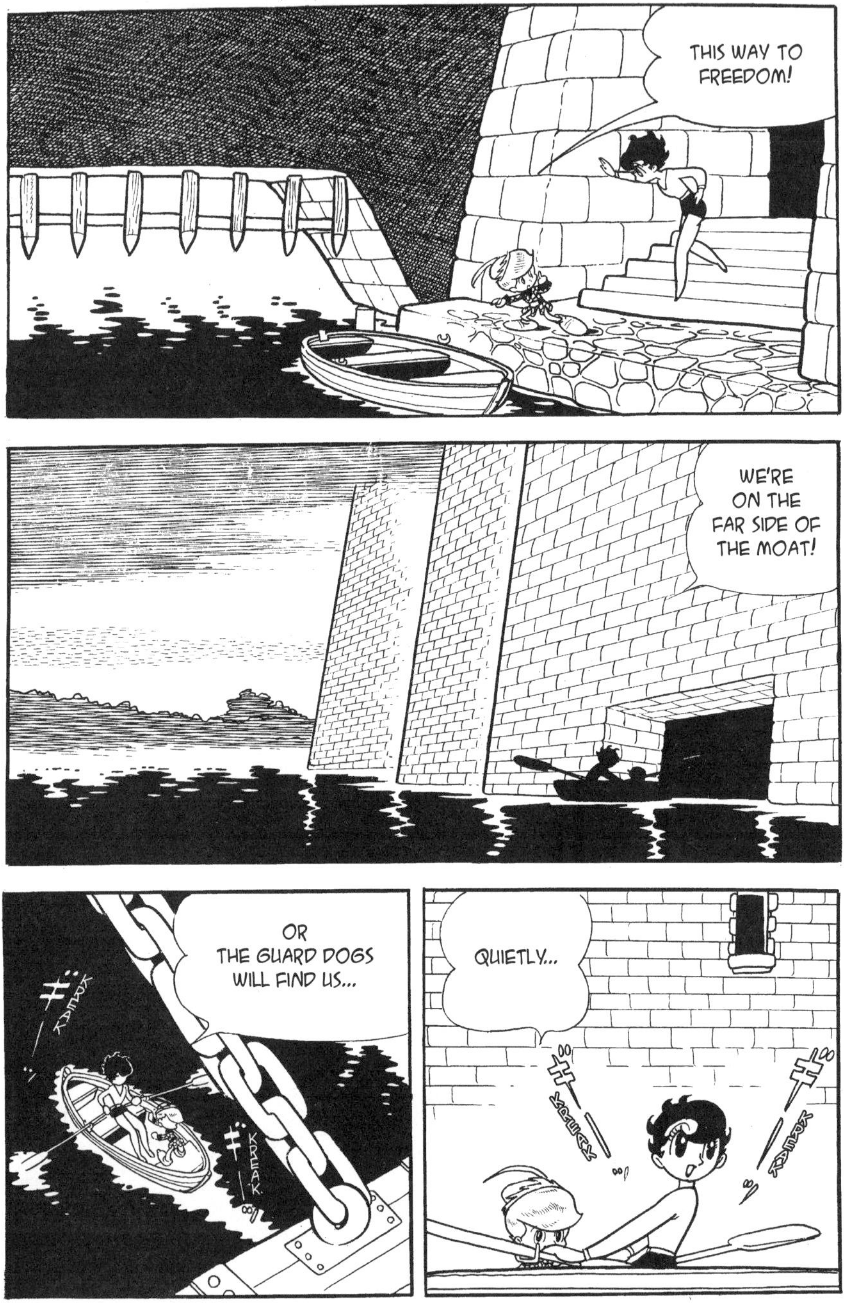
THIS WAY TO FREEDOM!
WE'RE ON THE FAR SIDE OF THE MOAT!
QUIETLY...
KREAK
KREAK
OR THE GUARD DOGS WILL FIND US...
KREAK
KREAK

Chapter 14

Two Hearts

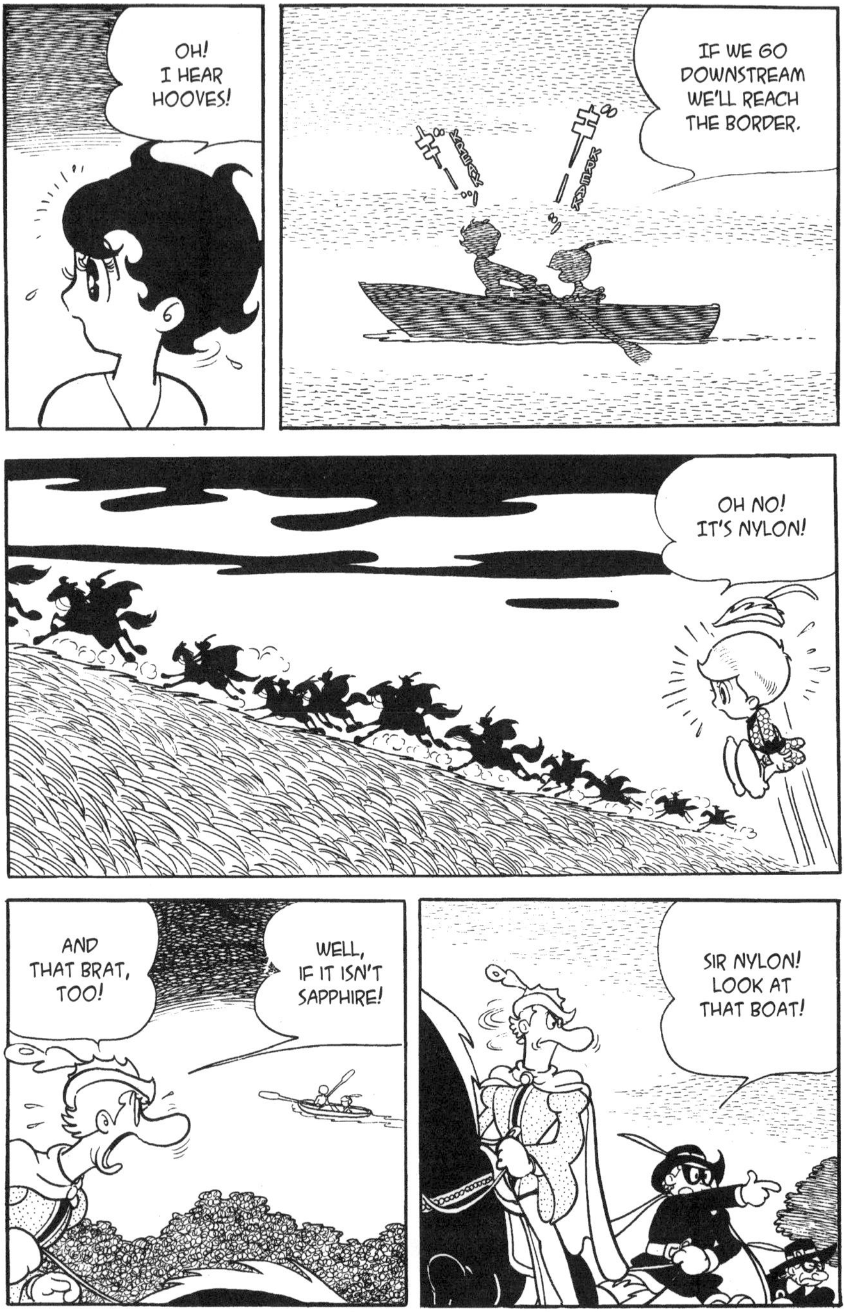
IF WE GO DOWNSTREAM WE'LL REACH THE BORDER.
KREAK
KREAK
OH! I HEAR HOOVES!
OH NO! IT'S NYLON!
SIR NYLON! LOOK AT THAT BOAT!
WELL, IF IT ISN'T SAPPHIRE!
AND THAT BRAT, TOO!

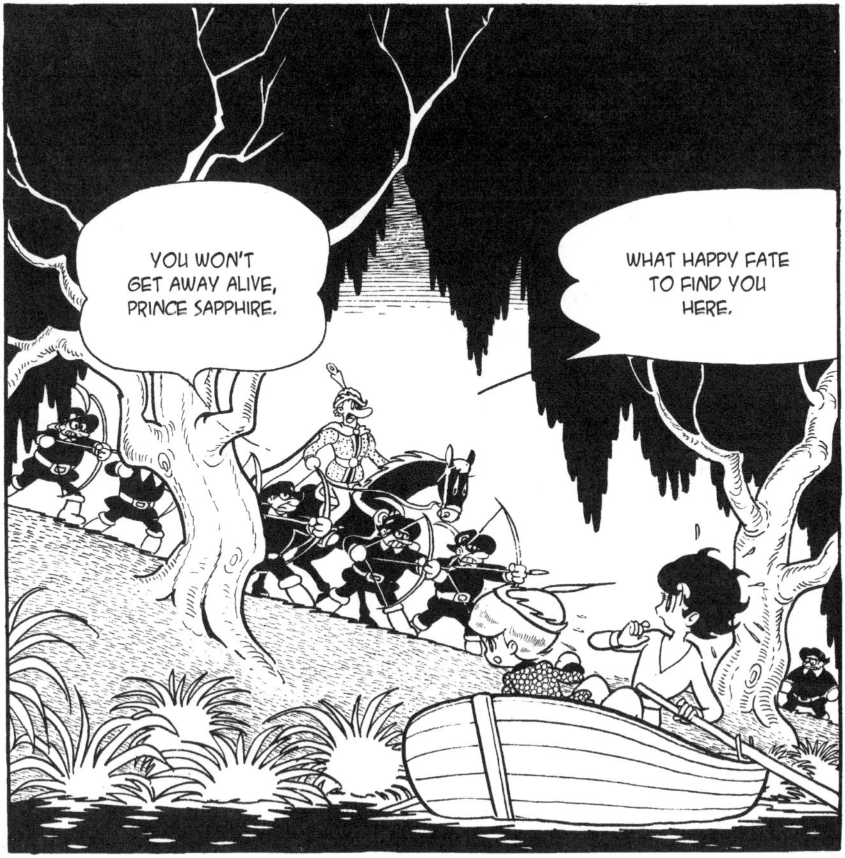
WHAT HAPPY FATE TO FIND YOU HERE.
YOU WON'T GET AWAY ALIVE, PRINCE SAPPHIRE.

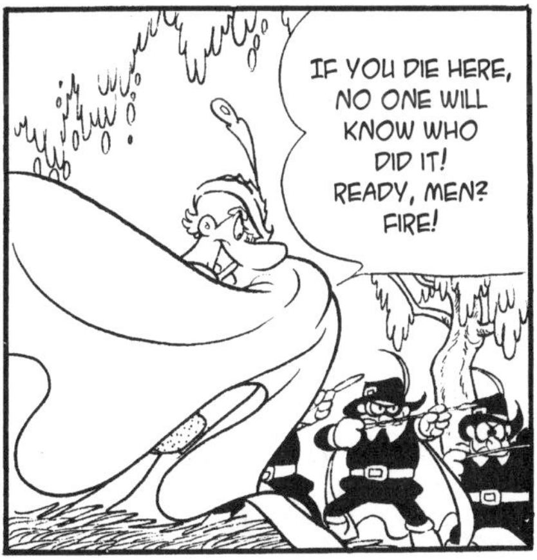
IF YOU DIE HERE, NO ONE WILL KNOW WHO DID IT! READY, MEN? FIRE!

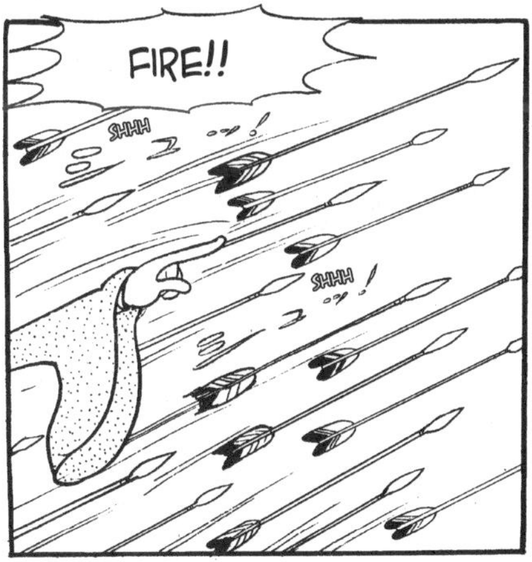
FIRE!!
SHHH
SHHH

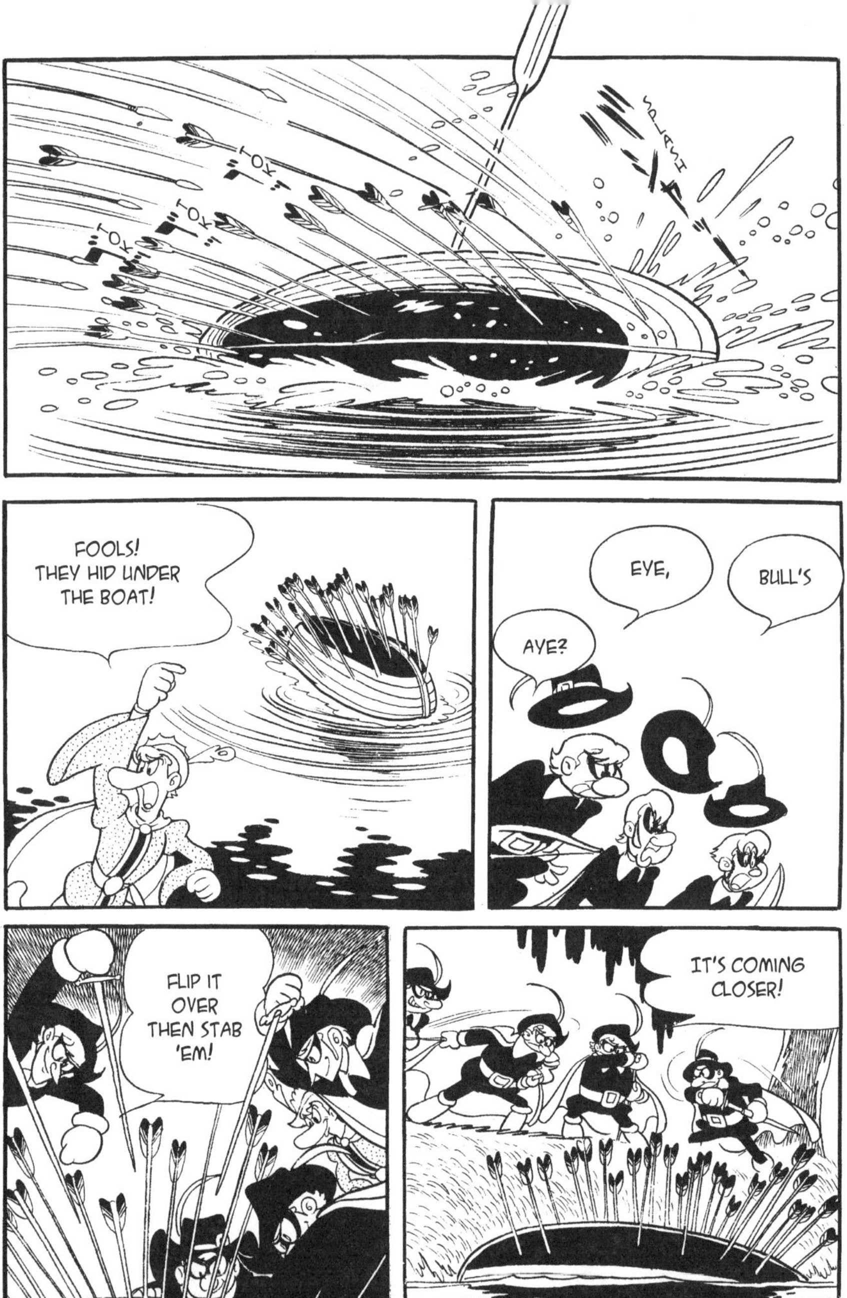
SPLASH
TOK
TOK
TOK
BULL'S
EYE,
AYE?
FOOLS! THEY HID UNDER THE BOAT!
IT'S COMING CLOSER!
FLIP IT OVER THEN STAB 'EM!

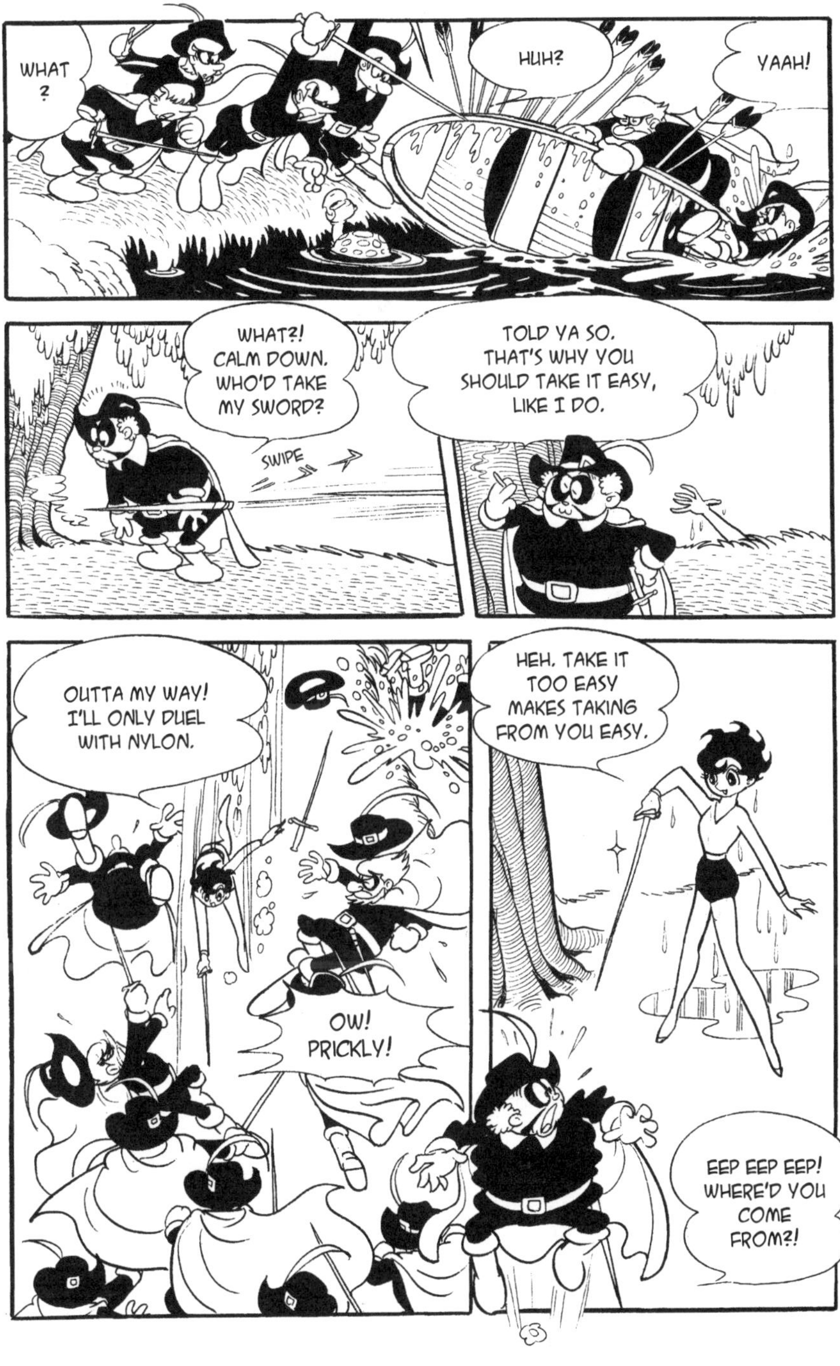
YAAH!
HUH?
WHAT ?
TOLD YA SO. THAT'S WHY YOU SHOULD TAKE IT EASY, LIKE I DO.
WHAT?! CALM DOWN. WHO'D TAKE MY SWORD?
SWIPE
HEH. TAKE IT TOO EASY MAKES TAKING FROM YOU EASY.
EEP EEP EEP! WHERE'D YOU COME FROM?!
OUTTA MY WAY! I'LL ONLY DUEL WITH NYLON.
OW! PRICKLY!

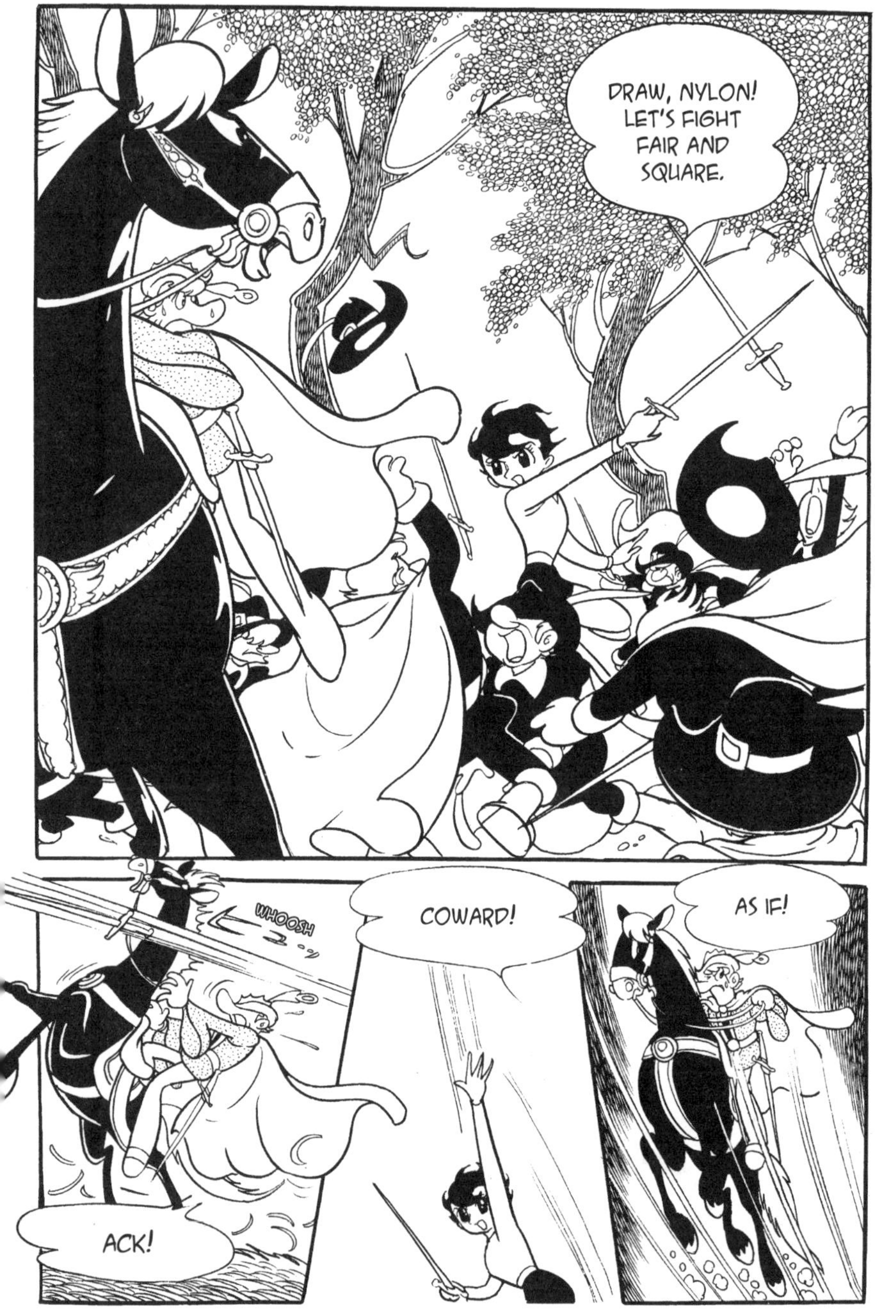
DRAW, NYLON! LET'S FIGHT FAIR AND SQUARE.
AS IF!
COWARD!
WHOOSH
ACK!

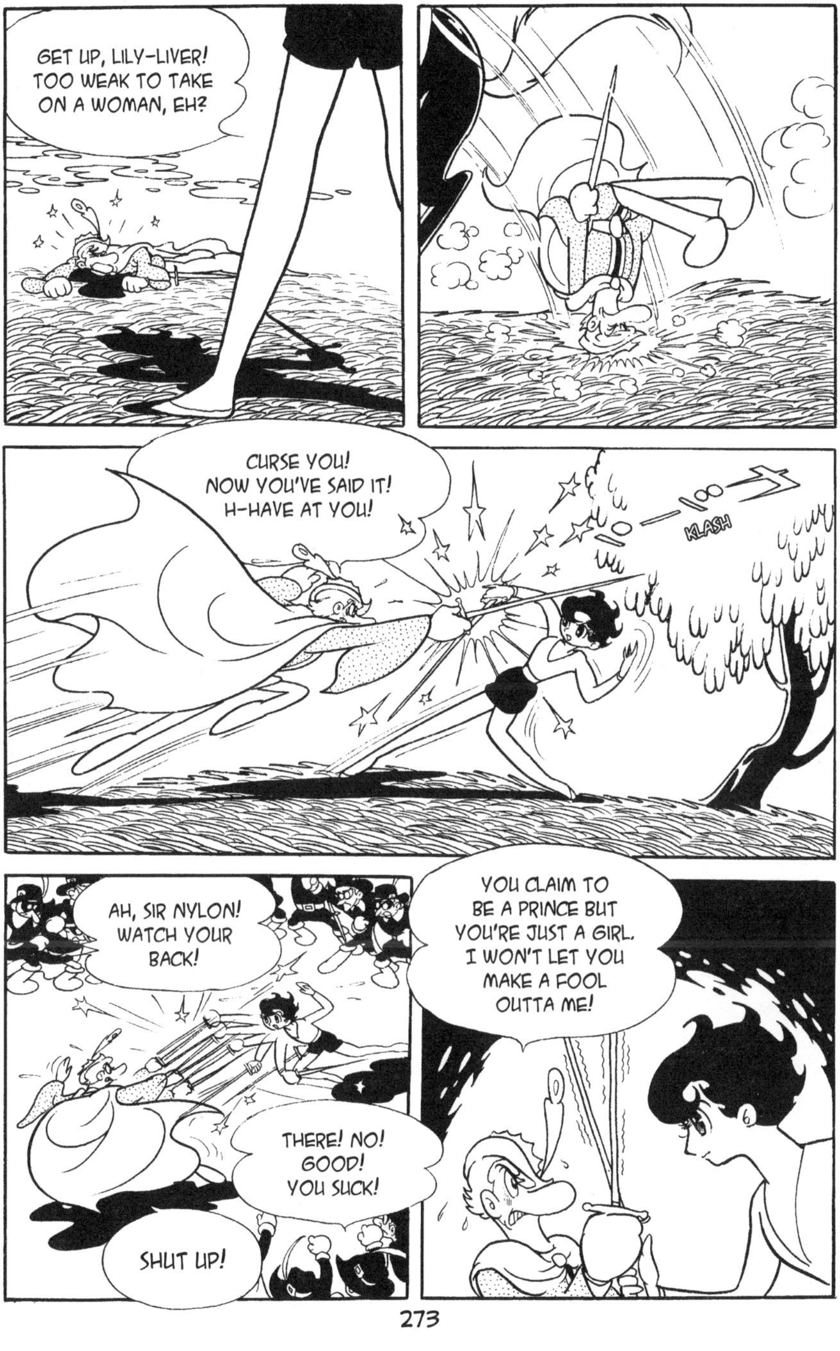
GET UP, LILY-LIVER! TOO WEAK TO TAKE ON A WOMAN, EH?
CURSE YOU! NOW YOU'VE SAID IT! H-HAVE AT YOU!
KLASH
YOU CLAIM TO BE A PRINCE BUT YOU'RE JUST A GIRL. I WON'T LET YOU MAKE A FOOL OUTTA ME!
AH, SIR NYLON! WATCH YOUR BACK!
THERE! NO! GOOD! YOU SUCK!
SHUT UP!

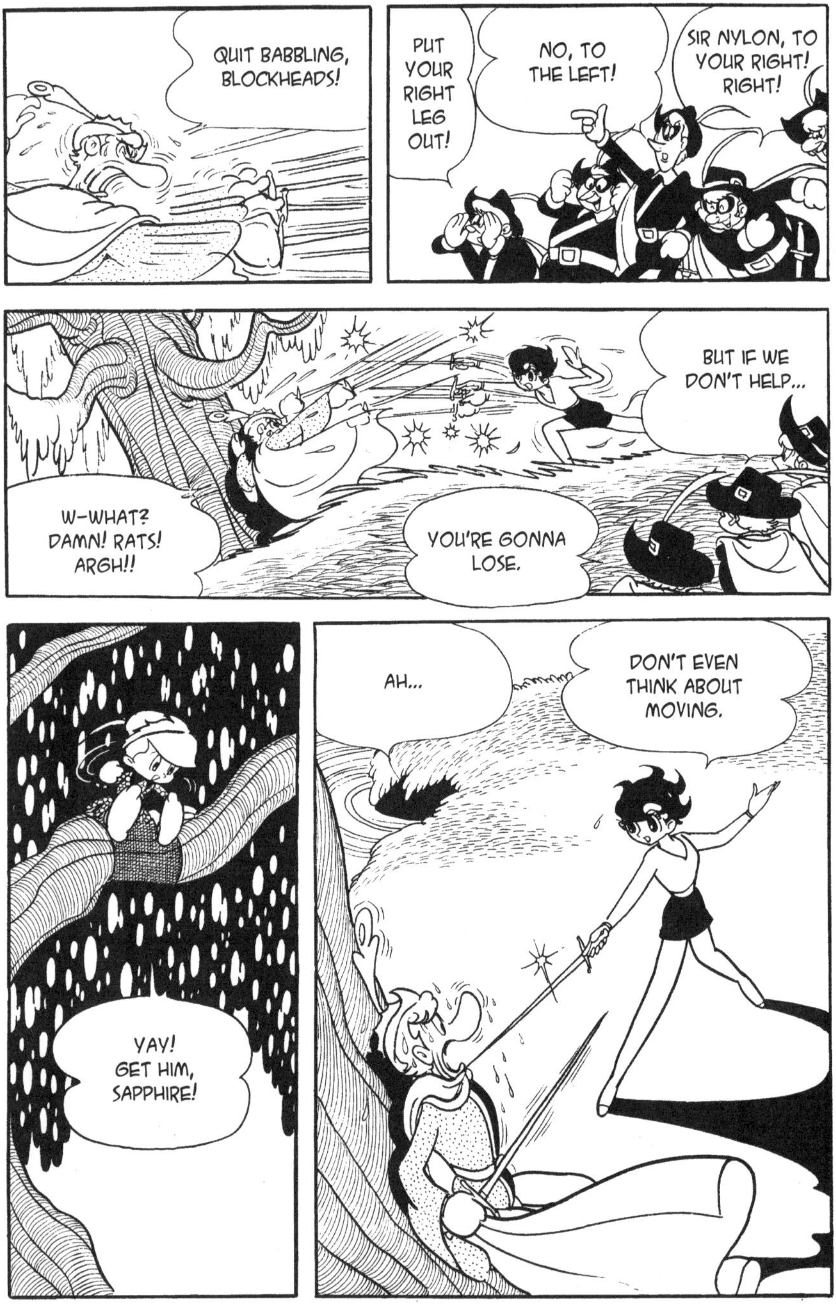

SIR NYLON, TO YOUR RIGHT! RIGHT!
NO, TO THE LEFT!
PUT YOUR RIGHT LEG OUT!
QUIT BABBLING, BLOCKHEADS!
BUT IF WE DON'T HELP...
YOU'RE GONNA LOSE.
W-WHAT? DAMN! RATS! ARGH!!
DON'T EVEN THINK ABOUT MOVING.
AH...
YAY! GET HIM, SAPPHIRE!

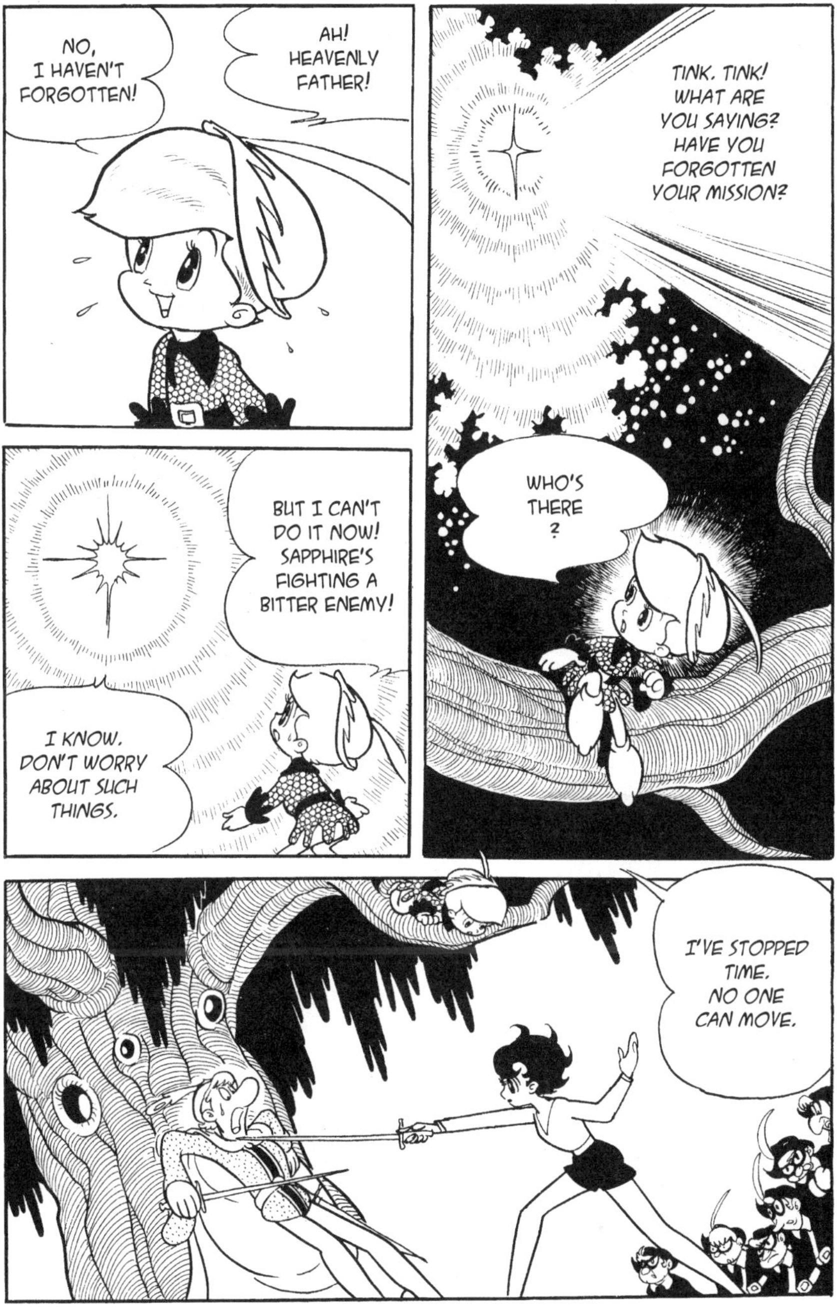
TINK. TINK! WHAT ARE YOU SAYING? HAVE YOU FORGOTTEN YOUR MISSION?
WHO'S THERE ?
AH! HEAVENLY FATHER!
NO, I HAVEN'T FORGOTTEN!
BUT I CAN'T DO IT NOW! SAPPHIRE'S FIGHTING A BITTER ENEMY!
I KNOW. DON'T WORRY ABOUT SUCH THINGS.
I'VE STOPPED TIME. NO ONE CAN MOVE.

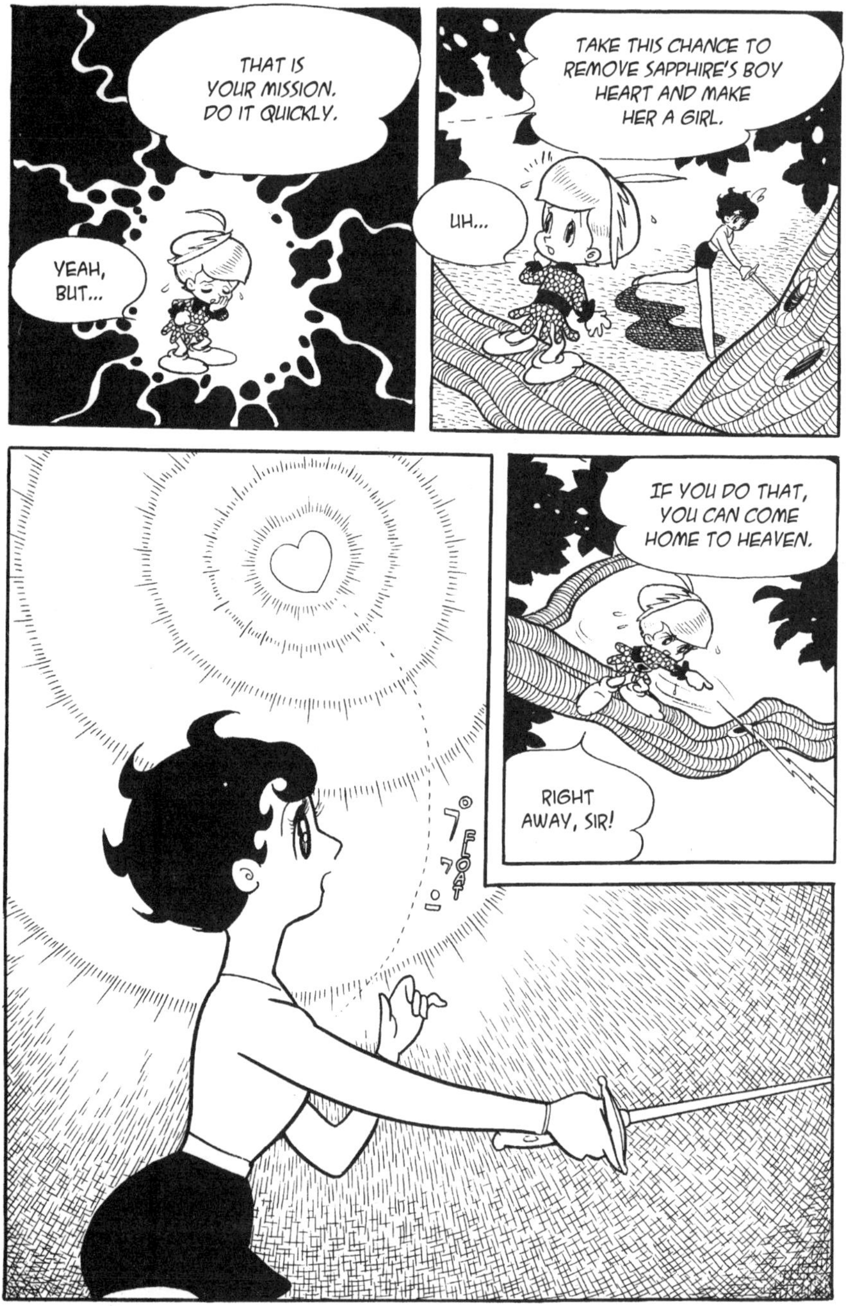
TAKE THIS CHANCE TO REMOVE SAPPHIRE'S BOY HEART AND MAKE HER A GIRL.
UH...
THAT IS YOUR MISSION. DO IT QUICKLY.
YEAH, BUT...
IF YOU DO THAT, YOU CAN COME HOME TO HEAVEN.
RIGHT AWAY, SIR!
FLOAT

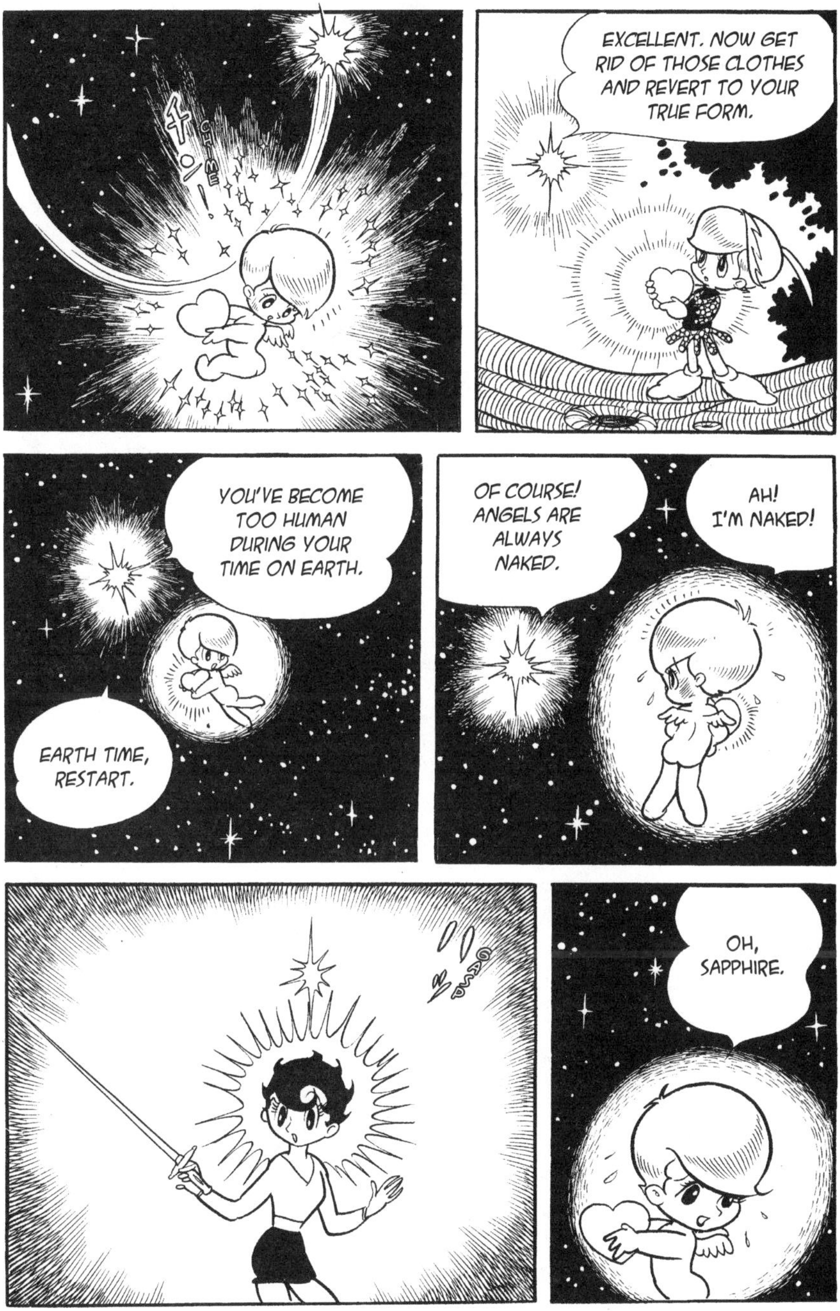
EXCELLENT. NOW GET RID OF THOSE CLOTHES AND REVERT TO YOUR TRUE FORM.
CHIME
AH! I'M NAKED!
OF COURSE! ANGELS ARE ALWAYS NAKED.
YOU'VE BECOME TOO HUMAN DURING YOUR TIME ON EARTH.
EARTH TIME, RESTART.
OH, SAPPHIRE.
GASP

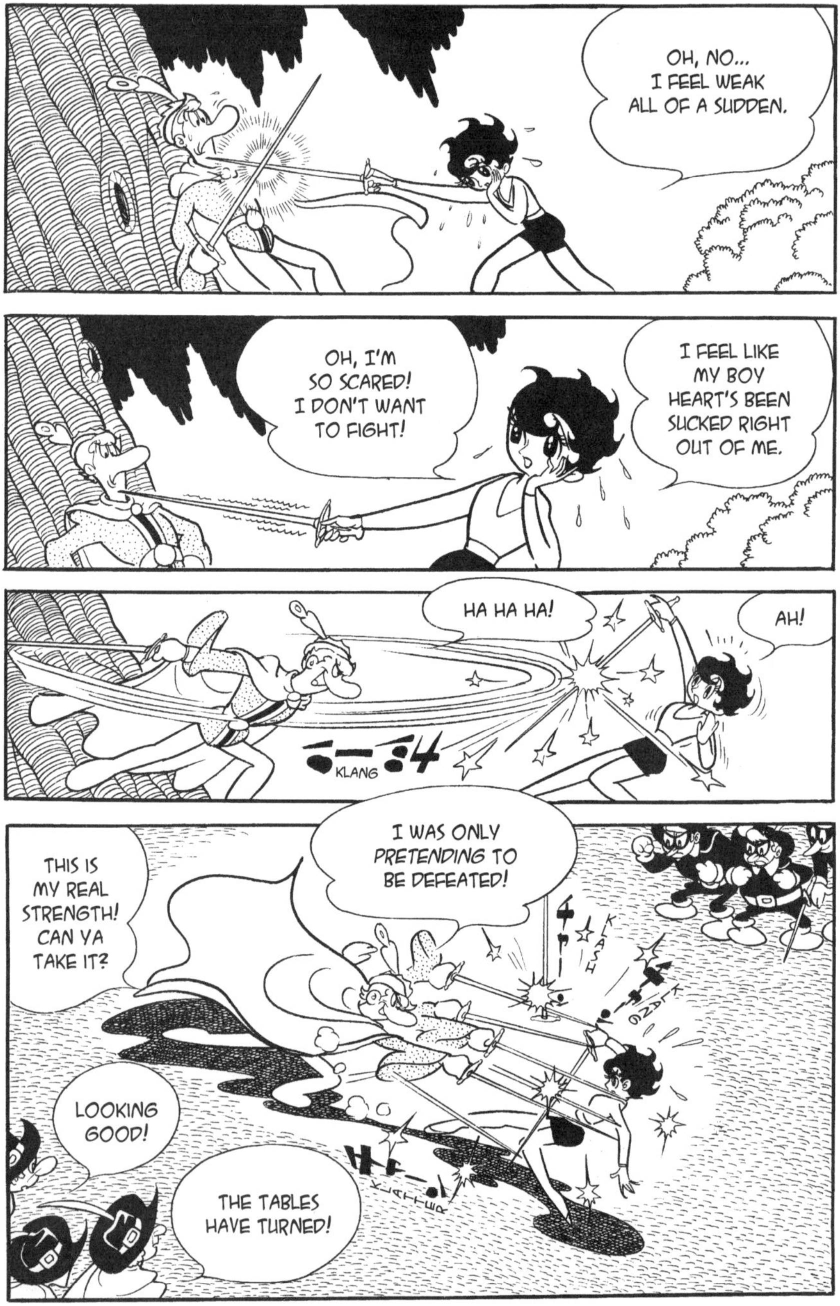
OH, NO... I FEEL WEAK ALL OF A SUDDEN.
I FEEL LIKE MY BOY HEART'S BEEN SUCKED RIGHT OUT OF ME.
OH, I'M SO SCARED! I DON'T WANT TO FIGHT!
AH!
HA HA HA!
KLANG
I WAS ONLY PRETENDING TO BE DEFEATED!
KLASH
THIS IS MY REAL STRENGTH! CAN YA TAKE IT?
LOOKING GOOD!
THE TABLES HAVE TURNED!
KLATTER

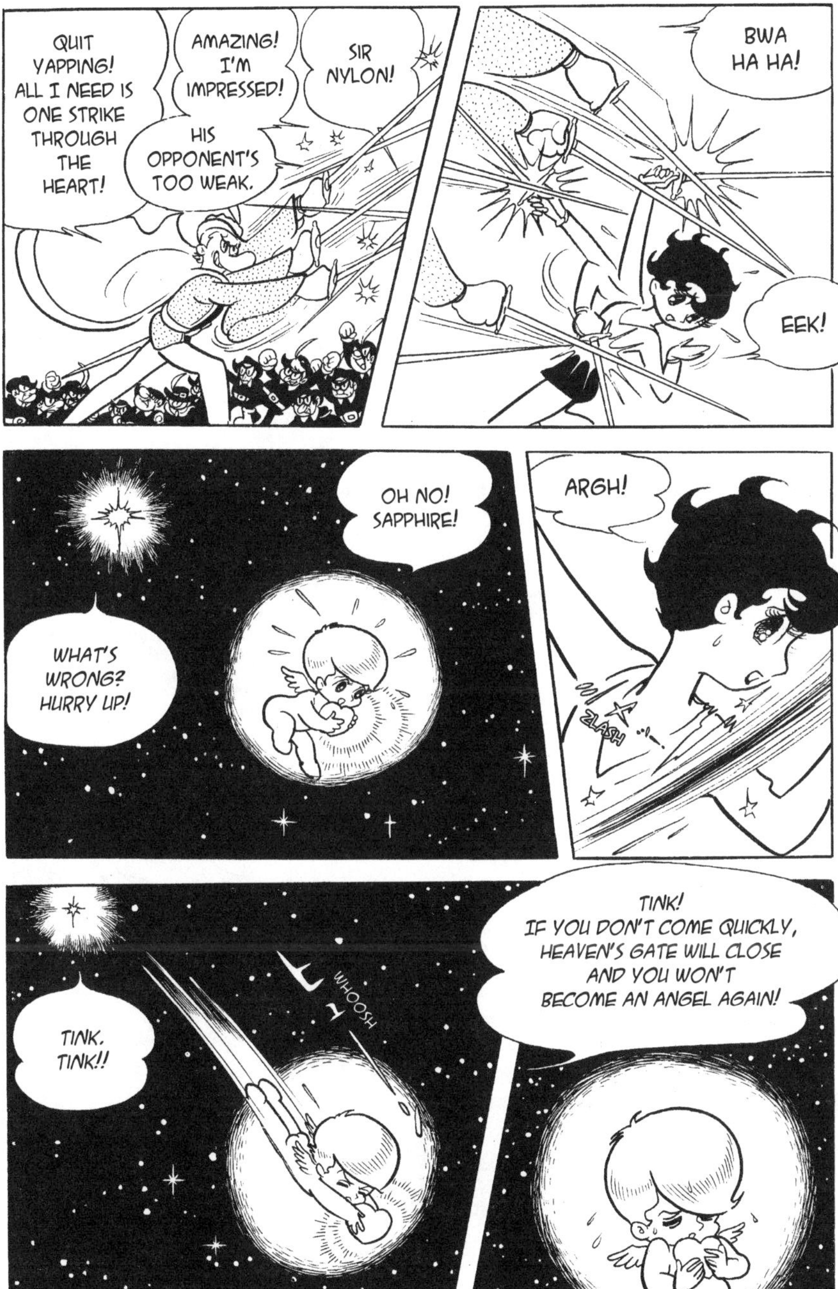
BWA HA HA!
EEK!
SIR NYLON!
AMAZING! I'M IMPRESSED!
HIS OPPONENT'S TOO WEAK.
QUIT YAPPING! ALL I NEED IS ONE STRIKE THROUGH THE HEART!
ARGH!
ZLASH
OH NO! SAPPHIRE!
WHAT'S WRONG? HURRY UP!
TINK! IF YOU DON'T COME QUICKLY, HEAVEN'S GATE WILL CLOSE AND YOU WON'T BECOME AN ANGEL AGAIN!
WHOOSH
TINK, TINK!!

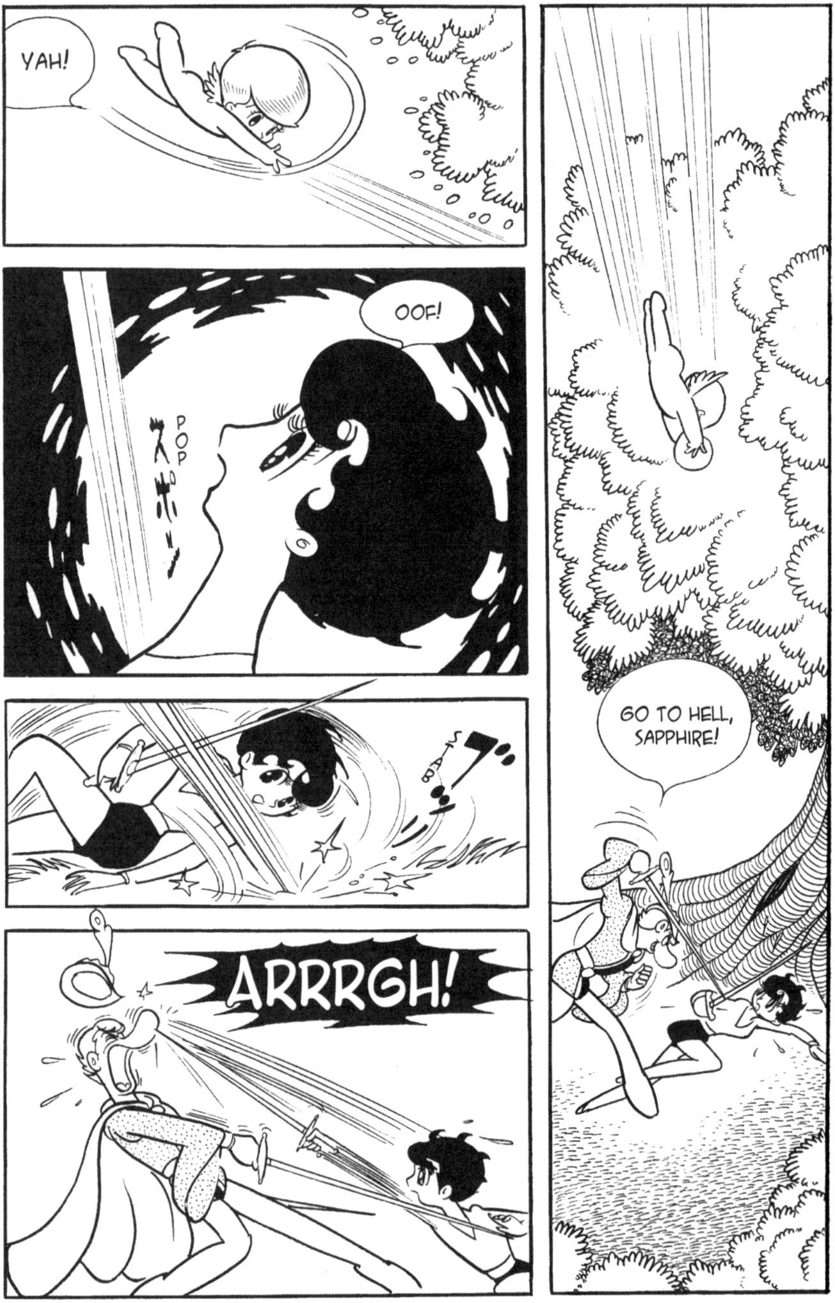
GO TO HELL, SAPPHIRE!
YAH!
OOF!
POP
STAB
ARRRGH!

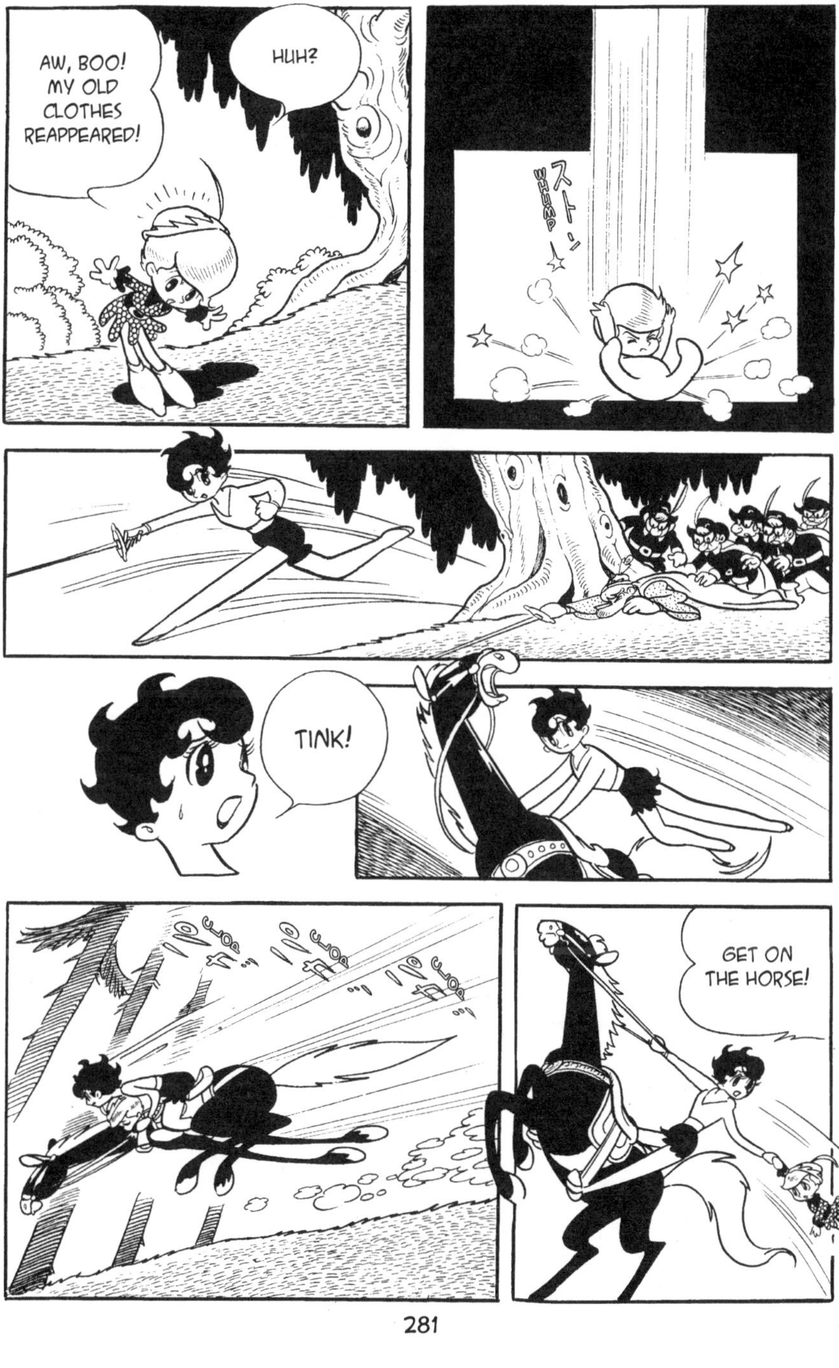
ストーン
WHUMP
HUH?
AW, BOO! MY OLD CLOTHES REAPPEARED!
TINK!
GET ON THE HORSE!
CLOP
CLOP
CLOP

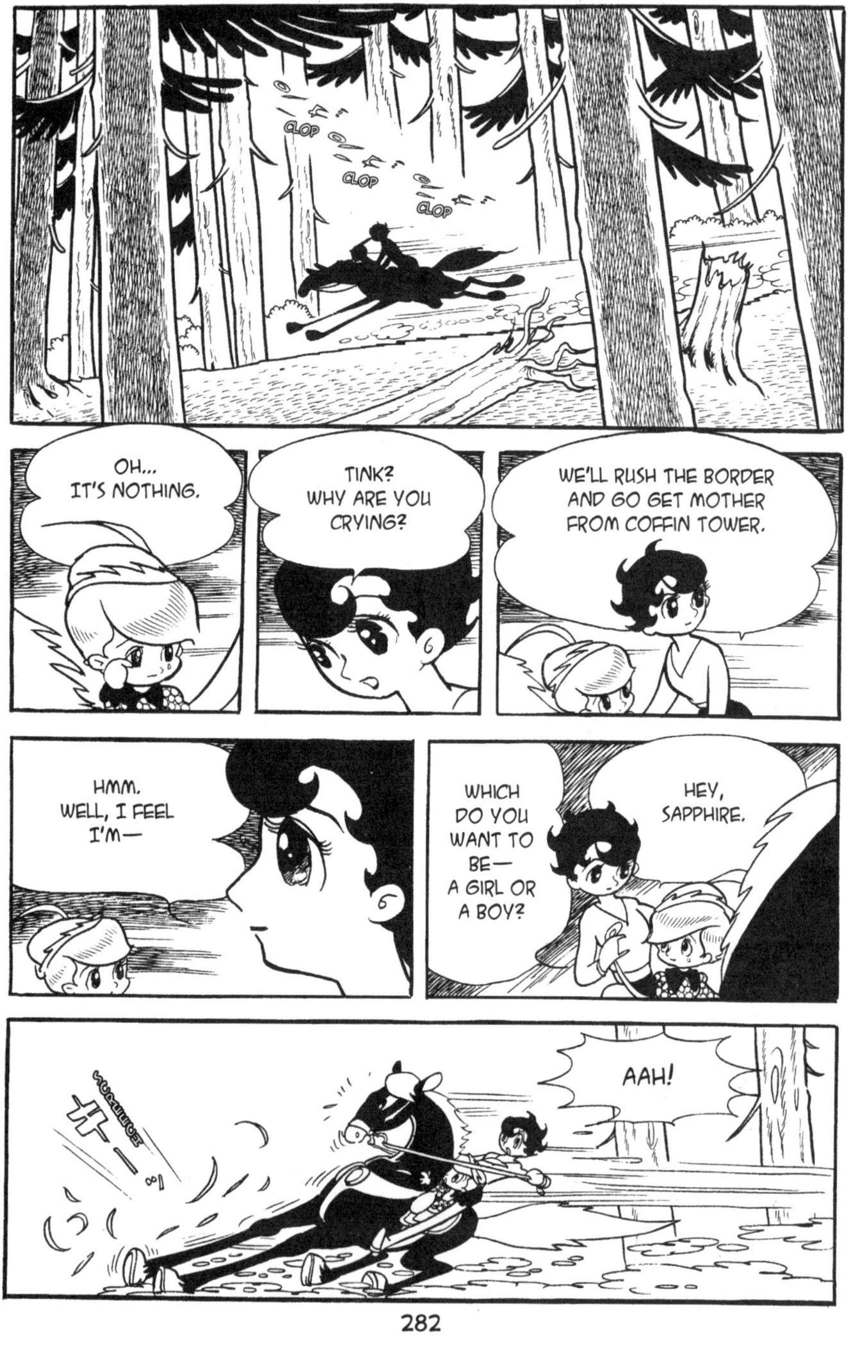
CLOP
CLOP
CLOP
WE'LL RUSH THE BORDER AND GO GET MOTHER FROM COFFIN TOWER.
TINK? WHY ARE YOU CRYING?
OH... IT'S NOTHING.
HEY, SAPPHIRE.
WHICH DO YOU WANT TO BE— A GIRL OR A BOY?
HMM. WELL, I FEEL I'M—
AAH!

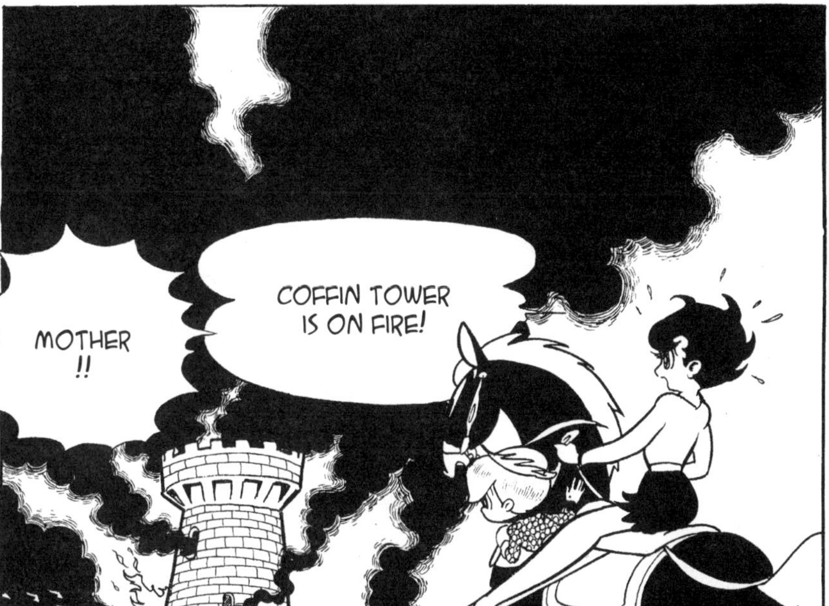
COFFIN TOWER IS ON FIRE!
MOTHER !!

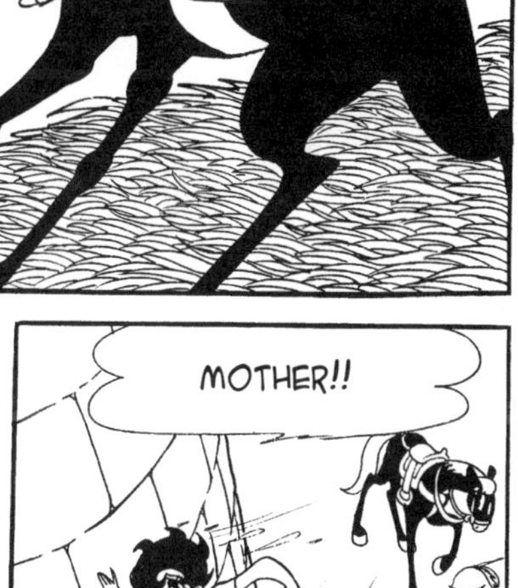
MOTHER!!

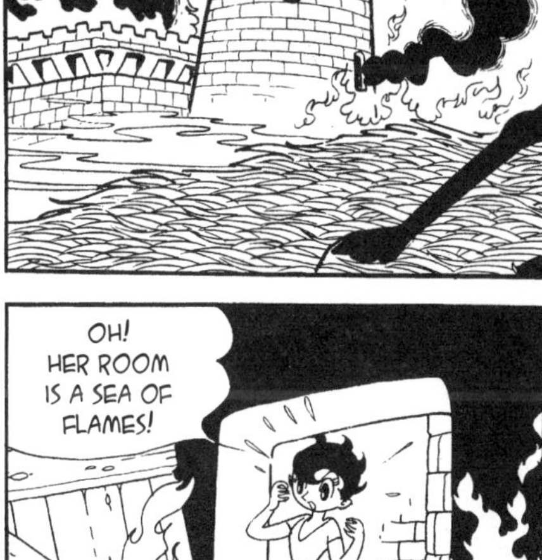
OH! HER ROOM IS A SEA OF FLAMES!

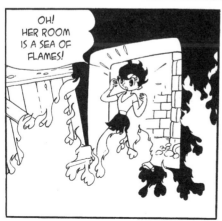

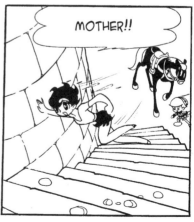

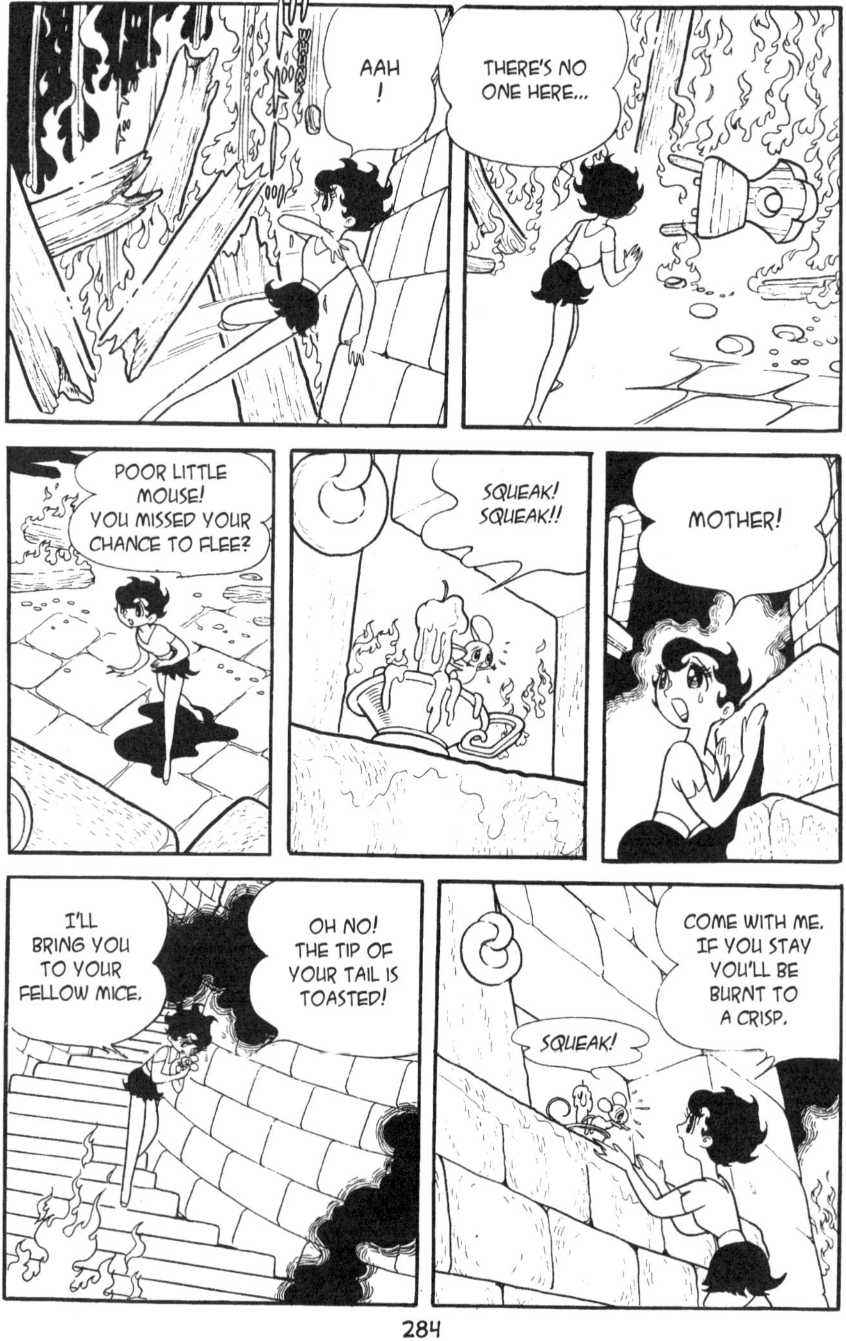
THERE'S NO ONE HERE...
AAH !
WHUNK
MOTHER!
SQUEAK! SQUEAK!!
POOR LITTLE MOUSE! YOU MISSED YOUR CHANCE TO FLEE?
COME WITH ME. IF YOU STAY YOU'LL BE BURNT TO A CRISP.
SQUEAK!
OH NO! THE TIP OF YOUR TAIL IS TOASTED!
I'LL BRING YOU TO YOUR FELLOW MICE.

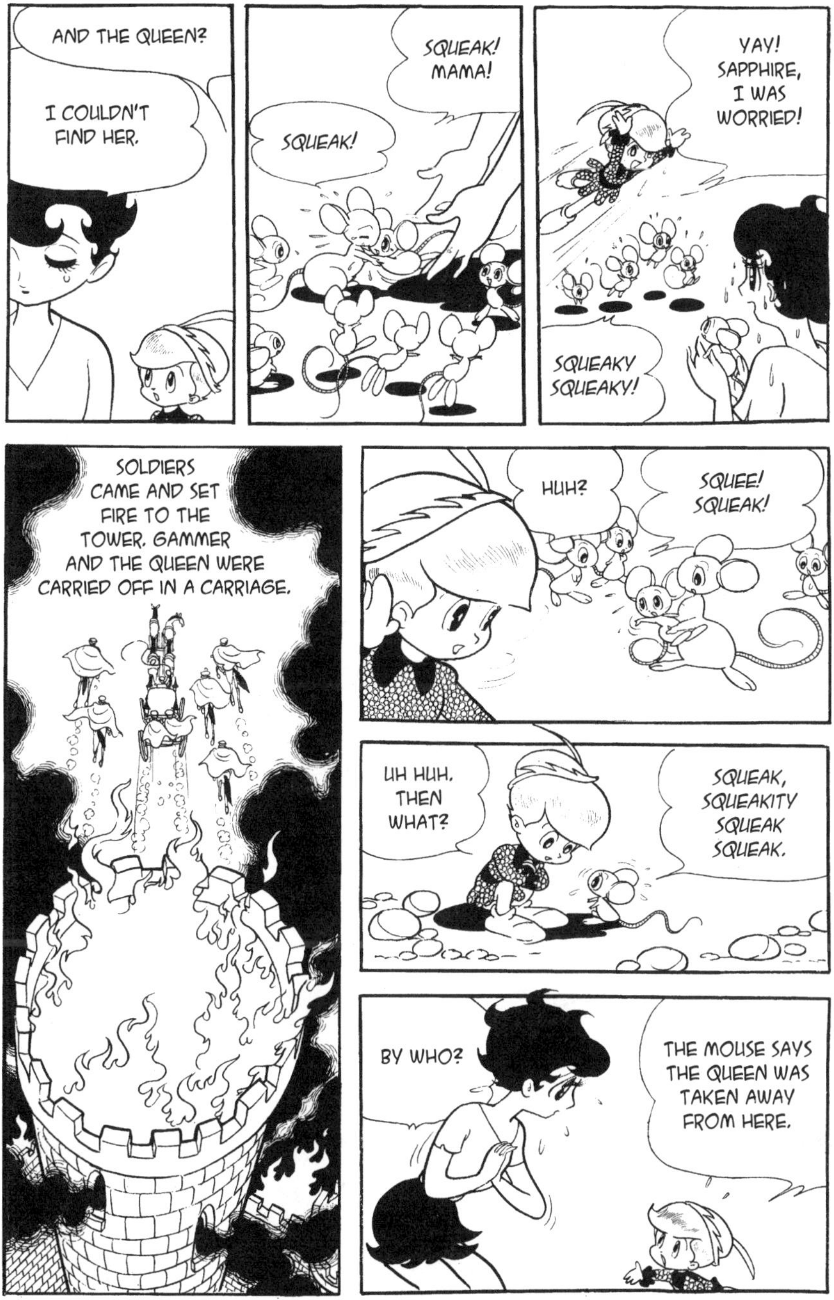
YAY! SAPPHIRE, I WAS WORRIED!
SQUEAKY SQUEAKY!
SQUEAK! MAMA!
SQUEAK!
AND THE QUEEN?
I COULDN'T FIND HER.
SQUEE! SQUEAK!
HUH?
SQUEAK, SQUEAKITY SQUEAK SQUEAK.
UH HUH. THEN WHAT?
THE MOUSE SAYS THE QUEEN WAS TAKEN AWAY FROM HERE.
BY WHO?
SOLDIERS CAME AND SET FIRE TO THE TOWER. GAMMER AND THE QUEEN WERE CARRIED OFF IN A CARRIAGE.

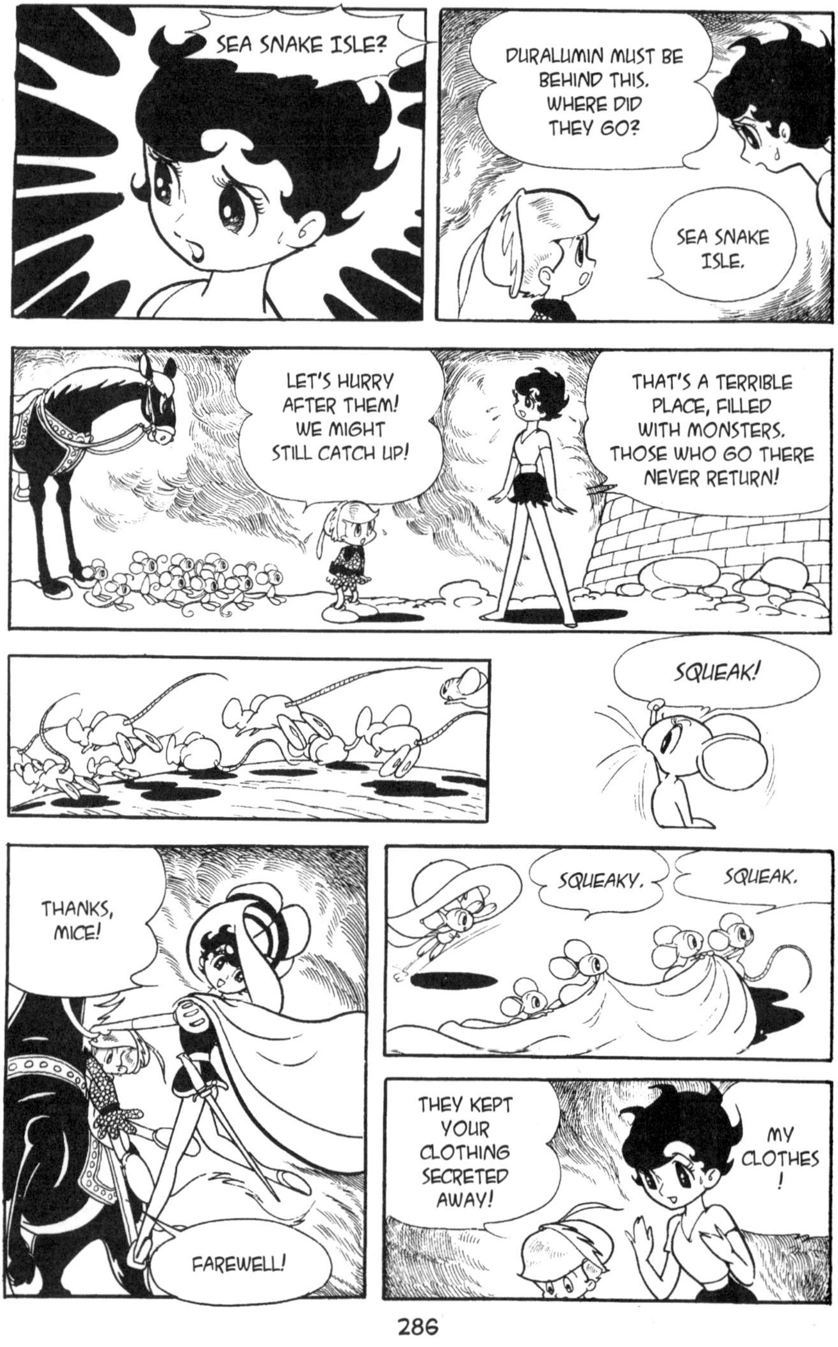
DURALUMIN MUST BE BEHIND THIS. WHERE DID THEY GO?
SEA SNAKE ISLE.
SEA SNAKE ISLE?
THAT'S A TERRIBLE PLACE, FILLED WITH MONSTERS. THOSE WHO GO THERE NEVER RETURN!
LET'S HURRY AFTER THEM! WE MIGHT STILL CATCH UP!
SQUEAK!
SQUEAK.
SQUEAKY.
MY CLOTHES!
THEY KEPT YOUR CLOTHING SECRETED AWAY!
THANKS, MICE!
FAREWELL!

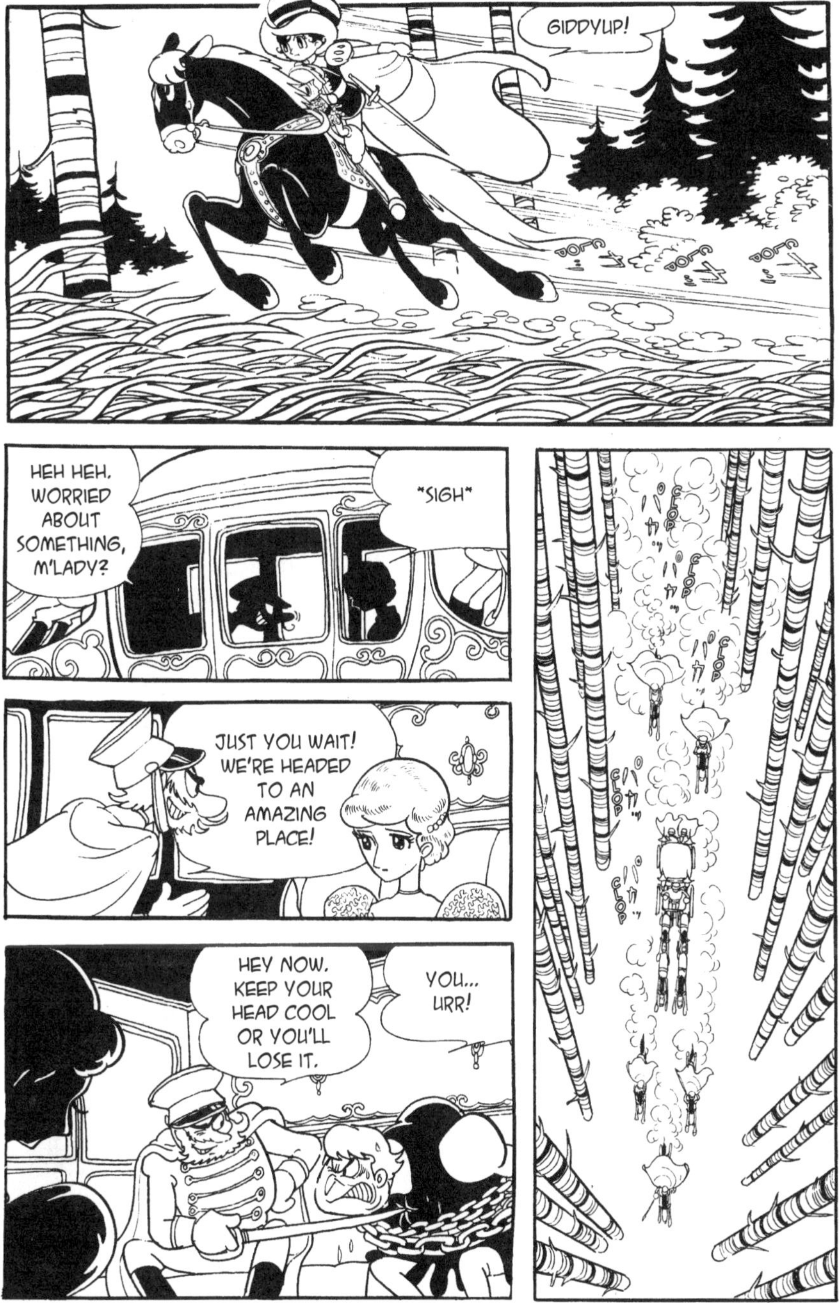
GIDDYUP!
CLOP
CLOP
CLOP
CLOP
CLOP
CLOP
CLOP
SIGH
HEH HEH. WORRIED ABOUT SOMETHING, M'LADY?
JUST YOU WAIT! WE'RE HEADED TO AN AMAZING PLACE!
YOU... URR!
HEY NOW. KEEP YOUR HEAD COOL OR YOU'LL LOSE IT.

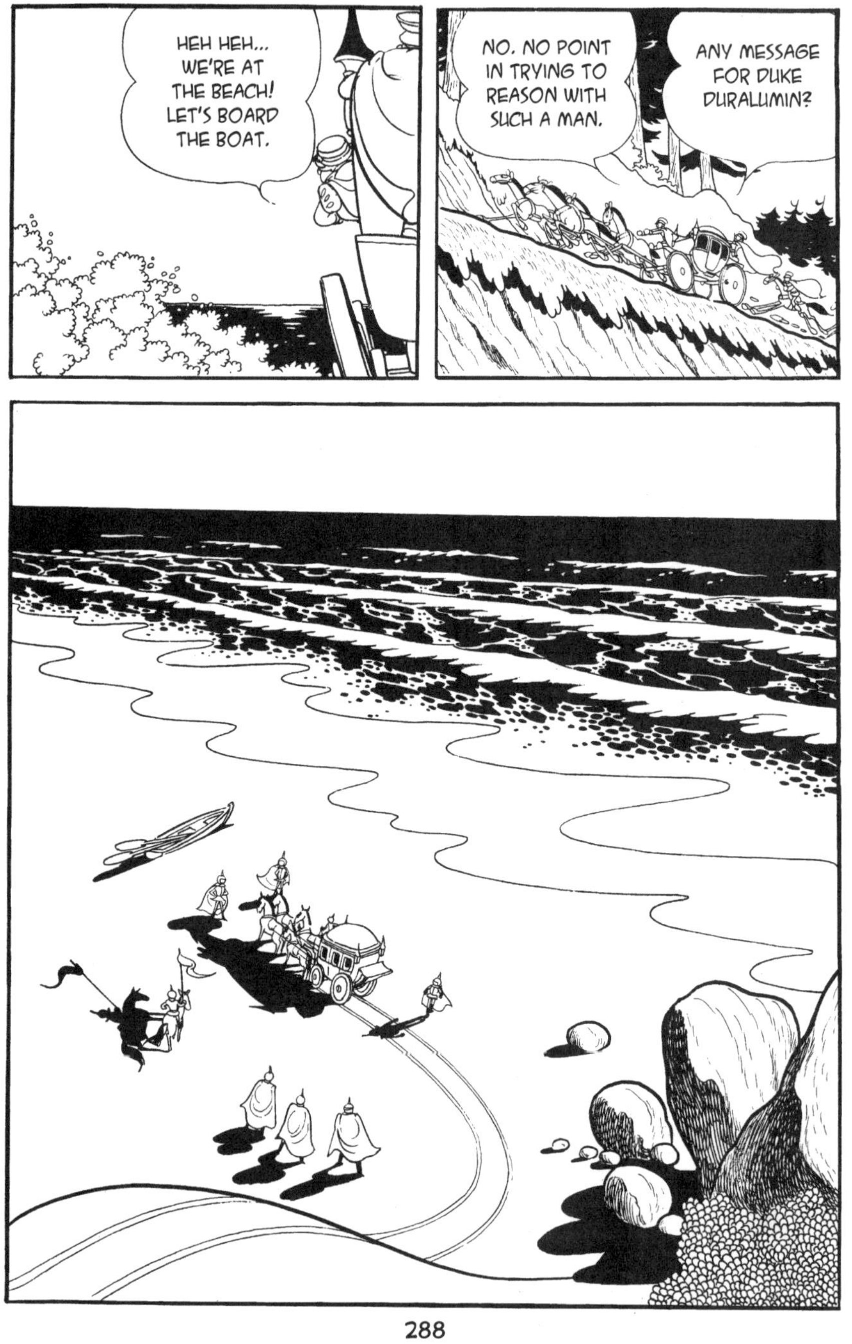
ANY MESSAGE FOR DUKE DURALUMIN?
NO. NO POINT IN TRYING TO REASON WITH SUCH A MAN.
HEH HEH... WE'RE AT THE BEACH! LET'S BOARD THE BOAT.

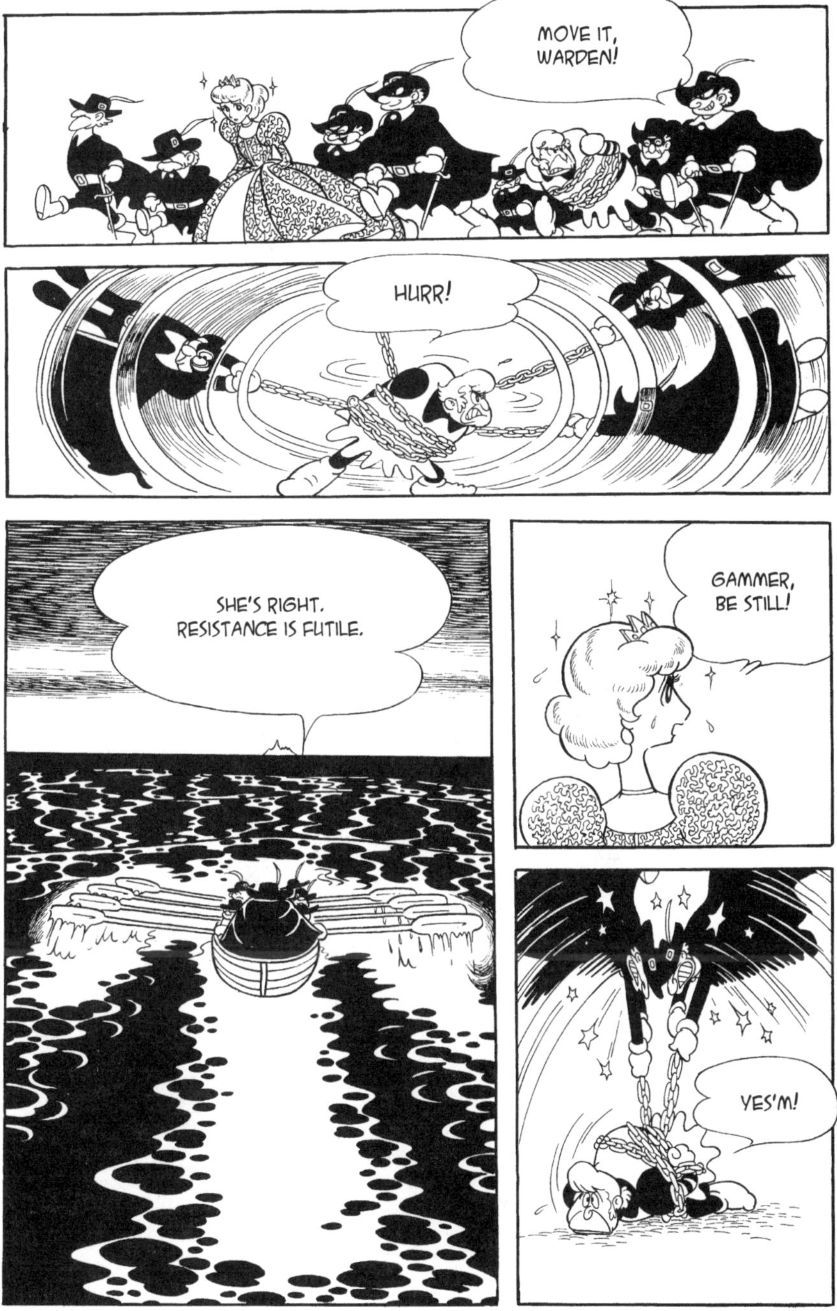
MOVE IT, WARDEN!
HURR!
GAMMER, BE STILL!
YES'M!
SHE'S RIGHT. RESISTANCE IS FUTILE.

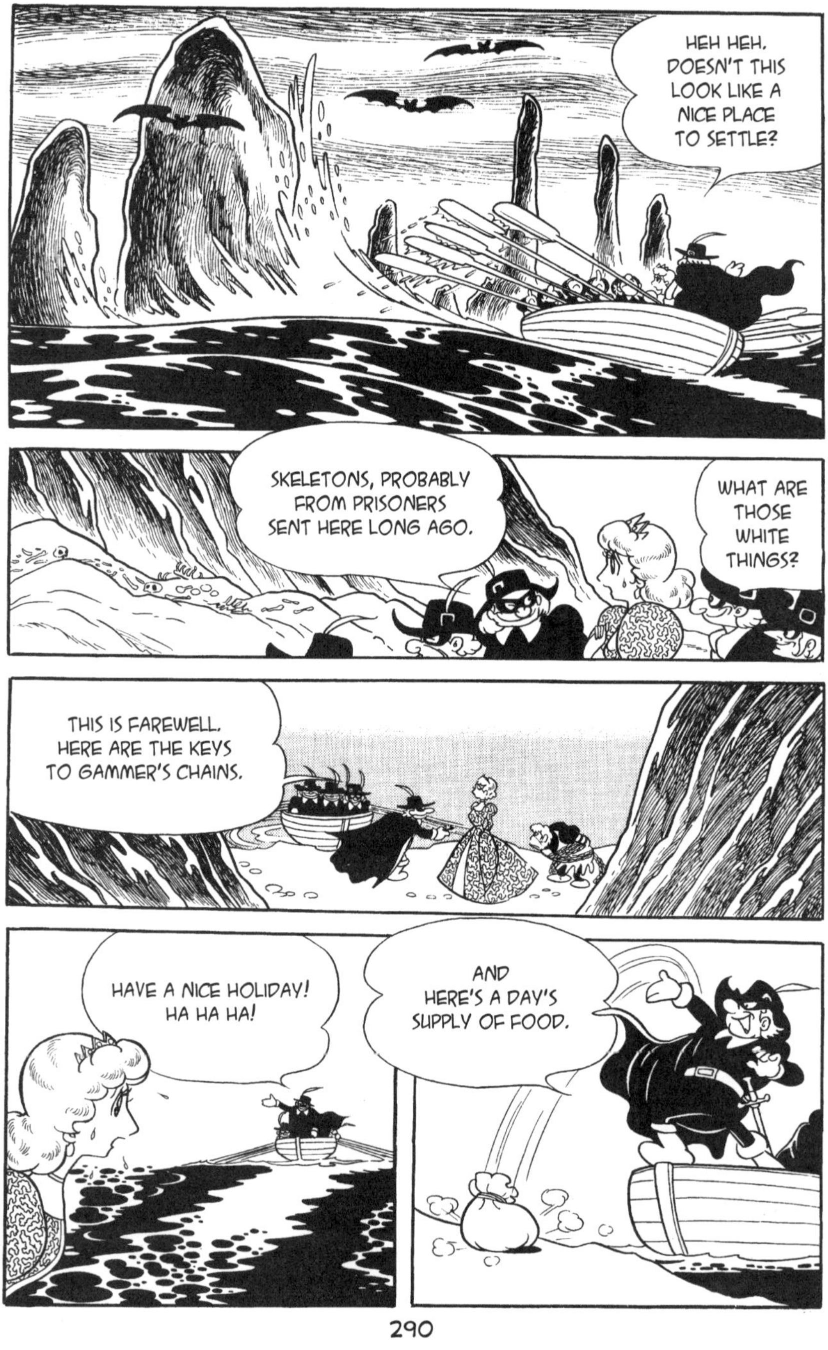
HEH HEH. DOESN'T THIS LOOK LIKE A NICE PLACE TO SETTLE?
WHAT ARE THOSE WHITE THINGS?
SKELETONS, PROBABLY FROM PRISONERS SENT HERE LONG AGO.
THIS IS FAREWELL. HERE ARE THE KEYS TO GAMMER'S CHAINS.
AND HERE'S A DAY'S SUPPLY OF FOOD.
HAVE A NICE HOLIDAY! HA HA HA!

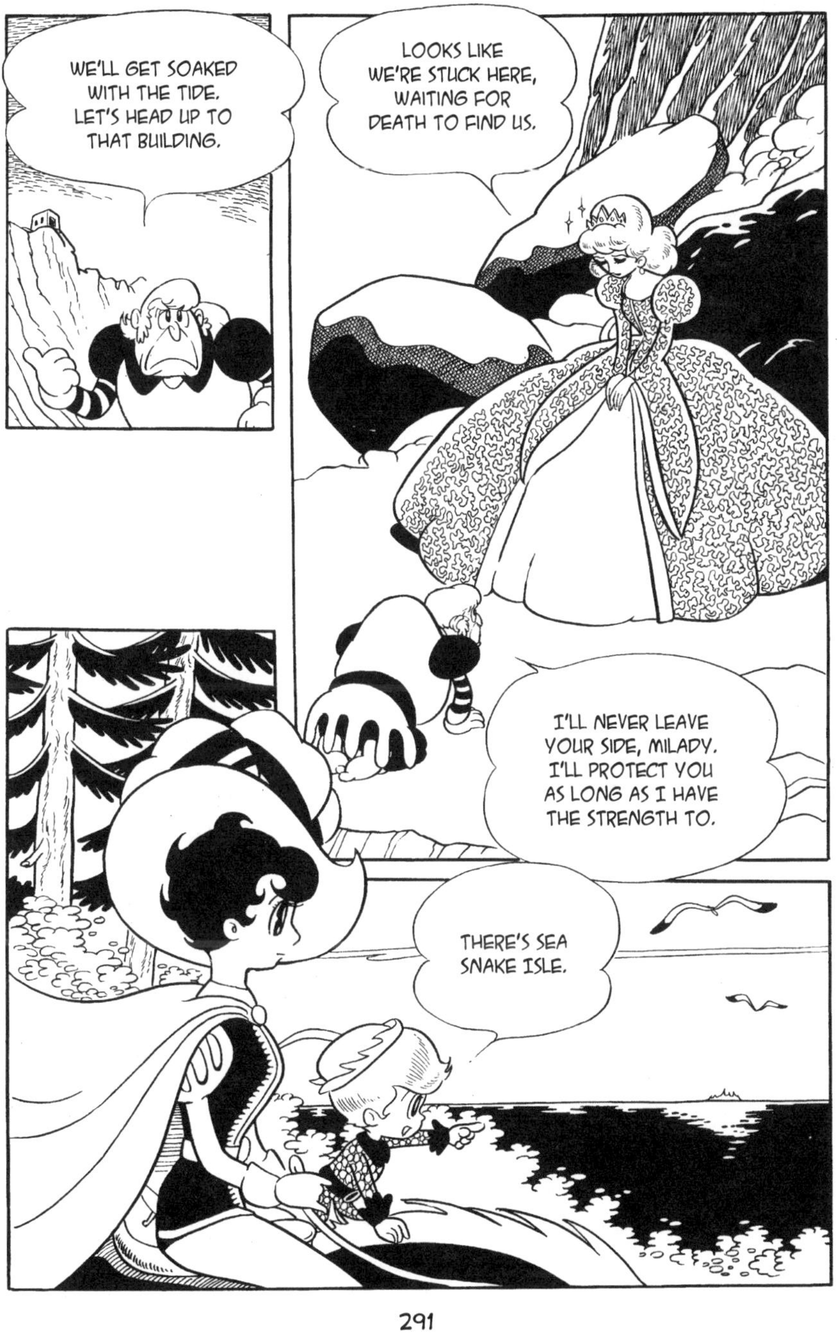
LOOKS LIKE WE'RE STUCK HERE, WAITING FOR DEATH TO FIND US.
I'LL NEVER LEAVE YOUR SIDE, MILADY. I'LL PROTECT YOU AS LONG AS I HAVE THE STRENGTH TO.
WE'LL GET SOAKED WITH THE TIDE. LET'S HEAD UP TO THAT BUILDING.
THERE'S SEA SNAKE ISLE.

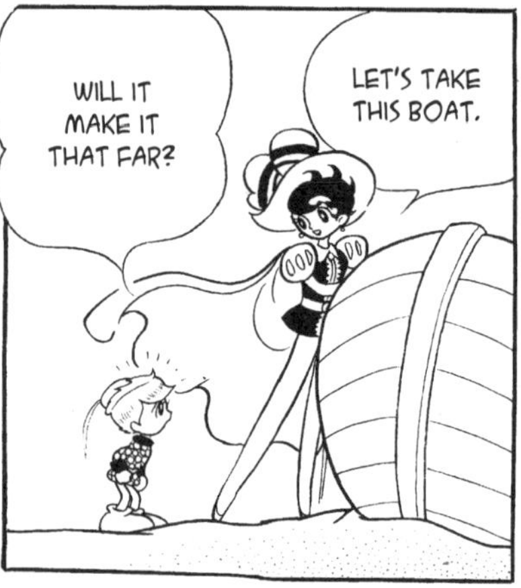
LET'S TAKE THIS BOAT.
WILL IT MAKE IT THAT FAR?

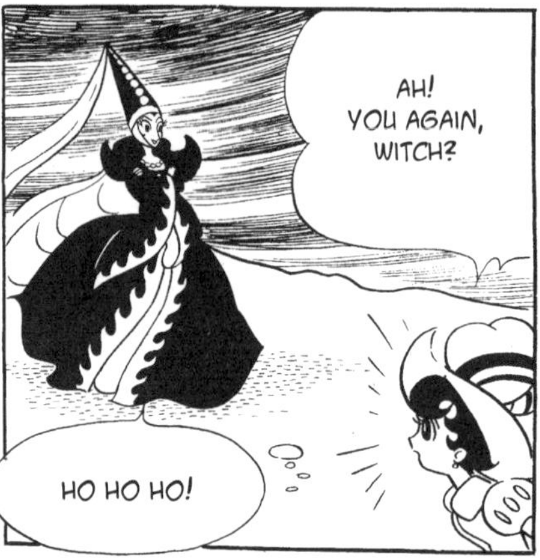
AH! YOU AGAIN, WITCH?
HO HO HO!

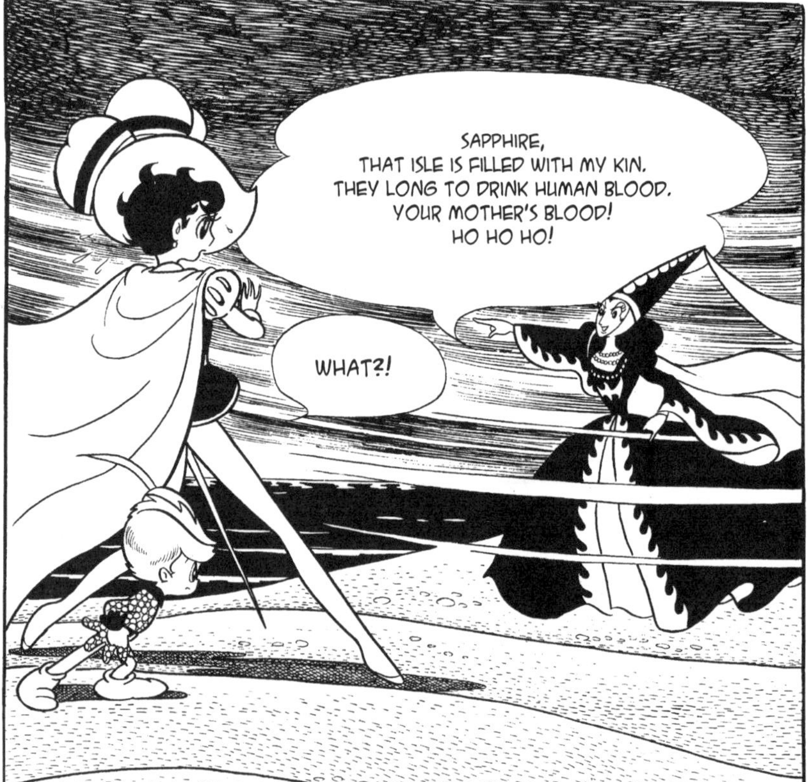
SAPPHIRE, THAT ISLE IS FILLED WITH MY KIN. THEY LONG TO DRINK HUMAN BLOOD. YOUR MOTHER'S BLOOD! HO HO HO!
WHAT?!

Chapter 15

Stone Queen

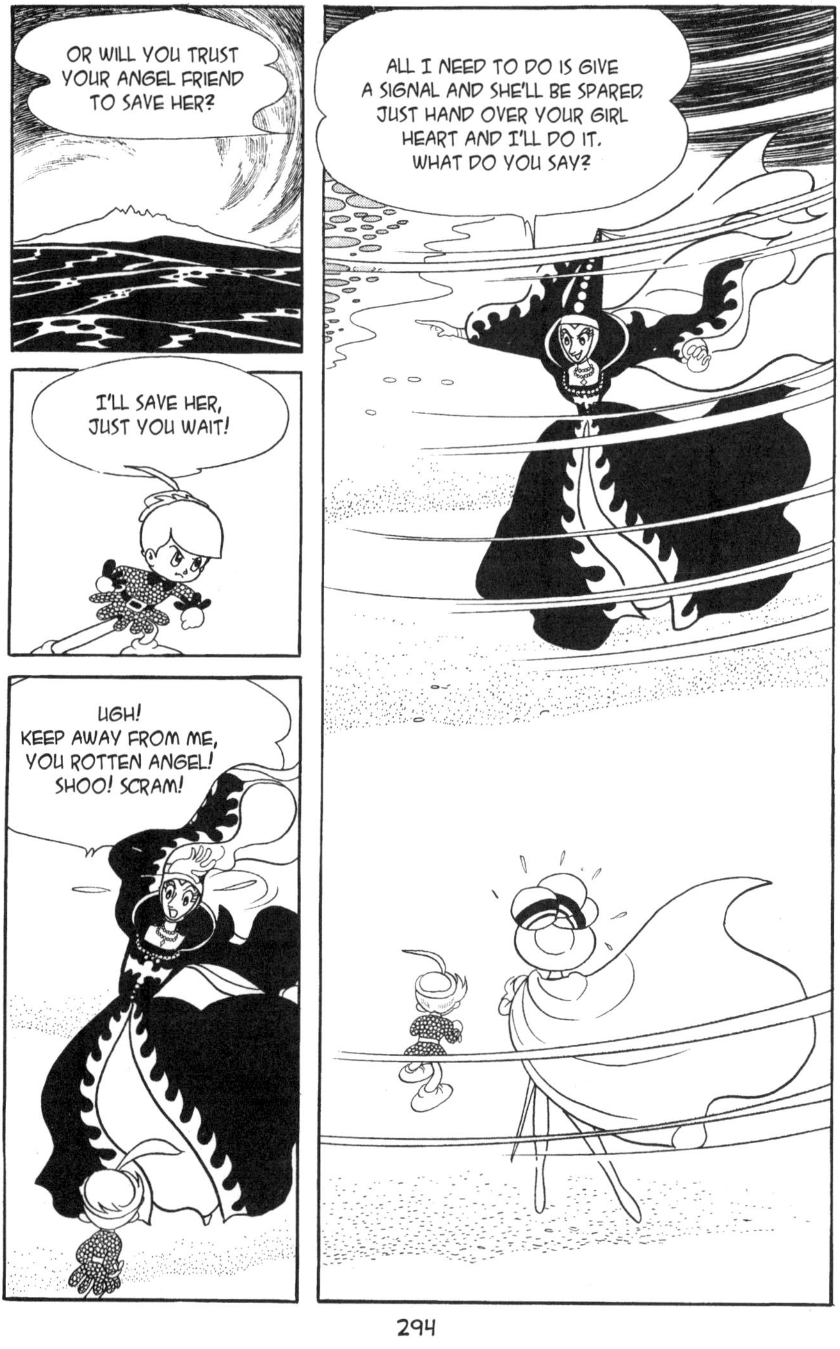
ALL I NEED TO DO IS GIVE A SIGNAL AND SHE'LL BE SPARED. JUST HAND OVER YOUR GIRL HEART AND I'LL DO IT. WHAT DO YOU SAY?
OR WILL YOU TRUST YOUR ANGEL FRIEND TO SAVE HER?
I'LL SAVE HER, JUST YOU WAIT!
UGH! KEEP AWAY FROM ME, YOU ROTTEN ANGEL! SHOO! SCRAM!

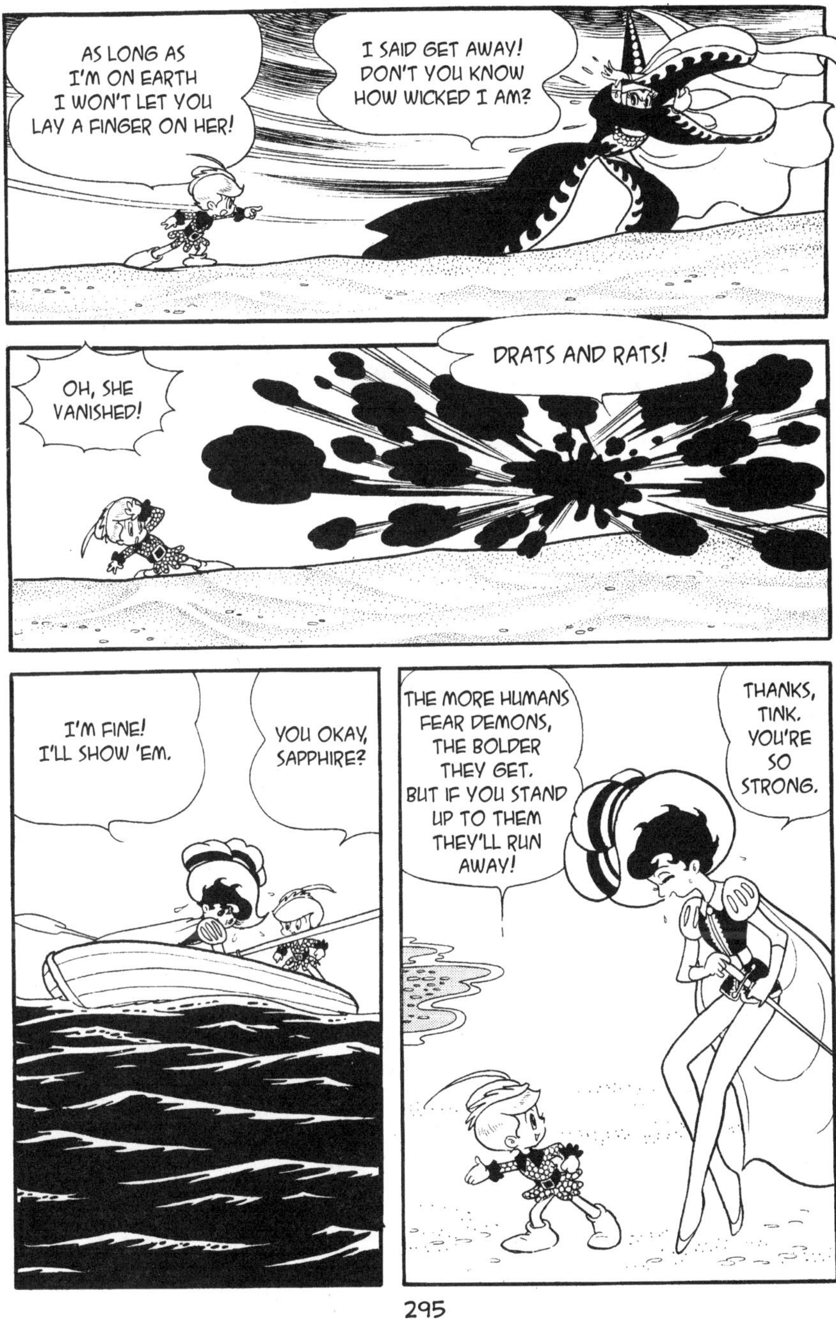
I SAID GET AWAY! DON'T YOU KNOW HOW WICKED I AM?
AS LONG AS I'M ON EARTH I WON'T LET YOU LAY A FINGER ON HER!
DRATS AND RATS!
OH, SHE VANISHED!
THANKS, TINK. YOU'RE SO STRONG.
THE MORE HUMANS FEAR DEMONS, THE BOLDER THEY GET. BUT IF YOU STAND UP TO THEM THEY'LL RUN AWAY!
YOU OKAY, SAPPHIRE?
I'M FINE! I'LL SHOW 'EM.

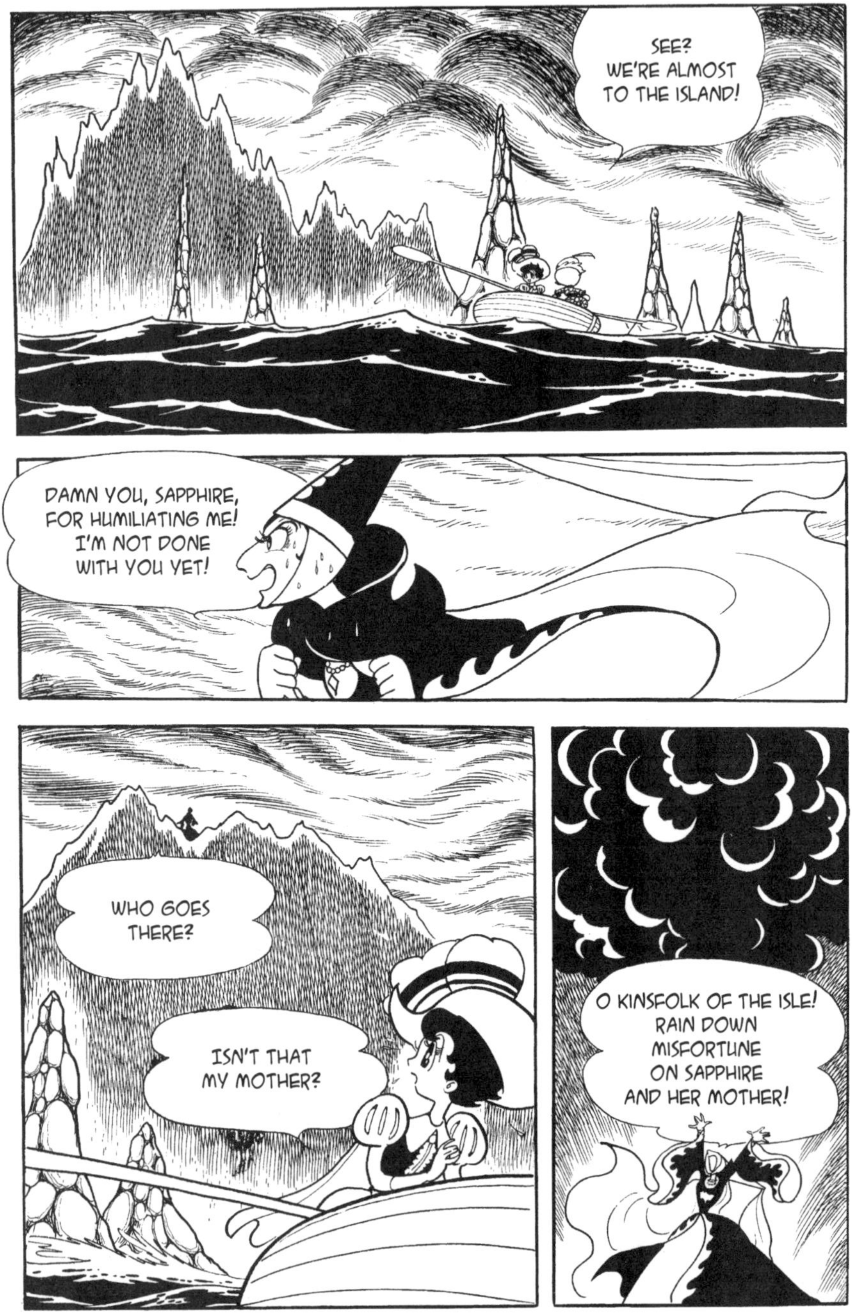
SEE? WE'RE ALMOST TO THE ISLAND!
DAMN YOU, SAPPHIRE, FOR HUMILIATING ME! I'M NOT DONE WITH YOU YET!
O KINSFOLK OF THE ISLE! RAIN DOWN MISFORTUNE ON SAPPHIRE AND HER MOTHER!
WHO GOES THERE?
ISN'T THAT MY MOTHER?

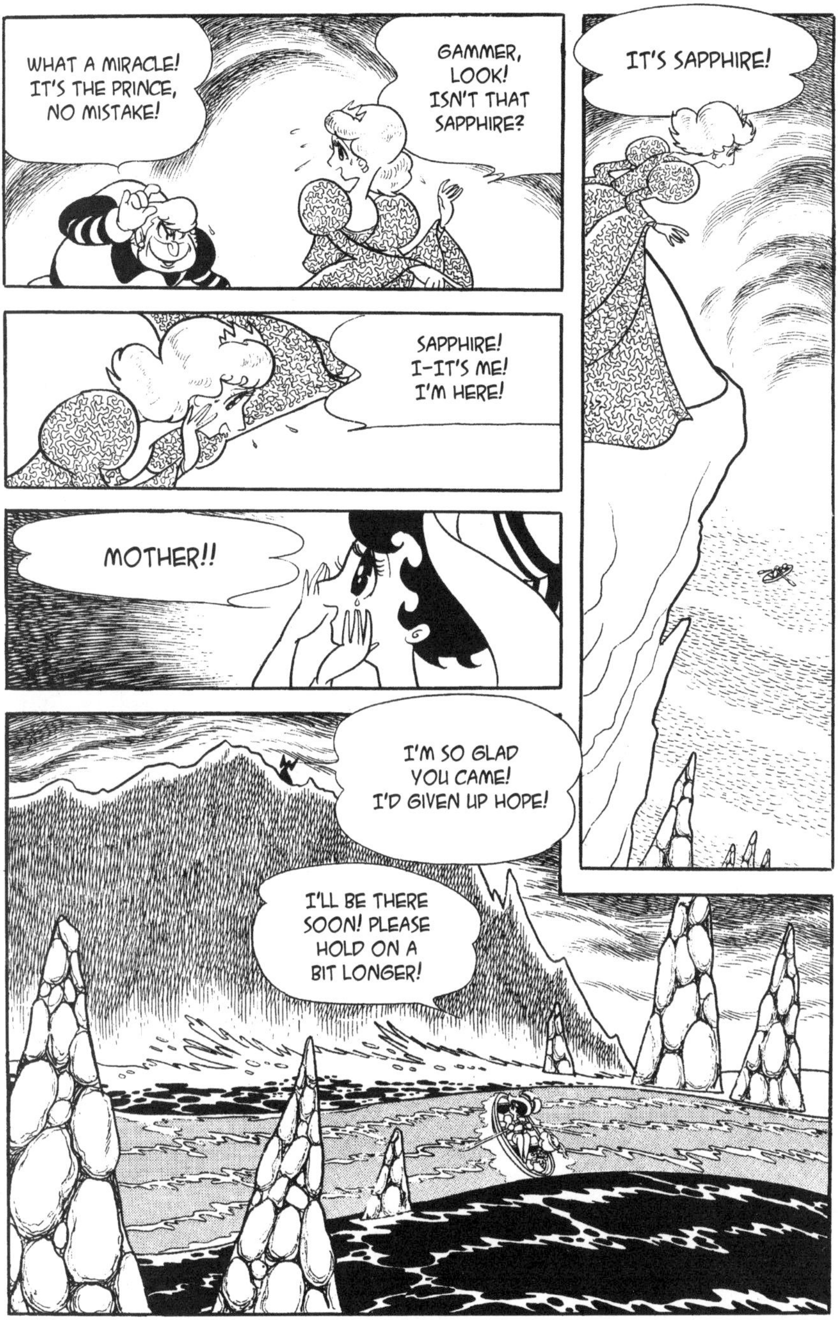
IT'S SAPPHIRE!
GAMMER, LOOK! ISN'T THAT SAPPHIRE?
WHAT A MIRACLE! IT'S THE PRINCE, NO MISTAKE!
SAPPHIRE! I-IT'S ME! I'M HERE!
MOTHER!!
I'M SO GLAD YOU CAME! I'D GIVEN UP HOPE!
I'LL BE THERE SOON! PLEASE HOLD ON A BIT LONGER!

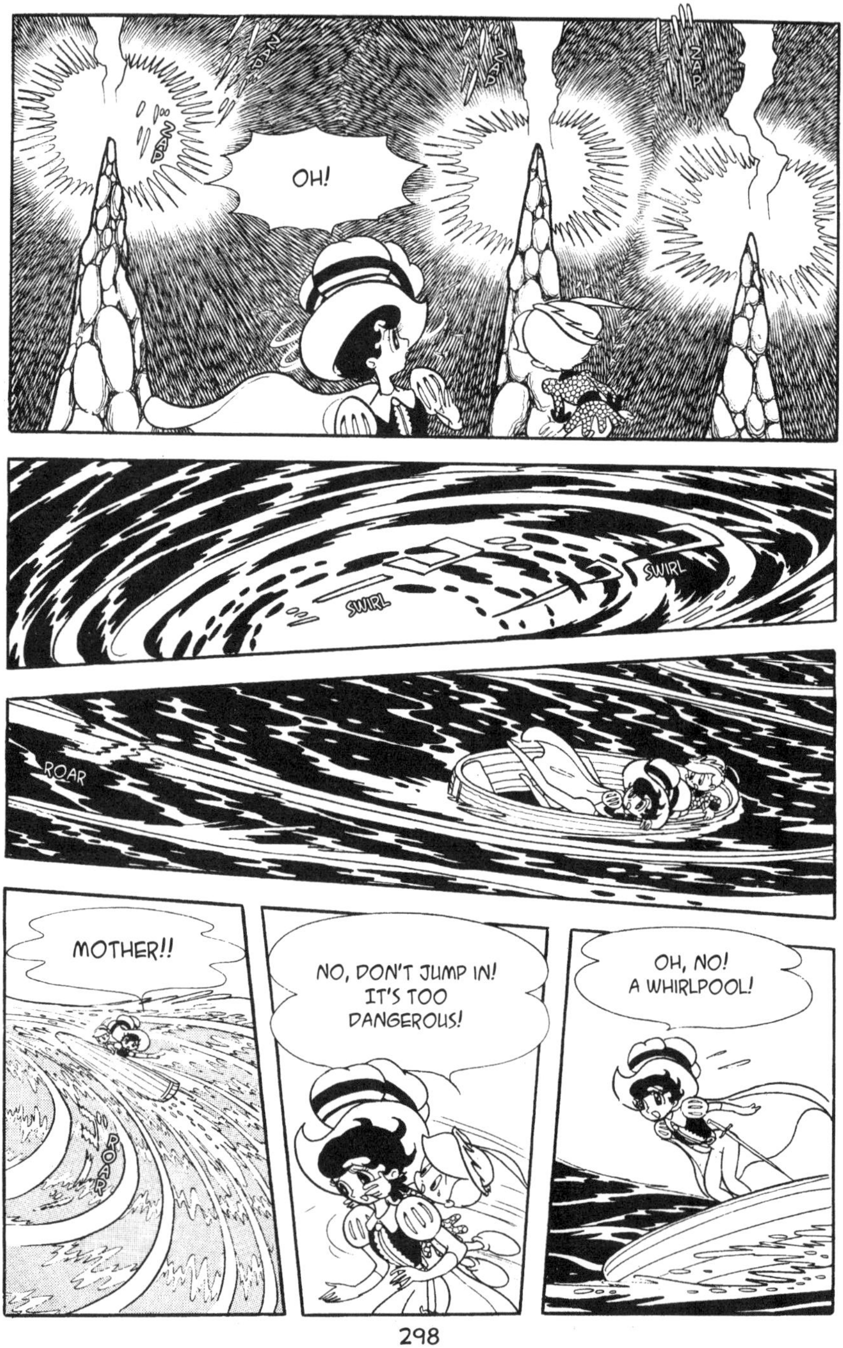
ZAP
ZAP
ZAP
ZAP
OH!
SWIRL
SWIRL
ROAR
OH, NO! A WHIRLPOOL!
NO, DON'T JUMP IN! IT'S TOO DANGEROUS!
MOTHER!!
ROAR

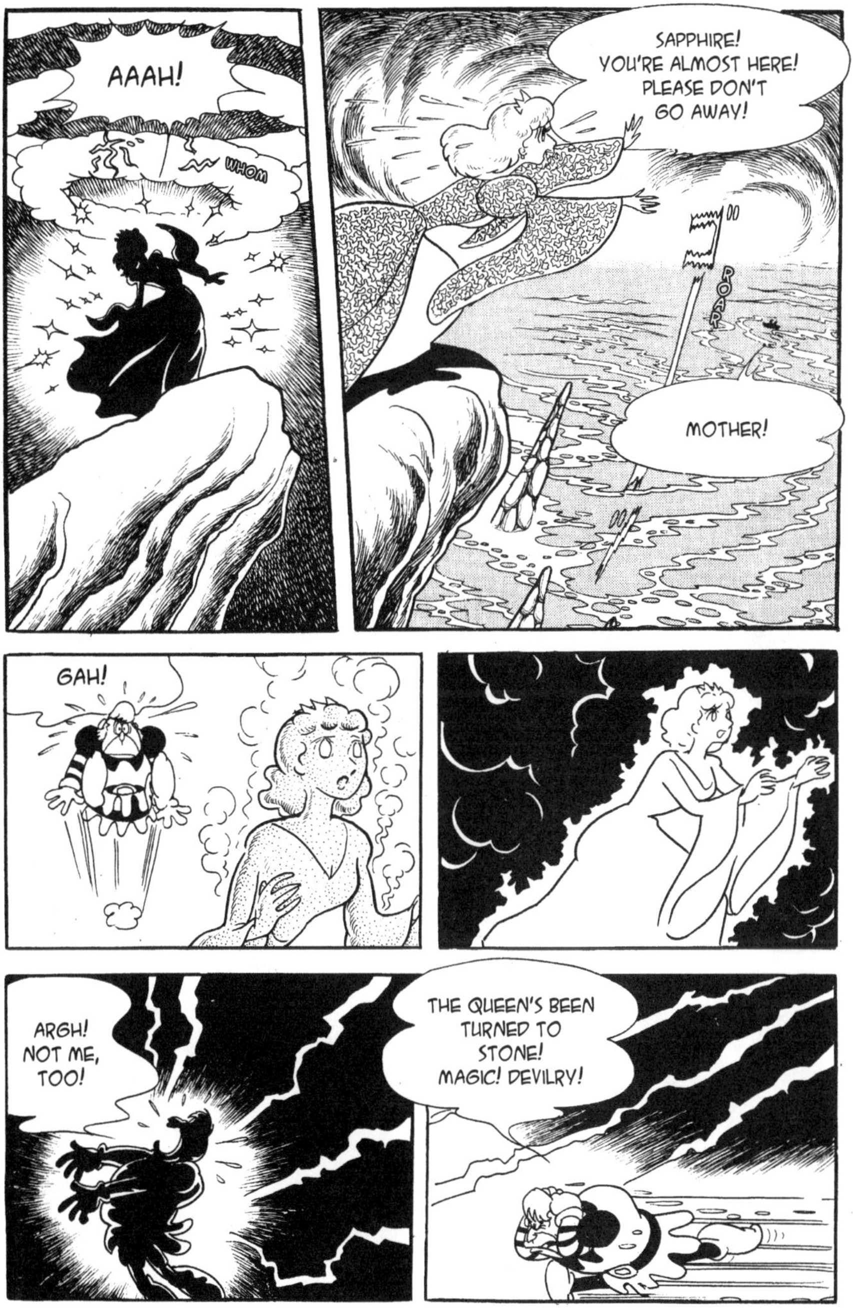
SAPPHIRE! YOU'RE ALMOST HERE! PLEASE DON'T GO AWAY!
ROAR
MOTHER!
AAAH!
WHOM
GAH!
THE QUEEN'S BEEN TURNED TO STONE! MAGIC! DEVILRY!
ARGH! NOT ME, TOO!

BE TURNED TO STONE, FROZEN IN PLACE AND PELTED BY STORMS FOREVER. ONLY RETURN TO YOUR TRUE FORM WHEN SAPPHIRE'S BLOOD IS SPILT UPON YOU. AT WHICH POINT, SAPPHIRE MUST DIE! HO HO HO!

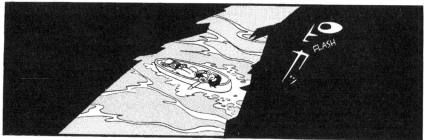

FLASH

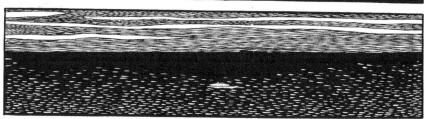

WHERE AM I?

"GASP"

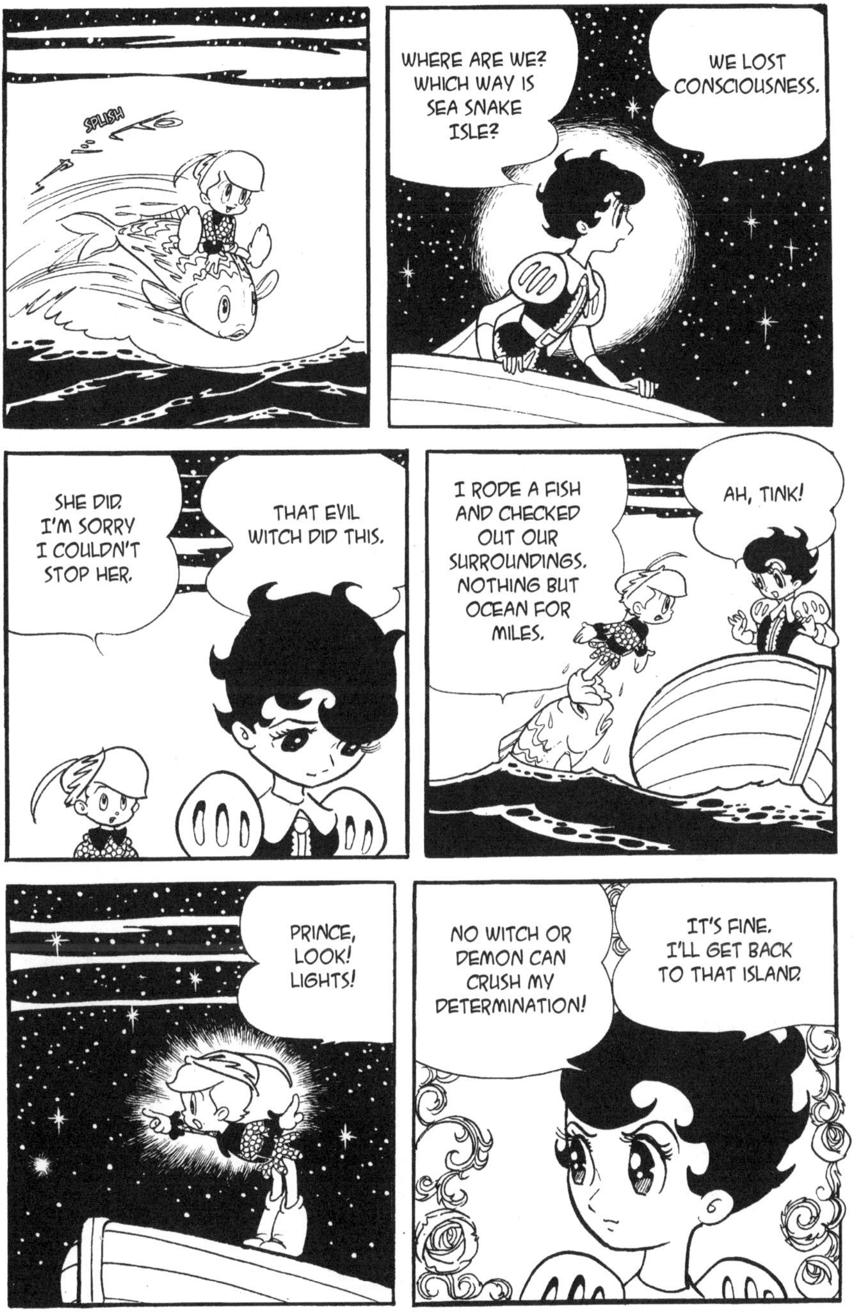
WE LOST CONSCIOUSNESS.
WHERE ARE WE? WHICH WAY IS SEA SNAKE ISLE?
SPLISH
AH, TINK!
I RODE A FISH AND CHECKED OUT OUR SURROUNDINGS. NOTHING BUT OCEAN FOR MILES.
THAT EVIL WITCH DID THIS.
SHE DID. I'M SORRY I COULDN'T STOP HER.
IT'S FINE. I'LL GET BACK TO THAT ISLAND.
NO WITCH OR DEMON CAN CRUSH MY DETERMINATION!
PRINCE, LOOK! LIGHTS!

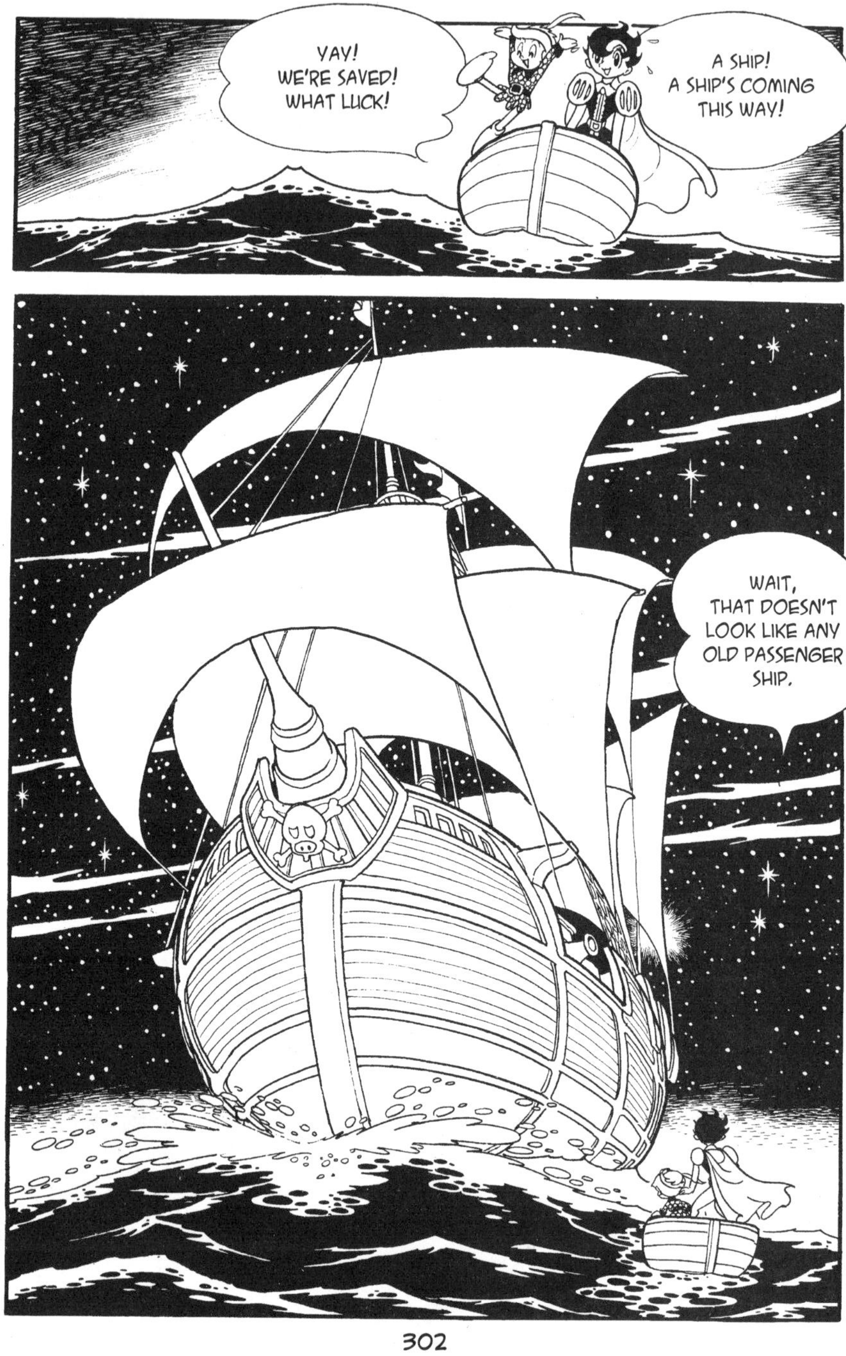
A SHIP! A SHIP'S COMING THIS WAY!
YAY! WE'RE SAVED! WHAT LUCK!
WAIT, THAT DOESN'T LOOK LIKE ANY OLD PASSENGER SHIP.

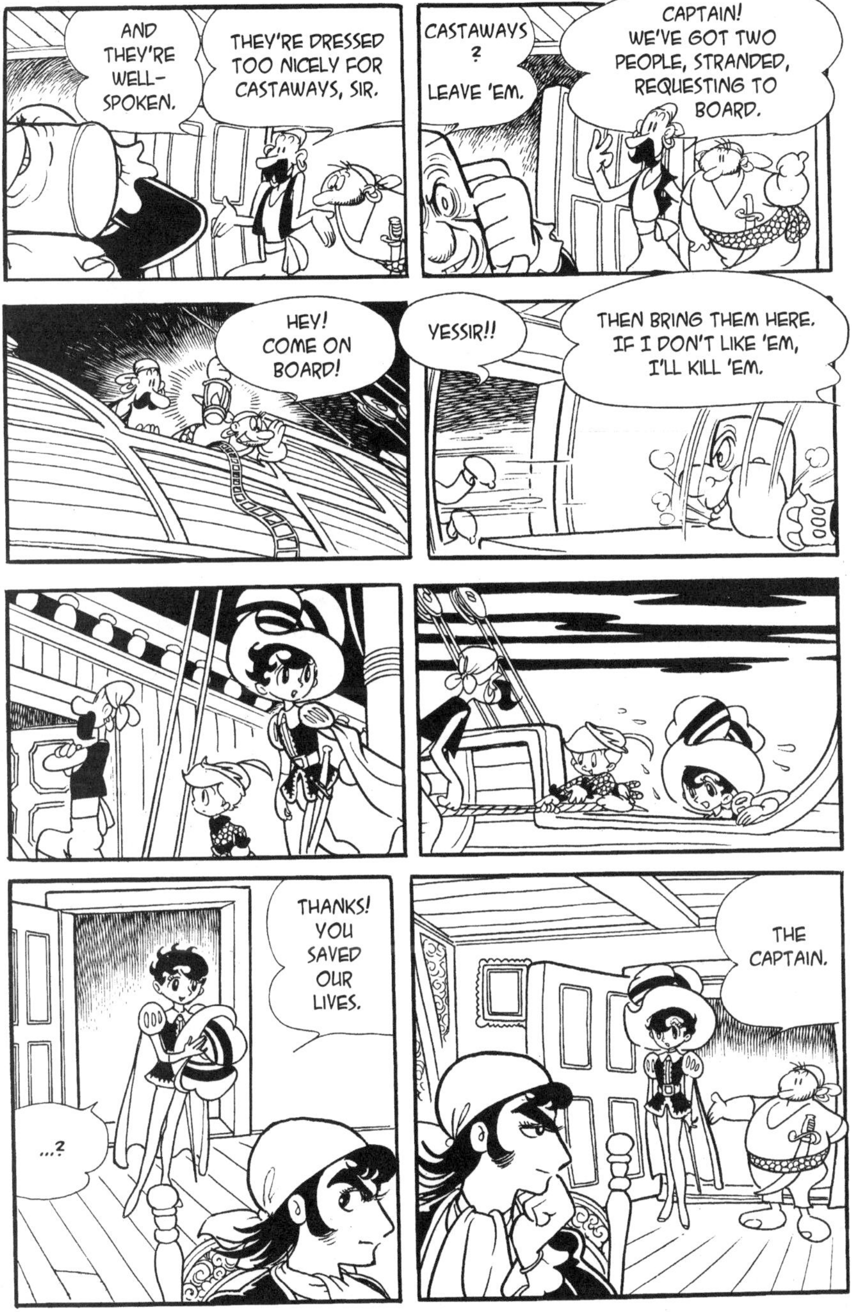
CAPTAIN! WE'VE GOT TWO PEOPLE, STRANDED, REQUESTING TO BOARD.
CASTAWAYS? LEAVE 'EM.
THEY'RE DRESSED TOO NICELY FOR CASTAWAYS, SIR.
AND THEY'RE WELL-SPOKEN.
THEN BRING THEM HERE. IF I DON'T LIKE 'EM, I'LL KILL 'EM.
YESSIR!!
HEY! COME ON BOARD!
THE CAPTAIN.
THANKS! YOU SAVED OUR LIVES.
...?

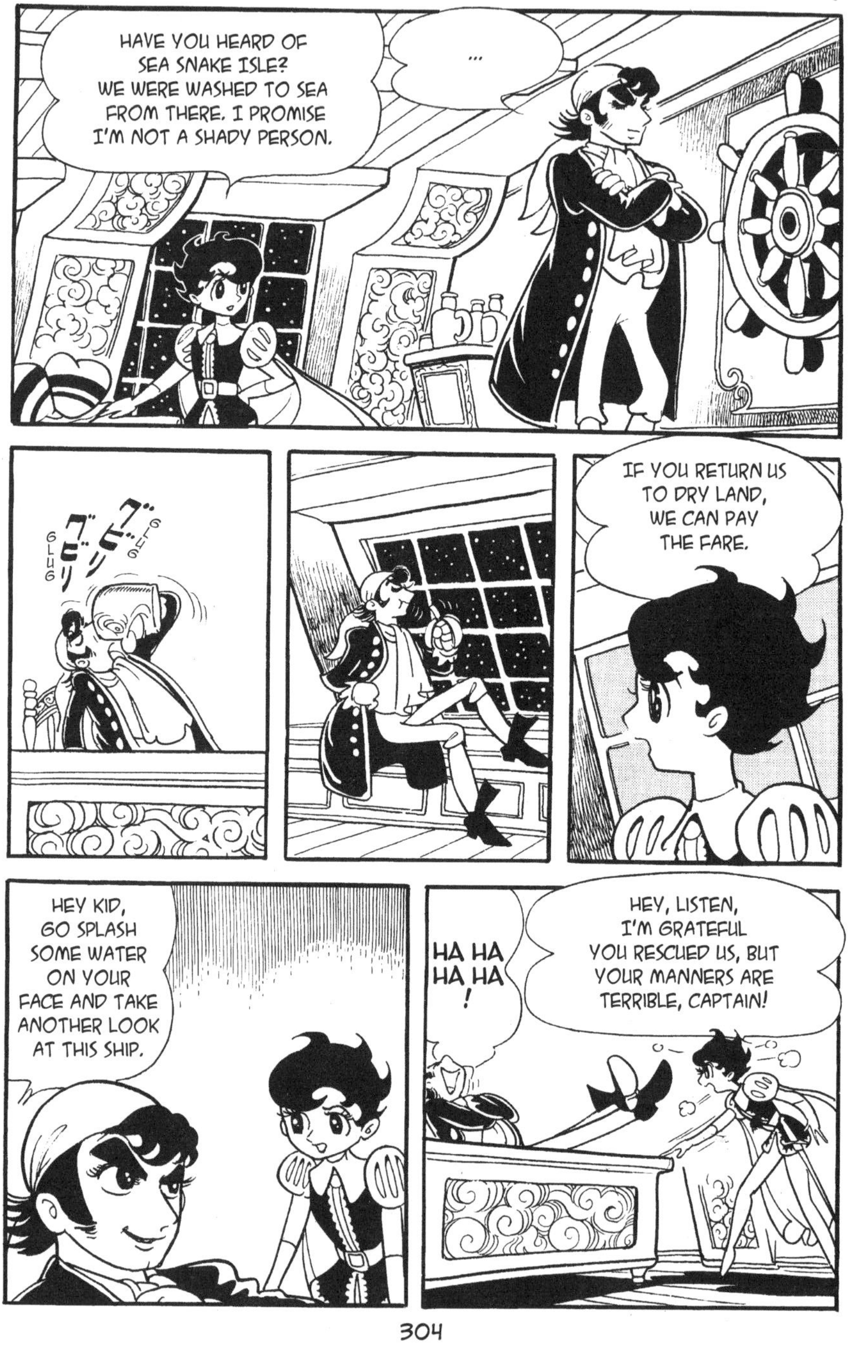
...
HAVE YOU HEARD OF SEA SNAKE ISLE? WE WERE WASHED TO SEA FROM THERE. I PROMISE I'M NOT A SHADY PERSON.
IF YOU RETURN US TO DRY LAND, WE CAN PAY THE FARE.
GLUG
GLUG
HEY, LISTEN, I'M GRATEFUL YOU RESCUED US, BUT YOUR MANNERS ARE TERRIBLE, CAPTAIN!
HA HA HA HA!
HEY KID, GO SPLASH SOME WATER ON YOUR FACE AND TAKE ANOTHER LOOK AT THIS SHIP.

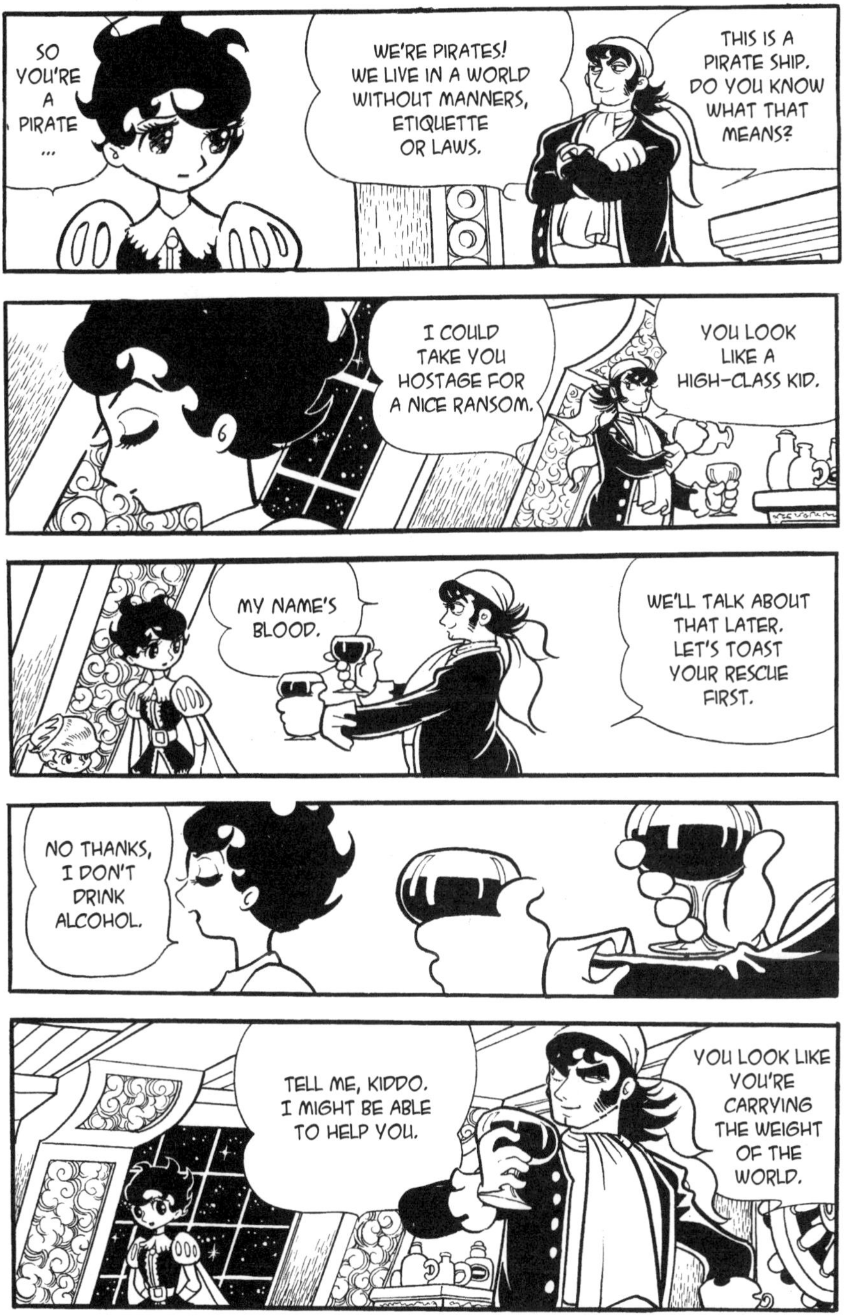
THIS IS A PIRATE SHIP. DO YOU KNOW WHAT THAT MEANS?
WE'RE PIRATES! WE LIVE IN A WORLD WITHOUT MANNERS, ETIQUETTE OR LAWS.
SO YOU'RE A PIRATE ...
YOU LOOK LIKE A HIGH-CLASS KID.
I COULD TAKE YOU HOSTAGE FOR A NICE RANSOM.
WE'LL TALK ABOUT THAT LATER. LET'S TOAST YOUR RESCUE FIRST.
MY NAME'S BLOOD.
NO THANKS, I DON'T DRINK ALCOHOL.
YOU LOOK LIKE YOU'RE CARRYING THE WEIGHT OF THE WORLD.
TELL ME, KIDDO. I MIGHT BE ABLE TO HELP YOU.

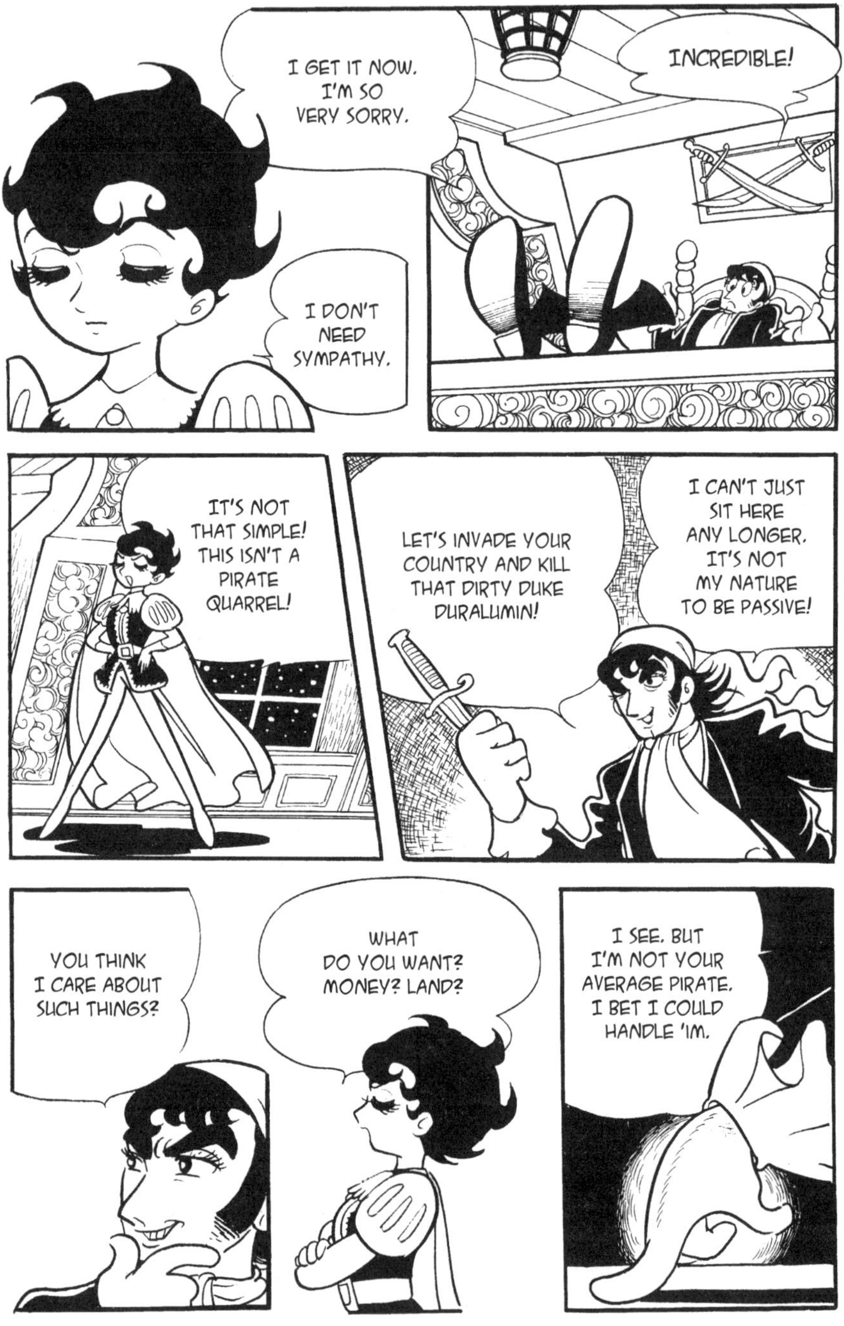

INCREDIBLE!
I GET IT NOW. I'M SO VERY SORRY.
I DON'T NEED SYMPATHY.
I CAN'T JUST SIT HERE ANY LONGER. IT'S NOT MY NATURE TO BE PASSIVE!
LET'S INVADE YOUR COUNTRY AND KILL THAT DIRTY DUKE DURALUMIN!
IT'S NOT THAT SIMPLE! THIS ISN'T A PIRATE QUARREL!
I SEE. BUT I'M NOT YOUR AVERAGE PIRATE. I BET I COULD HANDLE 'IM.
WHAT DO YOU WANT? MONEY? LAND?
YOU THINK I CARE ABOUT SUCH THINGS?

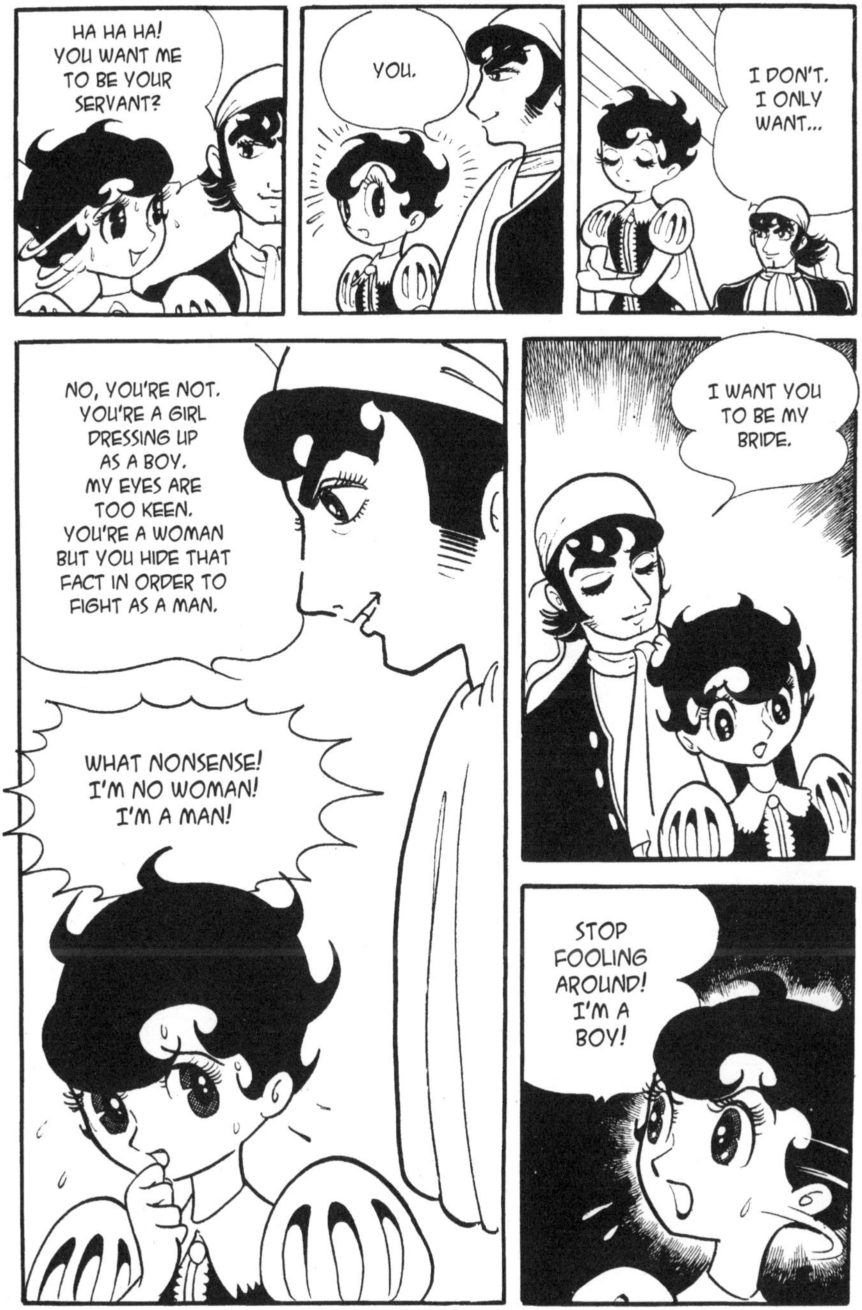
I DON'T. I ONLY WANT...
YOU.
HA HA HA! YOU WANT ME TO BE YOUR SERVANT?
I WANT YOU TO BE MY BRIDE.
STOP FOOLING AROUND! I'M A BOY!
NO, YOU'RE NOT. YOU'RE A GIRL DRESSING UP AS A BOY. MY EYES ARE TOO KEEN. YOU'RE A WOMAN BUT YOU HIDE THAT FACT IN ORDER TO FIGHT AS A MAN.
WHAT NONSENSE! I'M NO WOMAN! I'M A MAN!

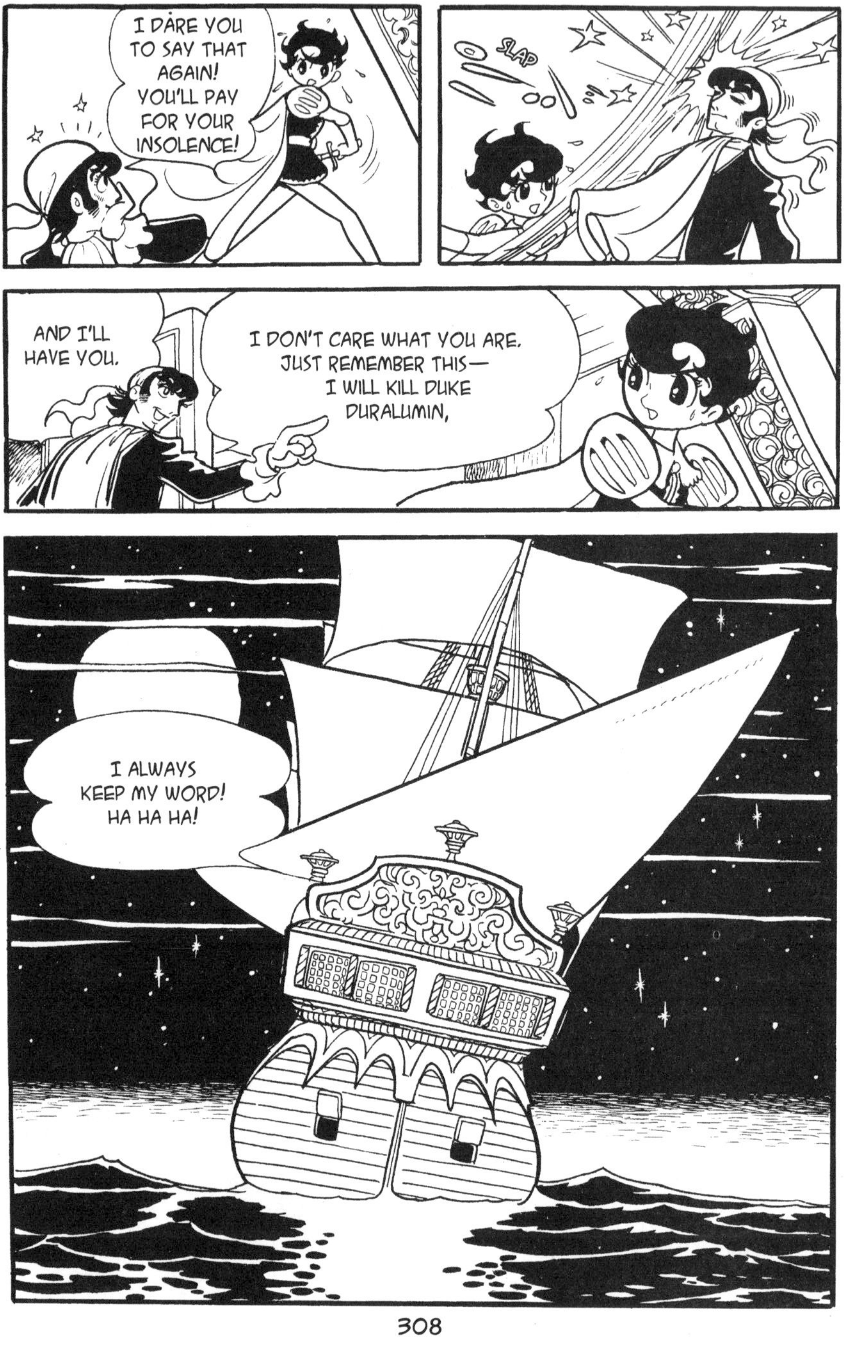
SLAP
I DARE YOU TO SAY THAT AGAIN! YOU'LL PAY FOR YOUR INSOLENCE!
I DON'T CARE WHAT YOU ARE. JUST REMEMBER THIS— I WILL KILL DUKE DURALUMIN,
AND I'LL HAVE YOU.
I ALWAYS KEEP MY WORD! HA HA HA!

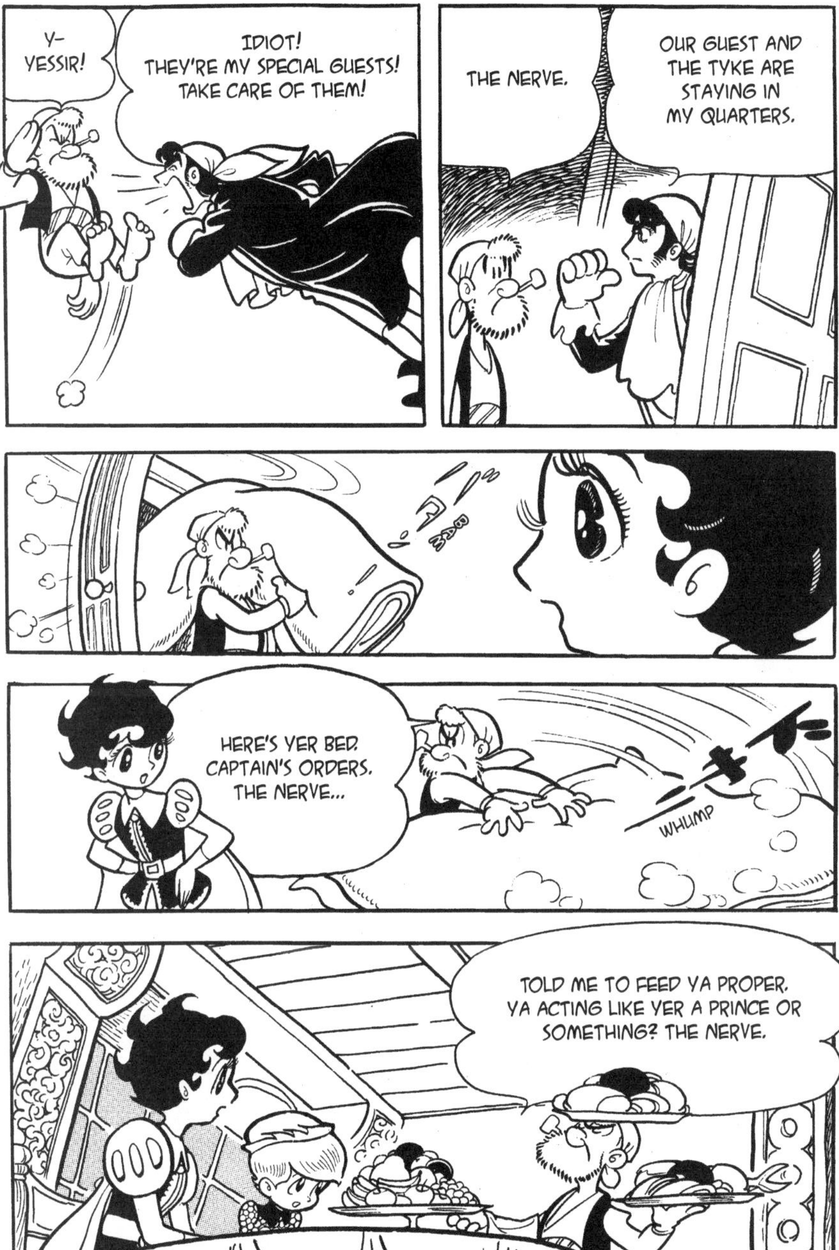
OUR GUEST AND THE TYKE ARE STAYING IN MY QUARTERS.
THE NERVE.
IDIOT! THEY'RE MY SPECIAL GUESTS! TAKE CARE OF THEM!
Y- YESSIR!
BAM
HERE'S YER BED. CAPTAIN'S ORDERS. THE NERVE...
WHUMP
TOLD ME TO FEED YA PROPER. YA ACTING LIKE YER A PRINCE OR SOMETHING? THE NERVE.

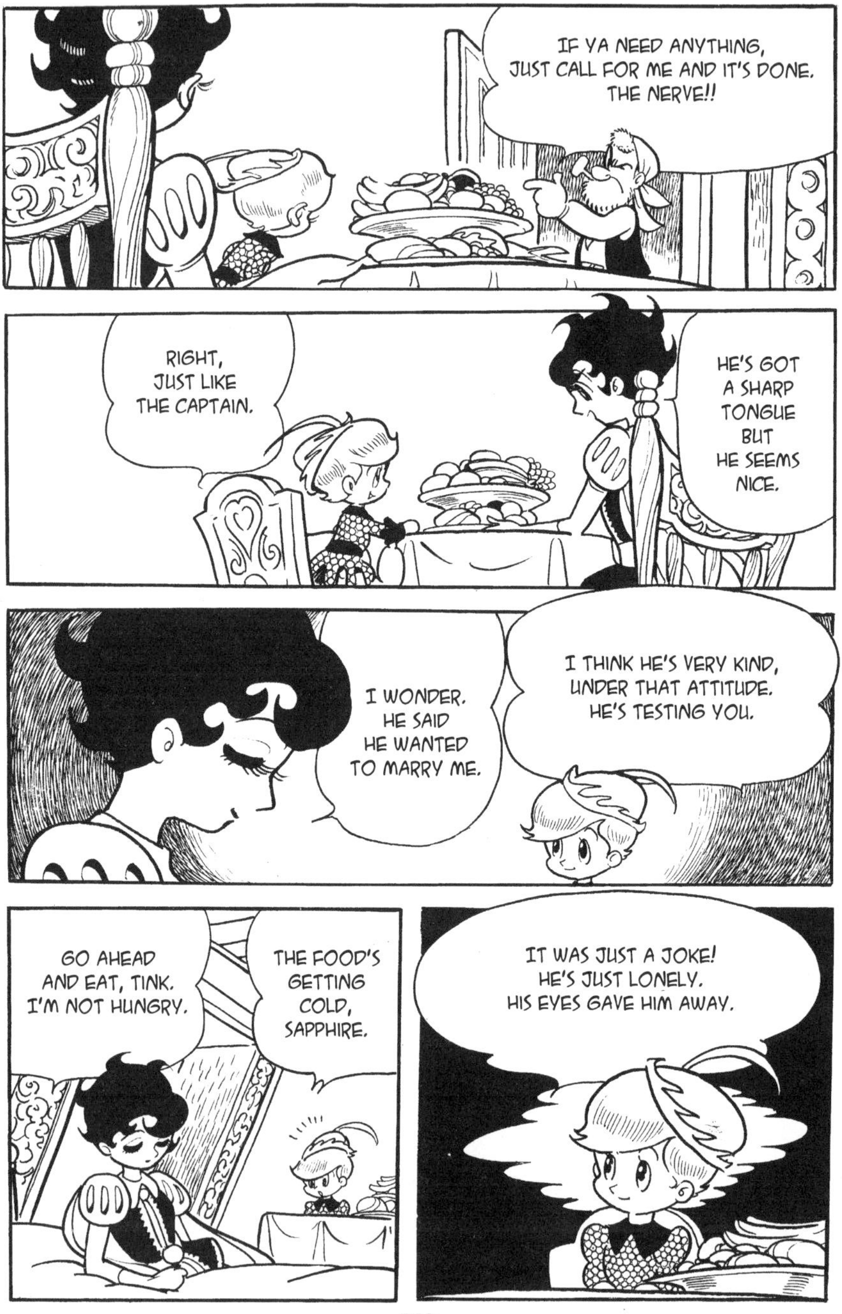
IF YA NEED ANYTHING, JUST CALL FOR ME AND IT'S DONE. THE NERVE!!
HE'S GOT A SHARP TONGUE BUT HE SEEMS NICE.
RIGHT, JUST LIKE THE CAPTAIN.
I THINK HE'S VERY KIND, UNDER THAT ATTITUDE. HE'S TESTING YOU.
I WONDER. HE SAID HE WANTED TO MARRY ME.
IT WAS JUST A JOKE! HE'S JUST LONELY. HIS EYES GAVE HIM AWAY.
THE FOOD'S GETTING COLD, SAPPHIRE.
GO AHEAD AND EAT, TINK. I'M NOT HUNGRY.

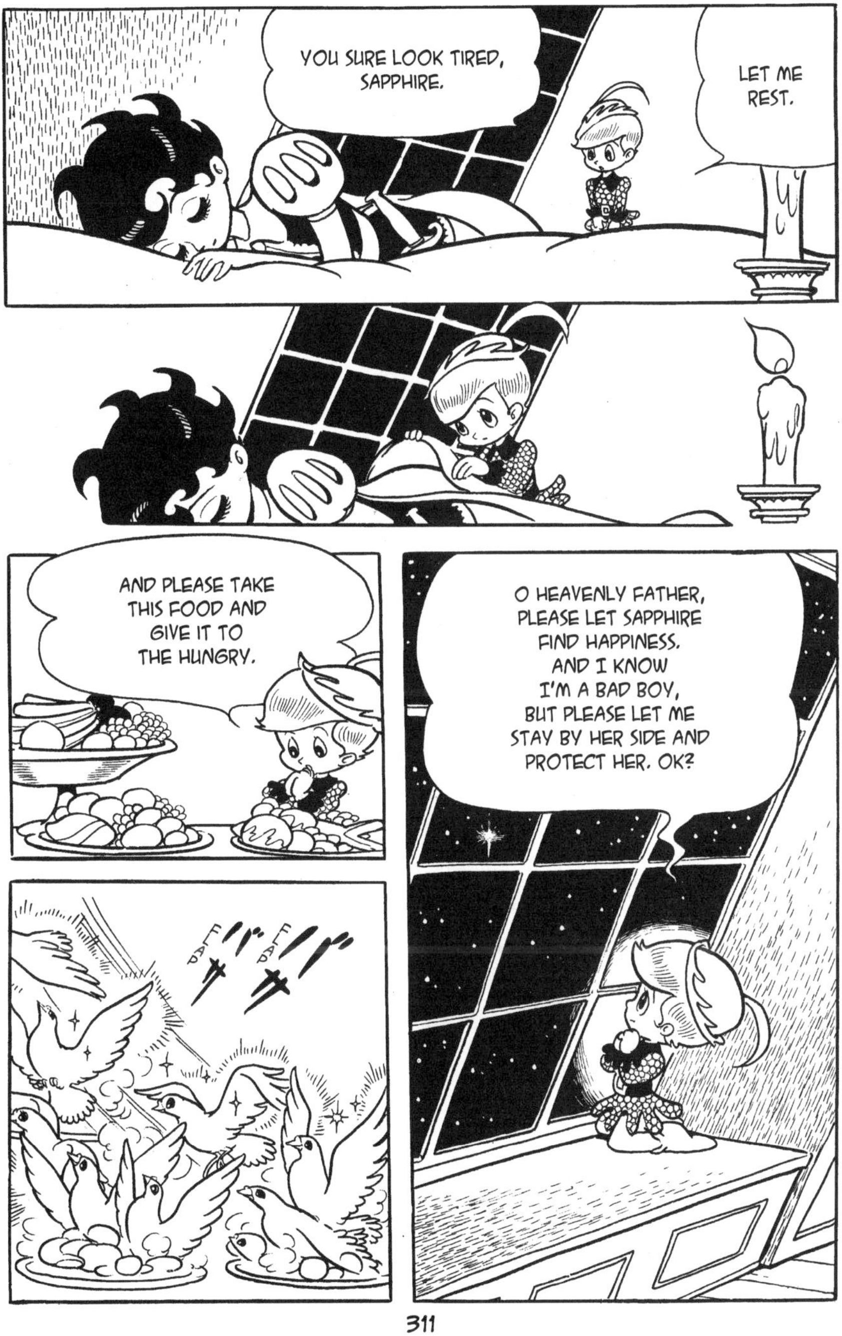
LET ME REST.
YOU SURE LOOK TIRED, SAPPHIRE.
O HEAVENLY FATHER, PLEASE LET SAPPHIRE FIND HAPPINESS. AND I KNOW I'M A BAD BOY, BUT PLEASE LET ME STAY BY HER SIDE AND PROTECT HER. OK?
AND PLEASE TAKE THIS FOOD AND GIVE IT TO THE HUNGRY.
FLAP
FLAP

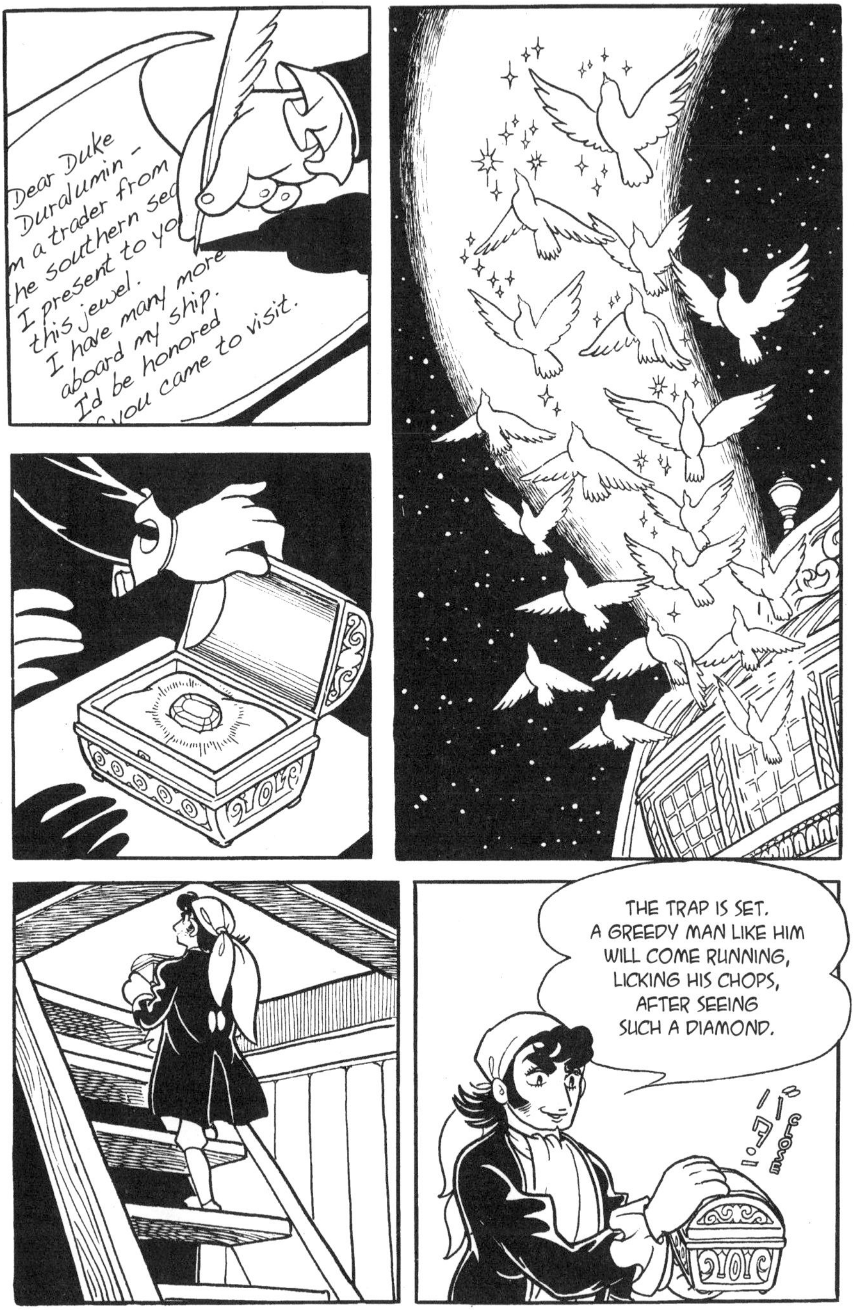
Dear Duke
Duralumin -
m a trader from
he southern sea
I present to yo
this jewel.
I have many more
aboard my ship.
I'd be honored
you came to visit.
THE TRAP IS SET. A GREEDY MAN LIKE HIM WILL COME RUNNING, LICKING HIS CHOPS, AFTER SEEING SUCH A DIAMOND.
CLOMP

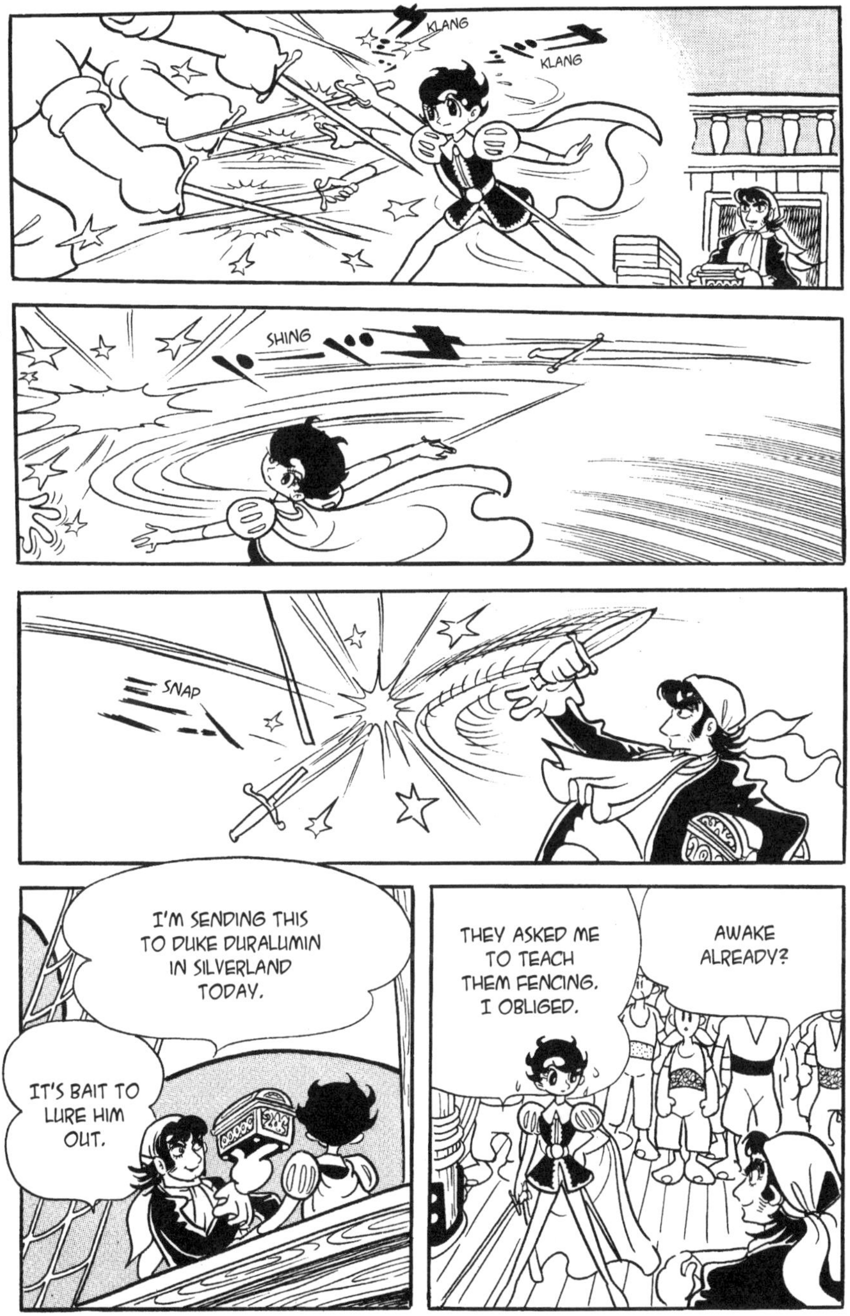
KLANG
KLANG
SHING
SNAP
AWAKE ALREADY?
THEY ASKED ME TO TEACH THEM FENCING. I OBLIGED.
I'M SENDING THIS TO DUKE DURALUMIN IN SILVERLAND TODAY.
IT'S BAIT TO LURE HIM OUT.

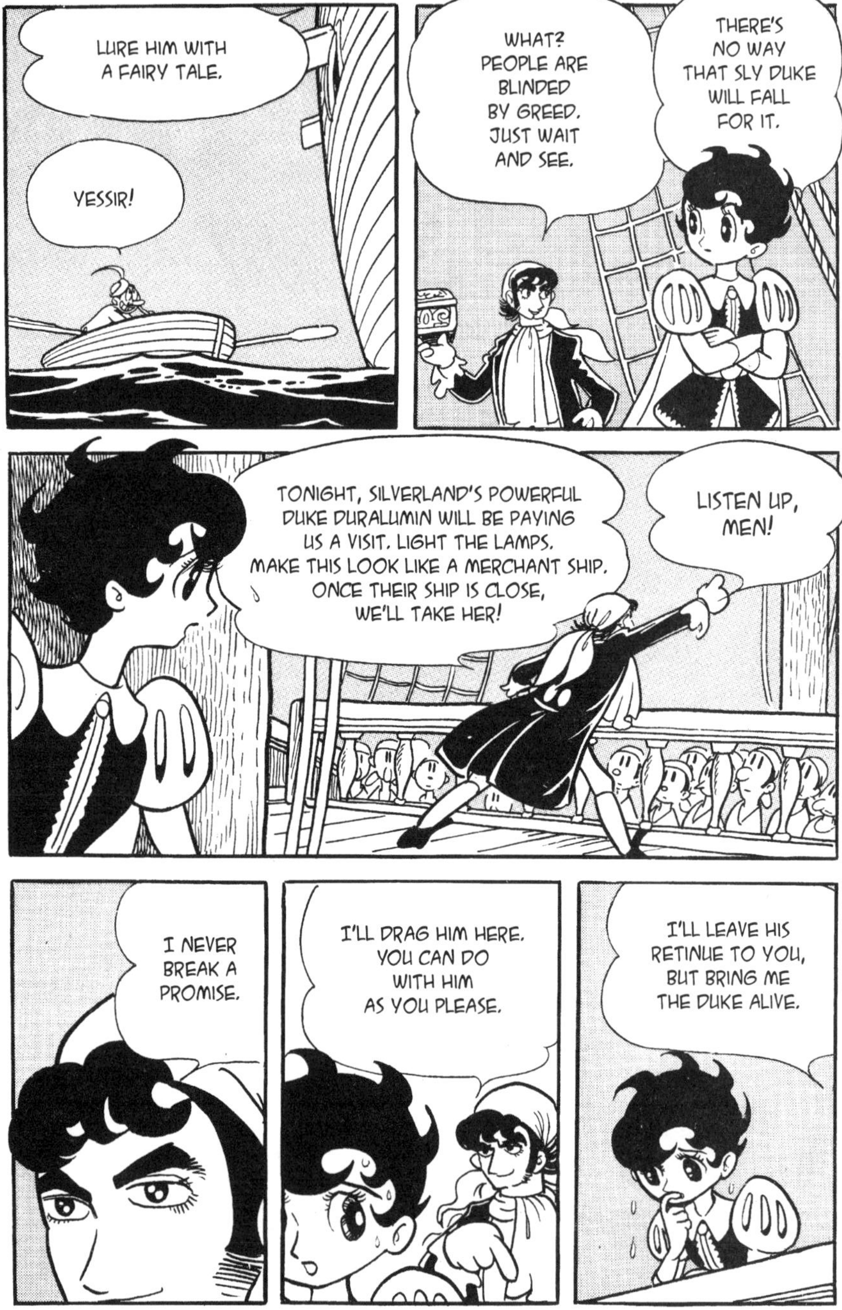
THERE'S NO WAY THAT SLY DUKE WILL FALL FOR IT.
WHAT? PEOPLE ARE BLINDED BY GREED. JUST WAIT AND SEE.
LURE HIM WITH A FAIRY TALE.
YESSIR!
LISTEN UP, MEN!
TONIGHT, SILVERLAND'S POWERFUL DUKE DURALUMIN WILL BE PAYING US A VISIT. LIGHT THE LAMPS. MAKE THIS LOOK LIKE A MERCHANT SHIP. ONCE THEIR SHIP IS CLOSE, WE'LL TAKE HER!
I'LL LEAVE HIS RETINUE TO YOU, BUT BRING ME THE DUKE ALIVE.
I'LL DRAG HIM HERE. YOU CAN DO WITH HIM AS YOU PLEASE.
I NEVER BREAK A PROMISE.

Chapter 16

Captain Blood, Pirate

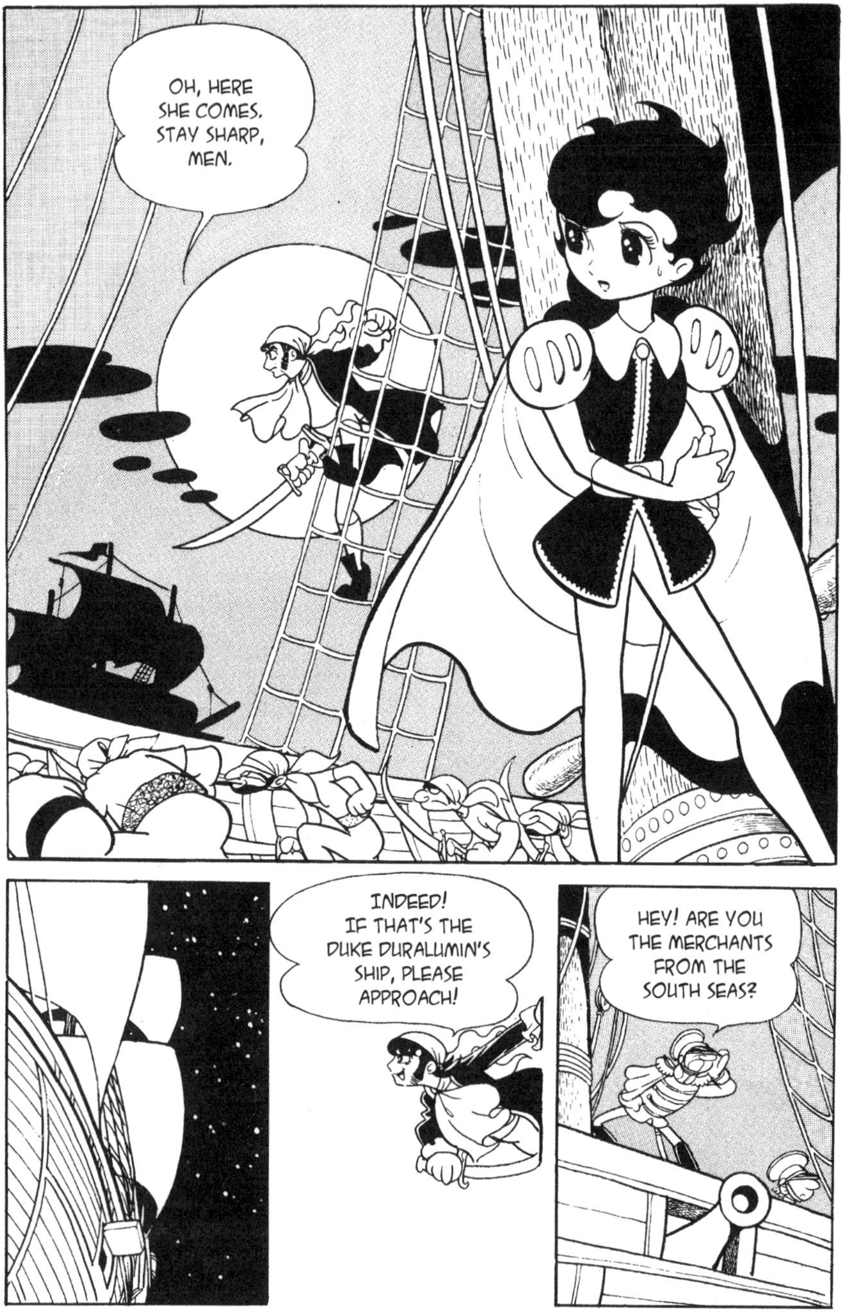
OH, HERE SHE COMES. STAY SHARP, MEN.
HEY! ARE YOU THE MERCHANTS FROM THE SOUTH SEAS?
INDEED! IF THAT'S THE DUKE DURALUMIN'S SHIP, PLEASE APPROACH!

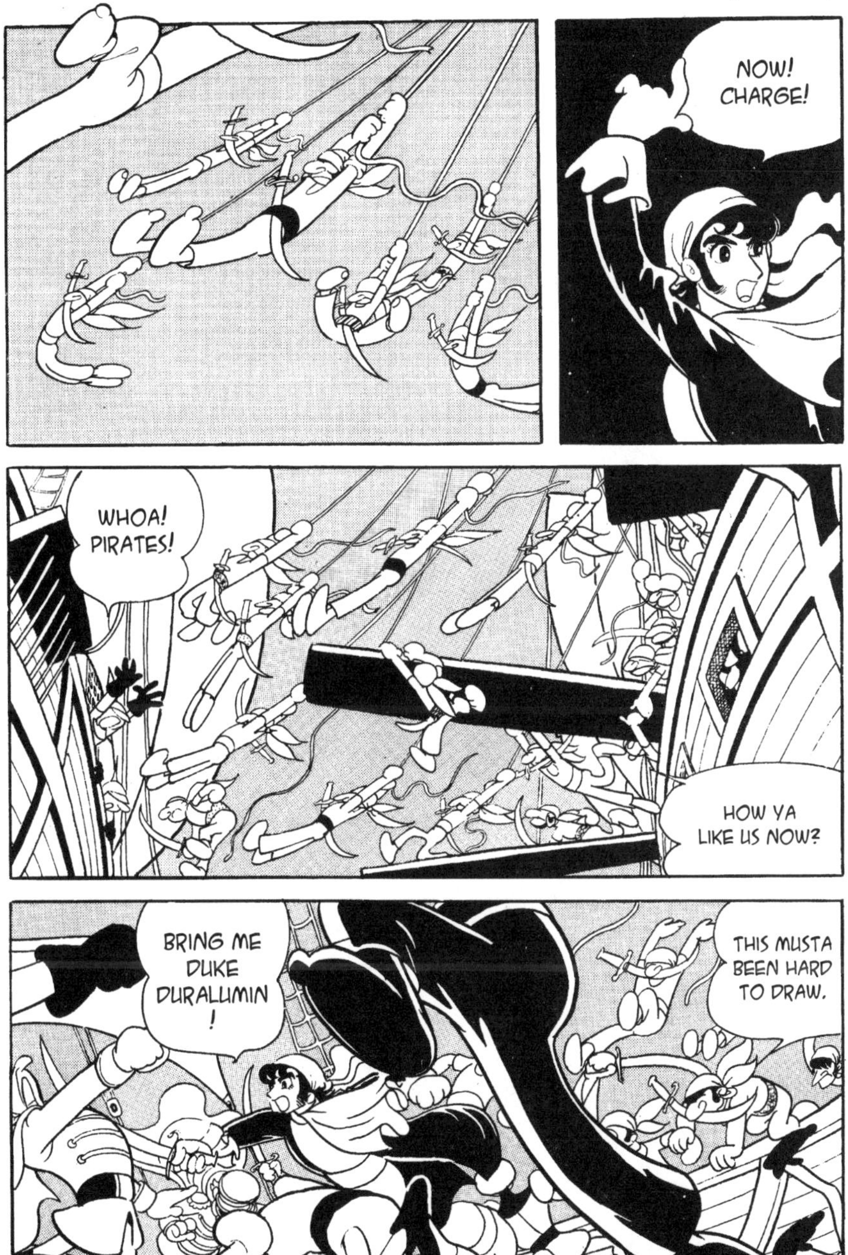
NOW! CHARGE!
WHOA! PIRATES!
HOW YA LIKE US NOW?
THIS MUSTA BEEN HARD TO DRAW.
BRING ME DUKE DURALUMIN !

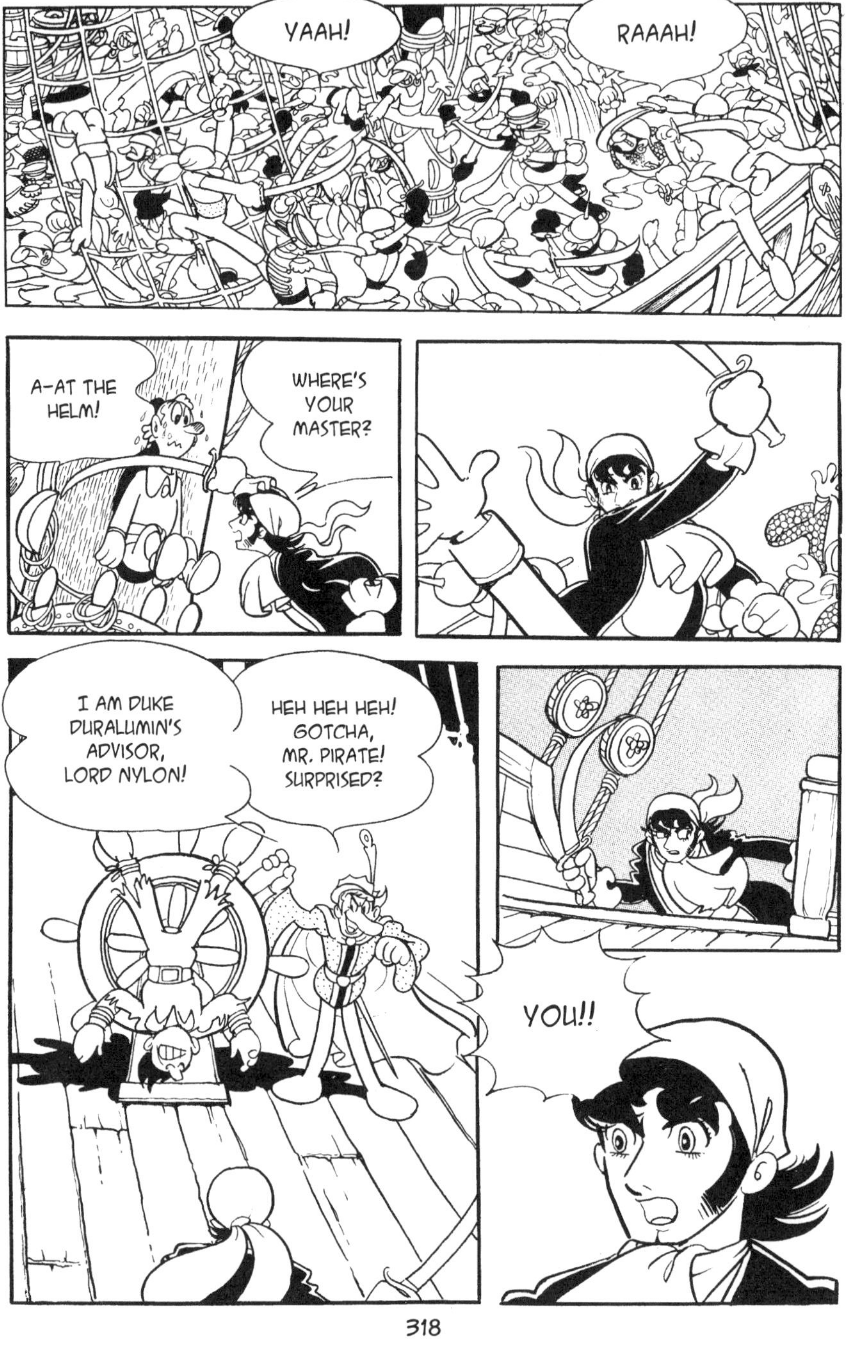
RAAAH!
YAAH!
WHERE'S YOUR MASTER?
A-AT THE HELM!
YOU!!
HEH HEH HEH! GOTCHA, MR. PIRATE! SURPRISED?
I AM DUKE DURALUMIN'S ADVISOR, LORD NYLON!

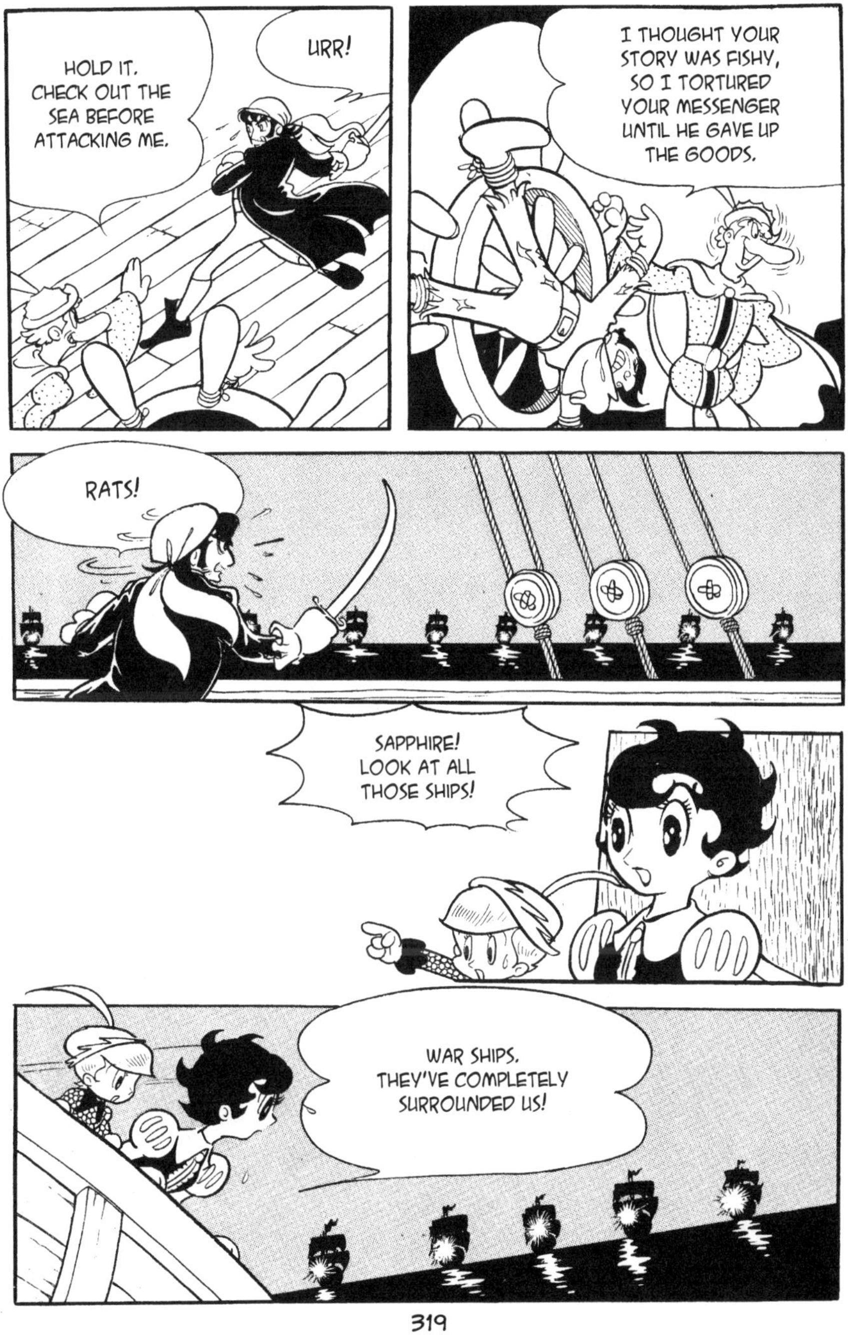
I THOUGHT YOUR STORY WAS FISHY, SO I TORTURED YOUR MESSENGER UNTIL HE GAVE UP THE GOODS.
URR!
HOLD IT. CHECK OUT THE SEA BEFORE ATTACKING ME.
RATS!
SAPPHIRE! LOOK AT ALL THOSE SHIPS!
WAR SHIPS. THEY'VE COMPLETELY SURROUNDED US!

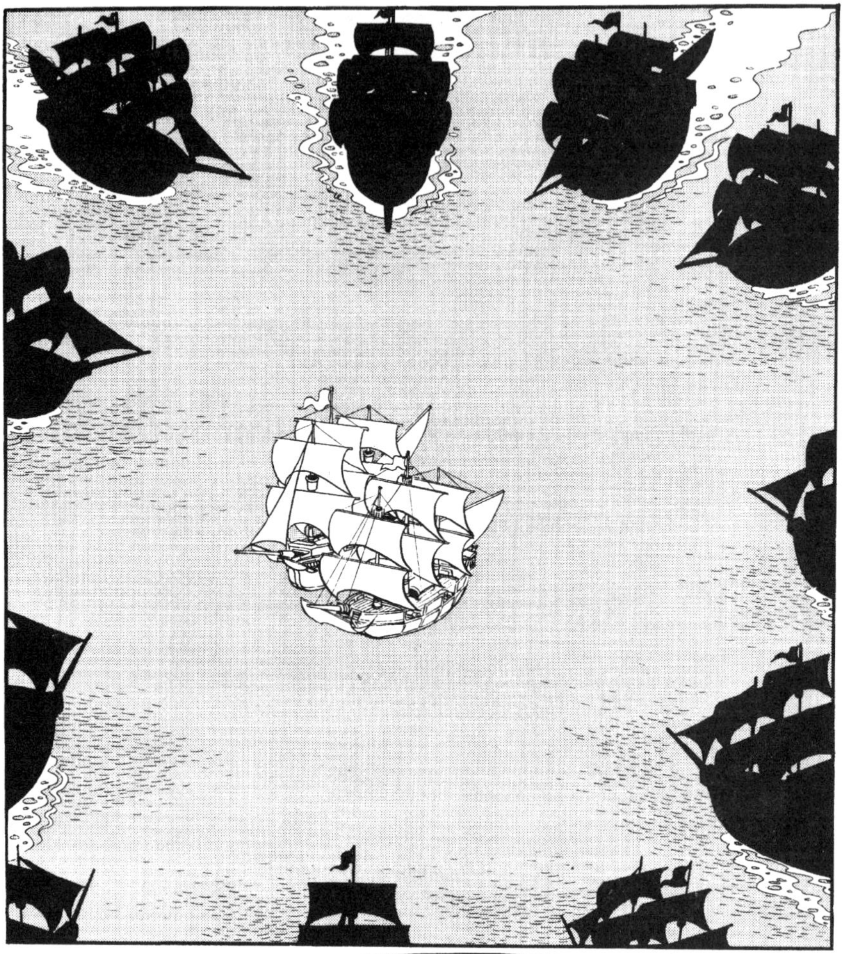

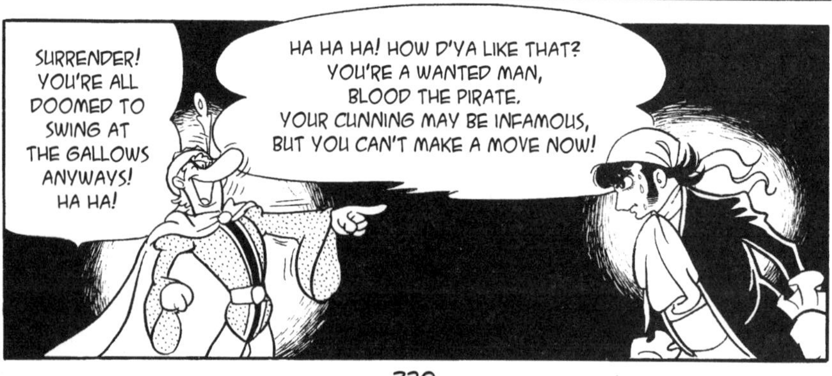
HA HA HA! HOW D'YA LIKE THAT? YOU'RE A WANTED MAN, BLOOD THE PIRATE. YOUR CUNNING MAY BE INFAMOUS, BUT YOU CAN'T MAKE A MOVE NOW!
SURRENDER! YOU'RE ALL DOOMED TO SWING AT THE GALLOWS ANYWAYS! HA HA!

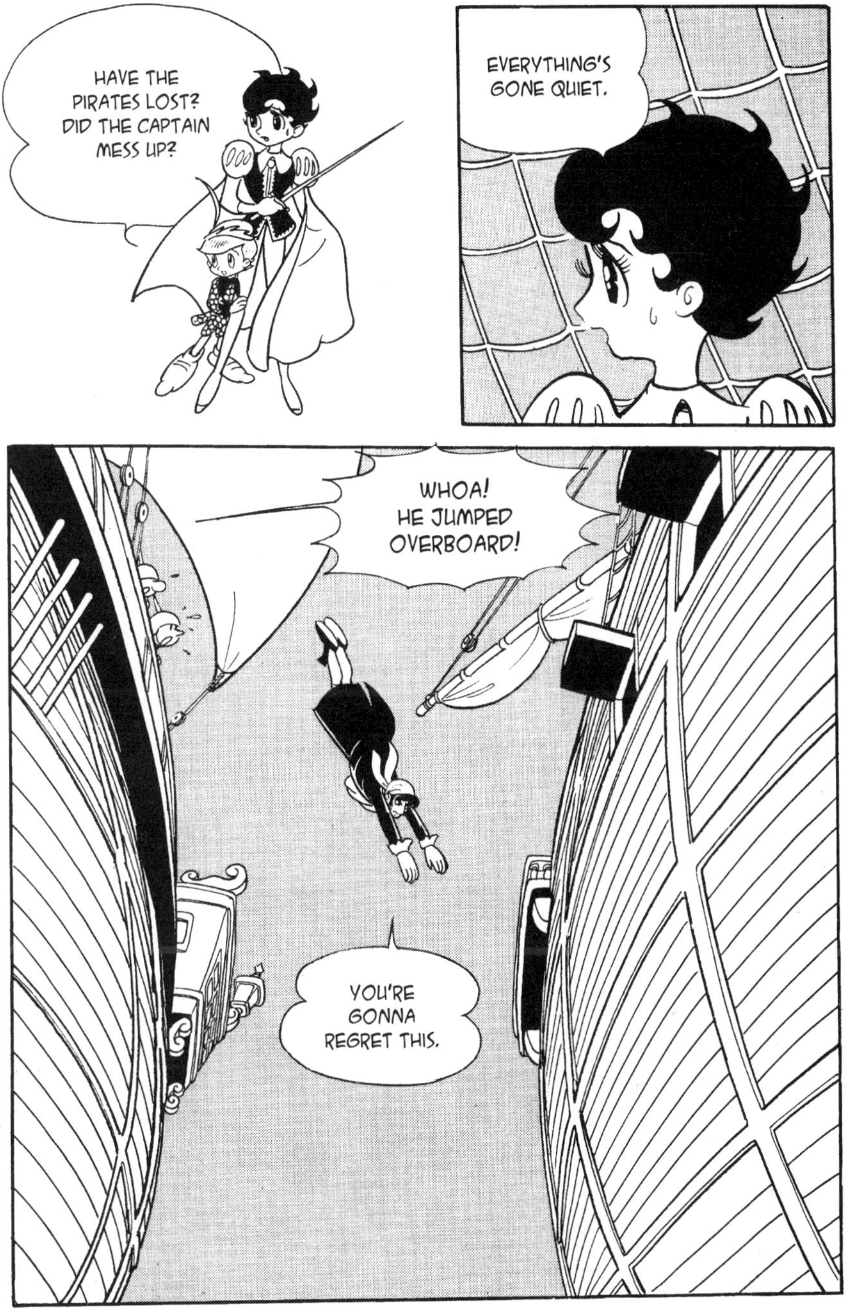
EVERYTHING'S GONE QUIET.
HAVE THE PIRATES LOST? DID THE CAPTAIN MESS UP?
WHOA! HE JUMPED OVERBOARD!
YOU'RE GONNA REGRET THIS.

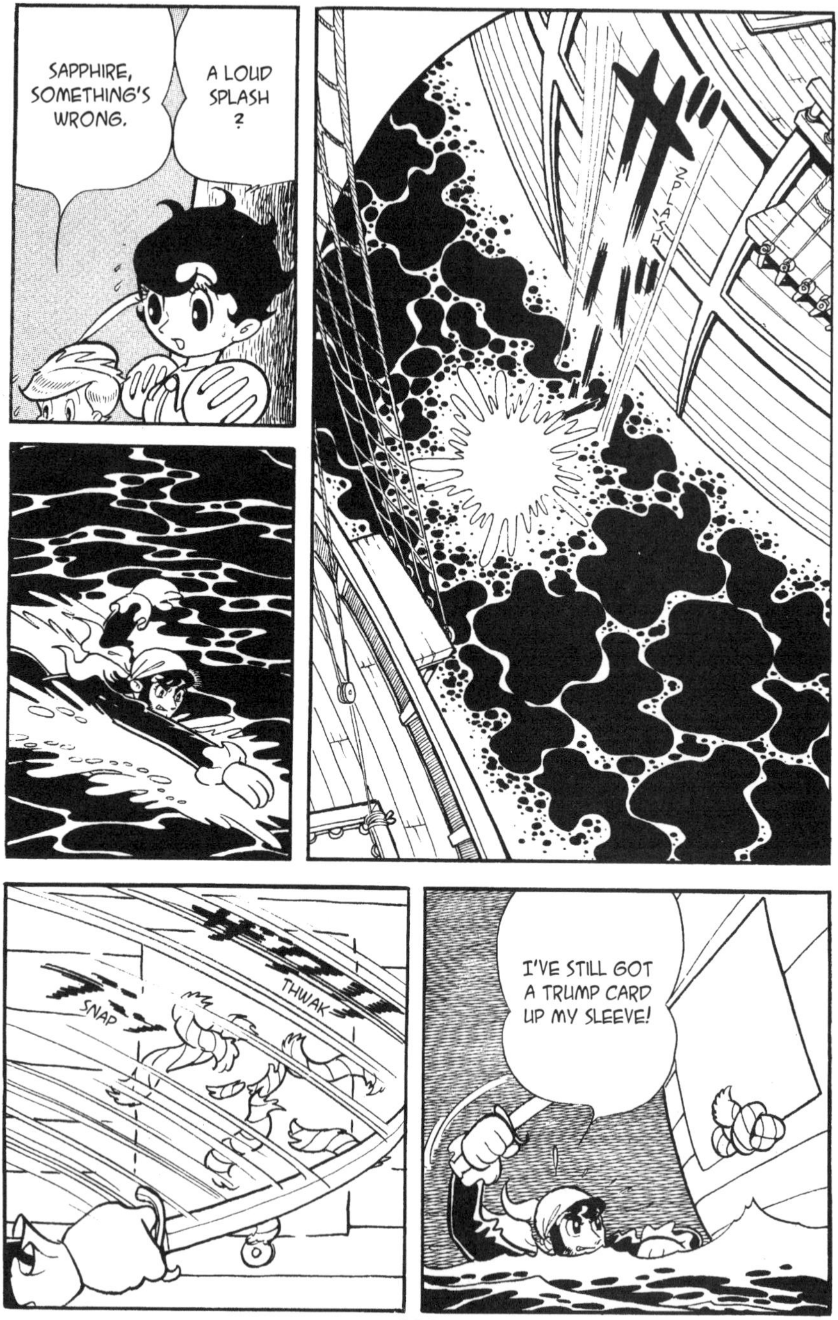
SPLASH
A LOUD SPLASH ?
SAPPHIRE, SOMETHING'S WRONG.
I'VE STILL GOT A TRUMP CARD UP MY SLEEVE!
THWAK
SNAP

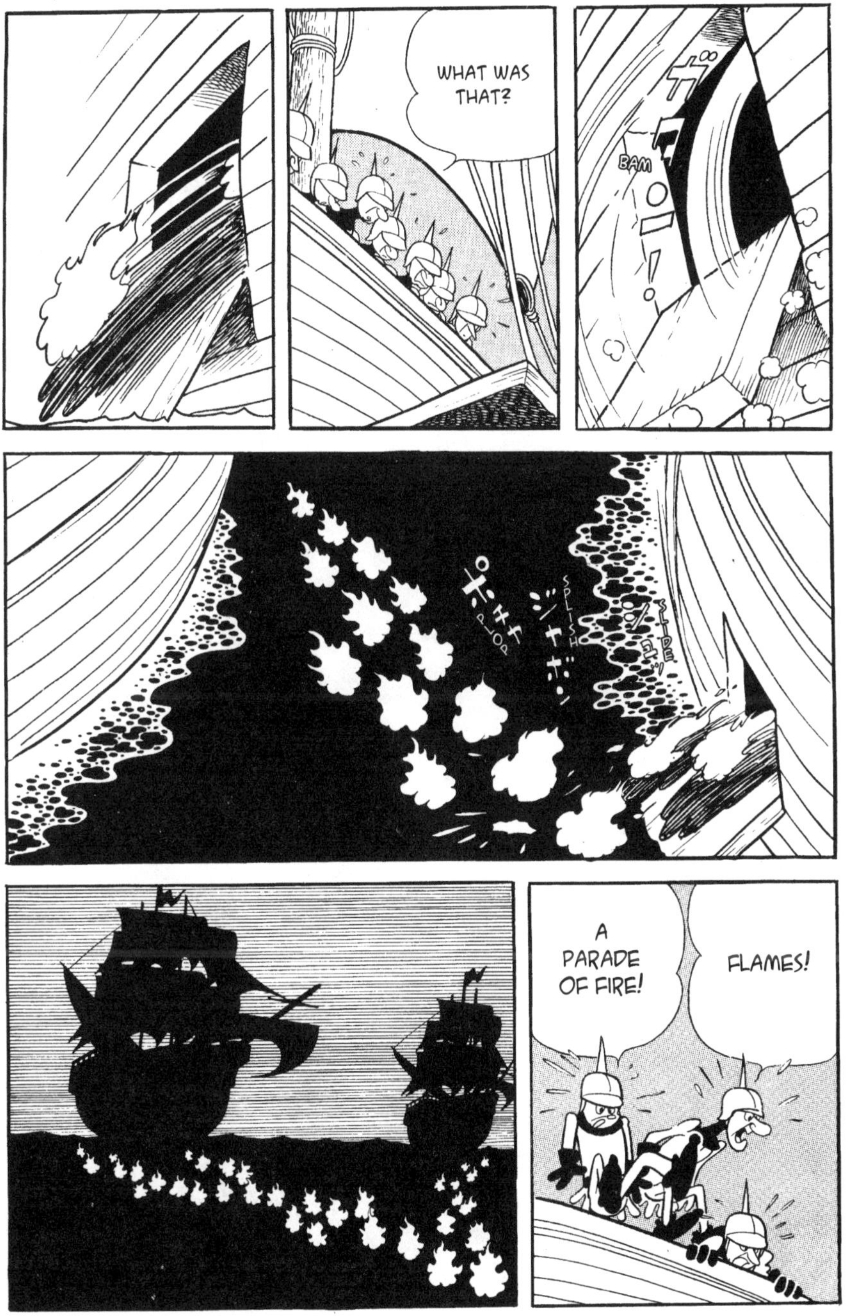
BAM
WHAT WAS THAT?
SLIDE
SPLISH
ジャボン
PLOP
ポチャ
FLAMES!
A PARADE OF FIRE!

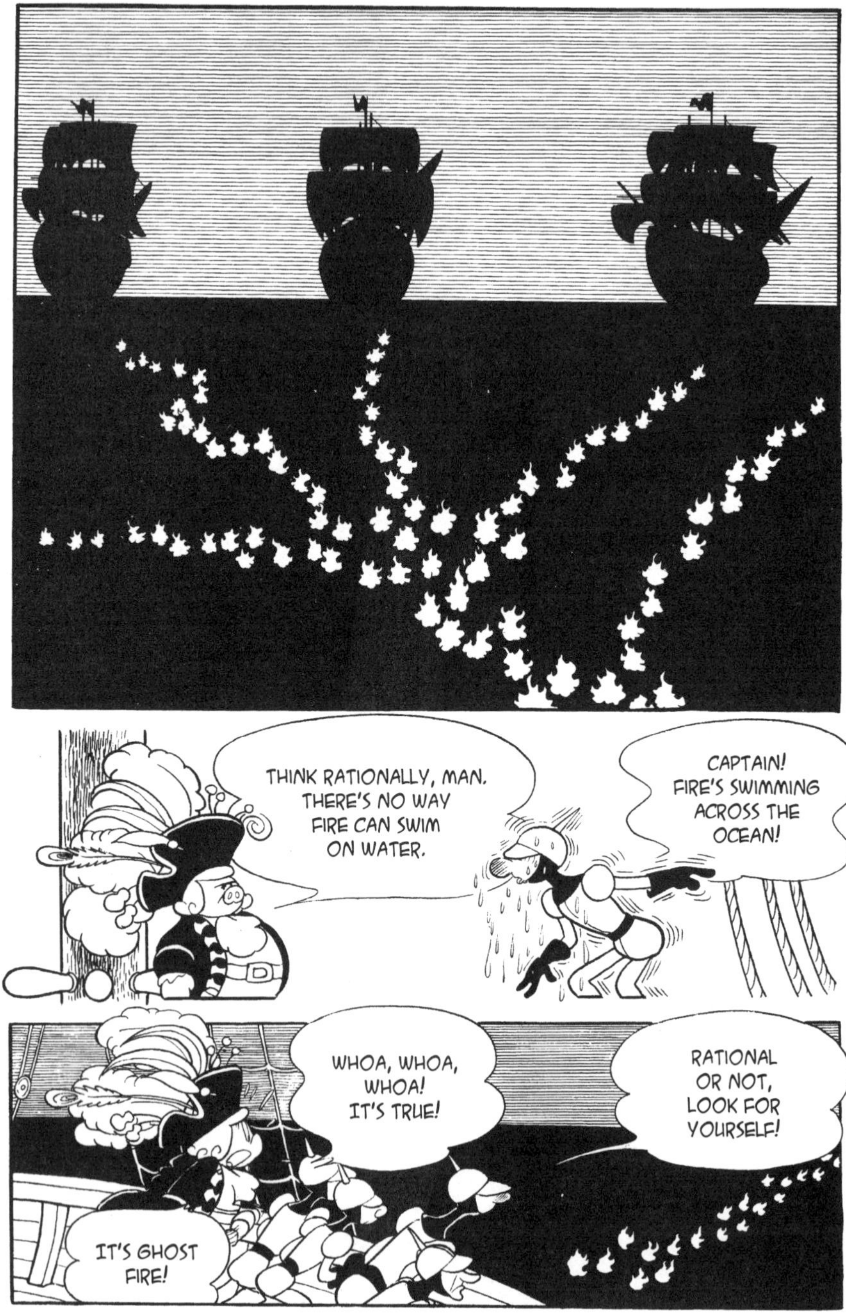
CAPTAIN! FIRE'S SWIMMING ACROSS THE OCEAN!
THINK RATIONALLY, MAN. THERE'S NO WAY FIRE CAN SWIM ON WATER.
RATIONAL OR NOT, LOOK FOR YOURSELF!
WHOA, WHOA, WHOA! IT'S TRUE!
IT'S GHOST FIRE!

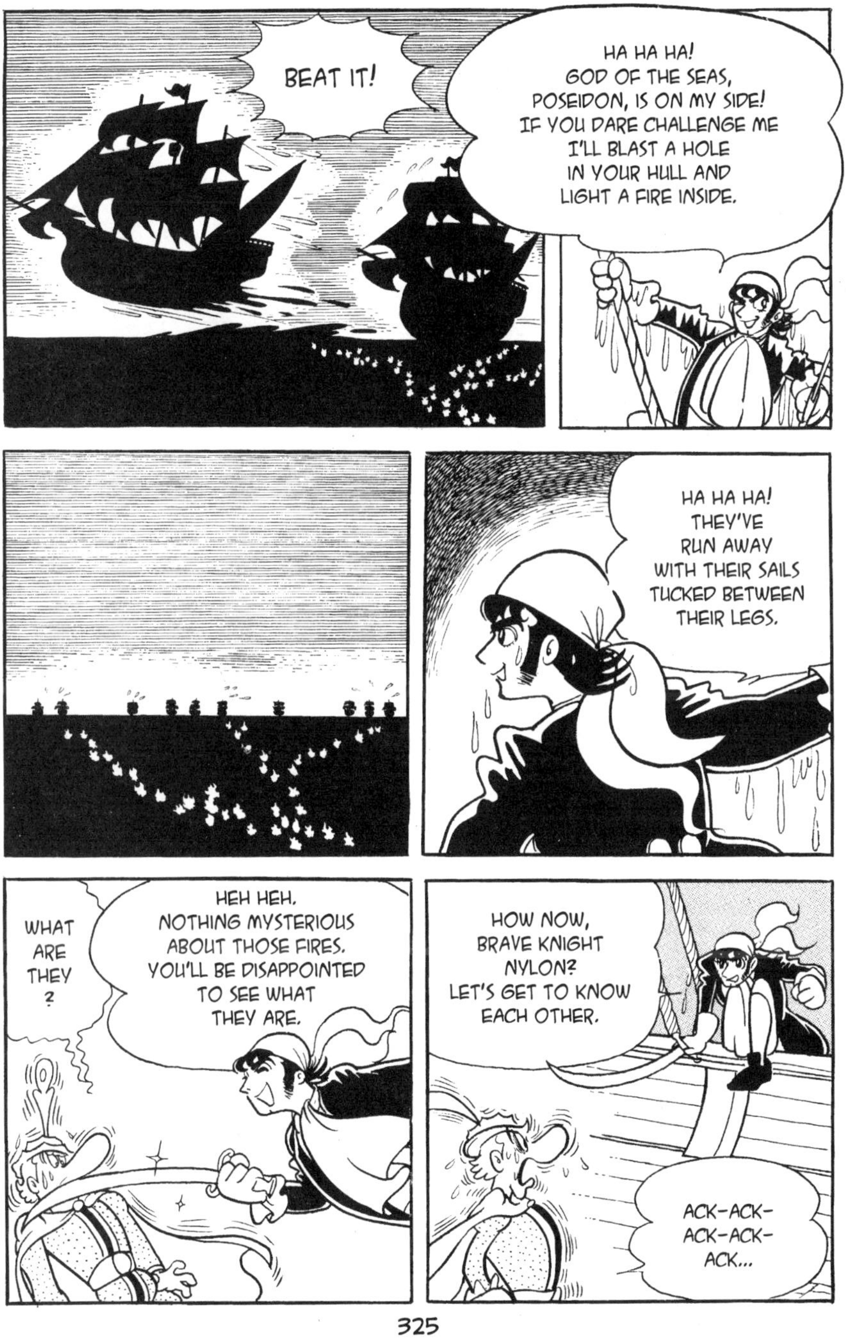
HA HA HA! GOD OF THE SEAS, POSEIDON, IS ON MY SIDE! IF YOU DARE CHALLENGE ME I'LL BLAST A HOLE IN YOUR HULL AND LIGHT A FIRE INSIDE.
BEAT IT!
HA HA HA! THEY'VE RUN AWAY WITH THEIR SAILS TUCKED BETWEEN THEIR LEGS.
HOW NOW, BRAVE KNIGHT NYLON? LET'S GET TO KNOW EACH OTHER.
ACK-ACK-ACK-ACK-ACK...
HEH HEH. NOTHING MYSTERIOUS ABOUT THOSE FIRES. YOU'LL BE DISAPPOINTED TO SEE WHAT THEY ARE.
WHAT ARE THEY?

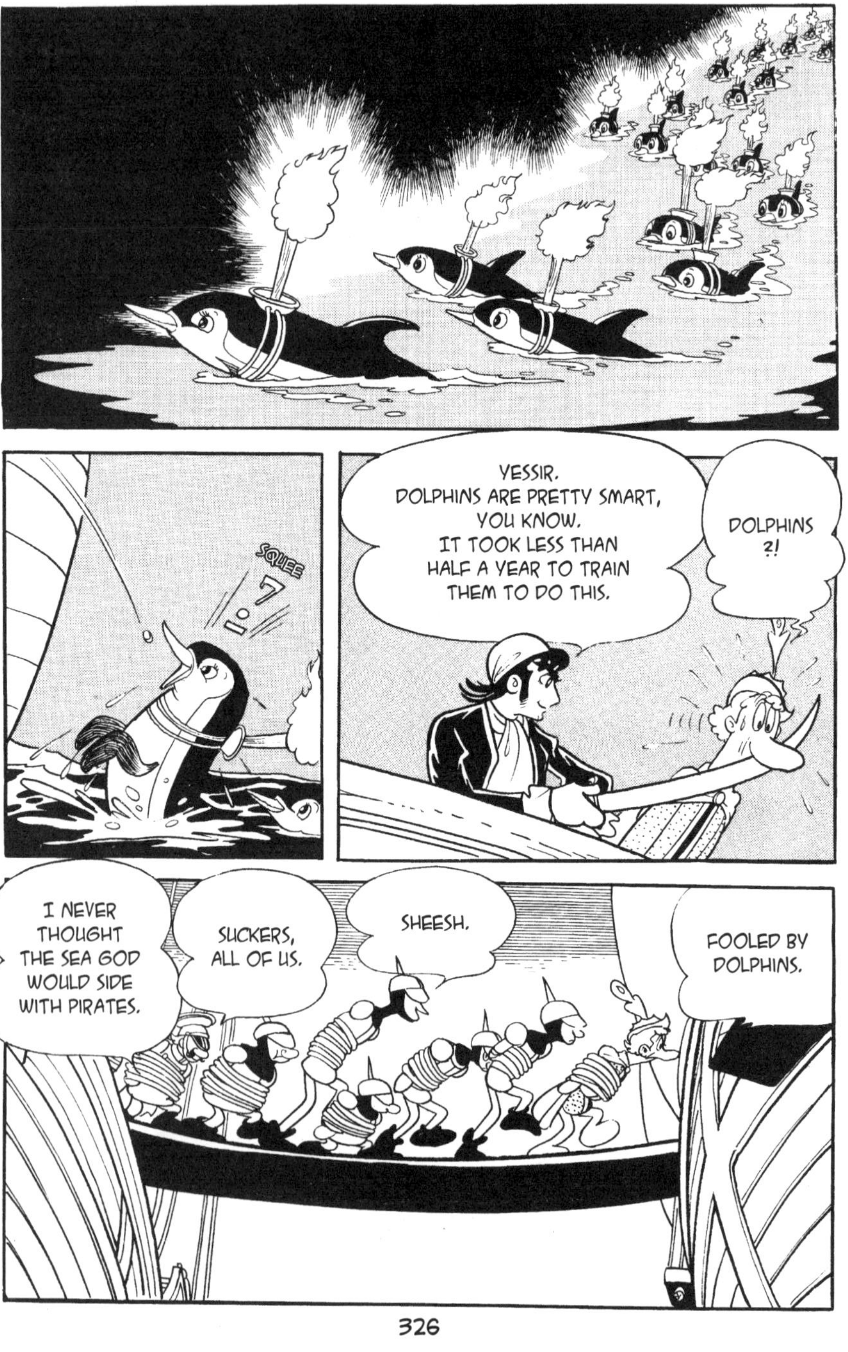
DOLPHINS ?!
YESSIR. DOLPHINS ARE PRETTY SMART, YOU KNOW. IT TOOK LESS THAN HALF A YEAR TO TRAIN THEM TO DO THIS.
SQUEE
FOOLED BY DOLPHINS.
SHEESH.
SUCKERS, ALL OF US.
I NEVER THOUGHT THE SEA GOD WOULD SIDE WITH PIRATES.

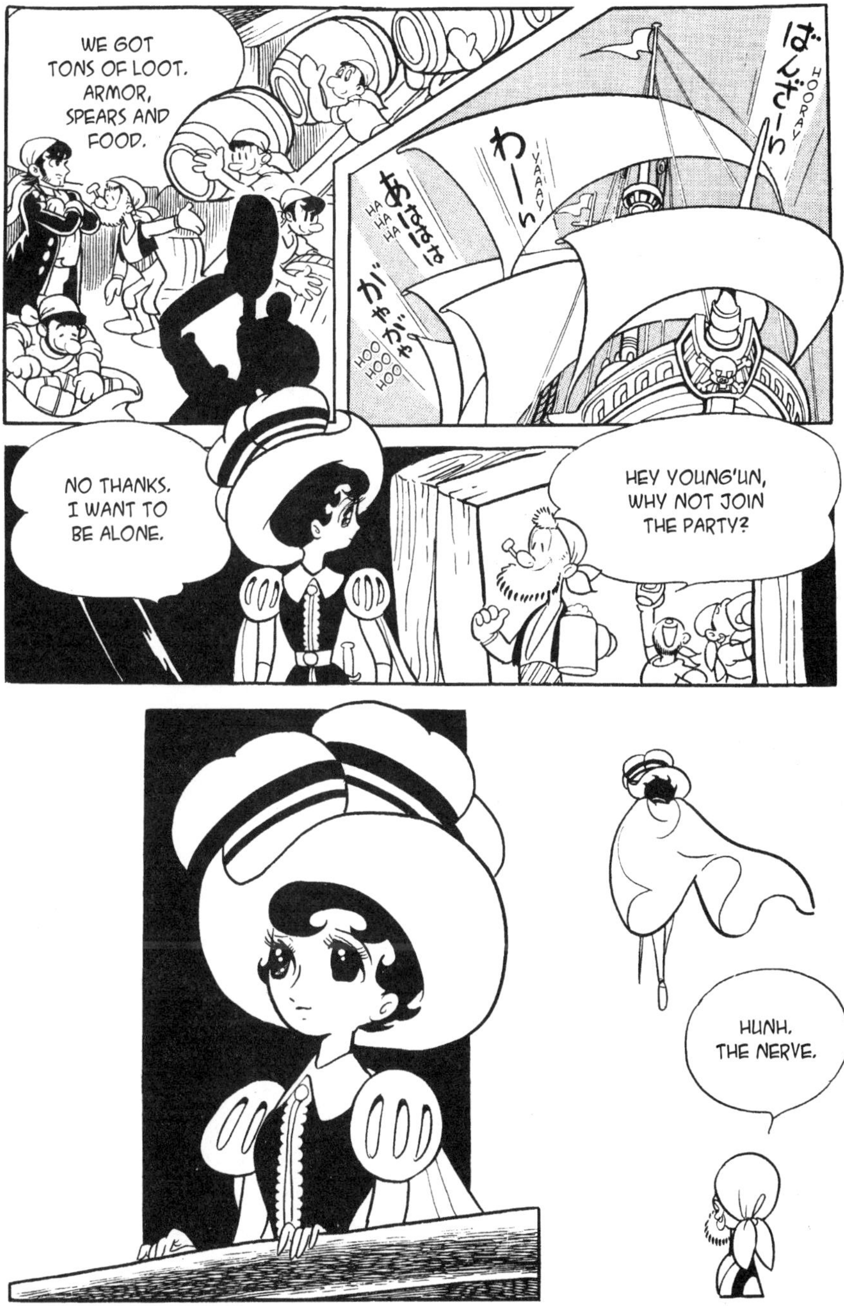
ばんざーい
HOORAY
わーい
YAAAY
あははは
HA HA HA
がやがや
HOO HOO HOO
WE GOT TONS OF LOOT. ARMOR, SPEARS AND FOOD.
HEY YOUNG'UN, WHY NOT JOIN THE PARTY?
NO THANKS. I WANT TO BE ALONE.
HUNH. THE NERVE.

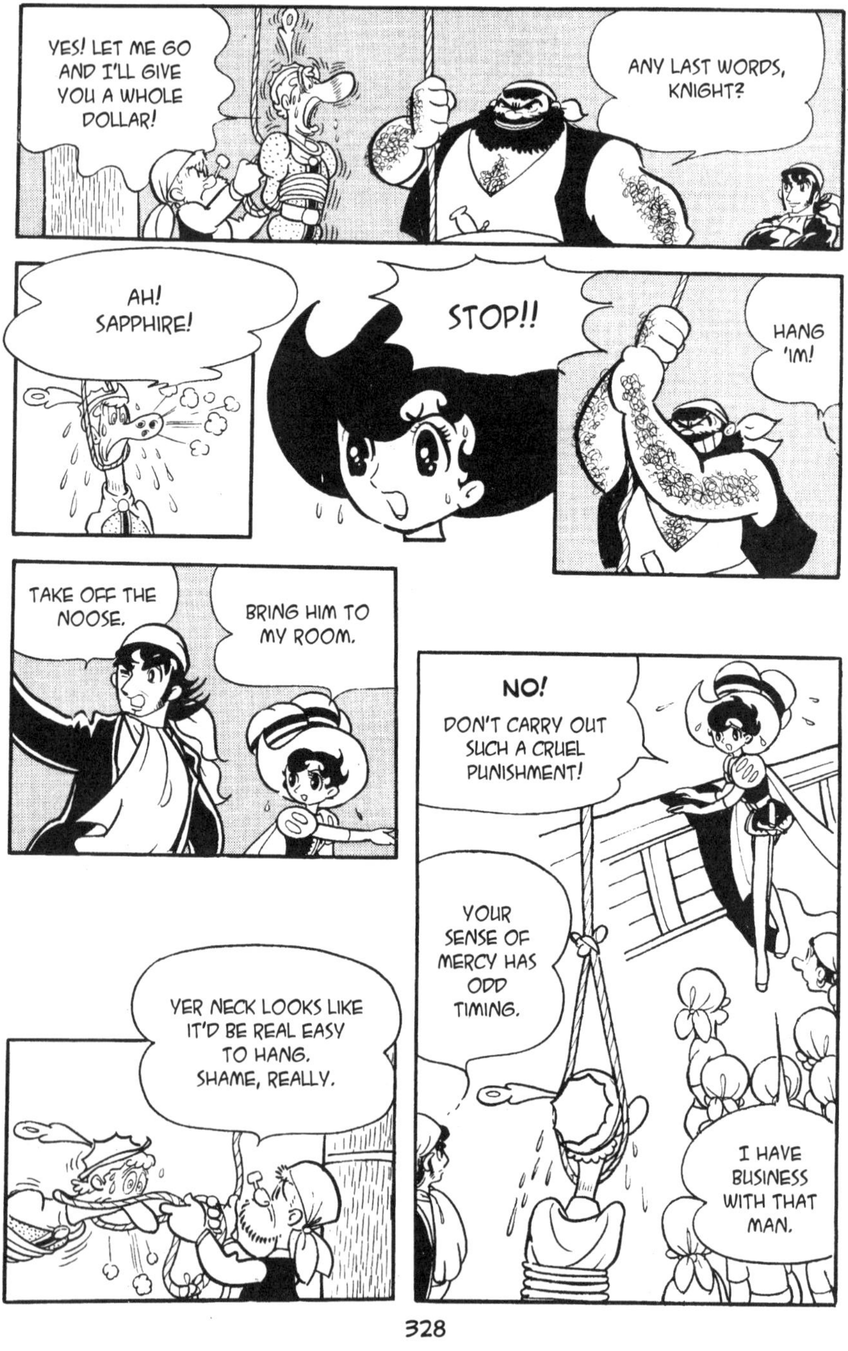
ANY LAST WORDS, KNIGHT?
YES! LET ME GO AND I'LL GIVE YOU A WHOLE DOLLAR!
HANG 'IM!
STOP!!
AH! SAPPHIRE!
NO! DON'T CARRY OUT SUCH A CRUEL PUNISHMENT!
YOUR SENSE OF MERCY HAS ODD TIMING.
I HAVE BUSINESS WITH THAT MAN.
BRING HIM TO MY ROOM.
TAKE OFF THE NOOSE.
YER NECK LOOKS LIKE IT'D BE REAL EASY TO HANG. SHAME, REALLY.

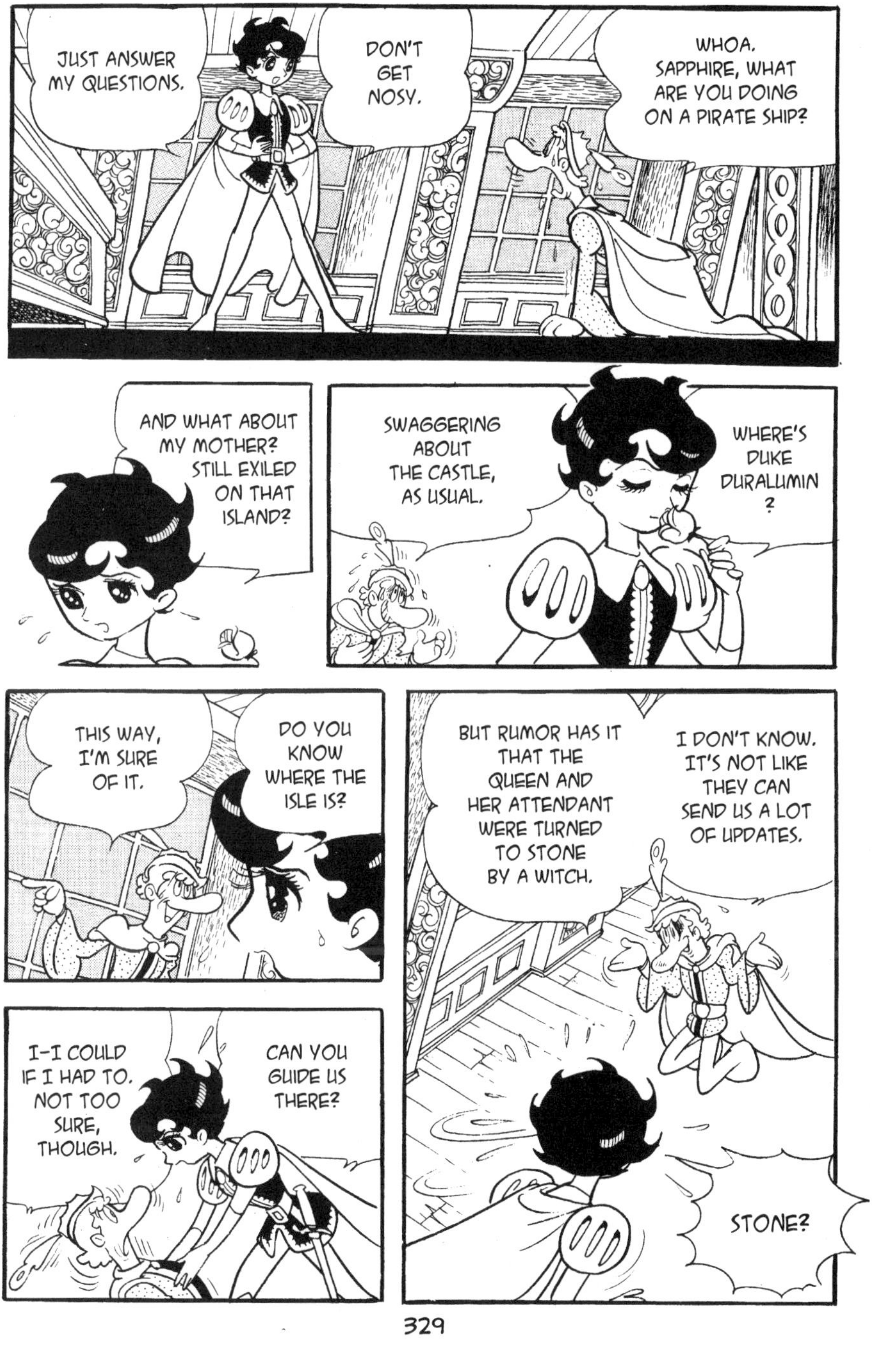
WHOA. SAPPHIRE, WHAT ARE YOU DOING ON A PIRATE SHIP?
DON'T GET NOSY.
JUST ANSWER MY QUESTIONS.
WHERE'S DUKE DURALUMIN?
SWAGGERING ABOUT THE CASTLE, AS USUAL.
AND WHAT ABOUT MY MOTHER? STILL EXILED ON THAT ISLAND?
I DON'T KNOW. IT'S NOT LIKE THEY CAN SEND US A LOT OF UPDATES.
BUT RUMOR HAS IT THAT THE QUEEN AND HER ATTENDANT WERE TURNED TO STONE BY A WITCH.
STONE?
DO YOU KNOW WHERE THE ISLE IS?
THIS WAY, I'M SURE OF IT.
CAN YOU GUIDE US THERE?
I-I COULD IF I HAD TO. NOT TOO SURE, THOUGH.

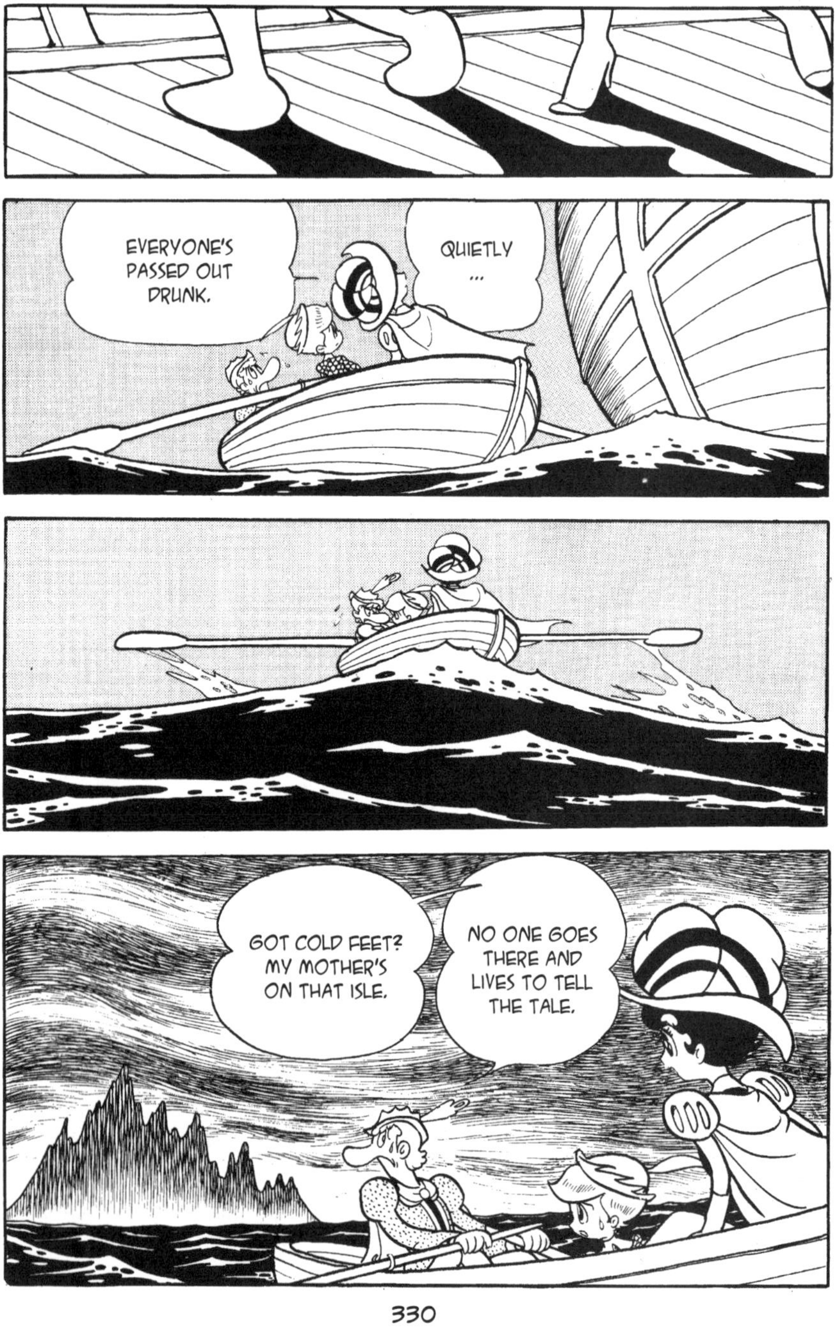
QUIETLY ...
EVERYONE'S PASSED OUT DRUNK.
NO ONE GOES THERE AND LIVES TO TELL THE TALE.
GOT COLD FEET? MY MOTHER'S ON THAT ISLE.

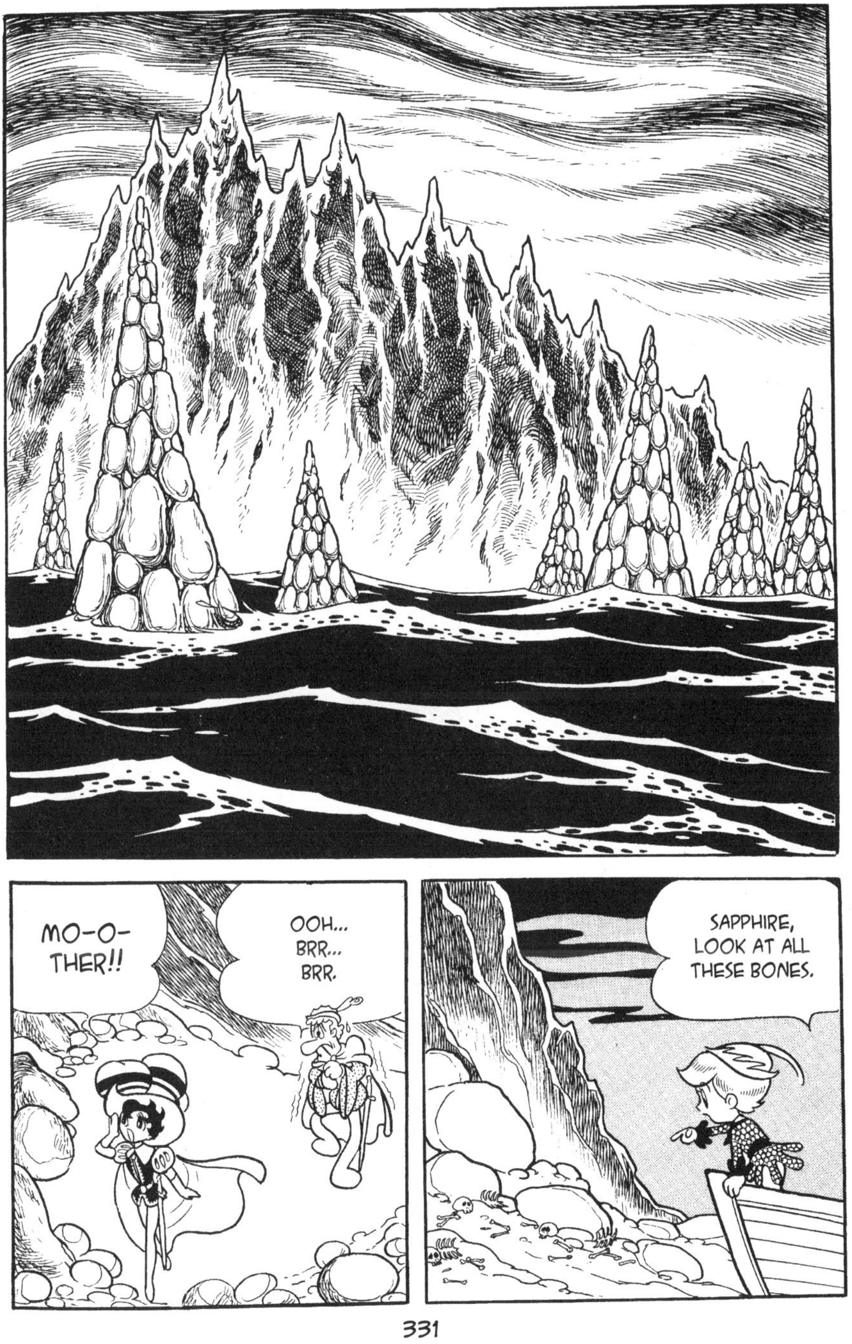
SAPPHIRE, LOOK AT ALL THESE BONES.
OOH... BRR... BRR.
MO-O-THER!!

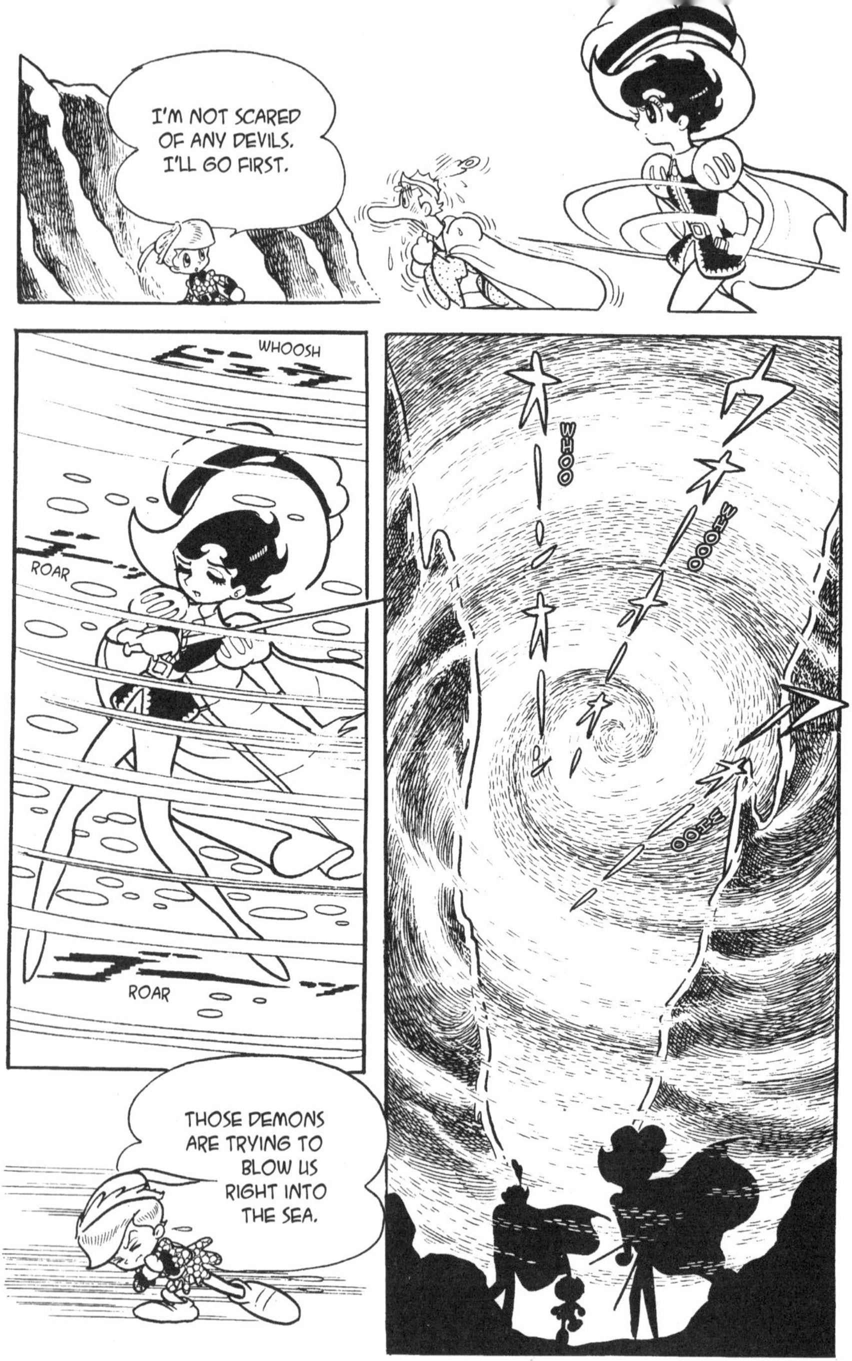

I'M NOT SCARED OF ANY DEVILS. I'LL GO FIRST.
WHOOO
WHOO
WHOO
WHOOSH
ROAR
ROAR
THOSE DEMONS ARE TRYING TO BLOW US RIGHT INTO THE SEA.

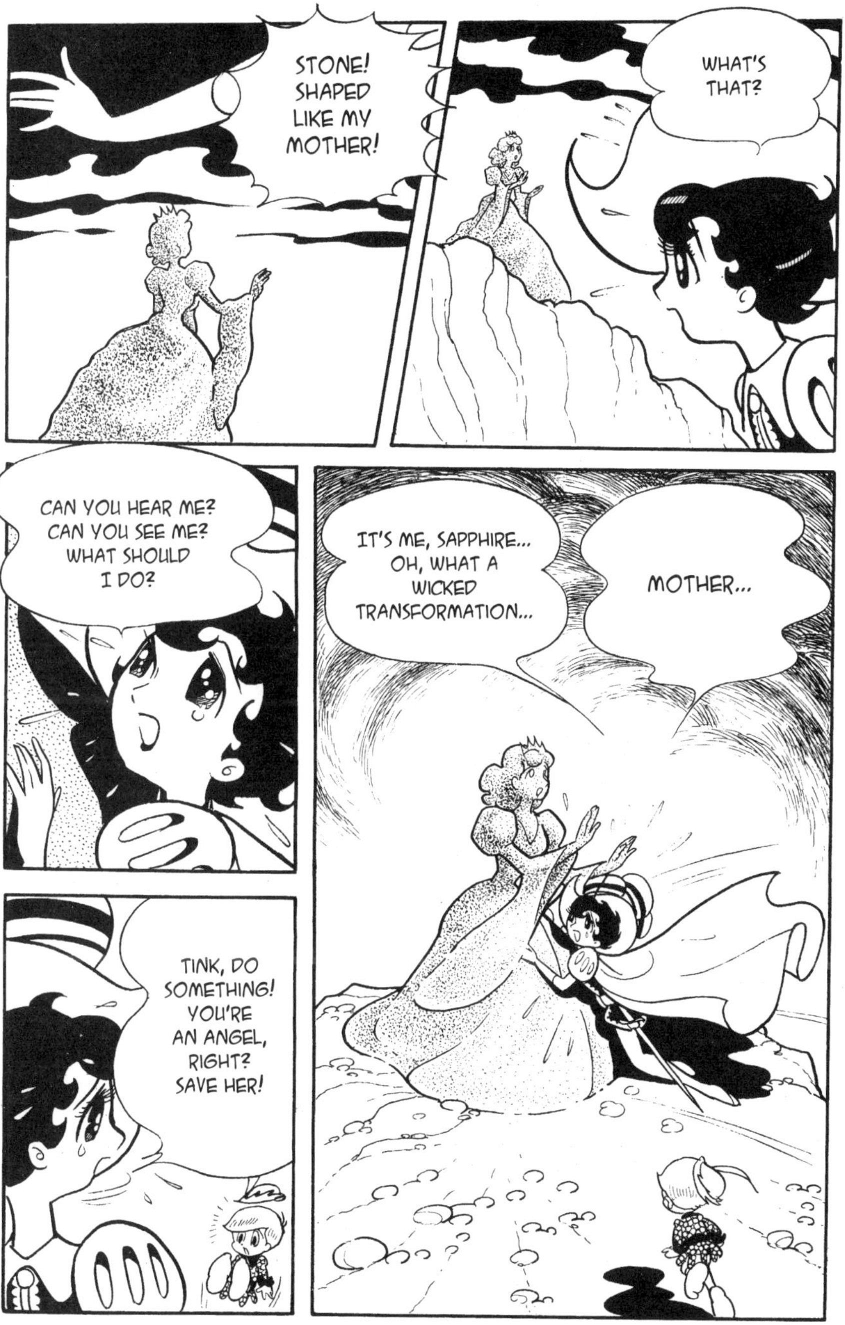
WHAT'S THAT?
STONE! SHAPED LIKE MY MOTHER!
MOTHER...
IT'S ME, SAPPHIRE... OH, WHAT A WICKED TRANSFORMATION...
CAN YOU HEAR ME? CAN YOU SEE ME? WHAT SHOULD I DO?
TINK, DO SOMETHING! YOU'RE AN ANGEL, RIGHT? SAVE HER!

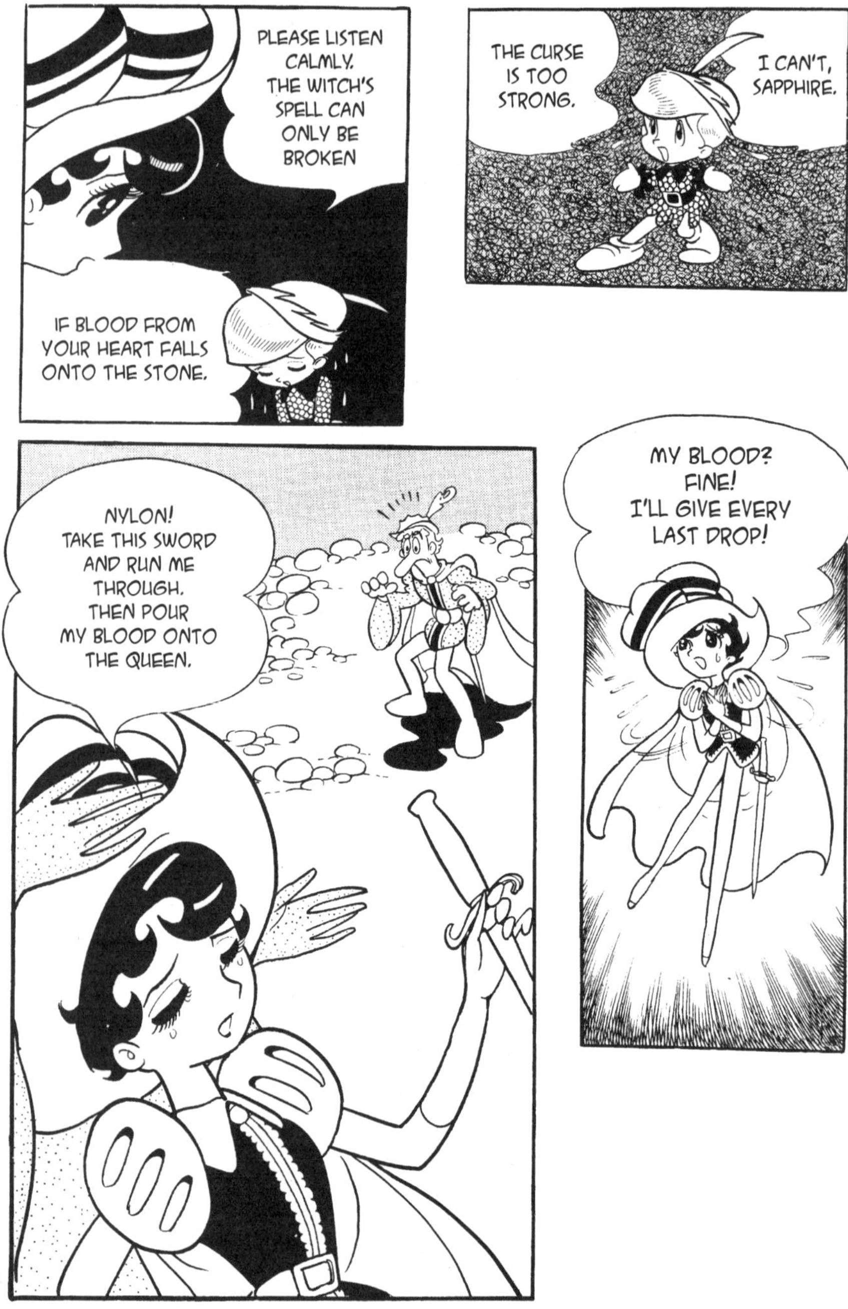
I CAN'T, SAPPHIRE.
THE CURSE IS TOO STRONG.
PLEASE LISTEN CALMLY. THE WITCH'S SPELL CAN ONLY BE BROKEN
IF BLOOD FROM YOUR HEART FALLS ONTO THE STONE.
MY BLOOD? FINE! I'LL GIVE EVERY LAST DROP!
NYLON! TAKE THIS SWORD AND RUN ME THROUGH. THEN POUR MY BLOOD ONTO THE QUEEN.

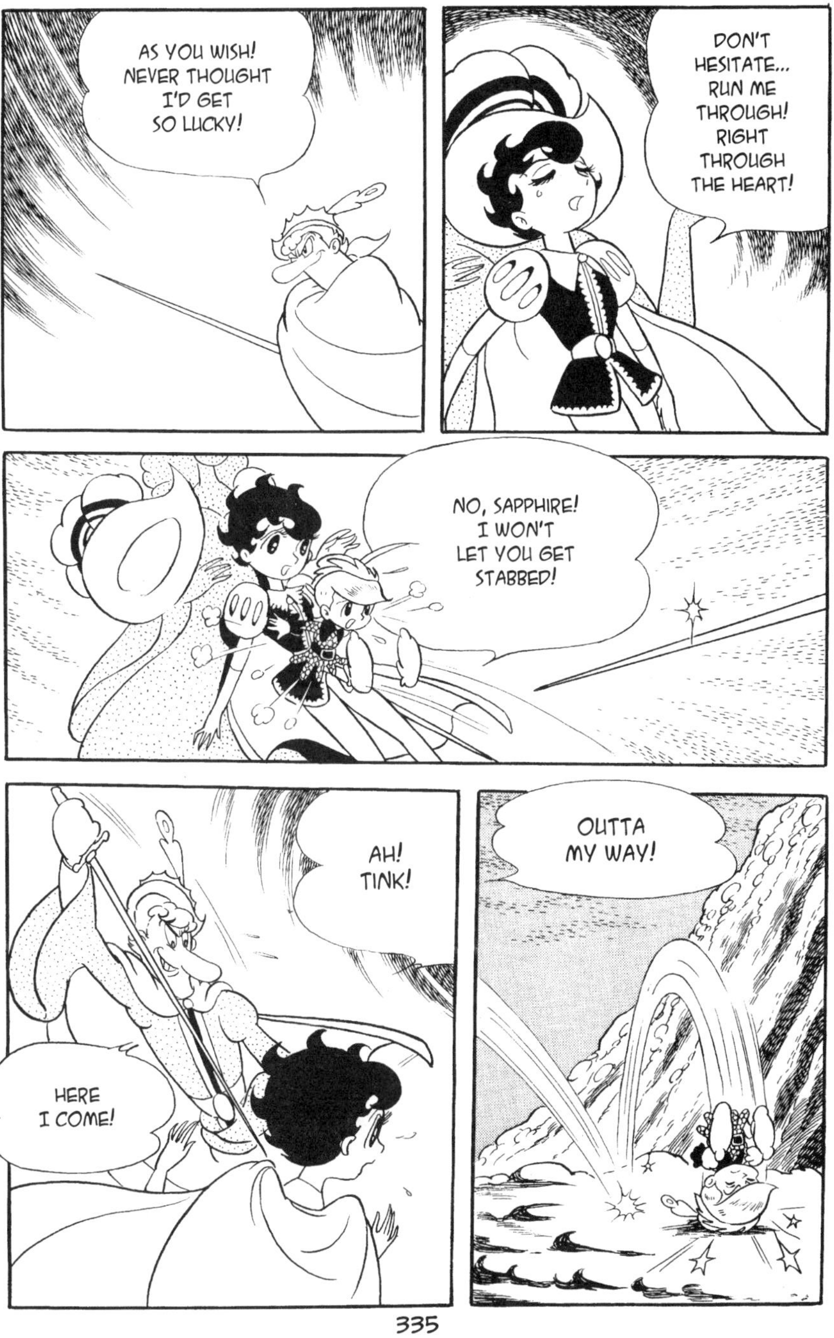
DON'T HESITATE... RUN ME THROUGH! RIGHT THROUGH THE HEART!
AS YOU WISH! NEVER THOUGHT I'D GET SO LUCKY!
NO, SAPPHIRE! I WON'T LET YOU GET STABBED!
OUTTA MY WAY!
AH! TINK!
HERE I COME!

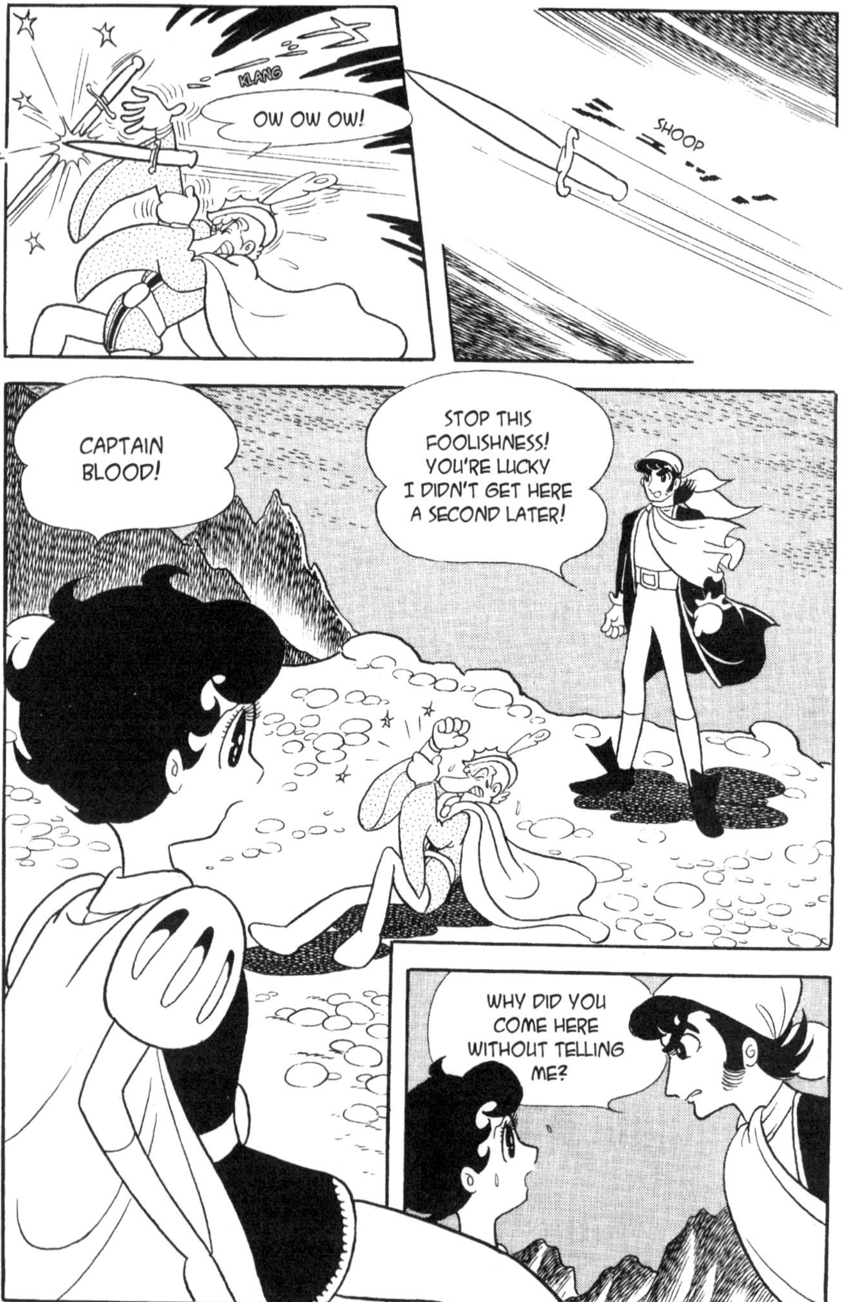
SHOOP
KLANG
OW OW OW!
STOP THIS FOOLISHNESS! YOU'RE LUCKY I DIDN'T GET HERE A SECOND LATER!
CAPTAIN BLOOD!
WHY DID YOU COME HERE WITHOUT TELLING ME?

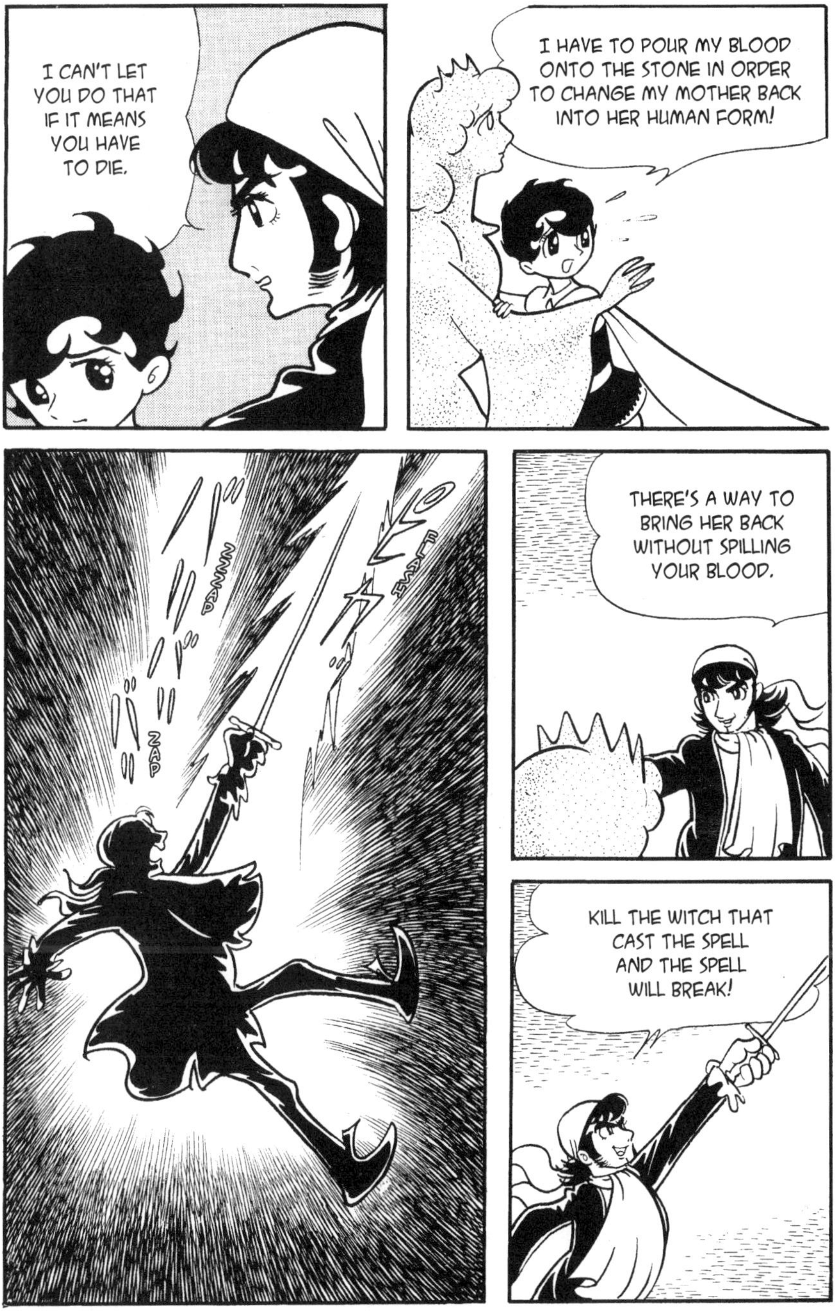
I HAVE TO POUR MY BLOOD ONTO THE STONE IN ORDER TO CHANGE MY MOTHER BACK INTO HER HUMAN FORM!
I CAN'T LET YOU DO THAT IF IT MEANS YOU HAVE TO DIE.
THERE'S A WAY TO BRING HER BACK WITHOUT SPILLING YOUR BLOOD.
KILL THE WITCH THAT CAST THE SPELL AND THE SPELL WILL BREAK!
FLASH
ZAP

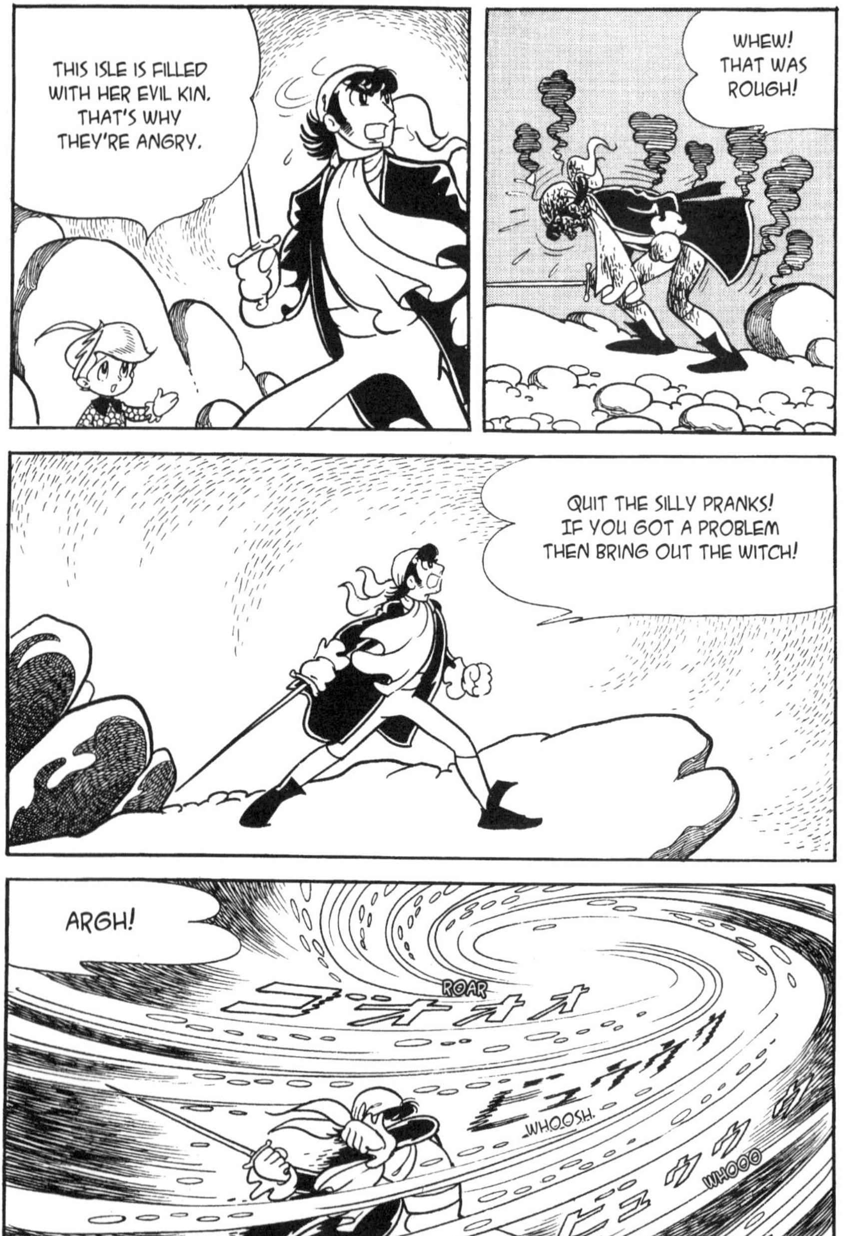
WHEW! THAT WAS ROUGH!
THIS ISLE IS FILLED WITH HER EVIL KIN. THAT'S WHY THEY'RE ANGRY.
QUIT THE SILLY PRANKS! IF YOU GOT A PROBLEM THEN BRING OUT THE WITCH!
ARGH!
ROAR
WHOOSH
WHOOO

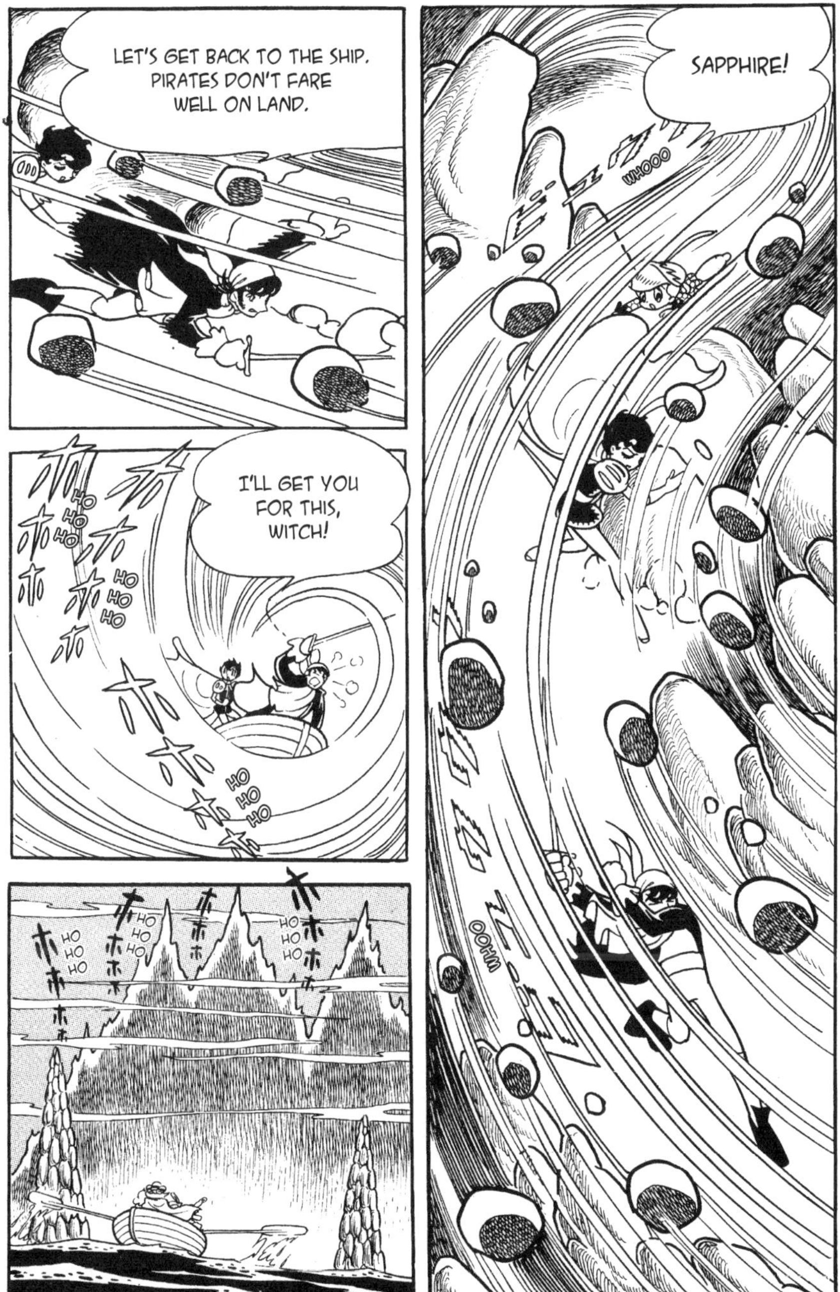
SAPPHIRE!
WHOOO
WHOOO
LET'S GET BACK TO THE SHIP. PIRATES DON'T FARE WELL ON LAND.
I'LL GET YOU FOR THIS, WITCH!
HO HO HO
HO HO HO
HO HO HO
HO HO HO
HO HO HO
HO HO HO

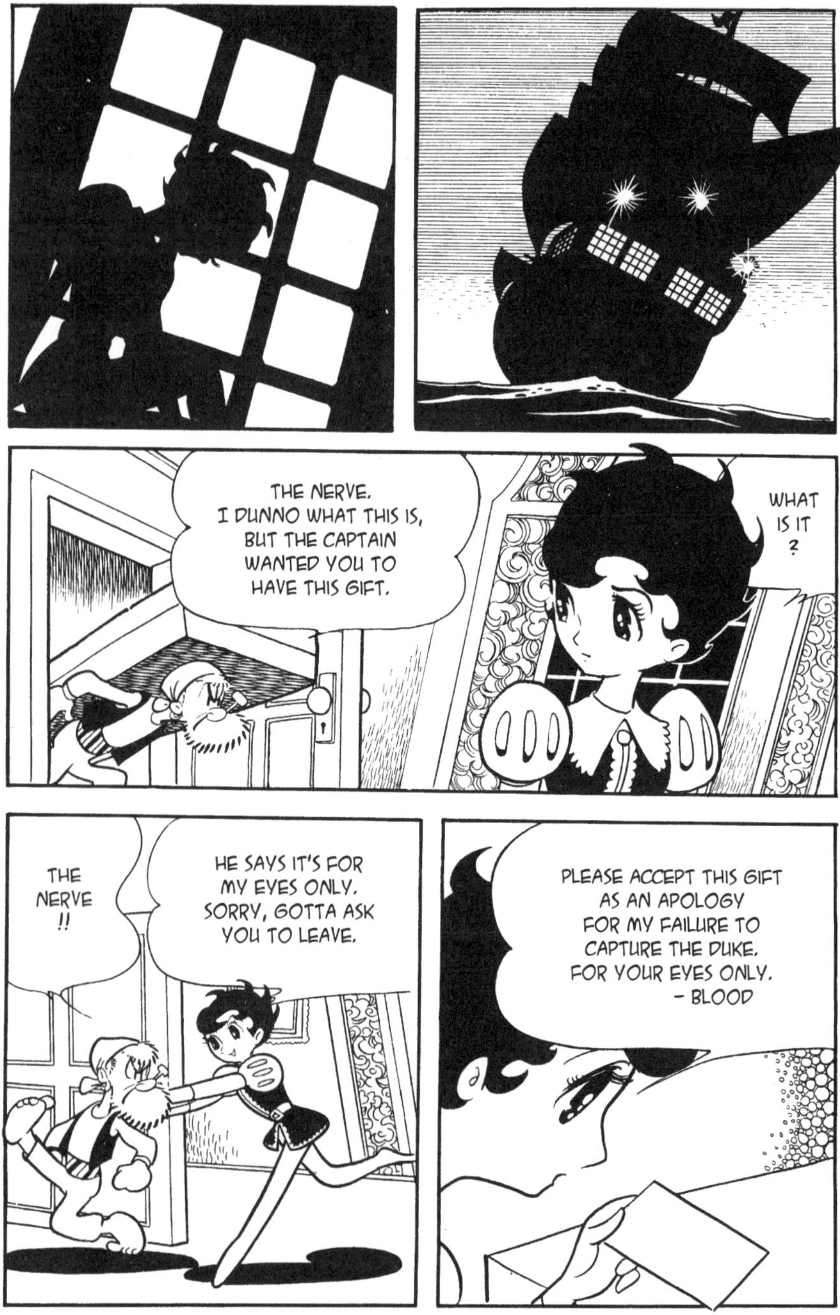
WHAT IS IT ?
THE NERVE. I DUNNO WHAT THIS IS, BUT THE CAPTAIN WANTED YOU TO HAVE THIS GIFT.
PLEASE ACCEPT THIS GIFT AS AN APOLOGY FOR MY FAILURE TO CAPTURE THE DUKE. FOR YOUR EYES ONLY. - BLOOD
HE SAYS IT'S FOR MY EYES ONLY. SORRY, GOTTA ASK YOU TO LEAVE.
THE NERVE !!

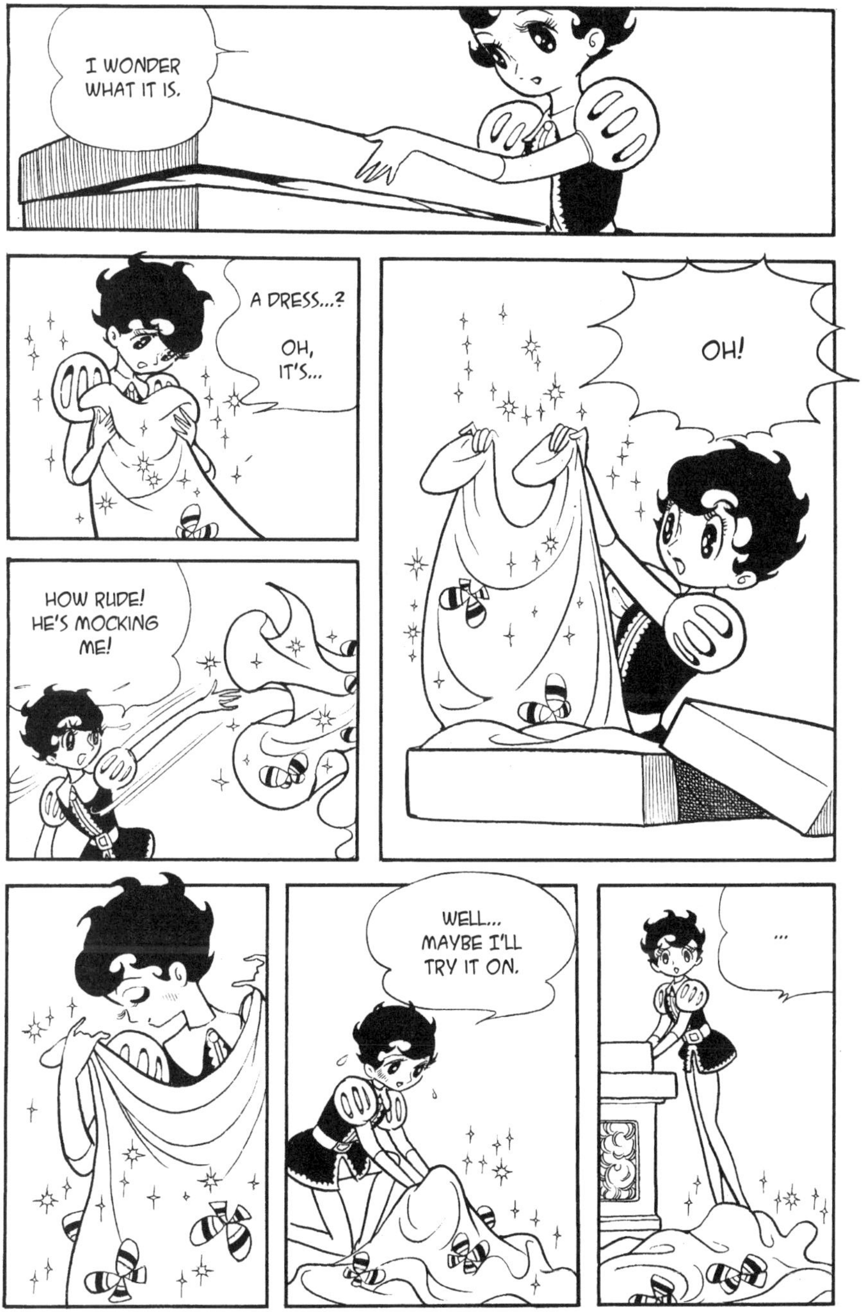
I WONDER WHAT IT IS.
OH!
A DRESS...?
OH, IT'S...
HOW RUDE! HE'S MOCKING ME!
...
WELL... MAYBE I'LL TRY IT ON.

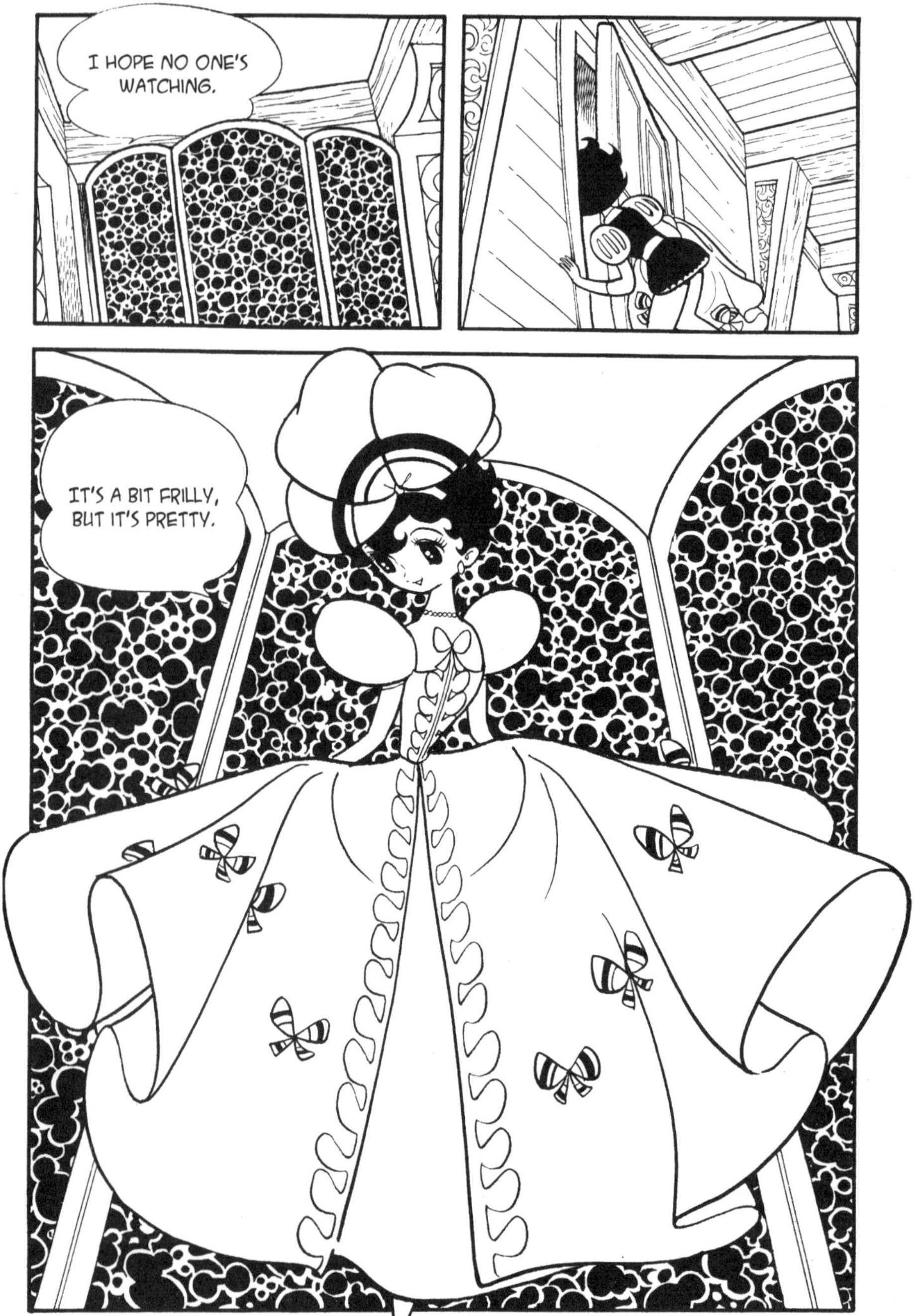
I HOPE NO ONE'S WATCHING.
IT'S A BIT FRILLY, BUT IT'S PRETTY.

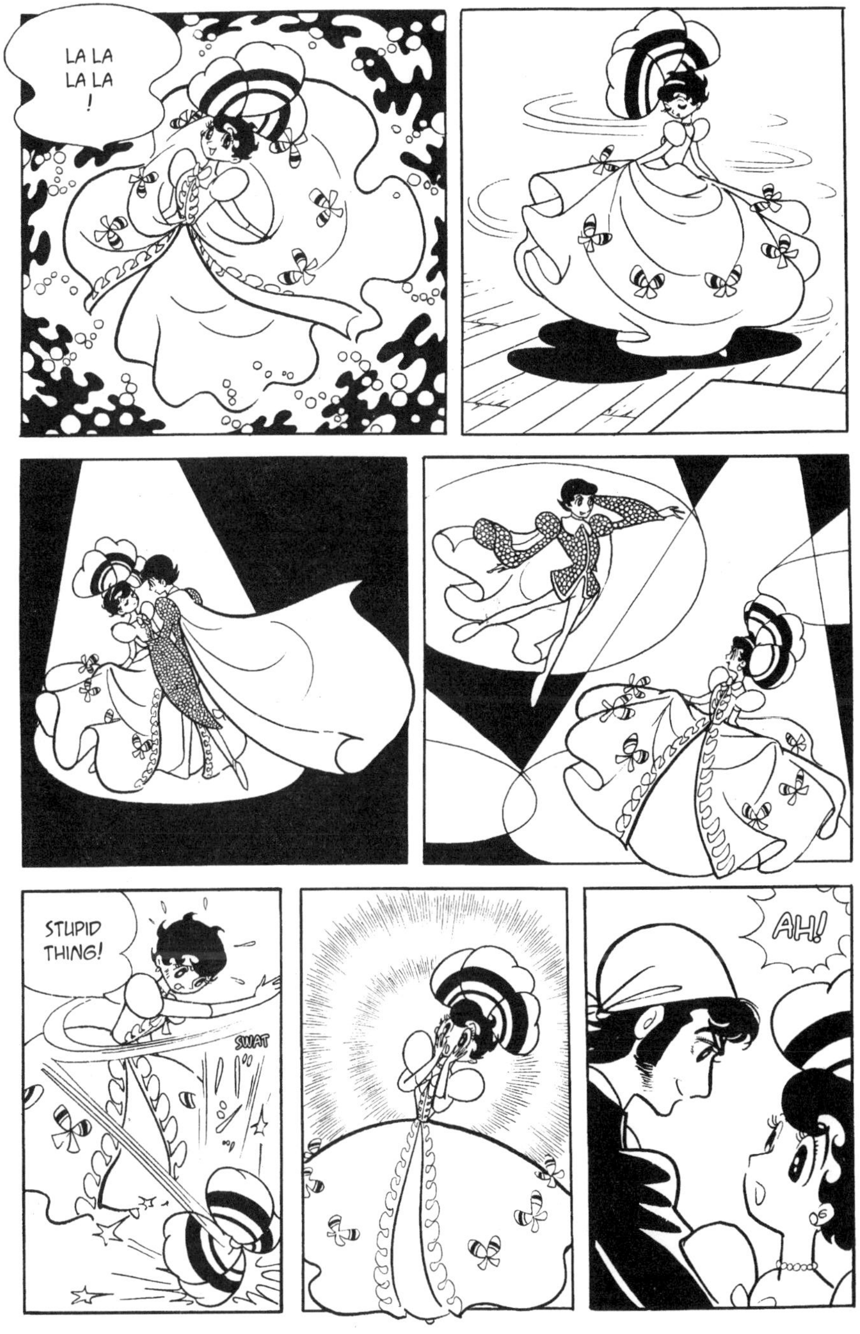
LA LA LA LA !
AH!
STUPID THING!
SWAT

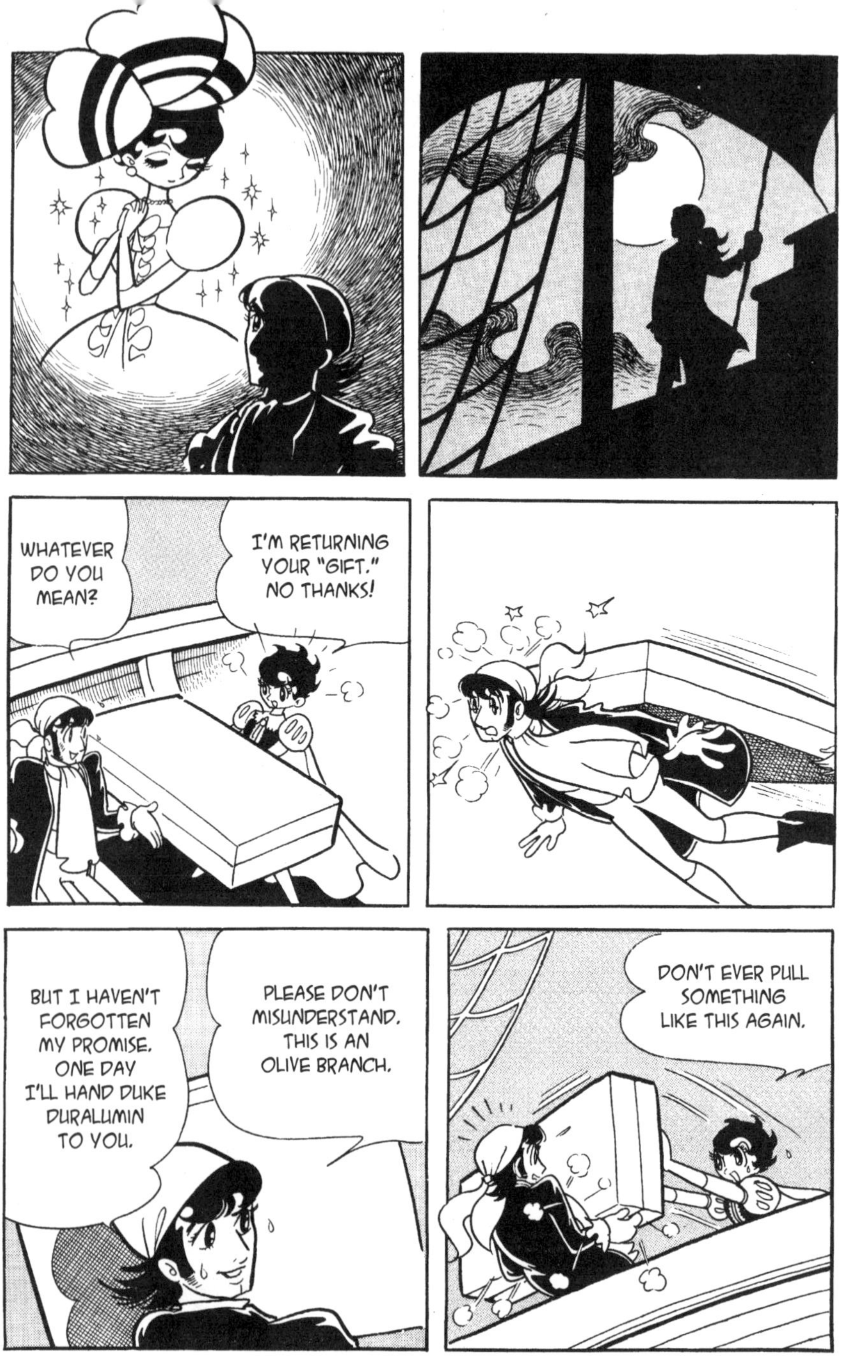
I'M RETURNING YOUR "GIFT." NO THANKS!
WHATEVER DO YOU MEAN?
DON'T EVER PULL SOMETHING LIKE THIS AGAIN.
PLEASE DON'T MISUNDERSTAND. THIS IS AN OLIVE BRANCH.
BUT I HAVEN'T FORGOTTEN MY PROMISE. ONE DAY I'LL HAND DUKE DURALUMIN TO YOU.

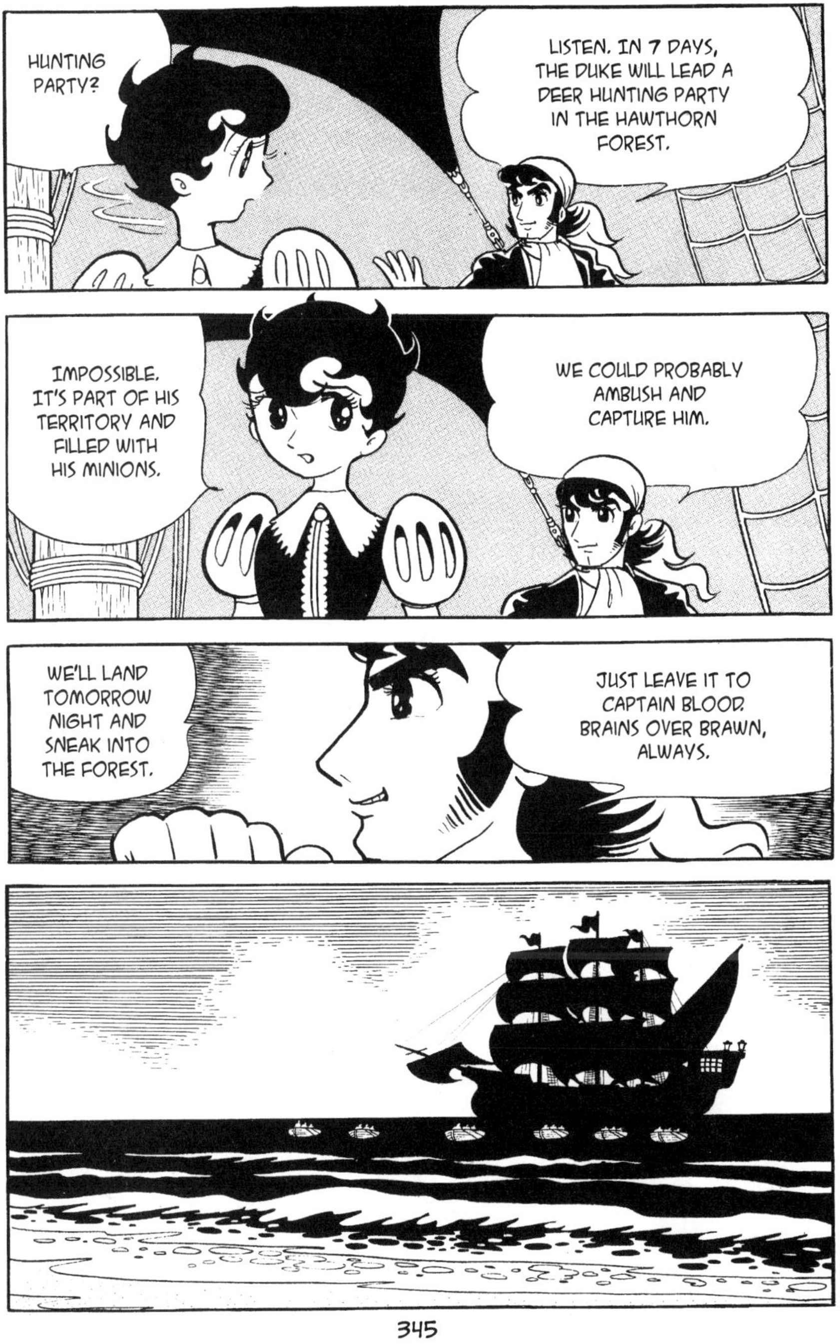
LISTEN. IN 7 DAYS, THE DUKE WILL LEAD A DEER HUNTING PARTY IN THE HAWTHORN FOREST.
HUNTING PARTY?
WE COULD PROBABLY AMBUSH AND CAPTURE HIM.
IMPOSSIBLE. IT'S PART OF HIS TERRITORY AND FILLED WITH HIS MINIONS.
JUST LEAVE IT TO CAPTAIN BLOOD. BRAINS OVER BRAWN, ALWAYS.
WE'LL LAND TOMORROW NIGHT AND SNEAK INTO THE FOREST.

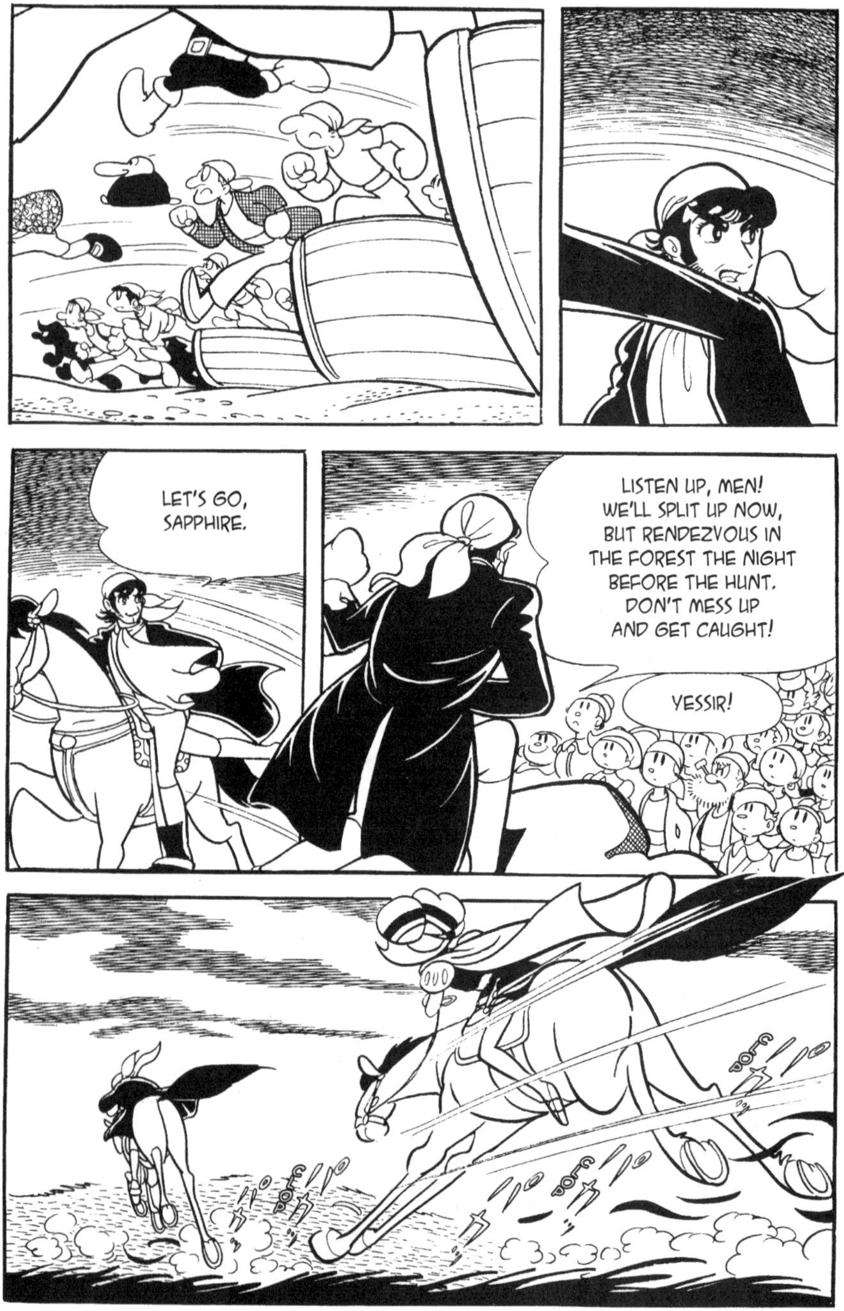
LISTEN UP, MEN! WE'LL SPLIT UP NOW, BUT RENDEZVOUS IN THE FOREST THE NIGHT BEFORE THE HUNT. DON'T MESS UP AND GET CAUGHT!
YESSIR!
LET'S GO, SAPPHIRE.
CLOP
CLOP
CLOP
CLOP

Continued in Part 2!

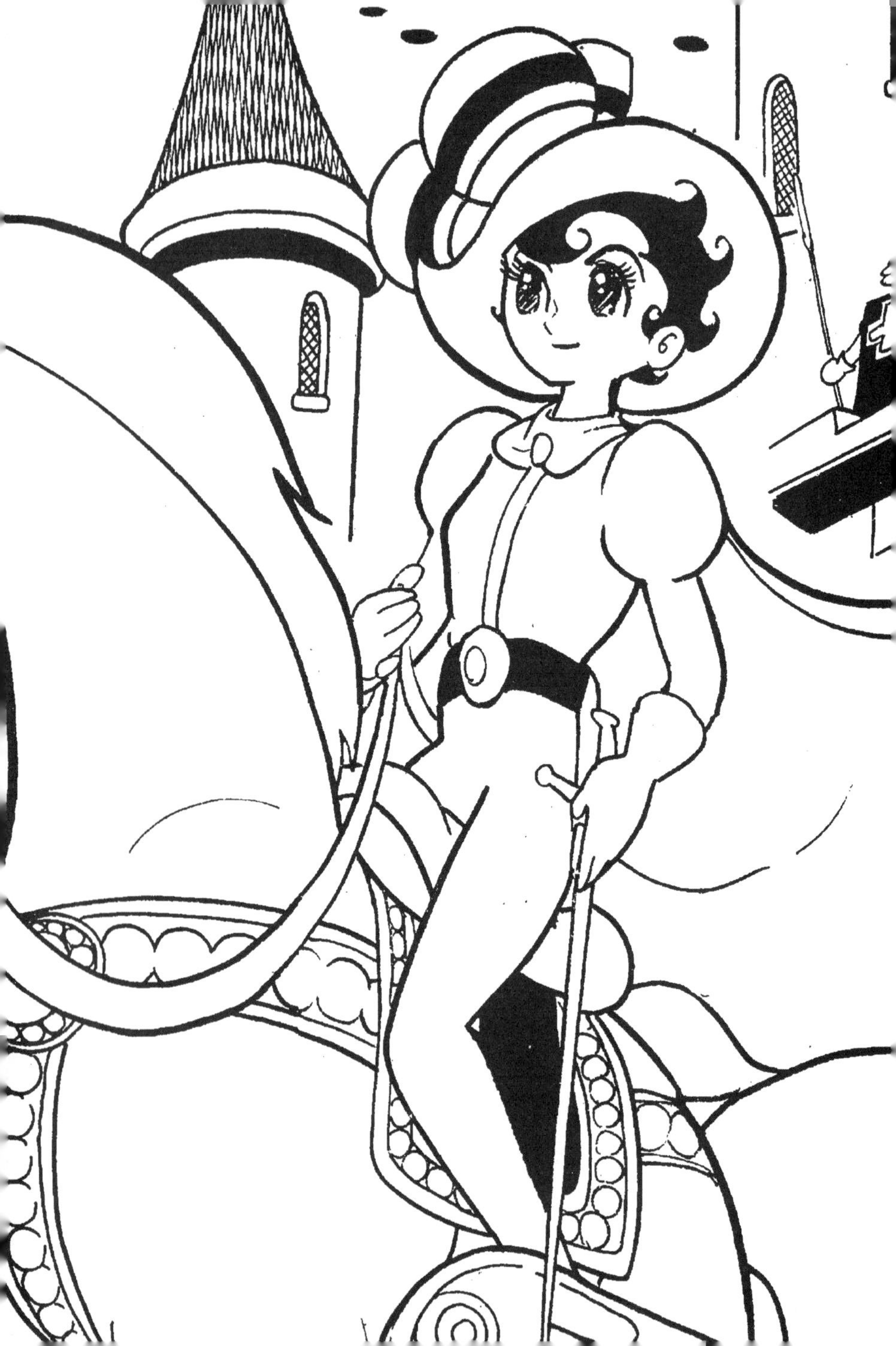

PRINCESS KNIGHT

by Osamu Tezuka

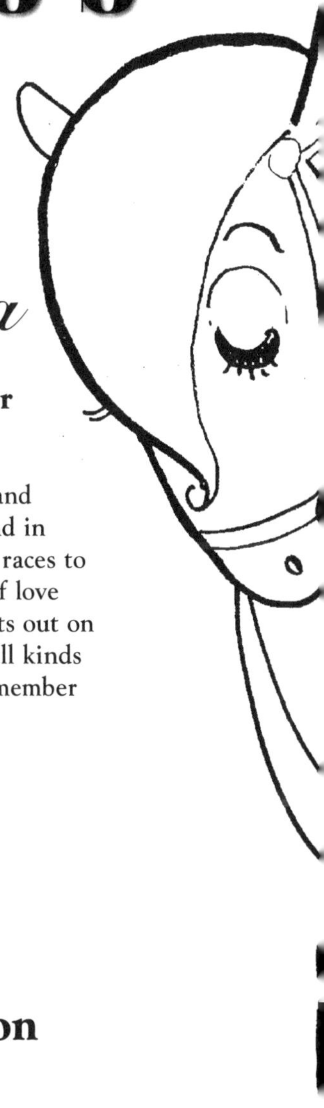

Follow Sapphire on her quest to rediscover herself and win back her Prince

A grave injury leaves Sapphire hovering between life and death. Madame Hell descends on the castle of Goldland in preparation for a devilish wedding. As Captain Blood races to find a way to save Sapphire's life, capricious goddess of love Venus meddles with Sapphire's memories. Sapphire sets out on a journey to find out who she really is, encountering all kinds of colorful characters along the way. Will Sapphire remember what's most important before it's too late?

PRINCESS
KNIGHT
part 2
Osamu Tezuka

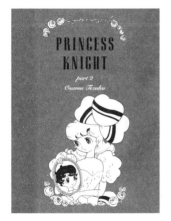

Part 2
the Conclusion

Coming
This Winter

PRAISE FOR *DORORO*, AN EISNER AWARD WINNER

"**Platinum Award**. Tezuka blends high-adventure plotting with deep and thoughtful themes in his inimitable style. It seems a shame it's only all been in Japanese until now." *—Advanced Media Network*

"**Grade: A**. Osamu Tezuka's ability to immerse his readers in the lives and hardships of his characters is staggering. An awesome action/adventure title with strong characterizations and a gripping setting." *—Manga Maniac Cafe*

"Tezuka's characters may be big-eyed and cute, but in *Dororo* they are up to serious business." *—Daily Yomiuri*

"Tezuka's drawing is as powerful and assured as ever... and the serious moments of the story have real power." *—ComicMix*

"A series you will surely see jump from those 'looking forward to' lists to the 'best of 2008' lists." *—Mecha Mecha Media*

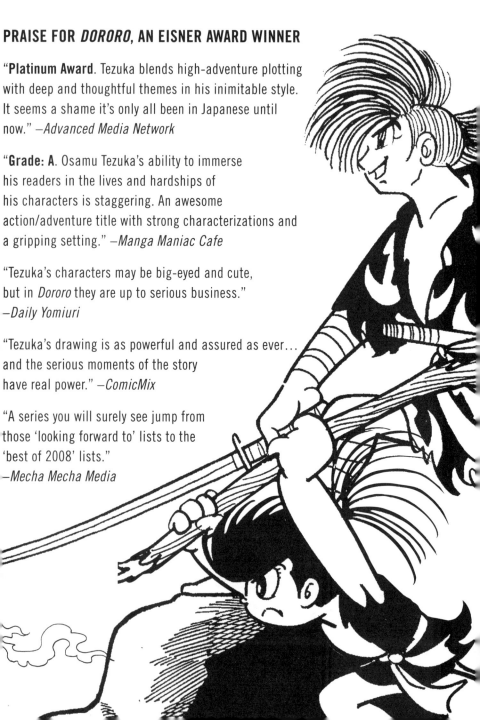

DOROR O by OSAMU TEZUKA

A young swordsman's hunt for the demons who stole his body parts and the tale of his little thieving friend takes the pair on an epic journey!

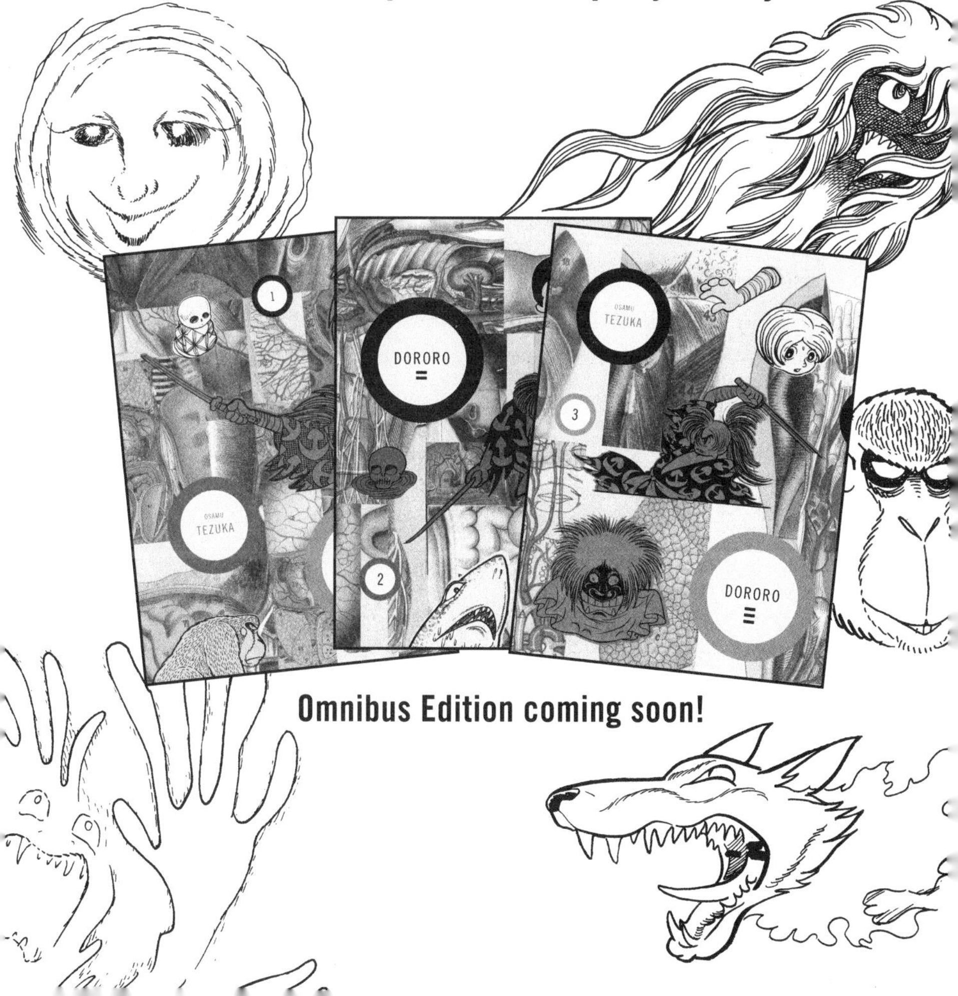
1
OSAMU
TEZUKA
DOROR O
2
OSAMU
TEZUKA
3
DOROR O

Omnibus Edition coming soon!

WRONG WAY

Japanese books, including manga like this one,
are meant to be read from right to left.
So the front cover is actually the back cover, and vice versa.
To read this book, please flip it over
and start in the top right-hand corner.
Read the panels, and the bubbles in the panels,
from right to left,
then drop down to the next row and repeat.
It may make you dizzy at first, but forcing your brain to do things backwards
makes you smarter in the long run.
We swear.